A LITTLE HATRED

By Joe Abercrombie

THE AGE OF MADNESS
A Little Hatred

THE FIRST LAW TRILOGY
The Blade Itself
Before They Are Hanged
Last Argument of Kings

Best Served Cold
The Heroes
Red Country
Sharp Ends: Stories from the World of the First Law

THE SHATTERED SEA TRILOGY
Half a King
Half the World
Half a War

A LITTLE HATRED

Book One of The Age of Madness

JOE ABERCROMBIE

www.orbitbooks.net

Copyright © 2019 by Joe Abercrombie

Cover design by Lauren Panepinto
Cover art by Sam Weber
Cover copyright © 2019 by Hachette Book Group, Inc.

Orbit
Hachette Book Group
1290 Avenue of the Americas
New York, NY 10104
orbitbooks.net

First Edition: September 2019
Simultaneously published in Great Britain by Gollancz

Orbit is an imprint of Hachette Book Group.
The Orbit name and logo are trademarks of Little, Brown Book Group Limited.

The Hachette Speakers Bureau provides a wide range of authors for speaking events. To find out more, go to www.hachettespeakersbureau.com or call (866) 376-6591.

Library of Congress Control Number: 2019933447

ISBNs: 978-0-316-18716-9 (hardcover), 978-0-316-42764-7 (signed edition), 978-0-316-42763-0 (Barnes & Noble signed edition), 978-0-316-42762-3 (Barnes & Noble Black Friday signed edition), 978-0-316-34186-8 (ebook)

Printed in the United States of America

LSC-C

10 9 8 7 6 5 4 3 2 1

For Lou,

With grim, dark

hugs

PART I

"The age is running mad after innovation;
and all the business of the world
is to be done in a new way."

Dr. Johnson

Blessings and Curses

"Rikke."

She prised one eye open. A slit of stabbing, sickening brightness.

"Come back."

She pushed the spit-wet dowel out of her mouth with her tongue and croaked the one word she could think of. "Fuck."

"There's my girl!" Isern squatted beside her, necklace of runes and finger bones dangling, grinning that twisted grin that showed the hole in her teeth and offering no help at all. "What did you see?"

Rikke heaved one hand up to grip her head. Felt like if she didn't hold her skull together, it'd burst. Shapes still fizzed on the inside of her lids, like the glowing smears when you've looked at the sun.

"I saw folk falling from a high tower. Dozens of 'em." She winced at the thought of them hitting the ground. "I saw folk hanged. Rows of 'em." Her gut cramped at the memory of swinging bodies, dangling feet. "I saw . . . a battle, maybe? Below a red hill."

Isern sniffed. "This is the North. Takes no magic to see a battle coming. What else?"

"I saw Uffrith burning." Rikke could almost smell the smoke still. She pressed her hand to her left eye. Felt hot. Burning hot.

"What else?"

"I saw a wolf eat the sun. Then a lion ate the wolf. Then a lamb ate the lion. Then an owl ate the lamb."

"Must've been a real monster of an owl."

"Or a tiny little lamb, I guess? What does it mean?"

Isern held a fingertip to her scarred lips, the way she did when she was on the verge of deep pronouncements. "I've no frigging clue. Mayhap the turning of time's wheel shall unlock the secrets of these visions."

Rikke spat, but her mouth still tasted like despair. "So . . . wait and see."

3

"Eleven times out of twelve, that's the best course." Isern scratched at the hollow above her collarbone and winked. "But if I said it that way, no one would reckon me a deep thinker."

"Well, I can unveil two secrets right away." Rikke groaned as she pushed herself up onto one elbow. "My head hurts and I shat myself."

"That second one's no secret, anyone with a nose is party to it."

"Shitty Rikke, they'll call me." She wrinkled her nose as she shifted. "And not for the first time."

"Your problem is in caring what they call you."

"My problem is I'm cursed with fits."

Isern tapped under her left eye. "You say cursed with fits, I say blessed with the Long Eye."

"Huh." Rikke rolled onto her knees and her stomach kept on rolling and tickled her throat with sick. By the dead, she felt sore and squeezed out. Twice the pain of a night at the ale cup and none of the sweet memories. "Doesn't feel like much of a blessing to me," she muttered, once she'd risked a little burp and fought her guts to a draw.

"There are few blessings without a curse hidden inside, nor curses without a whiff of blessing." Isern carved a little piece of chagga from a dried-out chunk. "Like most things, it's a matter of how you look at it."

"Very profound."

"As always."

"Maybe someone whose head hurt less would enjoy your wisdom more."

Isern licked her fingertips, rolled the chagga into a pellet and offered it to Rikke. "I am a bottomless well of revelation but cannot force the ignorant to drink. Now get your trousers off." She barked out that savage laugh of hers. "Words many a man has longed to hear me say."

Rikke sat with her back to one of the snow-capped standing stones, eyes narrowed as the sun flashed through the dripping branches, the fur cloak her father gave her hugged around her shoulders and the raw wind wafting around her bare arse. She chewed chagga and chased the itches that danced all over her with black-edged fingernails, trying to calm her mangled nerves and shake off the memories of that tower, and those hanged, and of Uffrith burning.

"Visions," she muttered. "A curse for sure."

Isern squelched up the bank with Rikke's dripping trousers. "Clean as new snow! Your only stench now shall be of youth and disappointment."

"You're one to talk of stenches, Isern-i-Phail."

Isern raised her sinewy, tattooed arm, sniffed at her pit and gave a satisfied sigh. "I've a goodly, earthy, womanly savour of a kind much

4

loved by the moon. If you're rattled by an odour, you picked the wrong companion."

Rikke spat chagga juice but messed it up and got most of it down her chin. "If you think I picked any part of this, you're mad."

"They said the same thing about my da."

"He was mad as a sack of owls, you're always saying so!"

"Aye, well, one person's mad is another's remarkable. Need I observe you're a long leap from ordinary yourself? You kicked so hard this time you nearly kicked your boots off. Might have to rope you in future, make sure you don't crack your nut and end up a drooler like my brother Brait. At least he can keep his shit in, mind you."

"My thanks for that."

"No bother." Isern made a little diamond from her fingers and squinted through it at the sun. "Past time we were on our way. High deeds are being done today. Or maybe low ones." And she dropped the trousers in Rikke's lap. "Best dress yourself."

"What, wet? They'll chafe."

"Chafe?" Isern snorted. "That's the limit o' your worries?"

"My head still aches so bad I can feel it in my teeth." Rikke wanted to shout but knew it'd hurt too much, so she had to whine it soft instead. "I need no more small discomforts."

"Life *is* small discomforts, girl! They're how you know you *are* alive." And Isern hacked that laugh out again, slapped happily at Rikke's shoulder and sent her stumbling sideways. "You can walk with your plump white arse hanging out if that's your pleasure, but you'll be walking one way or the other."

"A curse," grumbled Rikke as she wriggled into her clammy trousers. "Definitely a curse."

"So...you really think I've got the Long Eye?"

Isern strode on through the woods with that loping gait that, however fast Rikke walked, always left her an uncomfortable half-step behind. "You really think I'd be pissing my efforts away on you otherwise?"

Rikke sighed. "Guess not. Just, in the songs, it's a thing witches and magi and deep-wise folk used to see into the fog of what comes. Not a thing that makes idiots fall down and shit themselves."

"In case you never noticed, bards have a habit of dressing things up. There is a fine living, d'you see, in songs about deep-wise witches, but in shitty idiots, less."

Rikke sadly conceded the truth of that.

"And proving you have the Long Eye is no simple matter. You cannot force it open. You must coax it." And Isern tickled Rikke under the chin and made her jerk away. "Take it up to the sacred places where the old stones stand so the moon might shine full upon it. But it'll see what it sees when it chooses, even so."

"Uffrith on fire, though?" Rikke was feeling a weight of worry now they were down from the High Places and getting close to home. The dead knew she hadn't always been happy in Uffrith, but she'd no wish to see it in flames. "How's that meant to happen?"

"Carelessness with a cook-fire would do it." Isern's eyes slid sideways. "Though up here in the North, I'd say war's a more likely cause of cities aflame."

"War?"

"It's when a fight gets so big almost no one comes out of it well."

"I know what it bloody is." Rikke had a spot of fear growing at the nape of her neck which she couldn't shrug off however much she wriggled her shoulders. "But there's been peace in the North all my lifetime."

"My da used to say times of peace are when the wise prepare for violence."

"Your da was mad as a bootful of dung."

"And what does your da say? Few men so sane as the Dogman."

Rikke wriggled her shoulders one more time, but nothing helped. "He says hope for the best and prepare for the worst."

"Sound advice, say I."

"But he lived through some black times. Always fighting. Against Bethod. Against Black Dow. Things were different then."

Isern snorted. "No, they weren't. I was there when your father fought Bethod, up in the High Places with the Bloody-Nine beside him."

Rikke blinked at her. "You can't have been ten years old."

"Old enough to kill a man."

"What?"

"Used to carry my da's hammer, 'cause the smallest should take the heaviest load, but that day he was fighting with the hammer so I had his spear. This very one." Its butt tapped the rhythm of their walking on the path. "My da knocked a man down, and he was trying to get up, and I stabbed him right up the arse."

"With that spear?" Rikke had come to think of it as just a stick Isern carried. A stick that happened to have a deerskin cover over one end. She didn't like thinking there was a blade under there. Especially not one that had been up some poor bastard's arse.

"Well, it's had a few new shafts since then, but—" Isern stopped dead, tattooed hand raised and eyes narrowed. All Rikke could hear was whispering branches, the tap, tap of drips from the melting snow, the tweet, tweet of birds in the budding trees.

Rikke leaned towards her. "What's the—"

"Nock a shaft to your bow and keep 'em talking," whispered Isern.

"Who?"

"Failing that, show 'em your teeth. You're blessed with fine teeth." And she darted off the road and into the trees.

"My teeth?" hissed Rikke, but Isern's flitting shadow had already vanished in the brambles.

That was when she heard a man's voice. "Sure this is the way?"

She'd had her bow over her shoulder hoping for a deer and now she shrugged it off, fumbled out an arrow and nearly dropped it, managed to get it nocked in spite of a flurry of nervy twitches up her arm.

"We was told check the woods." A deeper, harder, scarier voice. "Do these look like woods?"

She had a sudden panic it might just be a squirrel arrow, checked it was a proper broadhead.

"Forest, I guess."

Laughter. "What's the bloody difference?"

An old man came around the bend in the road. He'd a staff in his hand, and he lowered it, metal gleaming in the dappled light, and Rikke realised it wasn't a staff but a spear, and she felt the worry spread out from that spot on her neck to the roots of her hair.

There were three of them. The old one had a sorry look like none of this was his idea. Next came a nervous lad with a shield and a short axe. Finally, there was a big man with a heavy beard and a heavier frown. Rikke didn't like the look of him at all.

Her father always said don't point arrows at folk unless you mean to see 'em dead, so she drew her bow halfway and pointed it at the road.

"Best hold still," she said.

The old one stared at her. "Girl, you have a ring through your nose."

"I am aware." And Rikke stuck her tongue out and touched the tip to it. "It keeps me tethered."

"You might wander off?"

"My thoughts might."

"Is it gold?" asked the lad.

"Copper," she lied, since gold is apt to turn unpleasant meetings into deadly ones.

7

"And the paint?"

"The mark of the cross is a goodly mark much loved by the moon. The Long Eye is the left eye and the cross will keep its sight true through the fog of what comes." She turned her head and spat chagga juice without taking her eyes off them, then added, "Maybe," since she wasn't sure the cross had done a thing but get smeared on her pillow when she forgot to wipe it off of an evening.

She wasn't the only doubter. "You mad?" growled the big man.

Rikke sighed. Far from the first time she'd fielded that question. "One person's mad is another's remarkable."

"Be a fine thing if you were to put that bow down," said the old one.

"I like it where it is." Though she definitely didn't, it was getting all sticky in her hand, shoulder aching from the effort of holding it half-drawn and a twitch in her neck starting up that she worried might jerk the string loose.

Seemed the lad trusted her to hold it even less than she did, peering at her over the rim of his shield. It was only then she noticed what was painted on it.

"You've a wolf on your shield," she said.

"Stour Nightfall's mark," growled the big man, with a hint of pride, and Rikke saw he had a wolf on his shield, too, though his was scuffed almost back to the wood.

"You're Nightfall's men?" The fear was spreading all the way into her guts now. "What you doing down here?"

"Putting an end to the Dogman and his arse-lickers, and bringing Uffrith back into the North where it belongs."

Rikke's knuckles whitened around her bow, fear turning to anger. "You're fucking not!"

"Already happening." The old man shrugged. "Only question for you is whether you'll be raised up with the winners or put in the mud with the losers."

"Nightfall's the greatest warrior since the Bloody-Nine!" piped up the young one. "He's going to take back Angland and drive the Union out o' the North!"

"The Union?" And Rikke looked down at the wolf's head badly daubed on his badly made shield. "A wolf ate the sun," she whispered.

"She is bloody mad." The big one stepped forwards. "Now drop the—" And he made this long wheeze, and his shirt stuck out, a glint of metal showing.

"Oh," he said, dropping to his knees.

The lad turned around.

Rikke's arrow stuck into his back, just under his shoulder blade.

Her turn to say, "Oh," not sure whether she'd meant to let go the string or not.

A flash of metal and the old man's head jolted, the blade of Isern's spear catching him in the throat. He dropped his own spear, grabbed for her with clumsy fingers.

"Shush." Isern slapped his hand away and ripped the blade free in a black gout. He wriggled on the ground, fiddling with the great wound in his neck as if he might stop it splurting. He was trying to say something, but fast as he could spit the blood out, his mouth filled up again. Then he stopped moving.

"You killed 'em." Rikke felt all hot. There were some red speckles on her hand. The big one was lying on his face, shirt soaked dark.

"You killed this one," said Isern. The lad knelt there, making these squeaky little gasps as he tried to reach around his back to the arrow shaft, though what he'd do if he got his fingertips to it, Rikke had no idea. Probably he'd no idea, either. Isern was the only one thinking clearly right then. She leaned down and calmly plucked the knife from the lad's belt. "Was hoping to set him a question or two, but he'll be giving no answers with that shaft in his lung."

As if to prove the point, he coughed some blood into his hand, and stared over it at Rikke. He looked a bit offended, like she'd said something hurtful.

"Still, no one ever gets things all their own way." Rikke jumped at the crack as Isern rammed the lad's knife into the crown of his head. His eyes rolled up and his leg kicked and his back arched. Just like hers did, maybe, when a fit came upon her.

The hairs were standing on Rikke's arms as he slumped down limp. She never saw a man killed before. All happened so fast she didn't know how she ought to feel about it.

"They didn't seem so bad," she said.

"For a girl struggling to penetrate the mists of the future, you don't half miss what's right in front of you." Isern was already rooting through the old man's pockets, point of her tongue wedged in the hole in her teeth. "If you wait till they seem bad, you've waited way too long."

"Could've given 'em a chance."

"To what? Put you in the mud? Or drag you off to Stour Nightfall? Chafing would've been the least of your worries then, that boy's got a bastard of a reputation." She caught the old man's leg and dragged him

9

from the path into the undergrowth, tossed his spear after. "Or were we going to invite 'em dancing through the woods with us, and all wear flowers in our hair and win 'em over to our side with my pretty words and your pretty smile?"

Rikke spat some chagga juice and wiped her chin, watching the blood work its way through the dirt about the lad's nailed head. "Doubt my smile's up to the task and I'm damn sure your words ain't."

"Then killing 'em was all o' the one choices we had, eh? Your problem is you're all heart." And she stabbed Rikke in the tit with one bony finger.

"Ow!" Rikke took a step away, holding her arms across her chest. "That hurts, you know!"

"You're all heart all over, so you feel every sting and buffet. You must make of your heart a stone." And Isern thumped her ribs with a fist, the finger bones around her neck rattling. "Ruthlessness is a quality much loved o' the moon." As if to prove the point, she bent down and heaved the dead lad into the bushes. "A leader must be hard, so others don't have to be."

"Leader o' what?" muttered Rikke, rubbing at her sore tit. And that was when she caught a whiff of smoke, just like in her dream. As if it was a tugging she couldn't resist, she set off down the path.

"Oy!" called Isern around a stick of dry meat she'd rooted out of the big one's pouch. "I need help dragging this big bastard!"

"No," whispered Rikke, the smell of fire getting stronger and her worry getting stronger with it. "No, no, no."

She burst from the trees and into cold daylight, took a couple more wobbling steps and stopped, bow dangling from her limp hand.

The morning mist was long faded and she could see all the way across the patchwork of new-planted fields to Uffrith, wedged in against the grey sea behind its grey wall. Where her father's old hall stood with the scraggy garden out the back. Safe, boring Uffrith, where she'd been born and raised. Only it was burning, just the way she'd seen it, and a great column of dark smoke rolled up and smudged the sky, drifting out over the restless sea.

"By the dead," she croaked.

Isern wandered from the trees with her spear across her shoulders and a great smile across her face. "You know what this means?"

"War?" whispered Rikke, horrified.

"Aye, that." Isern waved it away like it was a trifle. "But more to the matter, I was right!" And she clapped Rikke on the shoulder so hard she near knocked her down. "You *do* have the Long Eye!"

Where the Fight's Hottest

*I*n *battle*, Leo's father used to say, *a man discovers who he truly is.*

The Northmen were already turning to run as his horse crashed into them with a thrilling jolt.

He smashed one across the back of the helmet with the full force of the charge and ripped his head half off.

He snarled as he swung to the other side. A glimpse of a gawping face before his axe split it open, blood spraying in black streaks.

Other riders tore into the Northmen, tossing them like broken dolls. He saw one horse spitted through the head with a spear. The rider turned a somersault as he was flung from the saddle.

A lance shattered, a shard flying into Leo's helmet with an echoing clang as he wrenched away. The world was a flickering slit of twisted faces, glinting steel, heaving bodies, half seen through the slot in his visor. Screams of men and mounts and metal mashed into one thought-crushing din.

A horse swerved in front of him. Riderless, stirrups flapping. Ritter's horse. He could tell by the yellow saddlecloth. A spear stabbed at him, jolting the shield on his arm, rocking him in his saddle. The point screeched down his armoured thigh.

He gripped the reins in his shield-hand as his mount bucked and snorted, face locked in an aching smile, flailing wildly with his axe on one side, then the other. He beat mindlessly at a shield with a black wolf painted on it, kicked at a man and sent him staggering back, then Barniva's sword flashed as it took his arm off.

He saw Whitewater Jin swinging his mace, red hair tangled across gritted teeth. Just beyond him, Antaup was shrieking something as he tried to twist his spear free of bloody mail. Glaward wrestled with a Carl, both without weapons, all tangled with their reins. Leo hacked at the Northman and smashed his elbow back the wrong way, hacked again and sent him flopping into the mud.

He pointed at Stour Nightfall's standard with his axe, black wolf streaming in the wind. He howled, roared, throat hoarse. No one could hear him with his visor down. No one could've heard him if it had been up. He hardly knew what he was saying. He flailed furiously at the milling bodies instead.

Someone clutched at his leg. Curly hair. Freckles. Looked bloody terrified. Everyone did. Didn't seem to have a weapon. Maybe surrendering. Leo smashed Freckles on the top of the head with the rim of his shield, gave his horse the spurs and trampled him into the mud.

This was no place for good intentions. No place for tedious subtleties or boring counter-arguments. None of his mother's carping on patience and caution. Everything was beautifully simple.

In battle, a man discovers who he truly is, and Leo was the hero he'd always dreamed of being.

He swung again but his axe felt strange. The blade had flown off, left him holding a bloody stick. He dropped it, dragged out his battle steel, buzzing fingers clumsy in his gauntlet, hilt greasy from the thickening rain. He realised the man he'd been hitting was dead. He'd fallen against the fence, so it looked as if he was standing but there was black pulp hanging out of his broken skull, so that was that.

The Northmen were crumbling. Running, squealing, being hacked down from behind, and Leo herded them towards their standard. Three riders had a whole crowd of them hemmed into a gateway, Barniva in their midst, scarred face flecked with blood as he chopped away with his heavy sword.

The standard-bearer was a huge man with desperate eyes and blood in his beard, still holding high the flag of the black wolf. Leo spurred right at him, blocked axe with shield, caught him with a sword-cut that screeched over his cheek guard and opened a great gash across his face, carved half his nose off. He tottered back and Whitewater Jin crushed the man's helmet with his mace, blood squirting from under the rim. Leo kicked him over, tearing the standard from his limp hand as he fell. He thrust it up, laughing, gurgling, half-choking on his own spit then laughing again, his axe's loop still stuck around his wrist so the broken haft clattered against his helmet.

Had they won? He stared around for more enemies. A few ragged figures bounded through the crops towards the distant trees. Running for their lives, weapons abandoned. That was all.

Leo ached all over: thighs from gripping his horse, shoulders from swinging his axe, hands from gripping the reins. The very soles of his feet throbbed from the effort. His chest heaved, breath booming in his helmet, damp, and hot, and tasting of salt. Might've bit his tongue somewhere. He fumbled with the buckle under his chin, finally tore the damn thing free. His skull burst with the noise, turned from fury to delight. The noise of victory.

He almost fell from his horse, clambered up onto the wall. Something was soft under his gauntleted hand. A Northman's corpse, a broken spear sticking from his back. All he felt was giddy joy.

No corpses, no glory, after all. Might as well regret the peelings from a carrot. Someone was helping him up, giving him a steadying hand. Jurand. Always there when he needed him. Leo stood tall, the joyful faces of his men all turned towards him.

"The Young Lion!" roared Glaward, climbing up beside him and clapping a heavy hand on his shoulder, making him wobble. Jurand stretched out his arms to catch him, but he didn't fall. "Leo dan Brock!" Soon they were all shouting his name, singing it like a prayer, chanting it like a magic word, stabbing their glittering weapons at the spitting sky.

"Leo! Leo! Leo!"

In battle, a man discovers who he truly is.

He felt drunk. He felt on fire. He felt like a king. He felt like a *god*. This was what he was made for!

"Victory!" he roared, shaking his bloody sword and the Northmen's bloody standard.

By the dead, could there be anything better than this?

In the lady governor's tent, they were fighting a different kind of war. A war of patient study and careful calculation, of weighed odds and furrowed brows, of lines of supply and an awful lot of maps. A kind of war Leo frankly hadn't the patience for.

The glow of victory had been dampened by the stiffening rain on the long trudge up from the valley, doused further by the niggling pain from a dozen cuts and bruises, and was almost entirely smothered by the cool stare his mother gave him as Leo pushed through the flap with Jurand and Whitewater Jin at his back.

She was in the midst of talking to a knight herald. Ridiculously tall, he had to stoop respectfully to attend to her.

"...please tell His Majesty we are doing everything to check the Northmen's advance, but Uffrith is lost and we are giving ground. They struck with overwhelming force at three points and we are still gathering our troops. Ask him...no, *beg* him to send reinforcements."

"I will, my Lady Governor." The knight herald nodded to Leo as he passed. "My congratulations on your victory, Lord Brock."

"We don't need the king's bloody help!" snapped Leo as soon as the flap dropped. "We can beat Black Calder's dogs!" His voice sounded oddly weak in the tent, deadened by wet cloth. It didn't carry anywhere near so nicely as it had on the battlefield.

"Huh." His mother planted her fists on the table and frowned down at her maps. By the dead, sometimes he thought she loved those maps more than him. "If we are to fight the king's battles, we should expect the king's help."

"You should've seen them *run*!" Damn it, but Leo had been so sure of himself a few moments ago. He could charge a line of Carls and never falter, but a woman with a long neck and greying hair leached all the courage out of him. "They broke before we even got to them! We took a few dozen prisoners..." He glanced towards Jurand, but he was giving Leo that doubtful look now, the one he used when he didn't approve, the one he'd given him before the charge. "And the farm's back in our hands...and..."

His mother let him stammer into silence before she glanced at his friends. "My thanks, Jurand. I'm sure you did your best to talk him out of it. And you, Whitewater. My son couldn't ask for better friends or I for braver warriors."

Jin slapped a heavy hand down on Leo's shoulder. "It was Leo who led the—"

"You can go."

Jin scratched sheepishly at his beard, showing a lot less warrior's mettle than he had down in the valley. Jurand gave Leo the slightest apologetic wince. "Of course, Lady Finree." And they slunk from the tent, leaving Leo to fiddle weakly with the fringe of his captured standard.

His mother let the withering silence stretch a moment longer before she passed judgement. "You bloody fool."

He'd known it was coming, but it still stung. "Because I actually *fought*?"

"Because of *when* you chose to fight, and how."

"Great leaders go where the fight's hottest!" But he knew he sounded like the heroes in the badly written storybooks he used to love.

"You know who else you find where the fight's hottest?" asked his mother. "Dead men. We both know you're not a fool, Leo. For whose benefit are you pretending to be one?" She shook her head wearily. "I should never have let your father send you to live with the Dogman. All you learned in Uffrith was rashness, bad songs and a childish admiration for murderers.

I should have sent you to Adua instead. I doubt your singing would be any better but at least you might have learned some subtlety."

"There's a time for subtlety and a time for *action*!"

"There is never a time for recklessness, Leo. Or for vanity."

"We bloody *won*!"

"Won what? A worthless farm in a worthless valley? That was little more than a scouting party, and now the enemy will guess our strength." She gave a bitter snort as she turned back to her maps. "Or the lack of it."

"I captured a standard." It seemed a pitiful thing now he really looked at it, though, clumsily stitched, the pole closer to a branch than a flagstaff. How could he have thought Stour Nightfall himself might ride beneath it?

"We have plenty of flags," said his mother. "It's men to follow them we're short of. Perhaps you could bring back a few regiments of those next time?"

"Damn it, Mother, I don't know how to please you—"

"Listen to what you're told. Learn from those who know better. Be brave, by all means, but don't be rash. Above all, don't get yourself bloody *killed*! You've always known exactly how to please me, Leo, but you choose to please yourself."

"You can't understand! You're not..." He waved an impatient hand, failing, as always, to quite find the right words. "A *man*," he finished lamely.

She raised one brow. "Had I been confused on that point, it was put beyond doubt when I pushed you out of my womb. Have you any notion how much you weighed as a baby? Spend two days shitting an anvil and we'll talk again."

"Bloody hell, Mother! I mean that men will look *up* to a certain kind of man, and—"

"Like your friend Ritter looked up to you?"

Leo was caught out by the memory of that riderless horse clattering past. He realised he hadn't seen Ritter's face among his friends when they celebrated. Realised he hadn't even thought about that until now.

"He knew the risks," he croaked, suddenly choked with worry. "He chose to fight. He was proud to fight!"

"He was. Because you have that fire in you that inspires men to follow. Your father had it, too. But with that gift comes responsibility. Men put their lives in your hands."

Leo swallowed, pride melting to leave ugly guilt behind as pristine snow melts to show the world rotten and bedraggled. "I should go and see him." He turned towards the tent flap, nearly tripping on the loose strap of one of his greaves. "Is he...with the wounded?"

His mother's face had softened. That made him more worried than ever. "He's with the dead, Leo." There was a long, strange silence, and outside the wind blew up and made the canvas of the tent flap and whisper. "I'm sorry."

No corpses, no glory. He sank onto a folding field chair, captured standard clattering to the ground.

"He said we should wait for you," he muttered, remembering Ritter's worried face as he looked down into the valley. "So did Jurand. I told them they could stay with the ladies... while we handled the fighting."

"You did what you thought was right," murmured his mother. "In the heat of the moment."

"He has a wife..." Leo remembered the wedding. What the hell was her name? Bit of a weak chin. The groom had looked prettier. The happy couple had danced, badly, and Whitewater Jin had bellowed in Northern that he hoped for her sake Ritter fucked better than he danced. Leo had laughed so hard he was nearly sick. He didn't feel like laughing now. Being sick, yes. "By the dead... he has a *child*."

"I will write to them."

"What good will a letter do?" He felt the stinging of tears at the back of his nose. "I'll give them my house! In Ostenhorm!"

"Are you sure?"

"Why do I need a house? I spend all my time in the saddle."

"You've a big heart, Leo." His mother squatted down before him. "Too big, I sometimes think." Her pale hands looked tiny in his gauntleted fists, but they were the stronger then. "You have it in you to be a great man, but you cannot let yourself be swept off by whatever emotion blows your way. Battles may sometimes be won by the brave, but wars are always won by the clever. Do you understand?"

"I understand," he whispered.

"Good. Give orders to leave the farm and pull back towards the west before Stour Nightfall arrives in force."

"But if we fall back... Ritter died for nothing. If we fall back, how will that *look*?"

She stood. "Like womanly weakness and indecision, I hope. Then perhaps the rash heads on the Northmen's side will prevail and pursue us with manly smiles on their manly faces, and when the king's soldiers finally arrive, we'll cut them to pieces on ground of our choosing."

Leo blinked at the floor and felt the tears on his cheeks. "I see."

She had her soft voice, now. "It was rash, it was reckless, but it *was* brave, and... for better or worse, men *do* look up to a certain kind of man. I won't deny we all need something to cheer for. You gave Stour Nightfall a bloody nose, and great warriors are quick to anger, and angry men make mistakes." She pressed something into his limp hand. The standard with Nightfall's wolf on it. "Your father would have been proud of your courage, Leo. Now make me proud of your judgement."

He trudged to the tent flap, shoulders drooping under armour that felt three times heavier than when he arrived. Ritter was gone, and never coming back, and had left his weak-chinned wife weeping at the fireside. Killed by his own loyalty, and Leo's vanity, and Leo's carelessness, and Leo's arrogance.

"By the dead." He tried to rub the tears away with the back of his hand but couldn't do it with his gauntlets on. He used the hem of the captured standard instead.

In battle, a man discovers who he truly is.

He froze as he stepped into the daylight. What looked like a whole regiment had gathered in a crescent, looking up towards his mother's tent.

"A cheer for Leo dan Brock!" roared Glaward, catching Leo's wrist in his ham of a fist and hoisting it high. "The Young Lion!"

"The Young Lion!" bellowed Barniva as a rousing cheer went up. "Leo dan Brock!"

"I tried to warn you." Jurand leaned over to mutter in his ear. "She give you a roasting?"

"Nothing I didn't deserve." But Leo managed to smile a little, too. Just for the sake of morale. No one could deny they all needed something to cheer for.

It grew louder as he raised that rag of a standard, and Antaup swaggered forwards, throwing up his arms for more noise. One of the men, no doubt drunk already, dragged down his trousers and showed his bare arse to the North, to widespread approval. Then he fell over, to widespread laughter. Glaward and Barniva caught Leo and bundled him high into the air on their shoulders while Jurand planted his hands on his hips and rolled his eyes.

The rain had slackened off and the sun shone on polished armour, and sharpened blades, and smiling faces.

It was hard not to feel much better.

Guilt Is a Luxury

The snow had all melted and left the world cold and comfortless. The icy slop that stood for ground seeped into Rikke's boots and spattered up her sodden trousers. Cold dew dripped endlessly from the black branches, through her sopping hair, onto her soggy cloak and down her chafed back. The wet from above met the wet from below around her belt, which she'd been obliged to tighten on account of having hardly eaten anything in the three days since she killed a boy and watched her home burn.

At least it couldn't get any worse. Or so she told herself.

"Would be a fine thing to be on a road," she grumbled as she tried to tear her foot free of a tangle of clutching bramble and only succeeded in grazing herself worse.

Isern had an unnatural trick of finding only the dry parts of a bog to put her feet on. Rikke swore she could've danced across a pond on the lily pads and never got her feet wet. "Who else might be tiptoeing down the roads now, do we suppose?"

"Stour Nightfall's men," said Rikke, sulkily.

"Aye, and his uncle Scale Ironhand's, and his father Black Calder's. The thorns may scratch your downy-soft skin, but a lot shallower than their swords would."

Rikke cursed as the clutching mud near sucked her boot right off. "We could make for some high ground, at least."

Isern rubbed at the bridge of her nose like she never heard such folly. "Who else is having a high time on the high ground now, do you imagine?"

Rikke pushed her chagga pellet sourly from her top lip to her bottom. "Stour Nightfall's scouts."

"And Scale Ironhand's, and Black Calder's. And since they're there, swarming on the roads and the hills like lice on a log, where should we be?"

Rikke slapped an insect dead on the greasy back of her hand. "Down here in the valley bottom, with the brambles, and the mud, and the bloody shitty biters."

"It's almost like an unfriendly army swarming over your land is an inconvenience in all kinds o' ways. You're used to reckoning the world your playground. Beset by dangers now, girl. Time to act like it." Isern slipped on through the thicket as quick and silent as a snake, leaving Rikke to struggle after, pointlessly cursing.

She liked to think of herself as quite the rugged outdoorswoman, but in this company she was a towny oaf. Isern-i-Phail knew all the ways, that was the rumour. Even better'n her daddy had. Rikke had learned more from watching her the last couple of weeks than she had from that fool Union tutor in Ostenhorm in a year. How to build a shelter from ferns. How to set rabbit traps, even if they hadn't worked. How to reckon your course from the way the moss grew on the tree trunks. How to tell a man from an animal in the forest just by their footfalls.

Some folk said Isern was a witch, and no doubt she'd a witchy look and a witch's temper, but even she couldn't magic food out of rocks and bogwater at the arse-end of winter. Sadly.

As the sun sank behind the hills and left the valleys colder than ever, they wriggled like worms into a crack between boulders, pressed together for warmth, while outside the wind picked up and the slow drizzle turned to a stinging sleet.

"Reckon you could find a stick in this whole valley dry enough to take a flame?" whispered Rikke, rubbing her cold-fish hands together in her smoking breath then wedging them in her pits where, rather than getting warmed themselves, they only served to chill her whole body.

Isern hunched over the pack that held their dwindling supplies like a miser over his gold. "Even if I could, the smoke might bring hunters."

"Guess we'll stay cold, then," said Rikke in a small voice.

"That's the birth of spring for you, when your enemies have stole your daddy's hall so you've got no nice warm firepit to curl up beside."

Rikke knew what folk said about her, and maybe her head didn't have the right parts in the right places, but she'd always had a sharp eye for things. So in spite of the gloom and Isern's nimble fingers, Rikke saw the hillwoman only ate half as much as she handed over. She saw it, and was thankful for it, and wished she had the bones to insist on fair shares, but she was just so damn hungry. She stuffed her shred of dry meat down so quickly she swallowed her chagga pellet too without even noticing.

While she licked the wondrous taste of stale bread from her teeth, she found she was thinking of that lad she shot. That bit of dyed cloth around his scrawny neck, like mothers give sons to keep the cold off. That hurt, confused look he'd had. The same look she used to have, maybe, when the other children laughed at her twitching.

"I killed that lad." And she sniffed up a noseful of cold snot and spat it away.

"Aye." Isern trimmed off a chagga pellet and stuck it behind her lip. "You killed him all to bits, and robbed everyone who knew him, and cut all the good he might ever do out of the world."

Rikke blinked. "Well, you're the one split his skull!"

"That was a mercy. He'd have drowned on your arrow for sure."

Rikke found she was rubbing at her back, trying to get her thumb up to where that shaft had been, but she couldn't quite reach. No more than that boy had been able to. "Don't reckon he deserved it, really."

"Deserving won't make much difference to an arrow. The best defence against arrows is not a life nobly lived but to be the one who shoots them, d'you see?" Isern sat back against her, smelling of sweat and earth and chewed chagga. "They were your father's enemies. Our enemies. Wasn't as if there was any other choice."

"Not sure I even made a choice." Rikke picked at her sore fingernails as she picked at the memory, over and over. "Just fumbled the string. Just a stupid mistake."

"You could as well name it a happy accident."

Rikke hunched into her cold cloak and her bleak mood. "No justice, is there? For him or for me. Just a world that looks the other way and doesn't care a shit about either one of us."

"Why should it?"

"I killed that lad." Rikke's foot twitched, and the twitch became a quiver up her leg, and the quiver became a shiver all over. "However I turn it around... just doesn't feel right."

She felt Isern's hand firm on her shoulder, and was grateful for it. "If killing folk ever starts to feel *right*, you've a worse kind of problem. Guilt can sting, but you should be thankful for it."

"Thankful?"

"Guilt is a luxury reserved for those still breathing and with no unbearable pain, cold or hunger demanding all their fickle attention. Long as guilt's your big problem, girl..." Rikke saw the faint gleam of Isern's teeth in the gathering darkness. "Things can't be *that* bad."

She slapped Rikke's thigh and gave a witchy cackle, and maybe there was some magic in it after all because Rikke cracked her first smile in a day or two, and that made her feel just a bit better. Your best shield is a smile, her father always said.

"Why haven't you just left me behind?" she asked.

"I gave my word to your da."

"Aye, but everyone says you're the most untrustworthy bitch in the whole North."

"No one should know better than you what the things everyone says are worth. Truth is, I only care about keeping my word to folk I like. I seem untrustworthy because there are only seven of those outside the hills." She made a fist of her tattooed hand, trembling tight. "To those seven, I am a rock."

Rikke swallowed. "You like me, then?"

"Meh." Isern opened her blue fist and shook out the fingers with a clicking of knuckles. "About you, I remain to be convinced, but I like your father and I gave him my word. That I'd try to put an end to your fits and coax your Long Eye open and bring you back to him still breathing. The small matter of an invasion may have nudged him out of Uffrith, but the commitment still stands, far as I'm concerned, wherever Stour Nightfall's bastards might've driven him off to." Her eyes flickered to Rikke, cunning as a fox that sees the coop unguarded. "But I'll admit I've a selfish reason, too, which is a good thing for you, since selfish reasons are the only reasons you should trust."

"What reason?"

Isern opened her eyes very wide so they bulged from her filthy face. "Because I know there's a better North waiting. A North free of the grip of Scale Ironhand, and the one who pulls his strings, Black Calder, and the one who pulls *his* strings even. A North free for everyone to choose their own way." Isern leaned close in the darkness. "And your Long Eye will pick out our path to it."

Keeping Score

Sparks showered into the night, the heat a constant pressure on Savine's smiling face. Beyond the yawning doorway, straining bodies and straining machinery were rendered devilish by the glow of molten metal. Hammers clattered, chains rattled, steam hissed, labourers cursed. The music of money being made.

One-sixth of the Hill Street Foundry, after all, belonged to her.

One of the six great sheds was her property. Two of the twelve looming chimneys. One in every six of the new machines spinning inside, of the coals in the great heaps shovelled in the yard, of the hundreds of twinkling panes of glass that faced the street. Not to mention one-sixth part of the ever-increasing profits. A flood of silver to put His Majesty's mint to shame.

"Best not to loiter, my lady," murmured Zuri, fires gleaming in her eyes as she glanced about the darkened street.

She was right, as always. Most young ladies of Savine's acquaintance would have come over faint at the suggestion of visiting this part of Adua without a company of soldiers in attendance. But those who wish to occupy the heights of society must be willing to dredge the depths from time to time, when they see opportunities glitter in the filth.

"On we go," said Savine, boot heels squelching as she followed their link-boy's bobbing light into the maze of buildings. Narrow houses with whole families wedged into every room leaned together, a spider's web of flapping washing strung between, laden carts rumbling beneath and showering filth to the rooftops. Where whole blocks had not been cleared to make way for the new mills and manufactories, the crooked lanes reeked of coal smoke and woodsmoke, blocked drains and no drains at all. It was a borough heaving with humanity. Seething with industry. And, most importantly, boiling over with money to be made.

Savine was by no means the only one who saw it. It was payday, and impromptu merchants swarmed about the warehouses and forges, hoping to lighten the labourers' purses as they spilled out after work, selling small pleasures and meagre necessities. Selling themselves, if they could only find a buyer.

There were others hoping to lighten purses by more direct means. Grubby little cutpurses weaving through the crowds. Footpads lurking in the darkness of the alleys. Thugs slouching on the corners, keen to collect on behalf of the district's many moneylenders.

Risks, perhaps, and dangers, but Savine had always loved the thrill of a gamble, especially when the game was rigged in her favour. She had long ago learned that at least half of everything is presentation. Seem a victim, soon become one. Seem in charge, people fall over themselves to obey.

So she walked with a swagger, dressed in the dizzy height of fashion, lowering her eyes for no one. She walked painfully erect, although Zuri's earlier heaving on the laces of her corset gave her little choice. She walked as if it was *her* street—and indeed she did own five decaying houses further down, packed to their rotten rafters with Gurkish refugees paying twice the going rent.

Zuri was a great reassurance on one side, Savine's beautifully wrought short steel a great reassurance on the other. Many young ladies had been affecting swords since Finree dan Brock caused a sensation by wearing one to court. Savine found that nothing lent one confidence like a length of sharpened metal close to hand.

The link-boy had stopped at a particularly wretched building, holding his torch up to the peeling sign above its lintel.

"This really the place?" he asked.

Savine gathered her skirts so she could squat beside him and look in his dirt-smeared face. She wondered if he sponged the muck on as artfully as her maids did her powder, to arouse just the right amount of sympathy. Clean children need no charity, after all.

"This is the place. Our heartfelt thanks for your guidance." And Zuri slipped a coin into Savine's gloved hand so she could hold it out.

She was not at all above sentimental displays of generosity. The whole point of squeezing one's partners in private was so they could do the squeezing in public. Savine, meanwhile, could smile ever so sweetly, and toss coins to an urchin or two, and appear virtuous without the slightest damage to her bottom line. When it comes to virtue, after all, appearances are everything.

The boy stared at the silver as though it was some legendary beast he had heard of but never hoped to see. "For me?"

She knew that in her button and buckle manufactory in Holsthorm, smaller and probably dirtier children were paid a fraction as much for a long day's hard labour. The manager insisted little fingers were best suited to little tasks, and cost only little wages, too. But Holsthorm was far away, and things in the distance seem very small. Even the sufferings of children.

"For you." She did not go as far as ruffling his hair, of course. Who knew what might be living in it?

"Such a nice boy," said Zuri, watching him hurry away into the gloom with the coin in one fist and his sputtering torch in the other.

"They all are," said Savine. "When you have something they want."

"None more blessed, my scripture-teacher once declared, than those who light the way for others."

"Was that the one who fathered a child on one of his other pupils?"

"That's him." Zuri's black brows thoughtfully rose. "So much for spiritual instruction."

The grimy ale-hall fell silent as Savine swept in, as if some exotic jungle beast had wandered off the street.

Zuri whipped out a cloth and wiped down a vacant section of the counter, then, as Savine sat, she slipped out the pin and whisked away her hat without disturbing a hair. She kept it close to her chest, which was prudent. Savine's hat was probably worth more than this entire building, including the clientele. At a brief assay, they only reduced its value.

"Well, well." The man behind the counter was easing forwards, wiping his hands on his stained apron and giving Savine a lingering look up and down. "I'm tempted to say this is no place for a lady like you."

"We've only just met. You really have no idea what kind of lady I am. Why, you could be taking your life in your hands just talking to me."

"Reckon I'm brave enough if you are." By his squinty grin, he had somehow convinced himself he held some appeal to the fairer sex. "What's your name?"

She planted one elbow on the stretch of counter Zuri had wiped so she could lean closer and draw out both syllables. "Savine."

"That's a lovely name."

"Oh, if you enjoy the tip, you'll go mad for the whole thing."

"That so?" he purred at her. "How does it go?"

"Savine...dan..." And she leaned even closer to deliver the punchline. "Glokta."

If a name had been a knife and she had cut his throat with hers, the blood could not have drained more quickly from his face. He gave a strangled cough, took a step back and nearly fell over one of his own barrels.

"Lady Savine." Majir was coming from an upstairs office, wooden steps creaking under her considerable weight. "What an honour."

"Isn't it, though? Your man and I were just getting acquainted."

Majir glanced towards the ghost-faced barman. "Would you like him to apologise?"

"For what? Not being as brave as he claimed? If we executed men for that, I swear there wouldn't be a dozen left alive in the Union, eh, Zuri?"

Zuri clasped Savine's hat sadly to her breast. "Heroes are in lamentably short supply."

Majir cleared her throat. "If I'd known you were coming all the way down here yourself—"

"If I spent all my time shut up with Mother, we would *kill* each other," said Savine. "And I feel that business should be conducted, whenever possible, in person. Otherwise one's partners can convince themselves that one's eyes are not on the details. My eyes are always on the details, Majir."

In low company, Savine could be low. These were bullies, so they needed to be bullied. It was the language they understood. Majir's thick neck shifted as she swallowed. "Who would dare doubt it?" And she laid a flat leather pouch on the counter.

"It's all there?"

"A promissory note from the banking house of Valint and Balk."

"Really?" Valint and Balk had a dark reputation, even for a bank. Savine's father had often warned her never to deal with them, because once you owe Valint and Balk, the debt is never done. But a promissory note was just money, and money can never be a bad thing. She tossed the pouch to Zuri, who peered inside and gave the smallest nod. "It's coming to something when even the bandits are using the bank."

Majir mildly raised one brow. "Honest women have the law to protect them. Bandits must take more care with their earnings."

"You're a darling." Savine reached across the counter to pinch her fat cheek and give it an affectionate tug. "Thank you, Zuri. You're a darling, too." Her companion was already sliding the hatpin back into position.

"If you don't mind," said Majir, "I'll have a few boys follow you out of the neighbourhood. I could never forgive myself if something were to happen to you."

"Oh, come now. If something happened to me, your own forgiveness would be the least of your problems."

"True." Majir watched her turn away, big fists pressed into the counter. "Do pass my regards to your father."

Savine laughed. "Let's not demean ourselves by pretending my father gives a dry *fuck* for your regards." And she blew a kiss at the terrified barman on her way out.

Dietam dan Kort, famed architect, was a man who gave every appearance of being in control. His desk, scattered with maps, surveys and draughtsman's drawings, was certainly a wonder of engineering. Savine had moved among the most powerful men in the realm and still doubted she had ever seen a larger. It filled his office so completely, there was only the narrowest of passages around the edges to reach his chair. He must have needed help to squeeze himself through every morning. She wondered if she should recommend her corset-maker.

"Lady Savine," he intoned. "What an honour."

"Isn't it, though?" She made him lean dangerously far across the desk in order to kiss her hand. Savine studied his, meanwhile, big and broad with fingers scarred from hard work. A self-made man. His greying hair was painstakingly scraped across a pate quite obviously bald. A proud and a vain man. She noticed a slight fraying of the cuffs on his once-splendid coat. A man in straitened circumstances, intent on appearing otherwise.

"To what do I owe the pleasure of your visit?" he asked.

She settled herself opposite while Zuri whisked off her hat. A lady of taste should appear to make no effort. The right things simply happen around her. "The opportunity for investment you mentioned at our last meeting," she said.

Kort brightened considerably. "You have come to discuss it?"

"I have come to do it."

Zuri placed Majir's pouch on the desk as delicately as if it had been deposited by a summer breeze. It looked very small on that immense expanse of green leather. But that was the magic of banks. They could render the priceless tiny, the immense worthless.

The slightest sheen of sweat had sprung from Kort's forehead. "It's all there?"

"A promissory note from Valint and Balk. I hope that will suffice?"

"Of course!" He was unable to disguise a note of eager greed as he reached across the desk. "I believe we agreed a twentieth share—"

Savine placed one fingertip on the corner of the pouch. "You mentioned a twentieth. I remained silent."

His hand froze. "Then...?"

"A fifth."

There was a pause. While he decided how outraged he could afford to be, and Savine decided how little to appear to care.

"A fifth?" His already ruddy face turned positively volcanic. "My first investors received half as much for twice the money! I only own a fifth myself, and I near as damn it dug the thing with my own hands! A *fifth*? Have you lost all *reason*?"

To Savine, there was no more enticing invitation than a door slammed in her face. "One man's mad is another's perceptive," she said, her smile not even dented. "Your canal takes a clever route and your bridge is a wonder. Truly, I congratulate you on it. In a few years, they'll be building everything from iron. But it isn't finished and you've run out of money."

"I have two months' reserves!"

"You have two weeks' at best."

"Then I have two weeks to find a more reasonable investor!"

"You have two hours." Savine sent her brows up very high. "I am visiting with Tilde dan Rucksted tonight."

"Who?"

"Tilde, the young wife of Lord Marshal Rucksted. A wonderfully sweet-tempered girl, but *phew*, what a gossip!" And she glanced up for confirmation.

"It pains me to speak ill of one of God's creatures," admitted Zuri, with a pious fluttering of her long lashes, "but she is an abysmal blabbermouth."

"When I confide, in strictest confidence, that you are short of investment, lacking the necessary permissions and troubled by restless workmen, it will be all over town before sunup."

"Sure as printing it in a pamphlet," said Zuri, sadly.

"Good luck finding an investor then, reasonable or otherwise."

It had only taken a moment for Kort to go from bright red to deathly pale, and Savine burst out laughing. "Don't be silly, I won't do that!" She stopped laughing. "Because you are going to sign one-fifth of your enterprise over to me. Now. Then I can confide in Tilde that I just made the investment of a lifetime, and she won't be able to resist investing herself. She's not only loose-lipped, you see, but tight-fisted, too."

"Greed is a quality the priests abhor." Zuri sighed. "Especially the rich ones."

"But so widespread these days," lamented Savine. "If Lady Rucksted sees some gain in it, I daresay she can persuade her husband to make a breach in Casamir's Wall so you can extend your canal into the Three Farms." And Savine could sell the worthless slum buildings she had bought on the canal's likely route back to herself at an immense profit. "The marshal's notoriously stubborn for most of us but to his wife he's a pussycat. You know how it is with old men and their young brides."

Kort was trapped halfway between anger and ambition. Savine rather liked him there. Most animals, after all, look better in a cage. "Extend my canal...into the Three Farms?"

"The first to do so." Where it could service Savine's three textile mills and the Hill Street Foundry, incidentally, and sharply raise their productivity. "I daresay—for a friend—I could even arrange a visit of His Majesty's Inquisitors to a labour meeting. I imagine your troublesome workers will be far more pliable after a few stern examples are made."

"Stern examples," threw in Zuri, "are something the priests are *always* in favour of."

Kort was almost drooling. Savine thought they had better stop before he needed a change of trousers.

"A tenth part," he offered, in a voice rather hoarse.

"Pffft." Savine stood and Zuri eased forward with her hat, spinning the pin in her long fingers with the delicacy of a magician. "You're an architect to rival Kanedias himself, but you're entirely lost in the maze of Aduan society. You need a guide, and I'm the best there is. Be a darling and give the fifth before I take a quarter. You know I'd be a bargain at a third."

Kort sagged, his chin settling into the roll of fat beneath it, his eyes fixed resentfully upon her. Clearly, he was not a man who liked to lose. But where would be the fun in beating men who did?

"Very well. One-fifth."

"A notary from the firm of Temple and Kahdia is already drawing up the papers. He will be in touch." She turned towards the door.

"They warned me," Kort grunted as he slid Valint and Balk's note from the pouch. "That you care about nothing but money."

"Why, what a pompous crowd *they* are. Beyond a point I passed long ago, I don't even care about money." Savine flicked the brim of her hat in farewell. "But how else is one to keep score?"

A Little Public Hanging

"I hate bloody hangings," said Orso.

One of the whores tittered as if he'd cracked quite the joke. It was the falsest laugh he had ever heard, and when it came to false laughter, he was quite the connoisseur. Everyone was false in his presence, and he the worst actor of all.

"I guess you could stop it," said Hildi. "If you wanted."

Orso frowned up at her, perched on the wall with her legs crossed and her chin propped on one palm.

"Well...I suppose..." Strange how the idea had never occurred to him before. He pictured himself springing onto the scaffold, insisting these poor people be pardoned, ushering them back to their miserable lives to tearful thanks and rapturous applause. Then he sighed. "But...one really shouldn't interfere with the workings of the judiciary."

Lies, like everything that left his mouth, engineered to make him appear just a touch less detestable. He wondered who he was trying to fool. Hildi undoubtedly saw straight through it. The truth was, when it came to stopping this, as with so much else, he simply couldn't be arsed. He took another pinch of pearl dust, his heavy snorts ringing out as the Inquisitor in charge stepped to the front of the scaffold and the crowd fell breathlessly silent.

"These three...*people*," and the Inquisitor swept an arm towards the chained convicts, each held under the armpit by a hooded executioner, "are members of the outlawed group known as the Breakers, convicted of High Treason against the Crown!"

"Treason!" someone screeched, then dissolved into coughing. It was a still day, so a bad one for the vapours. Not that there were many good days for the vapours lately, what with the new chimneys sprouting up all over Adua. People at the very back must have been struggling to see the scaffold through the murk.

"They have been found guilty of setting fires and breaking machinery, of incitement to riot and sheltering fugitives from the king's justice! Have you anything to say?"

The first prisoner, a heavyset fellow with a beard, evidently did. "We're faithful subjects of His Majesty!" he bellowed in a hero's voice, all manly bass and quivering passion. "All we want is an honest wage for honest work!"

"I'd sooner take a dishonest wage for no work at all," grunted Tunny.

Yolk burst out laughing while swigging from his bottle and sprayed a reeking mist of spirits, which settled over the wig of a well-dressed old lady just in front.

A man with spectacular grey side whiskers, presumably her husband, clearly felt they were not treating the occasion with appropriate gravity. "You people are a damn disgrace!" he snapped, rounding on them in a fury.

"That so?" Tunny pushed his tongue into his grizzled cheek. "Hear that, Orso? You're a damn disgrace."

"Orso?" muttered the man. "Not—"

"Yes." Tunny showed his yellow grin and Orso winced. He hated it when Tunny used him to bully people. Almost as much as he hated hangings. But somehow he could never bring himself to stop either one.

The side-whisker enthusiast had turned pale as a freshly laundered sheet, something Orso had not seen in some time. "Your Highness, I had no *idea*. Please accept my—"

"No need." Orso waved a lazy hand, wine-stained lace cuff flapping, and took another pinch of pearl dust. "I am a damn disgrace. Notoriously so." He gave the man a reassuring pat on the shoulder, realised he had smeared dust all over his coat and tried ineffectually to brush it off. If Orso excelled at anything, after all, it was being ineffectual. "Please don't concern yourself over my feelings. I don't have any." Or so he often said. The truth was he sometimes felt he had too many. He was dragged so violently in a dozen different directions that he could not move at all.

He took one more pinch for good measure. Peering down through watering eyes, he noticed the box was getting dangerously empty.

"Hildi!" he muttered, waving it at her. "Empty."

She sprang down from the wall and drew herself up to her full height. Which put her about on a level with his ribs. "Again? Who shall I go to?"

"Majir?"

"Y'owe Majir a hundred and fifty-one marks. Said she can't give you more credit."

"Spizeria, then?"

"Y'owe him three hundred and six. Same story."

"How the hell did that happen?"

Hildi gave Tunny, Yolk and the whores a significant glance. "You want me to answer that?"

Orso racked his brains to think of someone else, then gave up. If he excelled at anything, after all, it was giving up. "For pity's sake, Hildi, everyone knows I'm good for it. I'll be coming into a *considerable* legacy one of these days." No less than the Union, and everything in it, and all its unliftable weight of care, and impossible responsibility, and crushing expectation. He grimaced and tossed her the box.

"You owe *me* nine marks," she muttered.

"Shoo!" Orso tried to wave her away, got his little finger painfully tangled in his cuff and had to rip it free. "Just get it done!"

She gave a long-suffering sigh, jammed that ancient soldier's cap down over her blonde curls and stepped off into the crowd.

"She's a funny little thing, your errand girl," warbled one of the whores, dragging too heavily on his arm.

"She's my valet," said Orso, frowning, "and she's a fucking treasure."

On the scaffold, meanwhile, the bearded man was bellowing out the Breakers' manifesto with ever more emotion. The noise from the crowd was growing but, much to the upset of the Inquisitor, he was starting to strike a chord. Calls of support were breaking through the mockery.

"No more machines!" the bearded man roared, veins bulging in his thick neck. "No more seizure of common land!"

He seemed a useful fellow. More useful than Orso, certainly. "What a bloody waste," he muttered.

"The Open Council shouldn't just be for the nobles! Every man should have a voice—"

"Enough!" snarled the Inquisitor, waving one of the executioners forward. The prisoner kept trying to speak as the noose was pulled tight, but his words were drowned by the rising anger of the crowd.

It was a riddle. This man, born with no advantages, believed in something so much he was willing to die for it. Orso, born with everything, could scarcely make himself get out of bed of a morning. Or, indeed, an afternoon.

"Bed is warm, though," he murmured.

"Certainly is, Your Highness," cooed the other whore in his ear. Her perfume was so sickeningly strong, it was a wonder pigeons didn't drop stunned from the sky around her.

The Inquisitor gave a nod.

31

Rather than needing strong men or horses to haul up the condemned, some enterprising fellow had devised a system whereby prisoners could be dropped through the scaffold floor at a touch upon a lever. There was an invention to make everything more efficient these days, after all. Why would killing people be an exception?

A strange sound rose from the crowd as the rope snapped taut. Part cheer of joy, part hoot of derision, part groan of discomfort, but mostly gasps of relief. Relief that it wasn't them at the end of the rope.

"Damn it," muttered Orso, working a finger into his collar. There was nothing even faintly satisfying in this. Even if these people really were enemies of the state, they hardly looked like very dangerous ones.

The next in line to receive the king's justice was a girl who might not yet have been sixteen. Her eyes, wide in bruised sockets, flickered from the open trapdoor to the Inquisitor as he stepped towards her. "Have you anything to say?"

She appeared hardly to comprehend. Orso found himself wishing the vapours were thicker, and that he could not see her face at all.

"Please," said the man beside her. There were tears streaking his dirty cheeks. "Take me but, please—"

"Shut him up," snapped the Inquisitor, not at all enjoying his part in this grisly pantomime. A few desultory vegetables were being tossed at the scaffold, but whether they were intended for the accused or those carrying out the sentence, it was hard to say. There was a dark stain spreading down the front of the girl's dress.

"Yuck," said Yolk. "She's pissed herself."

Orso frowned sideways. "*That's* what disgusts you?"

"I've seen you piss yourself often enough," sneered Tunny at Yolk, and the whores spilled more false laughter. The side whiskers of the man in front twitched as he ground his teeth.

Orso gritted his as he looked to the scaffold. Hildi had been right, he could stop this. If not him, who? If not now, when?

There was some problem with the girl's noose, the Inquisitor hissing furiously at one of the executioners as he dragged his hood up over his sweaty face to peer at the knots.

Orso was just about to step forward. Was just about to roar, *Stop!*

But circumstances always conspired to stop him doing the right thing. He heard a soft, high voice in his ear. "Your Highness."

Orso turned to see the broad, flat and decidedly unwelcome face of Bremer dan Gorst at his shoulder.

"Gorst, you tiresome bastard." The insult caused not the slightest re-action. Nothing ever did. "How did you track me down?"

"Just followed the stench of disgrace," said Tunny.

"It is quite powerful hereabouts." Orso reached for the pearl dust and realised it was gone, snatched Yolk's bottle from his hand instead and took a swig.

"The queen has sent for you," piped Gorst.

Orso blew out through his pursed lips to make a long farting sound. "Hasn't she better things to do?"

Yolk chuckled. "What could matter more to a mother than the welfare of her eldest son?"

Gorst's eyes slid across to him, and stuck there. All he did was look, but it was enough to make Yolk's laughter sputter into nervous silence. He might sound a clown, but His Majesty's First Guard was not a man you trifled with.

"Any chance I can bring the whores with me?" asked Orso. "I've paid for the whole day." It was his turn to face Gorst's fish-eyed stare. He sighed. "Would you conduct the ladies to their residence, Tunny?"

"Oh, I'll conduct a symphony with 'em, Your Highness." More false giggling.

Orso turned away without much reluctance. He hated bloody hangings, but the girls had wanted to go and he hated disappointing people, too. As a result of which, it seemed, he disappointed everyone. At his back, there was that strange sound between gasp and cheer as the next trapdoor dropped open.

Orso tossed his hat onto the bald head of a bust of Bayaz, congratulating himself that it came to rest on the legendary wizard at a pleasingly rakish angle.

The tapping of his boot heels echoed in the vast spaces of the salon as he crossed a sea of gleaming tiles to the tiny island of furniture in its centre. The High Queen of the Union sat fearsomely erect there, dripping with diamonds, growing out of the chaise like a spectacular orchid from a gilded pot. It hardly needed to be said that he'd known her his whole life, but the sheer regality of the woman still took him aback every time.

"Mother," he said, in Styrian. Using the tongue of the country they actually ruled only aggravated her, and he knew from long experience that aggravating Queen Terez was never, ever worth it. "I was just on my way to visit when Gorst found me."

"You must take me for a rare kind of fool," she said, angling her face towards him.

"No, no." He bent to brush one heavily powdered cheek with his lips. "Just the usual kind."

"Really, Orso, your accent has become appalling."

"Well, now that Styria is almost entirely controlled by our enemies, I get so little chance to practice."

She plucked a minute tuft of fluff from his jacket. "Are you intoxicated?"

"Can't think why I would be." Orso picked up the decanter with a flourish and poured himself a glass. "I've snorted just the right amount of pearl dust to even out the husk I smoked this morning." He rubbed at his nose, which was still pleasantly numb, then raised his glass in salute. "Bottle or two to smooth off the rough edges and it should be straight sailing till lunch."

The royal bosom, constrained by corsetry that was a feat of engineering to rival any wonder of the new age, inflated majestically as the queen sighed. "People expect a certain amount of indolence in a Crown Prince. It was quite winning when you were seventeen. At twenty-two, it began to become tiresome. At twenty-seven, it looks positively desperate."

"You have no idea, Mother." Orso dropped into a chair so savagely uncomfortable it was like being punched in the arse. "I have long been thoroughly ashamed of myself."

"You could try doing something to be proud of. Have you considered that?"

"I've spent whole days considering it." He frowned discerningly through the wine as he held it up to the light from the giant windows. "But *doing* it really feels like such a lot of effort."

"Frankly, your father could use your support. He is a weak man, Orso."

"So you never tire of telling him."

"And these are difficult times. The last war did...not end well."

"It ended pretty well if you're King Jappo of Styria."

His mother pronounced each word with icy precision. "Which you... are...*not*."

"Sadly, for all concerned."

"You are King Jappo's mortal enemy and the rightful heir to all he and the thrice-damned Snake of Talins have stolen, and it is high time you took your position seriously! We have enemies everywhere. Inside our borders, too."

"I am aware. I just attended the hanging of three of them. Two peasants and a girl of fifteen. She pissed herself. I've never felt prouder."

34

"Then I trust you come to me in a receptive mood." Orso's mother gave two sharp claps and Lord Chamberlain Hoff strutted in. With waistcoat bulging around his belly and legs stick-like in tight breeches, he looked like nothing so much as a prize rooster jealously patrolling the farmyard.

"Your *Majesty*." He bowed so low to the queen, he virtually buffed the tiles with his nose. "Your *Highness*." He bowed just as low to Orso but in a manner that somehow expressed boundless contempt. Or perhaps Orso only saw his own contempt for himself reflected in that obsequious smile. "I have positively *scoured* the entire Circle of the World for the most eligible candidates. *Dare* one suggest that the future High Queen of the Union waits among them?"

"Oh, good grief." Orso let his head drop back, staring up towards the beautifully painted ceiling of the peoples of the world kneeling before a golden sun. "The parade *again*?"

"Ensuring the succession is not a joke," pronounced his mother.

"Not a funny one, anyway."

"Don't be facetious, Orso. Your sisters both did their dynastic duty. Do you suppose Cathil wanted to move to Starikland?"

"She's an inspiration."

"Do you think Carlot wanted to marry the Chancellor of Sipani?"

Actually, she had been delighted by the idea, but Orso's mother loved to imagine everyone sacrificing all on the altar of duty, the way she was always telling them she had. "Of course not, Mother."

By then, two footmen were easing an enormous painting into the room, straining not to catch the frame in the doorway. A pale girl with an absurdly long neck smiled winsomely from the canvas.

"Lady Sithrin dan Harnveld," announced the lord chamberlain.

Orso sank lower into his chair. "Do I really want a wife who measures the distance from her chin to her tits in miles?"

"Artistic licence, Your Highness," explained Hoff.

"Call it art, you can get away with anything."

"She is quite presentable in the flesh," said the queen. "And her family can be traced back to the time of Harod the Great."

"A true *thoroughbred*," interjected the lord chamberlain.

"She's stupid as a horse, all right," said Orso. "And you can't have an idiot for both king *and* queen."

"Next," grated out Orso's mother, a second pair of footmen nearly colliding with the first as they carted in a painting of a slyly smirking Styrian.

"The Countess Istarine of Affoia is a proven politician, and would bring us valuable allies in Styria."

35

"From the looks of her, she's more likely to bring me a dose of the cock-rot."

"I had imagined you would be immune from constant exposure," observed the queen, waving the portrait away with an exquisite flourish of her fingers.

"Such a shame I never see you dance any more, Mother." She danced superbly. Sometimes she even seemed to enjoy it.

"Your father is an absolute oaf of a partner."

Orso gave a sad smile. "He does his best."

"This is Messela Sivirine Sistus," proclaimed the lord chamberlain, "younger daughter of the Emperor Dantus Goltus—"

"He doesn't even merit the older daughter?" demanded the queen, before Orso had the chance to raise his own objections. "I think *not*."

And so it went, as Orso marked the turning of morning into afternoon by the steadily decreasing level of wine in the decanter, and dismissed the flower of womanhood, one by one.

"How could I abide a wife taller than me?"

"She's a worse drunk than I am."

"At least we know she's fertile, she's borne two bastards that I know about."

"Is that a nose on her face or a prick?"

He almost wished he was back at the hanging. That, he could theoretic-ally have stopped. Over his mother, he was utterly powerless. His only chance was to wait her out. There were a finite number of women in the Circle of the World, after all.

Eventually, the last portrait was manhandled from the room and the lord chamberlain was left wringing his hands. "Your *Majesty*, Your *Highness*, I regret—"

"Finished?" asked Orso. "No portrait of Savine dan Glokta lurking in the hallway?"

Even at this distance, he felt the chill of the queen's displeasure. "For pity's sake, her mother is a low-born boor, and a drunk to boot."

"But an absolute scream at parties, and whatever you say for Lady Ardee, Arch Lector Glokta has the people's respect. Or at any rate their abject terror."

"A crippled worm," spat the queen. "A torturer!"

"But our torturer, eh, Mother? *Our* torturer. And I understand his daughter has made herself quite spectacularly rich."

"Money made through *trade*, and *dealings*, and *investments*." The queen spat the words as though they were criminal enterprises. For all Orso knew, Savine's dealings *were* criminal enterprises. He wouldn't at all have put it past her.

"Oh, come now, money shamefully made from trade fills the same holes in the treasury as the kind nobly wrung from the misery of the peasantry."

"She is too old! You are too old, and she is even older than you are."

"But she has impeccable manners and is still quite the celebrated beauty." He waved a loose hand towards the doorway. "She'd make a prettier portrait than any of those piglets, and the painter wouldn't even have to lie. Queen Savine sounds rather well." He gave a chuckle. "It even rhymes."

His mother was an icicle of fury. "Do you do this just to annoy me?"

"Not *just* to annoy you."

"Promise me you will have nothing to do with that ambitious worm of a woman."

"With Savine dan Glokta?" Orso sat back with a bemused expression. "Her mother's a commoner, her father's a torturer and she made her money from business." He shook the last drops from the decanter into his glass. "Quite apart from which, really, she's far too bloody *old*."

"Oh," he gasped. "Oh! Oh *fuck*!"

He arched his back, clutched desperately at the edge of the desk, kicked a pot of pens onto the floor, smacked his head against the wall and sent a little shower of plaster across his shoulders. He tried desperately to squirm away, but she had him by the balls. Quite literally.

He crushed his face up, nearly swallowed his tongue, coughed and hissed one more desperate, "Fuck!" through gritted teeth, then sagged back with a whimper, kicked and sagged again, legs shuddering weakly with aching after-spasms.

"Fuck," he breathed.

Savine looked around, lips pursed, then took Orso's half-full wine glass and spat into it. Even under those circumstances, he noticed, she held it by the stem in the most elegant manner. She scraped her tongue against her front teeth, spat again and set the glass down on the desk next to hers.

Orso watched his seed float around in the wine. "That...is somewhat disgusting."

"Please." Savine rinsed her mouth out from the other glass. "You only have to look at it."

"Such cavalier disrespect. One day, madam, I shall be your king!"

"And your queen will no doubt spit your come into a golden box to be

37

shared out on holidays for the public good. My congratulations to you both, Your Highness."

He gave vent to a silly giggle. "Why does someone as altogether perfect as you waste her energy on a dolt like me?"

She pushed out her lips discerningly, as though considering the mystery, and for a strange, stupid moment he almost asked her. The words tickled at his lips. There was no one better suited to him. She had all the qualities he wished he had. So sharp. So disciplined. So decisive. Besides, it would have been worth it just for the look on his mother's face. He almost asked her.

But circumstances always conspired to stop him doing the right thing.

"I can only think of one reason," she said, hitching her skirts up and wriggling onto the desk beside him.

His sweaty arse juddered against the leather as he slid down onto still-wobbly legs, trousers flopping about his ankles. He flipped the box open and sprinkled some pearl dust onto the back of his hand, sniffed half himself then offered her the rest.

"Let it never be said I think only of myself," he said as she covered one nostril to snort it up. She blinked at the ceiling for a moment, eyelids fluttering, as if she might sneeze. Then she dropped back on her elbows, working her hips towards him.

"Get to it, then."

"You really are in no mood for romance today, are you?"

She slid her fingers into his hair, then twisted his head somewhat painfully down between her legs. "*My* time is valuable."

"The naked gall." Orso gave a sigh as he hooked her leg over his shoulder, sliding his hand down the bare skin, hearing her gasp, feeling her shudder. He kissed gently at her shin, at her knee, at her thigh. "Is there no end to the demands of one's subjects?"

The Breakers

"What sort of a name is Vick, anyway?"

"Short for Victarine."

"*Very* fucking fancy," sneered Grise. Vick hadn't known her long, but she was already getting tired of her. "Daresay you've got a fucking 'dan' in your name, too, eh, your ladyship?"

She was joking. But things had to get pretty funny before Vick started laughing, and this didn't qualify.

She held Grise's eye. "I did have a 'dan' in my name, once. My father was Master of the Royal Mints. Had a great big apartment in the Agriont." And Vick nodded towards her best idea of where the fortress was, though the points of the compass were hard to tell apart in a mouldy cellar. "Right next to the palace. Big enough for a statue of Harod the Great in the hall. Life *fucking* size."

Grise had quite the frown on her round face now, light flickering across it as boots, and hoofs, and cartwheels clattered past the little windows high up near the ceiling. "You grew up in the Agriont?"

"You weren't listening. My father had an apartment there. But when I was eight years old, he trod on the wrong toes and the Inquisition took him. I hear it was Old Sticks himself who asked the questions."

That changed the atmosphere, Grise flinching a little and Tallow blinking into the shadows as if the Arch Lector himself might be loitering behind the dusty shelves with a dozen Practicals.

"My father was innocent. Of what they accused him of, anyway. But once Old Sticks got started..." Vick slapped the table with a bang, Tallow jumping so high he nearly hit the ceiling. "He leaked confessions like a broken drain. High Treason. They sent him to Angland. To the camps right up North." Vick didn't feel much like it, but she grinned. "And no one likes to split up a happy family. So they sent my ma with him. My ma, and my brother, and my sisters, and me. The camps, Grise. *That's* where I grew up. So don't question my commitment to the cause. Not ever."

You could hear the ill squelch as Tallow swallowed. "What are the camps like?"

"You get by."

Oh, the filth, pain, hunger, death, injustice and betrayal that she buried in that phrase. The black chill of the mines, the searing glow of the furnaces, the gnashing rage and sobbing desperation, the bodies in the snow. Vick forced her face to stay blank, pressed down the past like you might press down the lid on a box full of maggots.

"You get by," she said, firmer. When you tell a lie, you have to sound like you believe it. Goes double for the ones you tell yourself.

Grise spun around as the door squealed open, but it was only Sibalt come at last, Moor big and dour at his shoulder. He planted his fists on the table and took a heavy breath, that noble face of his sadly sagging.

"What is it?" asked Tallow, in a tiny voice.

"They hanged Reed," said Sibalt. "They hanged Cudber. They hanged his daughter."

Grise stared at him. "She was fifteen."

"What for?" asked Tallow.

"Just for talking." Sibalt put his hand on the boy's thin shoulder and gave it a squeeze. "Just for organising. Just for trying to get workers to stand together and speak with one voice. That's treason now."

"Then the time for talk's fucking past!" snarled Grise.

Vick was angry as anyone. But she'd learned in the camps that every feeling is a weakness. You have to lock your hurt away, and think about what comes next. "Who did they know about?" she asked.

"That all you can think of?" Grise stuck her fat fist in Vick's face and shook it. "Whether you're fucking *safe*?"

Vick looked from her fist to her eye. "Whatever names they knew, they'll have given up."

"Not Cudber. He wouldn't."

"Not even when they put the irons to his daughter?" Grise had nothing to say to that, shock gradually wiping the anger off her face. "Whatever names they knew, they'll have given up. Lots of other names, too, 'cause once you run out of truth, you start spilling lies."

Moor shook his big lump of a head. "Not Reed."

"Yes, Reed, Cudber, his daughter, yes, you or me or anyone. The Inquisition'll come for whoever they knew about, and soon. So who did they know about?"

"Just me." Sibalt looked at her calm and level. "I made sure of it."

"Then you have to get out of Adua. For your sake, for the sake of the cause."

"Who the fuck are you to give orders?" Grise leaned down over her with a stabbing finger. "You're newest here!"

"So maybe I'm thinking most clearly." Vick let her hand lie on her belt buckle where her brass knuckles were hidden. She didn't rate Grise much of a threat, for all her bulk. People who shout a lot tend to take a while working up to more. But Vick was ready to put her down if she had to. And when Vick put someone down, she made sure they went down hard.

Lucky for Grise, Sibalt laid a gentle hand on her shoulder and eased her back. "Vick's right. I have to get out of Adua. Just as soon as we strike our blow." And Moor slid out a dirty paper and unrolled it across the table. A map of the city. Sibalt tapped a spot in the Three Farms. Not far from where they'd started building that new canal. "The Hill Street Foundry."

"Though Hill Street's gone," said Moor, in that plodding way he had, "since they pulled it down to build the Foundry."

"They're fitting new engines there," said Sibalt.

Tallow nodded. "I passed 'em on the way. Engines that'll put two hundred men and women out of work, I hear."

"And what?" muttered Vick, frowning. "We're going to break 'em?"

"We're going to blow the lot to hell," said Grise. "With Gurkish Fire."

Vick blinked at her. "How much have you got?"

"Three barrels," said Sibalt. "That be enough, you think?"

"In the right places, maybe. You know how to use it?"

"Not really." Sibalt grinned at her. "But you do. Used it in the mines, didn't you? In Angland."

"I did." Vick narrowed her eyes at him. "Where did you get it?"

"What do you care?" snapped Grise.

"I care that your source is reliable. I care that it's going to work. I care that it's not going to pop too early and shower bits of us all over the Three Farms."

"Well, you can stop worrying, 'cause it comes straight from Valbeck," said Grise, smug as a king's tailor. "Straight from the Weaver himself—"

"Shush," hissed Sibalt. "Best if no one knows more than they have to. Don't worry, the powder's good."

Grise slapped her fist into her palm. "A blow for the common man, eh, brothers?"

"Aye," said Moor, slowly nodding his big head. "We'll strike a spark."

"And the spark'll start a fire," said Sibalt.

Vick sat forward. "If we do this, people get hurt. People get killed."

"Only those that deserve it," said Grise.

"Once the killing starts, it rarely sticks to those who deserve it."

"You scared?"

"If you're not scared, you're mad or stupid, and there's no place for either on a task like this. We need to plan every detail."

"I got a job there labouring," said Moor. "I can map it out."

"Good," said Vick. "More plans mean fewer risks."

Grise sneered her disgust. "All you ever fucking talk about is the risks!"

"Someone needs to. This has to be something we choose, not something we blunder into 'cause we're sore and can't think of anything better to do with ourselves." She looked around those four faces, strange in the flickering light of the cellar. "This is what you all want, is it?"

"It's what I fucking want," said Grise.

"It's what I want," said Sibalt.

"Aye," rumbled Moor.

She looked at Tallow last. He couldn't be older than fifteen himself, and might only have had three good meals in that whole stretch. Reminded her of her brother, a little. Those skinny wrists sticking from frayed sleeves just a touch too short. Trying to put a hard face on but beaming fears and doubts out like a lighthouse through those big damp eyes.

"There's a Great Change coming," he said, finally. "That's what I want."

Vick smiled a grim smile. "Well, if I learned one thing in the camps, it's that talking isn't enough." She realised she'd closed her fingers to make a fist. "You want a thing, you have to fight for it."

She stayed straddling him for a while afterwards, his chest pressed against hers with each snatched breath. Kissing at his lip. Biting at it. Then with a grunt, she slid off him, rolled onto her side next to him on the narrow bed, dragging the blankets up over her bare shoulder. It felt chill now they were done, frost showing in the smudges of lamplight at the corners of the little window.

They both lay silent, he staring at the ceiling, she staring at him. Outside the carts clattered by, and the traders offered their wares, and that drunk on the corner roared his meaningless pain and fury at nothing and no one. At everything and everyone.

Finally, he turned towards her. "Sorry I couldn't step in with Grise—"

"I can look after myself."

Sibalt snorted. "No one better. I'm not sorry 'cause I think you need my help. I'm sorry I can't give it. Better if they don't know we're..." He slipped his hand up onto her ribs, rubbing at that old burn on her side with his thumb, trying to dig up the right word for what they were. "Together."

"In here, we're together." She jerked her head towards the warped door in the warped frame. "Out there..." Out there, everyone stood on their own.

He frowned at the little gap of coarse sheet between them as if it was a great divide that could never be crossed. "Sorry I can't tell you where the Gurkish Fire comes from."

"Best if no one knows more than they have to."

"It'll work."

"I believe you," she said. "I trust you." Vick trusted no one. She'd learned that in the camps, along with how to lie. Learned to lie so well, she could take one tiny sliver of truth and beat it out, like the goldsmiths beating a nugget of gold into leaf, till it could cover a whole field of lies. Sibalt didn't doubt her for a moment.

"I wish I'd met you sooner," he said. "Things might be different."

"You didn't and they're not. So let's take what we can get, eh?"

"By the Fates, you're a hard case, Vick."

"We're none of us hard as we seem." She slipped her hand around the back of his head, through the dark hair scattered with grey, held it firm, looked him in the eye and asked one more time. "You're sure, Collem? You're sure this is what you want?"

"Don't really matter what we want, does it? Bigger things than our future to consider. We can strike a spark that'll set a fire burning. One day, there'll be a Great Change, Vick. And folk like you and me will get our say."

"A Great Change," she said, trying to sound like she believed it.

"When this is done, I'll have to get out of Adua."

She kept silent. Best thing to do when you've nothing to say.

"You should come with me."

She should've kept silent on that, too. Instead, she found she'd asked, "Where would we go?"

A grin spread across his face. Seeing it made her smile. Her first in a while. Hardly felt like her mouth should bend that way.

The frame groaned as he reached down beside the bed and came back up with a battered old book. *The Life of Dab Sweet* by Marin Glanhorm.

"This again?" asked Vick.

"Aye, this." It fell open at an etching across both pages. As though it was often opened there. A rider alone, staring out across a sweep of endless grass and endless sky. Sibalt held that drawing at arm's length as if it was a view spread out in front of them, whispered the words like a magic spell. "The Far Country, Vick."

"I know," she grunted. "It says under the picture."

"Grass for ever." He was half-joking. But that made him half-serious. "A place where you can go as far as your dreams can take you. A place where you can make yourself anew. Beautiful, isn't it?"

"Aye, I guess." She realised she'd reached towards that drawing with one hand, as if she might touch anything there but paper, and snatched it back. "But it's a made-up drawing in a book full o' lies, Collem."

"I know," he said, with a sad smile, like thinking about it was a fun game to play, but just a game. He flipped the book shut and tossed it back down on the boards. "Guess there comes a time you have to give up on what you want and make the best of what you're given."

She rolled over, pressing her back into his belly. They both lay silent, warm under the blankets, while the world went on outside, and the light of the furnaces across the street flickered orange beyond the misty windowpanes.

"When we strike that spark," he murmured, voice loud in her ear, "it'll change everything."

"No doubt," said Vick.

Another silence. "It'll change everything between us."

"No doubt," said Vick, and she slipped her fingers through his and pressed his hand tight to her chest. "So let's take what we can get. If I learned one thing in the camps, it's that you shouldn't look too far ahead."

Chances are you'll see nothing good there.

The Answer to Your Tears

Sometimes you wake from a nightmare, and there's a wonderful wash of relief as you realise the horrors you saw were just ghosts, and you're safe in your own warm bed.

For Rikke, it happened the other way around.

She'd been dreaming of something happy, somewhere happy, burrowing into feathers with a smile on her face. Then she felt the cold, creeping into her heart however tight she huddled. Then the aching in her sore legs as she shifted on the pitiless ground. Then the hunger, nagging at her gut, and it came back in a rush where she was, and she woke with a groan.

It was with great reluctance she opened her eyes, saw the cold, grey sky through branches creaking with the wind, and something swinging—

"Shit!" she squawked, scrambling from her clammy cloak. A man had been hanged from the tree right above where she'd been sleeping. If she'd stood up tall, she could've touched his dangling feet. When she lay down, it'd been too dark to see her own hands, let alone a corpse hung overhead. But there was no missing him now.

"There's a dead man," Rikke squeaked, pointing a trembling finger.

Isern barely spared him a glance. "On balance, I'd rather be surprised by dead men than living. Here." She pressed something into Rikke's cold hand. A soggy heel of loaf and a handful of those horrible bitter berries that left your teeth purple. "Breakfast. Savour it, for that is all the food it has pleased the moon to give us." She cupped her blue hand and her white and blew into them, ever so gently, like even breath was a resource to be rationed. "My da used to say you can see all the beauty in the world in the way a hanged man swings."

Rikke bit off damp bread, chewed it in her sore mouth, eyes creeping back to that slowly turning body. "Can't say I'm seeing it."

"Nor me, I will admit."

"Should we cut him down?"

"Doubt he'll thank us."

"Who is he?"

"Honestly, he's not had much to say for himself. Could be one of your father's men, hanged by Stour Nightfall's. Could be one of Stour Nightfall's, hanged by your father's. Not much difference now. The dead fight for no one."

One of her father's men? Had Rikke known him, then? How many folk she knew were killed, these last few days? She felt the ache of tears at the back of her nose, sniffed it up hard.

"How much more of this can we take?" And she knew her voice was getting shrill and cracked but couldn't stop herself.

"Can *I* take?" asked Isern. "I was six when my da first sent me to cut arrows from the dead. I can take as much as there is. Can *you* take? If you fall down and can't get up, we'll have riddled out your limit. Until then..." She looked off through the trees, picking at her berry-stained teeth with a fingernail. "We can't sit still. Nor make it up into the hills to my people. So we must find the Union, or your father's men, and they're all backing off towards the Whiteflow quick as goats before a wolf. We have to move faster than they are, and the enemy are between us and them, so the further we go, the more dangerous it gets. We'll be marching for days, still. Weeks, even."

Weeks of marching through bog and bramble, dodging bitter enemies, eating worms and sleeping under hanged men. Rikke felt her shoulders slump.

She thought of her father's hall in Uffrith. The faces carved in the rafters and the meat dripping gravy into the firepit. The hounds begging with their sad eyes and their chins on her knee. The songs sung of high deeds done in the sunny valleys of the past. Her father getting dewy-eyed at every mention of Threetrees, and Thunderhead, and Black Dow, even, raising his cup when a voice rumbled out the name of the Bloody-Nine.

She thought of the Named Men ranged along both sides of the firepit. All smiling at some joke of hers. Some song of hers. That Rikke, she's a funny one. You wouldn't want your own daughter wrong in the head, but she's funny.

She thought of wandering comfortably drunk into her room, and her own warm cot with the blanket her mother made, and the pretty things she'd found placed nicely on the shelf, and the pretty clothes all dry and beautiful in the chest.

She thought of the steep streets of Uffrith, cobbles shining from the rain, and the boats on the grey harbour, and the people gabbling in the market, and the fish sliding glistening from the nets as the catch came in.

She knew she'd been unhappy there. She'd said it so often, even she was tired of her moaning. Now she rubbed at the torn and stinking fur on her cloak and wondered how she could've been so hurt by cold words and sharp looks. Seemed foolish and childish and weak. But that's what growing up is, maybe. Realising what a fucking arse you've been.

By the dead, she wanted to go back to the safe and warm, and instead of being hunted just be scorned, but Rikke had seen Uffrith burn. It might be that the Long Eye can peek into the past, but of one thing there's no doubt—you can never go there. The world she'd known was gone and wasn't coming back any more than that dead man dangling, and the world she was left with was bitter chill and a mean bully besides.

She couldn't help herself. So hungry and cold and sore and scared and with more of the same the best she could hope for. She stood with her numb hands dangling, and her shoulders shaking, and the tears silently trickled down her face and dripped from her nose and brought the faint taste of salt to her waggling lower lip.

She felt Isern step close. Put a gentle hand on her shoulder. Take her chin, and tip it up, and speak in a softer voice than she'd ever heard her use before. "D'you know what my da would say, whenever I cried?"

"No," warbled Rikke, slobbery with snot.

With a sharp and shocking smack, Isern slapped her across the face.

Rikke blinked, jaw hanging open, putting one hand to her burning cheek. "What the—"

"*That's* what he would say." Isern shook her, hard. "And when that is the answer to your tears, you soon learn to stop mewling and attend to what has to be done."

"Ow," muttered Rikke, her whole face throbbing.

"Yes, you've had hardships. The sickness and the fits, and the being thought mad and blah, blah, blah. But you were also born with all your limbs and a fine set of teeth in your pretty face, the only child of a powerful chief, with no mother and a hall full of soft-headed old warriors doting upon you."

"That's not bloody fair—"

She gasped as Isern slapped her again, even harder, hard enough that salt blood joined salt tears on her lips.

"You are used to twisting the old men around your fingers. But if Black Calder gets his hands upon you, he will twist you around his. He will twist you until you are all broken apart and you will have no one but

yourself to blame. You have been *coddled*, Rikke. You are soft as pig fat."
And that merciless finger poked Rikke painfully in her tit again. "Lucky
for you, I am here, and I will pare the fat away and leave the iron which
I see beneath well sharpened." Poke, poke, in the same old bruise. "Lucky
for you, because out here that softness will kill you, and that iron can
save you." Poke, poke. "It may be just a needle now, but one day we might
make a dagger—"

"You cunt!" screeched Rikke and punched Isern in the mouth. It was a
decent punch, snapping her head back and sending specks of spit flying.
Rikke had always reckoned herself weak. More a weeper than a fighter.
Now a fury she never knew she had boiled up in her. It was a fine, strong
feeling. The first flicker of warmth she'd felt in days.

She raised her fist again but Isern caught her wrist, caught her hair,
too, and wrenched her head back, made her squawk as she was pinned
against the tree with fearsome strength.

"*There's* that iron!" Isern grinned, showing teeth blood- as well as berry-
stained. "Perhaps it is a dagger after all. One day, we might forge a sword
from it that strong men will cower at and the moon itself will smile upon."
She let go of Rikke's hair. "Now, are you warmed up and ready to dance
with me westwards?" Her eyes rolled upwards to the dangling body. "Or
would you prefer to dance beside our friend?"

Rikke took a long, ragged breath and blew it smoking out into the
chill air. Then she held up her empty hands, one now painfully throbbing
across the knuckles to add to her woes. "I'm all packed."

Young Heroes

"**B**astards," breathed Jurand, studying the valley through his eyeglass. Leo plucked it from his hand and trained it on the ridge. Through its round window, wobbling with his own barely controlled frustration, he could see the Northmen, their spears black pinpricks against the dull sky. They hadn't moved all morning. Maybe three score of them, thoroughly enjoying the sight of Angland's shameful retreat. Leo thrust the eyeglass at Whitewater Jin. "Bastards."

"Aye," agreed Jin in his thick Northern accent, lowering the glass and thoughtfully scratching at his beard. "They're some bastards, all right."

Glaward slumped over his saddle bow with a groan. "Who'd have thought war could be so bloody boring?"

"Nine-tenths of war is waiting," said Jurand. "According to Stolicus." As though quoting a famous source made it any easier to bear.

"You've two choices in war," said Barniva, "boredom or terror, and in my experience boredom's far preferable."

Leo was tiring of Barniva's experience. Of his talk of horrors the rest of them couldn't understand. Of his frowning off at the horizon as if there were haunting memories beyond. All because he'd spent eight months on campaign in Styria, and barely left Lord Marshal Mitterick's well-guarded command post the whole time.

"Not everyone's as fashionably war-weary as you." Leo loosened his sword in the scabbard for the hundredth time that morning then shoved it back. "Some of us want to see some *action*."

"Ritter saw some action." Barniva rubbed at his scar with a fingertip. "That's all I'll say."

Leo frowned, wishing he had a scar of his own. "If war's so terrible, why don't you take up farming or something?"

"I tried. I was no good at it." And Barniva frowned off at the horizon as if there were haunting memories beyond.

Jurand caught Leo's eye and rolled his to the heavens, and Leo had to smother a laugh. They knew each other's minds so well they hardly even needed words.

"They still up there?" Antaup reined his horse in beside them, standing in his stirrups as Jin handed him the eyeglass.

"They're there," said Leo.

"Bastards." Antaup tossed back that loose lock of dark hair that always hung across his forehead and right away it flopped down again. He was the one the girls couldn't leave alone, slick and quick and well groomed as a winning racehorse, but all of Leo's friends were fine-looking men in their own ways. Jin was fierce as the Bloody-Nine in a fight, but when that toothy grin split his red beard and those blue eyes twinkled, it was like the sun coming out. You couldn't deny Barniva made the brooding veteran act work for him, especially with the scar on his forehead and the white streak it had left in his hair. Then Glaward was a slab of good-humoured manliness, with the height, and the shoulders, and the stubble already thick an hour after he shaved.

As handsome a crowd of young heroes as you could hope to find. What a painting they'd make! Maybe Leo would get one commissioned. Who'd know an artist? He found himself glancing sideways.

The ladies in Ostenhorm might not see it, but Jurand was the best-looking of the pack. They might've called his features soft, beside Glaward's cleft chin or Antaup's sharp cheekbones, but Leo thought of them more as . . . delicate? Subtle? The slightest bit vulnerable, even? But you'd find no one tougher than Jurand in defence of his friends. The expressiveness he could pack into a glance. The little frown as he thought something through. The twitch at the corner of his lips as he leaned close to say it. And always something worth hearing. Something nobody else would've—

Jurand glanced sideways and Leo looked quickly away, back up towards those Northmen on the ridge.

"Bastards," he said, a little hoarse.

"And all we can do is sit here," grumbled Antaup, having a little rummage to unstick his balls. "Like caged lions."

"Like leashed puppies." Glaward wrestled the eyeglass from Antaup's hand. "Where the hell have you been, anyway?"

"Just . . . checking on the baggage."

Jin snorted. "With a woman?"

"Not necessarily." Antaup's grin seemed to have twice as many teeth as a regulation mouth. "Could've been several. A man has to find something to stave off the despair. Who'd have thought war could be so bloody boring?"

Barniva looked up. "You've two choices in—"

"Finish that sentence and I'll stab you," said Leo.

"Looks like we could all use a boost to morale." Glaward nodded towards a column of much less fine-looking men slogging along the valley bottom, clutching torn coats, tattered cloaks, threadbare blankets, spears drooping on hunched shoulders at every angle but straight.

Leo could usually rely on some cheering when the common soldiers saw him. A few shouts of, "The Young Lion!" so he could shake a fist and slap a back and bellow some nonsense about the king. Now the men struggled past in silence with their eyes on the mud, and with no help yet from Midderland, even Leo was a lot less inspired by royalty than he used to be. It seemed the days of warrior-kings like Harod the Great and Casamir the Steadfast were far in the past, and supplies of patriotic bluster were running dangerously short.

"I'd never argue with your mother on strategy," grunted Antaup, "but constant retreat is no good for men's spirits."

"Taste o' victory would soon perk 'em up," said Whitewater.

"Perk us up, too." Glaward nudged his horse closer to Leo, dropping his voice. "Be easy to teach those bastards a lesson." And he bunched one big, veiny fist and punched at the air with it. "Like we did at that farm."

Leo fiddled with the pommel of his sword, loosening it in the scabbard again. He could remember every detail of the charge. Ripping wind and thundering hooves. The axe-haft jolting in his hand. The fear-stricken faces of the enemy. The giddy joy as they broke and ran.

Jurand had that little crease of worry between his brows. "We've no idea what's behind that ridge."

Leo thought of Ritter's funeral. The words by the grave. The weak-chinned wife weeping by the fireside. Men's lives were in his hands. These men's lives, who'd ride through fire for him. His friends. His brothers. He couldn't stand to lose another.

"Jurand's right." He slapped his sword back, forced his hand away from the hilt. "We don't know what's behind that ridge. And mother would kill me."

"Ride up there, you'll save me the trouble."

Leo winced at that odd mix of reassurance and resentment that always came with his mother's voice, though every time, the reassurance was less and the resentment more.

"My Lady Governor." Jurand pulled his horse sideways to let her ride through next to Leo, her crowd of officers loitering on the slope.

"We did all right against Stour Nightfall's men last week," grumbled Leo.

"Nightfall is over on our right just now." She swished her baton towards the South, making him wince again. There was just something off about a woman waving a baton around, even if she was in command for now. "Those are Black Calder's men. And Calder is not a warrior, like his son." She raised one brow at Leo. "Or mine. Calder is a thinker, like me. You see those woods, over to the right? He has horsemen there, waiting for us to make a fool's mistake."

Jurand whisked his eyeglass out of Glaward's fist. "Metal," he murmured. "In the trees."

Leo should've been pleased at his own good judgement. Instead he felt angry at missing the obvious. "So we just sit here and let them laugh at us?"

"I wouldn't want them to miss the show." His mother nodded towards the straggling column, thrown into even more disarray by a puddle in the track. "I put our shabbiest men in this valley with orders to march as badly as they could."

"You did what?"

"Let them laugh, Leo. Their laughter will leave no widows weeping. We have our best companies out of sight in the valley behind. If they come, we'll be ready." She leaned from her saddle to push back his hair. "What's this?"

"Nothing," he said, brushing her hands away from the scab. "I was training. With Antaup and Barniva."

"Finally managed to land one on him," said Antaup, grinning.

Jurand cleared his throat and Leo's mother frowned. "Tell me he didn't fight you both at once."

Antaup's famous way with the ladies clearly didn't include lady governors. "Well...not as such—"

"When will you learn you'll never beat two strong men together?"

"I saw Bremer dan Gorst do it," said Leo.

"That man's no model for anything," she snapped. "Think of your father. He was brave, none braver, but between your grandfather's treason and the weakness of Angland when he took charge, he learned to be *patient*. He knew what he was good at. He never had too high an opinion of himself."

"You're saying I do?"

Jurand cleared his throat again and Leo's mother laughed. "You know I love you, Leo, but yes, painfully so. Still, it's hardly a surprise you turned out hotheaded. You were conceived on a battlefield."

Leo caught Glaward and Barniva grinning at each other and felt himself blushing. "Do you have to, Mother?"

"I don't *have* to. Honestly, every generation seems to think coupling is some grand new invention never thought of before. How they believe they came into being in the first place is entirely beyond me. High time you found a wife of your own. Someone to keep you out of trouble."

"I thought that was your job," he grumbled.

"I have a war to fight."

"That's the problem. You're not bloody fighting."

"Did you never read that Verturio I gave you? *Not* fighting is what war's all about." And taking the last word, as ever, she trotted off westwards with her retinue following.

Jurand cleared his throat yet again and Leo rounded on him. "Could you just bloody cough and get it over with?"

"Well, the lady governor always makes some very good points. And you really should read Verturio—"

"She's only governor until the king confirms me in my father's place." Three years since the funeral, and Leo was still bloody waiting. He glared across the valley at those bastard Northmen, watching from their ridge. "Then I can do things my way."

"Mmm." Jurand had that worried crease between his brows again.

"Whose side are you on?"

"The Union side, along with you *and* your mother."

Leo couldn't help grinning. "Very reasonable, as always."

Jurand grinned back. "Someone needs to be."

"Reasonable men might live longer." Leo pulled his gloves off and tossed them over, left Jurand juggling them as he swung down from his saddle. "But does anyone remember the bastards afterwards?"

The drummer boy at the head of the next company had given up playing altogether, shambling along with knees knocking against his drum, teeth chattering from the cold. He looked up as Leo came close and snatched his white hands from his armpits, but fumbled his sticks and sent them tumbling to the dirt.

Leo stooped and plucked them up before the boy could bend, gripped them in his teeth while he shrugged off his cloak and offered it out. "I'll swap you."

"My lord?" The boy could hardly believe his luck as he wriggled from the strap of his drum and swaddled himself in several dozen marks' worth of best Midderland wool.

Barniva had hopped down from his horse, smiling for once as he fell into step with the soldiers. Now Glaward and Jurand joined him, too, Whitewater Jin shaking his shaggy head but showing that grin as he muscled into the column.

"I'll just take the bloody horses back, then, shall I?" called Antaup, struggling to gather the reins.

"Mine's a mare!" shouted Glaward. "You're always saying how much the ladies love you!"

Some laughter through the column at that. The first in some time, by the look of things. Leo settled the drumsticks in his fingers, just like he used to when he marched the servants around the lord governor's residence as a boy.

A leader should share the hardships of his men, his father used to tell him. He'd have a dry tent, a warm fire and a good dinner this evening, while they'd be lucky to get a blanket and a bowl of soup. But if he could put a little spring in their step on the way, it would be something. Something for them, and something for him. Something to show those bastards on the hill.

That, and Leo had always been the worst man in the world when it came to doing nothing.

"I'll try to remember how to play," he called over his shoulder, "if you lot can remember how to march!"

"I'm no genius like Jurand," called Glaward, turning so he was trotting backwards, "but as I recall, it's one foot after the other!"

"We'll give it a try, my lord!" called a thickset sergeant, the men already moving faster.

Leo smiled as he started to tap out the rhythm. "That's all I ask."

The Moment

"You asleep?"

"No," grunted Clover. Only sort of a lie, since he had in fact just woken up. "Shut my eyes, is all."

"Why?"

He opened one and peered up at the boy. Hard to say which he was, with the sun flickering through the branches. Specially since Clover had forgotten their names again. "So I don't have to see the injury you two are doing to the noble art of swordsmanship."

"Doing the best we can," grumbled the other boy, whichever one he was.

"That'll be a comfort to your mothers when you're killed for not attending to my wisdom." Clover let his hand hover over the basket of apples, then plucked out one he liked the look of. Nice blush to it. He took a bite and sucked out the juice.

"Tart," he said, baring his teeth, "but tolerable. Like life, eh, lads? Like life." They stared at him blankly. He heaved a weary sigh. "Back to it, then."

They shambled unhappily out into the sun and turned to face each other.

"Yah!" The dark one dashed in, swinging his stick.

"Urgh!" The blond one parried, stumbling back.

Clack, clack, as the sticks knocked together. Coo, coo, went a cuckoo in the trees behind. Somewhere men were arguing over something, but so far off their voices were no more than a comforting burble. Clover wedged one hand behind his neck and wriggled back against the tree.

Sometimes, it could feel like life wasn't so bad.

Then he gave an unhappy grunt. Then a twitch. Then a grimace. Problem was, these students of his were about the most terrible swordsmen he ever saw. The blond one swung, swung, swung, teeth clenched, while the dark one snarled and burbled, more running away than defending, both already out of breath.

"Stop!" He sat up, tossing his half-eaten apple away. "For the dead's sake, stop!"

The boys stuttered to a halt, sticks wobbling down.

"No, lads, no." Clover shook his head. "Very much no. You're going at each other like a dog at a bitch. Wild and wayward. You've got to put more thought into this moment than any other. All your thought and all your effort, because everything you'll ever have is apt to be snatched away in the next breath. Your lives are hanging in the balance!"

"They're just sticks," said the blond one.

Clover rubbed at his temples. "But we're *pretending* they're swords, you halfhead. I'm not a bloody stick teacher, am I?" The dark-haired boy opened his mouth and Clover held up a silencing hand. "Don't answer that. Just take some time. Your dinner ain't getting cold, is it?"

"You said strike fast."

"Aye, once you strike, like lightning! But think *before* you strike, eh?"

"Why don't you come and show us?" asked the dark one.

"Out there in the sun?" Clover chuckled to himself. "I didn't become a bloody teacher so I could get up and do it my bloody self."

"But..." The blond boy shaded his eyes with his hand. If Clover had been the dark one, he'd have smashed him right then when he wasn't looking. But the dark boy just stood there picking his nose. No initiative, these little bastards. "Aren't you going to show us some...what do you call it...technique?"

"Technique." Clover laughed. "Technique is what we come to last. So far, you two are only just holding the sword by the right end."

"It's a stick," said the blond one, frowning at his stick. "The ends are the same."

Clover ignored him. "It's a *mindset* I'm trying to teach you. A winning way of *looking* at the world."

The dark boy was so baffled, he looked almost in pain. "It's about hitting him with a sword, ain't it?"

Clover took a slow breath in and slowly blew it out. "First of all, it's about deciding when to, and when not to. In the end...the only thing a man can really do...is pick his *moment*. Watch for the opening, and recognise it when it comes, and *seize* it." And Clover snatched at a handful o' nothing and shook his fist. "Picking your moment. That's the secret. You understand?"

The dark boy looked doubtful. "My da always said it was all in the grip."

"Aye. Well. If you had no grip, the sword would just drop out of your hand."

The boys stared blankly at him again. Clover sighed again.

"To it once more, lads, and this time pick your moment."

Clack, clack went the sticks. Tock, tock went a woodpecker in the trees behind. The snap of a stick in the brush and Clover slipped the knife from its sheath at his back and held it down behind his arm.

Another footstep and Clover reached out, without looking around, and tipped the basket of apples towards the newcomer.

"Apple?" he asked.

Black Calder was standing there, rubbing at that little scar on his chin as he watched the two boys swinging away and not picking their moment in the least. "No," he grunted.

"Hard day, Chief?"

"You get to my position, they all are."

Clover looked back to the demonstration of how not to use a sword, knife already put away and his hands clasped across his belly. "Reckon that's why I prefer my position."

"Huh." Calder worked his mouth, a little sourly in Clover's opinion, and said in a voice sharp with sarcasm, "Don't get up."

"I haven't."

Calder worked his mouth even more sourly. He was a sour sort these days, given how much life had given him, or how much he'd managed to claw from it, leastways. Time was he'd had a fine sense of humour, but the more men get, the sourer they tend to turn, and Black Calder had almost the whole North. His brother Scale might wear the king's chain, but everyone knew Black Calder made the king's choices.

"I meant do get up," he said.

"Ah."

Clover took his time. He considered it a point of principle to always take as much time as he could get away with. Then he shook out his aching legs, then slapped the dirt and dried pine needles from the arse of his trousers, then slapped his palms clean, too.

"There we go," he said. "I'm up."

"Let ring the bells," said Calder. "This here is Jonas Clover."

Clover looked around and got quite the shock to see someone had come up behind him and was leaning against the tree. A black-haired lad maybe twelve or thirteen years old with a cleft top lip and watchful eyes. He looked Clover up and down, and didn't say a thing.

"Used to be called Steepfield," added Calder, which made Clover scratch unhappily at the back of his head. "Maybe you heard of him."

"No," said the lad, looking over at the two fighting boys with his pale eyes narrowed. "Who're these?" They'd fallen to wrestling, lurching about with their sticks waggling at the sky.

"Those..." Clover considered denying any acquaintance with them, but doubted he'd get away with it. "Are my pupils."

The lad considered 'em a moment, then pronounced his solemn judgement. "They're no good."

"You've an excellent eye. They're shit. But that's how you know what a truly great teacher I am. Any fool can get results from the gifted."

The lad considered that. "So where's the results?"

"You have to trust they'll be along. Patience is a warrior's most fearsome weapon. Take it from me. I've been in a few fights."

"Did you win any?"

Clover snorted. "Oh, I like him, Calder. Did you come down here just to toss my hard-won reputation in the muck?"

"Not just that," said Calder. "I need your help."

"Thinking of learning some sword-work?"

"You ask me, swords are best swung by other men."

"Then...?"

Calder took an unhappy, growling breath. "My son."

"The Great Wolf? Our king-in-waiting? That peerless warrior Stour Nightfall? Thought he knew how to use a sword."

"He does. Too well, if anything. He's proving somewhat... wilful. Set fire to Uffrith, the bloody idiot. All those years I spent planning how to take the city, and the moment I get it, he sets fire to it."

"Once you call it a war, folk tend to get overexcited."

"My father used to say you point three Northmen the same way they'll be killing each other before you can order the charge. I've got Gregun Hollowhead and his boys from the West Valleys as like to join the Dogman as fight against him. How do I make them take my say-so when my own blood won't? If Stour weren't my son, I'd be forced to say the boy's a fucking prick."

"But he is your son, so...?"

Calder wasn't listening. "He cares about nothing but his own fame. His own legend. What's a bloody name worth at a market? *Warriors.*" He spat the word out like it tasted bitter. "I swear, the more they win, the worse they get."

"Defeat is good for the spirit." Clover scratched gently at his own scar with the little fingernail he left long for the purpose. "Learned *that* the hard way."

"He thinks he's bloody invincible. And his name draws fools like a turd draws flies and they give him fool advice. I sent Wonderful over to be his second, try to teach the Great Wolf some caution."

"Good choice. Good woman. Good judgement."

"Stour's got her tearing her bloody hair out."

Clover frowned. "Wonderful's got hair now?"

"It's a figure of speech."

"Ah."

"I want you to help her out. Keep Stour on the right path."

"I'm supposed to know where the right path is?"

"A damn sight better than my prick of a son. Maybe you can nudge him off a couple of wrong ones, anyway."

Clover scratched his beard, and watched the boys flounder in the meadow, and Calder's lad shaking his head in disgust, and he took a slow breath in and slowly breathed it out. "All right, then." He'd been around long enough to know when there was no squirrelling out of a thing. He grunted as he bent down and fished up his sword. Slowly, because why not? "I'll do what I can."

"Reckon that's all any of us can do, in the end. You're a straight edge, Clover. You've always been loyal."

"Doubtless. I was loyal to Bethod, then to Glama Golden, then to Cairm Ironhead, now to you."

"Well. You were loyal to them till they put themselves on the losing side."

"That sounds almost exactly like disloyalty."

Calder shrugged. "A man has to bend with the breeze."

"If I've got one talent, it's bending with the breeze. You keep the apples." And Clover nudged the basket towards the scar-lipped lad with his boot. "They make my tummy hurt."

"And all my dreams came true," said Clover, ambling up with his sword over one shoulder.

Wonderful turned her head, showing the white scar through the black and silver stubble on her scalp, and hacked out a laugh. A laugh without much joy in it.

"Look who it is," she said.

He glanced down at himself. "I recognise those boots! Jonas Clover has arrived and all wrongs shall be set right." He winked at her but she was not much charmed. "Must be your lucky day."

"I'm fucking due one." And she slapped her hand in his, and pulled him close by it, and they clapped each other around the back for good measure.

"You been eating well?" he asked, looking her up and down. "You're like hugging a bundle of spears."

"Always been lean."

"Oh, me too." And he patted his belly. "The body of a hero lies just below this carefully nurtured layer of fat."

She raised a brow. Clover loved to see things done well, and she'd a hell of a brow-raise, did Wonderful. "And what could possibly drag your fat this close to the fighting?"

"Black Calder. He tells me you need help."

"That I'll not deny. When does it get here?"

"You dare trifle with me, woman? I'm supposed to mind the future of the North, the king-in-waiting, the Great Wolf, Stour Nightfall."

Both her brows went up now. "You?"

"I'm to keep him on the right path. Calder's words."

"Good luck with that." She beckoned him close and lowered her voice. "Not sure I ever met a bigger prick than that boy, and I stood second to Black Dow."

Clover snorted. "For a day you did."

"A day was plenty."

"I do hear tell the Great Wolf can be somewhat prickish."

Wonderful jerked her head towards a column of smoke rising above the trees. "He's even now burning a village we just captured over yonder. He was going house to house when I left him. Making sure the flames got the lot."

Clover thought he'd caught that old burning-building whiff on the breeze. "Why fight for something if all you do is burn it?"

"Maybe the Great Wolf could tell you. For damn sure I can't."

"Well." Clover pushed his chin forward and scratched at the stubble on his stretched-out neck. "Luckily, I'm a man of heroic patience."

"You'll need to be." Wonderful nodded sideways. "Here comes the future."

And Stour came swaggering down the track. He'd been given the name Nightfall as a babe, on account of being born during an eclipse. It had been an hour before, in fact, but no one dared say so now. All part of the ever-inflating legend of the Great Wolf. He'd long, dark hair, and fine clothes buckled and riveted with gold, and these grey-blue eyes that looked always a little wet, as if he was about to cry. Tears of acid contempt, maybe, for the world and everything in it.

60

He was no giant, but there was a quick strength to the way he moved. A dancer's grace. And sneering confidence in crazed abundance. A surfeit of self-belief can get you killed, but Clover had seen it carry men through fire before as well. The old iron skin of arrogance. Here was a fellow who knew how to pick his moment, and to cut what he wanted from it with no hesitation and even less regret.

He had that crowd of cunts with him that famous fighters tend to gather, many of them proudly sporting the sign of the wolf on their shields. Men with no name of their own, drawn to the big name like moths to a bonfire. Clover had seen the wretched pattern a dozen times before. Glama Golden had a crew very similar, and the Bloody-Nine, too, and more than likely Skarling Hoodless had a glowering gaggle however many hundred years before.

Times change, but that crowd of cunts stays much the same.

Stour Nightfall fixed Clover with that wet, cold, hollow stare, quick hand sitting loose on the pommel of his sword, and his grin was full of good teeth and bad threats.

"Jonas Clover," he said. "What the fuck are you doing here?"

"Your father sent me. Black Calder."

"I know who my father is."

"He knows who his father is," sneered one of the sneerers. A heavy-muscled young bastard with a whole armoury strapped about him, made a sound on the move like a knife-seller carting too much stock.

Stour scowled sideways. "Shut your mouth, Magweer." Magweer bristled to be slapped down, a wearisome pattern of manly goings-on in which Clover, to his shame, had once been a keen participant. "What I want to know is—*why* did he send you?"

"To keep you on the right path." Clover gave a helpless little shrug. "His words, you understand."

"And you can tell the right path from a midden, can you?"

Stour's wolf-shield arse-lickers chuckled like that was some high wit, and Clover smiled along with 'em. If all a man can do is pick his moment, then this was no moment for pride. "I make no grand claims for myself, but I've chosen a few wrong paths down the years. Could be I can spare you from stepping in some of the turds that've made my boots so fragrant."

"I thought I could smell dung." And Stour sniffed, and licked his teeth, and wiped at his nose with a thumbtip. "So what'd be your first advice?"

"Never scratch your eyebrows with a sword." Clover grinned. No one else did, but that was their lookout. "Best to just leave 'em in the scabbard whenever possible, I'd say. Drawn swords are bloody dangerous, that's a fact."

Stour stepped a little closer and brought a little bubble of menace with him. "Wisdom fit for a hero," he whispered.

"I used to want to be a hero." Clover patted his belly. "Grew out of it. But I told your father I'd do what I could."

"So..." Stour swept his hand out towards the valley. "Care to point out the path?"

"Wouldn't presume. I know what I am, and I'm one of life's followers."

The king-in-waiting opened his wet eyes wide. "Try to keep up, then, old man." And he brushed past, eyes fixed on his next conquest, and Clover stepped out of the way of his scowling companions, bowing low. "I want to burn us another village or two before sundown!" the Great Wolf called over his shoulder, and the young glories competed with each other to laugh the loudest.

"What did I say?" Wonderful leaned close. "Absolute prick."

Break What They Love

Rikke wriggled her shoulders further back among the knotted roots, up to her neck in the icy river and her hair full of dirt, listening to the warriors of her enemy trudge past on the path above. By the sound of it, there were a lot of the bastards. She wondered, yet again, what would happen if they caught her. When they caught her. She tried to make her breath come slow, come even, come quiet.

What with the grinding fear for herself, and the chafing worry for everyone she knew, and the niggling pain of a hundred little knocks and scratches, and the gnawing hunger and gripping cold, it all added up to quite the shittest afternoon she'd ever had, and that with some recent savage competition.

She felt a fingertip under her jaw, pushing her mouth closed, and realised her teeth had started chattering. Isern was pressed against the bank beside her, river to her sharp chin and hair plastered to her frowning face, still as the earth, patient as the trees, hard as the stones. Her eyes rolled up from Rikke's to the root-riddled overhang above, and she quietly slipped one finger from the water and over her scarred lips for quiet.

"Shit," came a voice, so loud it seemed in Rikke's ear, and she startled, might've splashed from the bank on an instinct if Isern's hand hadn't clamped tight about her numb arm under the water.

"Shit...and..." A man's voice, getting on in years but soft and slow, like he was in no hurry. "*There* we go." A satisfied grunt, and a stream of faintly steaming piss came spattering into the water not a stride from Rikke's face. Sad thing was, she was tempted to stick her head under it just for the warmth.

"There's all kinds of pleasures in life," came the voice, "but I've come to think there's little better than a piss when you really need one."

"Huh." A woman's voice this time, picking each word careful as a smith

63

picks the nails for a rich man's horseshoes. "Not sure whether I've more respect for you or less following that little revelation."

"It's getting to the point..." The stream stopped, then started up again. "Where I sometimes hold on to it...so when I *do* go..." A few more little squirts. "It feels better than ever. How goes the noble clash of arms?"

"Union are pulling back as fast as they can. Some skirmishes but there's no real fight in 'em. No sign o' the Dogman's boys. Running, I reckon."

"Suits me well enough," said the man. "Any luck, they'll run all the way back to Angland and we can all have a lie down."

Rikke glanced over at Isern. She'd been right. She always was bloody right, specially when it came to disheartening predictions.

That morning they'd come upon a clearing full of corpses. A dozen or more. Men from both sides, all on the same side now. They say the Great Leveller settles all differences. Rikke had stared at those bodies, her wrist against her mouth, her breath crawling. Then she'd seen Isern, squatting over the dead like a corpse-eater from the songs, plucking at torn clothes, fiddling with buckles.

"What are you doing?"

"Looking for anything we can eat."

And Rikke had set to searching herself. Trying not to look at their faces as she rooted through pockets with numb fingers. Isern had been right about that, too. Your fear, your guilt, your disgust, they all vanish once you get hungry enough. The thing that really upset her as they crept away from the dead was that they hadn't found anything.

"Chief!" someone roared up on the road. "Nightfall! The king-in-waiting!" And there was an approving clatter of weapons on shields.

Rikke stiffened under the water. Stiffened far as she could given she was near enough a block of ice already, and Isern pressed against her and whispered, hardly more'n a breath, "Shhhhhhhh..."

"By the dead," she heard the woman mutter above, and then, with forced good cheer, "Chief! How's the day?"

"Bloodless so far, but it's still early." The voice of Stour Nightfall himself, then. A whining sort of voice for a famous warrior. Sounded like a boy on the edge of a tantrum. "They're thin sauce, these Southerners, always trickling away. The Bloody-Nine had Rudd Threetrees to fight, and Black Dow, and Harding Grim and all the rest. How's a man meant to win a great name without great enemies to weigh it against?"

A brief pause. "It's a tester, all right," said the woman.

"I've a task for you, Wonderful. There's a girl out in these woods." Rikke had a bad feeling in her stomach. Worse than the hunger, and she shrank against the bank like she could become one with the dirt. "I want her."

A snorting chuckle from the enthusiastic pisser. "Well, who wouldn't want a girl out in the woods?" There was a silence, like the jest had miscarried. Certainly Rikke wasn't fucking laughing. "How do we tell this girl from another?"

"They say she's got a twitchy way. She'll have a gold ring through her nose, maybe a cross painted over her eye."

Rikke touched the tip of her tongue to the ring through her nose and whispered, "Fuck."

"She might have some witch of a hillwoman with her. That you can kill. But the girl we need alive."

"Must be important," said the woman called Wonderful.

Nightfall gave a little hooting giggle. "Well, there's the thing. She's the Dogman's daughter."

"Double fuck," mouthed Rikke.

"Shhhhhhh," hissed Isern.

"What happens if we catch her?"

An unhappy grunt. "Well, if my father gets her, I daresay he'll ransom her back, dangle her as bait, use her to get his way when it comes to talking *peace*." And Nightfall spat out the word like it tasted bad. "You know my father. Plans within plans."

"Always been clever, Black Calder," came the man's voice.

"I see things different. How I see it, the way you break your enemy is you break what they love. Way I hear it, those old fools on the other side love that twitching bitch. Sort of a little mascot for 'em." Rikke heard the smile in his voice. "So if I get hold of her, I'll strip her, and whip her, and pull her teeth out, and maybe get some Thralls to fuck her, out between the lines where everyone can hear her squealing." Bit of a silence, and Rikke heard her own breath coming ragged, and Isern's hand tightening around her arm. "Or maybe I'd get my horse to fuck her. Or my dogs. Or...like, a pig, maybe?"

The older man sounded more than a touch disgusted. "How the hell would you do that?"

"There's naught you can't do if you've the imagination and the patience. Then I'll bind her up in the trees with brambles where everyone can see, and cut the bloody cross in her, and put a bucket underneath to catch her guts, and send 'em to the other side."

"What, her guts?"

"Aye, in a pretty box. Hardwood, nicely carved. With flowers, maybe.

65

Or no! Herbs. So those old fools won't smell what they're getting till they open it." And he gave a satisfied grunt, like he was talking about a nice fish he'd catch, or a nice meal he'd eat, or a nice sit on the porch he couldn't wait to have at sunset. "Imagine the looks on their faces." And he chuckled like her guts in a box would be quite the height of drollery.

"Fuck," breathed Rikke.

Isern just whispered, "Shhhhhhhhh . . ."

"But that's for later." And Nightfall gave a disappointed sigh. "Can't cook what you haven't caught, can you? My father's offering a big gild for her, that's sure. Whoever brings her in'll be a wealthy man."

The woman called Wonderful sounded like she was hardly enjoying this any more than Rikke was. "Right y'are, Chief. We'll be looking."

"Lovely. You can get back to your pissing now, Clover."

"That's all right. Won't need another for a while, I reckon."

Rikke heard soft footfalls moving away. Perhaps she should've been frozen with fear. The dead knew she'd a right to be. But what she felt instead was a boiling fury. A fury that warmed her through despite the icy water frothing to her chin. A fury that tempted her to slip from the stream with her knife between her teeth and cut the bloody cross in Stour Nightfall right then and there.

Rikke's father had always told her vengeance was a waste of effort. That letting it go was the strong thing, the wise thing, the right thing. That blood only led to more blood. But his lessons seemed far away now, meant for a warmer place. She clenched her jaw, and narrowed her eyes, and swore to herself that if she lived out the week, she'd make it her business to see Stour Nightfall fucked by a pig.

"I'll be honest, Wonderful," came the man's voice, the one called Clover, speaking soft like he was sharing a secret, "I'm finding that bastard increasingly troubling."

"Aye, I know."

"Took it for an act at first, but I'm starting to think he's everything he pretends to be."

"Aye, I know."

"Guts in a box? With herbs?"

"Aye, I know."

"He'll be king one o' these days, will guts-in-a-box over yonder. King o' the Northmen. Him."

A long pause, then a weary grunt. "It's a thing no right-thinking person could look forward to."

Rikke could only agree. She thought she saw a hint of their reflections, dancing among the black branches in the water.

"You see something down there?"

She stiffened, numb fingers curling tight around the grip of her knife. She saw the jaw muscles clench on the side of Isern's face, blade of her spear sliding from the water, smeared with pitch so it wouldn't catch the light.

"What? Fish?"

"Aye. Worth getting my rod, d'you think?"

The sound of Wonderful hawking up, then a glob of phlegm came spinning over from above and plopped into the water. "Nothing in this stream worth catching, I reckon."

It Was Bad

The sun was setting when he came home, just a pink glimmer over black hills. The valley was in darkness but Broad could've walked the way blindfold. Knew every rut in the track, every stone in the tumbledown wall beside it.

All so familiar. But all so strange.

After two years away, you'd think a man would run headlong towards a place he loved, the people he loved, with the biggest smile his cheeks could hold. But Broad trudged slow as the condemned to the scaffold, and smiled about as much, too. The man who left had feared nothing. The one coming back was scared all the time. He hardly even knew what of. Himself, maybe.

When he saw the house, huddled among those bare trees, lamplight showing around the shutters, he had this strange urge to walk on. This strange thought he didn't belong there any more. Not with what he'd seen. Not with what he'd done. What if he trod it in with him?

But the path leading past was a coward's path. He clenched his aching fists. Gunnar Broad was no coward. Ask anyone.

Took all the courage he had to knock on that door, though. More than it had to climb the ladders at Borletta, or lead the charge into those pikes at Mussella, or even carry those men dying of the grip in the long winter after. But he knocked.

"Who is it?" Her voice, beyond the door, and it made him wince worse than the points of those pikes had. Till that moment, he'd been afraid she wouldn't be there. That she'd have moved on. Forgotten him. Or maybe he'd been hoping she would've.

He could hardly find any voice at all. "It's me, Liddy. It's Gunnar."

The door rattled open, and there she stood. She'd changed. Not near as much as he had, but she'd changed. Leaner, maybe. Harder, maybe. But when she smiled, it still lit the gloomy world, the way it always had.

"What are you doing knocking at your own door, you big fool?"

And he just started crying. A jolting sob first that came all the way from his stomach. Then there was no stopping it. He fumbled his eye-lenses off with a trembling hand and all the tears he hadn't shed in Styria, on account of Gunnar Broad being no coward, came burning down his crushed-up face.

Liddy stepped forward and he shrank away, hunched and hurting, arms up as if to fend her off. Like she was made of glass and might shatter in his hands. She caught him even so. Thin arms, but a hold he couldn't break, and though she was a head shorter than him, she held his face against her chest, and kissed his head, and whispered, "Shhhh, now. Shhhhh."

After a while, when his sobs started to calm, she put her hands on his cheeks and lifted his head so she was looking straight up at him, calm and serious.

"It was bad, then, was it?" she asked him.

"Aye," he croaked out. "It was bad."

She smiled. That smile that lit up the world. Close enough that even without his lenses he could actually see it. "But you're home now."

"Aye. I'm home now." And he set to crying again.

The thunk of the axe made Broad flinch. He told himself it was the sound of honest work done well. He told himself he was home, safe, far from the battlefield. But maybe he'd brought the battlefield home with him. Maybe the battlefield was whatever dirt he stood on now. He tried to hide it under a joke.

"I still say chopping wood is man's work."

May set another log on the block and hefted the axe. "When the men sod off to Styria, it all becomes women's work."

When he left, she'd been boyish, quiet, awkward. As if her skin didn't fit her. She was bony still, but there was a quick strength in the way she moved. She'd grown up fast. She'd had to. Another thunk and two more neat pieces of wood went tumbling.

"I should've stayed here and sent you off to fight," said Broad. "Maybe we'd have won."

May smiled at him, and he smiled that he could make her smile, and wondered that someone who'd done all the bad he'd done could've had a hand in making something as good as she was.

"Where'd you get the lenses?" she asked.

Broad touched a finger to them. Sometimes forgot they were even on his face, till he took 'em off and everything beyond arm's reach became a smudge. "I saved a man. Lord Marshal Mitterick."

"Sounds fancy."

"Commander o' the army, no less. There was an ambush, and I happened to be there, and, well..." He realised he'd bunched his fists trembling tight again and forced them open. "He thought I'd saved him. But I had to admit I'd no clue who he was till after the business was done, since I couldn't see further than five strides. So he got me these as a gift." He took the lenses off, and breathed on them, and wiped them carefully with the hem of his shirt. "Probably cost six months of a soldier's pay. Miracle o' the modern age." And he hooked them back over his ears, and into the familiar groove across the bridge of his nose. "But I'm grateful, 'cause now I can appreciate my daughter's beauty even halfway across the yard."

"Beauty." And she gave a scornful snort but looked just a bit pleased at the same time. The sun broke through and was warm on Broad's smile, and for a moment it was like it had been before. As if he never went.

"So you fought, then?"

Broad's mouth felt dry of a sudden. "I fought."

"What was it like?"

"Well..." All that time spent dreaming of her face and now she was looking right at him, it was hard to meet her eye. "It was bad."

"I tell everyone my father's a hero."

Broad winced. The clouds shifted and cast the yard into shadow, and the dread was at his shoulder again. "Don't tell 'em that."

"What should I tell 'em?"

He frowned down at his aching hands, rubbed at one with the other. "Not that."

"What do the marks mean?"

Broad tried to twitch his shirt cuff down over the Ladderman's tattoo, but the blue stars on his knuckles still showed. "Just something the boys I was with did." And he slipped his hand behind him. Where May couldn't see it. Where he didn't have to.

"But—"

"Enough questions," said Liddy, stepping out onto the porch. "Your father just got back."

"And I've got plenty to do," he said, standing. They must've been working hard to keep the house presentable, but it was too much for three, let alone two, looked like it was crumbling back into the land. "Must be half a dozen leaks to mend."

"Be careful. Put your weight on the roof, I've a feeling the whole house might fall down."

"Wouldn't be surprised. I'll check on our flock first, though. I hear the price for wool's never better, what with all these new mills. They up the valley?"

May blinked over at her mother, and Liddy gave an odd kind of grimace, and Broad felt that dread pressing on him all the heavier. "What is it?"

"We don't have a flock no more, Gunnar."

"What?"

"I wanted to give you a proper night's sleep without having to worry." Liddy heaved up a sigh seemed to come right from her worn shoes. "Lord Isher fenced the valley in. Said we couldn't graze there any more."

Broad hardly understood what she was saying. "The valley's common land. Always has been."

"Not any more. King's edict. It's happening all over. Next valley, too. We had to sell the flock to him."

"We had to sell him our sheep so he could graze 'em on our land?"

"He gave us a good price. Some lords didn't give their tenants that much."

"So I get fucked when I go to war and I get fucked when I come back?" he snarled. The voice hardly sounded like his. "You didn't...*do* anything?"

Liddy's eyes were hard. "I couldn't think of anything to do. Maybe you could've, but you weren't here."

"None o' this works without a flock!" His father had raised sheep, and his grandfather, and his grandfather's grandfather. Felt like the whole world had come unravelled. "What'll we do?" He found he'd clenched his fists again. He was shouting but he couldn't stop. "What'll we *do*?"

And he saw May's lip trembling like she was about to cry, and Liddy put an arm around her, and all the anger drained out of him and left him cold and desperate.

"I'm sorry." He'd sworn never to lose his temper again. Sworn he'd live for the two of them, give them a good life, and he'd fucked it up a few hours through the door. "I'm sorry." He took a step towards them, lifting a hand, then saw the tattoos on the knuckles and jerked it back.

Liddy spoke soft and steady, looking him in the eye. "We've no choice, Gunnar. Isher offered to buy us out and we've got to go. Valbeck, I was thinking. There's work in Valbeck. In the new mills."

Broad could only stare at her. And in the silence, he heard the sound of horses, and turned towards the track.

There were three men coming up it. Coming slow, like they had all day to get there. One on a big chestnut. Two on a wagon with a creaky wheel. Gunnar recognised the driver. Lennart Seldom, the miller's younger brother. Broad had always reckoned him a coward and there was nothing in his shifty squint now to change his opinion.

"It's Lennart Seldom," he muttered.

"It is," said Liddy. "May, get inside."

"But Ma—"

"Inside."

The other two, Broad didn't know. A long, lean one sat by Seldom, swaying with the jolting of the cart, a big flatbow across his knees. Wasn't loaded, which was a good thing, as they'd a habit of going off at the worst times, but Broad couldn't see any reason for him to have it even so. A weapon for killing men. Or at least for threatening to.

He liked the look of the last rider even less. Big and bearded, with a fancy cavalry sword hanging low at his side, and a fancy three-cornered hat on his head, and a fancy way of sitting his saddle and looking around like this was his land.

He reined his horse in closer to the house than was polite, twisted his hat off, scrubbing at his flattened hair with his nails, considering Broad in thoughtful silence. Seldom brought the wagon to a halt behind him, between the two big lichen-spattered gateposts Gunnar's grandfather had carved on the boundary.

"Gunnar," he said, shifty eyes flicking to Liddy and back.

"Seldom."

Liddy tidied a stray strand of hair behind her ear, and the wind took it right away and set it flicking about her worried face again.

"You're back, then." If Seldom was trying to sound happy about it, he fell well short. "Where'd you get the lenses?"

"In Styria."

"How was it?"

"Bad," said Broad.

"Looks like you lost weight."

The one with the flatbow flashed a crooked grin. "How big did he use to be?"

"Even bigger," said the bearded one, barely giving Broad a glance as he settled his hat back on. "Evidently."

"Too little food and too much shitting, I guess," said Broad.

"The soldier's curse," said the bearded one. "Name's Marsh." He bit the words off short like he didn't care for talking and wanted to spend as little time at it as he could.

"I'm Able," said the thin one. "We work for Lord Isher."

"What kind of work?" asked Broad, though it was plain from the weapons.

"This and that. Buying up property, mostly. This is Isher's valley—"

"This bit of it ain't," said Broad.

Marsh gave an unhappy grunt, stretched his chin forward to scratch at his beard.

"You can't make a living here, Gunnar." Seldom gave a wheedling little chuckle. "You know that. Not now there's no grazing. To be fair to Isher, the king's hiked up his taxes neck high to pay for his bloody wars. There's land getting fenced in all over. Worked with machines."

"Efficiency," grunted Marsh, not even looking round.

His not caring a shit made Broad care all the more. "My father died on this land," he said, struggling to keep his voice down. "Fighting the Gurkish."

"I know. Mine, too." Seldom shrugged. "But what can I do?"

"You just do what you're told, eh?"

"If I don't, someone else will."

"Progress," grunted Marsh.

"Is it?" Broad frowned up the valley, towards the other houses, all sitting quiet. He'd thought it was strange, that there was no smoke from the chimneys. "Turned all these others out already, did you? Lant and his daughters, and the Barrows, and Old Neiman?"

"Neiman died, but the rest sold up."

"We made 'em see the sense in it," said Able, shifting that flatbow in his lap.

"So why's my wife still here?"

Seldom sneaked another shifty glance at Liddy. "Just wanted to give her some more time, 'cause we all know each other and—"

"You always liked her. I understand. I like her myself. That's why I married her."

Liddy had a worried, warning note in her voice. "Gunnar—"

"Why she married me, I couldn't say. But she did."

Seldom gave a watery effort at a smile. "Look, friend—"

"I wasn't your friend before I left." Felt suddenly like it was someone else speaking, and Broad was just watching. "I'm even less your friend now."

"That's enough." Marsh nudged his horse forward with his heels. Nudged her between Broad and the chopping block, where the axe was. A good horseman. He sat high on his saddle with the sky bright behind so Broad had to squint up at him. "Lord Isher's going to have his valley one way or another. No point being stubborn. Better for you to leave with a little money in your pocket."

"Better than what?"

Marsh took a heavy breath through his nose. "Be a shame if this lovely house o' yours were to catch fire one night."

His hand crept down. Not towards the peeling gilt basketwork of that fancy sword. To a knife, most likely. Thought he'd goad Broad into rashness, then he could just lean over and stab him, cut through a problem with one bit of sharp metal that a lot of talk couldn't seem to unravel. Maybe that'd worked for him before. Worked a lot of times.

"Catch fire, you say?" Funny thing was, Broad didn't feel angry. Such a relief to be able to let go, even for a moment, that he almost smiled.

"That's right." Marsh leaned down towards him. "Be a shame...if your lovely wife and daughter was—"

Broad caught his boot and flung him out of his saddle. Marsh gave a shocked grunt, flailed at the air as he went tumbling down.

He was snarling curses as Broad walked around the horse, trying to scramble up, but he had one foot still snarled in the stirrup.

Broad caught his wrist before he could right himself and twisted it up, forced his head down onto the chopping block. Marsh screamed as his elbow popped apart, knife dropping in the dirt, but only till Broad lifted one boot and smashed his face into the scarred wood with all his weight, bone crunching one, two, three times.

Able half-stood from the wagon's seat, eyes starting, fumbling with the string of his bow. Most men need time to act. Broad had the opposite problem. He was always loaded. Always.

Able had no time to draw the string as Broad strode to the wagon. No time to reach for a bolt, even.

He managed to swing the bow but Broad brushed it away with his forearm, caught Able by the front of his jacket. He gave a little hoot as Broad jerked him into the air and rammed him head first into the old gatepost, blood speckling the side of the wagon. He flopped down with one arm wedged through that creaky wheel, smashed skull bent all the way backwards.

Broad hopped up onto the seat while Seldom stared, reins still in his limp hands.

"Gunnar—" He tried to get up but Broad shoved him back down with his knee.

Wasn't sure how many times he hit him, fist up and fist down, fist up

74

and fist down, but when he stopped, Seldom's face was just a mess of glistening red.

Broad blinked down at him, a bit out of breath. Wind blew up cold on his sweaty forehead.

Broad blinked over at Liddy. She was staring, hand clapped over her mouth.

Broad blinked at his fists. Took a painful effort to uncurl the red fingers, and he started to realise what had happened.

He sat down beside Seldom's corpse on the wagon's seat, all weak and shaky. Spots on his vision. Blood, he realised, on his lenses. He fumbled them off, turned the world to a smear.

Liddy didn't say anything. Neither did he.

What was there to say?

A Sea of Business

"Welcome, one and all, to this thirteenth biannual meeting of Adua's Solar Society!"

Honrig Curnsbick, the great machinist, resplendent in a waistcoat embroidered with golden leaves, threw up his broad hands. The applause was the most enthusiastic this theatre could have heard since Iosiv Lestek gave his final performance on its stage.

"With thanks to our distinguished patrons—the Lady Ardee, and her daughter Lady Savine dan Glokta!" Curnsbick gestured towards Savine's box and she smiled over her fan as though her delicate feelings could hardly stand the attention. There were whoops, and calls of, "Hear, hear." From members who particularly wanted her money, she imagined.

"We never *dreamed*, when nine of us first met in Lady Savine's parlour, that only eight years later, the Solar Society would have more than four hundred members throughout the Union and beyond!" Curnsbick might not have, but Savine had always dreamed big. "We are living in bold new times! Times when only the lazy need be poor. When only the small-minded need be dissatisfied. Times when the world can be changed by the ingenuity and endeavour of a single man!" Or even, Fates help us, a single woman.

"Only yesterday, here in Adua, Dietam dan Kort completed a bridge made entirely of iron—of *iron*, mark you—that will bring a canal through Casamir's Wall and into the heart of the city." More applause, and down in the audience, Kort was clapped on the back by his peers. A back covered by a fine new coat paid for with Savine's money, as it happened. "With it will come boundless access to raw materials. Will come new industry and new commerce. Will come better jobs and better goods and better *lives* for the masses." Curnsbick flung his arms wide with a showman's flourish, eye-lenses flashing. "Will come prosperity for *all*!" But especially for Savine, it hardly needed to be said. What is the point in prosperity, after all, if everyone has it?

"And now to business! The business of *progress*! Our first address shall be by Kaspar dan Arinhorm, on the application of the Curnsbick Engine to the pumping of water from iron mines."

Savine rose to leave while Arinhorm was on his way to the lectern. The truth was she had never been very interested in the inventions. Her obsession was how they could be turned into money. And that particular alchemy was practised in the foyer.

A considerable crowd had already gathered beneath the three great chandeliers, buzzing with excited chatter, seething with prospects and proposals. Knots of soberly dressed gentlemen broke and re-formed, drawn into dizzying swirls and eddies, ladies' dresses bright dots of colour bobbing on the flood. Here and there, one could even spot the fabulous robes of some relic of the old merchant guilds. Savine's practised eye picked out those with money or connections, those without sucked spinning after them like rowing boats in the wake of great ships, desperate for patronage, involvement, investment.

It was a sea of business. Dangerous waters, swept by unpredictable storms, where fortunes could founder, enterprises be lost with all hands, reputations sink beneath the waves, but where a navigator with sufficient vision could be borne to spectacular success on the hidden currents of wealth and influence.

"God works for those who work themselves," murmured Zuri, checking her watch.

She was ever at Savine's shoulder, ready to guide the chaff away or, on occasion, make a note in her book for an informal meeting, perhaps an invitation to tea for the truly promising. Often at those pleasant interviews, she would make some passing observation about night-time habits, or questionable pasts, or illegitimate offspring, and how this or that scandal revealed might leave a promising career in ruins. There was almost no one worth noticing without a secret kept somewhere in her book. A dash of blackmail, tastefully administered, could always be relied upon to shift prices in the right direction. To win at this game, you had to keep one foot in the ballroom and the other knee-deep in the sewer.

"To work, then." Savine put on her most radiant smile, snapped out her fan and glided down the steps into the melee.

"Have you considered my proposal? Lady Savine? A new design for coal boats, if you recall? Both keels and colliers! We'll put coal in every household, however humble. Coal is the future!"

"My surveys show the hills near Rostod are *riddled* with copper, Lady Savine—why, you could scoop it up with your hands! Metals are the future!"

"I only need to convince the owner of the land, a relative of Lord Isher, and I know you are a close confidante of his sister..."

Savine might wear a sword, but on this battlefield she fought with a fan. A conspiratorial tap with it, closed, could coax out smiles more surely than a witch's wand. Snapped open with a flick of the wrist, it cut fruitless conversations off more sharply than an executioner's axe. Deftly raised, with a curl of the lip and a turn of the shoulder, it buried men deeper than a spade.

"Salt is the thing now, Lady Savine. Salt in quantity, for everyone. A partner could *triple* her money, within months, positively quadruple it..."

"Clocks are the thing! Accurate clocks! Affordable clocks! The *potential*, Lady Savine, you cannot be blind to the *potential*..."

"Why, a single word in the right ear at the Patent Office..."

One by one, she brought them forward with their schemes, their dreams, the light of certainty bright in their eyes. Her slightest smile lit their faces with delight. Her slightest frown doused them with horror. When she ended each interview with a snap of her fan, she thought of all the refusals she had endured, and relished her power.

"With your contacts in Styria, your patronage could make all the difference..."

"With your friends in the Agriont, it would only take an interview..."

"The *one* thing I need is investment!"

"*Quintuple* her money!"

"Lady Savine?" A woman, young, red-wigged, freckle-shouldered, with a way of peeking over her gaudy fan that was meant to be winsome but to Savine looked merely sly. "I am—forgive me—a *tremendous* admirer of yours."

Savine had a whole queue of tremendous admirers, and no idea what gave this girl the right to jump it. "How charming."

"My name is Selest dan Heugen."

"Boras dan Heugen's cousin?" Self-important oaf that he was. It appeared to run in the family.

"Only my second cousin," simpered Selest. "I fear I'm nothing but a tiny twig at the furthest reaches of the family tree."

"A prize bud just blooming, I am sure."

Selest blushed in the manner of an innocent country girl out of her depth in the big city. It made Savine think of a bad actress in a bad play.

"I knew you would be beautiful, but never dreamed you might be so kind. My father left me some money and I intend to invest it. Might I ask whether you have any advice?"

"Buy things that go up in value," said Savine, turning away.

"Lady Savine dan Glokta." A small man with curly hair and clothes that advertised both money and tasteful restraint. "I had been hoping to make your acquaintance."

"I believe you have the advantage of me."

"Certainly not in beauty." He was unremarkable, it was true, apart from his bright eyes. They were different colours, one blue, one green. "My name is Yoru Sulfur."

It was rare indeed for Savine to hear a name she had not heard before, and it always made her curious. New names meant new opportunities, after all. "And what is your business, Master Sulfur?"

"I am a member of the Order of Magi."

Savine was not easily surprised, but she could not stop her brows lifting at that. Zuri usually shepherded the cranks away, but she seemed for once to be elsewhere. "A wizard at a meeting of investors and inventors? Are you scouting the enemy?"

"Say rather that I am seeking new friends." His smile was full of clean, sharp, shiny teeth. "We magi have always been interested in changing the world."

"How admirable," said Savine, though in her experience, when men spoke of changing the world, they always meant to suit their own interests.

"There was a time, in the days of Euz and his sons, when magic was the best way to do it. But that time is long past. These days..." And Sulfur glanced about the heaving foyer and leaned close as if to share a secret. "I begin to think this is better."

"You go where the power is," murmured Savine, touching him gently on the wrist with her fan. "I am just the same."

"Oh, you should meet my master. I have a feeling the two of you would have a *great* deal in common. He is used to dealing with your father, of course. But no one lasts for ever."

Savine frowned. "Whatever can you—"

"Lady Savine!" Curnsbick was advancing on her, arms spread wide in a gesture of great affection. "When the *hell* are you going to marry me?"

"A few days after never. Besides, I swear I was at your wedding to someone else."

He folded her hand in his and kissed it. "Say the word and I'll throttle her myself."

"But she's such a lovely woman. I couldn't have that on my conscience."

"Don't pretend you have a conscience."

"Oh, I have one. But muzzled and kept well away from my business affairs. This is . . ." She turned to introduce Sulfur but he had already vanished into the crowd.

"Curnsbick, you old dog!" It was Arinhorm, the deliverer of the first address, blundering into their conversation like a hog into a rose garden.

"Arinhorm, my friend!" Curnsbick slapped him heartily on the shoulder. He was a genius where machines were concerned, but prone to give people far too much credit. "Might I introduce Savine dan Glokta?"

"Ah, yes." Arinhorm offered her a particularly mirthless smile. One of those insufferable men who thought everyone existed to service his needs. "I understand you have invested in several iron mines in Angland. Indeed, I understand you are perhaps the largest single owner in the entire province."

Savine did not like her affairs being discussed before an audience. Winning made people friendly. Winning too much made them nervous. "I believe I have some interests there."

"You should have heard my address. The main challenge to the efficiency of mines is how quickly water can be pumped from their depths. There are limits to what can be achieved by hand or horse, but with my adaptation of Master Curnsbick's engine, one can pump at ten times the speed and therefore dig further and deeper—"

There was sense in what he said, but Savine detested the way he said it. "My thanks, but it is not iron that interests me at the moment, but soap."

"Pardon me?"

"Soap, glass, crockery. Things which were once luxuries for the noble have become essentials for the wealthy and will soon be a staple for everyone. Clean bodies, and glazed windows, and . . . crockery. Find a way to pump dinnerware out of the ground and I would be delighted to discuss it."

"You must be joking."

"I save my jokes for those with a sense of humour. You understand I have to be careful in my choice of partners."

"You are making a mistake."

"It would hardly be my first. I struggle on regardless."

"One should never allow feelings to get in the way of profit," he snapped, slightly blotchy with anger about the collar. Zuri had slipped from the crowd now and was doing her best to ease him away but he refused to be moved. "This only strengthens my conviction that there really is no place in business for women."

"And yet here I am," said Savine, smiling all the wider. "And here you are, with your begging bowl. No doubt there are many parts of Union life in which there is no place for women. But you cannot stop me buying or selling a thing."

Curnsbick breathed on his eye-lenses and gave them a wipe. "Take care, my friend." And he placed them on his nose and looked up from under his brows. "Before Lady Savine chooses to buy and sell you."

"No need to worry." Savine flicked out her fan with a snap. "I only buy things with some profit in them."

"Master Arinhorm looks rather angry," murmured Curnsbick as they moved away through the crowd. "You might find, in the long run, that a little generosity can repay itself five-fold. Goodwill can be the best of investments—"

She dismissed his nonsense with a fond pat of his hand. "Generosity and goodwill sit well on you but they simply do not go with my complexion at all. A certain number of bitter enemies are an essential accessory for a lady of fashion."

"And it may be that he has procured an investor after all."

"Damn it." He was already deep in conversation with Selest dan Heugen. "Is she picking through my offcuts?"

"Do you know, I think she might be."

"Like a bitch at the butcher's bins."

"She seems quite popular with the gentlemen of the Society." Indeed, one could almost see the grey heads turning as she slipped through the room on Arinhorm's arm.

"Anything with a quim is popular with them," muttered Savine.

"Ouch. She reminds me of a younger you."

"Younger me was poison."

"Younger you was *nectar*. Almost as much so as older you. But I've heard it said that imitation is the most honest tribute. We have a whole theatre full of old fools trying to do a Curnsbick, after all. Do I complain?"

"Whenever you're not boasting."

"I've been boasting continuously for so long it hadn't come up." And Curnsbick gave her the mildest of grins. "The Circle of the World is wide, Savine. You can allow someone else to occupy one little plot of it."

"I suppose so," she grudgingly admitted, putting the distasteful union of Arinhorm and Heugen from her mind. "As long as they're paying me rent."

But Curnsbick was no longer listening. The eager chatter was falling silent, the crowd parting like soil before the plough. A man strode through the throng, his facial hair meticulously barbered and lavishly waxed, his crimson uniform festooned with gold braid.

"Bloody hell," whispered Curnsbick, gripping her wrist, "it's the bloody king!"

Whatever the criticisms of His Majesty—and there were many, regularly circulated in ever more scurrilous pamphlets—no one could have denied that King Jezal always looked the part. He chuckled, slapped arms, shook hands, traded jokes, a beacon of slightly absent good humour. A dozen fully armoured Knights of the Body clattered after him, and at least two score clerks, officers, servants, attendants and hangers-on after them, chestfuls of unearned medals glittering beneath the thousand dancing candle flames above.

"Master Curnsbick." His Majesty ushered the great inventor up from his knee. "So sorry I'm late. This and that at the palace, you know. Management of the realm. So much to take care of."

"Your Majesty," frothed Curnsbick, "the Solar Society is *illuminated* by your presence. I regret that we had to begin the addresses without you—"

"No, no! Progress waits for no one, eh, Curnsbick? Not even kings."

"Especially not kings, Your Majesty," said Savine, sinking into an even deeper curtsy. One of the royal party issued a choked splutter at her insolence, but no risk, no profit.

Curnsbick held out his hand to present her. "And this is—"

"Savine dan Glokta, of course," said the king. "It makes one very proud, to see one's subjects showing such . . . enterprise and determination." He gave a strange little shake of his fist. So strong a gesture, so weakly delivered. "I've always admired people who . . . *make* things."

Savine sank lower still. She had long ago become used to men staring at her. Had learned to tolerate it, to deflect it gracefully, to turn it to her advantage. But the look the king was giving her was not the usual kind. There was something awfully sad behind his blandly handsome grin.

"Your Majesty is far too kind," she said.

"Not kind enough." She wondered if he had somehow found out about her and his son. Had Orso let something slip? "With such young women to lead the way, the Union's future looks bright indeed."

Fortunately, there was a commotion further down the hall. A knight herald pushed through the crowd, winged helmet tucked under one arm. "Your Majesty, I have news."

The king looked mildly annoyed. "That's your job, isn't it? Could you be more specific?"

"News . . . from the North." He leaned in to whisper, and the king's fixed smile sagged.

"My apologies, Lady Savine. My apologies, everyone! I am needed at the Agriont." The gilt edge of His Majesty's cloak snapped as he spun on one highly polished heel, his retinue crowding after like a gaggle of self-important ducklings behind their mother, not a smile among them.

Curnsbick puffed out his cheeks. "Do you think we could call ourselves endorsed by His Majesty after a visit of half a minute?"

"A visit's a visit," muttered Savine. The chatter was already louder than ever, people flocking towards the doors, jostling one another in their haste to be first to learn the news. And to profit by it. "Find out what that knight herald had to say," she murmured to Zuri. "Oh, and make a note—I would like Kaspar dan Arinhorm to have troubles with his business in Angland."

Zuri slipped her pencil from behind her ear. "Rumours, regulations, or just no one answering his letters?"

"Let's start with a bit of each and see how we go."

Savine had not made society a snakepit. She was simply determined to slither to the top of it and stay there. If that meant being the most venomous reptile in Adua, so be it.

Fencing with Father

"Wake up, Your Highness." And there was the hideous scraping of curtains being flung wide.

Orso forced one eye open a slit, holding up a hand to block the savage glare. "I thought I said you shouldn't call me that." He lifted his head, but it began to throb in a most unpleasing manner, so he let it drop. "And how dare you presume to wake the heir to the throne?"

"I thought you said I shouldn't call you that?"

"I'm being inconsistent. The Crown Prince of the Union—"

"And Talins, theoretically."

"—can be as inconsistent as he damn well pleases." Orso's fumbling hand closed about the handle of a jug and he lifted it and took a swig, realised too late there was stale ale in it rather than water, and spat it over the wall in a mist.

"Your Highness will have to be inconsistent while dressing," said Tunny. "There's news."

Orso looked for water, couldn't see any, and swigged down the dregs of the ale after all. "Don't tell me that blonde from yesterday was carrying the cock-rot." He tossed the jug rolling across the floor and sagged back into bed. "The last thing I need is another dose—"

"Scale Ironhand and his Northmen have invaded the Protectorate. They've burned Uffrith."

"Pfft." Orso thought about grabbing a shoe and throwing it at Tunny but decided he couldn't be arsed, so he rolled over and cuddled up to that girl, what's-her-name, pressing his half-hard cock into the small of her back where it was warm and making her give a semi-conscious mew of upset. "That isn't funny."

"You're damn right it isn't. Lady Governor Finree dan Brock is fighting a brave rearguard action along with the Dogman and her son Leo, the big, bold Young Lion, but they're giving ground before the terror of the

84

Northmen and their fearsome champion Stour Nightfall, the Great Wolf, who's sworn to drive the damn Southerners out of Angland." There was a brief silence. "We're the damn Southerners, in case you're wondering."

Orso managed to get both eyes open at once. "You're not joking?"

"You'll know when I'm joking because Your Highness will be laughing."

"What the—" Orso felt a sudden stab of... *something*. Worry? Excitement? Anger? Jealousy? Some *feeling*, anyway. It was so long since he really had one it was like a spur in his backside. He scrambled out of bed, got one foot tangled in the sheet, kicked it free and accidently kicked what's-her-name in the back.

"The hell?" she mumbled as she sat up, trying to claw hair tangled with wine out of her face.

"Sorry!" said Orso. "Terribly sorry, but... Northmen! Invaded! Lions and wolves and whatever!" He grabbed his little box and took a pinch of pearl dust up each nostril. Just to blow away the cobwebs. "Someone should bloody do something." As the burning at the back of his nose faded, that feeling became sharper. So sharp it made him shiver, the hairs on the backs of his arms standing up. *You could try doing something to be proud of*, his mother had said. Might this be his chance? He had scarcely even realised how much he wanted one.

He looked from the empty bottles about the bed to Tunny, standing against the wall with his arms folded. "*I* should do something! Draw me a bath!"

"Hildi's already doing it."

"Where are my trousers?" Tunny tossed them over and Orso snatched them from the air. "I have to see my father right away! Is it Monday?"

"Tuesday," said Tunny as he swaggered from the room. "He'll be fencing."

"Then see if you can find my steels as well!" bellowed Orso as the door swung shut.

"For pity's sake, shut up," moaned what's-her-face, pulling the covers over her head.

"One touch a piece!" The king grinned hugely as he offered his hand.

"Well fought, Your Majesty." Orso let his father pull him to his feet, rubbing at his bruised ribs as he stooped to retrieve his fallen steel. He had to admit he was feeling the pace. His padded jacket seemed rather more padded than the last time he wore it. Perhaps his mother was right and he had passed the age where he could get away with anything. One sober day a week might be a good idea, from now on. A morning a week, at any rate.

But circumstances always conspired to stop him doing the right thing. By then, one of the servants was floating across the perfectly manicured lawn with two glasses on his polished tray.

The king wedged his long steel under his arm to sweep one up. "A little refreshment?"

"You know I never drink before lunch," said Orso.

They looked at each other for a moment, then both burst out laughing. "You've a hell of a sense of humour," said Orso's father, raising his glass in a little toast. "No one could ever deny that."

"To the best of my knowledge, they never have. It's every other good quality they accuse me of lacking." He took a swig, swilled it about his mouth and swallowed. "Ah, rich and red and full of sunshine." Osprian, no doubt, which made him wish, if only briefly, that they'd conquered Styria after all. "I'd forgotten what excellent wine you have."

"I'm the king, aren't I? If my wine's poor, there's something seriously wrong with the world."

"There are several things seriously wrong with the world, Father."

"Doubtless! I was visited by a delegation of working men from Keln, you know, just yesterday, with a set of grievances about conditions in the manufacturing districts there." He frowned across the beautiful palace gardens and shook his head in dismay. "Choking vapours on the air, adulterated food, putrid water, an outbreak of the shudders, awful injuries from the machinery, babies born deformed. Terrible stories—"

"And Scale Ironhand has invaded the Dogman's Protectorate."

The king paused, glass halfway to his mouth. "You heard about that?"

"I've been in a whorehouse, not down a well. Adua's buzzing with the news."

"Since when did you care about politics?"

"I care about a crowd of barbarians burning the cities of our allies, spreading blood and murder and threatening to invade the sovereign territory of the Union. I'm the heir to the bloody throne, aren't I?"

The king wiped his lustrous moustaches—grey shot with gold these days, rather than gold shot with grey—and wriggled his fingers back into his glove. "Since when did you care about being heir to the throne?"

"I've always cared," he lied, tossing the glass rattling back onto the tray and making the servant gasp as he weaved about trying to stop it falling. "I've just . . . had some trouble expressing it. Ready, old man?"

"Always, young pup!" The king sprang forward, jabbing. Their long steels feathered together, pinged and scraped. The king stabbed with his short steel but Orso caught it on his own, held it, turned. They broke apart, circling one another, Orso's eyes on the point of his father's long steel, but flicking occasionally to his leading foot. His Majesty had a habit of twisting it before he struck.

"You're a fine swordsman, you know," said the king. "I swear you've the talent to win a Contest."

"Talent? Possibly. Dedication, stamina, commitment? Never."

"You could be a true master if you practised more than once a month."

"If I practise once a year, it's a busy one." In fact, Orso practised at least once a week, but had his father known, he might have suspected that Orso was letting him win. You wouldn't have thought the monarch of the most powerful nation in the Circle of the World would care about beating his own son in the fencing circle, but throwing a touch or two was always the surest way for Orso to get what he wanted.

"So... what *are* we planning to do about the Northmen?" he asked.

"We?" The point of his father's long steel flicked against Orso's.

"All right, you."

"Me?" And flicked the other way.

"Your Closed Council, then."

"They plan to do precisely nothing."

"What?" Orso's steel drooped. "But Scale Ironhand has invaded our Protectorate!"

"That's in no doubt."

"We're supposed to be protecting it. Practically by definition!"

"I understand the principle, boy." The king lunged and Orso dodged aside, hacked with his short steel, the clang of their blades making the great pink wading birds in a nearby fountain look scornfully over. "But principles and reality are occasional bedfellows at best."

Like you and mother? Orso almost said, but thought that might be a little too much spice for the king's rather bland tastes in humour. Instead, he dodged another lunge and switched to the attack, catching his father's long steel on his, blade flickering around it and whipping it from his hand.

He caught a despairing thrust of the short steel, guards scraping, then the blade of his long flexed lightly as he jabbed the king in the shoulder.

"Two to one," said Orso, slashing at the air. Wouldn't do to let the old man win too easily. No one ever values what they get without trying, after all.

He beckoned one of the servants over with a towel while his father snapped his fingers impatiently at another to fetch his fallen sword.

"There will always be some crisis, Orso, and it will always be the worst ever. Not long ago, we were terrified of the Gurkish, and with good reason. Half of Adua was destroyed driving them out. Now their great Prophet Khalul has vanished, their all-powerful Emperor Uthman is deposed, and their power has drifted apart like smoke on the breeze. Instead of conquering armies, it is desperate refugees who spill from the South."

"Can't we take a moment to enjoy the fall of an enemy?"

"Some of us find little to celebrate in the violent overthrow of a monarch."

Orso winced. "I suppose it does strike a little close to home."

"All it shows is that great powers can fall as well as rise. Murcatto has almost all of Styria under her heel and the Old Empire grows in strength, challenging our hold on the Far Country and inciting yet more rebellion in Starikland. Now the bloody Northmen break our hard-won treaties and come to war again. There's no end to their appetite for blood up there."

"For other people's blood, maybe." Orso tossed the towel over the servant's head and found his mark again. "It's surprising how quickly the toughest men tire of the sight of their own."

"True enough. But it's the enemies inside our borders that cost me sleep. The wars in Styria have left everyone out of pocket and out of patience. The Open Council never stops complaining. If the nobles didn't hate each other even more than me, I swear they'd already be in open rebellion. The peasants may have quieter voices but they're every bit as dissatisfied. I face disloyalty everywhere."

"Then we must teach a sharp lesson, Your Majesty." Orso cut, cut, thrust and the king turned the cuts aside, sidestepped the thrust, blundered into a bush clipped to look like a storybook magus's tower and danced back into space. "A lesson delivered to the Northmen, but witnessed by your faithless subjects, too. Show our allies we can be relied upon, and our enemies that we won't be trifled with. A clutch of victories, a couple of parades and a dash of patriotic fervour! The very thing to bring the nation together."

"You're giving me the same arguments I gave to my own Closed Council, but the coffers are quite simply empty. They're beyond empty, in fact. You could fill the moat of the Agriont with the money I owe and still have debts left over. There's nothing I can do."

"But you're the High King of the Union!"

Orso's father gave a sad smile. "One day, my son, you'll understand. The more powerful you are, the less you can really do about anything."

The points of his steels appeared to wilt as he spoke, but it was quite clearly a ruse, Orso could tell he was ready by the way he held his back leg. Still, the king was so pleased with his trap it would have been rude not to blunder into it. Orso dived forward with a bark of triumph, then a highly convincing gurgle of shock at the parry he had known was coming. He suppressed his instinct to block the king's short steel, let it slip past his guard and groaned as it thudded into his training jacket.

"Two each!" cackled Orso's father. "Nothing like a bit of self-pity to bring the hothead rushing in!"

"Richly done, Father."

"Life in the old dog yet, eh?"

"Fortunately. I think we can both agree I'm not quite ready to take the throne."

"No one ever is, my boy. Why are you so interested in a Northern expedition, anyway?"

Orso took a deep breath and held his father's eye. "I want to lead it."

"You want to *what*?"

"I want to ... you know ... *contribute*. To something other than whores' purses."

His father gave a snort of laughter. "The last body of soldiers you led was that toy regiment the Governor of Starikland sent you when you were five years old."

"Then it's high time I gained some experience. I'm the heir to the throne, aren't I?"

"So your mother tells me, and I try never to disagree with her."

"I have to mend my reputation at some point." Orso stepped to his mark for their deciding touch, hacking a muddy divot out of the perfect lawn with his heel. "Poor thing's in a wretched state."

"Worried this Young Lion will steal all the glory, eh?"

Orso had heard that name too often for comfort lately. "I daresay he could spare a few shreds for his king-to-be."

"But ... fighting?" Orso's father worked his mouth unhappily and the old scar through his beard twisted. "The Northmen don't fool about when it comes to bloodshed. I could tell you some stories about my old friend Logen Ninefingers—"

"You have, Father, a hundred times."

"Well, they're bloody good stories!" The king straightened a moment, lowering his steels and giving Orso a quizzical little frown. "You really want this, don't you?"

"We have to do *something*."

"I suppose we do, at that." The king sprang forward but Orso was ready,

89

parried, twisted away, parried again. "All right. How about this?" Cut, cut, jab, and Orso retreated, watching. "I'll give you Gorst, twenty Knights of the Body and a battalion of the King's Own."

"That's nowhere near enough!" Orso switched to the offensive, almost caught his father with a jab and made him hop back.

"I agree." The king paced sideways, point of his long steel describing glittering little circles in the air. "The rest you'll have to find yourself. Show me you can raise five thousand more. *Then* you can rush to the rescue."

Orso blinked. Raising five thousand troops sounded worryingly like work. But there was an unfamiliar energy spreading through him at the thought of having something meaningful to *do*.

"Then I bloody well will!" He'd got all he'd get by losing. He felt like winning for once. "Defend yourself, Your Majesty!"

And steel scraped on steel as he sprang forward.

Fencing with Father

"Jab, jab, Savine," said her father, craning forward from his chair to follow her movements. "Jab, jab."

Her shoulder was on fire, the pain spreading down her arm to her fingertips, but she forced herself on, struggling to make every jab sharp, tight, perfect.

"Good," piped Gorst as he turned her efforts away, always balanced, always calm, the sounds of scraping steel echoing about the bare room.

Nothing was ever good enough for her father, though. "Watch your front foot," he snapped. "Keep your weight spread."

"My weight *is* spread." And she pumped out three more jabs, lightning-quick.

"Spread it more. I know how much you hate to do anything badly."

"Almost as much as you hate to see me do anything badly."

"Spread your weight, then. We'll both be happier."

She widened her stance and let go some more jabs, her steel scraping against Gorst's.

"Better?" asked her father.

It clearly was, but they both knew she would never concede defeat by admitting it. "We'll see. How are things in the North?"

"A procession of disappointments, like most of life. The Northmen advance, the Anglanders fall back."

"People say we can expect no better with a woman leading our troops." Savine lunged, steel clashing as Gorst caught her sword on his own and steered it wide.

"We both know what utter fools *people* are." Her father sneered the word as though the very thought of humans disgusted him. "Since the death of her father, I daresay Finree dan Brock is the Union's most competent general. You know her, don't you, Gorst?"

The king's hulking bodyguard, normally beyond expressionless, winced. "A little, Your Eminence."

"I wish I could have given her the command in Styria," said Savine's father. "We might have been counting our victories now, rather than our dead. Jab, then!"

"Brock against Murcatto, that would have been *something*." Savine hissed as she snapped out another flurry. "The two greatest armies in the Circle of the World, both commanded by women."

"They'd probably have decided there were better things to spend the money on and talked the whole thing out. Then where would we be? Enough with the point, let's see what you can do with the edge. And cut like you mean it, Savine, he's not made of glass."

She darted at Gorst as if to go right, switched to the left with a savage cut at head height. He dropped points and jerked away, fast as a snake in spite of his size, eyes focused on the blade as it whistled past his nose.

"Excellent," he squeaked.

She gave her steels a little flourish. "Can Brock beat the Northmen alone?"

"She's still gathering her forces in Angland," said her father, "and she has the Dogman with her, but Scale Ironhand has them well outnumbered. My guess is the Protectorate will be overrun but she'll hold the Northmen at the Whiteflow. Then, perhaps, circumstances will change here and we can swoop in next spring and reap the glory."

"The women do the hard work and the men reap the glory. Sounds familiar."

"Petulance is unbecoming in a swordswoman. Cut, girl. Put some blood into it."

Savine darted around Gorst, shoes squeaking on the wooden floor, slashing away from every angle. For all he scarcely seemed to move, his steels were always in the right place to parry.

"My daughter has quick feet, eh, Gorst?"

"Very quick, Your Eminence."

"That'll be your mother's dancing lessons. Sad to say, I don't dance much myself these days."

"A shame," said Savine as she circled, looking for an opening, sweat tickling at her stubbled scalp. "I imagine the Closed Council could use some clever footwork. If Brock loses, you'll look like cowards and fools."

"Even bigger cowards and fools than we do already."

"If she wins, she'll gild her own reputation. And her son's."

"Leonault dan Brock." Her father sneered, showing his empty gums again. "The Young Lion."

"Who comes up with these ridiculous names?"

"*Writers*, I daresay. I saw lions when I was on campaign in Gurkhul. Stupid beasts. Especially the males. That's enough. Break."

Savine took a hard breath, pulling her padded tunic open to let some air in. She had sweated clean through her shirt. She wondered, as she scrubbed her shaved head with a towel, whether the fine gentlemen of the Solar Society would recognise her now, without powder, jewels, dress, wig. More than likely they would smell money through the sweat and swarm around her just the same.

"We could adjust your grip a little." Her father leaned forwards, bones shifting under the pale skin of his hand as he gripped his cane to rise.

"No, no." She stepped over to put a gentle hand on his shoulder. "You're not hurting yourself just to show me how to grip a sword." She took the blanket from the arm of his chair and draped it over his legs, tucked it in carefully around him. By the Fates, he felt thin. It would have been unfair to call him skin and bone. There was scarcely any skin on him.

"How are you?" she asked.

His left eye twitched. "Have you noticed the nation falling?"

"Not this morning."

"Then I suppose I'm still alive today. You might want to check again tomorrow, though. I've enemies everywhere. In the palace. On the Closed Council. On the Open Council. In the fields and the factories. The Anglanders were furious with me before the war, they're downright incandescent now. I'm hated everywhere."

"Not here," she said. As close to a declaration of affection as she was ever likely to utter.

"That's more than enough for me." He gently touched her face, fingertips cold on her sweaty cheek. "And far, far more than I deserve."

"I suppose a few enemies are the price of one of the big chairs."

Her father gave a snort of disgust, bitter even for him. "The moment your arse hits the wood, you realise what they're worth. You think the Closed Council really rule? Or the king and queen? We're all no more than dancing puppets. There to draw the eye. To take the blame."

Savine frowned. "Then who pulls the strings?"

Her father's eyes met hers, bright and hard. "I have been asking questions all my life. I learned that some are better left unanswered." He let his hand drop and clapped it on top of hers. The one that held her steels. "Time to work on your defence."

"Three strikes?" asked Gorst.

Savine tossed her short steel up with her right hand and snatched it out of the air with her left. "Whatever you say."

He shuffled at her, jabbed and cut with no real venom. It was easy for her to block the jabs, to turn the cut away with a showy flick of the wrist.

"So, if the lady governor fights the Northmen to a stalemate, what does it mean for holdings in Angland?"

"Ah!" Her father grinned. "I was wondering when we'd get to money."

"We never left it." She parried, and again, sidestepped a sluggish lunge. For a man renowned for his ferocity, Gorst was scarcely hitting at all. "Prices are tumbling up there. Do I sell out or get deeper in?"

"The Union will never let go of Angland. If I were a man of business, I'd be snapping up the bargains. After all, danger and opportunity—"

"Often walk hand in hand," she finished for him, and out of the corner of her eye she caught his grin. There were few things that gave her the same satisfaction as making the Arch Lector smile. Aside from her mother, no one else could manage it. "I'll see about borrowing a little to expand my holdings in the mines up there." She could hardly keep the smile off her face. "There are excellent rates on offer from Valint and Balk—"

"Don't!" barked her father, with a wince that made her feel just a little guilty. "Don't even joke about it, Savine. Valint and Balk are vermin. Parasites. Leeches. Once they get stuck to you, there's no getting free of them. They won't be satisfied until they own the sun and can charge the world interest for letting it rise every morning. Promise me you'll never take a bit from the bastards!"

"I promise. I'll stay well away." Though it was not always easy. Like a greedy old willow tree, the twisted roots of that particular banking house burrowed into everything. "We're not talking about much. I already took a controlling share in the armoury in Ostenhorm at a price you would scarcely believe."

"Swords are always a good investment," admitted the Arch Lector as he watched her swat Gorst's away with her own.

"I'm told these fire-tubes are the future. These cannons."

"We had mixed results with them in Styria."

"But they're getting smaller all the time, more portable and more powerful." She stepped nimbly around a limp jab. "They've developed an exploding cannon-stone now."

"Explosions are always a good investment, too."

"Especially if I can arrange a contract or two with the King's Own."

"Oh? Do you know anyone with influence?"

"As it happens, I have arranged a little soirée with Asil dan Roth and a few other military wives. Her husband was recently appointed Master of the King's Armouries, I believe."

"What good fortune," murmured her father, drily.

Gorst's next lunge was positively belittling. "I'm not made of glass, either," said Savine, flicking irritably at the point of his steel. "Come at me like you mean it."

She had been fencing all her life, after all. As a girl, she had dreamed of winning the Contest disguised as a man, whipping off her cap to reveal her golden tresses to an ecstatic crowd. Then wigs had come into fashion and she had shaved her tresses off, which, honestly, had been a rather unprepossessing brown in any case. Then she had learned men never cheer for a woman who beats them at their own games, so she had left the fencing circle to the cocks and decided to count her victories at the bank.

She parried two efforts which were scarcely stronger than before and, this time, stepped neatly around the lazy cut that followed and gave Gorst a shove with the basketwork of her short steel. "Do you hit like a woman as well as talk like one?"

Gorst's eye gave the faintest twitch. "Ouch!" called her father. "A touch to the lady."

"I want to know how it feels to be attacked by a dangerous man who *means* it." Savine set herself again, confident in her stance, confident in her grip, confident in her abilities. "Otherwise what's the point?"

Gorst glanced at her father. The Arch Lector pressed his lips thoughtfully together, then gave the faintest shrug. "She *is* here to learn." There was a hardness on his face she was not used to seeing. "Teach her."

There was something ever so slightly different in the way Gorst took his mark, the way he twisted his feet into the faintly creaking boards, the way he worked his great shoulders and gripped his notched steels. His flat face hardly showed emotion, but it was as if a door had opened a chink, and beyond it Savine glimpsed something monstrous.

It is easy to smile at the bull you know is chained. When you realise of a sudden the chain is off, and its horns towards you, and its hoof scraping at the dust, the bull looks an entirely different animal.

She half-opened her mouth to say, "Wait."

"Begin."

She had been ready for his strength. It was his speed that shocked her. He was on her before she could draw a breath. Her eyes went wide as his long steel whipped down and she had just the presence of mind to sidestep, bringing up her short steel to parry.

She had not been ready for his strength after all. The force of it numbed her arm from fingertips to shoulder, rattled the teeth in her head. She stumbled back, gasping, but his short steel was already coming at her, crashing into her long, ripping it from her numb fingers and sending it skittering across the floor. She flapped blindly with her short, all training and technique forgotten, saw a flash of metal—

His long steel thudded into her padded jacket and drove her breath out in a burning wheeze, nearly lifted her off her feet and sent her tottering sideways. A moment later, his shoulder rammed into her body. Her head snapped forward, her face crunched against something. The blunt top of his skull, maybe.

Was she in the air?

The wall smashed her in the back, the bare room reeled and, to her great surprise, she found herself on hands and knees, blinking at the floor.

Spots of blood pit-pattered onto the polished wood in front of her face.

"Oh," she gasped.

Her ribs throbbed with each snatched breath, sick scalding the back of her throat. Her hand was all tangled up in the basketwork of her short steel, and she flopped it drunkenly around until the sword clattered onto the floor. The backs of her fingers were all grazed. She put them to her throbbing mouth and they came away bloody. Her hand was shaking. She was shaking all over.

It hurt. Her face, her side, her pride. But it was not the pain that really shook her. It was the powerlessness. The total misjudgement of her own abilities. The curtain had been twitched aside, and she saw just how fragile she was. How fragile anyone was, compared to a sword swung in anger. The world was a different place than it had been a few moments before, and not a better one.

Gorst squatted before her, notched steels in one hand. "I should warn you that I was still holding back."

She managed to nod. "I see."

There was no trace of guilt on her father's face. Constant pain, as he always liked to say, had cured him of that. "Fencing is one thing," he said. "Actual violence quite another. Few of us are made for it. It is healthy to be disabused of our self-deceptions every now and then, even if it hurts."

He smiled while she wiped the blood from her nose. Savine had given up trying to understand him. Most of the time, she was the one thing he loved in a world he despised. Then, on occasion, he treated her like a rival to be crushed.

"If you are attacked by a dangerous man who means it, my advice is to run away." Gorst stood, offering his broad hand. "I expect he will destroy himself before too long."

When he pulled her up, her legs were jelly. "Thank you, Colonel Gorst. That was...a very useful lesson." She wanted to cry. Or her body did, at least. She would not let it. She set her aching jaw and stuck her chin up at him. "Same time next week?"

Her father barked out a laugh and slapped the arm of his chair. "*That's my girl!*"

Promises

Broad lay awake, staring at the ceiling.

There was a crack, next to a yellowed blister on the limewash. Felt like he'd been staring at it all night. Staring at it as the sun crawled up over the narrow buildings, through the washing strung between them and into the narrow street, through the narrow window and into the one-room cellar they were living in.

Felt like he'd been staring at that crack for weeks. Turning things over in his mind. Fretting at them as if they were big choices he had to make. But they were big choices he'd already made, and he'd made the wrong ones, and now there was no changing them.

He took a heavy breath, felt it catch at the back of his throat. That oily scratch on the Valbeck air. That smell of shit and onions the cellar always had, no matter how Liddy scrubbed it. It was in the walls. It was in his skin.

Folk were setting off to work outside, boots tramping through the muck beyond the tiny window near the ceiling, shadows of their passing flickering on the mould-speckled wall.

"How are your hands?" murmured Liddy, twisting towards him on the narrow bed.

He winced as he worked the fingers. "Always sore in the mornings."

Liddy took his big hand in her small ones, rubbing at his aching palm, at his throbbing knuckles. "May up already?"

"She slipped out. Didn't want to wake you."

They lay there, she looking at him, he not daring to look at her. Not wanting to see the disappointment in her eyes. The worry. The fear. Even if it was only his own disappointment, and worry, and fear reflected back, like in a mirror.

"It's not fair on her," he whispered at that crack in the ceiling. "She

98

should be having a life. Dancing, courting. Not waiting on some rich bastard."

"She doesn't mind doing it. She wants to help. She's a good girl."

"She's the best thing I've done. She's the only good thing I've done."

"You've done good, Gunnar. You've done lots of good."

"You don't know what it was like, in Styria. What *I* was like—"

"Then do good now." An edge of impatience in her voice, and she gave his hand one last squeeze and let it go. "You can't change what's past, can you? Only what's next."

He wanted to argue but couldn't find a crack in her obvious good sense. He lay there sullen, listening to the shuffle of boots and the yammer of angry voices and a girl at the crossroads yelling out bad news for coppers. A bread riot in Holsthorm, and a plot to burn a mill in Keln, and unrest in every corner of Midderland, and war. War in the North.

"It's my fault," he muttered. Couldn't find a way to attack Liddy, so he ambushed himself. "I should never have gone to war."

"I let you go. I let the farm go."

"The farm was done anyway. That life was done. Would've been better for you and May if I'd never come back."

She put her hand on his cheek, firm. Turned his head so she was looking him straight in the face. "Don't ever say that, Gunnar. Don't *ever* say that."

"I killed 'em, Liddy," he whispered. "I killed 'em."

She said nothing. What could she say?

"I fucked it all," he said. "In one moment. Is there a thing I can't ruin?"

"There's nothing can't be ruined in a moment," said Liddy. "It all hangs by a thread, all the time. We've got to look forward now. That's what you do. You move on."

"I'll put it right," he said. "I'll find work here."

"I know you will." She forced out a smile. Looked like it took a lot of effort, but she forced it out. "You're a good man, Gunnar."

He winced at that, felt the pain of tears at the back of his nose. "No more violence," he said, voice thick and throaty. "I promise, Liddy." He realised he'd clenched his fists, forced them to open. "From now on I'll stay out of trouble."

"Gunnar," she murmured, soft and serious, "you should only make promises you know you can keep."

A little sprinkle of dust came floating down onto their bed. Along the street at the foundry, the engines were starting up, making the whole room tremble.

Wasn't until he got around the corner Broad even realised what he was queueing for.

Cadman's Ales was printed in gilded paint above the sliding warehouse doors, the bang and clatter of work booming from inside. A brewery. He'd spent half his time in Styria drunk and the rest aiming to get drunk. He'd promised no trouble, and he knew that for him, every bottle had trouble at the bottom.

Still, temptation was never far away in Valbeck. Every other building had a tap-house or a jerry-shop or a still in it, licensed or otherwise, whores and thieves and beggars buzzing around them like flies at a midden, and if you couldn't make it as far as next door to drown your misery, there were boys running the streets with barrels on their backs who'd bring the beer to you.

A brewery was a poor omen, far as Broad's promise to stay clear of trouble was concerned. But he'd seen no good omens in Valbeck, and he needed work. So he pulled his coat closed and hunched his shoulders against the thin rain that fell black out of the murky sky like ink, and shuffled forward another half-step.

"However early I get here, there's always a queue," said a grey-faced, grey-haired old man in a coat worn through at the elbows.

"More and more folk coming into Valbeck for the work," muttered one of the others.

"Always more folk wanting work. Never enough to go around. Used to be I had a house o' my own, up the valley near Hambernalt. You know it?"

"Can't say I do," muttered Broad, thinking of his own valley. The green trees in the breeze, the green grass soft around his ankles. He knew things were always better in your memory and the farm had been hard work for lean rewards, but it had been green. There was nothing green in Valbeck. Except the river, maybe, stained with great coloured smears from the dyeing works upstream.

"Beautiful valley, it used to be," the old man was droning. "Good house, I had, in the woods there, by the river. Raised five boys in it. Used to be good money in coppicing, burning charcoal, you know. Then they started making charcoal cheap in a furnace upstream and the river got full of tar." He gave a long, helpless sniff. "Prices just kept falling. Then Lord bloody Barezin cleared the forest for more grazing land anyway."

A big wagon clattered past, rattling wheels ripping muck out of the road and showering it across the queue, and men grumbled and shouted abuse at the driver and the driver grumbled and shouted abuse at the men, and they all shuffled forwards another half-step.

"My boys went off to other things. One died in Styria. One got married down near Keln, I heard. I had to borrow and I lost the house. Beautiful valley, it used to be."

"Aye, well," muttered Broad, feeling too sorry for himself to much enjoy anyone else doing the same. "Used to be gets you nowhere."

"True enough," said the old man, right away making Broad wish he'd never spoken. "Why, I remember back when I was a lad—"

"Shut your fucking hole, y'old dunce," snapped the man in front of Broad.

He was a big bastard with a star-shaped scar on his cheek and a piece out of his ear. A veteran, no doubt. The anger in his voice set Broad's heart thumping. A tickle of excitement.

The old man stared. "I'm not wanting to cause no offence—"

"That's why you should shut your fucking hole."

Just stay silent. Just stay out of it. He should've learned that lesson, shouldn't he? Learned it a dozen times and more. He'd promised Liddy. Just hours since he promised her. No more trouble.

"Leave him be," growled Broad.

"What'd you say?"

Broad took his lenses off and slipped them into his coat pocket, the queue behind the man's frowning face made a blur.

"I get it," said Broad. "You're disappointed. Don't reckon any man here had life turn out just the way he hoped, do you?"

"What d'you know about my hopes?"

Took everything he had not to smash this bastard's skull. But he'd promised Liddy. So Broad just took a step forwards, so the spit from his bared teeth flecked the man's scarred cheek.

"I know you'll find none of 'em facing this way." He lifted his fist. Turned his finger. "Now turn around 'fore I put your fucking head through the wall."

The man's scarred cheek twitched and, just for a moment, Broad thought he might fight. For one beautiful moment, he thought he could stop clinging on, and let go. The first time he'd felt free since he came back from Styria. Well, apart from when he smashed Lennart Seldom's face in.

Then the man's bloodshot eyes found Broad's fist. The tattoo on the back of it. He grumbled something and turned around. He stood, shifting his weight from one foot to the other. Then he pulled his shabby collar up, and cut out of the line, and stalked away.

"Thanks for that," said the old man, knob on the front of his scrawny throat bobbing. "Ain't many folk left will do the decent thing."

"The decent thing." Broad winced as he worked his fingers open. Seemed the only time they didn't hurt was when his fists were clenched. "Don't even know what that is any more."

He'd seen a lot of different men at the end of these queues, choosing who got work and who got nothing. Most had developed a liking for watching folk squirm. It had been the same with the officers in Styria. It's a rare man who's made better by a bit of power.

The foreman at the door of Cadman's Ales looked like one of the better ones, though, sat under a little awning with a big ledger in front of him. Grey-haired and solid, every movement slow and precise, like he'd taken his time and thought out just the right way to do it.

"My name's Gunnar Bull," lied Broad. He was a bad liar, and got the feeling this man saw straight through him.

"I'm Malmer." He gave Broad a careful look up and down. "Got any experience with breweries?"

"Guess I've drunk a fair bit o' their output down the years." Broad tried a grin, but Malmer didn't look like joining him. "But no experience with making it, no." Malmer just gave a slow nod, like he was used to disappointment. "I'll work hard, though." He'd had but two hours' work that week, raking out stables. This was his third stop today, and he couldn't go home empty-handed. "I'll shovel coal, or I'll sweep floors, or . . . well . . . whatever you want. I'll work hard, I promise you that."

Malmer gave a sad little smile. "Promises are cheap, friend."

"Shitting hell! Is that Sergeant Broad?"

A lean man with a sandy beard and a stained apron had come striding out of the brewery, hands on hips. Broad knew the face, but it took a while to riddle out where he'd seen it before and slot it into the world he lived in now. "Sarlby?"

"This is Bull Broad!" Sarlby grabbed Broad's hand and yanked it like he was trying to get water from a stiff pump. "Remember, Malmer, I told you all about him! Fought with him in Styria! Behind him, anyway, weren't such a good idea to be in front."

Malmer sat back, giving Broad that careful look again. "You told me a lot of stories about Styria. Must confess I somewhat stopped listening."

"Well, start fucking listening 'cause this is about the best man I know! First up the ladders at the siege of Borletta! First didn't fall straight back down, leastways. He was always the first man in. How many times? Five?" He caught Broad's wrist and pushed his sleeve up to show the stars on his knuckles. "Look at those bastards!" Like he was showing off some prize vegetable. "Look at *those bastards*."

Broad pulled his hand free, drew it up into his sleeve. "I put all that behind me."

"In my experience, the past don't drop back far," said Malmer. "You'll vouch for him?"

"Ain't a man he served with wouldn't vouch for him ten times over. By all the fucking Fates, yes, I'll vouch for him!"

"Then you're hired." Malmer dipped his pen, calmly tapped it off and let it hover over his ledger. "So... Bull? Or Broad?"

"Gunnar Bull," said Broad. "Put that down."

"Address?"

"We're in a cellar on Draw Street. Houses there don't have numbers."

"In the cellars?" Sarlby shook his head in disgust. "We'll get you out of there, don't worry." And he hooked a friendly arm around Broad's shoulders and led him through into the noisy, smelly warmth of the brewery. "What the hell are you doing here, anyway? Thought you had a farm somewhere."

"Had to sell it," muttered Broad, stumbling on the lie.

Sarlby just grinned. "Trouble, eh?"

"Aye," croaked Broad. "A little."

"Want a nip?" he asked, holding out a flask.

Broad did, in fact. A lot more than was healthy. Took an effort to force out the words. "Best not. I never could leave it at one."

"You weren't so shy in Styria, as I recall," said Sarlby, taking a swig.

"I'm trying not to make the same mistakes twice."

"That's all I ever bloody seem to do! What do you make of Valbeck?"

"It's all right, I guess."

"It's a fucking slag heap. It's a fucking meat grinder. It's a fucking *pit*."

"Aye." Broad puffed out his cheeks. "It's a pit."

"Fine for the rich folks up on the hill but what do we get? We who fought for our country? Open sewers. Three families to a room. Filth in the streets. The weak preyed on by the strong. There was a time folk cared about doing the right thing, wasn't there?"

"Was there?"

But Sarlby didn't hear. "Now all a man's worth is how much work can be squeezed from him. We're husks to be scraped out and tossed away. We're cogs in the big machine. But there's those who are trying to make it better."

Broad raised a brow at that. "I find men who prate a lot on making things better tend to make 'em a whole lot worse on the way."

Sarlby didn't hear that, either. He'd always been a great one for not hearing things he didn't want to. Maybe everyone is. He leaned close, like he'd a secret to share. "You heard of the Breakers?"

"Bandits, ain't they? Break machines. Burn mills. Traitors, I heard."

"Only the fucking Inquisition say so." Sarlby spat on the sawdust-scattered ground. He'd always been a great one for spitting, too. "The Breakers are going to change things! They don't just break machines, Broad, they break chains. Your chains and mine."

"I've got no chains on me."

"Says the man living in a cellar on Draw Street. I'm not talking about chains on your wrists, Broad. I'm talking about chains on your mind. Chains on your future! On your children's futures. The masters'll be brought low! Those who get fat on our sweat and our pain. The lords and ladies. The kings and princes." Sarlby's eyes glittered at the fine future he saw coming. "No more rich old bastards telling us how it's going to be. Every man with a say in how he's governed. Every man with a *vote*."

"So no more king?"

"Every man'll be a king!"

Broad might've called it treason once, but his patriotic feelings had taken quite the kicking the last couple of years. Now it just sounded like daydreams. "Not sure there's enough king to go around," he murmured. "I don't want trouble, Sarlby. Had more than my share."

"Some folk are made for trouble, Bull. You were always at your best with your fists clenched."

Broad winced at that. "At my worst, too."

"You were there, on the walls. You know how it is. Anything worth anything has to be *fought* for!" And Sarlby bared his teeth and punched at the air, a Ladderman's tattoo like Broad's showing on the back of his fist.

"Maybe." Broad felt a tickle of excitement, a stab of joy, but he pushed it away, twisted his own hand up into his sleeve as far as it would go. "But I've fought enough."

He'd made Liddy a promise. This time, he meant to keep it.

A Blow for the Common Man

"Everything ready?" asked Sibalt. Even in the darkness, Vick could sense his nerves, and it didn't help with hers.

She glanced up at Moor, a big outline on the wagon's seat, reins in his hands. She glanced at Tallow, perched beside him, rain beaded on his oversized oilskin. She almost asked again if they were sure they wanted to do this. But there's a time when doubts might do some good. A time to chew over the risks and the consequences. Then a moment passes. A moment you might not even notice. Then it's too late, and you've got to commit, and give it everything with no backward glances.

"It's ready," she said. "Let's go."

Grise caught her arm in the darkness. "What about them?" And she jerked her head towards the two bedraggled nightwatchmen either side of the foundry's gate, faces pinched in the light of their own lanterns.

"They're paid."

"You *paid* the fuckers?"

"It's easier to shift a man with gold than steel, and it almost always ends up cheaper." And before Grise had the chance to answer, Vick struck out across the street, head down, collar up.

She glanced each way, but the drizzle was on their side, the lane almost empty. The blood thudded in her head as she walked to the gate. Fear creeping up her throat and making her want to rush, want to shout. She told herself she'd been in tighter corners and knew it was true. She kept her breaths deep, her steps slow.

"Got a delivery for you," she said, shocked by how calm her own voice sounded.

The nightwatchman lifted his lantern to get a look at her and Vick narrowed her eyes at the glare. He knocked on the gates and there was the clatter of a bar being lifted. They took deliveries all night here. Nothing to remark upon.

"Let's go!" called Vick, and Moor gave the reins a flick, brought the wagon across the muddy street and through into the darkened yard. Coal heaps and wood stacks were gloomy ghosts, glistening with wet. The side of the shed loomed up, cliff-like, the angry gleam of fires beyond the windows.

Moor called softly to the big carthorse and slipped on the brake, handed the reins to Tallow. Sibalt clambered down from the back of the wagon, wiping his hands on his leather apron.

"Working so far," he muttered as he walked with Vick to the great foundry door.

"So far," she said. The big padlock had been left open and she slid it from the hasp, planted her hands on the big handle next to Sibalt's. His hands and hers, side by side. They heaved together, wheels clattering as the door slid open.

A waft of heat spilled from inside. The furnaces, and the engines, and the forges still giving off a welcoming glow. It'd never be cold in here, never be dark. Vick picked out the black outlines of the ironwork. The skeleton of the building. The pillars where they'd pack the powder.

She started back towards the wagon as Sibalt slid the door all the way open. Grise had already unlashed the tarp and dragged it away, the barrels showing underneath.

"All right," hissed Vick at her, "let's get that first one—"

Light flooded the yard and they all stood frozen, blinking in the glare. Hooded lanterns, suddenly opened all around them. Grise on the back of the wagon, rope in her hands. Moor with fingers hooked under the first barrel. Tallow holding the reins, his eyes bigger than ever. Sibalt in the wide doorway of the foundry.

That fast, their plans turned to shit.

"Hold!" bellowed a voice. "In the name of His Majesty!"

The big carthorse startled, dragged the wagon screeching forwards with its brake on. Grise tumbled over the side.

Moor stood, letting go of the barrel and snatching up a hatchet.

Tallow gave a high shriek. Not even a word.

There was a clicking, a fluttering. Bolts thudded into the wagon's side. Thudded into Moor, too.

Vick was already running. She caught Sibalt and dragged him into the foundry. They wove between the engines, the wagons, the rails, as they whipped up from the firelit gloom. Sibalt gasped as he slipped and went bowling into some crates, lengths of metal scattering across the stones with a clash and clang.

She helped him up, nearly falling herself, pulled him on, her breath and his hissing and wheezing, their slapping footfalls echoing from the roof high above. She glanced back, saw lights twinkling, a flicker of movement, heard shouts in the darkness.

She gasped as something caught her head—a dangling chain, left swinging in her wake. A few more steps and Sibalt grabbed her by the elbow, dragged her down into a shadowy space between two great iron tanks. She was about to ask why when she saw the lights ahead. Heard the footsteps. They were closing in from both sides.

"They were waiting," whispered Sibalt. "Knew we were coming."

"Who told 'em?" hissed Vick.

There was something strange about his face in the half-light. She was used to seeing him weighed with worries, now he looked like his load had been lifted. Vick glanced down and saw he had a dagger in his fist, the orange of the furnaces glinting along its edge. She drew away a little on an instinct. "You don't think it was me?"

"No. But it doesn't matter."

She could hear Grise screaming somewhere. "Come on, you fuckers! Come on!"

"You said it yourself," said Sibalt. "Once they get you, everyone talks. Sorry to leave you in the lurch like this."

"What are you saying?" Her voice didn't sound calm any more.

He smiled at her. That sad little smile. "Wish I'd met you sooner. Things might've been different. But the time comes...you have to stand up." And he rammed the dagger into his own neck.

"No," she hissed. "No, no, no!" She had her hands to his throat but it was ripped right open, blood welling black. Nothing she could do. Her hands were sticky to the elbows already. Her trousers soaked with blood as it spread in a great warm slick.

Sibalt stared up at her, spluttering black from his mouth, from his nose. Maybe he was trying to give her some message. Regret, or forgiveness, or hope, or blame. No way of knowing.

Grise's screams had turned to meaningless screeches, then muffled gurgles. The sounds of someone with a bag forced over their head.

Sibalt's eyes were glassy now, and Vick let go of his leaking neck. She sat back against iron still hot from the day's work, her red hands dangling.

And that's where she was when the Practicals found her.

Knowing the Arrow

Rikke crashed down the slope, trees and sky bouncing, all their careful plans flung away along with her cloak and her bow. That's the trouble with plans. Not many survive being chased through a downpour by a pack of dogs. Wet brambles clutched at her ankle, snatched it from under her and she reeled, howl cut off as she smashed face-first into a tree, fell and rolled helpless through thorn bushes, over and over, yelping with every bounce and giving a long groan as she slid on her face through a heap of sodden leaves.

She looked up to see a big pair of boots. She looked up higher and saw a man standing in them, looking down with an expression more of puzzlement than triumph.

"Quite the entrance," he said.

He wasn't tall, but solid as a tree, great meaty gut, great meaty forearms, great meaty neck and jowls, thumbs tucked into a weathered sword-belt. He might've been the same height as Rikke, but easily twice her weight. One of his cheeks was all puckered with an old scar.

She spat out some bits of leaf and whispered, "Fuck."

But instead of grabbing her around the throat, he just stepped back and bowed.

"Please." And he offered her the way with one broad palm, like one of those fancy footmen in Ostenhorm might've done.

No time to wonder about the gift, only to grab it with both hands. "Thanks," she wheezed as she clambered up, mouth tasting of blood. Her soggy shirt was hopelessly snarled on the thorns and she wriggled free of it, lurching on winded in her vest.

Dogs barked behind and she snatched blurred glances over her shoulder, shadows dancing in the rain-lashed forest, sure at every jolting step their teeth would sink into her arse and bring her down. Someone was crashing through the woods ahead, she heard Isern shout, "Rikke? You there?"

"Right…" she gurgled, "behind you!"

Then light flashed between trunks, the trees opening up. She felt a giddy surge of relief which, as usual, soon turned to horror. They'd seen the scar through the woods from higher up and thought there must be a river. But through the curtains of rain, there'd been no way of knowing it was cut into a deep ravine.

She knew it now. A rocky edge, sprouting with sick grass, clung to by stunted little trees, beaten water thundering below. She saw Isern spring, arching back in the air, spear over her head. She saw her clear the gap, a daunting four strides wide at least, roll through the wet moss and ferns clinging to the far side and come smoothly to her feet.

For an instant, Rikke thought about stopping. Then she thought about getting fucked by Stour Nightfall's horse and of a sudden, getting smashed to paste in the bottom of a gorge seemed a pretty fine outcome. Wasn't like she could stop anyway, belting full-tilt down a steep and slippery bank. She pushed herself faster, chest heaving, teeth rattling, and trusted to luck, however bad her luck had been lately.

The ravine yawned wide as she burst from the trees, a glimpse of jagged rock dropping away to white water.

She got a firm footing at the edge, which was lucky, and a decent push off with her right leg, which was good, and she went up something lovely, wind cold in her wide-open mouth, flying into the flitting rain.

It was just that she started coming down too soon. Maybe if she'd eaten something that day, there'd have been more spring in her. But she hadn't. She clawed at the air, like she might be able to drag herself closer, but she was dropping fast now and didn't need the Long Eye to see she'd fall short.

The terrible justice of the ground. Sooner or later, everyone who jumps must meet it.

The slick rocks came hurtling at her.

"Oh fu—"

Earth thudded into her stomach and drove all her wind out in a great spitty wheeze. She clutched desperately at wet leaves, wet roots, wet grass, no strength, no breath, dirt sprinkling in her eyes as she started sliding over the edge, fingernails uselessly scrabbling.

Then Isern's hand clamped around her wrist. Isern's face above her, screwed up with furious effort, scar white on her lips, tongue wedged into the hole in her clenched teeth. Rikke groaned as her shoulder stretched, feeling like her whole arm would rip from the socket.

Probably she should've told Isern to let her go, big dramatic gesture, time for a single tear before she plunged to her doom, but that's not how

109

it works when the Great Leveller's breathing on your neck. She clutched at Isern's sinewy arm like a drowning woman to the mast of a sinking ship, choking and struggling and kicking and like as not to drag them both over.

"You're heavier than you fucking—gah!"

Something flickered past and Isern gave a grunt, pulled even harder. Rikke's flailing foot caught on rock and she managed to shove herself upwards. Finally heaved a breath into her aching chest, growled as she pushed again and Isern went over backwards, dragging Rikke on top of her, the two of them rolling together into the soaking bracken.

"Move!" Isern staggered up, fell, crawled on, dragging her spear along with a handful of torn grass. There was an arrow through her leg. Rikke could see the bloody head sticking from the back of her thigh.

She looked over her shoulder, through the slackening rain saw dogs yapping and growling and prowling at the ravine's edge and, a few strides above them, a man kneeling in the trees. Close enough she could see the frown on his dirty face, the frayed edge of his archery guard, the bow drawn in his hand.

Her eyes went wide, and one burned hot. Hot as a glowing coal in her skull.

She heard the flapping click of the bowstring.

She saw the arrow.

But she saw it with the Long Eye.

And for an instant, like the dawn sun blazing into her room as the shutters were flung wide, the absolute knowing of that arrow burst upon her.

She saw where it was, all it was, where it had been and would be.

She saw its making, smith with teeth clenched as he hammered out the head, fletcher with tongue wedged in his cheek as he trimmed the flights.

She saw its ending, shaft rotted and head flaked away to rust among the brambles.

She saw it in the quiver hooked over the foot of the archer's bed as he kissed his wife Riam goodbye and hoped that her broken toe mended.

She saw its bright point cut through a falling raindrop and scatter it into glittering mist.

She knew with utter certainty where that arrow would be, always. So she flicked her hand out, and when it came to meet her, as she knew it must, it was the easiest thing to push it. Just to nudge it with her finger so it missed Isern as she limped away and spun off harmless into the trees, bouncing once and coming to rest in the undergrowth in its right place, in the only place it could be, where she'd seen it rot away among the brambles.

"By the dead," breathed Rikke, staring at her hand.

There was a bead of blood on the tip of her forefinger. Arrowhead must've grazed it. And a quivering shiver went all the way through her. She hadn't really believed it till this moment, not even when she saw Uffrith burning, just like in her dream. But now there was no denying it.

She had the Long Eye.

It still throbbed, warm in her clammy face. She stared at the archer, his brow knitted up in shock as he stared back, his jaw dropping lower and lower.

A great joyous, wondering giggle bubbled up at the impossible thing she'd done, and Rikke stuck her fist up and screamed, "Give my regards to Riam! Hope her toe mends!" Then she scampered after Isern, caught her under the armpit and helped her on into the dripping trees.

But not before she caught a glimpse of a rope bridge a hundred strides upstream, bouncing and twisting as men hurried across it, sharpened metal gleaming with wet. How many men, she couldn't tell. Enough, that was the number, and the joy of knowing the arrow was squashed straight out of her.

"Come on," she hissed as they blundered through the clutching, snagging, sodden bushes. Isern fell snarling and Rikke helped her up but she was slow, now, everything heavy with damp, her leg dragging.

"Go," she snapped. "I'll follow."

"No," said Rikke, hauling her on.

She thought she heard fighting behind them. Men screaming. Dogs whimpering. Scrape and clatter of steel. The trees echoed with it, everywhere and nowhere. Branches whipped at her and Rikke clawed them away, broke through into a boggy clearing. The rain was down to a drizzle, a broken wall of mossy rock ahead, slick with trickling water.

"Go." Isern turned towards the woods, growled in pain as her wounded leg gave and she slid onto her side. "Climb!"

"No," said Rikke, "I'm not leaving you."

"Better one of us live than neither. Go."

"No," said Rikke. She could hear someone crashing through the trees towards them. Someone big.

"Get behind me, then." Isern pushed Rikke back, but she could only stand leaning on her spear. She'd be fighting no one. Not winning, anyway.

"I've hid behind you long enough." Strange thing, but Rikke didn't feel scared any more. "I'm not much of a climber anyway." She peeled Isern's fingers from the shaft of her spear and helped her lean against the rocks. "Time for me to take a turn at the front."

Isern's bloody leg quivered as she sank back. "We're doomed."

Rikke gripped the spear tight and lowered it towards the trees, wondering whether to hold on to it or throw it when they came, wishing her Long Eye would open again so she didn't have to guess.

She thought of Nightfall's voice above her, while she hid in the stream. Her guts in a box, with some herbs, so her father wouldn't smell them till it was opened.

"Come on!" she screamed, spraying spit. "I'm fucking waiting!"

Wet leaves rustled and a man stepped into the clearing. A big man in a weather-stained coat, holding a scarred shield and a sword with a silver letter near the hilt. Even through the grey hair hanging lank across his face, Rikke could see the awful scar, from his forehead through his brow and across his cheek to the corner of his mouth, and in the misshapen socket of his left eye there was no eye at all, but a bright ball of dead metal, gleaming as the sun broke through above.

He raised his brows at the two of them, hunched and bloodied against the rocky wall. Or he raised the good one, anyway. The burned one just twitched a little. Then he spoke in a voice like the grinding of a mill wheel.

"Been looking for you two."

Rikke stood still, for a moment, just staring. Then she stepped towards him, letting out a long, shuddering breath, and she tossed the spear down in the grass and flung her arms around him.

"Took your fucking time, Caul Shivers!" Isern snarled through clenched teeth. "There's some of Nightfall's boys hunting us."

"Put 'em out o' your mind." And Rikke saw his sword was all dashed and speckled with red. He'd always been a man who could get a lot said in a few words. "Can you walk?"

"Without the arrow," hissed Isern, "I could run rings around you."

"Don't doubt it." Shivers puffed out cheeks scattered with silver stubble as he squatted beside her. "But you've got the arrow." And he poked at it with one big finger and made her grimace.

"You are not fucking carrying me," she growled.

"Ain't high on my list o' wants, believe it or not." Shivers slid his sword through the clasp at his belt. "But once you've a task to do, it's better to do it—"

"Than live with the fear of it," Rikke finished for him. It was one of her father's favourites.

Shivers pulled Isern up by one arm and hefted her over his shoulder as if she weighed nothing at all. With what they'd been eating, she probably wasn't far off.

"This is a bloody indignity," Isern grunted into Shivers' back as he started walking.

"What about me?" muttered Rikke. Now she was something close to safe her strength had all leaked away, and her face was twitching and her knees were knocking, and she felt like she might topple over right there and never get up.

"You always were a moaner." Shivers shook his head. "Come on. Your father's waiting."

Biding Time, Wasting Time

"Ever think maybe you drink too much?" asked Wonderful.

Clover smacked his lips. "Too much would, by definition, be too much. I find however much I drink is just the right amount." And he offered her the bottle.

She shook her head. "Drunks tend to say that."

Clover treated her to his aggrieved look. "As do the broadly sober." He'd a wonderful aggrieved look. Lots of practice. "I find myself aggrieved. Have you ever seen me lose a fight on account of drunkenness?"

"I've never seen you fight."

Clover slapped the cork back into the bottle. "A clear indication of reasonable drinking if ever there was one."

"Well, if I was you, I'd at least look sober." Wonderful pointed one of her brows off down the track. "The Great Wolf approaches."

And approach he did, with high drama. Storming and swaggering at once with his brow well creased and his brooding young stags at his back, making Thralls scatter from their path like chickens in a farmyard. Given all the damp still in the air, it was a wonder they weren't steaming.

"Here come the gods of war," mouthed Clover, and then out loud, as the Great Wolf stalked closer, "Drink, Chief?"

Stour slapped the bottle from his hand and it bounced away into the bushes.

Clover looked sadly after it. "I'll take that as a no."

"She got away!" snarled the king-in-waiting, in quite the fury even for him. "Fucking little bitch got away!"

"We're all distraught."

"She came through right where you were supposed to be!" snapped a bastard of Stour's called Greenway. If legends were built on sneering, he'd have had quite a place in the songs. "Did you see her?"

"Saw her shirt," said Clover, tossing the torn thing over. "At least, I'm guessing it was hers. Doubt it'll fit you, though. Bit tight under the arms, I expect—"

Greenway flung it angrily on the ground. "Did you see *her*?"

"If I had, I'd have caught her."

"You'd have had to fucking get up to do that," snarled Magweer, aiming for the same caged-wolf act as Stour but only managing a fraction of the menace.

"I'd have sung out, anyway," said Clover. "That I can do sitting down."

He wondered why he hadn't sung out. She'd just looked like such a desperate, ragged little scrap to have all these bastards chasing her, and when the hunt was on, he'd always secretly rooted for the fox. If you can't find a way to win that doesn't involve torturing some half-mad girl, then maybe you don't deserve to win at all. Or maybe that was all shit, and it was just 'cause she was pretty. The sad truth is that pretty people can slide through all kinds of scrapes that'd end very badly for the ugly.

Clover looked from Greenway to Magweer and shrugged. "Seems hunting girls just ain't my sport."

Stour stepped closer, staring at Clover with those ever-wet eyes of his. "Your sport is whatever I say it is."

Clover shrugged it off. "I'm eager to serve, great prince, but I can't just turn into a butterfly. Your father sent me for my cunning, not my running. Why, you might as well order the river to blow and the wind to flow."

"You're loyal, ain't you, Clover?" Magweer said it softly, like it was some brilliant trap of words.

"Reasonably so, I like to think. A man has to bend with the breeze."

"You turned on Glama Golden, I heard," said Greenway, climbing to new heights of sneer. "Cairm Ironhead, too."

"I was loyal to both," said Clover. "I was just more loyal to me. Truth is, men love to blab about loyalty till it might trap 'em on the losing side. Then there's a chorus o' silence on the issue. So I consider reasonably loyal to be a bit more loyal than most, and a lot more honest than most. It's a fool who makes folk choose too often between loyalty and good sense. How'd she get loose, anyway?"

"Caul Shivers was waiting on the other side of the river," hissed Stour, clenching his fists. "Killed four of my men."

"Shivers." Magweer was clenching his fists just the same way. "Wish I'd run into that old fucker."

Wonderful and Clover burst out laughing at the exact same time. He leaned forward, hands on his knees, and she leaned back, fist on his shoulder, and no doubt they made quite a picture chortling away but they really couldn't help 'emsleves.

"Good one," said Clover, with a sigh. "Good one."

"What's so fucking funny?"

Wonderful waved a finger at Magweer's collection of weapons. "My friend, if you'd run into Caul Shivers, you'd be wearing all those axes up your arse. You should take care charging at fights. Sooner or later, you'll trip over a bigger one than you wanted."

"There's no fight too big for me," he growled back.

"Really?" asked Wonderful. "What if it's just you and nineteen o' them?"

Magweer opened his mouth, strained, but couldn't find a reply. He was a child's notion of what a warrior should be, all scowl and muscle and carrying half a blacksmith's shop around. Clover gave a sigh. "You need to calm down, my friend."

"Or else what, old man?"

"Or else you'll make yourself sad, and ain't the world a grim enough place without another frown? Everyone stomping around like the Bloody-Nine, like they'd murder the whole world if they got the chance."

Stour narrowed his eyes. "The Bloody-Nine was the greatest warrior the North ever saw."

"I know," said Clover. "I watched him beat Fenris the Feared in the Circle."

Silence. "You saw that?" A hint of respect suddenly crept into Stour's whining voice.

Wonderful laughed again and thumped that fist down on Clover's shoulder. "He held a shield."

"You held a shield? When the Bloody-Nine fought the Feared?"

"On behalf of your grandfather, Bethod," said Clover. "Eighteen years old and knowing half o' nothing and thinking myself quite the hard bastard."

"Everyone says that was a great duel," breathed Stour, a faraway look in his wet eyes.

"It was a bloody one. Sadly, I walked away with the wrong lessons. Enough that I ended up taking a challenge or two myself..." Clover found he was scratching at his scar, and made himself leave it alone. "If you want my advice, stay out of the Circle."

"The Circle is where names are made!" barked Stour, thumping his chest with a fist. "I beat Stranger-Come-Knocking there! Carved him all to hell."

"And from what I heard, it was a fight for the songs." Though what Clover actually heard was that Stranger-Come-Knocking got old and slow and lived past his reputation, a tragedy that befalls every great fighter not killed in his prime. "But each time you step into the Circle, you balance your life on a sword's edge. Sooner or later, it won't fall your way."

Stour's young warriors scoffed like they never heard aught so contemptible as this eminent good sense. "Did Black Dow fear the Circle?" sneered Greenway.

"Or Whirrun of Bligh, or Shama Heartless, or Rudd Threetrees?" asked Magweer.

Wonderful rolled her eyes. No doubt she was about to point out that all four of those heroes died bloody deaths, and half of them in the Circle, too. Stour got in first, though. "The Bloody-Nine fought eleven duels and won 'em all."

"He beat the odds, that's true," said Clover. "For a time. He beat the Feared and he stole your grandfather's chain. But what did it get him? He lost everything, made nothing, and time'll just hand that chain to you. Who'd want to be like that bastard?"

Stour opened his arms wide, opened his eyes wide, put on the big act. "The only chain I want is a chain of *blood*!" Made not the slightest sense. How could you make a chain out of blood anyway? Terrible metaphor. But Magweer and Greenway and the rest of the arse-lickers gave a chorus of warlike growls and shaken fists. "I don't want to be *like* the Bloody-Nine. I want to *be* the Bloody-Nine!" Stour hitched his crazed smile a little wider in a reasonable impression of the Bloody-Nine in his worse moments. "*No* man more famed. No man more *feared*."

"He wants to be the Bloody-Nine," said Wonderful, deadpan, as the Great Wolf stalked off out of earshot, always hurrying to nowhere.

"To have women spit at the mention of your name. To sow death for years and reap naught but hate at the end. To walk all your days in a circle of blood." Clover could only shake his head. "I never will unpick the riddle of why men want what they want."

"You going to let that fool Magweer talk to you that way?" asked Wonderful.

Clover looked at her. "What's it to you how he talks?"

"Confirms these young idiots in their opinion they know best."

"We can't correct the misapprehensions of every idiot any more'n we can correct the tide." Clover frowned off into the damp undergrowth where Stour had slapped that bottle, wondering if there was enough left in it to justify the search. He decided most likely not, strolled to the nearest tree instead and slowly lowered himself beside it. "Words leave no wounds and I've run at feuds enough. I try to run the other way these days."

"Very wise. But like you said, you ain't much of a runner."

"True. If someone's fixed on feuding, I've come to realise there's only two realistic options." Clover wriggled back against the trunk until he found a comfortable position. "First, you just float over it, like dandelion seeds on a stiff breeze, and pay it no mind at all."

"Second?"

"Murder the bastard." Clover grinned up at the blue sky, where the sun was starting to finally show some warmth. "But I wouldn't want to spoil such a wonderful afternoon with murder, would you?"

"It'd be a shame, I'll admit." Wonderful watched Clover as he stretched out and crossed his legs. "What are you doing?"

"What we should all be doing." Clover closed his eyes. "Biding my time."

"What's the difference between biding it and wasting it?"

Clover saw no need to open his eyes. "Results, woman. Results."

The Bigger They Are

Glaward peeled his shirt off and tossed it over to Barniva, then growled as he brought his fists together, woody muscle flexing in his outsize chest. An appreciative mutter rose from the onlookers gathered at the fence, a few numbers tossed out. Leo's steadily lengthening odds, no doubt.

"I swear he's got bigger," murmured Jurand, eyes wide.

"So have I," growled Leo, trying to sound as big as he could.

"No doubt. Your legs are nearly as thick as his arms now."

"I can beat him."

"Easily. With a sword. So why fight him with your hands?"

Leo started unbuttoning his own shirt. "When I lived in Uffrith, the Dogman used to tell me stories about the Bloody-Nine. The duels he won in the Circle. I loved those stories. Used to dance around the garden behind his hall with a stick, pretending I was Ninefingers and the laundry post was Rudd Threetrees, or Black Dow, or Fenris the Feared." There was still a thrill in saying the names. Like they were magic words.

Jurand watched Glaward loose a few brutal practice punches. "The laundry post won't knock your teeth out."

Leo tossed his shirt over Jurand's head. "A champion never knows what he'll have to fight with. That's why I always let you bastards pick the weapons." It was a cold morning, so he started bouncing on his toes to get the blood moving. "That's why I beat Barniva with a heavy sword, and Antaup with a spear. Why I beat Whitewater Jin with a mace and you with long and short steels. That's why I test my archery against Ritter. Used to, that is." The poor dead fool. "But I never yet beat Glaward with my bare hands."

"Well, no," said Jurand, that worried crease between his brows. "He's built like a barn."

"The bigger they are—"

"The harder they hit?"

"Your defeats teach you more than your victories," muttered Leo, trying to slap some warmth into his muscles.

"They hurt more, too." Jurand dropped his voice a little. "At least tell me you'll fight dirty."

"With honour or not at all," grunted Leo. He thought Casamir the Steadfast might have said it in a storybook once. "Whose side are you on, anyway?"

"Yours." Jurand looked a little hurt by the question. "Always. We all are. That's why I won't enjoy seeing him choke you unconscious."

Leo narrowed his eyes. "What I need from my second is *belief.*"

Sinew popped from Glaward's arms as he raised his fists. Leo couldn't deny it was a majestic sight. Like some piece of exaggerated statuary. Even his teeth looked muscular. "I'm going to squeeze you out like a lemon," he growled.

"The Young Lemon!" barked Barniva, to much merriment from the onlookers.

Jurand leaned close. "If you die, can I have your horse?"

"*Belief,*" growled Leo, and dashed forward. Attack, always attack. Especially when the odds are against you.

He caught Glaward off guard, ducked under a wild fist, the wind of it catching his hair, and gave the big man the heaviest punches to the body he could. No doubt Glaward was carrying a little fat, but any hope he was soft underneath was long gone. Leo felt as if he'd punched a tree.

"Shit," he hissed through his fixed smile, shaking out his throbbing fingers.

"I'm going to make you eat this hillside," growled Glaward, and the growing audience whooped and laughed.

The dead knew Leo needed to watch Glaward's fists, but his eye kept being drawn to two of the oddest-looking women among the spectators. The older had a sharp, expressionless face, mouth twisted by a scar, trouser-leg slit open showing bandages underneath. The younger had a wide, almost over-expressive face, a thick gold ring through her broad, freckled nose and a tangle of red-brown hair so wild those behind had to lean around it to see.

"This is manly," she said, propping a muddy boot on the rail of the fence, its tongue flopping from bodged laces. "Do they charge for the spectacle?"

"Far as I can tell," mused the old one, "they take their clothes off for free."

The young one spread her arms and gave a huge smile. "What a public-spirited thing to do!"

Glaward was in no mood to give anything away. He kept pressing forward, one big fist flicking out in lethal-looking jabs. Leo dodged one, and another, but the third glanced his cheek and sent him staggering. He slipped on the wet grass, luckily, since Glaward's other fist lashed the air where his head had just been. He slid around the big man, gave him a petulant tap in the ribs as he passed to no effect at all.

Glaward gave a scornful snort. "Are we fighting or dancing?"

Over his heavy shoulder, Leo caught sight of the girl again, staring cross-eyed at a strand of hair in her face. She stuck her bottom lip out to blow it away, and it flopped straight back in her eyes along with three others. There was something familiar about her, like a name on the tip of his tongue.

"We're fighting!" he snarled, and ducked in with a flurry of punches, teeth bared and spit flying.

"That's it!" he heard Jurand shout. "Give him hell!"

But Leo's best efforts slapped harmlessly against Glaward's big arms, scuffed the top of his head, bounced from his sides. Then a heavy fist came from nowhere, caught Leo under the chin and sent him tottering. He whooped helplessly as he was hauled into the air by his belt.

Dark land and bright sky reeled, he flailed wildly, then the ground struck him hard in the side, rattled his teeth, tumbled him over and over and onto his face.

He gave a long groan as he dragged himself up and saw Glaward's great boot already rushing to meet him. He gasped as he rolled away, the big heel digging a great divot from the turf. He scrambled to his feet, lost his balance and fell against the fence.

"This blond one is pretty," the older woman was saying.

"I have eyes." The young one was watching him with her chin propped on her hands, head bouncing as she chewed something. She certainly did have eyes. Big, and very pale, and very piercing.

"He's like a hunting dog, all fierce and frisky."

Leo didn't feel too frisky as Glaward's fists came at him again. He covered up but the force in them was fearsome. A punch in the side slammed him against the fence and drove his breath out, a knuckle caught his jaw and turned his mouth salty.

"Get out of there!" he heard Jurand shout over his own gurgling, rasping breath.

He only just ducked a blow that would've knocked him right over the fence and shoved Glaward away with all his strength. The big man barely moved, but Leo bounced off at least, staggering clear of the fence with his face throbbing, lungs burning, knees wobbling.

Glaward could've knocked him down with a pointed finger. But he was fixed on milking his moment, throwing his great fists in the air, strutting like a cock in his own farmyard.

"Hit him!" Jurand hooted over the crowd. "Bloody hit him!"

But it was clear Leo would never beat Glaward with his fists. He had to beat him with his head. He thought, through the fog, of what his mother would've said. Less courage, more judgement. Putting their worst troops on show in the valley, marching as badly as they could. Even as his head cleared, he shook it as if he could hardly see straight, clutched at his ribs as if he could hardly get a breath. Even as the strength returned to his legs, he put on a drunken stagger.

"Are we fight?" he gurgled, showing his bloody teeth. "Or dance?"

He'd have won no laurels for his acting but Glaward was blessed with more muscle than imagination. He charged in with no caution at all, readying a punch they'd be talking about for years. But Leo had his wits back. He dropped under it, rolled smoothly, caught Glaward's big calf on the way past and sprang up, pulling the leg with him.

Glaward grunted with surprise, hopped once, waving his arms for balance, then his other foot slid from under him and he came crashing down on his face.

"Now who's eating the hillside?" crowed Leo. Glaward clawed helplessly at the turf, snapping and snarling, but Leo had Glaward's huge boot in a lock against his chest and wasn't letting go. "How does it taste?"

Leo twisted harder and the big man slapped at the ground. "All right! I'm done! I'm done!"

Leo let the boot fall and tottered back. He felt Jurand catch his wrist and lift his arm high.

"A victory for reasonably sized men everywhere!" he shouted, draping Leo's shirt over his shoulder.

"Don't get dressed on our account," called the older woman, and the younger threw her head back and gave a gurgling laugh.

"Leo!" someone shouted. One of the few optimistic enough to bet on him, probably. He tried to grin through the considerable pain. Was one of his teeth loose? "The Young Lion!"

The girl was frowning straight at him. "You're Leo dan Brock?"

"None other," said Jurand, clapping him proudly on the shoulder.

"Ha!" She sprang down from the fence and strutted towards him with a huge grin. "It's little Leo!"

Jurand raised his brows. "Little Leo?"

She looked him up and down. "Well, he has grown." And much to his surprise, she threw her arms around him, gripped him behind the head and pressed his face into her shoulder.

And that was when he saw, among a rattling mass of charms, bones, runes and necklaces she wore, a wooden dowel on a thong, all dented with tooth marks.

"Rikke?" He broke away to stare at her, looking for some trace of the sickly little girl he used to mock in her father's hall in Uffrith. "I heard you were lost!"

She threw her fists in the air. "I'm found!" Then she let them drop, and scratched at the back of her head. "To be fair, I was a little lost, but Isern-i-Phail knows all the ways. She steered me home."

"As a great sea captain steers a leaky skiff, d'you see?" The older woman's scar twisted the corner of her mouth and made her look like she had a constant frown. Or maybe she was constantly frowning. "I'm quite the hero, but let's not make too much of it."

"Black Calder's bastards were everywhere. And his son Stour fucking Nightfall." Rikke bared her teeth in a burst of fury so sudden, Leo nearly stepped back. "I'll see that prick back to the mud, I promise you!" And she spat, left a long string of it dangling from her lip and dashed it away. "Bastards."

"But...you're not hurt?"

Rikke stuck her fists in Leo's face and pushed a finger up for each point. "I've been starved, slapped, pissed on, shot at, chased by dogs, threatened with being fucked by a pig, slept under a hanged man, near fell down a gorge, killed a boy and shat myself, so, you know," and she shrugged, head falling to one side and her shoulders right up around her ears, "I'm hoping next week'll be easier going, let's say that."

"Sounds...trying." He hardly knew what she was talking about, but he liked hearing her talk. "It's good to see you again." He meant it. They'd been close once. As close as you could be, with someone as strange as she'd been.

"You remember the first time we met?" she asked.

Leo winced. "Hard to forget."

"You mocked my twitching and my foolish hair and my unusual way."

"Eager to prove myself in front of the boys."

She nodded towards Glaward, who was sitting on the hillside rubbing at his twisted ankle. "Some things never change."

"If it helps, I'm not proud of it."

"It helped when I knocked you down and sat on you."

Leo's turn to scratch at the back of his head. "Your defeats teach you more than your victories, I hear. And you were half a head taller than me." He drew himself up, looking down at her from as far above now as she'd looked down on him then. "Doubt you'd try it now."

"Oh, I don't know." She reached out and wiped the blood from his top lip with her thumb. Maybe her eye twitched. Or maybe she winked right at him. "I might be persuaded."

"Better'n being fucked by a pig, I reckon," said Isern-i-Phail, grunting softly as she lifted her bandaged leg from the fence and turned hobbling away. "I need to steer this leaky skiff back to her father before she drifts off course again. I gave my word!"

"I am in much demand." Rikke backed away, gave a bow that left one hand brushing the turf, then slipped up onto the rail of the fence. "See you later, little Leo." And she swung her boots over it and swaggered off, leaving Leo staring after her.

"My, my, *my*." Antaup had appeared, as he often did when women were around, sucking air through pursed lips as he watched Rikke go. "Who's the beauty with the ring through her nose?"

"*Three* mys?" murmured Jurand, drily. "Virtually a proposal of marriage."

"That," said Leo, "was Rikke."

"The Dogman's missing daughter?"

"We used to be close when I was in Uffrith. She's...grown."

"In *all* the right places," said Antaup. "Those eyes, though."

"Don't they say she can see the future?" asked Jurand, looking less than convinced.

Barniva's whisper was full of laughter in Leo's ear. "I've a suspicion she sees your cock in it."

Jurand turned away, shaking his head. "For pity's sake..." He was a great friend, and damned clever, but he could be a hell of a prude.

"Careful." Leo threw his arm around Barniva's neck and pulled him into a headlock. "I might have to make you eat the hillside next."

"Well, if you'd rather wrestle..." Antaup licked his finger and thumb and gave that loose curl at the front of his hair a little tweak. "It'd be a shame to leave such a promising field unploughed..."

It was then Leo made up his mind that he was interested. Antaup knew all about women. If he was impressed, everyone would be.

"Keep your plough to yourself." He caught Antaup with his free arm and dragged him into the good-natured tussle, giving Rikke's backside the same sort of hungry grin his friends were giving it. "And stay off my land."

Questions

She thought Tallow was in the room on her left. She'd recognised his voice burbling through the wall, and even if she couldn't hear the words, she could hear the fear. Grise was on her right. Vick had heard her screaming insults. Then just screaming. No questions yet, though. Softening her up. Vick wondered how soft she was, now.

Strange how quick you lose track of time when you can't see the sky. Just the windowless white room, too brightly lit, and the table with two chairs and three bloodstains, and the door. Was it hours since they were caught, or days? She might've dozed a while. Jerked awake with the sweat cold on her bare skin to hear someone begging in the corridor outside. But the door had stayed closed. They'd stripped her, and chained her to the chair, and left her there, gradually aching more and more to piss.

She was wondering whether she should just piss where she sat when the door opened.

A man came in. Or was brought in. He sat in a strange chair on wheels, pushed by a Practical of monstrous size. He was silver-haired, his skin almost as pale as his spotless white coat and deeply lined, as if stretched too tight over the bones. His face was twisted, left eye twitchily narrowed. On his little finger he wore a ring of office with a great purple stone, but even without it there was no mistaking him.

Old Sticks. The Cripple. The King's Skinner. The axle around which the Closed Council turned. His Eminence, Arch Lector Glokta.

"I like your chair," said Vick as it squeaked to a halt on the other side of the table.

The Arch Lector raised one brow. "I don't. But walking pains me more every year and my daughter tells me there is no nobility in suffering. She prevailed upon her friend Master Curnsbick to make it for me."

"The great machinist himself?"

"I hear he is a genius." Glokta glanced up at the vast Practical looming

126

over him, the chair's handles lost in his immensity of fist. "Now a use-less man can render a useful man useless wheeling him around. There's progress, eh? Remove her restraints, please."

"Your Eminence?" came muffled from behind the Practical's mask.

"Come, come, we are not animals."

The Practical took a little wedge from his pocket, knelt and slipped it under one of the chair's wheels with surprising daintiness. Then he lumbered around the table, manacles digging into Vick's skin as he un-locked them. Her wrists were chafed raw, but she made sure not to rub them. Made sure not to wince or flinch or stretch or groan. Not even when she put her hands on the table and saw Sibalt's blood still crusted under the nails. Show hurt, you're asking to be hurt. She'd learned that lesson in the camps. Learned it hard.

Arch Lector Glokta watched her, the trace of a smile on his twisted face, as though he guessed her every thought. "And the clothes, please."

The Practical unhappily placed a neatly folded shirt and pair of trousers on the table, and twitched one corner of the fabric like a fussy valet.

"You can leave us, Dole."

"Your Eminence?" The Practical's voice went squeaky with dismay.

"I have better things to do than repeat myself."

The Practical gave Vick one last frown, backed to the door, stooped beneath the lintel and pulled it shut. The latch dropped with a final-sounding *click*, leaving her alone in that bare, white room with the most feared man in the Union.

"So." He showed the yawning gap in his front teeth as he smiled. "It seems congratulations are in order again, Inquisitor Teufel. Ever so neatly done. I knew my confidence in you was not misplaced."

"Thank you, Your Eminence."

"Shall I turn my back while you dress?" He squinted down at the wheels of his chair. "I'm afraid it can take a while. Nowhere near so nimble as in my youth. I won the Contest without conceding a touch, you know—"

She made her own chair squeal as she stood, ignoring the ache in her stiff hip. "Don't worry." And she shook the shirt out and started pulling it on.

You strip a prisoner to make them feel vulnerable. Make them feel they've nowhere they can hide a secret. But it only works if you let it. Vick made sure she dressed just the way she would have if she was alone. When you grow up in the camps, sleeping beside strangers, sharing their warmth, their stink, their lice, hosed down in a cringing pack by the guards when the sickness comes through, modesty is a luxury you soon learn to live without.

"I can only apologise that it took me so long to reach you," said His Eminence, as unmoved by her nakedness as she was. "The government is in uproar over this fighting in the North. Did we get them all?"

"All except Sibalt. He…" Vick kept her face carefully expressionless as she thought of him ramming the blade into his neck. "He killed himself rather than be captured."

"Unfortunate. I know the two of you had become…involved."

The Arch Lector found out everything, of course. But it was as if his saying it, his knowing it, made it real. The feeling took her by surprise. She had to stop buttoning her shirt, look at the floor with her teeth gritted, stay silent in case her voice gave her away. Just for a moment. Then she carried on fastening the buttons with her blood-crusted fingers, mask back on. "Is that a problem, Your Eminence?"

"Not for me. We all yearn for a simple world, but people are imperfect, unpredictable, contradictory beasts with sympathies, and needs, and *feelings*. Even people like us."

"Feelings didn't come in to it," said Vick, pulling on the trousers.

She had a sense he saw through her. "If they did not, you have demonstrated your commitment. If they did, you have gone one better and demonstrated your loyalty."

"I know what I owe you. I don't forget."

"I try never to blame a person for what they think. Only for what they do. And you have done all I could have asked."

Vick sat back in the chair, facing him. "Sibalt was the leader. I doubt any of the others know much."

"We will soon see."

Vick looked him in his eyes. Those deep-set, fever-bright eyes. "They're not bad people. They just want a little more."

"I thought feelings did not come into it?" The Arch Lector's left eye had started to weep, and he pulled out a white handkerchief and gently dabbed it. "You grew up in the camps, Inquisitor Teufel."

"You know I did, Your Eminence."

"You have seen humanity in the raw."

"About as raw as it gets, Your Eminence."

"So tell me. These good people. If they get a little more, what will they want then?"

Vick paused a moment, but there was nothing else to say. "A little more."

"Because that is the nature of people. And their little more must be taken from someone else, and that someone else will be less than delighted. One cannot eliminate unhappiness any more than one can eliminate darkness. The goal of government, you see," and the Arch Lector prodded at the air with his bony forefinger, "is to load the unhappiness onto those least able to make you suffer for it."

"What if you misjudge who can make you suffer?"

"Misjudgement is as much a part of life as unhappiness. It is nice to hold the power and make the choices for everyone. But the risk of making any choice is always that you might make the wrong one. We must make our choices nonetheless. Fear of being a grown-up is a poor reason to remain a child."

"Of course, Your Eminence." There's only so much you can do. Then you move on. The camps had taught her that lesson, too.

"Where did they get the Gurkish Fire?"

"They spoke of friends in Valbeck."

"More Breakers?"

"A more organised group, perhaps. They mentioned the Weaver."

Glokta gave no reaction to the name. But then he buried his feelings even more deeply than Vick did. If he still had any. However hard the camps, they were soft beside the place where he learned his lessons.

"Valbeck is a large city," he said, "and growing every day. New mills. New slums. But it is somewhere to start. I shall ask your friends about their friends in Valbeck, and see if we can learn any more about this... Weaver."

Just one more try, maybe. Vick sat forward, clasping her hands. "With your permission—I think the boy Tallow might be turned."

"You can ensure his loyalty?"

"He has a sister. With her in custody..."

The Arch Lector flashed that toothless smile. "Very well. You can go next door and deliver him from his chains. I am glad someone will get good news tonight. No doubt you will want to be on your way to Valbeck. To rip this conspiracy up by the roots."

"I am eager to begin, Your Eminence."

"Don't work too hard. Practical Dole!" The door flew open, the hulking Practical almost filling the frame. "Wheel me out, would you?" Dole fished up the wedge, wheels squeaking as he pulled the chair away, but Glokta stopped him in the doorway with a raised finger and looked back. "You did the right thing."

"I know, Your Eminence," she said, meeting his sunken eyes. "I've no doubts."

When you tell a lie, you have to sound like you believe it.

Goes double for the ones you tell yourself.

Tallow stared at her with those big eyes, manacled hands on the table and his scrawny shoulders hunched around his ears. He really did look like her brother. There were no marks on him yet. That was something, she supposed.

"Did you escape from them?" he whispered.

Vick gave a sad smile as she sat down opposite him, in the chair for the one who asks the questions. "No one escapes from them."

"Then—"

"I am them."

He looked at her for a long moment, and she wondered if he might scream insults at her. If he might kick and scratch and go wild. But he was too clever or too scared. He just looked down at the stained tabletop and said, "Oh."

"Do you know who I was just talking to, next door?"

Tallow slowly shook his head.

"His Eminence the Arch Lector."

Those eyes went even bigger. "Here?"

"In his crippled person. You're a lucky boy. You've never seen him work. I have." And she gave a long, soft whistle. "Old Sticks, well, he'll be winning no footraces. But when it comes to making folk talk, believe me, there's no one faster. My guess is your friend Grise will already be telling him everything she knows about everything."

"She's strong," he said.

"No, she's not. But it doesn't matter. Once you're stripped and alone and he starts cutting, there's no strong that's strong enough."

Tallow blinked, tears glistening in his eyes. "But she's—"

"Put her out of your mind. She's already hanged. Moor's dead, and Sibalt..." Her throat was tight of a sudden.

"Sibalt?"

"He's dead, too."

"You say it like you're proud."

"I'm not. But I'm not ashamed, either. They made their choice, you heard me ask them. Just like I asked you."

Tallow paused a moment, licking his lips. No fool, this lad. "Grise is hanged, but...not me?"

"You catch on fast. For you there's a door still open. For you...and your sister." He blinked at that. Poor little bastard would've been the worst card player in the Union. It was as if his every feeling were written on his pinched-in face. "I told His Eminence maybe you could be saved. Maybe you could be of service to the king."

"What kind of service?"

"Whatever kind I pick."

He looked down at the table. "Betraying my brothers."

"I expect so."

"What choices do I have?"

"Just this one, and you're damn lucky to be getting it."

Now he looked up, a little unexpected hardness in his eyes. "Then why even ask?"

"So you understand what you owe me." She got up, slipping the key out, and unlocked his chains. Then she tossed him his clothes. "Get dressed. Then get some sleep. We'll be leaving for Valbeck in the morning. Need to know where those dullards got three barrels of Gurkish Fire."

Tallow just sat there, skinny wrists still in the open manacles. "Was any of it true?"

"Any of what?"

"What you told us?"

She narrowed her eyes at him. "A good liar lies as little as possible."

"So...you really did grow up in the camps?"

"Twelve years. Girl and woman. My parents and my sisters died there." She swallowed. "My brother, too."

He looked at her as if he didn't understand. "You've lost as much as anyone."

"More than most."

"Then how can you—"

"Because if I learned one thing in the camps..." She leaned down over him, baring her teeth, making him shrink back into his chair. "It's that you stand with the winners."

The Machinery of State

"Lord Marshal Brint," said Orso. "Thank you for seeing me at such short notice. I know you must be a very busy man."

"Of course, Your Highness." The lord marshal had one arm and no imagination, everything from his highly polished cavalry boots to his highly waxed moustache stiff, starched and according to regulation. "Your father is an old friend."

"Not to mention the High King of the Union."

The marshal's smile slipped just a fraction. "Not to mention that. How can I help?"

"I wish to speak to you concerning our response to the attack by Scale Ironhand and his Northmen."

Brint gave a bitter snort. "I only wish there'd be one! Those money-grubbing swindlers on the Closed Council refuse to release the funds. Can you believe it?"

"I cannot. But I have managed to persuade my father to give me command of an expeditionary force."

"You have?"

"Well—"

"That's excellent news!" The lord marshal sprang up, pacing to his maps, passing a highly polished suit of armour which he must have worn in his youth, if at all, as it still had both its arms. "We'll show these Northern bastards something, I can tell you!"

Orso had feared a career soldier might be upset to see a prince placed in command, but Brint looked positively delighted. "I realise I am without military experience, Lord Marshal, unless playing with toy soldiers as a boy counts." Or fucking whores in uniform, of course.

"That is why you employ officers, Your Highness." Brint was lost in contemplation of his charts, judging distances with spread thumb and forefinger. "I would suggest Colonel Forest as a second in command. He entered the army as an enlisted man long before me and has fought in every major war since. I cannot think of anyone with hotter experience or a cooler head."

Orso smiled. "I would be most grateful for his advice, and yours."

"Lady Governor Finree is holding the enemy most courageously. Hell of a woman. Old friend of mine, you know. If she can continue to do so, we could land here!" And he slapped the map so hard, Orso was concerned he might do injury to the one hand he still had. "Just near Uffrith, outflank the bastards!"

"Excellent! Outflank. Bastards. Wonderful." He really needed to find out what outflanking was, but other than that it was all coming together! The stern calls of a drill sergeant floated through the window from the yard outside, lending the interview an appropriately military flavour. Orso almost wished he'd worn his uniform for the occasion, though it was probably a little tight around the belly these days. He'd have to see about getting a new one for the campaign. "All I need now is the men."

Brint looked around. "Pardon me?"

"My father has promised me a battalion of the King's Own, as well as his First Guard, Bremer dan Gorst, who I understand is worth a company himself," and he gave a laugh which Brint by no means returned, "but I do require...somewhere in the region of, well, five thousand more?"

Silence stretched out.

"You don't have the men?" hissed Brint, spit flecking from his lips.

"Well...that's why I've come to you, Lord Marshal. I mean to say... you're a lord marshal." Orso winced. "Aren't you?"

Brint took a deep breath and regained command of himself. "I am, Your Highness, and I apologise. I find it difficult to keep my perspective where these Northmen are concerned." He frowned down at a ring on his little finger, pushed at it with his thumb-tip. A lady's ring, by the look of it, with a yellow stone. "Lost a wife to the savages, as well as two close friends. Not to mention a bloody arm."

"No need for apologies, Lord Marshal, I entirely understand."

"I hope you don't think that I resent your entirely reasonable request. I applaud it." Brint snorted, glancing towards his empty sleeve. "Or would, had I the equipment. I'm just embarrassed that I cannot give you the men, and ashamed not to have sent help to the lady governor already. Several regiments were disbanded following the war in Styria and what remains is spread thin. The rebellion in Starikland never ends." He waved the arm he had towards another map. "And now there's widespread unrest among the peasantry in Midderland. These bloody Breakers, curse them, making humble folk dissatisfied with their place in the world. Honestly,

I'm concerned about the battalion your father has already promised you. There's not the slightest possibility of my recruiting more without additional funds from the lord chancellor."

"Hmmm." Orso sat back, arms folded. It seemed, like most things in life, this was going to be a great deal more difficult than he had hoped. "It's a question of money, then?"

"Your Highness," and Lord Marshal Brint gave a sigh that bespoke an infinite weariness, "it is always a question of money."

"Lord Chancellor Gorodets, thank you for seeing me at such short notice. I know you must be a very busy man."

"I am, Your Highness."

There was a pregnant pause, during which the lord chancellor gazed levelly at Orso over the top of his gold-rimmed eye-lenses. He was a toad of a man with a taste for rich sauces, his many chins swelling expansively over his fur collar. Orso wished, not for the first time that day, that he was a great deal more drunk. But if he was to prevail against the impenetrable machinery of state, he would need every faculty.

"Let me get straight to the point, then," he said. "I am eager—as I am sure every right-thinking man in the Union must be—to rush to the aid of our hard-pressed brothers and sisters in Angland."

Gorodets gave a grimace of almost physical pain. "A war."

"Well, yes, but one forced upon us—"

"Those are no cheaper, Your Highness."

"No cheaper?" muttered Orso.

"Over the past twenty years, your father—encouraged by Her Majesty Queen Terez—has fought three wars in Styria for the sake of your birthright, the Grand Duchy of Talins."

"I wish he'd asked my opinion." Orso gave what he hoped was a disarming chuckle. "I scarcely want one nation, let alone two."

"That is just as well, Your Highness, since the Union lost all three wars."

"Come now, couldn't we call that middle one a draw?"

"We could, but I doubt anyone who fought in it would agree, and from a financial standpoint, victories are hardly to be preferred. To pay for those wars, I have been obliged to impose stringent taxes on the peasantry, on the merchants, on the provinces and, finally, with great reluctance, on the nobles. The nobles, in response, have consolidated their holdings, turned tenants off their estates and passed laws in the Open Council seizing and enclosing common land. People have flooded from the country into the cities and upset the whole system of taxation entirely. The Crown has been obliged to borrow heavily. *More* heavily, I should say. The debts owed to the banking house of Valint and Balk alone are..." Gorodets spent a moment scouring his vocabulary for a word of sufficient scale, and finally gave up. "Difficult to describe. Between the two of us, just the *interest* represents a significant proportion of the nation's expenditure."

"That much?"

"*More.* It is a thoroughly parlous situation, with acrimony boiling in every quarter. To find additional funds now is...unthinkable."

Orso listened with mounting horror. "Lord Chancellor, all I am asking for is the money for five thousand soldiers—"

"*All*, Your Highness?" Gorodets looked over his lenses like a tutor at a disappointing pupil, a look unpleasantly familiar to Orso from his actual tutors. Anyone in a position of authority, come to think of it. "Are you aware of how great a sum that is?"

Orso restrained his mounting frustration. "But you must see we have to do something about these Northmen!"

"I am afraid what *I* see is beside the point, Your Highness. I am a glorified accountant, and not even that glorified." He waved a hand at his cavernous office, every surface panelled with marble or encrusted with gold leaf, the plaster-cast faces of his predecessors gazing down smugly from up near the ceiling. "I manage the books. I try to make sure that what goes out in expenditure is equalled by what comes in through taxation. In this, like every lord chancellor before me, I habitually fail. It may be given to me to hold the purse strings but...I do not set policy alone."

"Alone?"

The lord chancellor gave a mirthless little chuckle as he wiped his lenses with a corner of his fur robe and held them up to the light. "I barely set policy at all."

"Who does?"

"It is His Eminence Arch Lector Glokta who takes the lead in setting the priorities of the Closed Council."

Orso sagged unhappily back into his chair. He remembered now why he had abandoned government and channelled his energies into women and wine. "It's a question of priorities, then?"

"Your Highness," and the lord chancellor perched his lenses back on his nose, "it is always a question of priorities."

"Your Eminence," said Orso. "Thank you so much for seeing me at such short notice. I know you must be a very busy man."

"To you, Your Highness, my door stands always open."

"Must cause a hell of a draught!" Arch Lector Glokta produced a false smile, displaying that hideous gap in his teeth. Orso wondered yet again how this monstrous remnant of a man could have had a hand in producing something so altogether magnificent as his daughter. "I wish to talk to you about the unfortunate situation in the North—"

"I would not call it unfortunate."

"You wouldn't?"

"Scale Ironhand, his brother Black Calder and *his* son Stour Nightfall have invaded our Protectorate and burned the capital of our long-standing ally. That is not misfortune. That is a calculated act of war."

"That's worse."

"Far worse."

"We should chastise these invaders, then!" said Orso, whacking his fist into his open palm.

"We should." Though something in the way the Arch Lector said "should" suggested he didn't think they would.

Orso paused, wondering how to frame it, but straightforward was usually best. "I wish to lead the expedition against them."

"Then I applaud your patriotic sentiments, Your Highness." To give Glokta his due, he showed not the slightest trace of mockery. "But this is a military matter. Perhaps you should raise it with Lord Marshal Brint—"

"I did. He led me by a roundabout route to Lord Chancellor Gorodets, who led me by a roundabout route to you. I followed the power, you might say, to your door." And he grinned. "Which stands always open to me."

The Arch Lector's narrow left eye twitched and Orso inwardly cursed. These flourishes of cleverness never did him the slightest good. He would get further with powerful men if they thought they were indulging an idiot. They probably were, after all.

"My father has given me leave to go," he went on. "Lord Marshal Brint can supply the officers. What I am lacking are the men. Or, more precisely, the money to pay and outfit them. Five thousand of the blighters, to be precise."

His Eminence sat back and regarded Orso with those sunken, feverishly bright eyes. Not a pleasant gaze to endure, by any means. Orso was glad he had only to endure it here, on the ground floor of the House of Questions, and not below.

"Do you know my daughter, Your Highness?"

A chilly breeze drifted through the Arch Lector's stark, hard office then, making the great heaps of papers on the tables shift and crackle like restless spirits. For a moment, Orso found himself wondering how many of them were the confessions of guilty traitors. Or innocent ones. But he was decidedly pleased with the way he kept his face blank, despite the sudden surge of guilty horror, not to mention healthy fear, produced by the question. Orso might not have excelled in all the areas his mother would have liked, but at feigning ignorance he was a master. Perhaps because he had so much real ignorance to draw on.

"Your daughter...Sarene, is it?"

"Savine."

"*Savine*, of course. I believe we've met...somewhere." Indeed, his tongue had met her quim and her mouth his cock not long ago and they had all got on bloody famously. He cleared his throat, aware of a swelling in his trousers by no means appropriate during a meeting with the most feared man in the Union. "Charming girl...as I recall."

"Do you know what she does?"

"Does?" Orso was starting to wonder if His Eminence had found out all about their little arrangement, in spite of the exhaustive precautions Savine insisted on. He was a man whose job it was to find things out, after all, and he was very, very good at his job. And that was not the sum of his job. Orso was confident the heir to the throne would not be bobbing to the surface of a canal any time soon, bloated by seawater and horribly mutilated, but...the Arch Lector would be a bad man to upset. The worst. "Young ladies do a lot of sewing, I understand?"

"She is an investor," said Glokta.

Orso played the dunce, waving one hand so his lace cuff flapped about the fingers. "A kind of...merchant?"

"A merchant in inventions. Machines. Manufactories. Better ways of doing things. She buys ideas and makes them real."

Orso could not, in fact, have been more awed and mystified by what Savine did if she had been a magus practising High Art, but he thought it might suit the role better if he barked out a mildly contemptuous laugh. "How thoroughly...*modern*."

"*Thoroughly* modern. In my youth, for someone to make a considerable fortune in that way, let alone a woman, would have been unthinkable. Savine may be a pioneer, but there are others following. We are entering a new age, Your Highness."

"We are?"

"My daughter recently helped finance the building of a large mill near Keln." And His Eminence pointed with one pale, knobbly finger across the map of the Union carved into the tabletop between them, towards what looked like nothing so much as an old, stained nail mark. "In that mill is a machine, operated by one man and powered by a waterwheel, that can card as much wool in a day as nine men could the old way."

"I suppose that's a fine thing for the wool trade?" offered Orso, baffled.

"It is. A fine thing for my daughter and her partners, too. But it is not so fine a thing for those other eight men, who used to card wool and are now looking for a new way to feed their families."

"I suppose not."

"And the very clever man who came up with that machine—a Gurkish refugee by the name of Masrud—has just come up with another that spins the carded wool into thread. Each one of those puts six women out of work. And they're not happy about it."

"Arch Lector, fascinated though I am by your daughter's exploits," and he bloody was, he was having to cross his legs at the thought of her to prevent embarrassment, "I'm not sure how they relate to our Northern troubles—"

"Change, Your Highness. At a pace and of a kind that has never been seen before. An order that has stood for centuries buckles and twists. Traditional barriers, however we might try to shore them up, collapse like sandcastles before the tide. Men fear to lose what they have, covet what they do not. It is a time of chaos. Of fear." The Arch Lector shrugged, tentatively, as though even that gave him pain. "A time of opportunity, if you are as clever as my daughter, but a time of great danger, too. Not long ago, the Inquisition rooted out a scheme, devised by a group of disaffected labourers, to burn down that mill I told you of and raise the workers against your father's government."

"Ah."

"Every day, threats are sent to the owners of manufactories. Every night, workers with soot-smeared faces cause wanton damage to machinery. In Hocksted, yesterday morning, the funeral of an agitator devolved into a full-scale riot."

"Ah."

"Below us, in the cells, are members of the group called the Breakers, apprehended only last night in the act of blowing up a foundry not two miles from where we sit. We are even now persuading them to help us uproot a conspiracy that spans the breadth of the nation."

Orso's eyes rolled down towards the floor. "That sounds...bad." He wasn't sure whether he was thinking of the plot or the fate of the plotters. Perhaps both.

"There is disloyalty everywhere. Treason everywhere. People love to say that things have never been so bad—"

Orso smiled. "They do, they do."

"But things really have never been so bad."

Orso's smile vanished. "Ah."

"I wish we were free to do what we thought right. I truly do." The Arch Lector glanced up at a huge, dark portrait on the wall. Some fearsome bald bureaucrat of the past, glowering down watchfully upon the little people. Zoller, maybe. "But we simply cannot risk any overseas adventures, however well intentioned, however deeply desired, however apparently necessary." He clasped his long, thin hands and gazed levelly at Orso, eyes glittering in skull-like sockets. "Put simply, the government of the Union hangs by a thread and must look first to its own security. To the legacy of the king. To the position of his heir."

"Well, I wouldn't want to interfere with your making *his* position comfortable." Orso gave a helpless shrug. He was quite out of ideas. "It's a question of politics, then?"

"Your Highness," and Arch Lector Glokta smiled, once again displaying that yawning gap in his front teeth. "It is *always* a question of politics."

Orso shuffled through his hand again, but it was as awful as it had been when it was dealt.

"I fold," he grunted, tossing his cards down in disgust. "What a pig of a day. Makes you wonder how anything gets done."

"Or realise why nothing does," said Tunny as he raked in the pot.

"It gives me scant enthusiasm for the job of being king, that's sure."

"Not that you had much in the first place."

"No. One begins to understand why my father is... how he is."

"Ineffectual, you mean?" Yolk chuckled. "He must be the most ineffec—"

Orso grabbed a fistful of his shirt and dragged him half out of his chair. "I get to mock him," he snarled in Yolk's shocked face. "You fucking don't."

"There's no point bullying that idiot," said Tunny, managing to smoke a chagga pipe, stare at Orso through narrowed eyes and deal expertly all at once. "He's an idiot."

Yolk spread his palms in mute agreement, and Orso gave a disgusted hiss and dumped him back in his chair, sweeping up his new hand and casting a lazy eye over it. It was every bit as awful as the last. But perhaps good card players are the ones who can win with bad cards.

"Forget those old bastards in the government." Tunny pointed at Orso with the stem of his pipe. "They've no vision. No audacity. We need to look at this another way. We need to frame it as a *bet*." And he tossed a couple of silvers into the empty centre of the table. "You need someone with money. With ambition. With patience. Someone who'll see a few favours from you down the line as a solid gamble."

"Won't be me," said Yolk, sadly, tossing his hand away.

"Rich, ambitious and patient," mused Orso, frowning at those two glinting coins. "A gamble. Or...an investment? Pass me that pencil." And Orso scrawled a few words across one of his playing cards, folded it and held it out. "Could you take this to the usual place, Hildi?" And he gave her a meaningful waggle of the brows. "An invitation to Sworbreck's office. Ten bits in it if you're quick."

"Twenty and it'll be there yesterday," said Hildi, hopping off the settle and sticking her chin up at him as though it was a loaded flatbow and she a highwayman.

"Twenty it is, you bandit. How much do I owe you now?"

"Seventeen marks and eight bits."

"Already?"

"I'm never wrong about numbers," she said solemnly.

"She's never wrong about numbers," said Tunny, shifting his chagga pipe from one side of his mouth to the other using only tongue and teeth.

"She is *never* wrong about numbers," said Orso, counting out the coins.

Hildi snatched them from his hand, stuck them into her cap, twisted it down hard onto her mass of blonde curls and slipped out through the door nimbly as a cat.

"How're we going to play with a card missing?" grumbled Yolk.

"You manage it without looks, wits or money," said Orso, sorting through his hand again. "You can manage without one card."

Sore Spots

"**H**ow the *hell* did you get that bruise?"

Savine put her fingers to her mouth. She had powdered carefully but her mother, while oblivious to so much, had an uncanny eye for injuries. "Don't worry, it's nothing. I was fencing. With Bremer dan Gorst."

"Fencing? With Bremer dan bloody *Gorst?* For such a clever girl, you do some witless things."

Savine winced at the pain through her ribs as she shifted in her chair. "I'll admit it was far from my best idea."

"Does your father know about this?"

"He presided over it. I've a feeling he was thoroughly tickled, in fact."

"He bloody would be. The only thing he enjoys more than his own suffering is other people's. Why you play with swords is quite beyond me."

"It's fine exercise. Keeps me strong. Keeps me…focused."

"What you need is less focus and more fun." Her mother drained her glass with a practised toss of her head. "You should get married."

"So I can be ordered around by some idiot? Thank you, no."

"Then don't marry an idiot. Marry a rich man who likes men. At least you'll have that in common." She peered thoughtfully up at the ceiling. "Or at least marry a pretty idiot, then you've something nice to look at while you regret it."

"That was your plan, was it?" asked Savine, sipping her own drink.

"Actually yes, but when I got to the counter, all they had left was the crippled mastermind."

Savine laughed so suddenly she blew wine out of her nose, had to jerk from her chair so she didn't spatter it down her dress, and ended up flicking it on the carpet in a most unladylike manner.

Her mother chuckled at her discomfort, then sighed. "And do you know?" She gave the monstrous diamond on her wedding band a lopsided grin. "I haven't regretted a day of it."

There was a sharp knock at the door and Zuri slipped through with the book under one arm, leaning close to murmur in Savine's ear. "A few decisions to be made, my lady. Then dinner with the loose-tongued but tight-fisted Tilde dan Rucksted and her husband. An opportunity to discuss their investment in Master Kort's canal."

Savine's turn to sigh. Another of the lord marshal's tales of derring-do on the frontier and she might be obliged to drown herself in the canal rather than extend it. But business was business.

Savine's mother was pouring herself another glass of wine. "What is it, darling?"

"I have to dress for dinner."

"Now?" She stuck her lip out in a needy pout. "How bloody tiresome. I was hoping we could talk tonight."

"We just did."

"Not like we used to, Savine! I've a hundred cutting comments just as funny as the last one."

Savine set down her glass and followed Zuri to the door. "Keep them dry for next time, Mother. It's business."

"Business." Her mother wiped the drip from the side of the decanter and sucked her finger. "These days, you are *all* business."

"Tighter," hissed Savine through gritted teeth, fists clenched on her dressing table, and she heard Freid hiss with effort as she hauled on the laces.

It was an informal event, so it only took four of them to dress her. Freid was handling the wardrobe on her own. Lisbit was face-maid, on paint, powder and perfume. Metello—a hatchet-featured Styrian who had once been chief dresser to the Duchess of Affoia—barely spoke a word of common but expressed herself with unmatched eloquence through the medium of wigs. Zuri, meanwhile, attended to book and jewels and ensured that the others did not make a mess of anything all at once.

"Master Tardiche writes to say the foundry cannot be competitive without another five thousand marks for new machinery," she said, meeting Savine's eye in the mirror.

Savine frowned. "I did not care for the way he spoke to me last time he visited. Great tall fellow, declaiming from on high." She lifted her chin so Lisbit could lean in, different shades of powder smeared on the back of her hand like an easel, and set to work on her eyelids with the tip of a little finger. "Let him know I am selling my share. If he comes grovelling,

I might reconsider." She gasped as Freid gave another tug at her corset and near dragged her off her feet. "Some men just look better on their knees. Tighter, Freid."

"Everyone looks better on their knees. It was my favourite thing about attending temple." Zuri set the book down to step in, winding the laces tight around her hands and pushing one knee into Savine's back. "Breathe out."

Savine's lungs were emptied in a faint groan as Zuri pulled. She might have been slender as a willow switch but, by the Fates, she was strong as a docker. The feeling of constriction was, for a moment, quite terrifying. But great results require great pains.

People liked to think of beauty as some natural gift, but Savine firmly believed that just about anyone could be beautiful, if they worked hard at it and spent enough money. It was merely a question of emphasising the good, disguising the bad and painfully squeezing the average into the most impressive configuration. Very much like business, really.

"That's it, Zuri," croaked Savine, shifting her shoulders back and letting everything settle. "Unless you feel like it's cutting you in half, it isn't doing the job. Knots, Freid, before they loosen."

"Master Hisselring called." Zuri took up the book again. "He asks for another extension on his loan."

Savine would have raised her brows had Lisbit not been in the midst of shaping them. "Poor old Hisselring. It would be a shame to see him lose his house."

"The scriptures hold much praise for charity. But they also say only the thrifty will enter heaven."

"A cynic might observe that the scriptures can be used to support both sides of every argument."

Zuri had the tiniest smile at the corner of her mouth. "A cynic might say that is the point of them."

When Savine felt herself softening, even for a moment, she found it effective to taunt herself with the things other people had that she did not. At that moment, the fine, rosy blush to Lisbit's cheek was in her eyeline. It made the girl look like a peasant, but it was fashionable. One can always find some small, irrelevant thing to be jealous of. The moment you lose your murderous edge, after all, could be the moment you lose altogether.

Some might have said that made her self-serving, shallow and poisonous. She would have replied that the self-serving, shallow, poisonous people always seemed to come out on top. Then she would have laughed ever so sweetly, and whispered to Zuri to place a note in the book for their future destruction.

Savine considered her face in the mirror. "A touch more blush. And I think I have given Hisselring quite long enough. Call in the debt."

"My lady. Then there is Colonel Vallimir, and the mill in Valbeck."

Savine gave the loudest groan of frustration she could while pushing her lips out for Lisbit's brush. "Still making a loss?"

"Quite the reverse. He reports a large profit this month."

Savine could not help glancing sharply around, causing Lisbit to cluck with annoyance as she smudged, then lean in so close to correct it with a fingertip that Savine could smell her oversweet breath.

"Blessed are the thrifty...does Vallimir explain his sudden success?"

"He does not," said Zuri, slipping a necklace around Savine's neck so gently she barely felt it. The new emeralds from her man in Ospria. Just the one Savine would have picked.

"Suspicious."

"It is."

"We should pay him a visit. Make sure our partners realise that our eyes are always on the details. And we have plenty of other interests in Valbeck. There never was a city so ill-conceived, ill-built and ill-tempered, but there really is a great deal of money to be made there. Zuri, clear a few days somewhere in the next month so you and I can—"

"I am afraid...I will not be able to accompany you." Zuri said it as she did everything. Gently. Gracefully. But very firmly.

Savine stared at her in the mirror, momentarily lost for words. Lisbit swallowed. Metello glanced up from the wig on its stand, comb frozen in her hand.

"Things in the South are...worse than ever," said Zuri, eyes to the floor. "Some say the Prophet was killed by a demon. Some say he overcame her and is recovering from the battle. The emperor has been cast down, and his five sons struggle with each other. The provinces declare their independence and look to their own survival. Warlords and bandits spring up everywhere. It is chaos." Zuri looked up at her. "Ul-Safayn, my family's home, has become lawless. My brothers are in danger. I have to help them get out."

Savine blinked. "But Zuri...you're my rock."

And she was. She was beautiful, tasteful, discreet, spoke five languages, had a refined sense of humour and an effortless mastery of the workings of business, and yet somehow never stole the attention for herself. She would no doubt have held as high a place in Gurkish society as Savine did in the Union's, had Gurkish society not crumbled into madness, causing refugees to flood across the Circle Sea and dark-skinned ladies' companions to become so terribly fashionable in Adua.

Since Savine's father first introduced her, a friendless exile in desperate need of a position, Zuri had made herself indispensable in a dozen ways. But it was more than that. Savine's acquaintance was immense. A great web of favours, partnerships and obligations that stretched across the Union and beyond. But the truth was she had no friends at all. Apart from the one she paid.

"You'll be back soon?" she found she had asked.

"As soon as I can."

"Should I send some men with you—"

"I will be safer alone."

Savine caught a glimpse of herself in the mirror and realised, even with the elaborate powdering, she looked quite crushed. That would not do at all.

"But of course you must go," she said, a little too brightly. "Family comes first. I'll pay for your passage."

"Lady Savine, I—"

"You could check on our agents in Dagoska on the way. Make sure they are not fleecing us. And perhaps, under the circumstances, there might be some bargains to be had on the shores of the Gurkish Sea."

"I would not be surprised," said Zuri, frowning over at Freid.

She was clutching Savine's dress like a shield, wide eyes showing over its embroidered collar. "Aren't you worried about...*Eaters?*"

Zuri sighed. "God knows I have enough real worries without inventing more."

"My aunt says the South is *teeming* with them," said Lisbit, always keen to jump into any gossip with both feet.

"My father saw one," said Freid, breathless. "Years ago, at the Battle of Adua. They can steal your face, or turn you inside out just by looking at you, or—"

"Tall tales spread by people who should know better," said Savine, sternly. "Lisbit, you will be my companion while Zuri is away. You'd enjoy a trip to Valbeck, wouldn't you?"

Lisbit's rosy cheeks went even rosier. "I'd be honoured, my lady!"

As though her honour was Savine's concern. Without making a sound, Zuri screamed that she was a peerless lady's companion, and therefore that the lady she accompanied must also be peerless. Lisbit sent no such message. She was pretty enough, but she would be worse than worthless with the book and she had no taste at all. Still. *We must work with the tools we have*, as Savine's father was forever saying. She smothered her disappointment with a smile.

"And, of course, if any of your family need work, or a place to stay, they will always be welcome with me."

"You are too generous," said Zuri. "As always."

"I daresay Master Hisselring would not agree. If your brothers are half as useful as you, it will be the best investment I ever make."

There was a knock at the door and Lisbit opened it a crack, a moment later leaned close while Freid and Zuri were easing Savine's dress on. "That girl's here, my lady." Her lip wrinkled with distaste. "With a message from Spillion Sworbreck."

Savine felt that familiar flutter in her stomach, that familiar heat in her face. "When am I due at the Rucksteds'?"

Zuri consulted the watch. "Two hours and ten minutes."

Savine thought about that, but not for long. "Please send Tilde my deepest regrets, but I cannot attend. I have a headache. Show Sworbreck's girl in."

She was, of course, not Sworbreck's girl at all, but Prince Orso's. Most princes would have employed some lord's son as a valet, but he, with characteristic disregard for the rules, had a thirteen-year-old waif whose last job had been laundering soiled sheets in a brothel. Orso did love to surround himself with curiosities. Probably to distract as much attention from his being the heir to the throne as possible.

The girl stood there now, freckle-faced and threadbare with a battered soldier's cap pulled all the way down to her eyes, as incongruous in Savine's perfumed dressing room as a rat on a wedding cake. She watched Metello clamber up onto the stool to seat Savine's wig with horrified amazement, as though she had happened upon a coven of witches about some arcane ritual.

"Hildi, isn't it?" said Savine, watching her in the mirror.

She nodded. Quick eyes, she had. "My lady."

"Master Sworbreck has asked for me?"

The girl gave an impressively guarded wink. "At his office, my lady."

"Take your cap off in front of Lady Savine," said Lisbit, already putting on airs now she felt she had a promotion. Savine wondered if she would have throttled her by the time Zuri returned, and gave it about evens.

Hildi sourly pulled her cap off. She had a surprising mass of pinned-up, pale-blonde hair underneath. Metello gave a hum of interest, hopped from her stool to poke at it with a comb, rubbed a lock between finger and thumb, finally made Hildi squawk as she jerked a strand from her head and held it up to the light. She gave Savine a significant look from under her grey brows.

"Such beautiful hair you have," said Savine.

"Thanks," grumbled Hildi, still rubbing her head. "I guess."

"I'll give you three marks for it."

"For my hair?" Her surprise did not last long. "Ten."

"Five. You won't miss it under that cap."

"The cap won't fit without it. Ten or nothing."

"Oh, I like this girl. Give her twelve, Zuri."

Zuri slipped out that curved knife of hers. "Hold still, child."

Savine watched as Zuri neatly cropped her hair to stubble. "Like sunshine in a bottle," murmured Savine as Metello laid out the lengths. "We can stop into my wig-maker's on the way. You run on ahead, girl." The thought of seeing Orso had quite chased away her upset over Zuri's forthcoming absence, and she caught Hildi's eye in the mirror and gave her the very same wink. "Tell Master Sworbreck I'll be *delighted* to see him."

"Shit," she gasped, knocking over a heap of Sworbreck's papers as she sagged back, spent, an avalanche of notes spilling onto the floor behind her. She unclenched her aching hand, the edge of the desk imprinted white across her palm.

"You..." She untangled the fingers of her other hand from Orso's hair and patted him on the cheek. "Have been practising."

"As often as possible." Orso grinned as he wiped his face and shrugged her leg off his shoulder.

"I really should tell Sworbreck..." her breathing still ragged as she fished a niggling letter opener from under her shoulder and tossed it away, "to get a bed in here."

"Oh, I'd miss this desk." Orso leaned towards her, but not quite far enough, making her crane up to kiss him. "So many memories."

She pushed down her skirts and reached for his belt. "Your turn."

"Can we...talk first?"

"Talk *first*?" She narrowed her eyes. She was still pleasantly soft, flushed and shuddery all over, but if he thought to slip something by her, he would have a rude awakening. "What are you after?"

"It's this business in the North." He knelt in front of her, looking earnestly up. "We can't leave Finree dan Brock to fight our battles for us. We're supposed to be a bloody Union."

"Supposed to be—"

"There has to be a response!" He thumped the desk, hard enough to make the glasses rattle. "And...I feel I should be the man to lead it."

She burst out laughing, saw he did not, and petered out into uncertain silence. "You're serious?"

"Deadly. I went to see my father. Then I went to see yours—"

She jerked up. "You did *what?*"

"Give me some credit, Savine, I didn't lead with, 'Your Eminence, I had my tongue up your daughter last night.' He doesn't suspect a thing."

"You'd be a brave man to bet on what my father suspects."

"And I'm not one, is that it?"

He looked a little wounded, and she felt a little sad for him. "Oh, you poor baby." She put her arms around his neck, drew him close and kissed him softly. "After twelve years of drinking, gambling and fucking anything with a hole in it, does no one take you seriously?"

"Plainly you don't." And he stood up and started to button his shirt.

In fact, she thought she might be the only one who did. "I'm here, aren't I?" She pulled him back down, and pushed her hand through his hair, and held his head against her chest. "What did the great men tell Your Highness?"

"My father gave me a battalion and said I can have command if I raise five thousand more men, but...for that I need money." He let a fingertip trail down her collarbone to the hollow at the bottom of her throat. "You know people. Rich people. People who might consider me... an investment."

Savine frowned. If she judged an opportunity to be poor, she would not damage her reputation by passing it on. If she judged an opportunity to be good, she wanted it for herself. But five thousand soldiers meant a vast expense. Uniforms, weapons, armour, bedding, provisions. Then there was the army of men and women needed to get those men to the field and keep them there. The host of carts, wagons and beasts of burden. The food and supplies for *them*.

And, however much she wanted to be generous, Orso was beyond unreliable. He kept a brothel's laundry girl instead of a servant, for pity's sake. He scarcely understood the rules of business, let alone could be expected to observe them. If she was to lend him money, she would need guarantees. A crystal-clear understanding of what she expected in return. A contract. One so tightly binding, not even a king could wriggle free of it.

Perhaps encouraged by her thoughtful silence, he gave the slightest, uncertain smile. "What do you think?"

Her mouth smiled in return. Then, entirely independently of her mind, it said, "I'll give you the money."

There was a silence. As the expression gradually formed on his face, he looked more suspicious than grateful. And who could blame him? What the hell was she doing? "Just...like that? All of it?"

"Why have money at all if you can't help...a friend." Somehow she almost choked on the word.

"No repayment plan? No favours in kind? No speak-to-this-fellow about that-piece-of-business?"

"It's all in a good cause, isn't it? Patriotic." Good causes? Patriotism? It was as if some other person was speaking with her voice.

He reached up and gently stroked her cheek. He could be so delicate when he wanted. "Just when I think my opinion of you can't get any higher...you surprise me. I have to go! There's so much to organise."

It wasn't until he whisked his hand away that she realised she'd been pressing her face against it. She still felt the heat in her cheek. She was blushing like a child and turned away, embarrassed. Furious with herself, in fact.

"Of course." She smoothed her dress, fiddled with her necklace, adjusted her wig. "I've a dinner to attend myself. With Marshal Rucksted and his wife—"

"Sounds an absolute riot. Now, you're sure about this?" He slipped an arm around her waist from behind, held her tight against him. "You're absolutely sure?"

"I always say what I mean." And she did. Except now, for some reason.

"I'll be in touch," he whispered in her ear, making her neck tingle. "Or Sworbreck will, at least." And the door clattered shut behind him.

Savine stood there, in silence, in Sworbreck's cramped office, trying to understand what she had done. She loved to gamble, but she always knew the game. This was reckless. This broke all her rules.

All those awfully intimate friends who she knew really envied and hated her would have a ready answer, of course. *There is no more ambitious snake in Adua than Savine dan Glokta. That bitch hopes to ride the worthless crown prince's cock all the way into the palace. She wants to steal the throne. Then she really can be above us all instead of merely acting like it.*

Perhaps they would have been right. Perhaps she was harbouring some childish dream of becoming High Queen of the Union. Zuri had a point, after all: everyone looks better on their knees. Had Orso not been crown prince, she would have had no interest in him. What was there to be interested in?

Apart from his looks, of course. And his easy confidence. And the way he made her laugh. Really laugh, without a shred of pretence. That little twitch at the corner of his mouth as he thought of a joke that set hers twitching in sympathy as she wondered what it would be, never quite able to guess. No one could surprise her like he could. No one understood what she needed like he did. She thought of how dull everything was while she waited for the message from Sworbreck. The dressing, the dinners, the teas, the profits, the dressing, the gossip, the strategising, the marks in the book. Then how everything exploded with colour when the message arrived. As if she was in prison when she was not with him. As if she was buried and only came to life when—

"Shit," she breathed.

She felt suddenly as weak at the knees as she had when Bremer dan Gorst rammed her into the wall. She had to slump back on Sworbreck's desk, staring down at her discarded drawers, rumpled on the floor.

Everyone knew he was a vain, lazy, useless waste of flesh. A man she should not want. A man she could never have.

And she was totally in love with him.

PART II

"Progress just means
bad things happen faster."

Terry Pratchett

Full of Sad Stories

"**B**e sure to sweep the chimneys on the east side first," said Sarlby, leaning on his broom. "These ones only just got doused. Still hot as the Maker's forge."

The sweep was a quivery old drunk with a squinty eye and a stink halfway between a tap-house and a mass grave. Two smells Broad knew better than he'd like. "I know my business," he grunted, not even looking up as he led his boys past. Four of them, soot-smudged and hungry-looking, loaded with brushes and rods. The littlest whistled as he went, gave Broad a grin with a couple of teeth missing. Broad tried to grin back, but he didn't have much of a grin in him.

"I swear that fucker's more drunk every time I see him," muttered Sarlby, frowning after the sorry little procession.

"If I hadn't sworn off drink already, the sight of him'd be a winning argument for temperance," said Broad.

"It's a damn shame, lads that age sent down chimneys. How old was that youngest one, you reckon?"

Broad kept sweeping. He'd learned in Styria there's a lot of things that are better just not thought about. Couldn't be a coincidence that the happiest men Broad ever knew were generally the stupidest.

"They buy 'em, you know, from the pauper houses. Lads with no kin and no hopes. They're hardly better'n slaves." Sarlby wiped his forehead and leaned down close. "They scrub their knees with brine. Elbows, too. Scrub 'em raw, morning and night, toughen 'em up like boot leather so they can stand those hot chimneys."

"It's a damn shame." Broad lifted his lenses to rub at the sweaty bridge of his nose, then settled them back. Summer outside and the kettles cooking all day inside and the brewhouse was hot as an oven. "But the world's full o' sad stories."

"No doubt." Sarlby gave a joyless little chuckle. "I know one poor arsehole lives in a cellar by the river over on Meadow Street, leaks so bad he has to bail it out every morning like his home was a sinking skiff. Where's your family now?"

"Malmer found us a set of rooms halfway up the hill."

"Oh, my *lord*." Sarlby stuck his nose in the air and put on his idea of a nobleman's voice. "A whole *set*?"

"If you can call two a set. They cost, but my daughter's got work as a maid and my wife's bringing some money in stitching. Funeral clothes, mostly."

"All the best clothes around here are funeral clothes."

"Aye." Broad gave a sigh. "Always been good with a needle, Liddy. Good at whatever she turns her hand to. She's the one with the talent."

Sarlby grinned. "Not to mention the looks, the brains, the sense o' humour... What is it you bring to the marriage, again?"

"Honestly, I've no bloody idea."

"Well, good for you, and good for your family. Things aren't so bad halfway up the hill, where the vapours are a little thinner. Someone's got to come out on top, I guess. Someone's got to do well while others suffer."

Broad gave Sarlby a look over his lenses. "Will you ever stop pricking at me?"

"It's your conscience doing that."

"Oh, aye, you just hand it the ammunition."

"You get tired of the stabbing feeling, you know what you can do." Sarlby put a hand on Broad's shoulder, murmured in his ear. "The Breakers are gathering, brother. More of us every day. There's going to be a Great Change. Just a matter o' when."

Maybe it was the breath on his neck, or the sense of a secret shared, or the risk of what they were discussing, or just the sticky heat, but something gave Broad a shiver. He'd wanted to change things once. Before he went to Styria and learned things don't change easy. " 'Course," he grunted. "And they'll give every man his own dragon to ride and a candy castle to live in. Then when we get hungry, we can just eat the walls."

"I'm no fool, Bull. I know what the world is. But maybe we can spread the wealth *about* a little. Maybe we can take some rich bastards out of those palaces on the hill and some poor families out of those cellars on Meadow Street. Maybe we can give each man an honest wage for an honest day's work. Stop the false clocks and the fines and the girls pressed into night work. Put an end to the butchers selling tainted meat, and the flour bulked out with chalk, and the ale watered down with rotten water.

Maybe we can make sure there's no little boys being scrubbed with brine any more, at least. That'd be worth something, wouldn't it?"

"Aye. That'd be worth something." Broad had to admit there wasn't much in Sarlby's little speech he could argue with. "Never had you marked down for an orator."

There was a clatter somewhere, further down the brewhouse floor. "I stole the words from better men," said Sarlby. "You like that, you should come to a meeting, listen to the Weaver. He'd soon have you thinking our way."

Broad could hear someone shouting, muffled. "Can't afford to think your way," he said, with some regret. "I gave up putting the world right a while back. First time we climbed those ladders, maybe. Second time, for sure. I've enough trouble at my back. Got to keep my head down. Look after my family."

Another clatter, louder, and a cloud of soot came belching from one of the fireplaces they'd just doused.

"What the hell?" Sarlby took a step towards it. "We're trying to sweep up down here!"

A scraping, slithering sound echoed from that fireplace, and another puff of soot, and a high wail came from inside. Broad went cold all over at the sound of it—shrill with pain and panic.

"I can't get out!" Had to be one of the sweep's boys. "I can't get out!"

Broad and Sarlby stared at each other, Broad seeing his own helpless horror mirrored in his old comrade's face.

"He's trapped in there!" squawked Sarlby.

Broad dashed to the chimney, dropping his broom, clambering up onto a bench beside the flue. The fires had been burning all day. Even on the outside, the bricks were hot to touch.

There was another clatter, the sound of something sliding, and the boy's cries turned to mindless, wordless shrieks.

The flue had been built no better than most of Valbeck, and Broad tore at its crumbling mortar with his fingertips, with his fingernails, as if he could rip it apart with his bare hands and get to that boy, but he couldn't.

"Here!" Malmer had run over, was shoving a crowbar at him, and Broad snatched it from his hands and started digging at the loose mortar, stabbing, hacking, brick chips flying while he hissed curses.

He could hear the boy inside, no screams for help any more, just coughs and whimpers.

A brick came grinding free and the wash of heat made Broad jerk his face away. He wedged the bar in the gap, used it as a lever, popped more bricks out.

Soot came billowing with them and he coughed, dust across one side of his lenses. He saw Sarlby grab at the side of the ragged hole, gasp at the heat, tear his apron off and wrap it around his hands.

Broad rammed his bar into the chimney and heaved with all his weight, trembling with effort, growling through gritted teeth. A great wedge of bricks tore free and tumbled down, the black flue opened up and Broad saw something wedged in there. Two black sticks. One had a boot on the end.

So hot inside. Oven hot. Broad could feel the sweat springing out of his face. The boy's trousers were smouldering, smoking, the flesh of his legs all slick and bubbled. At first, Broad thought it was ash that slid off when he grabbed them. Then he saw it was skin.

"Damn it!" snarled Sarlby, digging again with the crowbar. Bricks and mortar tumbled down and the boy slithered out into Broad's arms in a shower of soot.

He was hot, too hot to touch. It was a painful effort not to let him drop.

"Set him down!" rasped Malmer, sweeping a bench clear and slapping embers from the boy's smouldering hair.

"Fuck," whispered Sarlby, back of his arm across his mouth.

The boy didn't move. Didn't breathe. Burned as he was, maybe that was a good thing. There was a smell like cooking. A smell like bacon in the pan of a morning.

"What do we do?" shouted Broad. "What can we do?"

"Naught we can do." Malmer's grey-fuzzed jaw worked as he stared down. "He's dead."

"Cooked," whispered Sarlby. "He fucking cooked alive."

"I thought you said the west side..." Broad turned to see the sweep standing there, the little lad next to him, staring. "I thought you said—"

It was cut off in a gurgle as Broad caught him by his collar, lifted him, rammed him into the broken chimney. He fumbled helplessly at Broad's fists, the tendons standing stark from the tattoo on the back of his hand.

"I didn't know..." Tears wet on his face and his breath stinking of drink and rot. "I didn't know..."

"Easy," Broad heard someone saying. A deep voice, soft and soothing. "Easy, big man. Let him go."

Broad was like a flatbow cranked too tight, all that strain running through him, far easier to let the bolt fly than not. Took a mighty effort

156

not to break the sweep's back over the chimney, to unclench his hands and let go of his dirty coat, to step away from him, let him slide down to sit blubbing on the floor beside the boiler.

Malmer patted Broad on the chest. "There you go. Nothing to gain with violence. Not now."

Not ever. Broad knew that. He'd known that for years. But what he knew and what he did had never had much to do with each other.

He looked back at the boy, lying there all blackened, all reddened. He made his aching fists unclench. He fumbled off his dirty lenses and stood breathing. He looked up at Sarlby and Malmer, two blurs now in the lamplight.

"Where are these meetings?"

Surprises

Rikke flopped down, misjudged it and sat so hard she bit her tongue and gave her backside quite the bruising. Isern had to shoot out a quick hand to stop her chair going over backwards.

"You're drunk," she said.

"I *am* drunk," said Rikke, proudly. She'd hit the chagga pipe as well and everything had a lovely glow. Faces all shiny and smeary and happy in the candlelight.

"You're proper shitted," said Isern. "But people are forgiving of you because you're young, foolish and strangely lovable."

"I *am* lovable." Rikke took another drink, which met just a smidge of burp-sick coming up the other way and made her half-choke and splutter ale everywhere. Would've felt extremely undignified if she'd been less drunk. As it was, she just laughed. "And being drunk, well, that's the *point* of a feasht."

Isern's eyes slipped slowly towards her over the rim of her cup. "The word is *feast*."

"That's what I said," said Rikke. "Feasht." Bloody word, she couldn't quite get her numb teeth all the way around it. The hall—or the barn, in fact, because they had to use what they could get these days—was falling quiet. Rikke's father was getting up to give a speech.

"Shush!" hissed Rikke. "Shush!"

"I didn't speak," said Isern.

"I said *shush!*" Her cracked voice rang out across the now-silent barn, and her father cleared his throat, and Rikke felt all eyes on her and her face burned and she squashed herself down as low as she could go and took a stealthy slurp from her cup.

"Might be Calder and Scale and their bastards have us on the run!" called Rikke's father. "So far."

"So far, the bastards!" someone bellowed, and others seized the chance to growl insults of one kind or another at the enemy and Rikke curled her lip and spat onto the straw.

"Might be my garden's been trampled to muck!"

"Was naught but brambles anyway!" someone called from the back.

"Might be I'm giving a speech in some fool's barn rather'n my hall in Uffrith!"

"That hall smelled o' dog!" came a voice, and there was a scattering of laughter from the hundred or more Named Men wedged around tables made from old doors.

Rikke's father looked grave, though, and they soon shut up. "Lost a lot of things, in my life," he said. "Lost 'em, or had 'em taken. Lot of good folk gone back to the mud these past few weeks. Lot of empty spaces, here, now, where friends should be sitting. Spaces that can't ever be filled." And he raised his cup, and so did everyone else, and a solemn murmur went around the barn.

"To the dead," growled Shivers.

"To the dead," echoed Rikke, sniffing back a sudden wave of sadness and anger mixed.

"But I've been blessed with loyal allies!" Rikke's father nodded towards Lady Finree, doing her best to look comfortable, bless her. "And now my daughter's come back to me." He grinned down at Rikke. "So, in spite of some sorrows, I count myself lucky!" And he hugged her tight, and kissed her head, and while the barn rang to its ancient rafters with cheers and whoops, muttered softly, "Luckier'n I deserve, I reckon."

"I'd like to raise a cup myself!" Rikke clambered onto the table with a hand on her father's shoulder and held her cup over her head. Ale slopped out and spattered on the wood, though it was already so ale-spattered no one could've noticed the difference. "To all o' you sorry bastards who were so hopelessly lost, but thanks to the tender guidance of Isern-i-Phail, were able to find your way back to me!"

"To lost bastards!" someone roared, and everyone drank, and there was laughter, and a fragment of song, and a fight broke out in a corner and someone got punched and lost a bit of a tooth, but all in good humour.

"By the dead, I'm glad you're back safe, Rikke." Her father cupped her face in his gnarled old hands. "Anything happened to you…" Seemed like he had tears glimmering at the corners of his eyes, and he smiled, and sniffed. "You're all the good I've done."

The way he looked worried her—washed-out and grey, years older than when she'd last seen him just a few weeks ago. The way he talked worried her—sappy and sentimental, always looking back like he'd nothing ahead to look to. But the last thing she wanted was to let him see she was worried, so she clowned more than ever.

"What're you talking about, you silly old bastard? You've done piles of good. Mountains. Who's done more good for the North than you? Not a one o' these fools wouldn't die for you."

"Maybe. But they shouldn't have to. I'm just not sure..." He frowned out at the barnful of drunk warriors like he hardly saw them. Like he was staring through them with the Long Eye and saw something horrible beyond. "Not sure I got the bones for the fight any more."

"Now listen." She caught his deep-lined face and dragged it back towards her, growling the words at him, fierce. "You're the Dogman! There's *no* man in the North got more bones than you. How many battles you fought in?"

He gave a faint smile at that. "Feels like pretty much all of 'em."

"It *is* pretty much all of 'em! You fought beside the Bloody-Nine! You fought beside Rudd Threetrees! You beat Bethod in the High Places!"

He licked at one pointed tooth as he grinned. "I don't like to boast, you know."

"Man with your name doesn't need to." She raised her chin, puffed herself up, showed him how proud she was to be his kin. "You'll *beat* Stour Nightfall and his arse-lickers, and we'll see him hanged with brambles, and I'll cut the bloody cross in him and send his fucking guts back to his daddy!" She realised she was snarling the words, spraying spit, shaking her fist in his face, and she made the fingers uncurl and wiped her mouth with them instead. "Or something..."

Her father was somewhat taken aback at her bloodthirstiness. "You never talked like that before."

"Aye, well, I never had my home burned, either. Never understood why feuds were such a popular pastime in the North but I reckon I'm getting it now."

Her father winced. "Hoped my scores would die with me and you could walk free of 'em."

"Weren't your fault! Or mine. Scale Ironhand attacked us! Black Calder burned Uffrith! Stour fucking Nightfall chased me through the woods. They trampled your garden..." she finished, lamely.

"The beauty o' gardens is that they grow back."

"Changes your feelings," she growled, the anger bubbling up again at the memory, "when you're sunk to your neck in a freezing river, starving and shitting yourself and quite fucking chafed as well, actually, and hearing some bastard brag on the horrors he'll inflict on you. Break what you love, he said, and they've fucking broken everything. Well, I'll break what *they* love, then we'll see. Swore to myself I'd see Stour killed, and I *swear* I will."

Rikke's father gave a sigh. "The beauty o' making yourself a promise is that no one else complains if you break it."

"Huh." Rikke realised she had her fists clenched again, decided to keep 'em that way. "Isern says I'm soft. Says I'm coddled."

"There's worse you could be."

"Isern says ruthlessness is a quality much loved o' the moon."

"Might be you should be careful what lessons you learn from Isern-i-Phail."

"She wants what's best for me. What's best for the North."

Her father gave a sad smile at that. "Believe it or not, we all want what's best. The root o' the world's ills is that no one can agree on what it is."

"She says you have to make of your heart a stone."

"Rikke." And he laid his hands on her shoulders. "Listen to me, now. I've known a lot of men did that down the years. Men who had plenty in 'em to admire. Men who turned their hearts hard so they could lead, so they could win, so they could rule. Did 'em no good in the end, nor anyone around 'em." He gave her shoulders a squeeze. "I like your heart how it is. Might be if there were a few more like it, the North'd be a better place."

"You reckon?" she muttered, far from convinced.

"You've got bones, Rikke, and you've got brains. You like to hide it. Even from yourself, maybe." He looked out at the room, and the shouting men that filled it. "I reckon they'll need your bones and your brains, when all this is over. But they'll need your heart, too. When I'm gone."

Rikke swallowed. Turned her fear into a joke, as usual. "Where you going, the shit-pit?"

"Shit-pit first. Then my blanket. Don't get too drunk, eh?" He leaned close to murmur in her ear. "Be a shame to make o' your heart a wineskin, either."

She frowned as she watched him go. He'd always been thin, but wiry-strong like a bent bow. Now he looked crooked, brittle. She caught herself wondering how long he had left. Wondering what would become of her when he was gone. What would become of them all. If they were counting on her bones and her brains, they were in bigger trouble than she'd thought.

Shivers sat frowning into the room, bit of a space around him. He had a reputation made most folk keep their distance, even drunk. There were too many bad men in the North and Caul Shivers, by most accounts, was one of the very worst. Bad men are a terrible curse, no doubt, right

161

up until you're in bad trouble and there's one on your side. Then they're the best thing ever.

"Hey, hey, Shivers!" She slapped him on the shoulder and nearly missed. Lucky thing it was a big shoulder. "Not sure you're really getting this whole feast thing. We are rejoicing in my heroic return. You're meant to smile." She looked at his ruined face, the lid sagging around his metal eye and the great burn across his cheek. "You can smile, can't you?"

He looked at her hand on his shoulder, then up at her, and didn't smile at all. "Why were you never scared of me?"

"You just never seemed all that scary. Always found your eye sort of pretty. Shiny." Rikke patted his scarred cheek. "You always just seemed... lost. Like you lost yourself and didn't know where to look." She put her hand on his chest. "But you're in there, still. You're in there."

He looked as shocked as if she'd slapped him, and there was a gleam of damp in his real eye, or maybe it was just her own sight that was smeary, as Caul Shivers wasn't really known as a big weeper, except when his bad eye dribbled, which was a different thing.

"Lot o' teary old men about today," she muttered, pushing herself away from the table. "I need another drink." Probably another drink wasn't a good idea, but for some reason she'd always found bad ideas the more appealing kind. She was sloshing ale into her cup, tongue pressed into the dent in her lip where the chagga usually sat with the effort of not spilling, when she caught sight of Leo dan Brock.

He usually had a few of his friends with him, and the one with all the teeth wasn't far away, grinning at a serving woman like his smile was a gift she was lucky to get, but it looked like the rest had been scared off by his mother. To be fair, Lady Finree was a pretty fearsome woman, and she was delivering a pretty fearsome lecture to her son, if her wagging finger and his screwed-up face were a guide.

"...but I shan't cramp you any longer," Rikke heard her say as she came closer. "*Someone* has to manage this retreat, after all."

Leo glared daggers at his mother as she strode away, then tossed his head back and drained his cup, then threw the cup across the rubbish-strewn table and started drinking straight from the jug, little rivulets running down his hard-working throat.

"I sometimes think more ale gets spilled than drunk at these things," said Rikke in the Union tongue, both hands on the table beside him with her shoulders up around her ears.

He lowered the jug and peered at her over the rim, answered in Northern. "If it isn't the Dogman's missing daughter. Glad to be back?"

"I'd prefer to be back in Uffrith, but Uffrith's burned, and the people scattered. The lucky ones, anyway. Always thought I hated the place, but now it's gone I miss it…" She had to swallow another lump of sadness. "Still, this is an awful lot better'n being hunted through a freezing forest by a crowd of horrible cunts, so there's that. Lot o' bastards in the North, but that Stour Nightfall." And she bared her teeth at a sudden stab of hate. "By the dead, he's a bastard for the songs."

"You Northmen love to make songs about bastards."

"I'm a North*woman*," she said, poking at her chest with a thumb.

"I noticed," he said, raising his brows at it. Her thumb, not her chest. Though maybe he was taking a sly look at that, too. She somewhat hoped so but was too drunk to tell. Seemed every word between them had an edge to it. A little danger, like the jabs in a duel. A little thrill, like each breath was a gamble.

"Not easy," she grunted, dropping on the empty stool where his mother had been sitting, thumping her boot down on the table and rocking carelessly back. "Being in the shadow of a famous parent."

"No. I miss my father." Leo frowned into his ale-jug. "Three years, he's been gone. Still feels like yesterday. Didn't get nearly so much of my mother's attention when he was alive."

"You should be glad of your mother's attention. Never knew mine."

"I'll be lord governor soon," said Leo, trying and largely failing to sound lord governor-ish, though it was a failure Rikke found endearing. She was finding everything about him endearing right then. Specially his collarbones, for some reason. Strong, bold collarbones, he had, with a hard dimple between she reckoned her nose would nuzzle into just right. "The king'll send an edict, and I'll be able to do whatever I want."

Rikke opened her eyes very wide. "So…you only have to do what your mama tells you till a man with a golden hat gives you permission?" She puffed out her cheeks. "That's impressive. That is really quite fucking something."

He'd been frowning at first, but she was pleased to see it crumble into a sheepish smile. "You're right. I'm being a prick."

She was thinking that sometimes a prick is the very thing you need, but she just about stopped herself saying it. A girl should maintain *some* mystery, even when drunk.

Leo leaned close and she felt a guilty flush of heat on the side facing him, like he was made of hot coal and she was sitting too close to the fire. "They say you were raised by witches."

Rikke snorted as she glanced over at Isern-i-Phail. "Bitches, maybe."

"They say you've got the Long Eye."

She took the chance to lean a bit closer, turning her left eye towards him. "That's right." Their faces couldn't have been more than a few inches apart, and the space between felt hot as an open oven. "I can see your future."

"What's there?" Doubt, and laughter, and curiosity in his voice, and did she catch just a husky hint of desire as well? By the dead, she hoped so.

"Trouble with seeing the future is you don't want to spoil the surprise." She stood up, nearly tripping over her own stool, but steadying herself masterfully by clutching at the edge of the table. "I'll show you."

She caught him by the arm, started trying to drag him up, but got distracted halfway and ended up just thoughtfully feeling it. All hard in his sleeve. Like it was made of wood.

"That's a lot of arm," she murmured, and pulled him towards the big barn doors, open wide now men were filtering off to their tents and their bedrolls. Leo's cautious friend, Jurand or whatever, was watching them from a place near the wall with this disapproving expression, but she couldn't be arsed to be disapproved of right then. Isern-i-Phail was stood next to Shivers, her bare, bandaged leg propped up on a stool.

"*That* is a leg." Isern gestured at it proudly, sinews standing from her white thigh. "That, d'you see, is all a leg should be and more."

Shivers gave the leg in question a careful examination. "No doubt."

"The other one," said Isern, "is even better."

Shivers' eyes, or his eye, at any rate, shifted from Isern's leg to her face. "You don't say?"

"I do." She leaned down towards him. "And as for what's betwixt the two..."

"Excuse us," said Rikke, slipping past and dragging Leo after, both trying to stifle their giggles. The night air was like a slap after the warmth inside, and it pinched her nose and made her head spin. Fires pricked at the night, hint of tents in the darkness, snatch of someone singing some old song about some dead hero. She led Leo by the elbow, heading nowhere, both of them laughing whenever they took a wobble.

He grabbed at her shoulder. "Where are you taking—" And he grunted as she shoved him back against a crumbling wall, pushed her fingers into his hair and pulled him towards her. She held him there, their faces just a few finger-breadths apart. She dragged the moment out, his hot, eager, ale-smelling breath tickling at her cheek. She dragged the moment out, distant firelight gleaming in the corners of his eyes. She dragged the moment out, getting closer, getting closer, until he was pushing his smiling lips towards her and she brushed them with hers, one way, then the other.

Then they were kissing, hungry, messy, lips sucking and teeth scraping and tongues lapping and Rikke reflected that she was quite an excellent kisser even if she did say so herself and he wasn't at all bad either. No point pecking away like a sparrow at the seed. You've got to get stuck in. They broke apart to catch their breath and he swayed a bit and wiped his mouth, his eyes darting all over her face in a slightly flustered, slightly excited, slightly drunk sort of way that made her feel flustered and excited and drunk as well. Then he took a long breath and blew it out.

"So...where's this surprise, then?"

She grinned. "You bastard." A rickety door stood with a crack of darkness showing and she shouldered it wobbling open and bundled him through. He tripped over his own feet and went tottering, a thud as he fell, then silence.

"Leo?" she hissed, shuffling forward. It was close to pitch-black, her hand out and feeling for him. Then she felt her wrist caught and she yelped as she was dragged down, fell into something soft, a heap of straw, smelling of earth and animals and rot, but Rikke had never been all that picky and she was feeling even less picky than usual right then. Picky Rikke. She gave a little snort of laughter as Leo slid on top of her, kissing her again, making eager little grunts in his throat that made her grunt back, his mouth hot in the darkness.

One of his hands slipped under her shirt, up her waist, up her ribs, and she grabbed his wrist.

"Wait!" she hissed.

He froze. "What?" Silence, and she could hear his quick breath over the sound of her own thudding heartbeat. "You all right?"

"Shouldn't we...get your mother's permission first?"

She saw the faint gleam of his teeth as he smiled. "You bastard."

"Or maybe His Majesty's? A royal edict probably overrules a lady governor—"

"You're right," he said propping himself up. "I'll send a message to Adua. They'll want to discuss it in the Closed Council, but we should get a knight herald back with an answer before—"

"Not sure I'll be this drunk by then," she said, already wriggling out of her trousers. Before she got them past her hips, her hand slipped and she flopped over and got a mouthful of straw, hissed and spat, giggled and burped, and they were kissing again, both her hands on his face, his jaw sharp and the stubbled skin rough under her fingertips.

His hand slipped down between her thighs and she tried to open her legs but was all tangled with her belt, straw prickling her arse as she pushed herself against him, rubbing, rubbing, her tongue in his mouth and his breath fast and sounding like he was smiling. She was smiling, too, smiling right to the corners of her face, and this surely beat being chased through the woods when it came to entertainment.

Didn't need the Long Eye to see where things were going now. Nothing like being wanted, is there? Wanted by someone you want. Always seems like magic, that something can feel so good but cost nothing.

She rolled over on top of him, partly thinking she'd take charge, partly quite annoyed by the straw in her arse. Managed to work her trousers down around her ankles so she was straddling him, started wrestling with his belt but couldn't see a thing and the darkness was all spinning and she'd half a thought she might fall over even though she was only kneeling up and in hay too and her fingers were all clumsy and it was like trying to unpick stitching with gloves on.

"Fuck," she hissed. "Your mother put a lock on this? Where's the buckle?"

"Usual place," he whispered, and his hot breath tickled her ear and gave her a funny shudder. "Where else would it be?" And there was a faint jingle as he eased it open and she pushed her hand down inside.

"Oh," she said, stupidly. They always surprised her, somehow, cocks. Strange bloody piece of anatomy. Still, she knew her way around one, even if she did say so herself. No point flicking away like you're scared of it. You've got to get stuck in.

"Ah!" And he jerked up from the straw. "Gently."

"Sorry." Maybe she was a little rusty after all and the shed surely felt like it was spinning now, spinning like a boat going down a whirlpool, but a decidedly pleasant whirlpool, warm and sticky and smelling of animals, and his hand was busy between her spread legs, not quite in the right spot but close enough, and she shifted her hips until it was in the right spot and started grunting in his ear, rocking back and forth, back and forth, back and forth.

"Shit," he whispered in the blackness, fumbling at her, voice on the edge of laughter. "Where's your..."

"Usual place," she hissed back at him, spitting in her hand, catching hold of his cock and wriggling closer. "Where else would it be?"

The Lion and the Wolf

If anyone asked, he'd always say he loved the ladies. The chase. The conquest. The bawdy jokes. But the truth was, Leo had never been comfortable around women. Men made sense. Slapped backs and firm shakes and blunt talk and wrestling. But women were a bloody mystery. He never quite knew what to make of their chatter and their feelings and their strange, soft bodies. Tits. Men talked a lot about tits. So Leo did, too. Nudge in the ribs, look at the cargo *she's* carrying. But if he was entirely honest, he didn't really understand the appeal. To Leo, tits were just...there. He'd get the job done in bed, of course. He'd lead the bloody charge! No problems in *that* department. But some of the most awkward moments of his life had been mornings-after.

He reached for his trousers, picked some straw out of them, painstakingly pulled them on, wincing as his belt-buckle clinked. He fished up his shirt and his boots, took a step towards the chink of light down the edge of the door, and looked back.

Rikke lay in the hay, arms flung heedlessly wide, gold ring through her nose gleaming with the morning light, tangled mass of chains and runes and talismans shifting as she breathed, a stray strand of hair across her face. In spite of his headache, he found he was smiling.

Leo had never been comfortable around women. But perhaps his problem had been finding the right one. Rikke was nothing like the ladies his mother would manoeuvre into his path in Ostenhorm. They always seemed to say one thing but mean another, like talking was a game you won by making the other player totally confused. Rikke had known him for years. There was no need for fumbling small talk. And every moment with her felt like an adventure. She could kidnap a conversation and in a breath carry it off into strange territory. You never knew where you'd end up, but it was always *honest*.

He tossed his boots away and slipped down beside her again. He lifted his hand, paused a moment then, grinning all the while, gently pushed that strand of hair off her face. Her eyes didn't open, but her mouth curled into a smile. "Decided not to slink away after all?"

"Realised there's nowhere I'd rather be."

It gave him an odd little shiver when she opened those big grey eyes and looked at him. "Fancy another go around, eh?" And she stretched out, arms over her head, wriggling back into the straw.

"No word from the king yet," he said, leaning close to kiss her.

She pulled her chin away from him. "And the lady governor?"

"Nothing in writing," he murmured, "so I'm taking it they approve." Her breath was sour, her lips scummy at the corners, and he didn't care.

She slid a hand into his hair, gripped him hard and kissed him deep. Hungry, tonguey kisses that left nothing to the imagination. She rolled him over, getting up onto one elbow, biting at her lip as she started undoing his belt and he squirmed back into the hay, breath coming fast again, headache forgotten—

She stopped, frowning. Pushed herself up to sitting, wrinkling her nose. "Can you smell that?"

"They keep animals in here."

"No. Smells sweet. Smells like..." Rikke sniffed, wafting air at her nose. Her little finger was twitching. "Oh no." Her face fell as she stared at it. "Always the worst times." All her fingers were twitching now. "Get Isern-i-Phail!" And she dropped back in the straw, her whole arm shaking.

"What?"

"Get Isern!" Rikke grabbed the dowel on its thong around her neck and bit down hard on it. Next moment, she arched back like a full-drawn bow. She made a great, long, hollow wheeze as if all the breath was being squeezed out of her. Then she dropped, hay flying as she writhed, muscles madly jerking, kicking heels hacking at the dirt floor.

"Shit!" squeaked Leo, one arm out towards her, the other out towards the door, wanting to hold her down so she didn't smash herself, wanting to help her and not knowing how. His first thought, much to his dismay, was to run for his mother. His second was to do as he'd been told and get Isern-i-Phail.

He flung the door open and charged across the yard, chickens scattering, between tents, past men picking at their breakfast, sharpening their weapons, moaning at the wet and the food and the state of things, staring at him as he dashed by half-naked. He saw Glaward sitting by a fire, grinning as Jurand whispered something in his ear. They both spun wide-eyed as Leo pounded up, then broke apart and he sprang between them over the flames, knocking a pot of water bouncing away.

"Sorry!"

He nearly fell as his bare foot slid on the other side, tottered a few steps and was charging on, through the Northmen's campsite, smoky fires and the smell of cooking and someone singing in a rumbling bass as he pissed into the trees.

"Where's Isern-i-Phail?" he screeched. "Isern-i-Phail!"

He followed a pointed hand towards a tent, hardly even knowing whose hand it was, lashed at the flap and ripped his way through.

He'd half-expected to find her bent over a cauldron, but the hillwoman was sitting in her tent in a tattered Gurkish dressing gown, her bandaged leg propped on an old crate, a smoking chagga pipe in one hand and a jug of last night's ale in the other.

She glanced at him as he tried to catch his breath. "I rarely turn down a half-naked man first thing in the morning, but—"

"She's having a fit!" he wheezed out.

Isern dropped the pipe in the jug with a hiss, hauled her injured leg off the crate and stiffly stood. "Show me."

There she lay, not thrashing like she had been but still squirming and making that wheezing moan, spit around the dowel turned to froth and flecked across her twisted face. She must've caught her head against the wall, there was blood in her hair.

"By the dead," grunted Isern, kneeling beside her and putting a hand on her shoulder. "Help me hold her, then!" And Leo knelt, too, one hand on Rikke's arm and one on her knee while Isern rooted through her hair to look at the cut. It was then he realised Rikke was stark naked and he wasn't far off.

"We were just..." Maybe Antaup could've pulled out an innocent explanation. He'd had the practice. But Leo had never been much of a liar and this needed a true master of the art. "We were just..."

"I am a woman of the world." Isern-i-Phail didn't even bother to look at him. "I can hazard a mad guess at what you were about, boy." She leaned down over Rikke, wiping the froth away with her fingers, smoothing her hair back from her face. "Shhhh," she breathed. Sang it, almost. "Shhhhh."

Ever so gently she held her. Ever so softly she spoke. More gently and more softly than Leo would've thought that hard-faced hillwoman could have.

"Come back, Rikke. Come on back."

Rikke gave a feeble grunt, a last flurry of twitches running through her legs and up to her shoulders. She groaned, slowly pushed the spitty dowel out of her mouth with her tongue.

"Fuck," she croaked.

"There's my girl!" said Isern, the edge back on her voice. Leo closed his eyes and gave a sigh of relief. She was all right. And he realised he was still gripping her tight even though she'd stopped jerking, and he let go quickly, saw the marks of his fingers pink on her arm.

Isern was already working Rikke's trousers over her limp feet and up her legs. "Help me get her dressed."

"Not sure I know—"

"Got her undressed, didn't you? Same thing, d'you see, but in reverse."

Rikke gave a long groan as she slowly sat up, clutching at her bloody head.

"What did you see?" asked Isern, wrapping Rikke's shirt around her shoulders and squatting beside her.

"I saw a bald weaver with a purse that never emptied." Rikke's voice sounded strange. Rough, hollow. Not like her voice at all. It made Leo feel a little afraid, somehow. And a little excited.

"What else?" asked Isern.

"I saw an old woman whose head was stitched together with golden wire."

"Huh. What else?"

"I saw a lion...and a wolf...fight in a circle of blood. They fought tooth and claw and the wolf had the best of it..." She stared up at Leo. "The wolf had the best of it...but the lion was the winner." She caught him by the hand, staring into his face, dragging him close with a shocking strength. "The lion was the winner!"

Till that moment, Leo had been sure it was all guff. The Long Eye. Old tales and superstitions. What else could it be? But looking into Rikke's wild, wet eyes, pupils swollen up so big there was no iris left at all but only black pits with no bottom, he felt the hairs on his neck rise and the skin on his spine tingle. Suddenly he began to doubt.

Or maybe he began to believe.

"Am *I* the lion?" he whispered.

But she'd closed her eyes, sagged back in the straw, her limp hand dropping from his.

"Out you go, now, boy," said Isern, shoving his boots and his shirt into his arms.

"Am I the lion?" he called again, for some reason desperate to know.

"Lion?" Isern laughed as she pushed him out into the yard. "Ass, maybe." And she kicked the door shut.

No Unnecessary Sentiment

"**M**y father thinks very highly of you."

Inquisitor Teufel's permanently narrowed eyes swivelled from the sunny country slipping past the window to Savine, but she said nothing. To have called her hard-looking would have been an epic understatement. She appeared to be chiselled from flint. Her chin and cheekbones jutted, her nose was blunt and slightly bent with two marked creases above the bridge from constant frowning, her dark hair was shot with grey and bound back tightly as a murderer's shackles.

Savine flashed her artfully constructed artless smile, the one people usually could not help returning. "And he's not a man who gives praise lightly."

Teufel acknowledged that with the faintest nod, but kept her silence. Compliments can coax more from some people than torture, and Savine had found compliments relayed from some respected third party most effective of all. But Teufel's locks were not so easily picked. She swayed faintly with the jolting of the carriage, face as guarded as a bank vault.

Savine could not help shifting at a sudden pang. With impeccable timing, her menses were starting early, the familiar dull ache through her belly and down the backs of her thighs with an occasional sharp twinge into her arse by way of light relief. As usual, she struggled with every muscle to look perfectly relaxed and forced her grimace into an ever-brighter smile.

"He tells me you were raised in Angland," she said, trying a different tack.

Finally, Teufel spoke, but only the minimum. "I was, my lady." She reminded Savine of one of Curnsbick's engines: stripped back, angular and unapologetic. No unnecessary flesh, no unnecessary ornament, and for damn sure no unnecessary sentiment.

"You worked in a coal mine."

"I did." And had not changed her clothes since, by the look of it. A worn shirt with sleeves rolled up to the elbows and those leather braces workmen wear. Coarse trousers tucked into tightly laced work boots, one of which was thrust defiantly out into the centre of the carriage floor, as if staking a claim to the territory. Scarcely a gesture towards femininity anywhere. Had there ever been a woman who took less care over her appearance? Savine subtly shifted her new dress in a vain attempt to move a chafing seam away from her damp armpit. She would never have admitted it but, hell, how she envied her, especially in this heat.

"Coal is changing the world," she observed, nudging the window down to get a little more air in and swishing her fan a touch faster.

"I heard."

"Is it changing it for the better, though?" muttered the boy, wistfully. "That's the question."

He glanced up, and a flush spread across his pale cheeks, and his big, sad, frog-like eyes flickered over to Teufel. She gave him the same calm, critical stare she gave Savine. A look that let him judge for himself whether he should have opened his mouth. The lad looked at the floor and folded his arms even tighter about himself.

They certainly made an odd couple. The woman of flint and the boy of wax. She not showing a hint of feeling, he with every emotion written right across his face. They seemed the very last people one would suspect of being agents of the Inquisition. But Savine supposed that was rather the point.

"Are you expecting trouble in Valbeck?" she asked.

"If I was," said Vick, "I imagine your father would've told you not to come."

"He did. I ignored him. And I hardly think he would be sending you if there was not at least a *little* trouble there. Am I right?"

Vick did not even blink. There really was no rattling the woman. "Are *you* expecting trouble?" she asked, answering a question with another.

"I find it's always wise to expect it. I own a share in a textile mill in the city."

"Among other things."

"Among other things. I have a partner there, one Colonel Vallimir."

"Once commander of the King's Own First Regiment. Too inflexible to work under Mitterick. Is he flexible enough to work under you?"

Apparently, Vick not only knew her own business, but everybody else's. "Where would be the fun in bending flexible people to your whims?" asked

Savine. "And partners are useful. Someone to oversee operations. Someone to share the risks."

"Someone to take the blame."

"You should go into business."

"Not sure I'm ruthless enough. I'll stick with the Inquisition."

Savine rewarded that with her exhaustively practised spontaneous laugh. "The mill was losing money. Troubles with the workers, I expect. I always used to say that textiles are for wearing, not investing in." She flicked an infinitesimal speck of dust from the embroidered cuff of her travelling jacket. "There are lots of ex-soldiers among the weavers, violent men prone to grudges. When the guilds were broken up, they were left rudderless, injured in their pockets and their pride."

"What changed your mind?"

"The usual. I realised how much money was to be made. And now, of a sudden, I find my mill is in profit."

"Which is a *wonderful* thing, of course," said Lisbit, who never had anything worth saying but could never stop saying it anyway, and to make matters worse was saying it in an ever more affected accent since she was made temporary companion. At this rate, Savine would have throttled her before they reached Valbeck, let alone by the time Zuri returned from the South.

"Which *is* a wonderful thing," said Savine. "But profits so fast and so large make me...suspicious."

"You should go into the Inquisition."

"In this corset? I hardly think so."

Now Teufel smiled. Just a little curl at the corner of her mouth. Considered, like every expression of hers. As though she had been over her budget and decided she could afford one.

"You don't give much away, do you?" said Savine.

That smile curled up a little more. "Comes from not having much, maybe."

It was not mockery, exactly. They simply both knew that Teufel had seen things, suffered things, overcome things that Savine would never have to. Would never dare to. She needed no wigs or powder to hide behind. She sat safe in the certainty that she was carved from fire-toughened wood, and could break Savine in half with those veined coal miner's hands if she pleased.

Savine found she was shifting a little to hide her sword. She wished she had not worn it. How absurd an affectation it seemed, sitting opposite someone who cut people for a living.

Vick sat with her leg stretched out. The old niggle in her hip was acting up, and every bump in the road sent a jolt through the carriage and a jab of pain from her knee right to her back, but she wasn't about to squirm for a comfortable position she knew she'd never find.

Savine dan Glokta looked serenely comfortable, one leg carelessly crossed over the other, the shiny toe of one immaculate boot showing beneath the embroidered hem of a dress that probably cost more than the carriage, and the carriage was an expensive one. Vick had never seen a woman who took more trouble about her appearance, and she'd once spent a horrible half-hour lurking at the back of one of Queen Terez's functions.

Not a hair of Savine's eyebrows, not a thread of her clothes, not a speck of her powder was out of place, even in the heat. All so porcelain-perfect it was a surprise whenever she moved, talked, breathed like ordinary humans. She wore a ridiculous little sword with jewels on the hilt. She wore a tiny, pointless hat fastened with a crystal pin. She fluttered a fan made from fillets of iridescent seashell gracefully back and forth, back and forth. She had a nest of golden braids which only a dunce could've imagined was her real hair. Or anyone's real hair. Had there been any justice in the world, she would've looked absurd. But Vick knew well there was no justice, and she looked spectacular.

Might Vick have looked like that herself, if her father hadn't been taken by the Inquisition? If her family hadn't been sent to Angland along with him? Might she have been sitting there, in a wig that took a month to weave, tapping the toe of those wonderful, horrible boots, as smugly satisfied with herself as a cat by the kitchen fire?

Vick learned long ago that might have is a game with no winners. Few games do have winners, in the end.

"Do you have those sweets, Lisbit?" asked Savine.

Lisbit, who was only slightly less well groomed than her mistress, slipped a polished box from her travelling bag. Perfume wafted out as she revealed no more than a dozen little sugared fruits, nestling in crushed paper. Vick's mouth flooded with spit. When you've starved, food comes to touch a special place, and you can never quite go back.

"Can I tempt you?" murmured Savine.

Vick glanced from her overpriced sweets to her overpriced smile. In the camps, everything had a cost, and usually with painful interest, too. Looking into Savine dan Glokta's eyes, hard and shiny as the eyes of an expensive doll, Vick doubted you could find a more merciless creditor if you scoured the whole of Angland.

Owing one Glokta was far too many. "Not for me."

"I entirely understand. Can't eat them myself." Savine sighed as she arched her back, pushing one hand into her impossibly slender side. "I'm like a weight of sausage meat squeezed into a half-weight skin already."

It wasn't mockery, exactly. They just both knew that Savine had more manners, money and beauty in one quim hair than Vick could've dug from her whole acquaintance. She sat safe on invisible cushions of power and privilege, knowing she could buy and sell Vick on a whim.

Savine offered the box to Tallow. "How about you, young man?"

A blotchy flush spread across his cheeks. As if a goddess had floated from the heavens to offer him eternal life. "I . . ." He glanced at Vick. "Can I take one?"

"If Lady Savine says you can take one, you can take one."

Savine smiled wider than ever. "You can take one."

He reached out with a trembling hand, prised one from the fancy paper, then sat staring at it.

"That sweet probably cost more than your shoes," said Vick.

Tallow lifted up one dirty boot, its creased tongue hanging out like a thirsty dog's. "They were free. Got 'em off a dead man." And he stuffed the sweet in his mouth. "Oh." His eyes went even wider. "Oh." He closed them, and chewed, and melted into his seat.

"Good?" asked Lisbit.

"Like sunshine," he mumbled.

"You really should say thank you."

"Don't worry." Savine hid it well, but Vick noticed the twitch of annoyance on her face. She offered the box again. "You're sure?"

"Not for me," said Vick. "But you're very kind."

"I doubt everyone would agree."

"If everyone agreed, I'd be out of a job." Vick forced herself not to wince as she drew in her outstretched leg and slid the window all the way down. "Pull up!" she called to the driver. "We'll go on foot from here."

"It's true one *must* be careful who one is seen with." Savine opened her eyes very wide as the carriage rattled to a halt. "My mother likes to tell me a lady's reputation is all she has. Ironic, really. Her reputation is dismal."

"Sometimes you don't value a thing till you've thrown it away," muttered Vick.

Valbeck was hidden behind the hills to the north as she hopped down into the rutted mud, but she could see the smoke from the city's thousands of chimneys, spreading on the breeze to make a great dark smudge across the sky. Maybe she could smell it, too. Just an acrid tickle at the back of her throat.

"Is that all your luggage?" asked Savine as Tallow dragged their stained bags down from the mass of boxes on the roof.

"We travel light," said Vick, pulling on her battered coat and giving her shoulders the labourer's hunch that went with it.

"I envy you that. It sometimes seems I can't leave the house without a dozen trunks and a hat stand."

"Wealth can be quite a burden, eh?"

"You've no idea," said Savine as Lisbit swung the door shut.

"Thanks for the sweet, my lady," croaked out Tallow.

"Such wonderful manners deserve a reward." And Savine tossed the box through the window.

Tallow gave a little gasp as he caught it, fumbled it, managed to stop it falling and finally clasped it tight to his chest. "Don't know what to say," he breathed.

Savine smiled. Open, and easy, and full of opulently polished pearly teeth. "Then silence is probably your best option." It nearly always was, in Vick's opinion. Savine touched her fan to the brim of her perfect little hat. "Happy hunting."

Fan snapped, whip cracked and the carriage lurched on towards Valbeck. Tallow watched it go in sad silence, shading his eyes against the midday glare. Vick shook her hair out, stuck her hand in the ditch beside the road and made sure she combed dirty water through to the ends.

"You really have to do that?" asked Tallow.

"We're among the desperate now, boy," she said, putting some labourer's gravel in her voice. "Need to look like it." And she reached out and smeared mud down his cheek.

He sighed as Savine's carriage was lost behind some trees, that fancy box still clasped tight.

"Never met anyone like her," he whispered.

"No." Vick slapped some life into her stiff leg, sniffed, hawked and spat on the road. Then she snapped her fingers at Tallow. "Give us one of those sweets, then."

Friends Like These

The Vallimir residence, high on the hill where most of the affluent citizens of Valbeck had their houses, was a lesson in the dangers of excessive wealth and inadequate taste. Everything—furniture, cutlery and guests most of all—was too weighty, too fancy, too shiny. Mistress Vallimir's dress was a misjudged purple, the curtains a garish turquoise, the soup a lurid yellow. The colour of urine with a taste not far removed.

"I've never known such a hot spell!" clucked the lady of the house, fanning herself ever more vigorously.

"Oppressive," said Superior Risinau, head of Valbeck's Inquisition, dabbing a dewy sweat from his plump cheeks that instantly sprang back. "Even for the season."

It was very far from helping that Savine's menses were now in full and particularly brutal first-day flow. Drawers like a battlefield, as her mother delighted in saying. Even bundled in a triple napkin, she would not have been at all surprised, on getting up, to find she had left a great bloody smear across the Vallimirs' tasteless upholstery. A contribution to the party to live long in the memory. She had to suppress a wince at a particularly sharp pang, set down her overembellished spoon and slid her bowl away.

"Not hungry, Lady Savine?" asked Colonel Vallimir, peering down from the head of the table.

"Everything is delicious but, alas, as I get older, I must take ever greater pains over my figure."

Risinau gurgled out a chuckle. "Not a consideration *I* trouble myself with!"

Savine plastered a smile over her disgust as she watched him slurp from his spoon like a hog from a trough. "How fortunate for you." And how repugnant for everyone else.

Lord Parmhalt, the city's mayor, teetered on the verge of slumber.

Mistress Vallimir pretended not to notice as he drifted towards her, in imminent danger of slumping into her lap. The draught from her fan had loosened some strands of grey hair previously plastered across his bald pate and they now floated from his head to an impressive height. For the tenth time that evening, Savine wished she had stayed in Adua. Probably curled up in an aching ball with the curtains closed, giving vent to a torrent of obscenities. But she flatly refused to be a slave to her tyrant of a womb. Business came first. Business always came first.

"And how is business?" she asked.

"Positively booming," said Vallimir. "The third shed is up and running and the mill working at full capacity. Costs down, profits up."

"The very directions for costs and profits that I like."

Vallimir gave something between a cough and a chuckle. He was a man with a fragile sense of humour. "All good news. As I told you in my letter. Nothing to worry about."

"Oh, I can always find something to keep me awake at night," said Savine. Even if it was only a constant grinding ache through her stomach and down the backs of her legs.

Perhaps it was her presence, but there was a nervous edge to the gathering. The talk too urgent, the laughter too shrill, the staff twitchy as they whisked the soups away. Savine's eye was caught by the glint of metal at the window: a pair of guards patrolling the grounds. There had been four of them at the door when she arrived, accompanied by a sullen monster of a dog.

"Are all the armed men really necessary?" she asked.

She was gratified to note the twitch of dismay on Vallimir's face. As if he had sat on a pin. "Given your position in society, given the envy that might be directed towards you, given... who your *father* is, I thought we could not be too careful."

"One can *never* be too careful," echoed Superior Risinau, leaning close to touch Savine's shoulder with entirely too much familiarity. "But you need have no fear, Lady Savine."

"Oh, I am not easily intimidated. I receive at least a dozen threats a day. The most vivid fantasies of my degradation and violent murder. Angry competitors, jealous rivals, disgruntled workers, scorned business partners, disappointed suitors. If there was money in threats, I would be..." She paused a moment to consider it. "Even richer, I suppose. I swear, I receive more venom even than my father. It has made me realise there is only one thing men hate more than other men."

There was an expectant pause. "Which is?" asked Mistress Vallimir.

"Women," said Savine, shifting in her uncomfortable chair. If a man was struck in the balls during a fencing match, he would be expected to howl and weep and roll around, while his opponent gave him all the time he needed and the crowd murmured their sympathy. If, during days of monthly agonies, a woman once let her smile sour, it would be considered a disgrace. She forced her own smile wider while the sweat sprang out of her. "I suppose the bars on the windows were installed for my benefit, too?"

"Here on the hill…" Mistress Vallimir leaned around the nodding mayor, picking her words as carefully as mossy stepping stones on the way across a river, "we are all obliged to take great care over our security."

"Three weeks ago," squeaked Condine dan Sirisk, mousy wife of a mill owner kept away by business, "a factory owner was *killed*. Murdered in his own house!"

"A robbery." Risinau licked his lips as little purple jellies began to be delivered to the far end of the table. "A botched burglary, plain and simple." He leaned across to give Savine a reassuring pat on the forearm, enveloping her in his rosewater and sour-sweat scent. "We'll ferret out the perpetrators, don't worry about *that*."

"So…there are no Breakers in Valbeck?"

Every face turned towards Savine, then silence, the only movement the wobbling of those horrible little jellies.

"Only a few weeks ago, a plot was foiled in Adua to blow up a foundry using Gurkish Fire," she went on. Mistress Sirisk pressed a hand to her chest and gasped. Less fear at the news, by the look of things, than near-sexual delight at the prospect of sharing it with her entire social circle by noon tomorrow. Savine gave her a conspiratorial wink. "I have some contacts in the Inquisition."

"Well," grumbled Vallimir, looking rather put out. He appeared to be one of those men who was put out whenever a woman opened her mouth. "We have no troubles of that kind here in Valbeck."

"None," frothed Risinau, dabbing a new sheen of sweat from his forehead. He was quite obviously hiding something. "There are no Breakers, no Burners—"

"Burners?" asked Savine.

Vallimir and his wife exchanged a worried glance. "Worse scum even than the Breakers," said the master of the house, reluctantly. "Madmen and fanatics, delighting in destruction. The Breakers desire…" and he wrinkled his lip with disgust, "to reorder the Union. The Burners desire to destroy it."

"Even if you believe such monsters exist, you will find none *here*," said Risinau. "The workers of Valbeck are without grievances."

"In my experience, workers can weave a grievance from the most unpromising thread," said Savine, "and you have a vast number of workers here. Can a city grow so fast without troubles?"

Lord Parmhalt jolted awake. Possibly as a result of Mistress Vallimir's carefully applied elbow. "Great strides have been made, Lady Savine. Thanks in part to generous loans from the banking house of Valint and Balk. Recently opened a new branch in the city, you know." He shook himself, then began once more to sag towards slumber. "You should visit...the new part of town."

"New streets," said Vallimir.

"*Model* streets," said Risinau.

"Closed-in drains," said the mayor, rousing himself for another heroic effort, "and running water to every house, and all manner...of innovations."

"In Gurkhul, they build temples," observed Savine, "in Styria, palaces. Here we build drains." There was a round of polite laughter. She glanced up at the maid, just manoeuvring a jelly into place before her with desperate concentration. "Might I ask your name, my dear?"

She blinked at Savine, then at Mistress Vallimir, then blushed bright pink and tidied a loose strand of hair behind her ear. "May, my lady. May Broad."

"Tell me, May, do you like Valbeck?"

"Tolerably well, my lady. I'm still...getting used to the air."

"The air can be terribly harsh, away from the hill. Worse vapours even than in Adua."

May swallowed. "So I'm told, my lady."

"Don't worry, you can speak your mind," said Savine, "I insist on it. There's really no point otherwise, is there?"

"Well...my family have a good place on the slope of the hill, now. Very grateful for it."

"And what about the old town?"

May nervously cleared her throat. "We were there when we first arrived. The old town's very full, begging your pardon. There are families of six to a cellar."

"Six to a cellar?" Savine glanced at Vallimir, and he gave that wince again.

"And the walls running with damp, and children playing in the open sewers, and pigs kept in the alleys, and the water from the pumps is far from healthy." She was warming to it now, waving her arms in jerky gestures. "More people come in every day, and there isn't work for all of them, and prices for everything are high—"

Her hand caught Savine's glass, sent it teetering. She shot her hand out as though jabbing with a short steel and caught it before it fell.

The maid stared down in horror. "I'm...I'm so sorry—"

"No harm done. Thank you so much. You can go."

"Foolish, wayward girl," snapped Mistress Vallimir, the moment she had pulled the overpolished door shut, her fanning turned positively savage.

"Nonsense," said Savine, "it was entirely my fault."

"Loose hands and a looser tongue. I will let her go in the morning."

Savine's voice had a sudden sharpness. "I would rather you did not."

Mistress Vallimir bristled. "Pardon me, Lady Savine, but in my own house—"

"A beautiful house in which I am honoured to be a guest. But I asked for honesty. I will not see her punished for it." The pain had quite ground away Savine's patience. She set her smile aside for once, and made sure she held Vallimir's eye. "Please don't make me insist. Not when we are having such a lovely evening. If I had been punished every time I spoke truth to an investor, why, I would never have been able to make you so rich."

There was a long silence, then Risinau leaned close to Savine and put his fat, moist hand on hers. It was like having one's fingers smothered in old dough. "Lady Savine, I give you my personal guarantee, the workers are content and there is *nothing* to worry about."

It was his bad luck that this patronising reassurance coincided with a particularly savage cramp, as if there was a fist clenching around her guts. Savine leaned towards him, cupping her mouth to keep anyone else from hearing, and whispered in his ear. "Touch me again and I will stab you with my fork. In your fat fucking neck. Do you understand?"

The Superior swallowed and carefully peeled his hand from hers. Savine looked back to Vallimir. "You said business is good at the mill?"

"It is."

"Then I would very much like to look at the books. I *so* enjoy the successful ones."

Vallimir gave that twitch again. "I will have them brought to you."

"Better if I go to them. Having come all this way, I must see the improvements you have made first hand."

"A visit in person..." ventured Vallimir, wincing.

Risinau took up the challenge. "It might not be the best—"

"You'll hardly know I'm there." And their wanting her to stay away meant she absolutely had to go. "I find, when it comes to business, there is nothing like the personal touch." She took up the absurdly long spoon, delved deep into the jelly and slurped it through pursed lips with great relish.

"My compliments, Mistress Vallimir, such a delicious jelly." It was a vile jelly. Perhaps the worst Savine had ever had the misfortune to consume. She weathered another stab in her belly and presented the gathering with her most glittering smile. "You simply *must* give my maid the recipe."

Sinking Ships

They ate in an overpriced chophouse where the windows were thick with sooty grime and the plates hardly cleaner. Tallow wolfed his meat and gravy down then watched as Vick ate hers, only just short of drooling like a hungry dog. She didn't like eating with those big sad eyes on her, but she took time cleaning her plate even so. Another habit from the camps. A habit from never having enough.

Relish every mouthful, it feels like it goes further.

They waited for dusk, though with the smoke over Valbeck it wasn't much darker than day and felt even hotter, the sunset an angry, molten-metal smear behind the great chimneys they were building in the west. Then they worked their way into the teeming, steaming backstreets like rats into a dungheap, asking roundabout questions, trying to winkle out hints of where the Breakers might be.

Vick had picked over her story a hundred times. Picked over Tallow's, too, until the lies were like a second skin, more familiar than the truth. She had an answer for every question, a story for every suspicion, a set of excuses that left her looking good but not too good. The one thing she hadn't been prepared for was the one thing she found.

"The Breakers?" said a boy-whore, not even bothering to lower his voice. "Expect you'll find 'em meeting on that little alley off Ramnard Street." He called out to a girl-whore busy arranging the straps of her dress over a bare shoulder dotted with pox-marks. "What's the name o' that alley where the Breakers meet?"

"Don't know that it's got a name." And she went back to smiling for the passing trade.

All careless as if the Breakers were a sewing circle rather than a mob of renegades ripping up the fabric of society. Old Sticks had called Superior Risinau a fat man prone to folly, with no imagination but plenty of loyalty. From the careless way folk spoke of treason here, he'd let things get far out of hand in Valbeck.

The whores nodded them towards a smirking pimp. After a little bargaining, the pimp pointed out a beggar with one arm. For a few bits, the beggar sent them to an out-of-work smith selling matches from a stall on wheels. The smith nodded them down an alleyway towards an old warehouse. A big man stood outside its door, light from an upstairs window reflected in a pair of round eye-lenses that looked tiny on his broad skull.

Vick knew right off he could be trouble. The size of him, yes, almost a head taller than her, and his threadbare jacket stretched tight over great brawny shoulders. But it was more the look he had when he saw her coming. Apologetic, almost. None of that peacock strut men who think themselves hard put on. That hint of guilt the really dangerous ones tend to have.

She knew it from the mirror, on her bad days.

And if she'd had any doubts, there was the tattoo on his fist, before he twisted it up into his sleeve. Axe and lightning, crossed over a shattered gatehouse. Blue stars on the knuckles. On all the knuckles. So he'd been a Ladderman. First up the walls in a siege. Front of the storming party. He'd done it five times and lived to tell the tales. Or, more likely, to never speak of it again.

It was a habit from the camps to think about how she'd bring a man down. This one you'd make sure was on your side. Or run away from him, fast as you could. Whole thing felt like a trap to Vick. But then everything did, and she told herself that was a good thing. It's the moment you feel safe that you make your last mistake.

"My name's Vick. This is Tallow." The Breakers kept to first names, in the main.

The big man looked them over, those guilty eyes made small by his lenses. "I'm Gunnar."

"We've come from Adua." She leaned close to murmur, "We were friends of Collem Sibalt."

"All right." He looked more puzzled than suspicious, as if it wasn't really his business. "Good for you."

"Aren't you guarding the door?"

"Just came out for some air. Getting too hot for me in there." And he tugged at his collar. "That Judge woman makes me..." He paused, mouth open, like he couldn't quite work out what this Judge woman made him.

"Well, can't say I like the way things are. Wouldn't be here otherwise. But I can't see her making 'em better."

Vick leaned close to him, dropping her voice. "Aren't you worried about the Inquisition?"

"Must admit I am, but no one else seems to be." And he nudged the door open with his tattooed hand, and offered them the way.

Vick didn't speak much, but that was a choice. Actually being lost for words was rare with her. All she could manage as she stepped over the threshold of that warehouse, though, was, "Shit."

"Aye." Tallow's eyes had gone wider than ever. "Shit."

Must've been five hundred people crowded close in there. It was hot as an oven and noisy as a slaughterhouse and it smelled of old tar, unwashed bodies and rage. It was ill-lit by torches and the flickering of fire lent everything an edge of madness. Against one wall, someone had unfurled a huge banner made from old bedsheets, the words *Now or Never* daubed across it.

Some children had climbed up to sit on the high rafters, legs dangling, and for a moment, Vick thought they had a row of hanged men below them. Then she saw they were straw dummies, with leering painted faces. The king and queen, with wooden crowns over their eyes. A bloated Lord Chancellor Gorodets, a twisted Arch Lector Glokta. The bald one with a stick in his hand she reckoned must be Bayaz, First of the Magi. The great and good of government, mocked in the open.

They'd drawn up an old wagon to serve as a stage, and a woman stood there now giving as wild a performance as any actress, one thin hand clutching at the rail while she tore at the air with the other.

Judge, Vick reckoned, and she had a sense for theatre. She wore an old, scarred breastplate rusty at the rivets over a ragged red dress that might once have been some noblewoman's wedding gown. She had a mass of flame-red hair all braided and coiled and pinned into a mad tangle. Her eyes bulged, huge in her bony, blotchy face, black, and empty, catching the torch flames so it looked as if she had fire in her skull. Maybe she did at that.

"The time for talk's long *past!*" she screamed in a wild, piercing voice that made Vick wince. "*Nothing* was ever got with talk..." Judge let it hang there a moment, head cocked to one side, a brittle smile quivering on her lips. "That couldn't be got with *fire*."

"Burn 'em!" someone shouted.

"Burn the mills!"

"Burn the owners!"

"Burn it all!" squealed one of the children from the rafters, so excited she nearly fell, and others took up the chant.

"Burn it! Burn it! Burn it!" Fists punched at the air, tattooed writing on bared forearms. Like the rebels in Starikland used to have. Treasonous slogans, proudly on display. Weapons, too, thrust up from the crowd in time with the chanting, and not just workmen's tools sharpened for a show. Polearms. Swords. At least one flatbow. Soldiers' weapons, made for killing.

"What did I tell you?" The man called Gunnar was standing next to her, shaking his head as he watched Judge prowl the stage, urging the crowd louder.

"If I'd known it was fancy dress," murmured Vick, "I'd have made more effort."

She could dig out a smart comment when she had to, but in truth she was way off balance. She'd been expecting the Breakers in Valbeck to be a dozen blowhard fools like Grise, hiding in a cellar and arguing over what colour to paint a fine new world that'd never come. Instead she found them armed and organised in numbers, preaching open rebellion. She was off balance, and she wasn't used to it, and her mind raced to catch up.

"Hold up, now!" And an old man hauled himself onto the wagon beside Judge. "Hold up!"

"That's Malmer," said Gunnar, leaning down towards Vick's ear. "He's a good man."

He was Judge's opposite. Big and solid and dressed in plain work clothes, face lined from years of labour and his balding hair iron-grey, all ice-water calm to her burning fury. "You can always find folk keen to start fires," he said, turning to the sweltering warehouse. "Finding folk to build in the ashes is harder."

Judge folded her arms across her battered breastplate and sneered at Malmer down her nose, but the rest of the crowd settled to hear him speak.

"Everyone's here 'cause they don't care for the way things are," he said. "Who could?" And Gunnar grunted and nodded along. "I was born in this city. Lived here all my life. You think I like the way it's changed? Think I like the river running with filth or the streets knee deep in rubbish?" With each phrase his voice grew louder, with each phrase an answering grumble swelled from the crowd. "Think I like to see good folk put out of work at the whim of some bastards born to privilege? Our rights stripped away for the sake o' their greed? Good folk treated like cattle?"

"Fuck the owners!" screeched Judge, and the crowd cheered and jeered, wailed and grumbled.

"There's men here turn out miles of cloth a day but can't afford a shirt for their backs! Women whose highest ambition is to con the factory inspector that her son's old enough to work! How many fingers missing here? And hands? And arms?" And people held up stumps and crutches and mangled hands, veterans not of battles but endless shifts at the machinery. "There are folk dying o' hunger just a mile from the palaces on the hill! Boys who can hardly breathe for the white lung. Girls who catch some owner's fancy and are forced into night-work. You know the sort o' work I mean!"

"Fuck the owners!" screeched Judge again, and the crowd's rage came back louder than ever.

"There'll be a reckoning!" Malmer clenched his fists as he glowered at the crowd, his grinding anger every bit as worrying as Judge's stabbing fury. "I promise you that. But we need to think. We need to plan. When we spill our blood—and blood'll be spilled, depend on that—we need to make sure it *buys* us something."

"And we will! No less than everything!" A smooth voice rang out, a cultured voice, and the crowd fell quickly silent. A mood of expectation, people hardly daring to breathe.

Judge grinned as she held out her hand to pull someone up onto the wagon. A plump man in a dark, well-tailored suit, soft and pale, oddly out of place in this rough company.

"Here he is," murmured Gunnar, folding his arms.

"Here who is?" whispered Vick, though from that silence she already guessed the answer.

"The Weaver."

"Friends!" called the plump man, stroking gently at the air with his thick fingers. "Brothers and Sisters! Breakers and Burners! Honest folk of Valbeck! Some of you know me as Superior Risinau of His Majesty's Inquisition." And he held up his pink palms, and gave a sorry smile. "For that I can only apologise."

Vick could only stare. If she'd been off balance before, she was knocked on her back now.

"Fucking shit," she heard Tallow breathe.

"The rest of you know me as the Weaver!" The crowd gave a jagged murmur, part anger, part love, part anticipation, as though they'd come to see a prizefight and the champion had just strutted into the circle.

A fat man prone to folly, Glokta had said. No imagination, but plenty of loyalty. For the first time in Vick's memory, it appeared His Eminence had made a most serious misjudgement.

"I wrote to the king a few weeks ago," called Risinau, "laying out our grievances. Anonymously, of course. I did not deem it appropriate to use my given name." Some laughter through the crowd. "The ever-dwindling pay. The ever-swelling cost of living. The appalling quality of lodgings. The foul air and water. The sickness, squalor and hunger. The cheating of workers through false measures and hidden deductions. The oppression of the employers."

"Fuck the employers!" shrieked Judge, spraying spit.

Risinau held up a flapping sheet of paper. "This morning I received a reply. Not from His foolish Majesty, of course."

"The cock in the Agriont!" sneered Judge, grabbing hold of her groin to much laughter among the crowd while the children jumped on the rafters and made the dummy king dance.

"Not from his Styrian queen," continued Risinau.

"The cunt in the palace!" screamed Judge, thrusting her hips at the crowd, and someone worked a thread that pulled the dummy queen's skirts up, showing a great fleece muff to gales of merriment.

"Not from his dissolute son, Prince Orso." Risinau glanced expectantly over at Judge.

She shrugged her bony shoulders. "There's nothing to say about that waste o' fucking flesh." And a wave of boos and jeering swept the crowd.

"Not from the figureheads," called Risinau, "but from the pilot of the ship! From Old Sticks himself, Arch Lector Glokta!" The fury at the name was the loudest yet by far. Just ahead, Vick saw an old man with a bent back curl his lip and spit at Glokta's twisted dummy in disgust.

"He offers no help, you will be surprised to hear." Risinau peered down at the letter. "He cautions against disloyalty, and warns of stiff penalties."

"Fuck his penalties!" snarled Judge.

"He tells me the market must be free to operate. The world must be free to advance. Progress cannot be chained, apparently. Who knew the Arch Lector was so firmly set against manacles?" Some laughter at that. "When one man knowingly kills another, they call it murder! When society causes the deaths of thousands, they shrug and call it a fact of life." Growls of agreement, and Risinau crushed the letter in his fist and tossed it away. "The time for talk is *done*, my friends! No one is listening. No one who counts. The time has come for us to throw off the yoke and stand as free men and women. If they will not give us what we are owed, we must rise up and take it by force. *We* must bring the Great Change!"

"Yes!" shrieked Judge, and Malmer nodded grimly as men shook their weapons.

Risinau held up his hands for quiet. "We will take Valbeck! Not to burn the city," and he wagged a disappointed finger at Judge, and she stuck her tongue out and spat into the crowd, "but to *free* the city. To give it back to her people. To stand as an example to the rest of the Union." And the audience gave an approving bellow.

"Wish it was that easy." Gunnar slowly shook his head. "Doubt it will be."

"No," muttered Vick. She made Tallow wince, she squeezed his arm so hard as she marched him over towards the wall to hiss in his ear.

"Get out of town now, you hear? Head for Adua."

"But—"

She pressed her purse into his limp hand. "Quick as you can. Go to my employer. You know who I mean. Tell him what you saw tonight. Tell him…" She glanced around, but folk were too busy cheering Risinau's mad speech to mind her. "Tell him who the Weaver is. I'm trusting you to get it done."

She let him go but he didn't move, just stared at her with those big eyes that were so like her brother's. "You're not coming?"

"Someone has to try to handle this mess. Go." She shoved him away, watched him totter towards the door.

Vick wanted to follow. Badly. But she had to get to the hill and find Savine dan Glokta, maybe there was still time to put out a warning—

"This must be Victarine dan Teufel!" She froze at that strangely prim voice. "I had heard you were in Valbeck." Risinau came smiling through the crowd, dabbing his shining face with a handkerchief, Judge at one shoulder, Malmer at the other.

There was a hollow feeling in Vick's guts as dozens of pairs of hard eyes turned towards her. Like that moment in the mines, in the dark, the day her sister drowned. When she hissed for quiet, and heard the water rushing, far off.

They had her. She was done.

Risinau wagged one plump finger. "Collem Sibalt told me all about you."

Her heart was thudding so hard she could hardly breathe. Hardly see. The children had pulled down the dummy of Bayaz and were beating it with its own staff, straw flying. She couldn't believe how calm her voice sounded. Like someone else's. Someone who knew exactly what they were doing. "Good things, I hope."

"*All* good things. He said you were a woman with a hard heart and a level head. A woman as committed to our cause as any. A woman who could keep her wits on a sinking ship." And Risinau stepped forward and folded her in a smothering hug while she stood there, damp with cold sweat and her flesh creeping. "Collem Sibalt was a dear friend. Any friend of his is a friend of mine."

Judge was staring at her with those black, empty eyes, head dropped to one side. Vick couldn't tell whether she was putting on a hell of an act or if she really was as mad as she looked.

"I don't trust this one," she growled.

"You don't trust anyone," grunted Malmer.

"Yet folk still disappoint me."

Risinau held Vick out at arm's length, smiling. "You've come at just the right moment, sister."

"Why?" asked Vick. "We on a sinking ship?"

"By no means." The Superior-turned-revolutionary threw an arm around her shoulders. "We are aboard a ship embarking for shores of prosperity, shores of equality, shores of freedom! A ship headed for a Great Change! But the voyage will not be easy. At midday tomorrow, our fair city will pass through quite the storm. Yes, my friends!" He turned towards the crowded warehouse, throwing up his hands. "Tomorrow is the day!"

And the Breakers and Burners broke into thunderous applause.

Welcome to the Future

The spike-topped wall seemed better suited to a prison than a manu-factory, and Savine felt far from comfortable stepping through its iron-faced gate. Her monthly agonies had dwindled to a nagging ache, but the summer heat was more oppressive even than yesterday, and her sense of unease had been steadily growing all the way through Valbeck from the hill as her carriage clattered down murky streets strangely empty, oddly quiet, towards the river.

The three towering sheds were unlovely buildings of soot-streaked brick-work with few windows and no adornments. Even through the thick-soled boots she had chosen, Savine could feel the cobbles of the yard buzz with the movement of the great machines inside. Men slouched sullen about the yard, loading and unloading wagons, grey-clothed and grey-skinned, hard eyes turned rudely towards the new arrivals. Savine met the stare of one and he made a great show of spitting. She was reminded of the charming reception Queen Terez received on her rare appearances before the commoners. At least no one was screaming *Styrian cunt!* at her. But only, she suspected, because she was not Styrian.

"The workers appear less than delighted by my visit," murmured Savine.

Vallimir snorted. "If there is a way to delight the workers, I have yet to find it. Managing soldiers was considerably more straightforward."

"One can have perfectly cordial relationships with one's competitors, but rarely with one's employees." Savine glanced over her shoulder at the ten armoured guards filing through the gate after them, fingers tickling their weapons. It did nothing for her nerves that heavily armed men looked even more nervous than she did. "Do we really need such a conspicuous escort?"

"Merely a precaution," said Vallimir as he led Savine, Lisbit and the rest of their party across the yard. "Superior Risinau suggested you have a dozen Practicals about you at all times."

"That seems...excessive." Even for the daughter of the Union's most hated man.

"I felt their presence would only inflame tensions. In order to make the mill profitable, certain...efficiencies have been necessary. Longer hours and shorter breaks. Reductions in the budgets for food and living quarters. Punishments for talking or whistling."

Savine nodded approvingly. "Sensible economies."

"But several of the older hands banded together to oppose them and had to be laid off. There was some violence. It became necessary to forbid any organising among the workers, though that was made easier by the king's new laws against congregation." Savine's father's new laws, in fact, which she had taken a personal hand in drafting. "Then the new methods instituted in our third shed have caused..." Vallimir frowned towards the newest of the three buildings, longer, lower and with even narrower windows in its already grubby walls. "*Considerable* ill will."

"I often find the more effective the method, the more ill will it causes. Perhaps we should begin our tour there."

Vallimir winced. "I am not sure you would be...comfortable inside. It is extremely noisy. Very warm. Not at all a suitable place for a lady of your standing."

"Oh, come now, Colonel," she said, already striding towards it, "on my mother's side, I am from tough common stock."

"I am aware. I knew your uncle."

"Lord Marshal West?" The man had died before she was born, but her mother sometimes spoke of him. If you counted the sentimental platitudes one used about family long in their grave.

"He once challenged me to a duel, in fact."

"Really?" Her interest piqued by that flash of an honest recollection. "Over what?"

"Rash words I have often regretted. You remind me of him, in a way. He was a very driven man. Very committed." Vallimir glanced towards her as he produced a key and unlocked the door. "And he could be quite terrifying." The hum of machinery became a roar as he pushed it wide.

Inside, the whole place shook with the endless anger of the engines. The slap of belts, the clatter of cogs, the rattle of shuttles, the shrieking of metal under furious pressure. The manufactory floor was dug deep into the ground so they stood at a kind of balcony. Savine stepped to the rail, frowning down at the workers, and paused, wondering if there was some trick of perspective.

But no.

"They are children." She let no emotion enter her voice at the word. Hundreds of children, lean and filthy, gathered in long rows about the looms, darting among the machines, rolling spindles of yarn as tall as they were, bent under bolts of finished cloth.

"If Valbeck has one commodity in abundance," shouted Vallimir in her ear, "it is orphaned and abandoned children. Paupers, serving only as a burden to the state. Here we provide them with useful occupation." He gave a grim smile. "Welcome...to the future."

In one corner of the shed there were large shelves, five or six high, equipped with sliding ladders but holding only rags. As Savine watched, a tangle-haired girl crawled from one. Their beds, then. They lived in this place. The smell was nauseating, the heat crushing, the noise thunderous, the combination positively hellish.

She stifled a cough as she tried to speak again. Even up here on the balcony, the air was heavy with dust, the shafts of light from the narrow windows swarming with motes. "Wages are minimal, I imagine?"

Vallimir gave a strange grimace. "That is the beauty of this scheme. Aside from a stipend to the poor house from which they are acquired, and minimal expenditure on food and clothing, they receive no wages. They can, in effect...be purchased."

"Purchased." Savine let no emotion enter her voice at that word, either. "Like any other piece of machinery."

She looked down at her new sword-belt. She had been delighted when it was delivered the other day. Quite the masterpiece. Sipanese leather, with gem-studded silver panels showing scenes from the Fall of Juvens. How many children could she have bought for the same money? How many *had* she bought?

"We used to employ skilled hand-weavers, but in practice there is little need. Children can learn to mind the machines just as quickly, and with one-tenth the fuss." Vallimir gestured towards the whirring engines, the little figures crawling around them. Though more the gesture of a judge towards a crime than a showman towards a spectacle. "With the improved machinery, plus the lower costs of labour and housing, this shed is more profitable than the other two combined. And far more easily controlled."

Vallimir nodded down towards a heavyset foreman patrolling the floor. Behind his back, Savine saw that he held a stick. Or would one describe it as a whip?

"How long do they work here?" she croaked out, over the hand she had unconsciously pressed across her mouth.

"Shifts are fourteen hours. Any longer has proved unsustainable."

She had boasted of her toughness, but a few moments in there was enough to make Savine feel dizzy, and she clutched at the rail. Fourteen hours' hard labour in that dust and noise, day after day. And hot as the Maker's forge, as her father liked to say. She could already feel the sweat tickling at her scalp beneath her wig. "Why is it so hot?"

"Any cooler and the yarn becomes sticky, the machines can be fouled."

She wondered if so much wilful human misery had ever been created in one space before. She put a hand on Vallimir's shoulder. "When it comes to business, profit is the only right. Loss the only wrong."

"Of course."

Something told Savine they both had their doubts. But she could blame him, the bloodless bastard, and he could blame her, the flint-hearted bitch, and no doubt the profits would lubricate any grinding gears in both their consciences. If they did not make efficiencies, after all, there would always be some other owner whose stomach had been strengthened by failure. Would their workers weep for them when they went out of business? Or would they rush to find some new employer to whine their petty grievances at?

"Well done," she shouted in Vallimir's ear, though her voice sounded somewhat strangled. The heat, of course, and the noise, and the dust. "I asked you to make a profit and you have done so, regardless of sentiment."

"Sentiment is even more dangerous in a mill owner than a soldier."

They were cooking something somewhere, and Savine caught a whiff of it. Like the food they gave her mother's dogs on the estate. She pressed one hand to her still-aching stomach, but hardly felt it through the bones of her corset. She wondered about her button and buckle manufactory in Holsthorm, where little fingers were best suited to little tasks. Was it like this? Was it worse? She licked her lips, swallowed sour spit.

"You might consider improving their conditions, however. Perhaps some separate living quarters could be constructed in the yard? Somewhere clean for them to sleep. Better food."

Vallimir raised one brow.

"Luxury is wasteful," said Savine, "but hardship can reduce productivity. In my experience, there is a balance to be struck. With better conditions, you might manage longer shifts after all."

"An interesting suggestion, Lady Savine." Vallimir nodded slowly as he looked down at the children, jaw-muscles working. It should have been a heartbreaking spectacle. But there is no room in business for hearts. Not ones easily broken, anyway.

She hitched up the corners of her smile. "If I might look over the books now?"

A great frame occupied the middle of the first and largest shed, a spinning shaft through its centre that brought power from the river, via an engineer's nightmare of cogs, gears, cranks, belts, to the great looms that ran in two rows along the floor. A web of thread was reeled in from giant spindles, cloth of different patterns and colours grinding off the rollers. Around the looms the men were gathered, sweat-beaded and grease-smeared, tight-lipped and hard-eyed. If the occupants of the third shed had been apt to break her heart, she imagined the occupants of the first would rather smash her skull.

Savine did not expect affection from the workers. She had made her reputation from flagrant displays of wealth, after all, and those tended to sit badly with the poor. But there was something about the way these particular men watched her. A cold, quiet focus to their fury more troubling than any outburst. Rather than too many guards, she began to wonder whether they had brought too few.

She touched Lisbit gently on the elbow. "Would you mind stepping outside and bringing the carriage to the gate?"

The heat had turned Lisbit's rosy cheeks an angry, blotchy red. "Sure we shouldn't leave now, my lady?" she muttered, worried eyes darting to the workers.

Savine kept blandly smiling. A lady of taste always smiles. "Better not to show weakness. To our employees or our partners." She was not a woman to be deterred by hatred: not from her workers, not from her rivals, not from the men she bullied, bribed or blackmailed to get her way. It is when they truly hate you, after all, that you know you have won. So she met the seething dislike with effortless superiority, paraded past with her shoulders back and chin high. If she was to be cast as the villain, so be it. They were always the most interesting characters anyway.

Vallimir's office was at the very end of the shed, a kind of box up on a frame with barrels and crates stacked haphazardly beneath, a balcony outside from which an owner might look down upon their employees like a king upon his subjects. Or an empress upon her slaves.

The colonel bowed stiffly as he offered her the way up. "Take as long as you need." He turned to frown at the scores of sullen workmen. "Though perhaps no longer."

The door was fitted with two locks and a heavy bar, so sturdy it was an effort for Savine to swing it shut. She tore open the hook at the collar of her jacket, trying to flap some air onto her sweaty neck, but the atmosphere in the office was hardly less stifling than on the manufactory floor, the nerve-shredding chatter of the machines hardly less oppressive.

A loose board groaned under her boot as she made her way to Vallimir's desk and its cargo of ledgers. She hated to see anything shoddily made, especially in a building she had helped pay for, but at that moment she had larger worries. She slipped past the desk to the window, one hand rubbing at her throat where the worry had become an almost painful pressure.

The street outside was deserted. All at work, of course, and what but work would bring anyone to this lane of spiked walls and barred gates, of towering mills and rumbling machinery? Yet there was something wrong about the quiet. A weight on the air, like the calm before a thunderstorm. Savine frowned out at the empty lane, biting at her lip, wondering if she could leave now without—

A man slipped around the brick corner of the next mill. Others followed, a group of twenty or more. Working men in colourless clothes, much like the ones Savine had seen in Holsthorm, in Adua, in all the cities of the Union. Much like the ones at work below, but moving furtively, as if they were one animal with one purpose.

Then she caught a glint of bright steel and became aware, with a strange shiver, that they were all armed. Some carried sticks beside their legs, some heavy tools. The leader had what was quite clearly an old sword. He knocked at a gate in the wall; it swung open as if by prior arrangement and the men rushed inside.

She spun around at a shout from the shed behind her, then more, and louder. A commotion even over the roar of the engines. She crept to the door, put a tentative hand to the latch, wanting to open it, fearing to open it.

"Back!" she heard Vallimir roar as she eased it open. "Back, damn you!"

The workers had abandoned their tasks and crowded towards that end of the mill, a solid mass of men all facing her, faces twisted with anger, tools, iron bars and stones gripped in their fists. Her jaw dropped.

Vallimir's guards were holding them back in a desperate crescent at the bottom of the steps but they were outnumbered twenty-to-one. Savine's eyes darted in horror over that ugly swarm. That mob.

Vallimir stood facing them on the balcony, the back of his neck turning red as he bellowed at them. "Step away *at once*!"

A man in a stained vest whose arms looked like they were made from old rope pointed at Vallimir with a club and screamed, "*You* step away, you old fucker!"

Things began to flicker up from the crowd: thrown stones, thrown tools, thrown bits of machinery, bouncing from the walls of the office, clattering from the guards' armour.

Something knocked Vallimir's hat off and he sank down with his hand clapped to his bloody scalp. A bottle shattered next to the door and Savine heaved it shut, dropped the heavy bar and backed into the room. In spite of the stifling heat, she felt cold to her shaved scalp. She had expected an ugly scene on the way out, perhaps, insults hurled and surly men dragged to the cells while she glided back to luxury, unruffled. How could she have expected this? An armed insurrection!

She could hear her own snatched breath. The breath of a hunted animal. Foolishly, with fumbling fingers, she drew her sword. That was what one was supposed to do when one's life was in danger. Was her life in danger? The noise was louder outside, closer. Over the endless whirr of the machinery she heard screaming, swearing, mindless growling, the clash of steel. A long, high shrieking started which would not stop.

She needed to piss, needed to piss terribly. The sword's grip was slippery in her suddenly sweaty palm. Her eyes darted to the windows. Fitted with heavy grates. To the furniture. Nowhere to hide she would not be found in an instant. To the floor...and the loose board.

She threw herself onto her knees, prising at the wood with her fingertips, with her polished fingernails. She clenched her teeth as she worked her fingers under the board, heedless of the tearing splinters, worked the point of her sword into the gap, hammering at the pommel with the heel of her hand.

Savine jerked her head up at a voice outside. "Open the door, darlin'." Syrupy, but with an edge of menace. The voice of a slaughterman coaxing a piglet back into the pen. "Open the door, we'll be gentle. Make us break it, maybe we break you, too." Rough giggling, and Savine jumped at a blow that made the bar shudder.

She hauled at the hilt of her sword, every sinew tensed and trembling. With a squealing complaint, the nails gave and Savine went sprawling on her back, sword bouncing away bent across the floor.

She scrambled to the hole. A glimpse of the dusty boxes below between two joists. Wide enough to wriggle through? She fumbled at the buttons on her jacket, bleeding fingertips leaving red smears on the material, and tore it off. She wrestled the silver buckle of her lovely sword-belt open and flung it away. The sword she dropped through the hole, its clatter drowned out by the clattering of the machines. No time for preparations. No time

198

for doubts. She swung her legs into the gap, started to slide through. Far from ladylike, but there is no ladylike way to escape from a gang of killers.

"I'm going to count to five, bitch!" That voice from outside the door, boiling over with violence now. "Five, then we're coming in!"

"Count to a thousand, you cunt!" she snarled as she worked her hips into the hole, tight, too tight, boards digging at her through her clothes.

"One!"

She was stuck fast. She clenched her teeth, squirmed desperately, clutched at the joists and tried to haul herself through.

"Two!"

She gave a growl and with a mighty ripping of cloth tore through, scraped one shoulder, caught her chin on timber as she fell, flopped down on her side below, head cracking against the rim of a barrel.

"Three!" she heard faintly through the ringing in her ears.

She pushed herself up, groggy. She couldn't see, felt a stab of panic. Touched a trembling hand to her eyes. Her wig was skewed across them. She ripped it off, threw it down. She was trapped by something. Her torn skirt, snagged on a nail head above. She clawed at the laces and slithered free of it, left it hanging behind her.

"Four!"

She saw her sword gleaming in the shadows, closed her fist around the grip and started to crawl, keeping low, slithering along in the dust behind the barrels. That unearthly shrieking was still going on, pausing every now and then for a whooping breath then starting again.

"Five!" She heard the door of the office tremble from a blow, the bar rattle in its brackets.

She'd cut her palm, somehow, torn two of her fingernails half-off, was leaving blood on everything she touched, dabs and smears of it across her petticoats. That would be hell to get out. Hell to get out. She had to get out.

She crawled on, head pulsing, shoulder throbbing, jaw aching, hips grazed raw, crawled as fast as she could, tongue pressed into her teeth, crawled, blood tickling at her eyebrow, catching glimpses between the barrels as she went.

Vallimir being dragged away, bloody head lolling. A worker cackling as he waved the colonel's hat around, impaled on the end of a huge knife. One of the guards, lying still, helmet torn off, hair matted and a dark pool around his broken head. Another on hands and knees, men gathered around, hitting him lazily with sticks which clanged off his dented armour.

He stumbled up, putting out a groggy arm to steady himself, was jerked off his feet as his hand was caught between two cogs, dragged into the midst of the machinery. He gave a great high-pitched scream as his arm was crushed, hauled into the gears up to the shoulder, blood spattering his face. Savine felt spots of it on her own cheek, but no one heard her gasp over the noise of the tortured machinery, of the tortured man.

There was a lurch, a slow grinding, the guard's scream turning to a bubbling wail, then the machinery lurched on, wheels turning. Savine tried not to look. Keep her eyes ahead. This wasn't happening. None of it was happening. How could it be happening? Men were shouting. Barking like a pack of dogs. She couldn't make out words, only anger and the shuddering blows on the door above.

She followed the main driveshaft with her eyes, saw it disappear through a dark hole in the brickwork on the other side of the looms. Perhaps she could crawl to it, in the shadowy, dusty space below the gears. Through there. Perhaps through there.

She wriggled under the rollers on her belly. Ambitious as a snake, now she slithered like a snake, like a worm, wet with sweat in the sticky heat, prickling with fear as the frames rattled and whirred around her. She could see a lad through the turning machinery, chink of light across his eager face, but he was staring towards the office. They all were. Staring like wolves at the henhouse. Waiting for the door to give. So they could drag her out.

She crawled on, broken fingernails clutching, on through a great spatter of that guard's blood, on under the great shaft that brought power into the shed, twinkling with grease as it madly spun, dust puffing from the floor with her every whimpering breath.

At any moment, she expected the delighted scream. *There she is!* At any moment, she expected rough hands to close around her ankle. *Bring the bitch out!* Her sweating back tingled in anticipation of it. Her chest heaved, coughing and shuddering from the dust as she struggled on, biting her tongue, trying to smother the desperate fear.

When she finally reached the hole in the wall, she almost sobbed with relief. Clutched at the ragged bricks and dragged herself through, tumbled into a dark passageway, sprawled in ankle-deep water and took a fetid mouthful, spat it out, retching.

The place was dark, only a flickering glimmer at the edges of damp bricks, throbbing with the noise of machines, echoing with distorted screams. There was light ahead, a winking light, and she eased towards it, sodden boots slopping and slurping in the mud, the clattering growing louder, something moving up ahead.

One of the great waterwheels that turned the driveshaft. Whirring, creaking, thrashing timbers, light stabbing between the black beams, water foaming as the slats of the wheel plunged into the river, showering spray as they thrust out again in a rain of shining drops.

The wheel might have been four times as high as a man. There was no way through it. But between its endlessly moving timbers and the slimy wall of the mill, there was a gap. A gap beyond which she saw muddy daylight, the faintest hint of a shingle beach.

She glanced back down the shadowy tunnel. No sign of pursuit. But the door would not hold for ever. They would be coming. And if they caught her...

Could she slide between the wheel and the wall? Was it possible?

She pressed her tongue into the roof of her mouth as she tried to judge the gap. What if she did not fit? Would she be dragged under and drowned? Dragged into the gears and ripped limb from limb? Would her skull be crushed like a walnut between wheel and supports? Would she be slashed, cut, nipped and nibbled as she struggled to get free, bleeding to death from a hundred wounds while she was spun helplessly over, and over, and over? She thought of that guard's despairing wail as his arm was crushed by the machinery. But there was no other choice.

She pressed herself against the wall, breath shuddering through her teeth with fear and exhaustion, and slowly, by tiny degrees, eased one shoulder around the corner. She lowered one filthy boot into the river, fishing for the bottom, fishing, sodden petticoats clinging to her trembling leg as she eased in to the thigh and found mud. She wormed herself on, sticking to the corner, clinging to it with her shoulder blades as if her life depended on it. Which it did.

She tried desperately, pointlessly to suck herself in, suck herself flat, clutching at the sodden grip of her sword, chewing on her lip with fearsome concentration, sunlight flashing and flickering through the spinning bars. She trusted to her footing on the muddy river bottom and gradually, gradually slipped her other leg in, taking a fistful of her petticoats and dragging them hard against her in case they floated into the wheel and snatched her to her death. Killed by her own clothes fleeing a textile mill. There was a joke there somewhere.

She gasped as a bolt sticking proud of the wood caught her chest, ripped some embroidery free and nearly dragged her into the thrashing timbers of the wheel. She just managed to keep her balance, broken fingernails scrabbling at the crumbling mortar behind her, teeth rattling with terror. She edged sideways, the clammy weight of her sodden petticoats clinging to her legs, water showering her, hardly able to breathe for the rotten acid stink of the river, one cheek scraping the bricks and her eyes squeezed almost shut, her skull fit to burst with the wheel's clatter, hammer, whirr, its mindless rage.

And with a whimper she slid free, plunged face down into the river, floundered away sobbing, gurgling, half-swimming and half-crawling. She dragged herself up onto wet shingle on quivering hands and knees. For a moment, she wanted to kiss the ground. Until she saw the foamy filth that covered it.

She looked up, wiping her wet face on the back of one trembling hand.

The river slurped past, purple and orange and green with great blooms of unnatural colour from the dye-works upstream, bobbing with refuse, churned to stinking froth by dozens of hammering waterwheels. On the left bank was a kind of beach, streaked with tidemarks of dead brown weed, scattered with the city's flotsam, with rags and skins and broken chairs and splintered glass and rusted wire and things too far rotted to be identified, all vomited up by the tortured waters and pecked at by flocks of birds bedraggled to winged rats.

A bent-backed woman was picking through the rubbish. She stared at Savine with wild eyes, stared at the sword she still held in one hand, then scuttled away with a bloated sack over one bloated shoulder.

Savine tottered up the shingle, sodden clothes clinging to her, slapping at her. She had to find something she could hide in. She stumbled along, turning over tree branches draped with rags, plucking up broken boxes, coughing at the stink of watery rot. Flies buzzed near a corpse—pig or sheep or dog, all matted hair and dirty bone.

Savine caught sight of something beside it. An old coat, one arm torn off and the lining hanging out like offal from a carcass, but she seized on it with far greater delight than she might have the latest silks in the clothiers of Adua. Those, after all, would not save her life. This might.

Her boots were so caked with dirt, no one could have told they cost more than a house in this neighbourhood, but her petticoats, filthy with river scum, heavy as armour with river water, might give her away. She fumbled at the fastenings with bloody fingertips, ended up sawing at them with her bent sword. She was left squatting on that vile riverbank in her clinging drawers. Her corset had to stay, ripped open and with one of the bones poking out. There was no way she could reach the laces.

She dragged the muddy coat over it, a thing not even the old beggar woman had seen any value in. It stank of rot with a chemical edge that caught in her throat, but she was grateful for it. At least no one could mistake her for that leader of fashion, that scourge of ballroom and parlour, that terror of inventors and investors, Savine dan Glokta.

She wanted nothing more, right then, than to burrow into the refuse and hide. But they would be coming for her. They knew who she was. Who her father was. They would have broken down the office door by now, found the loose board. They would be following her bloody trail, through the machines, past the wheel. Any moment now, they would find her.

She scraped muck from the beach, smeared it across her stubbled scalp, down her face. She hunched over the way the old beachcomber had, dragging one filthy boot behind her. She hardly had to pretend at a limp, she had wrenched her ankle somewhere and it was starting to throb. Everything hurt. She clutched the stinking coat around her, sword tucked out of sight inside, and hobbled away leaving two hundred marks' worth of the finest Gurkish linen slashed and ruined on the shingle.

She clambered up a low wall, into the lane behind the mill. The lane where she had seen the armed men earlier. She felt something tickle her neck. By the Fates, her earrings! The gaudy ones Lisbit had picked. She plucked them out, was about to fling them away when she realised what they might be worth. She stuffed them into the torn lining of her corset.

The sound of the machines had stopped. Now there was only a faint din of crashing metal, ripping cloth, shattering glass. They were the Breakers, after all. They could smash the whole city for all she cared, as long as they left her in one piece.

She crept to the corner of the wall, peered around it towards the gate of the mill.

There was the carriage, looking just the way it had when she got into it that morning, driver sitting with his chin squashed into his scarf, one of the horses tossing its head, harness faintly jingling. All strangely safe and normal in the empty street.

With a whimper of relief, she stumbled towards it.

The Little People

Lisbit practised her sitting-up-straight. She wasn't sure how Lady Savine made her neck look the way she did. She couldn't have more bones in it than anyone else. But Lisbit had been studying her, every spare moment, and she'd get the trick of it. You had to work your shoulder blades back till it felt like they'd touch, then not lift your chin exactly, but sort of lift your whole throat…

She slumped back, wriggling her shoulders. Bloody hell, it was hard work. She opened the watch, spent a moment working out what the time was, then snapped it shut with that lovely *click*. Lady Savine was taking a while, but she'd wait, of course, that's what a lady's companion did. She'd wait until the sun went out if she had to. That's how faithful she was. Better than that brown bitch Zuri, looking down her nose and giving orders to decent people like she was better than them. Well, she wasn't better than Lisbit, and she'd prove it. She'd finally got her chance and she meant to take it. She straightened one of the very fine lace cuffs on the very fine new dress she was wearing, gave the watch a little pat where it sat above her heart, looking so grand on its beautiful chain. Lisbit Beech, lady's companion. It just sounded *right*. She deserved it. More than that bloody Zuri. What kind of a name was that, anyway? A name you'd give a doll.

Bloody brown witch had everyone convinced she knew best. And now she was bringing her brothers back, too. And Lady Savine had just said, "Bring 'em in! Let 'em live here, where the decent folk have to live!" Lisbit couldn't believe it. As if there weren't enough of them in Midderland already. She wanted to be kind. She was a generous person. Big-hearted, ask anyone. Always giving bits to the tramps when she had one spare. But there had to be a limit. Folk in the Union had their own problems, without a crowd of brown bastards flooding in and bringing more. They were everywhere now in Adua! There were places in the city a decent person hardly dared tread.

She slipped her little mirror out to check her face. This damn heat was the worst thing for powder. While she was tutting at the colour in her cheeks, she caught a glimpse through the window of some beggar limping up the street, making right for the carriage. Some beggar in a filthy coat with one sleeve missing, scrawny arm sticking out. She thought it might be a woman, and her lip curled with disgust. Filthy, she was, stubble hair caked with shit and blood and who knew what else. She looked diseased. The last thing Lisbit needed when Lady Savine got back was some sick cripple with her hand out.

She snapped the window down and snarled, "Get the *fuck* away from here!"

The beggar woman's red eyes slid sideways, and she veered away from the carriage and hobbled off, hunching down.

A moment later, there was a clatter as the door on the other side of the carriage was ripped open. A man ducked in. A big man in worn work clothes with a great smear of soot down the side of his face. Barging into Lady Savine's carriage, bold as you please.

"Get out!" snapped Lisbit, furious. But he didn't get out. More men crowded in behind him, leering faces at the windows, dirty hands reaching for her.

"Help!" she shrieked, cringing against the door. "Help!" And she kicked furiously at the one with the sooty face, caught him a good one on the jaw, but one of the others grabbed her ankle and they dragged her shrieking right out of the carriage and into the gutter and all of a sudden it was like she was drowning in a clutching, stomping sea of hands and boots and furious faces.

"Where is she?"

"Old Sticks' daughter?"

"Where's that Glokta bitch?"

"I'm just the face-maid!" she squealed, no idea what was happening. A robbery! A riot! They'd dragged the driver down from his seat and were kicking him, kicking him while he huddled on the ground with his bloody hands over his head.

"We'll give you one chance—"

"I'm just—"

Someone hit her. The dull thud of it and her head cracked the pavement, blood in her mouth. Someone pulled her up by her hair. Rip of stitching. The arm of her jacket was half torn off, lace dangling. Someone was rooting through her bag, flinging the pretty pots of paint and powder away, stomping her brushes into the pavement.

"Get her inside, we'll soon find out what she knows."

"No!" she squealed, watch chain scraping her face as someone tore it off. "No!" They were laughing as they started to drag her through the gate. "No!" She tried to cling to the frame, but one had her left arm, another her right, a third her left ankle. "No!" Her right shoe kicked helplessly at the ground. Such a nice shoe. She'd been so proud to put it on.

"I'm just the face-maid!" she shrieked.

"Stop!" roared Kurbman, shoving one man out of his way, then another. "Stop!" He grabbed one lad, who'd eagerly stuck his hand up the girl's torn skirt, by the throat and threw him to the ground. "Have you forgotten who we are? We're not animals! We're Breakers!"

In that moment, as their maddened faces turned towards him, he had his doubts. But he kept on shouting anyway. What else could he do?

"We done this so *we* wouldn't be victims. Not so we could make victims o' them. We're better'n that, brothers!" And he tore at the air with his hands, trying to make 'em see. "We done this to bring the Great Change! For justice, remember?"

He knew better, o' course. Some done it for justice, some for vengeance, some for profit and some for the chance to run riot, and it wasn't like there was no room for a mixture. At a time like this, all flushed with victory and violence, even the better ones could turn dark. Still, there were just enough o' the first group to get some doubts going.

"You thinking to let 'er go?" someone asked.

"No one's letting anyone go," said Kurbman. "They'll be judged with the others. Judged fair. Judged proper."

"I'm just the face-maid," gasped the girl, her powder streaked with tears.

At that moment, two of the others came out dragging Vallimir between them, his clothes torn and his face bloody and his eyes barely open. One of the lads spat on him. "Fucking bastard!" growled another.

Kurbman stepped in front of him, hands up. "Easy, brothers. Let's not do anything we'll regret."

"I'll be regretting nothing," snapped someone.

"And I ain't your brother," said another.

"If you've not got the guts for this, leave it to those who do," said a third, like making yourself part of a mob was quite the act o' courage.

Things might've turned ugly then, or uglier, at any rate, if it hadn't been for some prisoners brought rattling up the street. Two dozen, maybe, a lot of fine clothes in disarray and a lot of proud faces bruised, shocked and tear-tracked, shackled in pairs to a great length of chain. Five Breakers minding 'em, home-made manacles hanging from their belts, a hard-faced old bastard at the front Kurbman knew from meetings, though he didn't think he'd ever heard him talk.

"Brother Lock!" he shouted, and the man held up his shuffling column. "You taking these to the Courthouse?"

"I am."

"Got two more for you." Kurbman pulled the girl free and, in spite of the grumbling from his comrades, gave her over to a man with a blond beard who started shackling her to the chain. Bloody hell, but one of the prisoners was Self, the foreman from the third shed at Resling's Glassworks, eyes down and a great bloody welt on his cheek. He was a good man, Self. Always done his best for his people. Kurbman swallowed. Getting these folk shackled was the best he could do. Getting anyone unshackled would more'n likely see him dead.

"I'm just the face-maid," whimpered the girl as they chained Vallimir beside her, head lolling and his hair matted with blood.

Kurbman turned back to the workers, his voice cracking. "We've a chance to make a better world, brothers! A *better* world, you understand? But we have to do it *right*."

With a jerk on the chain, Resling and the rest were set marching again. Or stumbling, tottering, weeping and groaning, anyway, watched over by half a dozen sinewy men in workmen's clothes, sticks in their dirty fists.

"Bastards," he muttered to himself.

He was Karlric dan Resling, and he would see them all hanged.

They were dragged past the burning shell of a carriage. Rubbish scattered the street. Broken timbers, broken glass. He flinched as something burst from an upstairs window—a great desk, tumbling down and shattering, papers spilling across the cobbles.

Some men stood near it, watching. One ate an apple. Another laughed. A shrill, nervous kind of laughter.

They had burst onto the bridge. His office, that was, but he called it the bridge. He'd always loved a maritime metaphor. "Get out, damn you!" Shouting always made them lower their eyes. "Get *out*!" But not this time. He had not *believed* it! He *still* could not! He was the admiral! He was Karlric dan Resling!

They had dragged him from behind his desk. "Damn you!" Dragged him across his own deck. The factory floor, that was, pelted with rubbish by his own employees, who were working with more vigour than they ever had before, destroying the machines he had hired them to operate! "Curse you all!" After everything he had done for these men, for this city. They had manacled him to this damn chain, shackled to two dozen other helpless unfortunates like slaves in bloody Gurkhul. "How *dare* you?"

It was a motley group. The man up ahead with the torn coat Resling knew by sight. A lawyer, perhaps? Beside him was that idiot's wife, what was his name? Sirisk? The girl they had just added to the chain looked more like a bloody maid than a lady. Her tear-streaked cheeks were pink as a farm girl's. Where were they even being taken? There was no sense to it. There was no sense to any of it.

A woman with a gaudily painted face leaned from a window above, laughing, laughing, flinging great heaps of papers into the air. Accounts. Receipts. Deeds. Fluttering like demented confetti, coating the cobbles, swirls of elaborate calligraphy smudging in the filth.

It was more than a strike. More than a riot. It was not just his mill, or the mill next door. The streets were infected by revolution! It was everywhere. The world run *mad*.

What would his darling Seline have thought to see her beloved city brought to this? She who spent her evenings giving soup to the destitute. Feeding the bloody scroungers. Perhaps it was a good thing the grip had taken her in that bitter winter, in spite of all the money he lavished on doctors. For the best. Just as they had said at the graveside.

Down a side street, he saw men pushing over a wagon, its cargo of barrels bouncing across the cobbles.

"These *bastards*!" he snarled at the nearest guard. The nearest Breaker. The nearest traitor. The nearest *animal*. "I am Karlric dan Resling, and I'll see you all—"

The man punched him. It was so utterly unexpected, he stumbled back and sat down hard in the road, nearly dragging the woman in front of him down, too. He sat in the dirt, astonished, blood bubbling from his nose. He had never been punched before. Never in his life. He felt, very strongly, that he never wanted to be again.

"Get up," said the man.

Resling got up. There were tears in his eyes. What would his darling Seline think if she could see him now?

He was Karlric dan Resling. He was the admiral. Wasn't he?

He wasn't sure any more.

*

"Bastards," whimpered the man beside her, but it was a plaintive little bleat now. Even so, it was tempting fate.

"Stop it!" Condine hissed at him through her tears. "You'll only make it worse."

Could it be worse, though? Men clattered past, snarling faces, clenched fists, sticks and axes. They shouted, whooped, animal noises that hardly sounded like words. One ducked towards her, snapped his teeth at her, and she cringed as they whirled past.

The tears were streaming down her face. They had been ever since the men kicked in the door of the tea shop where she had been spreading Savine dan Glokta's gossip. They had not needed to kick it in. They could have opened it. Such a charming tinkle the bell always made.

Her father had always been so impatient when she cried. "Toughen up, girl." Furious, as though her tears were an unfair attack on him. Sometimes he had cuffed her around the head, but the blows seemed to have made her less tough, not more. Her husband had opted for a kind of benign neglect instead. The idea of his being interested enough to hit her was absurd. Being shackled to a chain was the most attention anyone had paid her in years.

The line of prisoners shambled past a great manufactory on fire, smoke roiling up into the darkening murk, a popping crash as a window shattered, showering glass, gouting flame, smouldering rubbish and laths and bits of slate tumbling into the street, and Condine held up a hand against the heat of it, drying the tears on her face as fast as she could shed them.

A workers' uprising had formed the backdrop to one of her favourite books, *Lost Among the Labourers*, in which a beautiful mill-owner's daughter is saved from a fire by one of her father's roughest hands. The edges of the pages in the passage where she finally yields to him among the machinery had become quite dishevelled. Condine had always particularly enjoyed the description of his arms, so strong, so gentle.

There were strong arms here. Gentle, no. She saw men kicking wildly at the door of a shop. Others were dragging a carpet from a house. Her smarting, weeping eyes darted to yells, squeals, mad sounds. Petty horrors everywhere. No trace of romance in it.

Some beggar in a filthy coat was skulking along after them. Why? They were going to hell. They had already arrived.

"Bastards," sobbed the man behind her.

"Shush!" Condine snarled furiously at him.

The man in front frowned over his shoulder. "Both o' you shush."

*

Colton turned away from the blubbing, whining pair of 'em, shaking his head. There was the trouble with rich folk, they'd no idea how to cope with hardship. No practice. He scratched at the sore skin under the shackles. Home-made they were, with some rough edges, prone to chafe. But Colton was used to things chafing.

He hadn't wanted to be a guard. But they'd been offering a coat. Plus meals, even if they were bad ones, and pay, even if it was shit. And by then, what choice did he have? He'd have been a fucking guard *dog* if they'd offered a kennel. Principles are fine, but only once you've got a roof.

They passed three hunched shapes on the ground. Red jackets ripped, stained dark. Soldiers. If the army couldn't stop this madness, what hope for the rest of them?

Always thought he'd be a weaver, like his old man. There'd been these golden years, just after Curnsbick patented his spinning engine, when yarn came spooling out of the new manufactories so cheap they were giving it away, and weavers were suddenly in high demand. Dressed like lords, they'd been, and walking with a swagger. And, aye, the spinners had faced some lean times, poor bastards, but that was their problem.

Then, around the time Colton finished his apprenticeship, along came Masrud's weaving engine, and in the length of three summers, the weavers got the way the spinners had before them, which was to say thin. Only made it worse that a lot o' the spinners had turned their hands to weaving, since that was where the money was, and there was no money there no more.

So Colton was out o' work. Came to Valbeck, where everyone said there was always work, but everyone had the same idea. So he'd become a guard. Folk looked at him like that was treachery. But he'd needed the coat. He'd needed the meals. And now he was shackled to a chain along with a load of rich bastards. In a cruel joke, they'd even stolen his coat. Hardly seemed fair. But then ask the spinners about fair.

A dog was barking as they shambled up onto the bridge. Frisking maddened around a ruined wagon a bunch of boys were stealing the crates from, barking at no one, barking at everyone. That woman was still sobbing just behind him. No idea how to cope with hardship, the rich. No practice. They'd get some practice now, he reckoned.

"Wait," said the Breaker in charge o' the chain, and the column staggered to a halt on the bridge. Strange thing was, Colton knew him. Lock was his name, he thought. He'd been a weaver, way back when. Remembered him and Colton's old man laughing together at a meeting o' the guild, before his old man died and the guild got broke up. He was a grim-looking bastard now. But a lot of weavers were. Mostly on account of Masrud's weaving engine.

Lock walked to the parapet and frowned down at the water.

Filthy water, full of foam and rubbish, streaked with glistening oil. He'd stood here often. This very spot. Considering the waters. After his wife died. Hard to imagine, in this hot summer, how bitter that winter had been.

Maybe it was the cold done it, or the hunger, or the grip, or maybe it was just the hope bled out of her. Got so she just couldn't be warmed. Got sicker and sicker and then she never woke. His son followed two nights after, eight years old. His daughter was last to go, just before the thaw. He couldn't remember what they'd been like, really. Couldn't remember 'em living. But he remembered 'em dead. He'd slept next door to 'em a few nights, while the ground softened. A few last nights together.

He remembered the burying. One grave, and he'd been lucky to get it, there were so many going in the ground. His wife on the bottom, the children on top, like she was holding 'em, maybe. He'd looked down, and thought they were the lucky ones. Wished he was with 'em. He hadn't cried. He didn't know how. The gravedigger had put a hand on his shoulder and said, "You should come to a meeting. Hear the Weaver speak."

He remembered looking over and seeing some rich folk walking past, laughing. Not laughing at him and his sorrows. Not even noticing 'em. Like they lived in a different world from him and his.

They didn't now.

He turned to look at 'em.

A few men bleeding and a few women blubbing but Lock felt no pity. Didn't feel anything. Hadn't felt anything for a long time.

"What are you doing?" one of them asked. The man with the bloody mouth. "I demand to know what—"

"Shut up!" shrieked the girl with the ripped dress and the red cheeks. "Shut your fucking hole, you fucker!"

Lock looked at the heavy chain. No way any of 'em were swimming shackled to that. All he had to do was push the first couple in and the lot would be dragged after, and down to the bottom of the river, and that'd be that.

He knew it wouldn't be justice.

But he wondered if it might be close enough.

Two men chased another past with sticks, laughing as they hit him, sent him stumbling, dragged him back up, hit him again. There was some beggar, crouching in a doorway at the foot of the bridge, watching Lock with bright eyes.

The old Breaker who led the column looked right at her and Savine edged away around the corner, huddling into her stinking coat.

She dared not go up onto the bridge, where she would be hemmed in and helpless. She had only followed the prisoners because she hardly knew what else to do. At least with them ahead, it felt as if she was not quite alone. But she could not help them. They could not help her. There was no help for anyone.

Her body wanted desperately to run, every muscle aching with tension, but there was nowhere to run to. All she could do was slink down streets scattered with torn papers, with upended wagons, slaughtered horses, broken machinery, sword clutched under her fetid rag of a coat, casting about for somewhere to hide. Some hole where she could reason out what had happened, and some way to escape it. Some place the madness had not reached. But soon enough she realised it was everywhere. Spread like sickness. Like wildfire. The whole city had lost its reason. The whole world.

She flinched at a woman's scream, quickly muffled. Saw bodies moving in an alley, someone forced into a gutter, kicking legs, one stockinged foot, one scuffed shoe. "Help me! Help me!"

She could have done something. She had a sword. But instead she hurried on, the wild shrieks quickly lost in the shouts, the crashes, the barking of dogs. She heard a creaking and glanced up, recoiled against the wall. A body swung from a gib on the side of a building. A well-dressed body, hands tied, grey hair in wild disarray. Some mill owner? Some engineer? Some acquaintance of hers, who she had laughed with at some function?

She hobbled on, eyes fixed on the ground as it turned from new paving, to old cobbles, to straw-scattered dirt, to rutted mud. Narrower streets, further from the river, away from the manufactories. The buildings closed in until she crept down stinking man-made gullies paved only with the slops from the cellars, mean windows down by her boots, wretched garments flapping overhead like bunches of mad flags, little patches of the street made into pens where pigs honked and squealed and burrowed in the rubbish.

A murk even more hellish than usual had descended on the city as the sun sank and smoke from burning buildings billowed into the streets.

Shapes loomed and vanished, phantoms in the soupy gloom. Savine was utterly lost. Valbeck was become a maze of horrors from which there was no escape. Could this be the same world as the one in which she presided over meetings of the Solar Society, changing lives with a flick of her fan?

Suddenly people were scattering like a shoal of fish, squealing in terror. She had no idea what they were running from but the panic was more contagious than the plague and she fled, fled mindlessly to nowhere, snatched breath sharp in her raw throat, rotten coat flapping at her skinned knees. She saw a man duck into an alleyway and followed, nearly ran straight into him as he spun about, a broken-off chair leg in his hand.

"Get back!" His face was so deranged, he hardly looked human. He shoved her and she fell, biting her tongue, sprawling in the street, nearly cutting herself on her sword as she rolled in the gutter. Someone kicked her in the side as they ran past, tumbled over her. She scrambled up, limping on, wincing at new bruises.

Could it have been only that morning she swapped small talk at Mistress Vallimir's overdecorated breakfast table? Such a fragrant tea, who is the importer? Could it have been only an hour ago she had mused on the price of children with the colonel? Her lovely new sword-belt, such craftsmanship! Now the colonel and his wife were more than likely murdered and Savine dan Glokta was a memory. An unlikely story she once heard.

If fate let her live through this nightmare, she would be better. She would be the good person she had always pretended to be. No longer a gambler. No longer an ambitious snake. If fate would only let her live. Soon enough, she realised she was muttering it to herself with every whimpering breath.

"Let me live... let me live... let me live..."

Like a poem. Like a prayer. She used to laugh when Zuri spoke of God. How could someone so clever believe something so silly? Now she tried to believe herself. Wished she could believe.

"Let me live..."

She limped into a square of buckled cobbles, a grand building burning at one end. Fire spouted behind black columns, ash fluttering down against the bloody sunset. An old statue of Harod the Great stood in the centre. Figures were gathered around the pedestal, beating at the legs with hammers. Others had tied ropes about its shoulders, straining to drag it down. A gleeful crowd watched, torches in their hands, screeching with joy and fury, swearing in rough voices. Music was playing, a pipe and a fiddle tooting and sawing, a woman crazily dancing, ragged skirts and ragged hair whirling. And a man. A naked, fat man lumbering about. An air of mad carnival.

Savine stood staring, beyond desperate, beyond exhausted. She was filthy as a pig. She was thirsty as a dog. She almost wanted to laugh. She almost wanted to cry. She almost wanted to join the dancers, and give up. She sagged against a wall, trying to breathe. Trying to think. But that mad music left no room for it.

Figures, black against the fires, shimmering with their heat. A tall man in a tall hat, pointing, screaming.

"Rip it *down*!" bellowed Sparks.

He was a fucking king, and this square was his kingdom, and he'd suffer no other king within its borders. "Rip it down!"

Might be he'd get a new statue up there in due course. A statue of him, wearing the tall hat he'd just stolen that made him look quite the fine article.

Sparks was scared of nothing. The more he said it, to everyone else and to himself, the more true it became. Acres had been scared of everything. Had hidden crying in the cupboard when men came to visit his mother. Sparks hated that weak little cringing bastard, scared of everything. So he'd shrugged him off like a snake sheds its skin. Sparks was scared of nothing.

He grinned at the dancers, waddling and lurching, variously stripped, whipped and humiliated. "Might be we should hang one o' these bastards!" He shouted it louder'n ever, so everyone could see nothing scared him. "Teach the others a lesson."

"Shouldn't we wait for Judge?" asked Framer.

Sparks swallowed. He was scared of nothing, but Judge was something else... not only mad herself, but she had a way of turning other people mad. Like she was a match, and they were the kindling. And you never knew quite what she'd think. Might love what he'd done with the square. Might find it tasteless. Those black eyes of hers might slide towards him, pointed tip of her tongue showing between her teeth. "Ain't this all a bit fucking tasteless, Sparks?" she'd say, and everyone would be looking at him, and his mouth would get dry and his knees all trembly, like Acres' used to, when he hid in the cupboard.

"You *what*?" he screamed. Like always, the fear made him angry. He grabbed Framer by his threadbare jacket. The idiot lacked even the presence o' mind to steal better clothes from one of the gentleman callers. "I'm the fucking boss here, idiot! This is *my* fucking square, understand?"

"All right, all right, it's your square."

"That's right! I'll burn what I please!" Sparks strutted up the heap of papers to the top of the pyre, threw his arm around the bastard they'd tied to the stake in the middle of it. "I'll burn *who* I please." And he lifted his torch high, and the fire in the darkness made him feel brave again. "I'm the king o' this fucking square! You understand?"

And he scrubbed the bastard's hanging head with his hand and then, 'cause his hair was all full of wine and blood, had to wipe it on his bloody shirt front. Then he hopped down, and grabbed the bottle out of Framer's hand, and took a pull. The spirits helped him feel brave. Helped him feel like Acres was far away, and the cupboard, too, and Judge even.

He grinned around at his handiwork. Hadn't decided whether to burn that bastard yet. He'd been thinking not, but as night came on, he started to reckon a man on fire might make a nice centrepiece.

"Help me..." whimpered Alinghan.

But there was no one to help him. Everyone had gone mad, all mad. Smiles full of glistening teeth. Eyes full of pitiless fire. They were like devils. They *were* devils.

When they dragged him from his office, he had been sure the city watch would come. When he was tied to the stake, he had no doubt the Inquisition would arrive to deliver him. As darkness fell and the great riot became an orgy of destruction, he had still hoped that soldiers would tramp into the square and put an end to it.

But no one had come, and a great heap of legal papers, and engineers' drawings, and official pronouncements, and lewd etchings, and broken furniture from the offices around the square had built up to his thighs.

A pyre.

He did not suppose they would actually light it. They could not possibly mean to light it. Could they?

He had wondered if it was a questionable neighbourhood in which to lease an office. But to be taken seriously, an engineer needs an office, and the rents in the better parts of Valbeck were out of all compass. They had said the Breakers were entirely under control. Had been taught harsh lessons. That the Burners were just a rumour spread by pessimistic moaners intent on talking down the city. They had pointed out the brand-new and thoroughly modern branch of Valint and Balk, and talked of gentrification.

Now flames spurted from the windows of the brand-new and thoroughly modern branch of Valint and Balk, ash and flaming promissory notes drifting down across the square, and the Burners had vomited forth from the shadows, in person, a demented legion, capering about him with their torches and their lamps.

Someone slapped him across the face, laughing, laughing. Why did they hate him? He had made the world better. More efficient. Countless small improvements to the machinery and operating practices at several manufactories. He had been steadily building a name for himself as a diligent worker. Why did they hate him?

"What a day!" someone was screaming. "The Great Change, come at last!"

He caught a choking waft of smoke, stared desperately about to see if his pyre had caught light, but no. So many bonfires, glimmering through the desperate tears in his eyes.

"Help me..." he muttered, to no one. All it would take was a stray torch. A stray burning paper on the capricious breeze. A stray spark. And the longer this went on, the wilder they became, the more likely his destruction.

A woman ripped down her dress and another poured wine over her bared breasts and a man shoved his face between them like a pig into a trough, all shrieking with desperate laughter, as if the world would end tomorrow. Perhaps it had ended already. The fiddle-player capered past, sawing discordant music, broken strings dangling from the neck of his instrument.

Alinghan closed his eyes. It was like some story of the Fall of Aulcus, chaos and debauchery on the streets. He had always thought of civilisation as a machine, cast from rigid iron, everything riveted in its proper place. Now he saw it was a fabric gauzy as a bride's veil. A tissue everyone agrees to leave in place, but one that can be ripped away in an instant. And hell lurks just beneath.

"Stack it up, you bastards!" roared the one they called Sparks, the chief Burner, the chief demon, the temporary Glustrod of this square, and men and women flung more papers in Alinghan's face, and they fluttered and curled and whirled on the hot breeze.

"Help me..." he whispered, to no one.

Of course they would come. The city watch. The Inquisition. The soldiers. Someone would come. How could they not?

But Alinghan was forced to concede, as he looked down in horror at the steadily growing heaps of paper about his legs, that they might come too late for him.

"The Great Change!" someone shrieked, cackling with mad delight. "What a day!"

"What a day!" bellowed that bastard with the squint. Mally could never remember his name. Nasty little bastard, she'd always thought. The sort that's always peering in at windows, looking for something they can snatch.

"We're fucking free!" he shrieked.

Mally wanted to be free. Who doesn't? In principle. It's a pretty dream, to go running through the flower garden with your hair down. But she didn't want to be free of getting paid. She'd tried that, and it hurt like you wouldn't believe. That's how she'd ended up whoring in the first place. No one had forced her to it, exactly. It was just that a choice between whoring and hunger weren't no choice at all.

They'd broken down the door o' the tapping house and dragged out the gentleman callers by the feet, made 'em dance for everyone's amusement in the glare of the burning bank, dressed, or undressed, however they'd been at that moment. One portly old gent shuffled about the heap of papers with his hat still on but his trousers around his ankles. Another fellow, a lawyer, she thought, that one who was always going on about charity and liked to cover his face while he was having his cock sucked, was naked as a babe, whip marks on his hairy back glistening in the firelight.

Watching the regulars dance for her made a nice change, she had to admit, and she wasn't the least bit arsed if the bank turned to ashes, but there was a worry looming about who was going to pay for her broken door. And a bigger worry looming behind that one. If they burned all the regulars, who'd pay for anything tomorrow?

"The Great Change!" The squinty bastard caught Mally by the arm, painfully tight, almost dragged her over. Funny how, whenever men talked about freedom, they never really meant for the women. "What a day, eh?" he shrieked in her face, blasting her with foul breath.

"Aye," she said, smiling as she twisted her arm free. "The Great Change."

Was it a change for the better, though? That was her concern. Maybe she'd wake tomorrow and the world would suddenly have turned sane, and someone would've fixed her broken lock, too. She had her considerable doubts. But what could she do but smile through it and hope for the best? Least at that she had plenty of practice.

She saw Sparks watching her. Felt like she had to do something cruel, show she was one of them. The naked lawyer blundered past and she stuck out a boot and tripped him. He tumbled over, rolling in the dirt, and she pointed at him and howled with forced laughter.

She didn't like it any, but a choice between getting hurt and doing the hurting weren't no choice at all. She'd sat at the shitty end o' that see-saw often enough.

"Up, pig!" someone snarled.

Randock staggered to his feet, clutching at his side, trying to hold up a weak hand and dance at the same time. He'd never been much of a dancer. Even with his clothes on. And he was exhausted now, sweating like a hog in spite of his nakedness, the old dyspepsia burning up his throat. But dyspepsia was the least of his worries.

That girl Mally had tripped him, he thought. Now she was pointing, screeching with laughter. He could not understand it. He had *helped* her, often. Financial assistance, from the good of his heart. That was why he kept coming here. To *help* these poor girls, driven into lives of debauchery by the harsh times. If they wished to express their natural gratitude, he would not demean them by refusing. He had a strong social conscience. And *this* was how they repaid him, the ingrate bitches. Fucking filthy whores, the lot of them!

He lumbered past the hill of documents they were heaping up around that poor fellow in the cheap suit, tied to a stake like some heretic by fanatics in the savage South. Perhaps there were some of Randock's cases in the pyre, ready to be sent up in smoke. The waste of it. The folly! He had given his life to the law. More charity, on his part. He had sweated on behalf of his clients. So conscientious! You're in good hands with Randock! He had built a reputation on it. Thus the thriving partnership of Zalev, Randock and Crun. Zalev died some years ago, of course, taken by the grip in that cold winter, but Randock wasn't paying for a new sign just on his account, and Crun was away doing patents. Lot of money in patents these days.

With paper and ink one could level mountains, he had always said, if given the time and appropriate connections about the Courthouse. Nothing was stronger than the law! Now it seemed that fire was stronger still. Law alone, without enforcement, is just breath. He flinched as part of the bank's roof sagged inwards, flames spurting up, sparks whirling. Never cross Valint and Balk, Zalev had told him the day he entered the law. *Never.* By the Fates, if they with all their wealth and secrets and power could be burned, what was safe? The fire was already spreading towards the narrow building where his own offices were located.

He had spent his life's work on that firm. Built it up with his own hands. Well, his and Zalev's and Crun's, he supposed, but mostly his, since Zalev had died and Crun was concentrating on patents.

He lurched to a halt, wheezing, groaning, bending over with hands on knees as the horrible music sawed on, and the whores pointed and laughed and drank. The injustice! He came here to *help* these girls. He was their benefactor. Their patron. A father figure! Well, no, more a kindly uncle. He was *loved* in this neighbourhood. And now they mocked him while he blundered about naked. Like a sad bear he once saw with a travelling show.

Still, it could have been worse. It could have been him tied to the stake with all that legal kindling about his ankles. He put a hand over his mouth, trying to swallow his dyspepsia.

Someone hit him and he squealed in agony. A line of fire across his bare buttocks.

"Please!" he wheezed, holding up that desperate hand. "Please!"

A little fellow with a nasty squint leered at him, held up a coachman's whip.

"Dance, you fat shit!" he snarled. "Or you'll be the one in the fire!"

Randock danced.

"What a day!" screamed Moth, 'cause the Great Change had finally come and everything was turned upside down, and the folk who'd been on the bottom all their lives were suddenly on top, the scum made lords, and all the things he'd wanted but knew he'd never get he could just reach out and take. Who'd stop him? "What a *day!*"

And he lashed at the lawyer again with his whip and caught him across the thighs, made him stagger, fall on his knees, the fat bastard. Fat bastard who'd barely even looked sideways at him when he'd asked for a coin a few days before. Like he was an insect. Who was the insect now, eh? He knew 'em all. He saw 'em, even if they didn't see him. He had a tally of all the slights they'd given him and today was the day to pay the bill.

"Dance, you fat shit!" And he kicked the lawyer in the jaw as he tried to stagger up and knocked him on his back, threw the whip down and snatched up a hammer in both hands, started beating at the statue again.

"Fuck yourself!" he snarled at it. Some king, some big man. "Not so big now!" He smashed a bit of the inscription away. He'd no idea what it said. There'd be no need for letters after the Great Change.

"Give me some o' that!" Ripping a bottle from Framer's hand while he was in the middle of trying to drink and making him spill spirits all over that stupid cap of his.

"You bastard," said Framer, wiping his face, but Moth just laughed and took another swig. He saw a little girl in a doorway, watching at him. A little brown girl with great dark eyes, tear tracks glistening on her face.

He shoved the bottle in the air and laughed. "What a *day*!"

Hessel turned away from the madness in the square. It scared her too much. She shuffled back into the doorway, where her father was lying.

"Father," she whispered, tugging at his arm. "Please wake up!"

He wobbled with her shaking, but he did not wake. One of his eyes was a little open, just a slit of white showing. But he did not wake.

Once when they were out walking in the public gardens in Bizurt, where the Emperor Solkun was said to have planted ten thousand palms, her father had told her it was always wise to carry a cloth, to keep oneself clean and presentable. She pulled hers out now, and licked it, and tried to dab the blood from his forehead, but the more she dabbed, the more there was. The cloth turned red with it. His grey hair turned black with it.

"Oh God," she whispered as she dabbed, not sure if she was swearing or praying. In spite of the priests' long efforts at instruction, she had never quite been able to tell the difference. "Oh God, oh God, oh God."

He had said things would be better here. Dawah was not safe any more. First, the emperor's soldiers had been driven out of the town, and there was chaos, and that had been very bad. Then the Eaters had come, to bring back order, and that had been far worse. She had seen one of them, in the main street, at sunset. A terrible light had shone from it. She still saw it, in her dreams, the black eyes, and the empty smile, and the blood on its fine robes. So they had fled from Dawah. Her father had said things would be better here.

"Oh God, oh God, oh God..."

But things had not been better here. There was no work. People spat at them in the street. They had gone from one town to another, and the little money that had not been stolen from them by the sailors on the voyage had gradually leaked away. They had heard there was work in Valbeck, so they had banded together with a dozen other Kantics for safety on the road. It had been a hard journey, only to find there was no work in Valbeck, either. Not for pale faces, let alone for dark. People looked at them like they were rats. And now everything had gone mad. She did not understand what had happened. She did not even know who had hit her father, or why.

"Oh God, oh God..."

The priests said if she prayed every morning and every night and was pure within then good things would happen. She had prayed every night and every morning. Had she done it wrong? Was she rotten inside, that God should punish her?

"Oh God," she whimpered, shaking her father's shoulder. "Please wake up!"

She did not know what to do. There was no one here she knew. They had taken her father's shoes. His shoes, God help her, his bare feet flopped out sideways, and she touched one of them gently with a trembling hand, tears in her eyes.

"Oh God," she whispered. What should she do?

She heard scraping footsteps. Someone had edged around the wall into the doorway, hunched over in a ragged coat missing an arm, staring fearfully out into the square where figures writhed and lurched to the deranged music.

Hessel crouched, showing her teeth, not sure whether to fight or to cry. Sometimes, the priests had said, one must rely on the kindness of strangers.

"Please," she said. It came out a desperate squeak.

The beggar spun about. It was a woman. A pale woman with a shaved head. She looked mad. Streaks of dried blood from a scab on her scalp, dark paint smeared from one staring, red-rimmed eye.

"My father...won't wake up," said Hessel, the unfamiliar words clumsy in her mouth.

"I'm sorry." The woman's bloody neck shifted as she swallowed. "There's nothing I can do."

"Please!"

"You have to be quiet!" hissed the woman, eyes sliding terrified towards the square.

"Please!" shouted Hessel, grabbing at her bare arm. "Please! Please!" She started to scream it, louder and louder, she could not stop herself. She was not even sure if she was saying it in the Union tongue or the Kantic.

The beggar pulled away, dragging Hessel after her.

"Please! Please! Please!"

"Shut your mouth!" shrieked the woman, and flung her against the wall, and Hessel heard her scramble away, out into the square.

She picked herself up, rubbing at the sore spot where her head had struck the stone. She crawled over to her father and touched him gently on the arm.

"Father," she begged. "*Please* wake up."

221

Something of Ours

Savine stumbled from the alleyway. Behind her, the child was still wailing.

The music had screeched to a halt. The dancing, too. Eyes turned towards her. Black eyes, glinting with flames in the darkness.

She saw the outline of the tall man with the tall hat, a burning torch in one hand, his other raised to point at her.

"Bring me that one!"

She fled, forcing her trembling legs to another effort, ducked down a side street, slid in filth, went over in the gutter and scrambled up again. She plunged past a staring old woman, through a court crammed between tiny houses, a great heap of ash and dung and bones piled in the midst, crawling with vermin.

Shouts behind her, jagged shouts and jagged laughter, slapping footfalls echoing off the peeling walls. She flung herself desperately at doors as she passed, locked, locked, locked, then one flew open and she tumbled through the guts of a squalid building.

A room with a sagging ceiling where rags were heaped, people stretched out sleeping. Drunk, husk-addled, half-dressed, mouths hanging heedlessly open, spilling drool. The stench was indescribable. Someone had broken a hole in the floor and used it for a privy, flies crawling. Savine retched as she staggered between the bodies, hand over her mouth, blundered through a door at the back and into an alleyway.

"There you are." Two men ahead of her. She reeled away, boots skittering on the cobbles, and found herself facing a dead end. A blank wall of mouldy brick, not even a door to try. She slowly turned, breath crawling in her throat. They closed in with the cocky swagger of men who know they've won. One had an ugly squint and a stick with a nail through it. The other had a cap drawn low over a bent face.

"Get back!" hissed Savine, holding up her hand. It might have been more impressive had it not been trembling so badly.

"It's a woman," said Squinty, starting to grin.

The one with the cap peered down his bent nose at her coat, held tight over her sword. "What're you hiding?"

"None of your business." Savine tried to make her voice effortlessly confident, the way it used to be. Sound in command, you're halfway to being there. It came out a quavering croak. But her accent was plain, even so.

Squinty's smile spread further. "Not just a woman. A real *lady*." And he slapped his stick gently into his palm, fingered at that nail through it. "Fallen on hard times?"

"Lot of ladies have, today," said the one with the cap, easing forwards.

Savine shuffled back in a crouch, eyes darting between them. "I'm warning you—"

Squinty had turned thoughtful. "Might be it's her."

"Her? Who her?"

"Savine dan—"

"Shut your *mouth*!" she shrieked. Her eyes went wide. She realised she had run him neatly through the chest with her sword. A textbook lunge Bremer dan Gorst could have been proud of.

"Fuck," said the one with the cap, stepping back, eyes wide.

Squinty gave a strangled cough, dropped his stick and pawed at his chest where the blade was. He tried to say something but had no breath.

She pulled the sword back and it sliced a deep gash through the side of his hand. Blood welled, a black stain spreading down his jacket.

The one with the cap reeled away and Savine darted forward, slashing him across the back of the thigh. She fumbled the sword and it caught him with the flat, didn't even cut through his ragged trousers, but it was enough to make him stumble and he sprawled in the gutter.

"Please!" he squeaked, wriggling up onto his hands, staring over his shoulder, as scared as Savine had been a moment before. "Please!"

He gave a little whoop as the blade punched through his ribs, arched back, squirmed over, face twisting in agony. Savine knelt on top of him, trying to drag her sword free, but it was stuck right through him and he was wriggling, groaning, wriggling. She heard shouting up the street. Echoing footfalls.

She let go of her sword and ran, every muscle aching now, her lungs on fire. She snatched a look back. Figures in the murk, huge, distorted. Whoops and laughter, like huntsmen after a fox. A great shape loomed ahead, a monster with a thousand bristling limbs, and she skittered to a halt. A barricade, thrown up across the street, the limbs the legs of chairs, and desks, and tangled timbers. A man stood on it. A huge man with hardly any neck, hair clipped to stubble, features hidden but for lenses flashing orange, the new kind, mounted in thin wire, tiny on his heavy, stubbled face.

"Help me!" Holding out her bloody hand, her voice a desperate squeak. "I'm begging you!"

He folded Savine's wrist in an irresistible grip. For a terrible moment, she wondered if she had made the worst mistake of her life.

He hoisted her effortlessly up beside him. She saw torch flames bobbing, could hardly breathe for fear, hardly move for it. She shrank down trembling behind a broken chest of drawers, clung to a chair leg.

Her pursuers slowed as they came close. Six of them, breathing hard from their run, sticks and clubs and torches in their clenched fists, and at the front the tall one swaggered forward, tall hat skewed at a rakish angle.

"That's far enough," said the big man. A calm voice, very deep, very slow. How could he be calm? How could anyone be calm ever again?

"Nice wall you've built," said Tall Hat, sneer across a sweat-beaded, pockmarked face, his eyes wild, wide, burning with the reflected fire of his torch as he held it high.

"Thanks," said the big man, "but I'll ask you to admire it from a distance." He unhooked his lenses from his ears and ever so carefully folded them. "I'll ask nicely." He rubbed at the bridge of his nose with finger and thumb. "But I'll only ask once."

"Can't." Tall Hat gave a big grin. "You've got something of ours."

The big man pushed his folded lenses into Savine's limp hand and gently curled her fingers shut around them. He sounded almost sad. "Believe me, there's naught here you want."

"Give her up!" barked Tall Hat, voice turned suddenly so sharp, Savine flinched at it.

The big man hopped down from the barricade and walked forward, not worried, not hurried. Savine could hardly understand what he was doing.

Tall Hat had his doubts, too. He raised his torch. "I'm not scared o'—"

The big man darted at him, caught the swinging torch on his shoulder and shrugged it off in a shower of sparks. His fist sank into Tall Hat's side, a short, quick blow, but Savine heard the thud of it, felt the force of it. It folded Tall Hat over and left him tottering.

The big man took him by the coat and jerked him off his feet. Lifted him high, as if he was no more than a sack of rags, then flung him down on the cobbles so hard his hat bounced off.

He gave a shuddering groan, stretched out a quivering hand, and the big man calmly lifted his big boot and stomped his face into the road.

Savine stared, hardly breathing.

The big man looked up at Tall Hat's companions, brushing a few embers from his shoulder. They stood in a shocked half-circle. Five men, but none of them had moved the whole time.

"We can have him," said one, though he sounded far from certain. He licked his lips, took a hesitant step forward.

"Ah." A second man had climbed up onto the barricade. Or maybe he'd been there all along, so still Savine hadn't noticed. A stringy man with a drooping moustache. He held a loaded flatbow, something drawn on the back of the hand on the trigger. Tattooed. "*Ah*, I said." He eased towards them, pointing the bow with more intent, head of the bolt gleaming. "Don't you bastards understand fucking *ah*?"

It seemed they did. They began to retreat. The one who'd worn the hat gave a faint gurgle. One of them dragged him up, head lolling, his face a mass of black blood.

"Aye!" shouted the stringy man, lowering his flatbow as they disappeared into the sweltering night. "And don't come back!" He wiped his sweaty forehead with his tattooed hand as his companion clambered back onto the barricade. "Damn it, Bull, this wasn't part o' the plan."

Bull was an apt name for the big man. He frowned at Savine, and she cringed away until her back hit a wall. "Well," he said, wincing as he rubbed at his knuckles, "you know what happens to plans when the fighting starts."

"Fucking Burners!" snarled the bowman, loosening his string and slipping out the bolt with a practised air. "Bastards have gone mad. Just want to burn everything!"

"That's why they call 'em Burners, Sarlby." There was a woman there, too. A girl with a tough, bony face, squatting down beside Savine, all business.

"She hurt?" asked Broad.

"I think just scared, mostly." Savine felt her hand prised open, and the girl took the lenses out and offered them up. "Who could blame her for that?" Savine realised who she was. The Vallimirs' maid. What had been her name? Dinner on the hill felt like a thousand years ago. May. May Broad.

She put gentle fingertips on Savine's cheek. "What's your name?" She didn't recognise her. No surprise. Savine barely recognised herself.

"Ardee," she whispered. Her mother's name was the first she could think of, and she felt a burning pain building at the back of her nose, and gave a great snotty sob, and started to cry. She couldn't remember the last time she cried. She wasn't sure she ever had. "Thank you," she blubbered. "Thank you—"

The girl was frowning down at her chest and Savine realised her foul coat had fallen open. Ruined though it was, one of the bones poking from torn silk, there was no mistaking the quality of her corset. Only a fool could doubt this belonged to a very rich lady, with servants to get her into it. And one look in this girl's sharp eyes told Savine she was no fool.

She opened her mouth. To blurt some story. Puke some lie. But all that came out was a stuttering croak. She had nothing left.

May's eyes moved up from that ruined embroidery that had been a month of some poor woman's labour. Then she calmly pulled the coat closed over it.

"You're safe now," she said. "I'll take her inside." And she helped Savine to her feet, and towards a doorway. "Reckon she's had quite a day."

Savine clung to her and blubbed like a baby.

The Man of Action

The Steadfast Standard snapped majestically, such miraculous needlework that its white horse rampant seemed to rear upon the breeze against a sun of cloth-of-gold, the names of glorious Union victories glittering about its edge. The very flag under which Casamir the Steadfast had conquered Angland, now held perfectly straight in Corporal Tunny's gnarled fist, martial prowess distilled into a square of cloth.

There was a rousing rattle of arms and armour as the men spun towards Orso, stomped down their left heels and saluted in perfect unison. Five hundred soldiers, moving as one, sun glinting from their freshly forged equipment. A mere tenth part of his newly raised expeditionary force, fully prepared to sail north and give Stour Nightfall a resounding kick up the arse.

Orso probably shouldn't have said it himself, but it was quite a stirring spectacle.

He returned their salute with a flourish he had been perfecting in front of the mirror. He had to admit he liked wearing a uniform. It gave him the novel feeling of being a man of *action*. Furthermore, as well cut and starched as this one was, no casual observer could have suspected his paunch had been on the increase lately.

Colonel Forest grinned as he looked the soldiers over. That open, honest grin that seemed to represent the very best of the Union common man. Earthy, dependable, loyal. A stout yeoman if ever there was one, with his stocky build, and his pronounced facial scar, and his lustrous grey moustaches, and his campaign-worn fur hat.

"As fine a body of fighting men as I ever saw, Your Highness," he said. "And I've seen a few."

They had chosen to call themselves the Crown Prince's Division. Well, Orso had let them choose the name and Forest had no doubt suggested it. Or more likely insisted on it. Even so, Orso was hugely pleased by the

227

compliment. Perhaps because, for once, he felt he had done the slightest something towards deserving it.

"What d'you think, Hildi?" he asked.

"Very shiny," she said. With characteristic enterprise, she had wangled an embroidered drummer-boy's uniform to go with her battered cap and now looked quite the soldier. Why not? She had, after all, no less military experience than Orso.

"What d'you think, Gorst?" he asked.

"A fine body of men, Your Highness." Orso had to stop himself wincing. However often one heard that piping voice, one never quite got comfortable with it. "You are to be congratulated."

"Nonsense. All I did was stand here." And spend Savine's money, and smile, and develop a top-quality salute, anyway. "You're the one who did the work, Colonel Forest!"

"*Colonel* bloody Forest," muttered Tunny, shaking his head as if at unbearable affectations, while Yolk, always keen to follow his leader, gave a sneer to match.

Forest ignored them. At ignoring Tunny, as at so many things, he appeared steeped in experience. "They've all served before, Your Highness. Some fought in the North. Most fought in Styria. All I did was remind 'em how to go about the business, and that's no more than my job."

"Men can do their jobs badly but you've done yours bloody well. I'm lucky to have you." And Orso gave Forest the special smile. The one he reserved for moments of actual happiness.

The two of them had formed a winning partnership, so far. Forest provided the experience, judgement, warmth, discipline, courage, facial scarring and, of course, superb moustache. Orso supplied the sparkle, the... Well, his facial hair had always been wretched and he had no noticeable scars, so honestly the sparkle was about all. Perhaps that was what the historians would call him. The King of Sparkle. He gave a helpless snort of laughter. People could have called him worse, he supposed. Indeed, they often had.

"A king's job is not to do things well." Orso gave the slightest wince at the Styrian words, pronounced at ostentatious volume among hundreds of men who had been fighting Styrians for the last ten years—and losing. He had forgotten his mother had come to observe. She sat in her folding chair in the shade of a portable purple awning, her ladies arranged about her on the grass like the gilt frame to a masterpiece. "It is to pick the people who will do them well on his behalf."

"You sound almost impressed, Mother," said Orso, switching to Styrian himself, but at least doing it quietly. "I hadn't realised your voice could actually take that tone."

"Nonsense, Orso. You have heard me be impressed with other people on occasion."

He sighed. "True enough."

"And it is hardly as though you have done anything you could expect to impress me since you went over to solid food."

He sighed again, more deeply. "Also true enough."

"A future king has no business fighting."

"All the greats were warriors, no? Harod, Casamir, Arnault—"

The queen waved the weighty names away. "No doubt the common folk swoon over a conquering king, but it's the coupling kings who found the dynasties."

"I've spent years coupling. That's never impressed you, either."

"It's *who* you couple *with*, Orso, as you very well know. I'd much rather you were getting married." She sat back, giving him a thorough examination, tapping at the arm of her folding chair with one exquisitely manicured fingernail. "But if you *must* play soldiers in the meantime, I will admit…" And she allowed the corner of her mouth to bend by an infinitesimal fraction. "I *am* impressed."

Orso often told himself that he long ago gave up caring about his mother's opinions. The glow of satisfaction that warmed him to the roots of his hair revealed that for one of his many lies. "I suppose everyone grows up sooner or later," he said, turning away so she would not see him blush.

The queen stood, her folding chair instantly whisked away by one of her liveried footmen. "Perhaps you could help your father do it." And she turned back towards the palace, her ladies-in-waiting forming a glittering spearhead of which she was the diamond point.

"Her Majesty looked almost…pleased," muttered Tunny, lowering the Steadfast Standard and rolling the royal heirloom up with superb skill. Say what you like about the man, and people often did, but he knew his way around a flag. "And I've a feeling that's not easily done."

Orso raised his brows. "She'd rather I was getting married, apparently."

"You could marry Colonel Forest," said Tunny. "I definitely sense love blooming between you two."

"A man could do a lot worse. Forest is experienced, organised, dependable, considerably more intelligent than me yet defers to me anyway. Aside from a quim, he has every quality one could ask for in a bride."

Tunny glanced over at Forest, face reddening beneath that fine fur hat as he bellowed orders at the men. "That bloody hat of his looks like a quim."

Orso choked back a laugh. It actually did, a little. "Watch your mouth, Corporal. I may be forced to promote you."

"Anything but that." Tunny had been offered the role of sergeant major but flatly refused to consider anything above corporal. Some men are like water. No matter how high they are lifted, they always yearn to return to the appropriate level. He squinted up at the blazing sun. "Hope you've packed some warm clothes, Your Highness. Hard to imagine now, but it gets bitter up there in the North."

"It's what the place is known for, after all."

A knight herald was striding over, past the footmen busily dismantling the queen's awning. "Your Highness!" he thundered at entirely unnecessary volume, snapping his armoured heels together. "His Majesty wishes to see you *at once!*"

"At the palace?"

"At the House of Questions, in the company of Arch Lector Glokta."

Orso winced. "Can't they see I have an army to lead to glory?" He thought about that for a moment. "Or to watch Colonel Forest lead to glory?"

Tunny leaned in to mutter, "You've made glory wait twenty years. Daresay another hour won't make the difference."

"At last!" snapped the king as Orso stepped through the door, plainly very far from his usual good-humoured self.

His Eminence sat behind his desk in his wheeled chair, a blanket over his knees in spite of the heat, looking even more grim, gaunt and pale than usual, which took some doing. Orso had once seen a three-day-old plague corpse with better colour to its cheeks. Standing at Glokta's shoulder was perhaps the one man in the entire Union more hideous than he: his deputy, Superior Pike, whose entire face was obliterated by monstrous burns. Pike's expression was hard to read, but overall the mood was far from encouraging.

As was his long-established habit, Orso began with deflection. "I've got quite the busy day, Father. If you want to see me off, you—"

"You're not going to the North," growled the king.

"I'm...what?" Orso was robbed of the chance to move on to evasion and forced straight to entitled upset. "Father, I worked for this—"

"Other men work for things all the time! What makes you special?"

I'm the crown prince of the bloody Union! was on the very tip of Orso's tongue, but luckily Pike spoke first, his soft voice betraying no more emotion than his burned face.

"Your Highness, there has been an uprising in Valbeck."

Orso swallowed. "Uprising?" The word was a decidedly ugly one to use before someone of royal blood. Could Pike not have gone for something a bit more neutral, like *incident*? Even *riot* would have been preferable. Then he realised the fact that the Superior *was* using it, in front of a king, a crown prince and their Arch Lector, might be a good guide to the severity of the situation.

"It is coordinated, well organised and on a considerable scale. It would appear the workers at several mills rose up simultaneously, overpowering foremen, guards and owners."

"They're in control of these mills?"

The Arch Lector's left eye began to twitch and he dabbed away a tear. "It would appear that they are in control of the whole city. They may well have infiltrated the town watch, too. Perhaps... even the Inquisition."

"They have thrown up barricades," said Pike, "taken hostages and are issuing demands."

"Good grief." Orso sank numbly into a chair. Valbeck had grown to be one of Midderland's largest and most modern cities. *Uprising* was beginning to sound like a euphemism. This was a short step from outright revolt! "How could this *happen*?"

"A damn good question!" snapped the king, frowning towards his Arch Lector.

"The Breakers are at the heart of it," said Glokta. "And the Burners."

"Who the hell are they?" asked Orso.

A muscle was working angrily on the side of His Majesty's head. "The Breakers want to force concessions from me. The Burners want to see me and the entire nobility and government of the Union hanged so they can impose a new order, probably one on fire."

Orso swallowed again. It felt as if there was a lump in his throat he could not force down. "I take it their opinion of me is less than glowing?"

"You think your mother's a harsh critic? Wait until you hear what *these* bastards say about you."

"I have an agent in Valbeck," said Glokta. "She sent a boy back to Adua with a warning, but too late to act on, and since then... nothing. We simply have no idea of the situation inside the city."

"Chaos," growled Orso's father, clenching his fists.

"The success of these traitors will encourage other malcontents," said Glokta. "Other plots against His Majesty and His Majesty's subjects. We

231

are stretched to the limit keeping the peace. Prince Orso, yours are the only troops available."

"I will accompany you to Valbeck, Your Highness," said Pike, "to provide the full support of the Inquisition."

Orso blinked. "But what about the North? I was—"

"For pity's *sake!*" the king burst out with uncharacteristic violence, ripping open the top button of his braid-heavy jacket and dashing sweat angrily from his forehead. "Not everything is about *you*! The Arch Lector's own *daughter* is caught up in this!" He seemed to remember himself, cleared his throat self-consciously. "And many others, of course. Many sons and daughters—"

"Wait, what?" Orso struggled to supress a surge of utter horror. "Your daughter...Savine?" Though he knew full well the Arch Lector had no others. That lump in his throat had swelled so much he could scarcely speak around it.

Glokta sagged into his chair. "She was in Valbeck. Visiting one of her manufactories." His grey lips peeled back from his ruined teeth. "I have not heard from her. I do not know if she is free, or a prisoner. I do not know if she is alive, or—"

"Damn these treacherous bastards!" burst out the king, grinding one fist into his palm. "I've more than half a mind to lead the Knights of the Body out there myself!"

"It would be beneath the king's dignity." Orso stood, the legs of his chair shrieking across the tiles. "I'll go." Savine needed him. "I'll go at once." And the rest of the Union, of course, but, bloody hell, Savine needed him! "Tunny!" he roared, striding for the door. Almost a shriek, in truth. "Tell Colonel Forest we march for Valbeck immediately!"

Ugly Business

S he lay on her side, her cheek on his shoulder and both legs wrapped around one of his, pressed against him, huddled against him, burrowed into the blankets beside him.

Leo was always so warm, like having one of those lovely glowing winter logs from the old firepit in bed with her. Not long ago, she'd spent weeks bitter cold, not to mention hungry, chafed and terrified, so lying warm and safe, nicely balanced between sleeping and waking, was contentment to feel awfully thankful for in Rikke's mind. Would've been perfect, really.

If he could've just kept his mouth shut.

"She won't let me do a bloody *thing*," he was grumbling. "She treats me like . . . a puppy on a short leash!"

"Lion on a leash," she mumbled.

"It's a wonder she doesn't have me packed in a box at night."

If his mother could've packed his head in a box but left the rest of him available, it would've suited Rikke just fine, but he probably didn't want to hear that.

"All we do is prod at them," he snapped, "loiter around their supply lines, nibble little victories here and there."

"Uh," grunted Rikke, stroking absently at those nice grooves in his stomach and hoping vainly that might shush him up. No such luck.

"We need to get to *grips* with them." An uncomfortable jolt went through his shoulder as he clenched his fists. "Need to *hurt* the bastards!"

"Isn't that the point?" Rikke reluctantly opened one eye and lifted her head to peer at him through it. "Scale and Calder and Stour between 'em have more men than us. So we slow them down. Keep them split up. Keep them guessing. Every mile we draw them on, they get weaker." It was somewhat troubling that she, who'd never drawn a sword, was having to explain to him, a famous warrior, how their strategy worked. "We wait for our moment. *Your* moment." She let her head drop back onto his shoulder and wriggled into his warmth again. "Wait for your friend Prince Orso to arrive—"

He jerked up, dumping her head onto the mattress and bringing her fully and unpleasantly awake.

"Oh, yes," he sneered, "the Prince of Drunkards will totter to our rescue."

"Well, not on his own." Rikke tried to pick the sleep out of her eyes. "My father says he's bringing five thousand men with him."

"Five thousand whores, maybe. They say that's how many he's bedded."

"How old is he? Twenty-five?" Rikke screwed her face up as she went over the sums. "If he really got going at seventeen, that's eight years of fucking so...what...a couple every day? Provided none of 'em tempt him back for seconds. And he never has a day off. I mean, we all have moments when we're not in the mood. Has he got 'em queueing down the palace corridors?" She gave a snort of laughter. "His cock must be *sore*."

"Perhaps it's only four thousand," said Leo, sourly.

"More likely his reputation's run way ahead of the truth." Rikke raised one brow at Leo. "I hear that can happen with some young men."

"Perhaps Crown Prince Orso's the exception. Maybe he'll fuck the Northmen to death for us."

"Fine by me, if it gets the bastards to go home."

She tried to ease him back down beside her but he wouldn't be moved. "It'd hardly be a surprise, since he's got a Styrian degenerate for a mother."

"A Styrian what?"

Leo's lip curled like it might've at a dead dog in bed with them. "The rumour is she lies with *women*."

Rikke had never been able to understand why you'd care a shit who someone you'd never even met lay with. How few problems do you need to have before you count that among 'em? "Would've thought you'd understand. You spend most o' your time with men."

"What does that mean?"

"Well...tight-knit group, your friends, aren't they?"

Leo frowned, not quite getting all her point yet. "We've known each other for years. I grew up with Jurand and Antaup. And I met Jin in Uffrith, you know that. We're brothers-in-arms."

"And such strong arms, too!" And she squeezed one of his. "No wonder you all enjoy a wrestle."

"It's good exercise, and..." His eyes went wide and he twisted away from her. "That's disgusting!"

"Not to me." He'd some towering opinions, all right, but rarely built

234

on much. She quite liked digging at their foundations and watching 'em totter. "Can't think of anything more wholesome than all those muscular male bodies, glistening with sweat, grunting and straining and slithering around together—"

"Do you have to drag everything into the gutter?"

"I don't *have* to." She caught his shoulder and pulled him back beside her. "But it is warm down here." She tried to nuzzle up against him but he was already on to his next grievance.

"I don't blame Orso, really." As if that was doing the man quite a favour. "Stealing other men's glory is what princes are for." As if this was all about who got the glory, not who got home alive. "It's my bloody mother I blame, for letting him get away with it!" He'd have blamed his mother for letting the rain fall. "Why can't she just *trust* me?"

"Ugh," said Rikke, rolling away to stare up at the flapping tent cloth. It was plain her favourite part of the day was fully ruined. She'd no notion why he was so keen to rush into a battle he'd most likely lose. The boy had many fine features—bravery, honesty, good humour, a fine-shaped face and an even better-shaped arse, and so constantly, reliably *warm*. But imagination was not a strong point. Nor was he labouring under a low opinion of himself. Maybe losing was not a thing he could conceive of. Maybe to him, every delay was just wrong-headed shits throwing themselves in the way of his certain triumph.

"...let me off the leash, I'd show these bastards something..."

The memory floated up, as it did at least once a day, of hiding under that riverbank while Stour Nightfall laughed about what he'd do to her. She thought of Uffrith in flames, and all the good folk hurt or killed, and she clenched her fists at the usual rush of fury. No one wanted that bastard dead more than she did, but even she saw they had to be patient. Whether you waited for all the help you could get seemed like no kind of question at all.

"...I'm supposed to be her son, and she treats me like—"

Rikke puffed out her cheeks and gave a sigh that made her lips flap.

"Sorry," said Leo sulkily, "am I boring you?"

"Oh, no, no, no." She rolled her eyes towards him. "Nothing gets a girl wet like hearing a man complain about his mother."

He grinned. Say one thing for Leo, he might get sulky, but he cheered up quick. He pushed the blankets back and wriggled next to her, his hand sliding across her chest, and down her stomach, and around her backside, and onto the inside of her thigh, and giving her quite the pleasurable shiver. "What does get a girl wet?" he whispered in her ear.

"For me, it's pretty boys with too much courage and too little patience..." Seemed the morning might not be a total loss after all. She pushed her fingers into his hair and dragged his face down towards hers, straining up to kiss him, his breath a touch fierce with the overnight smell, but—

"Leo!" came a call from outside.

"Ah, shit," she hissed, head dropping back.

"There's a knight herald in the camp!" Jurand's voice, sharp with excitement.

"Bloody hell!" Leo squirmed free of Rikke despite her attempts to wrap her legs around him, jumped out of bed and started dragging his trousers on. "Might be the Closed Council!" Grinning over his shoulder as if that was just the news she'd been waiting for. "Making me lord governor!"

"Grand," grunted Rikke, upending her boot and shaking it till the chagga pellet fell out, then wedging it behind her lip.

There was quite the mood of expectation outside, half-dressed men shuffling between the tents, still chewing their breakfasts, breath smoking as they asked for news and got no answers. Everyone was drifting one way, like leaves on a current, towards a pair of gleaming wings bobbing up ahead. The helmet of a knight herald, striding through the rain-sodden camp towards the forge Lady Finree had borrowed for her headquarters.

Leo hurried after him, pulling on his cloak, while Rikke hopped along behind with Jurand, one of her socks already full of mud.

"Is your message for me?" asked Leo. "For Lord Brock?"

Maybe not everything was about him after all. The knight herald strode on up the muddy hillside without even a sideways glance, a satchel over his shoulder stamped with the golden sun of the Union.

"Might be Prince Orso's arrived with his men," said Rikke hopefully, trying to get her other boot on and follow both at once.

"I wouldn't count on it." Jurand didn't look at her, a jaw muscle working on the side of his face.

"You don't like me much, do you?"

He glanced across, surprised. "Actually, I do." And he offered her his elbow so she could stop hopping. "You're hard not to like."

"I am, aren't I?" she said, finally dragging her boot on.

"I'm just...protective." He frowned towards Leo as they set off again, still failing to get a word out of the knight herald. "We grew up together, and, well...he's nowhere near so tough as he pretends to be."

She snorted. "We did some growing up together, too, and believe me, I know."

"He doesn't have the best luck. With women."

"Maybe I'll be the exception."

"Maybe." He gave a smile that looked like it took some effort. "I just don't want to see him get hurt."

"Senior staff only," growled a soldier at the door of the forge. Rikke barged Jurand with her shoulder so he lurched into the guard's arms. While they were busy getting disentangled, she sidestepped, slipped around them and was in.

She'd never been in a council of war before but, like fucks and funerals, her first time was something of a let-down.

The forge was stuffed with people, warm and damp from their nervous breath. Leo's mother had her gloved fists planted on a table spread with maps, a litter of anxious officers clustered about her. Lords Mustred and Clensher were among 'em, two dour old noblemen of Angland who'd brought some reinforcements in the day before. Rikke wasn't sure which was which, but one had a thick grey moustache, the other whiskers all around his jaw but his top lip shaved. Like they only had one whole beard between 'em.

Rikke's father was scratching uneasily at his own silvery stubble, his War Chiefs around him. Hardbread looked concerned, as usual. Red Hat looked grim, as usual. Oxel had his usual shifty sideways squint like the knight herald was another man's sheep he was thinking of making off with. And Shivers just looked like Shivers, which was probably the most troubling of the lot.

In fact, the least worried man in the forge was the smith who owned it, who simply looked angry to have been stopped working so a bunch of fools could argue under his steadily leaking roof. But that's war for you. An ugly business that only leaves bad men better off. Why folk insisted on singing about great warriors all the time, Rikke couldn't have said. Why not sing about really good fishermen, or bakers, or roofers, or some other folk who actually left the world a better place, rather than heaping up corpses and setting fire to things? Was that behaviour to encourage?

"World's full o' mysteries, all right," she muttered to herself, and shifted her chagga pellet from one side of her mouth to the other.

"My Lady Governor!" boomed out the knight herald, painfully loud in that little space, bowing low and nearly poking Shivers' good eye out with one of the wings on his helmet. "A communication from His August Majesty!" And he whipped that satchel open, produced a scroll and shouldered through the damp press to hand it over with a showman's flourish.

Silence, then, as Finree dan Brock broke the great red seal and began to read, stony face giving nothing away. Rikke knew her letters. Had learned the bastards at great personal pain during her horrible year in Ostenhorm. But she couldn't make a thing out of these ones, the writing was so flourished and flounced.

"Well?" snapped Leo, eager voice harsh in the breathless silence.

"Has Prince Orso arrived?" growled Mustred. Or Clensher.

"He has not," she said, still reading.

"Tell me he's embarked, at least!" growled Clensher. Or maybe Mustred.

"He has not." The lady governor's jaw worked as she looked up. "Nor will he." She passed the letter to Leo, noticed for the first time that his shirt was hanging out, undone, then frowned over at Rikke, whose shirt was hanging out, too, all the buttons in the wrong holes.

Rikke looked down at the ground, chewing hard at her chagga and her face on fire. Lady Finree often spoke about forging stronger connections between the Union and the North but she doubted Rikke fucking her son was quite what she'd had in mind.

"There has been a serious uprising in Valbeck," grated out Leo's mother. "The Breakers have seized the city. There are fears it could turn into a general revolt."

Leo's eyes flickered across the paper. "The crown prince has been sent to recapture the city. Even if he succeeds... he won't be here for weeks!"

There was silence in the little forge then, but for the patter of a new shower on the roof, the plop and trickle of a leak into a bucket. Silence, while each man or woman chewed over the implications. Then everyone started shouting at once.

"By the dead," whispered Hardbread, pulling at his sparse grey hair.

"Fucking Union!" sneered Oxel. "I told you we're fools to trust 'em."

"So what?" sneered Red Hat back. "You'll kneel to Black Calder?"

Shivers just stood and looked like Shivers, which was worrying enough, and Rikke's father rubbed at the bridge of his nose and gave a weary groan.

"Is it for *this* that Angland's been near bankrupted by taxes?" fumed Mustred, or maybe Clensher.

"What's the damn point of a king who won't defend his kingdom?" bellowed Clensher. Or Mustred.

"This is disgusting! Outrageous! Unprecedented—"

"My lords, please!" Lady Finree held up her palms, trying to calm the uncalmable. "This does not help us!"

The only person who looked happy was the Young Lion, his smile growing wider and wider as it dawned on him what this meant.

Rikke puffed out her cheeks. "Reckon we'll have to save ourselves."

In the Mirror

Scale Ironhand, King of the Northmen, was at least twenty years past his best.

He'd been a great warrior, but then he'd lost his hand and had an iron one wedged onto the stump. He'd been a great War Chief, but now he was happy to follow along in the rear and eat all the spoils. Eat 'em messily, since he was missing his two front teeth as well as his hand. Clover remembered him when he'd still been a tower of brawn. Now he was a mountain of blubber, pale jowls spread over his fur collar, a tuft of grey hair sprouting from his sweat-beaded pate, his beard full of grease and his swollen cheeks full of broken veins. Two painfully skinny girls haunted his elbows with a platter and a jug and the hardest jobs in the North—making sure their king never ran out of ale.

A set of old warriors were gathered at his right side with well-polished armour but long-faded names. Scale would've called them his closest Named Men, his royal retinue, his king's bodyguard. But their main purpose was to remind him of old victories, and insist he was still the man he'd been when he had half the belly and twice the hands, in spite of all the evidence.

The firepit was banked high, the tables crammed with warriors, the stolen hall sweaty as a forge and noisy as a battle, women kicking and cursing as they shoved through the press with platters of meat. Clover sat with Wonderful at Black Calder's table, in the shadows further from the firepit. There was less gold over here, and less laughter, and less ale, but a lot more power. Scale Ironhand might wear the king's chain, but everyone who mattered knew it was his brother who made the king's choices.

Calder had an odd guest today, though. A small man in travel-worn clothes who carried no weapon but a staff he'd left leaning against the wall. As strange a thing in this hall bristling with blades as a hen playing among foxes. Clover had seen Black Calder entertain some strange, proud, grand guests. Styrians, and Union men, and dark-skinned Southerners drawn into his spider's web of schemes. But he never saw him treat anyone with as much respect as this nothing-looking little unarmed man.

"He'll be along, Master Sulfur," said Calder, laying a humble hand on the tabletop between them. "You can depend on it."

"You have never given me cause to doubt," said Sulfur. "Yet." And he gave that hand a familiar pat.

Calder swallowed and drew his hand back. "A shame your master couldn't be here."

"Oh, indeed." Sulfur smiled about at the grease-smeared, ale-spattered gathering. "He does love sophisticated conversation. But, sadly, he is detained in the West."

"Nothing serious, I hope?"

"A disagreement with two other members of our order. His brother Zacharus and his sister Cawneil have...their own ways of seeing things."

"Families, eh?" grunted Calder, frowning at his brother. "Our best friends and our worst enemies." And there was a clatter as the doors were heaved open.

Stour Nightfall swaggered in with chin hefted high and sword slung low, oozing so much scorn it was a wonder he didn't tramp through the firepit and dare the flames to burn him. The warriors at his back swept the benches with fighters' contempt as the hall fell silent. Magweer aimed a baleful glare at Clover, and Clover saluted him with a piece of half-eaten meat.

"You come *late?*" rumbled Scale, sucking the last shreds from a bone and tossing it down for his dogs to fight over. "To dine with your *king?*"

The old king and his old cunts glowered at the young heir and his young cunts, naught praiseworthy on either side but all jealous of what the others had even so. Matching groups, in many ways; Clover could almost see each warrior squaring up to his counterpart. The mean one, the handsome one, the one who hardly spoke, the one who spoke too much.

"Like looking in a mirror," he muttered.

"A mirror that makes you old," said Wonderful.

"I come whenever it *fucking* pleases me." Stour hoisted his sneer up from the king's impressive collection of stripped bones to the king's fat face. "After all...my guess was...you'd be dining...*a while.*"

The chill moment stretched a little longer, then Scale broke out in a roar of wheezy laughter and struggled with an effort to his feet, almost upending the table as he caught it with his mighty belly. "Tell me of your victories, Nephew!" And he spread his arms wide, iron hand dangling limp from the end of the withered right one.

Stour gave that wolf grin as he danced around the table. "None to sing of lately, Uncle," and he flung his arms around the king, and they clapped each other on the back with a great show of manly affection. "This Union bitch and this Dogman coward are still fighting over who can run away from me fastest."

"Ha! Keep pushing 'em, boy, keep pushing 'em! Don't give those bastards a chance to breathe!" Scale jabbed weakly with his iron hand as if it was an army, while he drained his cup with the other and held it out for more.

"He should get himself a bigger cup," murmured Clover.

"Maybe two," said Wonderful. "He could empty one while his servants filled the other. The poor girls would never have to stop pouring."

The Great Wolf was still bemoaning the lack of murder. "At this rate, they'll fall back beyond the Whiteflow and we'll win without ever drawing our swords."

Scale clapped Stour on the shoulder so hard he nearly knocked him over the table. "You're like a fighting dog, can't wait to slip the leash! So was I, once. So was I." And the King of the Northmen stared off into the firepit, eyes shining with reflected fire, and drained his cup again, and held it out again, and made the girl shrug back her long braid and dart forward with the jug. Again.

Clover took a sip from his own cup. "Don't ever let me drift along on past glories, Wonderful."

She gave a grunt. "You'd have to have some glories to do that."

"Tell me how you beat Stranger-Come-Knocking one more time!" roared Scale. He was one of those men couldn't say anything quietly. "By the dead, I wish I could've been there!" And he knocked his iron hand against the table with a clonk. "Where's that girl? Fill a cup for my heir!"

Stour sat back and flung one boot up on the table. "Well, Uncle, when I crossed the Crinna with a thousand Carls, I knew we were far outnumbered..."

Wonderful rubbed at her temples. "Must've heard this story ten times the last ten weeks."

"Aye," said Clover, "and every telling makes Stour a bigger hero. Soon he'll be beating a thousand barbarians with his hands behind his back and his sword tied to his cock."

"Warriors." Sulfur gave a heavy sigh, as if at a spell of bad weather. "It seems the Great Wolf is in no mood to discuss the future of the North tonight."

"No, Master Sulfur!" If it had been any other man, Clover would've called the note in Black Calder's voice a wheedle. "Like all storms, he'll soon blow himself out."

"Alas, I have so much other business." Sulfur's eyes shifted to Clover for a moment. Different-coloured eyes, he noticed, as they glittered in the torchlight. "Never the slightest peace, eh, Master Steepfield?"

"I reckon not," muttered Clover, no idea who this bastard was or how he knew his old name, but judging it always wise to agree with a dangerous man. And any man Black Calder feared was a dangerous man, whether he wore a sword or not. "They call me Clover these days, though."

"Calling a wolf a cow will not make him give milk. The same could be said of calling chaos order." Sulfur put aside his cup and stood, looking down at Calder. "My master appreciates that we must sometimes have a little chaos if a better order is to emerge. There can be no progress without pain, no creation without destruction. That is why he has indulged this little war of yours." He looked up as Scale roared with laughter at some new flourish of Stour's, and the warriors about them competed with each other to blast the spittiest peels of merriment. "My master loves to see the earth ploughed, from time to time."

Calder nodded. "That's all I'm trying to do."

"Provided the soil settles quickly and a new seed is sown. Otherwise how can he reap a harvest?"

"Tell him this war will be done soon," said Calder, "and the harvest richer than ever. We'll win. He'll win."

"Whoever wins, he wins. You know that. But too much chaos is bad for everyone's business." Sulfur plucked his staff from the wall. "It is often the doom of men blessed with greatness that they are cursed with short memories. Your father, for instance. I advise you to keep that pit always in your mind. The one outside Osrung." And Sulfur smiled as he turned away. A toothy little bright-eyed smile, but it seemed to Clover there was somehow a threat in it.

He leaned close to Wonderful. "Everyone serves someone, I reckon."

"Looks that way," she said as she watched Sulfur slip from the hall. "And they're usually a prick."

The moment he was gone, Calder thumped furiously at the table. "By the fucking *dead*!" He glared over at his son, still boasting to his king's great delight. "He's worse than ever and my brother only encourages him! Didn't I tell you to keep him on the right path?"

Clover helplessly spread his hands. "There's only so much even the best shepherd can do with a wilful ram, Chief."

"At this rate, he'll end up as mutton! What did Stolicus say? Never fear your enemy, but always respect him? This Brock woman's for damn sure no fool and the Dogman's for damn sure no coward."

"Reckon they're just waiting for their moment." Clover sighed. "Sooner or later, they'll be setting a trap for us."

"And at this rate, these two heroes will be blundering right into it." Calder frowned harder than ever at his son. "How did he end up with so little of me in him?"

"Never had to face hard times," said Wonderful, softly.

Clover wagged a finger at her. "There speaks the stern voice of experience. Defeats do men far more good than victories." And he reached up and scratched gently at his scar. "Best gift I was ever given. Taught me humility."

"Humility," scoffed Calder. "Can't think of a man with a higher opinion of himself than you."

Clover raised his cup to Magweer, who'd picked him out for another dose of glaring as Stour's manly legend reached its climax. "The world's brimming with folk keen to break me down. Don't see any reason to do their work for 'em."

"You don't see any reason to do any work at all."

There was no point denying it. Luckily for Clover, the King of the Northmen chose that moment to struggle up, raising his iron hand for silence.

"Here comes the wisdom," murmured Black Calder, without much relish.

"My father, Bethod!" Scale roared at the gathering, swaying from good ale and bad knees. "Made himself King of the Northmen! He built cities, and bound them with roads. He forced the clans together, and carved out a nation where there was none before." No mention of the thirty years of bloodshed that had got it done. But that's the nice thing about looking backwards. You can pick out the bits that suit your story and toss the unhappy truths to the wind.

Scale was frowning down into the firepit now. "My father was betrayed. My father was struck down! His kingdom torn up like meat between greedy dogs." His dewy eyes rolled up, and he pointed to Stour with his good hand. "But we'll put right the wrongs of the past. We'll finish the Dogman's fucking Protectorate! We'll drive the bloody Union out of the North! Stour Nightfall, my nephew and my heir, will rule supreme from the Whiteflow to the Crinna and beyond!" And he held up his cup, ale slopping over the rim and spattering down his front. "Bethod's dream lives on in his grandson! The Great Wolf!"

And all raised their drinks and competed with each other to roar out Stour's name the loudest, and Clover and Wonderful raised theirs just as high as anyone else.

"Still say he's a prick," whispered Clover, smiling wide.

"More so with each day," forced Wonderful through clenched teeth, and they tapped their cups together and took a swallow, because Clover had never worried much over what he drank to, as long as he drank.

Calder didn't join the toast. Just frowned at his brother as he sagged back down on his bench and bellowed for more ale. "Some men never learn," he murmured.

"We all learn." Clover watched those old warriors and those young, and ever so gently scratched at his scar. "Just some of us have to learn hard."

A Deal

"You promised me, Gunnar." Liddy's voice came muffled through the flimsy wall, but easily understood. "You promised me you'd stay out of trouble."

"I've tried, Liddy. I haven't looked for it, it's just... it's found us out."

"Trouble has a habit of finding you out."

Savine looked across the little room at May, light from outside the ill-fitting window catching her clenched jaw, head turned away from her parents' voices as if to pretend she could not hear them.

"I'm just trying to get from one day to the next," came Gunnar's voice. "Trying to keep things together."

Keeping things together was no easy task in Valbeck. The riots might mostly have stopped but the heat, and the anger, and the fear hung over the city thick as the vapours had when the furnaces were still lit. Fear of violence. Fear of hunger. Fear of what would happen when the authorities returned. Fear that they might not. Who was in charge depended on who you asked, which part of town you were in, whether it was day or night. If there was any plan in all this madness, all this destruction, Savine could not see it. No one was safe in Valbeck now. Perhaps no one ever truly was. Perhaps safety was a lie people told themselves so they could carry on.

She closed her eyes, and thought of the feeling as she stabbed that squinting man through the chest. As she ran the one with the cap through the back. A slight pressure in her palm. A slight tugging at the grip of the sword. So shockingly easy, to kill a man. She told herself they had given her no choice. And yet she saw their faces whenever she closed her eyes, and felt her breath coming fast, the sweat prickling, her heart thumping the way it had then, rubbing over and over at her itchy, greasy neck with her fingertips.

"So you're a Breaker now?" came Liddy's voice through the wall.

"Malmer's doing the best he can for folk so I'm doing the best I can for him. Stand on the barricades. Hand some food out. I'm not a soldier no more. I'm not a herder no more. What should I be?"

"My husband. May's father."

"I know. That's all that matters, but... what should I do?" It was strange to hear that wheedling, almost tearful note in the voice of a man Savine knew to be so very dangerous. "I can't just sit and do nothing, can I, while people are getting hurt?"

There was no weakness in Liddy's voice. Her strength amazed Savine, the way she kept going, working, smiling, making the best of this nightmare. "It's a fine line, Gunnar, between helping people and hurting 'em. You're prone to wander all over it."

"I'm trying to do the right thing, it's just... the right thing ain't always easy to know." And their voices dropped to a soft burble, lost as someone started shouting outside. A fight, maybe. Savine shrank back until it drifted off down the street and was gone.

She licked her lips as the silence pressed in on her. She did not want to speak. But it was better than seeing those faces again. "My parents used to argue, sometimes."

May's eyes met hers. "What about?"

"My father's work. My mother's drinking. Me. I was always their favourite argument." Were they arguing about her even now? Savine looked down at the cheap boards, full of splits and splinters. It was better not to think about her old life. Better to pretend to be a new person, who belonged where she was. Who knew she was lucky to be here.

Liddy had given her a dress, if you could call it that. A shapeless bag of coarse cloth, carefully mended and smelling of cheap soap, and she was grateful for it. Gunnar had found her a mattress, or some scratchy sacking that the straw poked through. Savine had no doubt it swarmed with lice, and she was grateful for it. She shared a room with May no bigger than a cupboard in her house in Adua, with laths showing through the cracked plaster and a bloom of mould about the flaking window frame. She scarcely ever had a moment to herself, but she was grateful for that, too. When she was alone, the things she had seen and done the day of the uprising rushed into her mind, like filthy water into a holed boat, and dragged her down so quickly she felt she was drowning.

She had thought of trying to get out of the city, but the truth was she scarcely had the courage to look out of the window, let alone to risk the streets again. She found she had a great deal less courage altogether than she had smugly supposed while blackmailing investors, or choosing a wig, or pronouncing social death sentences in the salons of Adua. She had always reckoned herself such a gambler. No more audacious woman in the Union. Now she realised the games had always been rigged in her favour. She never had to gamble with her life before, and the stakes had risen suddenly far too high for her taste.

They had a candle the first few nights but now it was gone, and the only light came from distant fires, always burning somewhere in the city. Everything was running out. The shops had been looted, the rich houses stripped back to the rafters. The Breakers brought some food around, but every day there was less.

She had always known life was hard in these slums, but if she had thought about it at all, she had pictured a romantic version. A version that was easy to live with. Pretty children, giggling as they frolicked in the gutters. Old women cackling as they boiled bones in a pot. Strapping men slapping one another on the back, singing good old work songs in harmony as they sat around a fire made from their last sticks of furniture. Oh, the sisterhood, the spirit, the nobility of poverty!

It turned out there was nothing romantic about shitting in a bucket while someone else watched. Nothing spirited about hoarding the bones from the chicken for tomorrow's dinner. Nothing sisterly about the women who tore at each other over scraps scavenged on the great rubbish heaps. Nothing noble in the cramps you got from rotten water at the pump, or the lice you picked from your armpits, or being endlessly cold, endlessly hungry, endlessly scared.

And yet living this way did not make Savine sorry for the people who were forced to do it every day. Who did it in the many buildings just like this one she profited from all across the Union. It only made her desperate never to live this way herself again. Perhaps that made her selfish. Wicked. Evil, even. While she fled whimpering through the city on the day of the uprising, she had sworn to a God she did not believe in that she would be good, if it meant she could live.

Now she was happy to be evil, if it meant she could be clean.

"You were in Colonel Vallimir's house," said May. Savine stared at her, caught off balance and failing to hide it, the constant nagging ache of fear turned suddenly, terribly sharp.

"What?" she croaked.

"The night before the uprising." May could not have looked calmer. "I served you jelly."

Savine's eyes slunk to the door. But there was no way out of this room without going through the other. Where a man she had seen stomp

247

another man's head into the road was arguing with his wife. "Horrible jelly," she muttered.

"I was trying to work out how much your dress cost," said May. Far more than this room. Probably more than this whole building. "Your hair was different." She glanced up at the mousy fuzz starting to grow back on Savine's scalp. "A wig?"

"Lots of us wear them. In Adua." So she knew who Savine was. She had always known. But she had not told. Savine took a deep breath, trying not to let the fear show. Trying to think. The way she used to in a meeting with partners. A negotiation with rivals.

May nodded slowly. As if she guessed Savine's thoughts. "Beautiful dresses. Horrible jellies. Different world, isn't it? You asked me what I thought about the city."

"You were...very honest."

"Little too honest for my own good, I expect. Always been a problem of mine. You stood up for me, though. I listened at the keyhole, and you stood up for me."

Savine cleared her throat. "Is that why you took me in?"

"Wish I could say yes." May sat forward, thin hands dangling over her knees. "But that wouldn't be entirely honest. Fact is, Vallimir's whole house was buzzing with news of your visit. Everyone desperate to get a look at you. I know who you are, my lady."

Savine twitched. "You don't have to call me that."

"What should I call you? Savine?"

Savine flinched. "Best for both of us if you don't call me that, either."

May lowered her voice to a whisper. "Lady Glokta, then?"

Savine grimaced. "Best not to even think the name." There was a long silence while they looked at each other. Next door, someone had started singing. Always happy songs, because there was misery enough here without singing up more. "Might I ask...whether you're thinking of telling anyone?"

May sat back. "My father thinks you're just some waif got lost. My mother guesses you're somebody, but she'd never guess who. Best we keep it that way. If news got out..." She left that hanging. It was nicely judged. There really was no need to say more. Savine remembered the crowd of men in her mill, all looking at her. The mob. The hate in their faces.

She carefully licked her lips. "I would...appreciate your discretion. It would put me... *very* much in your debt."

"Oh, I'm counting on it."

Savine turned up the hem of her dress, heartbeat thud, thud, thudding in her ears, and dug down inside the fraying seam with a finger, hooking out the earrings she had been wearing the day of the uprising. First one, then the other, the unfamiliar gleam of gold in the shadows.

"Take these." Her voice was far too eager for a negotiator of her experience. "They're gold with—"

"Don't think they'd go with my ensemble." May's eyes flicked down to her own threadbare dress, then back up to Savine. "You keep 'em."

Silence stretched out. Clearly May had planned this. Waited for her moment and already set her price.

"What is it you want?" asked Savine.

"I want my family taken care of. When this is over, there'll be hell to pay."

Savine closed her hand around the earrings and let it drop. "I expect so."

"I want no trouble with the Inquisition. A full pardon for my father. I want you to find somewhere for us to live, good jobs for my parents. That's all I want. For you to keep us safe. The way we've kept you safe." May held her eye for a long time. Trying to judge whether she could be trusted. Just as Savine would have, in her worn-out shoes. "Can you do that?"

A refreshing change, to go into a negotiation holding none of the cards. "I think that is the very least I could do," said Savine.

May spat in her palm and offered it out. The room was so small, she barely had to lean forward. "Deal, then?"

"Deal."

And they shook.

The New Monument

"**D**o you know how many peasant labourers died building King Casamir's roads?" asked Risinau.

He shaded his eyes against the angry sun to look up at the monument that dominated Casamir's Square. Or its remains, anyway. All that was left on the eight-stride-high pedestal, cobwebbed with wobbly scaffolding, were a pair of enormous boots sheared off at the calf. Aropella's famous statue of the legendary king himself, who'd defeated the Northmen and added Angland to the Union, lay in scarred chunks on the cobbles, daubed with messy slogans. A gleeful urchin was trying to prise His Majesty's nose off with a crowbar.

Vick only broke a silence when she knew she could improve on it. Risinau was the sort of man who'd soon answer his own questions.

"Thousands! Buried in the loam of Midderland in unmarked pits beside the roadways. And yet Casamir is remembered as a hero. A great king. And all those marvellous roads. What a gift to posterity." Risinau gave a snort of contempt. "How often have I walked through this square and gazed up at this paean to a tyrant, this symbol of oppression?"

"No doubt it's a stain on the Union's past." Risinau turned somewhat reluctantly to Malmer, who stood behind them with Gunnar Broad looming at his shoulder. "But it's the present that's worrying me."

Most of the Breakers still had the fervour of true believers, or at least pretended to, but Broad pushed his lenses up and frowned at the ruined monument as if he was harbouring some doubts. What happened when the rest began to doubt was anyone's guess. Risinau didn't seem worried, though. He was fixed on higher things.

"And only look at what we have achieved today, brothers!" He clapped Malmer and Broad on their shoulders as if he'd fold them in a great hug. "We have cast Casamir down! In his place we shall raise a new monument to the workers who died for his vainglory!"

Vick wondered how many workers would be dying for Risinau's vainglory. No small number was her guess. Casting down a king two centuries dead was one thing. The one currently on the throne might raise stiffer objections. She was starting to think the ex-Superior was at least half-mad. But then sanity was a rare commodity in Valbeck lately, and didn't look to be coming back into fashion any time soon.

Practicals were always loitering around Risinau like the dogs around the city's baking rubbish. They'd put aside the black and taken off the masks, but a sharp eye could still pick out the telltale tan marks around the mouth. They were swarming in the streets near the House of Questions, optimistically renamed the House of Liberty, hunting for anyone disloyal. Or perhaps for anyone loyal. Loyalty had become quite the fluid concept.

The uprising had changed some things, but others seemed wearily familiar. The workers were still working, the Practicals were still watching, the big hats might have moved around, but the men wearing them were still lecturing everyone else on the way things should be while doing none of the work themselves.

Some Great Change.

"Ever since its founding by that charlatan Bayaz, the Union was always built on the backs of the common folk," Risinau was spouting. "The coming of the machines, the ever-swelling avarice of investors, the raising up of money as our god and the banks its temples, these are only the latest, bleakest appendices to our sorry history. We must dig new theoretical foundations for the nation, my friends!"

Malmer made another effort at hauling him down to earth. "Honestly, I'm more worried over feeding folk. One of the big granaries got burned that first day. Another's empty. And this heat's not helping. Few o' the pumps in the old town are already running dry. The water from some of the others I wouldn't give to a dog—"

"The mind needs nourishment, too, brother." Risinau waved away a fly, the only things prospering in the stifling city, then grinned at Vick. "No doubt Sibalt told you that."

If Sibalt had told her that, she'd likely have broken his nose. It was the sort of shit only someone who's never starved could serve up.

"He was a fine man." Risinau struck his fist against his heart. "I miss him as one might miss a part of oneself. I think... that must be why I so enjoy conversing with you, sister. It is as close as I can come, now, to talking to him."

Vick rarely allowed herself the luxury of not liking people. No more often than the luxury of liking them. Either one could get you killed.

But she was starting to truly despise Risinau. He was vain as a peacock, selfish as a toddler, and for all his high-flown language, she was starting to suspect he was a fool. Truly clever things are said with short words. Long ones are used to hide stupidity. She could see no way this fat dreamer could have organised this uprising alone. Someone a great deal more formidable had done the heavy lifting. And Vick wanted very much to know who. So she nodded along to his nonsense as though she'd never heard such profound revelations.

"I arrested him for organising here," said Risinau, gazing into the distance. "Twenty years ago, just after I joined the Inquisition, and the foundations of the first mills were being laid in Valbeck. We both were young men, then. Idealistic men. I arrested him, but in the end, I could only agree with him. That the workers would be ground down." Risinau gave a heavy sigh, the plump hand on his plump gut rising and falling with his breath. "I released him. To be my informant, I thought. I told myself that I had turned him, but the truth was...he turned me. We turned each other, maybe. Just the two of us, talking late into the night about the blows we would strike for the common man! Just the two of us...and the Weaver."

Vick frowned. "Aren't you the Weaver?"

"A title I borrowed from a better man," mused Risinau, before his fickle attention was snatched away. "We should draw up a manifesto, don't you think? Demand a workers' representative on the Closed Council!" He had that gleam in his eye again, as though he was gazing off towards a better tomorrow. "Sibalt would have loved that idea..."

"Look, brother." Malmer made one more desperate effort at waking the dreamer, stepping in close, making Risinau's Practicals bristle. "I knew Sibalt, too, and he was a good man, but he's dead. There's lots of good living folk in need. People are hungry, people are sick, people are scared." He dropped his voice. "I'll be honest, *I'm* bloody scared."

"You don't have to be! No one does. We've stopped the riots, haven't we?"

"In daylight. But there have been beatings. Hangings, even. And not just owners. Foreigners. Servants. Folk are taking the chance to settle scores. To just grab whatever they want. We need order."

"And we will have it, brother! Some of the workers have been so long oppressed they were sure to be carried away with their new freedom. But our prisoners are safe in the House of Questions—of Liberty, I should say, the House of *Liberty*. The mayor, the commander of the city watch, various leading citizens, by which I mean the most greedy and debased—"

"What about Savine dan Glokta?" asked Malmer. "I heard she was in the city."

"She was." Risinau gave a shudder of distaste. "A most acid, arrogant and impolite young woman. The exploitative avarice of the modern age, personified. Scarcely to be preferred to her father as a dining companion."

"It's not her manners that interest me, it's what she could buy us."

"It would appear she slipped through our fingers. The day of the uprising was rather chaotic, as I say, even more so than expected..."

Broad gave Malmer a worried glance over his lenses. "Let's hope Judge doesn't have her."

Vick felt a surge of worry even above the usual. "Why would Judge have her?"

"The Burners took charge of a big chunk of the old town," said Broad. "We had to put barricades up. They aren't too picky over who they hurt."

"We've no notion what's going on over there," said Malmer, "but they've taken hostages. I hear Judge set herself up in the Courthouse—"

"Where else would Judge take up residence?" Risinau gave a little titter, but no one joined him.

"She says she's going to start trying her prisoners for crimes against the people."

Vick felt the horror creeping up her throat. "How many does she have?"

"Two hundred?" Malmer gave a hopeless shrug. "Three? Some owners, some rich folk, but plenty of poor folk, too. Collaborators, she's calling 'em. Anyone ain't zealous enough for her taste. And her taste is for the very zealous."

"We have to get those prisoners," said Vick. "If we're ever going to negotiate—"

"Judge has never been the most reasonable." Risinau shrugged as though all this was a natural disaster in which he was entirely helpless. "Since the uprising, she has turned positively *caustic*."

"Don't the Burners answer to you?"

"Well...they're unpredictable people. Fiery. That's why they call them Burners, I suppose!" He snorted up another a little titter, then, when he saw Vick had never looked less like laughing, cleared his throat and went on. "I suppose I could ask for her prisoners..."

"Or you could send me to ask," she said, catching his eye and holding it. "That's what Sibalt would've done. We need you to work on what really matters. Our manifesto. Our principles. Let me talk to Judge."

Risinau liked that. His little eyes twinkled at the thought of paragraphs of neat script. Of high-minded declarations. Of rights and freedoms.

"Sister, I begin to see why Sibalt thought so highly of you. Take some men along."

"Definitely." From what she'd seen of Judge, Vick thought she'd better take a lot of men and those ready for violence. As luck had it, her first pick was close by.

"Brother Gunnar?" She glanced down at the tattoo on Broad's fist. "I've a feeling you could find a few men who know how to fight."

He frowned at her over his lenses. "Made a promise to my wife I wouldn't take any risks."

"The bigger risk is if we *don't* do it. If the Arch Lector's only daughter gets hurt, His Eminence won't rest until every one of us is dangling." She looked over at Risinau, explaining to his unmasked Practicals how he wanted his new monument to look, living in a dream that was apt to become everyone's nightmare. "At this rate, his new monument will be our tomb."

All Equal

The Burners ruled here, and it showed.

There were houses plundered, their broken doors dangling from twisted hinges. There were houses burned out, their windows yawning empty, the fire-blackened brickwork of a fallen chimney stack left in pieces across the sun-baked mud of the roadway. Rubble and glass were scattered, torn clothes and broken furniture flung around as if a great wind had ripped through the neighbourhood. The place stank, worse the further they went. Stank of rot and piss and charred wood and stale smoke, all cooking in the sticky heat.

Sarlby held his flatbow tight, hard eyes flicking between the doorways. "Weren't many rich folk around here before the uprising."

"Weren't any," said Broad.

"Got robbed and burned out anyway."

"Poor folk never feel comfortable around the rich. Given the choice, they'd much rather rob other poor folk."

Vick turned to hiss over her shoulder. "Keep up. Keep together."

"Can't say I care much for taking orders from a woman," grumbled Sarlby, though he took 'em anyway.

"This one seems to know what she's doing," said Broad. "More'n I can say for most of the officers in Styria."

"You've a point there."

"Looking back at the last five years, truth is I make shit decisions. These days I tend to do what the women tell me and assume it's for the best. Liddy says build a barricade, I build one. May says take in the girl came over it, I take her in."

"The one with the clipped head? She's living with you?"

"Ardee's her name, and she can't do a damn thing. Liddy asked her to help cook and she looked at the pot like she never saw one before." Broad puffed out his cheeks. "But May's taken a liking to her, so she stays."

"Hard times, I guess," said Sarlby. "Everyone's got to do what they can."

"Hard times," echoed Broad. "When do they get softer? That's the question."

All felt far too quiet. He saw a figure lurking in an alleyway, a face at a window quickly vanished, a couple fighting over a bone who scurried away as they came close. Someone had been busy with a paintbrush, there were slogans smeared and spattered everywhere. Painted across whole terraces in letters three strides high. Scrawled across front doors in letters tiny as in a book.

"What do they say?" asked Sarlby.

Broad pushed his lenses up his sweaty nose and squinted so he could spell them out. "Fuck the king. Fuck the queen. Fuck them all. Rise up. Take what's yours. That type o' thing."

"Might steal your clothes," muttered Sarlby, shaking his head, "but they'll leave you with a fine slogan. Fucking Burners. Just another kind of arsehole."

"That's politics for you," grunted Broad. "Arseholes digging up excuses to be arseholes."

"High ideals and reality are like oil and water," muttered Vick. "They don't mix well." She squatted at a corner, beckoning them over. "Quiet now. We're here."

Valbeck's Courthouse had been a grand building, stately steps of coloured marble with stately columns at the top. Someone had been on the roof and torn some copper from the dome, a spider's web of rafters showing on one side. The big new bank next door must've been even grander than the Courthouse not long ago. Now it was just a burned-out shell. Ashes chased each other around Broad's boots in little swirls as they crossed the empty square in front.

"Someone tried to hold 'em off here," he said as they eased up the steps. The doors were battered, one half-torn from its hinges and hanging loose.

"Let's hope we do better," said Sarlby, fingering his bow.

A pair of statues flanked the entrance. Impossibly stately ladies in noble poses no person ever struck, one holding a book and a sword and the other a broken chain. Justice and freedom, Broad reckoned. The Burners had smashed Freedom's head off and put a dead cow's where it used to be, flies crawling at the glassy eyes, dried blood in streaks down the hacked marble. Justice had a great red smile daubed over her frown, and *We'll give you fucking justice* painted in drippy letters across her chest.

Vick strode between them. "Some sense of humour, these Burners."

"Oh, aye," said Broad. "They're a hoot."

The door of the great courtroom wasn't guarded, but the public benches were scattered with Burners. Or perhaps they were just thieves, pimps, gamblers and drunks. Hard to tell the difference. Some hooted and jeered, shook their fists. Others were passed-out, surrounded by empty bottles. A couple had made a nest from some old curtains and the slurping sound of their hungry kissing echoed about the chamber. A dark-skinned Kantic was huffing so hard on a husk-pipe, Broad wondered if he was trying to replace the Valbeck vapours single-handed. Flies buzzed in the soupy heat and the place stank of unwashed bodies. Someone had daubed a childish cock across the mosaic floor in red paint, but rain had come through the hole in the dome and washed half of it into a rusty puddle.

Judge sat up on high in the judge's box, the lunatic ringleader of this carnival of fools, a judge's four-cornered black hat perched on her riot of red hair. She'd wreathed herself in stolen jewels: fingers crusted with rings and one arm dripping with bracelets, guildsmen's chains and strings of pearls and ladies' necklaces in a tawdry tangle across her battered breast-plate. She had one long, thin leg slung lazily over the arm of the gilded chair, tattooed writing scrawled blue around and around her bare white thigh. The sight of that leg gave Broad a guilty tickle, deep inside. The same one he got when he felt violence coming.

The dock held a bony old prisoner, hands tied behind his back, wispy hair stiffened with blood, chin covered with white stubble. The two guards by him wore clown's motley but the swords they carried were no joke.

"Ricter dan Vallimir!" sneered Judge. "Quite apart from anything else, you stand accused of having a fucking 'dan' in your name—"

"Guilty!" There were ten whores in the jury box, eight women and two boys, plus a thickset man in an apron who looked decidedly puzzled to be there. One of the whores had leaped up, night bell tinkling around her neck, painted face twisted in a mad snarl. "Shitting guilty!"

"Ladies of the jury!" Judge whacked at her desk for order with a hatchet, sending splinters flying. "How many times? *Fucking* silence till I'm done with the charges!"

"I reject this court," growled Vallimir, puffing up his chest. "I denounce it!" Someone on the public benches flung rotten fruit at him. It missed, burst against the far wall, spraying slime across the fine old panelling. "You scum have no authority over me!"

"Wrong!" shrieked Judge. "Show him our credentials!"

One of the men in motley clubbed Vallimir across the head and knocked him gasping against the rail. The other dragged him up again, blood from a fresh cut streaking his face.

Judge shook her ring-covered fist at him. "We have the authority of the *fist*! We have the authority of *sharpened metal*! We have the authority of *force*, you blubbing cunt, which is the only real authority there is." Some light cheering from the few members of the audience still conscious. "You should know that. You were a soldier. Counsel for the defence? Where's that fucker Randock?"

A man rose trembling from behind a table covered with ash, empty bottles and a flyblown chicken carcass. He was stripped naked apart from a pair of broken lenses clinging to his broken nose, hands clasped defensively around his fruits, his back a mass of purple bruises. "No defence, your honour," he gabbled out, "what defence could there be?" And he gave a hysterical little titter and shrank back into his broken chair which rocked on three legs and nearly dumped him on the floor, much to the amusement of the jury.

Judge wasn't laughing. She'd caught sight of Vick and her Breakers as they filtered through the door and spread out around the public benches. Her black eyes seemed to linger on Broad and made that guilty tickle spread all over him. He told himself she was lethal as a scorpion, but that didn't help. Just the opposite.

"I don't remember calling witnesses," she said, lip curling. "I might have to find you lot in contempt."

"That's one word for it," said Vick, glancing around. "Risinau sent us. He wants your prisoners."

Judge reached for a bottle and took a long pull. Seeing folk drink always made Broad thirsty, but there was something about the way she wrapped her tongue around the glass neck made him especially want to be in her place. Or maybe it was the bottle's place he wanted.

Judge narrowed her eyes at Vick. "If Risinau wants a favour, he should've come himself."

"He sent me."

"Should I be scared?" The Burners were waking up to the new arrivals now, staring blearily over, hands creeping towards weapons.

Vick didn't step forward, didn't step back. "Not if you give me the prisoners."

"My prisoners have charges to answer, sister, but don't worry!" Judge waved towards the jury. "They deliberate like lightning, these bitches. Sometimes I have to stop 'em giving the verdict before I've even named the accused! If they were in charge in Adua, we'd soon have the case backlog cleared and every lawyer out of work."

"They'd be selling their arses in the gutter!" squealed one of the whores, to gales of laughter from her fellow jury members, and the naked lawyer flinched, and looked down at his feet.

Judge leaned forward, smile turning to a snarl. "We didn't throw down our masters just to raise up another! Far as I can see, Risinau's setting himself up like an owner above his workers, like a king above his subjects, like—"

"A judge above her jury?" offered Vick.

"Ouch!" Judge pushed out her lips in a pantomime of upset. "Cut with my own razor, you cunning fucker." She leaned from her box to shriek at the tiny clerk's desk below, where a bent old beggar-woman was sitting. "Strike that from the record!"

"Can't write anyway," muttered the beggar, and went back to drawing scribbles in the ledgers.

"I get it." Vick stepped forward. "You want to see someone pay. No doubt there's plenty to pay for." Broad didn't know how she could stay so cool with all this sweltering madness around her. "No one wants to see them pay more than me. But we've a city full of people to think about. We need something to bargain with."

It was a good effort. Very calm. Very reasonable. But Broad didn't reckon this was the place for calm or reason. Strip it all back, it's the authority of the fist that counts. Judge was right about that, and Broad knew it better than anyone. Beside him, Sarlby eased the dowel from the trigger of his flatbow.

Judge slowly stood, clenched fists on her scarred desk, bony shoulders hunched around her neck, stolen chains swinging. "Oh, I *see*. You're going to march my prisoners up to our oppressors and swap 'em for a better world. Just you and your honeyed tongue." She stuck out her tongue and made the pointed end wiggle in a way Broad found disgusting and strangely exciting both at once. She was trouble made flesh. Everything he'd sworn he was done with. Felt he was breaking his word just looking at her. And he couldn't take his eyes off her.

"*Please*," she spat. "You can't buy freedom." And she snatched up her hatchet and hacked at the desktop, making everyone jump. "You have to *cut* it out of them! You have to *burn the bastards*, then dig through their ashes for it! Look at you sorry fuckers. A crowd o' cowards, playing at change. Someone get these fools out o' my sight."

"Your honour!" One of the motley clowns stepped towards Vick. "She says out you go, so—" He was cut off in a squawk as Broad caught him by the neck and flung him across the room. He crashed into the witness box, staving in the panelling with the side of his head and going down in a tangle of limbs and splinters, his sword clattering away across the floor.

One of those long, silent moments, then. Broad heard some hard breaths behind, the scrape as men stood, the rattle as Sarlby brought his bow to his shoulder, the soft ring of steel as weapons were drawn. Broad unhooked the lenses from his ears, folded them, slid them into his coat pocket. Ready to let go. Always ready.

"Oooooooooh." Judge's throaty voice had gone all purry-soft, and even though she was just a sparkly blur now, Broad knew she was staring straight at him. "*You* I like. You've got a devil in you. Takes one to know one, eh?"

Felt like Broad stood at a precipice, and all it would take was a nudge to tip him over. His voice seemed to come from a long way off. Hardly sounded like his at all. "I don't want to hurt no one—"

" 'Course you fucking do! It's written all over you. 'Cause you're not much at anything else, are you? But at hurting people you're the best! Don't apologise for it! Don't snuff your candle, bad man, let it *burn*! You belong with us. You belong with *me*. Don't want to hurt anyone?" She clicked her tongue. "Your mouth says you don't but your fists say you do."

Then Broad felt a hand on his shoulder. Gentle. But firm. "We just want the prisoners." Vick's voice. Solid as a wall. "Then no one gets hurt."

That wonderful, awful moment stretched out just a little longer. Then Judge slumped back into her seat, stuck out her tongue and blew a long fart. "You're one o' those stubborn bitches, aren't you? Once you've latched your teeth into something, no amount o' beating will get you off. You know why they call me Judge?"

"Can't say I do," said Vick.

"Used to settle the disputes among the whores, down on the docks in Keln. Judge who had the right of it. Judge what was fair. Those girls can dispute fucking anything, believe me. And in that game, well, sometimes you've got to find a compromise. We're all on the same side, aren't we, after all? All seeking a better world? A world where we're all equal?"

"That's right," said Vick, her hand still on Broad's prickling shoulder. "All equal."

"Even if our methods are different, meaning mine might fucking work and yours most assuredly fucking won't." Judge gave a generous wave of her hand, ring-covered fingers twirling. "Take the prisoners. But if you think you're getting anything for 'em from Old Sticks, I reckon you'll learn a bitter lesson. Warden of the court?"

A man stepped forward and planted his gilded halberd on the tiles

260

with a bang, smiling hugely, stark naked apart from a filthy sock over his fruits. "Your fucking honour?"

"Conduct these worthies to the yard where the majority of our prisoners are taking their ease. And mind your foul mouth, you rogue, you, our guests have delicate sensibilities." She waved Vallimir away. "Take him down and give him into the custody of the Breakers, the lucky fucker. The fucky lucker. Ha! Case dismissed."

No more violence today, then. Broad wasn't sure whether it was relief or disappointment he felt as he fumbled his lenses back on to see Judge pointing down at him, lips split in a mad smile. "As for *you*, you beautiful bastard, you get tired o' pretending, my arms are *always* open." She whipped her hat off and tossed it spinning at the Kantic smoker. "Don't hog that pipe, you shit! Stoke it up and give me a suck."

Broad stood staring at her a moment longer, pulse still thudding in his skull, then let Vick steer him after the warden's hairy buttocks and out of the courtroom. The jeers of the jury followed him but they were half-hearted. It seemed, for now, the Burners had drunk their fill of justice.

He thought he could hear the creaking of rigging as he followed Vick down the shadowy steps behind the courtroom. The sound he'd heard when he looked up at the billowing sails on the voyage to Styria. But there was no reason for that much wood and rope behind a courthouse.

"Bloody hell," whispered Sarlby as they stepped out into the light.

Across the cobbled yard, between the broken windows to either side, the Burners had set up a dozen great beams, stolen from some half-built mill, maybe. From those beams, at neat intervals, bodies hung. Might've been a hundred. Might've been more. Swaying just a little with the breeze. There were men and women. There were young and old.

All equal now, all right.

"Bloody hell," whispered Sarlby again.

None of the other Breakers said a word. Vick stood staring. Broad stood staring. High ideals, like the ones that'd led him to Styria. They surely can take you to some dark places.

"There's a few haven't been tried yet, down in the cells." The warden sniffed and adjusted his dirty sock. "Guess you can have them, too."

Young Men's Folly

"**P**rince Orso isn't coming," said Leo, stomping up the crumbling stairway after his mother with the Dogman behind him. "We have to *fight*."

Her only reply was a frustrated sigh as she stepped onto the moss-speckled roof of the tower. From the top there was a fine view of the valley below the ruined holdfast, the road threading along its bottom and the high fell on the far side, crowned by red bracken. Off to the west, the road met a fast-flowing stream and crossed it by an ancient-looking bridge. There must've been a village beyond, the houses out of sight but the smoke from their chimneys faintly smudging the sky.

Cries drifted over as the wind picked up. Thousands of men, hundreds of horses, dozens of wagons trickling down the road between the two hills and over the bridge in a glittering ribbon. The army of Angland pulling back steadily to the south and west. Just as it had been for weeks.

"Mustred and Clensher brought two thousand men from Angland. We won't get any more." Leo stepped up next to his mother, planting his fists on the crumbling parapet. "Hold off now...we'll look like *cowards*."

His mother gave a dry little laugh. "The one advantage of being a woman in command of an army is that you don't have to worry about looking cowardly. Everyone expects it."

"We'll bloody *be* cowards!"

The Dogman snorted. "Your mother was a prisoner of Black Dow, and faced him down, and didn't only talk her own way free but saved sixty men besides. I'll hear her given no lessons in courage, boy. There's a world o' difference between being scared to fight and waiting till you can win."

"As long as you stop waiting!" Leo waved off in a direction he hoped was south-west, past the bridge towards Angland. The direction the Union men were retreating. Always retreating. "We're no more than eighty miles

262

from the border, and if we're pushed all the way to the Whiteflow we'll never push back. The Protectorate will be *finished*."

He might've hoped for some support from the Dogman. His bloody Protectorate, wasn't it? And he'd stood beside the Bloody-Nine, the greatest champion the world ever saw, who won eleven duels and claimed the crown of the North in the Circle!

But the old Northman only frowned into the valley, and thoughtfully rubbed at his pointed jaw, and quietly said, "Well, you have to be realistic. Naught lasts for ever."

"I understand the stakes," said Leo's mother, turning from the road to frown at the dark woods to the north, fussing absently at that bald patch she had under her hair. You could see the footprint of the fortress on the hilltop below them, the walls little more than heaps of rubble, loose stones scattered down the hillside, the forest pressing in at the base. "If you think all we do is run away, our enemies might, too."

Creases spread around the corners of the Dogman's eyes as he grinned. "You're going to fight 'em here."

"You approve?"

"Ground's good." He considered the steep-sided trough of a valley with its grey thread of a river, its brown thread of a road, the rocky hills to either side. "Could be very good, if luck's with us."

"You're going to fight them here?" asked Leo, eyes wide.

"This is a war, isn't it? Stour Nightfall has moved ahead of his father and his uncle. Perhaps as much as a day ahead. His men are scattered, tired, undersupplied and exposed."

The Dogman grinned. "Touch reckless of him."

"A mistake I hope we can make fatal."

"If we put a fat enough worm on the hook."

"You know how warriors are about their flags." Leo's mother turned to look at him. "Your standard should be the very bait he needs. Especially after you stung his pride by stealing one of his. We'll make it look as though our rearguard is caught in a tangle on the bridge. Hopefully, it'll be a temptation he can't resist."

"You want me here in the ruin?" asked the Dogman.

"Hidden and waiting for my signal. Angland's forces will be concentrated behind that hill to the south. Once Nightfall is committed, we fall upon him from both sides and catch him against the river. If we manage it well, we might destroy him in one throw."

"That'd do a lot to even the odds."

"And make me feel a great deal better about all this retreating. Believe it or not, Leo, I enjoy it no more than you do."

Leo couldn't stop the smile spreading across his face. "We're going to fight them here."

"The day after tomorrow, I hope. Do either of you have an opinion on the plan?"

Leo was too busy imagining the victory. The two hills would be the jaws of their trap. The Great Wolf, lured into the valley between them by his own arrogance, surrounded at the bridge and crushed against the water. What a *song* that would make! He was already wondering what they'd call the battle, when the history books were written.

"I like it," said the Dogman. "If there's one thing you can rely on, it's young men's folly. I'll send word for Uffrith's warriors to gather here and be ready for a battle." He paused, wind stirring the grey hair about his craggy face. "Lady Finree... I've fought beside great warriors. Great War Chiefs. Against some, too. But I rarely saw an army better handled than by you. Might be men who think there's something weak in what you've done, the last few weeks." He curled his tongue and spat over the battlements. "Those men know less'n nothing about war. Would've been easy to break faith with us. Let us be swallowed up. But you kept your word. Aren't many who do, once they see it'll cost them." And he held out his hand.

Leo's mother blinked, evidently moved, and took it. "I'll have kept my word when you are back in your garden in Uffrith, not a moment before."

He broke out a great toothy grin. "Then we'll drink to our victory there." And the Dogman turned and trotted down the crumbling stair with a new spring in his step.

It gave Leo a flush of pride, to see the respect the old Northman had for his mother. The respect they had for each other. He took a breath of sharp air through his nose and let it sigh happily out. "I'll lead those men at the bridge—"

"No," said his mother. "I want your standard there to draw him on. But not you."

"The first wave of reinforcements, then—"

"No." And she gave him that look down her nose that always made him feel like he was still a little boy. "We'll keep our cavalry in reserve in the village of Sudlendal." She nodded towards the faint smoke rising beyond the bridge. "I want you with them."

"With the *reserves*?" He waved a hand towards the valley. Towards the glory. Towards the songs. "Finally we fight and you leave me with the *baggage?*"

"It's not as if I'm sending you back to Ostenhorm." The muscles at her temple squirmed as she clenched her jaw. "If something goes wrong, as it very well might, you can ride in and save the day. That's why we're all here, isn't it? To bear witness to your legend?"

"That's *so* unfair!" he whined, the niggling thought that it might be entirely fair making him even angrier. "When you're fighting for your life, you don't leave your best sword on the mantelpiece and charge in with a bread knife!"

"There are other men in this army who can fight." She spoke with icy calm, but there was an angry colour spreading across her face. "Experienced men who understand the value of caution, and planning, and of doing as they're bloody told. You're *reckless*, Leo. I can't risk it."

"No!" he snarled, thumping the crumbling battlements with his fist and sending stones clattering down the wall. "I'll be lord governor soon! I'm not a boy any more—"

"Then fucking act like it!" she snarled, with such violence he shrank back a little. "This isn't a negotiation! You'll stay with the reserves, and that's the end of it! Your father's dead! He's dead, and I can't lose you, too, do you understand?" She turned her back on him to look into the valley. "I can't lose you, too."

There was the slightest quaver in her voice, and somehow that cut him down more sharply than any sword blow. He stood staring, suddenly guilty and ashamed and feeling an utter fool. She'd carried him, when his father died and he fell all to pieces. She'd stood dry-eyed and stern by the grave, and through his tears Leo had thought how heartless she was. But he saw now she'd stayed strong because someone had to. She'd been carrying them all, ever since. Instead of being grateful, being a good son, helping her lift this impossible weight, he'd moped, and whined, and picked at her as if there was nothing bigger at stake than his pride.

He had to blink back tears himself, and he stepped up and put a gentle hand on her shoulder. "You won't lose me, Mother," he said. "You'll never lose me."

She laid her hand on his. An old hand, it seemed, suddenly, frail, the skin on the back wrinkled around the knuckles.

"I'll lead the reserves," he said.

They stood together in the wind, looking down into the valley.

The Party's Over

The clatter of the handle, the gurgle of filthy water as it surged into the bucket, the slop and trickle as she lifted it, breath wheezing, legs, arms, shoulders trembling, and passed it to May, and took an empty bucket from the old man on her left, handle clattering, and bent to the water again.

She stood hunched, up to her knees in the river, soaked dress rolled and tucked into a belt made from knotted rope, all thought of propriety long gone. All thought of propriety had gone the moment she staggered from this sewer of a river the first time, shivering in her drawers.

Clatter, gurgle, slop and trickle. How long had she been filling buckets now? It felt like hours. As blue evening turned to grey twilight turned to mad darkness lit by the glow of fires. As the distant tang of burning became a tickling reek then an endless scratching of smoke that even with a wet rag across her face made her want to choke with every breath. How long had she been filling buckets now? It felt like days. It felt as if she had always been filling buckets, and always would be.

The women made a chain, passing slopping pails, cans, pots from hand to hand up the shore, children darting back through the rubbish with the empties so Savine could take them and fill them again, clatter, gurgle, slop and trickle.

On the other side of the river, mills were burning, flames towering into the night, the great chimneys black fingers against the brilliance, their reflections wriggling in the slow-flowing water. Burning things drifted from the sky into the streets, onto the beach, into the river, little flaming birds that sputtered and popped, dancing lights floating on the black mirror for a moment before they were gone.

Up among the burning buildings, at the end of the chain of buckets, men struggled with the fires, shouting, bellowing, yelling at one another. Anger, maybe. Desperation, maybe. Encouragement, maybe. Savine was too tired to tell the difference. So tired she could hardly remember how to speak. How to think. She had become a machine herself. A machine for filling buckets. What would her important connections at the Solar Society think if they could see her now? She gave a weary snort that caught in her throat and nearly made her retch. Serve the arrogant bitch right, more than likely.

The clatter of the handle, the gurgle of water as it filled, the slop and trickle as she passed it to May, her legs, her arms, her shoulders trembling with the effort. Was it the cold, or the exhaustion, or the fear that made her shake so? What was the difference?

Her breath snagged and she was caught with a coughing fit, sudden as a punch in the gut. She doubled up, wasted ribcage buzzing with each choking gasp, tore the rag from her face and was sick. All she had to be sick with, anyway, bitter bile and bad water, her own little contribution to the river's filth.

She wrested back control of her lungs, then stooped to fill the bucket. Clatter, gurgle, slop and trickle—

There was a hand on her shoulder. Liddy. "It's out," she said.

Savine stared dumbly at her, then up the bank towards the buildings. Smoke still rolled skywards, but the flames were gone. She waded from the river and flopped on the slimy shingle on her hands and knees, utterly spent. She arched her back, one way then the other, aches stabbing right through into her heels, right up into her neck. The faintest shadow of what her father felt, perhaps, every morning. Maybe it should have given her sympathy for him. But as he was so fond of saying, pain only makes you sorry for yourself.

"It's out," rasped May, sinking down on the shore beside her.

Savine groaned as she came up to sitting, winced as she tried to work her fingers, cracked and wrinkled by cold water, ripped raw by the rusted handles of the buckets.

"It's out over here," she whispered, staring across to the great blaze still raging on the far bank.

"All we can worry about is here. Over there..." The orange glow of the fires across the river picked up the hollows of Liddy's face even more starkly than usual. Savine understood. Over there was lost. Over there was gone.

When she arrived in the city, she had smiled to see the building sites everywhere, the cranes and scaffolds, the stuff of creation. But Valbeck was one vast demolition now.

She caught some fragment of her mind trying to calculate the scale of the investments gone up in smoke. The buildings and machinery destroyed, the people ruined. What were her own losses, for that matter? None of it felt very important, compared to the pain in her hands.

There was a breeze, at least, carrying the haze of smoke down the river. Enough that Savine could get a proper breath into her raw chest.

"What happened?" she whispered.

"Reckon the Burners set some fires on their way out of town." Liddy wiped her face on the back of her sleeve and only succeeded in smearing ash across it. "A little parting gift."

"Their way out?"

May ran her tongue around the inside of her mouth and spat. "They say the crown prince is coming with five thousand soldiers. Rumour is they'll be outside the city tomorrow."

"Orso is here?" she whispered. She had hardly thought of him since the uprising. Hunger, cold and the constant threat of death rather blunted one's appetite for romance. Now his grin came up in her memory, painfully sharp, and she felt weak with a sappy welling of relief.

"Guess they managed to prise him out of the whorehouse," said Liddy. "No doubt he'll be bringing the Inquisition with him."

"Oh," said Savine, stupidly. For most people here, a horrifying prospect. For her, the best news in weeks.

"Seems the party's over," murmured May.

There was a rumble and Savine jerked up. On the other side of the river, the roof of a burning mill was falling in, fountains of sparks towering into the night, smoke boiling as half of one wall toppled inwards. The brave new age collapsing on itself.

Crown Prince Orso was riding to her rescue. Perhaps she should have laughed at that. Perhaps she should have wept at it. But she had no laughter and no tears left. She was a husk.

She sat on the bank and watched the flames dance in the water.

Eating Peas with a Sword

"Should we attack, Your Highness?"

"Attack, Colonel Forest?" Orso did not blame the man. Violence is very much the job of a career soldier, after all. But the limits of his imagination were becoming clear. "Attack who? The city itself is an asset, not an enemy. As for the inhabitants, we really have no idea who is loyal and who disloyal. Who a rebel and who a hostage. Making war on our own citizens...it would look dreadful. We would create more rebels than we killed."

Orso peered through his eyeglass towards Valbeck again. He could see tiny buildings, towers, pinprick chimneys, dark columns rising from the stricken city that he feared was the smoke of destruction rather than of industry.

How he would have loved to order a glorious charge. To put rebels to the sword, to root through every house until he found Savine. To whisk her off her feet and kiss her fiercely and so on, much to her great delight. To be, for once, the one to rush to *her* rescue. But Orso knew he had to put the children's stories to one side and think.

She was tough. A great deal tougher than he was. She was resourceful. A great deal more resourceful than he was. Her best chance—everyone's best chance—was for him to move slowly, cautiously and very, very boringly. He blew a sigh from puffed cheeks, itchy with the beginnings of a beard he hoped might look military but suspected would prove to be another of his many mistakes.

"Attacking the city with an army would be like eating peas with a sword," he said. "Messy, frustrating and you've a good chance of stabbing yourself in the face. We need to be measured. Calm. The firm but necessary hand of authority. We need to be the grown-ups." For once in his life.

Orso snapped his eyeglass decisively closed. Vital to look decisive, especially when you haven't a bloody clue what you're doing. He had been making it up as he went along all his life, of course, but never before had the fates of many thousands of other people depended so directly on his total ignorance. Perhaps that's what makes a hero, though. The towering self-confidence to dance at the brink of disaster and never consider the drop.

"Surround the city," he said, tapping the eyeglass thoughtfully into his palm and letting his eyes wander across the fields around Valbeck. "Deploy our cannons where they can be clearly seen but *not* used. Block every route in or out, cut off their supply, make it abundantly clear that we are in charge."

"Then?" asked Forest.

"Then find out who's leading the rebels and..." He shrugged. "Invite them to parley."

"War is only ever a prelude to talk," came a voice. A man stood nearby, in neat civilian clothes. A man who Orso had, as far as he was aware, never laid eyes upon before. A nondescript man with curly hair and a length of wood in one hand. He smiled at Orso. "My master would thoroughly approve, Your Highness."

As a crown prince, Orso was used to forgetting nine-tenths of the people he was introduced to, as well as to total strangers sticking their noses into his business, and so he remained scrupulously polite. "Pardon me, but I am not sure we have met...?"

"This is Yoru Sulfur," offered Superior Pike. "A member of the Order of Magi."

"I was just now struggling to put out a fire in the North when the unmistakable tang of the Union in flames reached my nose." Sulfur smiled wider. "Never any peace, eh? Never the slightest peace."

"His Eminence the Arch Lector," said Pike, "as well as His Majesty your father, were *very* keen that Master Sulfur should join us."

"Merely to observe." Sulfur waved it away as if the favour of the Union's two most powerful men was nothing to comment on. "And perhaps offer some trifling advice, if I can. As a representative of my master, Bayaz, First of the Magi. Pressing business detains him in the West, but the stability of the Union has ever been a prime concern of his, even so. Stability, stability, he's always saying. A stable Union means a stable world. This business..." And he shook his head sadly as he looked towards the smoke over Valbeck. "Is *quite* the opposite. Why, the very first thing they did was burn the bank."

"I...see," said Orso. Meaning that he did not see at all. He turned back to Forest, where things made at least a little more sense. "What was I saying?"

"Surround the city, Your Highness."

"Ah, yes. Proceed!"

Forest gave a stiff salute and the orders rang out, followed by the tramp and jingle as the latest column of the Crown Prince's Division left the road and fanned out into the fields to begin the encirclement.

"Master Tallow?" said Orso.

The boy crept forward. "Yes, sir, I mean, Your...er..."

"Highness," threw in Tunny, grinning ever so slightly.

"You've been in the city?"

He nodded, those great luminous eyes fixed on Orso.

"And you observed a meeting of these Breakers?"

He nodded again.

"Any notion who's in charge in there?"

"Risinau, the Superior of the Inquisition. Called himself the Weaver. Seemed like he was leading them, but he talked like a madman. Then there was a woman called Judge." He gave a little shiver. "But she seemed even madder'n Risinau. Then there was an old fellow. Mulmer. Molmer. Something like that. He seemed...decent, I reckon."

"Mulmer it is, then, I suppose." Orso frowned at Tallow. "Have you eaten today? You look bloody famished."

Tallow blinked.

"You like chicken?"

He slowly nodded.

"Yolk?"

"Your Highness?"

"Go to my cook and get the boy a chicken with...well, with whatever he wants."

Yolk looked a little sour.

"Sour about that, Yolk? Think the task's beneath you?"

"Well—"

"Any task I could give is far above you. Get the boy a damn chicken, then I want you and him to go out towards Valbeck under a white flag —have we got a white flag, Tunny?"

Tunny shrugged. "Stick a shirt on a stick, job done."

"Chicken first, then shirt on a stick, then head up to the nearest barricade and tell them Crown Prince Orso would very much like to speak to Mulmer of the Breakers. Tell them I am ready to negotiate. Tell them I am *keen* to negotiate. Tell them I feel about negotiation the way a stallion feels about a mare."

"Yes, Your Highness," said Yolk, still looking somewhat sour.

"Yes, Your Highness," said Tallow, his eyes still wide. Narrowing them simply did not appear to be an option for the boy.

Orso stood frowning towards the city as they walked away, one hand on his stomach. "Hildi?" he called.

The girl was sitting cross-legged in her drummer-boy's uniform, making a chain of daisies. "Little busy here."

"Get me a chicken, would you?"

"I could eat."

"Get everyone a chicken, then. Chicken, Master Sulfur?"

"Very kind, Your Highness, but I must keep to a very specific diet."

"The discipline of the magical arts, eh?"

Sulfur grinned wide, showing two rows of shiny white teeth. "We all must make sacrifices."

"I suppose so. Never been much good at it, though."

"Lack of practice, probably," said Hildi.

Orso snorted up a laugh. "I can hardly deny it. I fear I want everyone to like me, Master Sulfur."

"We all do, Your Highness, but he who tries to please everyone pleases no one at all."

"I wish I could deny that, too, but I've certainly pleased no one so far." He looked over at the magus who, aside from the staff, was about the least magical-looking man one could have asked for. "Don't suppose you could solve all this with...I don't know...a spell?"

"Magic can level mountains. I have seen it. But there is always a cost, and it rises with each passing year. In my experience, swords offer considerably better value."

"You speak more like an accountant than a wizard."

"A sign of the times, Your Highness."

"Superior Pike? Can I tempt you to chicken?"

The superior did not look pleased by the thought of chicken. Indeed, it was the most Orso could do to stand his ground as the man's hideously burned face advanced on him. "You mean to treat with the rebels?"

"I do, Superior." Orso gave a false chuckle. "After all, what harm can talk do?"

"A very great deal. I am not sure His Eminence will approve."

"Is there anything His Eminence does approve of?" Orso grinned, but Pike's face remained impassive. Perhaps it was the burns. Perhaps he

272

was thoroughly tickled but physically unable to smile. Perhaps he was chortling away on the inside the whole time. It did not seem likely. "Look, Superior, the wonderful thing about being crown prince is you can talk and wheedle and promise and bluster and everyone has to listen." He leaned close to murmur in the melted remnants of Pike's ear. "But you never have the power to actually *do* anything."

Pike raised one brow. Or looked as if he would have, had he any to raise. Then he gave the faintest nod, perhaps even a nod of approval, and faded back to confer with Sulfur.

Orso was left alone in the wheatfield with Tunny, the Steadfast Standard resting covered in the crook of one arm.

"What is it, Corporal?"

"I never saw more harm done than by the heroes who couldn't wait to get started."

Orso popped open his top button. Uniforms were a great help around the belly but they could get awfully tight at the throat. "Well, if I excel at anything, it's doing nothing."

"You know what, Your Highness? I'm starting to think you might make a better-than-average king."

"So you're always telling me."

"Yes." Tunny had a knowing smirk as he watched the men of the Crown Prince's Division steadily spread out around the city. "But I never actually *meant* it before."

The Battle of Red Hill

"How's your leg?" asked Rikke.

"Sore," said Isern, wrinkling her nose as she picked at the stitches with a fingernail, "and somewhat crusty." She straightened with a sigh. "But sore and crusty is about as good as one could hope for from an arrow wound."

She stuck two fingers in a pouch and started smearing something on the pink and puckered skin. It was Rikke's turn to wrinkle her nose. The smell of it was quite impossible to describe. "By the dead," trying to hold her breath, "what is that?"

Isern started to wind a fresh bandage around her thigh. "Better you don't know. I might have to spread some on you if you get arrow-pricked, and I wouldn't want you arguing." She slipped a pin through the bandage and stood, wincing as she rubbed at her thigh with her thumb, flexing her knee, testing her weight on it. "Knowledge isn't always a gift, d'you see? Sometimes it's better we be swaddled in the comforting darkness of ignorance."

She pushed a pellet of chagga up behind her lip, then rolled another between finger and thumb and handed it over. Rikke chomped on it, savoured that sour, earthy taste which she'd found so vile when she started chewing it but that now she could never get enough of, and pushed it down behind her lip.

It was cold. No fires in case Stour's scouts saw them and spoiled the trap, and she'd hardly slept and she was aching and hungry but sick at the same time and bloody hell she felt nervous. Kept fussing with her fingers, fussing at the chagga pellet with her tongue, fussing at the runes around her neck, fussing at the ring through her nose—

"Stop fussing," said Isern. "Neither of us'll be fighting."

"I can feel worried for those who will, can't I?"

"Meaning your Young Lion?" Isern grinned, tip of her tongue showing through that hole in her teeth. "Can't spend your whole life fucking, you know."

"No." Rikke gave a smoky sigh. "Something to aim for, though."

"I've heard less noble goals, 'tis true."

The silence stretched. The silence, and the nerves, and somewhere someone started up a song in a deep bass. That one about the Battle in the High Places, where her father laid Bethod low. Old battles. Old victories. She wondered whether some time in the future, folk would sing songs about the Battle of Red Hill, and if they did, who'd be the winners and who the losers.

"When will they get here?" she asked for the hundredth time.

Isern leaned on her spear and frowned off to the east. The sun was rising there, a brilliant crescent over the hills that set the edges of the clouds on fire. The valley bellow was dark still, here or there a glitter on the stream, mist hanging over the trees that marched off to the North. "Could be soon," mused Isern. "Could be later. Might be they change their mind and don't come at all."

"In other words, you've no notion."

Isern glanced sideways. "If only someone could just look into the future and tell us how it'll all unfold. That'd be handy."

"Aye." Rikke planted her chin in her palms and sagged. "It would."

"Bravery," said Glaward, staring gloomily at the fire, "audacity, loyalty... yes. But I never guessed patience would be the soldier's most important virtue."

Barniva rubbed at his scar with a thumbtip. "Fighting and soldiering are two very different things."

They were starting to seem like opposite things to Leo. He frowned at the sun, the slightest pink smudge in the east. He could've sworn the damn thing was rising at a tenth the normal speed. No doubt it was somehow in league with his mother.

"Patience is the parent of success," murmured Jurand, with so gentle a touch on Leo's shoulder he only just felt it. "Stolicus."

"Huh." Normally, as the sun rose, Leo would've been training. He'd heard Bremer dan Gorst, well into his fifties, still trained for three hours every day, so he'd determined to do the same. But what's the point of training if you end up stuck on your arse in a village miles from the fight? He took a hard breath and let it smoke away. His thousandth of the morning so far.

"Nothing to do but wait." Whitewater Jin carefully pushed his sausages around the pan and made them sizzle. The fork looked tiny in his paw of a hand. "Wait, and eat."

The smell was making Leo's stomach rumble, but there was no way he could think of eating. He was too nervous. Too impatient. Too frustrated.

"By the *dead*!" He flung an arm towards the men scattered about the village, already in their armour. Angland's cavalry. The best and the brightest, sitting idle. "She should be letting us fight! What's she thinking?"

"I saw an army mishandled in Styria," said Barniva. "This is not what it looks like."

"If you ask me," said Jurand, "the lady governor's a hell of a general."

"No one did ask you," snapped Leo, even though he just had.

Jurand heaved out a sigh, and Barniva drew his blanket tight about his shoulders, and they went back to watching the sausages sizzle.

Leo frowned up at the sound of hooves. One rider trotting down the rutted track that led from the bridge. Antaup, loose in his saddle.

"Morning!" he called, scraping that lock of dark hair back with his fingers.

"Any news?" Leo couldn't keep the eager little warble out of his voice, though it was perfectly clear there was no news at all. He was needy as a jilted lover, unable to stop pining no matter how often he was turned down.

"No news," said Antaup, swinging from his saddle. He peered over Jin's big shoulder at the pan. "Don't suppose you lads have a sausage spare?"

Barniva grinned up. "For a boy with a smile as pretty as yours? I think we can find a sausage."

"Do you have to?" snapped Leo, curling his lip with disgust. "What did mother say?" He right away regretted his choice of words, but how does a man make taking orders from his mother sound good?

"She said sit tight." Antaup leaned on Jin's shoulder, made him turn, then reached around his blind side and nimbly stole the fork from his plate. "She said she'd let you know if anything changed." And he stretched over to fork one of the sausages from the pan.

"Oy!" snapped Jin, elbowing him away.

Leo frowned up towards the red-topped hill, a black lump against the pinking sky, here and there the telltale glint of metal where the men were getting ready for battle. Or for just another day of waiting.

The waiting, the waiting, the endless bloody waiting. He really was the worst man in the world at doing nothing.

"I'm going up there!" And he grabbed his helmet and strode for his horse.

"And she said don't go up there!" called Antaup with his mouth full.

Leo froze for a moment, angrily clenching his jaw. Then he strode on. "I'm bloody going anyway!"

"I'll come with you," said Jurand. "Keep a sausage for me!"

"For a boy with such delicate features as yours," said Barniva, laughter in his voice, "I'll *always* have a sausage."

"By the dead," grumbled Leo, hunching his shoulders.

"I've got a feeling about today," said Wonderful.

Clover was fully occupied trimming a blister on his big toe. "Good feeling or bad?"

"Just a feeling. Something's going to happen."

"Well, *something* happens every day."

"Something big, you fool."

"Ah," said Clover. "Well, I hope I'm left out of it. I like little things, mostly."

"You must be pleased wi' your cock, then." Magweer, sneering down from his horse with the sun behind.

Clover saw no pressing need to look away from his feet. "A cock's not for pleasing yourself, boy, it's for pleasing others. Maybe that's where you're going wrong."

Magweer bristled. Always the ones quickest to insults got the thinnest skin, for some reason. "You spend more time on your blisters than your weapons."

"My blisters are more important," said Clover.

Magweer's ill-favoured face crunched up in a clueless scowl.

"If you're lucky, you might get through a whole campaign without drawing your sword." Clover gave his blister one last shave with the point of his little knife, then sat back to admire the results. "But you will, without question, be using your feet."

"The man has a point," said Wonderful.

Magweer spat. "No fucking idea why, but Stour wants the two o' you up front with him."

"Oh, aye?" asked Clover. "Has he not got all the wise counsel he needs with you lot o' heroes?"

"You mocking me, old man?"

Clover puffed out a weary breath. That boy seemed determined to butt heads with him. You let things go with most men, they let things go, too. But some are just fixed on taking offence. "Wouldn't dare, Magweer," he said. "But wars are depressing things, whatever the songs say. We must lighten the mood where we can, eh, Wonderful?"

"I smile whenever possible," she said, stony-faced.

Magweer looked from one of them to the other, then gave a sour hiss, spat once more for luck and wrenched his horse roughly around to the west. "Just get up there with the scouts soon as you can or there'll be trouble." And he rode off, mud flicking from his horse's hooves, nearly riding down some poor woman who'd been off fetching water and making her drop her buckets in the mud.

"I like that boy a lot. Reminds me of me as a young man." Clover shook his head. "If I'd been an absolute cunt."

"You were an absolute cunt," said Wonderful. "And I've observed no significant changes in that regard."

Clover started pulling his boot on. "Or, indeed, in any other."

Wonderful scrubbed worriedly at the back of her shaved head as she frowned off down the road to the west. "Damn it, though," she said, "I've got a feeling about today."

"No sign," said Rikke's father, offering her his battered eyeglass.

"If you say there's no sign," she said, "I daresay there isn't any. You're the War Chief. I'm...I don't know, a seer, maybe?" Sounded like a bloody presumptuous title. "Just...a really shit one."

"Sooner or later, you'll have to stop hiding your talents, girl. Your Long Eye may be patchy but your short ones are still way sharper'n mine."

Rikke sighed, and took the eyeglass, and peered over the weed-sprouting old battlements, keeping low just in case. Spots of gorse on the hillside. Fast-flowing water in the stream. Sheep dotted about the yellow-green grass. Sunlight and shadow chasing each other down the valley as the gusting wind dragged clouds across the sky. There were a couple of hundred Union men gathered around the bridge, where a wagon had been carefully positioned to look like it had just that moment broke an axle and was blocking things up halfway across.

The bait on their hook. Seemed a laughably obvious trick right then, but tricks always do when you know how they're managed. Fish keep biting, even so.

"No sign." Rikke handed back the glass, and clapped her father on the shoulder, and slipped down the steps.

The yard of the ruin was crammed with Oxel's and Red Hat's Carls, checking their gear, passing food, talking softly to one another. You'd think men would get fired up before a battle but more often they get maudlin.

When you feel the Great Leveller's shadow cold on your back, it's not your hopes you come back to, but your regrets.

Isern had set her bony arse on the heap of crumbled masonry that was once the north wall of the fortress, spear across her knees, giving the blade a few licks with the whetstone.

"No sign?" she asked, not even looking up.

Rikke thought she caught a glint of metal among the trees at the bottom of the slope, but there was nothing there now. "No sign." And she perched on the tumbledown wall and wriggled till she found a comfortable spot, then started to arrange the fronds of a surprisingly pretty weed growing out of it. "The songs don't say much about all the time spent sitting down, do they?"

Isern winced as she stretched her hurt leg out. "The skalds give disproportionate attention to the sword-work, it's true. Truth is, battles are more often won with spades than blades. Roads, and ditches, and trenches, and proper shit-pits. You'll dig your way to victory, my da always told me."

"Thought you hated your da?"

"Being an utter fucker didn't make him wrong. Quite the opposite, far as fighting goes."

"It's a sad fact that the..." Rikke trailed off, staring.

A man had stepped from the trees below them. A tall man with pale brows and pale hair in a spiky riot, shoulders hunched and elbows stuck out wide and short beard jutting. He had a sword in one hand and an axe in the other and he was frowning up the slope. Not at her, but at the tower beyond.

"Who's that?" she said.

"Who's who?"

The pale man beckoned with his axe, and Rikke's jaw fell open as a couple of dozen others slipped from the trees around him, all well armed. She jumped up, near falling over that pretty weed, and pointing wildly down towards them.

"There's men in the trees!" she screeched.

A few Carls scrambled onto the crumbling wall, staring down. Oxel was one. Rikke was waiting for him to roar out for more men, but all he did was turn his shifty sneer from the trees to her and spit.

"What the hell you talking about, girl?" he growled. "There's no one there."

"Fucking mad bitch," she heard one of the others mutter as they drifted back into the ruin, shaking their heads.

Rikke wondered if she was going mad. Or more mad, maybe. Men were flooding from the trees now. Hundreds of the bastards. "You see 'em, don't you?" she asked Isern in a small voice.

The hillwoman leaned on her spear, calmly chewing. "The men are rude, but the men are right. There's no one there." She gave Rikke a painful jab with her sharp elbow. "But maybe someone *will* be."

"Oh, no." And Rikke covered her eyes with a hand and the left one was hot. "Wanna be sick." She bent over and coughed out an acrid little mouthful, but when she looked up, the men were still there, too brightly lit since the sun was still low, a great standard in their midst, flapping hard even though the breeze had died. "They even got a flag."

"What flag?"

"Black with a red circle."

Isern's frown got harder. "That was Bethod's standard. Now it's Black Calder's."

Rikke was sick again. Just a little string of drool this time, and she spat and wiped her mouth. "Thought he...was way off north."

"You cannot force the Long Eye open," murmured Isern. "But when it opens by itself, it's a fool who doesn't see." She turned and limped quick across the rubble-strewn yard of the fortress, making men grumble as she shouldered past. "Black Calder's always had a bad habit of turning up where he shouldn't."

"So what're you doing?"

"Warning your father."

"You sure?" muttered Rikke as she followed Isern up the crumbling steps, still glimpsing those men out of the corner of her eye. An army of 'em now. "I mean, what if they're going to turn up next week? Or next month? What if they turned up years ago!"

"Then we'll look like a right pair o' fools." Isern grinned at her as she limped up onto the roof of the tower. "But at least we won't be two corpses in a big heap of corpses. Dogman!"

"Isern-i-Phail," muttered Rikke's father with a sideways glance. "Make it good, I've got a battle to—"

"Black Calder's in those woods." She nodded off to the North. "Planning to sneak men around you, I reckon."

"You seen 'em?"

"I must confess, I did not. But your daughter did." She slapped a heavy hand down on Rikke's shoulder. "The moon has smiled upon us all and blessed her with the rare gift o' the Long Eye. We should make ready for blood."

"You're not joking." Rikke's father pointed in the opposite direction.

"Stour Nightfall might be coming down that road any bloody minute and Lady Brock's counting on us to be one-half of a trap for him! We don't arrive, the whole plan's in the shit."

Isern grinned like this was all quite the lark. "Not half as deep as if Black Calder sidles up our arses while we're facing t'other way, though, d'you see?"

Rikke's father pressed at his temples. "By the dead. I can't turn around just on your say-so, Rikke. I can't."

"I know," she said, shrugging her shoulders high as they'd go. "I wouldn't."

"You seen 'em, though?" croaked Shivers.

Rikke glanced sideways and there they still were, a great long line just in front of the trees, hundreds of Carls, their shields bright blobs of colour, gathered around Black Calder's standard. "I see 'em now. The one at the front's smiling right at me."

"Describe him."

"A long, lean, pale bastard with an axe and a sword, sort of hunched over, all elbows. Ugh." And she had to bend over herself, hands on her knees, head spinning.

"Sounds a lot like the Nail," said Shivers, frowning down towards the woods. "If Black Calder sent a man around the back, the Nail's the sort o' man he'd send."

Rikke's father gave a low grunt. "Maybe."

"Give me a few Carls," said Shivers. "I'll have a root around those woods. I find nothing, nothing lost."

Rikke's father looked from Shivers, to Isern, to Rikke, and back. "Root around, then, but quick. If we're called for, we can't wait."

Shivers nodded and slipped down the crumbling steps. The sun was getting higher, and down in the valley on the brown strip of the road, men were moving. A few, and coming carefully. "Oh, by the dead." Rikke covered her eye with her hand, felt it still throbbing hot against her palm. "Tell me you see them?"

"Oh, aye. Stour Nightfall's scouts, I reckon." And Isern spat. " 'Course I see *them*."

Muddy grey dawn had become muddy grey morning by the time Leo rode up through the red bracken on the hillside. The men of Angland sat in massed ranks where they were hidden from the valley, armed and ready. Some stood to salute, a few held up their swords. Others called out, "The Young Lion!" against their orders to stay quiet. Seemed the soldiers approved of him a lot more than his mother did.

She was kneeling in the bracken just beyond the summit, an eyeglass trained on the valley, a whispering group of scouts and officers around her.

She shook her head as he crept over, keeping low. "I thought I gave Antaup orders that you shouldn't come up here?"

"Yes, and I came anyway..." He trailed off. There were men in the valley. Mounted men, spread out, watching their little show of incompetence down at the bridge. Northmen, without a doubt. "Nightfall's scouts?" he asked in an eager whisper.

She handed him her eyeglass. "And his main body is following close behind. Head of the column is there at the farm."

Leo trained the glass on a few pale farm buildings higher up the valley. Metal gleamed on the brown strip of road. Mail and spear points. A column of armed men, moving towards the bridge. Carls, from the little spots of bright colour which must be their shields. Like seeing one ant in the grass and suddenly seeing dozens, Leo became aware of another column, and another.

"Bloody hell," he squawked, excitement surging up his throat and nearly choking him. "They're taking the bait!"

He squinted harder. There was something waving beside the farm. A tall grey flag, and though he couldn't be sure at this distance, he'd a feeling there was a black wolf on it.

"Nightfall's standard," he whispered.

"Yes." His mother pulled her eyeglass from his limp grip and set it to her own eye again. "And this time, I've no doubt, the Great Wolf is here in person."

"What did these bastards do?" asked Clover, frowning up at the bodies.

"They was on the Dogman's side," said Greenway, nodding like a family dangling from a tree was a job well done.

Couple of Thralls had dragged a cupboard from the farmhouse, now they shoved it over in the dirt and started hacking at it with axes. Clover squinted at 'em, bemused.

"What is it they think an axe will reveal that opening the doors won't?"

"Hidden stuff. Gold, maybe."

"Gold? You're having a laugh."

Greenway frowned a pouty frown—aside from sneers, it was his one expression. "Silver, then."

"Silver? If these bastards had silver, let alone gold, why the hell would they be up here farming for a pittance? They'd be in town, drunk, which is where I should bloody be."

"Best to be sure," said one of the men.

"Oh, aye," said Clover. "Daresay you'll be burning the house once you've found nothing, 'cause fire is pretty."

The man glanced over at Greenway, somewhat sheepish, and scratched his head. Seemed that was exactly what he'd been planning.

"And if Stour wants somewhere to sleep tonight, he can curl up in the ashes, can he?" Clover strolled past, shaking his head. What a waste. Waste of people, waste of things, waste of effort. But that was war for you. Nothing he hadn't seen a dozen times before. If the Great Wolf wanted to decorate his new land with corpses and have creaking ropes for music, then who was he to complain?

The king-in-waiting was a little further on with Wonderful, considering the view while he chewed on a stolen apple.

"Don't like the looks of this," said Clover, folding his arms tight. "Not one bit."

"No," said Wonderful. "It fucking stinks."

The road dropped into a grassy valley ahead, a steep hill on either side. One had some old ruin clinging to its rocky top, the other was bigger and shallower, red bracken giving the crown a dried-blood look Clover didn't much care for.

Between the two fells, down in the valley's bottom, a little bridge crossed a stream. Looked like there might be a few Union men tangled up on both sides of it. Clover's eyes weren't all they once had been, but he thought he could see a flag waving above them.

Stour's eyes were sharper, and thoughtfully narrowed in its direction. "You reckon that's Leo dan Brock's standard down there?"

Clover felt his heart sinking. It was getting to be a familiar feeling around Black Calder's son. "Could be someone else's?" he tried, hopefully. "No one's in particular?"

"No, it's his." Stour worked the words around and spat 'em out. "The Young Lion. What kind o' name is that?"

"Ridiculous." Clover held up his hands and fluttered the fingers. "The Great Wolf! Now *that's* a name."

Wonderful made a little squeak. She had her lips pressed together tight like she was trying not to shit herself. Stour frowned at her, then at Clover.

"Are you making light o' me, you old fucker?"

Clover looked dumbstruck. "Man like me, make light of a man like you? I wouldn't dare. I'm agreeing the Young Lion is a stupid name for a man to have. For one thing, he's not a lion, is he? For another he's, what, twenty-ish?"

"About that," said Wonderful.

"So...considering the lifespan of a lion..." Clover squinted up at the grey sky, no idea how long a lion lived, "probably...maybe...he'd be quite an old lion, would he?"

He kept his face blank as fresh snow, counting on the short attention span common to famous warriors and, indeed, soon enough, the Great Wolf forgot all about it, fully occupied glowering down the valley, towards that bridge. Towards that standard. He gave a great sniff. "Let's have a poke at those bastards."

All of a sudden, Wonderful looked like shitting herself for very different reasons. "Don't know about that, Chief. You sure?"

"Ever known me to not be sure?"

In Clover's experience, only idiots were ever sure about anything. He nodded up towards that ruined tower above the bridge, the red-topped fell on the other side. "Could be a trap. If they've got men waiting on those hills, we'd be putting ourselves in a right pickle."

"No doubt," said Wonderful, jaw set tight.

Stour gave an irritated hiss. "Everything looks like a trap to you two."

"Act that way," said Clover, "you'll never be surprised."

"You'll never surprise your enemy, either. Bring up a couple of hundred Carls, Wonderful." And Stour bunched his fists, white-knuckle tight, like he couldn't wait to start throwing punches. "Let's give those bastards a poke."

She pointed that brow of hers at Clover but he could only shrug, so she turned and bellowed at one of the scouts to bring up more men. What else could she do? Getting folk to do what your chief says is what being a second is all about. Whether or not your chief's a prick is beside the point.

Rikke crouched on the roof of the broken tower, twitching, chewing, fretting, even more nervous than before. Almost too nervous to bear.

First the Union had been forced back over the bridge, then more Union men had come up and driven the Northmen back, then more Northmen had come up, and now there was a great clog of warriors crowding in on either side of the river, more of Nightfall's Carls flooding down the road towards it. Strange sounds floated up, twisted by wind and distance.

"That bloody fool's stumbled right into it!" Rikke's father was licking his lips, but she couldn't share his joy. Couldn't twitch free of the feeling it was them stumbling into something. She glanced towards the trees again. The men she'd seen with the Long Eye had faded now. Maybe she caught their ghostly after-images. Maybe nothing.

"We can't wait any longer. Red Hat?"

"Aye, Chief?"

"Send Oxel and Hardbread the word—"

"Wait!" hissed Rikke. There was something moving in the woods. Branches thrashing, a glimmer of metal through the leaves. "Tell me you see that!"

Her father's face had turned grim. "I see that."

Shivers burst from the trees, running full tilt for the fortress. Some of his scouts shot from the woods around him, one looking back as they started to scramble up the grassy hillside.

"Man the walls!" roared Shivers. Arrows flitted from the trees, twittering about him. One of his men took a shaft in the back and slipped, tottered up, carried on running with the shaft sticking from his shoulder. "Woods are full o' the bastards!"

Rikke's father stood up tall at the crumbling battlements, bellowing down into the yard. "Man the walls! Black Calder's coming from the North!"

Then Rikke saw that pale man step out of the trees, right to the spot she'd already seen him in. He beckoned with his axe, just the way she'd already seen him do, and men started to spill from the woods around him.

"It's the Nail!" roared Red Hat, waving his sword, and warriors swarmed towards the ruined walls, falling over each other in their haste to shift from the south side of the fortress to the north.

Now came the standard, black with the red circle. Bethod's standard. Black Calder's standard. Suddenly the treeline was alive with men.

Isern gave a sigh. "There's the problem with looking for a fight." And she pulled the deerskin cover from the bright blade of her spear. "Sometimes you get more fight than you wanted."

Seemed the Nail was smiling right at Rikke now. Just the way she'd known he would.

Without taking her eyes from the valley, Leo's mother held up a finger. "Get the troops on their feet."

Leo heard the calls of the officers spreading out across the back of the hill. The great scrape and rattle as the men stood, took up their weapons, began to form ranks.

The valley was flooded with Northmen now. Hundreds of them. Thousands. An iron plague, spreading steadily down the road towards the bridge. Leo felt utterly useless. All he could do was kneel in the dirt, the steadily thickening drizzle seeping through his armour, and watch.

"The men are ready, Lady Finree," said an officer. "Should we advance?"

She shook her head. "Just a little longer, Captain. Just a little longer."

The time stretched, slow, silent, unbearably tense. A bird hovered, high overhead, feathers ruffling in the wind, poised and ready to swoop.

"Knowing the right moment." Her eyes flickered over the disorganised fighting at the bridge, across the columns of Northmen in the valley, up to the farm, and back. "My father always told me that was half a general's job."

"The other half?" asked Leo.

"Looking like you know the right moment." And she stood up tall and slapped the dirt from the knees of her skirt. "Ritter?" A freckled little boy stepped up with a bugle clenched tight in one fist.

"Your Grace?"

"Sound the advance."

It rang out over the valley, piercingly loud, and there was an almighty clattering as several thousand armoured men began to march.

"Shit," said Wonderful, frowning at the red hill.

Clover felt that familiar sinking feeling as he followed her eyes. That feeling he'd got at least once in every battle he'd ever fought in. Spear tips showed over the brow, against the spitting sky, then helmets, then men. Ranks and ranks of men. Union foot, well armed and organised and coming down from the high ground on their flank.

They didn't seem to trouble the Great Wolf any. Quite the reverse. "Lovely," he purred, grinning like an eager groom watching his bride shown in. "Fucking beautiful. Form a shield wall facing that fell and we'll get to grips with these Union bastards."

"Lovely? We don't know where the Dogman is!" Clover pointed up towards the ruined fortress with a stabbing finger. Even his old eyes could pick out figures on the roof of that tower. "What if there's men up there? We'll be showing 'em our bare arses!"

"I guess." Stour looked back to the bridge, in no hurry. It was a right mess down there now, corpses scattered, arrows flitting, spears tangled, men struggling in the water, even. Stour tapped a finger against his pursed lips as he watched, like a cook judging whether to toss a pinch more salt in the pot, rather'n a War Chief sending men to their deaths. But maybe that's just the kind o' carelessness with other men's lives a general needs. "Bring everyone up. I think I'll have that bridge."

Wonderful looked stunned, and well she might've. "You're playing their bloody game!" she said. "It's a fucking trap!"

Stour's wet eyes rolled towards her. " 'Course it is, but who's caught in it?"

"We are," snapped Clover, "and tripping over our cocks on the way. What'll your father say to this?"

"He'll be fucking delighted." The wolf-grin spread across Stour's face. "The whole thing was his idea."

Clover blinked. "What?"

Stour nodded towards the old fortress. "He's on the other side o' that hill, ready to attack. These fools think they'll catch us with our trousers down." He leaned close to Clover. "But it's us who'll catch them. Come on, you old bastards!" And he drew his sword, spun it around in his fingers lightly as an eating knife. "We've a fucking battle to win!"

Rikke never saw a battle before, and she hoped she never saw another.

Black Calder's men pressed in on every side. The tumbledown wall had become a mass of straining men, a great tangle of shields and clattering, sliding, stabbing spears. One had a flag on it that had got all wrapped around a Carl's arm, and he was shrieking with fury as he tried to drag it free and only got himself more tangled. Rikke saw a spear blade poking into his cheek and he twisted and shouted but couldn't be heard, couldn't be moved, was eased onto that spear by the weight of men behind, the trickle of blood becoming a bubbling rush and Rikke looked away, the breath crawling in her throat.

She saw her father on the steps of the tower, veins standing from his neck as he roared words she couldn't hear over the screams of pain and screams of rage. How could anyone bring order to this chaos? Might as well command a storm to stop blowing.

She saw a boy with curly hair just staring, taking a step one way, then the other way, face white and pale and his jaw hanging open, not knowing what to do. Rikke wondered if he was going to die here. Wondered if she was going to die here.

The rain was coming heavier now, on a chill wind, beading weapons and armour, sticking hair to snarling faces, turning ground churned by boots and bodies to sticky mud.

"Heave!" The shield wall was no more than ten strides from her, buckling and twisting, shields shrieking and scraping, boots sliding as men tried desperately to shove the attackers back. One stood tall to lash over the top of the wall with his axe. Stood again and squealed as a spear caught him under the rim of his helmet. He fell back, shrieking, thrashing, blood leaking between the fingers clapped to his face. "My eye! My eye!"

Arrows flitted down, clicked from the ground, bounced from a dead campfire. A man sank to his knees, leaning on his mace, face all crumpled, drooling, wheezing, a shaft in his back.

"Careful," said Isern, easing Rikke behind a broken pillar, mossy old devil faces carved around the head. "Careful," and Rikke felt something cold brush her palm, and saw that Isern had slipped a knife into her hand, and she stared at it as if she'd never seen such a thing before.

She saw a man sitting on the ground, cursing as he fiddled with his bloody sleeve, blood in his beard, axe dangling from one wrist. She saw a man stomping on someone's head, spots of blood across his mad snarl as he lifted his boot and rammed it down, lifted it and rammed it down. "Can you save my leg?" A lad with yellow hair turned dark by the drizzle and the rags of his trousers all oozing black. Another man gibbered, mail pulled up to show a little slit that welled blood and when the healer wiped it welled again and she wiped it again but the blood came too fast to stop, too fast.

There was a kind of groan, and at the crumbling wall where that pretty weed had grown the shields buckled, gave, and Rikke stared as Black Calder's men surged into the fortress.

A knot of them, mail rain-glinting and mud-spattered. A wedge of them, bristling with sharpened steel. A dagger-thrust of them, screaming their war cries, and at their very front a man with gold on his helmet and a green tree on a shield all scored and dented. He rushed right at Rikke with an axe held high.

That would've been a good moment to run, but maybe she'd run enough. Maybe the madness was catching. Without thinking, she dropped into a crouch, and bared her teeth, and raised her knife to meet him.

He twisted at a mad screech and Isern sprang from the crumbling steps on one leg, point of her spear darting over his shield-rim, catching him under the jaw and ripping his throat wide. He wobbled another step or two, blood showering down that green tree and turning it red, then his knees went and he fell on his face, gold-chased helmet bouncing off and rolling right between Rikke's boots.

She saw Shivers snarling, hacking, snarling, metal eye shining. She saw Red Hat shooting arrows into the midst. She saw other men she knew, some of her father's closest, good men, gentle men, screeching hate, shoving with shields, chopping with swords and axes.

That wedge of Black Calder's men was choked off, and hemmed in, and cut down one by one, stabbed with spears, shoved over with shields, stomped on the ground. One huge warrior was left, wearing battered plates of armour, swinging a great axe around in heedless circles, rattling and clattering against the spears that stabbed at him.

Then a snarling Thrall sprang onto his back, caught him around the throat, hacking at him with a knife. Another darted in and chopped at his leg, brought him lurching onto one knee. Then they were all around him, Oxel using his sword like a pick in both hands to chisel his helmet off, chisel his skull open.

She saw Isern, tongue pressed into the hole in her teeth as she stabbed one stricken warrior after another with her spear. One crawled towards Rikke, crying through a faceful of mud, and Shivers stepped on his neck and took the top of his head off with a swing of his sword.

That assault was made into a heap of dead, their bravery all come to nothing, but Black Calder's men still pressed in all around. Through waving spears she saw the Nail, up on the wall, shaking his axe, blood-dotted face twisted with fury and laughter at once, screaming, "Kill the fuckers! Kill the fuckers!"

Arrows flickered over, the noise of fighting like hail on a tin roof. Rikke saw ghosts now, among the fighting, among the killing, among the dead. Ghosts of men fighting, killing, dying. Battles long done, maybe, and battles yet to come, and she slid down the pillar until her backside hit mud, knife dropping from her hand into the dirt, and sat there trembling with her smarting eyes squeezed shut.

Leo stood at the top of the hill, hands helplessly clenching and unclenching.

It was the greatest battle he'd ever seen. The greatest the North had seen since the Battle of Osrung, where his mother loved to say he'd been conceived.

Nightfall's shield wall had bent back when the Anglanders first charged. It had buckled, looked ready to give under the strain, but it had held. More Northmen had filtered down the road to shore it up and pushed the Anglanders back to the base of the red hill. Now there was a boiling engagement all the way along the valley bottom, the mad clamour echoing from the fells, the carnage at the bridge at one end.

If the Dogman swept down from the other side of the valley now, it would all be over. Nightfall would be surrounded, shattered, they could take every one of his men prisoner. Perhaps they could even capture the Great Wolf himself and make the bastard kneel.

But the Dogman didn't appear, and the glee of the officers on the hilltop turned to concern, then grim worry.

"Where the hell is the Dogman?" muttered Leo's mother. The ruin on the far side of the valley was just a ghost through the thickening rain. "He should be attacking."

"Yes," said Leo. He couldn't say more. His mouth was too dry.

"Can't see a thing in this damn rain," she fretted.

"No," said Leo. He'd always been a doer. Sitting idle while other men fought was torture.

"If he doesn't come soon..."

They could all see it. Some of Nightfall's Thralls were still dribbling onto the battlefield. If the Dogman didn't come soon, they might get around the flank and the Union line would crumble.

A rider came lurching up the back of the hill, pushing his mount hard. A Northman, rattled and dirt-spattered.

Leo's mother strode up as he slithered from the saddle. "What's become of the Dogman?"

"Black Calder came out o' the woods," he said, breathing hard. "We're only just hanging on at the ruin. No way we can help with the attack."

One officer swallowed. Another stared down into the valley. A third seemed to deflate, like a punctured wineskin.

"Black Calder was supposed to be a day away," breathed Leo's mother, her eyes wide.

"He tricked us," muttered Leo. They were caught in their own trap, outnumbered and facing destruction. He stared towards the bridge. That was where he belonged, where the names were made and tomorrow's songs written. He could make the difference. He knew he could.

Strategy had failed. It was time to fight.

"We have to send in the reserves." He stepped close to his mother. No whining now, no wheedling. Just the simple truth. "There's no choice. We're committed."

She frowned down into the valley, a muscle on the side of her head constantly working, and said nothing.

"If we pull back, we leave the Dogman at Black Calder's mercy. We have to *fight*."

She closed her eyes, her mouth a hard, flat line, and said nothing.

"Mother." He put one hand gently on her shoulder. "Wars may be won by the clever, but battles have to be fought by the brave. It's *time*."

She opened her eyes, and took a hard breath, and puffed it out. "Go," she said.

It was as if that one soft word lit a fire in Leo's belly and set his body tingling, from the roots of his hair to the tips of his toes. He felt a great smile spread across his face as he turned. "Jurand!" he barked out, voice quivering with excitement. "We're going in!"

Jurand sprang up. "Yes, sir!" And he hurried for his horse.

"Leo?"

He turned back. His mother stood there against the grey sky, fists clenched tight.

"Give those bastards hell," she snarled.

"Come on!" screamed Stour. He hadn't bothered with a helmet, which seemed a prime slice of folly to Clover, but if men can't see your face, how can they tell everyone afterwards who did all the high deeds? "I want me that bridge!" snarled the Great Wolf, wet hair plastered to his forehead and his teeth bared as a wolf's teeth should properly be. "That's *my* fucking bridge!"

It was all quite the mess now. Stour's Carls had only just held the Union at the foot of that red hill, their shield wall twisting back on itself and threatening to burst. But they'd held them, and now there was a mad fight all along the valley, the bridge at one end the fiercest spot, Leo dan Brock's golden standard fluttering above the carnage. It was a temptation Stour couldn't ignore

"Let me at that bastard!" He was near frothing at the mouth. "I'll slit this Young Lion from his fruits to his throat!"

That bridge really didn't seem worth all the effort to Clover. If it hadn't been for all the rain the last week, you could've just stepped around the bloody thing without getting your feet wet. He started to slow. Let Stour and his eager young stags charge on ahead. He'd fought enough battles. The fresh lads could claim their share of the action, and the costs, and the lessons.

He stopped, hands on knees, then nearly tripped over his own feet as someone shoved him in the back. He turned with a curse on his lips, but grinned when he saw the culprit.

"Magweer!" And with an even stormier look than usual. Like he'd caught Clover fucking his mother rather than just snatching a breather. "Thought you'd be up front with the rest o' the firebrands, pumping your name up with glory."

"Seems I'm needed here," snarled Magweer, "making sure you fight, you fucking old coward!"

"A coward's just a man with the proper respect for sharp metal," said Clover, waving him down. "A battle's no place for a warrior."

"What the *fuck*?" spluttered Magweer, all his weapons rattling with upset.

"No room to swing. More men killed by bad luck than good sword-work. It's all just shove and grunt, at the mercy of choices made miles away and hours before by men you'll never meet. Your trouble is you've got yourself an idea about how life should be, but it's just not how life *is*." Magweer twisted his mouth open to spit some rejoinder, but Clover stopped him by bending down to fish a spent flatbow bolt from the grass. Horrible-looking thing, rain gleaming on its barbed head. "Let me show you what I mean. Imagine if one of these bastards fell on you."

Magweer's voice had gone shrill with fury. "Wouldn't be a battle without—" His eyes bulged as Clover caught his shoulder and rammed the bolt through his throat, so hard and so sudden the head punched right out of the back of his neck.

Clover caught him as his knees went, lowering him gently. He glanced both ways, but no one was looking. Man dying on a battlefield is hardly suspicious, after all. Magweer fumbled for one of his many knives but Clover caught his hand and held it tight. "I warned you." He sadly shook his head as Magweer stared up at him, blood bubbling from his nose. "A battle's a dangerous place."

Clover grabbed a fistful of bloody mail and hauled Magweer over his shoulder, put on a look of shocked concern, then set off quick as he could for the rear. Wasn't all that quick, being honest. Been quite a while since he last carried a man. After a few steps, he was puffing hard, specially with all Magweer's weapons dangling about. Just goes to show, hardly matters how many swords you carry if someone else strikes first.

Up the muddy road he struggled, away from the bridge where the fight was going harder than ever, away from the great shield wall that was stretching up the valley, past frowning Carls flooding the other way. More flatbow bolts flickered down from the high ground, peppered the grass.

Clover gritted his teeth and hefted Magweer up his shoulder, feeling the blood seeping warm through his shirt. He kept on, uphill, past a War Chief urging his men to fight harder. Kept on, past a pair of stretcher-bearers with a wounded Thrall wailing between 'em. Kept on, like there was nothing more important than saving this poor arrow-stuck lad on his back. By the dead, it was hard work, but he kept on, all the way up to that farm and its tree with the four bodies still swinging.

The wounded were laid out beside the house, groaning and mewl-ing and squealing for water, or mercy, or their mothers. All the things wounded folk tend to squeal for, they're highly predictable in that regard.

Songs about the glory of it all were thin on the ground right then and there. Clover wished he could've shown this to Magweer while he was still alive. Maybe then he'd have seen. But he doubted it. More often than not, men only see what they want to.

He hefted Magweer off his shoulder and down onto the wet grass where one of the healers was working, bloody to her elbows. She took a quick glance across. "He's dead."

That was no great revelation to Clover. When he chose to stab a man, he aimed to do it in such a way that he'd never need another stabbing, and practice had made him very good at it. But he put on a show of sad surprise even so.

"What a shame." He planted hands on hips and shook his head at the pointlessness of it all. "What a waste."

But, you know. Nothing he hadn't seen a hundred times before.

He stretched out his aching back, frowning at the way he'd come. Battle was still going strong, misty through the falling rain, a great seething mass of bloodshed in the valley's bottom.

"Shit." He wiped his sweaty forehead. "Daresay it'd all be over by the time I got back down there."

The healer didn't answer. Busy tending to the next man in line, who'd a nasty-looking gash out of his shoulder, blood welling down his limp arm in streaks.

Clover found a rock to sit on and set his sword beside it, still sheathed. "Probably best if I just stay up here."

Settle This Like Men

Leo wound the thong tight around his wrist, took a firm grip on the haft, then turned to the riders behind him, rain pattering on their armour and the wet coats of their mounts. He lifted his axe high. "For the Union!" he bellowed, and there were nods and murmurs. "For the king!" Not that anyone was too pleased with His August Majesty these days. "For Angland!" Louder now, manly growls, angry calls, clenched gauntlets thumped on shields. "For your wives and your children!" He put a hand on Jurand's shoulder and stood in his stirrups, trying to make them all feel the same boiling anger, burning eagerness, seething joy he did. "For your honour and your pride!" An answering cheer, smoking from helmets on the wet air, weapons thrust high. "For a piece of fucking vengeance!" A furious roar now, hooves pawing at the mud, men crowding forward, straining to be released.

"For Leo dan Brock!" Glaward punched at the sky, huge as some knight of legend. "The Young Lion!"

That brought the loudest cheer of all, and Leo had to grin. The men found his name almost as inspiring as he did.

"Forward!" And he slapped down his visor and dug in his heels.

First at a walk, down the rutted track from the village, rain-pricked puddles shattered by his horse's hooves. Barniva came level, and through the open face of his helmet Leo could see his eager smile, that fashionable war-weariness burned away in the fire of action. Leo smiled with him and urged his horse on. On, to the very point of the spear, where a leader belonged.

Now at a trot, Antaup bouncing up beside him couched low, Whitewater Jin on the other side, red beard jutting. The valley came up grey through the rain ahead, the stream and the two hills, bouncing with the movement of Leo's horse. Between them the bridge, men crowding onto it from both sides under a tangle of spears.

His smile grew wider. Jurand was beside him, and there was nothing he couldn't do. Finally, he was free of his shackles! He could take his fate in his own hands. Carve out a place in the legends. The way Harod the Great had done, or Casamir the Steadfast. The way the Bloody-Nine had done.

Now at a jolting canter, the thunder of hooves as the best men in Angland followed, charging into battle. A battle ill-suited to horsemen, though, it had to be admitted.

The Union forces were crumbling. They'd been forced back onto the near bank of the stream and now they were starting to break, battle-weary men running in panic, Carls screaming their war cries as they poured across the bridge.

Leo pounded heedless past the scattering Anglanders, fixed on one of the pursuing Northmen. As he saw Leo bearing down, his yellow grin became a circle of surprise. He turned, slipping and falling, hunter become prey. He was still scrambling up when Leo's axe caught him between the shoulders and flung him on his face.

Leo gave a roar of triumph, heard Antaup's shrill whoop over the hammering of hooves, over the wind through his visor. He swung at a Carl, missed as the man threw himself aside, leaned over his saddle to chop down another, sent him reeling into the mud.

Everything simple. No grinding worry, no chafing frustration, no wasted days slipping past. Only the beautiful, terrible now.

"Forward!" he roared, pointlessly. Where else can charging cavalry go? Some Northern horsemen had forced their way across the bridge and he spurred his horse towards them, riding down a fleeing Carl who bounced from his horse's flank and was crushed under the hooves of Barniva's.

He crashed into the midst of the shocked riders, his mount far bigger and better-trained than theirs, flinging them aside like a plough through loose soil. A lovely jolt up his arm as his axe glanced from a Northman's helmet, making him reel in the saddle, thudded into his horse's neck, spattering blood and making the beast totter sideways.

Leo twisted the other way, his helmet hot with his own breath as he snarled and spat and swore. He hacked at a shield, knocked it clear, hacked at the man who held it, ripped his shoulder open and hurled him from his saddle, blood and mail rings flying, hacked at the leg left caught in the stirrups and chopped a great gash in it.

A spear screeched down his shield and Leo caught the haft, wrestled with it, slobbering meaningless curses. He reared up in his saddle, brought his axe up and over in a great arc and smashed the spearman's helmet right in with a hollow thud.

He swung sideways at a rider with silver rings in his beard, missed, got tangled with him, punched at him with his shield hand and snapped his head back. He lived for this! He lived for—

"Gah!" His axe was stuck in something. "Bah!" Its bearded head caught in the straps of a saddle and it was pulling away, dragging him sideways. "Shit!" He struggled to twist his hand from the loop of the axe but he'd made sure it was fast and he was dragged backwards, leg wrenched as his foot was ripped from the stirrup. He tumbled down, the world reeling, took a glancing blow on the helmet from a flailing hoof as a horse dropped beside him.

He rolled, groggy, helmet full of drool. He crawled onto all fours, shook his shield from his arm and fixed on the thong around his wrist, plucking at it, fingers clumsy in his gauntlets. Like trying to sew with mittens on. Something made his ears ring—or were they ringing already?

Suddenly his wrist tore free and he almost stumbled over backwards. The rider with the silver in his beard was lying just next to him, mace in his hand, one leg caught under his horse.

"Bastard!" he was snapping in Northern. "Bastard!" He swatted at Leo with the mace but couldn't hope to reach him. Leo stood, swaying. Mud showered him as a horse thundered past. He realised his hands were empty. Sword! Draw sword.

He pawed at the hilt, trying to shake the fuzz from his head. Faint scrape of steel as it slid from the scabbard. He stabbed at the rider, stumbled, missed, point of the sword sliding into the mud beside him.

"Bastard!" He hit Leo's leg with his mace, but weakly. He hardly even felt it.

Leo was getting less dizzy. He aimed better this time, slid his sword through the man's chest. He sat up and made a long fuffing sound. Fuff. All wheezy and clownish. Leo pulled his sword free and the rider fell back.

He wasn't sure which way he was facing, world a dizzy mess through the slot in his skewed visor. Damn thing must've got bent when the horse kicked him. His head was throbbing. Felt like he could hardly breathe. He fumbled the buckle open, dragged his helmet halfway around before he could finally twist it off.

The chill wind hit his sweaty face like a slap and the world rushed at him, the roar of battle furiously loud.

"Leo!" Someone had him by the arm and he almost swung before he saw it was Barniva, unhorsed and mud-smeared. Dead horses everywhere. Dead men. Wounded men. Broken weapons. Leo wobbled down and clawed up a shield. A Carl's round shield. Shoved his arm through the straps. A Northman was crawling through the mud with a broken spear sticking from his back. Leo chopped his head open.

"Regroup!" he roared, hardly knowing who he was shouting at, hardly sure if there was anyone left to regroup except him and Barniva. It didn't matter. They could do it together. He could do it alone.

The rain was coming hard, fat drops pinging from his armour, soaking into the padding beneath, turning it to cold lead. "To the bridge!" And he started to slog in the direction he thought it was, trusting that men were following. He'd retreated for long enough.

He caught sight of his standard. The white field, the golden lion. Hanging sodden at the near end of the bridge. And there was Stour Nightfall's. The slavering wolf on grey. Drooping in the rain at the far end. A lion fought a wolf in a circle of blood, and the lion won.

Leo bared his teeth, squelching forward through mud battered and mashed by countless boots advancing and retreating, advancing and retreating. The fighting had been fiercest here. Bodies everywhere. Bodies from both sides. Men still and men still moving, crawling, crying, pawing at the ground, pawing at themselves. Leo stepped between them, stepped over them, teeth clenched, head throbbing, pushing on towards the bridge.

"Leo!" Barniva grabbed him, dragged him down, shield across his face. Something rattled from it. An arrow. Another bounced from Barniva's armoured shoulder, more flickered into the grass. Someone fell, hands clapped to his throat. Leo peered over the rim of his shield, saw the archers, kneeling in a long row before the bridge, nocking arrows.

Barniva sat down. "Lo," he said, tongue strangely clumsy.

There was an arrow sticking out of his face. In the hollow between his eye and the bridge of his nose. It looked ridiculous. Like a joke. Like a child wedging his wooden sword between his arm and his ribs and standing sideways on. I'm stabbed! I'm stabbed!

But it was no joke. The white of Barniva's eye had turned red. Blood-stained.

Leo caught him by the shoulders as he dropped backwards. "Luh," he said, red eye rolling off to look sideways. The other was slightly crossed, peering at the shaft poking from his face, a look of confused surprise.

"Uh." A long streak of blood leaked from the shaft and down his cheek, like a red tear.

"Barniva?" said Leo. But he didn't move.

"Barniva?" He was dead.

Leo stood, numb. More arrows flitted down around him with the rain. He lifted his sword, anger boiling up with it.

"Charge!" he bellowed, though it came out just a mad gurgle. Other men roared behind him. Glaward's voice, and Jin's, and Jurand's, war cries, mad screams. They were all running. An arrow flickered past. Another rattled off Leo's breastplate.

"Fuckers!" he screeched, spraying spit. "Fuckers!" He caught his foot and went sliding on his face, took a mouthful of grass, near stabbing himself with his own blade. He scrambled up and charged on, throwing his stolen shield away and lifting his sword in both hands.

A glimpse of the stream, full of bobbing bodies. A glimpse of the archers as he clattered closer. Some old men. Some young men. One had a leather hood. One a shock of curly red hair. One's face was bent sideways by some old wound. He saw Leo pounding towards him, faltered as he drew an arrow from his quiver, let it fall, turning to run. The one with curly hair loosed a shaft from only a few strides away but he fumbled it in his panic and it went spinning high into the air.

He ducked gasping under Leo's sword but Leo crashed into him with his shoulder, knocked him on his back, started hacking at the others, ears full of their squeals and gibbers and his own growls and the smashing and cracking of metal and flesh.

"Die!" Glaward roared in his ear. "Die!"

The archers had no armour and Leo's sword thudded into them like a butcher's cleaver into meat, opening great spitting and spurting wounds. One man fell screaming with his side laid right open. Leo broke a man's bow as he tried to block his sword with it and took his arm off, too, tottered past all off balance, bounced off Antaup as he stabbed a man on the ground with his spear. He fell, rolled, saw an archer with a knife ready to spring on him, lifted a clumsy arm to fend him off, then he was smashed out of the way by a great mace. Whitewater Jin, and he grabbed Leo's wrist and dragged him up.

The archers were running, being hacked down, floundering into the stream, and Leo wobbled on towards the bridge.

A man was stumbling away, clutching at his shoulder, blood bubbling between his fingers, and Leo hit him across the side of the head with his sword, caught him with the flat and knocked him sprawling, trampled over him.

His chest was on fire now, his limbs numb and floppy. Every step was a mountain.

Onto the bridge. He could feel the stones slippery with mud and blood, slick with the falling rain.

There were Carls here, desperately trying to organise a shield wall. A

Named Man with a fox-fur around his shoulders pointed with a thick finger. Leo didn't so much charge at him as fall onto him, his weary swing clattering harmlessly off the Named Man's shield. He caught his chin on the rim, mouth filling with the salt taste of blood.

The Northman lurched back a pace but didn't fall, and they twisted into an awkward, exhausted embrace, shuffling, snarling, wrestling, shouldering and elbowing while armoured men clobbered away at each other around them.

Leo heard the Northman's desperate, whistling breath in his ear, grunted and clawed at him, wet fur in his mouth. His sword was tangled with something, couldn't move it. He managed to draw his dagger with his other hand, stabbed, but the blade only scraped uselessly on mail. No room. No breath. No strength, the dagger twisted from his grip, fell in the mud.

They lumbered about in a pawing circle, bounced off the bridge's parapet, enough room for Leo to force his free hand up under the man's chin, push his gauntleted thumb into his mouth, shove it through so he caught a fistful of his cheek, ripping his lip open, tearing his face open, and the man screamed and grabbed Leo's wrist, letting Leo's sword loose. With a last growling effort, Leo shoved him away, smashed him on the side of the head, flinched as blood spotted his face, something bouncing off his cheek. A tooth, maybe. The man went reeling over the mossy parapet and splashed into the stream with the other corpses. Bloody thing was more corpse than river now. No corpses, no glory.

Leo flopped down on all fours, clawed up his sword along with a fistful of mud. Up to one knee, with a groan to his feet and he stood swaying, grasping at the slick stones, every muscle throbbing, dragging in air in great wheezing gasps, like a fish hooked and hauled helpless from the river.

"Have...to pull back." It was Jurand, with hardly the breath to talk. Helmet off and his face spotted with blood. He hugged Leo, half holding him up, half leaning on him. "Get you to safety."

"No," growled Leo, gripping him tight, their wet armour scraping, then trying to struggle free, to press on. "We *fight*."

The rain was hammering down, pinging and spattering. The empty bridge stretched away, a rutted hump scattered with arrow-pricked and spear-pierced corpses, sprawled beside the parapets, heaped against them, draped over them. And at the far end, beneath that wolf standard, more Northmen were gathered.

A group as muddy, bloody and sodden as Leo, teeth bared with hate but weapons drooping from weariness. They faced each other across the rain-drenched bridge, Leo and his friends at one end, this knot of Named Men at the other, and in their midst a tall man, long hair plastered to his snarling face by the rain.

"Leo dan Brock!" he shrieked, wet eyes wild with battle-madness, and Leo knew from the gold on his sword and the gold on his belt and the gold on his armour who he had to be.

"Stour Nightfall!" Leo roared back, spit flying from his bared teeth. He tried to drag himself forward but Jurand held him back, or maybe held him up, it was only fury stopped Leo's knees from buckling.

"We won't settle this on the field!" snarled Nightfall.

That was true enough. They were all fought out. Up on the red hill, vague through the rain, the Union were pulling back, but Stour's men were in no shape to follow and the rain had turned the battlefield to glue.

Stour fought free of his warriors and stood tall, pointing across the bridge with his blood-slathered sword. "Let's settle it like men! In the Circle! You and me!"

Leo hardly even gave a shit about the terms. All he wanted was to fight this bastard. To rip him apart with his bare hands. To bite him with his teeth.

A lion fought a wolf in a circle of blood, and the lion won.

"In the Circle!" he bellowed into the rain. "You and me!"

PART III

"Love turns, with a little indulgence,

to indifference or disgust;

hatred alone is immortal."

William Hazlitt

Demands

Forest stepped into the room wearing his hallmark fur hat and ruggedly grave expression. The hat he removed. The grave expression he kept in place. "The Breakers should be here soon, Your Highness."

"Good," murmured Orso. "Good." He expressed the exact opposite of his feelings so often, one might have hoped he would be better at it. In fact, the thought of the Breakers' arrival left him desperately wanting a drink. But dawn was probably considered too early at a peace negotiation, even for a small beer or something. He puffed out a worried sigh.

A local worthy had offered up his dining room as the venue, and though the table was highly polished, Orso found the chairs exceedingly uncomfortable. Or perhaps he simply found himself uncomfortable in the role of negotiator. Or any responsible role, really. He nervously straightened his jacket for the thousandth time. It had fit him perfectly in the safety of Adua, but suddenly it was tight about the throat. He leaned towards Superior Pike with an apologetic smile.

"I think it might be useful if, when they arrive...you were to play the villain?"

Pike subjected Orso to that withering stare. "Because of my hideous burns?"

"That and all the black."

The faint twisting of Pike's face might almost have been a smile. "Don't worry, Your Highness, I have had some practice in the role. Feel free to slap me down if I become too dastardly. I look forward to seeing you as the hero of our little piece."

"I hope I can convince," murmured Orso, tugging his jacket smooth yet again. "I fear I missed all the rehearsals."

The double doors swung open and the Breakers strode in. Orso's ever-fertile imagination had built them up into red-handed zealots. In the flesh, they were a slightly disappointingly, then perhaps a rather reassuringly, ordinary group.

In the lead came a weighty old man: brawny shoulders, broad hands, heavy-lidded eyes that settled on Orso and stayed there, immovable. Next came a fellow with a scarred face whose eyes settled on nothing, darting twitchily around the room to windows, doors, the half-dozen guards about the panelled walls, meeting no one's eye. Finally, there was a woman with a stained coat and an unkempt shag of lank hair, one of the hardest frowns Orso ever saw showing beneath. The look of implacable scorn in her blue eyes actually reminded him more than a little of his mother.

"Welcome!" He aimed at a balance between warm indulgence and effortless authority, but no doubt ended up with prickly weakness. "I am Crown Prince Orso, this is Colonel Forest, commander of the four regiments currently encircling Valbeck, and this—"

"We've all heard of Superior Pike," said the old man, dropping heavily into the middle chair and frowning across the table.

"Only good things, I hope," whispered Pike, oozing menace. Orso felt the hairs on his neck bristling even though he sat on the same side. When it came to playing the villain, he was clearly in the presence of a virtuoso.

"My name is Malmer." The old Breaker's voice was as weighty as his frame, each word placed as carefully as a master mason fits his stones. "This is Brother Heron, fought a dozen years in your father's armies." He nodded towards the scar-faced man, then to the hard-faced woman, who appeared to be reaching greater heights of epic contempt with every breath Orso took. "This is Sister Teufel, spent a dozen years in your father's prison camps."

"Charmed?" ventured Orso, more in hope than expectation, but Pike was already sitting forward, lips curling back.

"You will address the Crown Prince of the Union as your—"

"Please!" Orso held up a calming hand and made Pike sit back like a hound called off. "No one will die because of a defect of etiquette. It is my ardent hope that no one will die at all. I understand . . . hostages have been taken?"

"Five hundred and forty-eight at the last count," grated out the woman, Teufel, as if delivering a mortal insult to a lifelong enemy.

"But we'd like nothing better than to see 'em released," said Malmer.

Orso burned to ask whether Savine was among them but, incompetent negotiator though he was, even he saw that could only put her in more danger. He had to bite down on it. Had to stop following his cock from one disaster to another and use his head for once. "In which case you could simply release them?" he ventured.

Malmer gave a sad smile, leathery skin creasing about his eyes. "I'm afraid we've got some demands first."

"The Crown does not negotiate with traitors," grated out Pike.

"Please, gentlemen, please." Orso held up that calming hand again. "Let us set the blame aside and concentrate on a resolution that gives everyone some of what they want." He was surprised by how well that came out. Perhaps he wasn't so bad at this after all. "By all means, present your demands—"

His satisfaction was quickly cut off as Teufel flung a folded paper so it spun across the polished table and into his lap. He winced as he unfolded it, expecting insults scrawled in blood.

But there was only small, neat writing in a tightly controlled hand.

Show no surprise. Pretend you are looking at a list of demands. In spite of appearances, I am your friend.

Caught off guard, Orso glanced up at the woman. She glared back at him even more angrily than before, hard lines forming between her brows.

"You can read, can't you, *Your Highness?*" she sneered.

"I must have worn out a dozen tutors, but my mother was most insistent that I learn." Orso frowned down at the paper, trying to look like a man baffled by what he saw there. It required no great effort of acting on his part.

Superior Risinau was the prime instigator of the uprising but fled the city before you arrived, along with the Burners, who caused most of the death and damage. Malmer is in charge now, if anyone is. He is not a bad man. He does not wish to see the hostages hurt. His main concern is for the safety of civilians, and for the Breakers and their families. He has demands but he is becoming desperate. Food is scarce and order is collapsing.

This information was, to say the least, as useful as it was unexpected, but Orso kept his face carefully blank. He acted as if he had drawn a winning hand at the gaming table, and now had only to drag the biggest bets possible from the other players.

Malmer knows he has little left to bargain with. Offer him too much and he will become suspicious. He feared you would attack at once. Now he fears you will surround the city and starve the Breakers out. He expects you to be an arrogant liar. My advice is to treat him with honesty

305

and respect. To seek a peaceful solution and avoid bluster. But to firmly
refuse any demands and make him aware that you know time is on your
side. If you were to offer amnesty for the Breakers, I believe he could be
persuaded to surrender. He knows that is more than he could hope for.

The Breakers' demands were laid out next: changes to labour laws, controls on wages and the price of bread, sanitation and housing, things Orso scarcely understood, let alone could grant.

Superior Pike held out his melted glove of a hand. "May I, Your—"

"You may not." Orso folded the paper, sharpened the crease in it with his thumbnail and slipped it inside his jacket.

Then he smiled—always begin with a smile—and he leaned towards Malmer as though sharing a confidence with an old friend. As though the fates of thousands in no way hinged on their coming to an agreement.

"Master Malmer, I judge you to be an honest man, and I want to be honest in return. It would be easy for me to offer you the world, but I do not wish to insult you. The truth is, the Closed Council is in no mood to negotiate and, even if I agreed to all your demands..." He spread his hands in the same gesture of cavalier helplessness he used with jilted lovers, frustrated creditors and outraged officers of the law. "I'm the crown prince. There would be nothing to stop my father or his advisors refusing to honour my promises. I suspect, frankly, that's the very reason they sent me. And I suspect, frankly...you're well aware of that."

"Then why are we even here?" snapped Heron.

Forest had managed to crank his scarred face a notch graver. "Troops stand ready to move into the city at your order, Your Highness—"

"The *very* last thing we want is further bloodshed, Colonel Forest," said Orso, giving him the calming palm now. He had enough calming palm for everyone. "We are all citizens of the Union. We are all subjects of my father. I refuse to believe we cannot find a peaceful solution."

He might not have spent much time negotiating for hostages, but at convincing people he could be trusted, whether in a gaming hall, a lady's bedroom or a moneylender's shop, he had almost bottomless experience to draw on. He softened his voice, he softened his face, he softened everything. He held Malmer's eye and made himself all syrupy sympathy.

"I am aware that the author of this unfortunate situation...was Superior Risinau. I note that he has not come forward to negotiate, however. Perhaps as the danger grew, his commitment to his own cause shrivelled?" Did Orso detect the slightest twitch on Malmer's stony face?

"I know that type of man. Let us be honest, I have often seen him in the mirror. A man who makes a mess and leaves others to mop up."

Nobody leaped to his defence, which was disappointing, but nor did they leap to Risinau's.

"I understand what it's like..." he gave his three opponents each a sympathetic look, "to be left with the blame. I appreciate that those of you still in the city are those who chose to stay and try to salvage the situation. The authors of this disaster will be tracked down and punished, of that I assure you."

"Of that there is no question," hissed Pike.

"But I have no interest in punishing you for their crimes," said Orso. "My concern—my *only* concern—is the safety of the men, women and children of Valbeck. All of them, regardless of where their loyalties may have lain. I can bring your demands to my father. I can relay your demands to the Closed Council. But, in the end, you and I both know I cannot promise to meet them." Orso took a long breath and gave a long sigh. "I can, however...promise you amnesty. A full pardon to every Breaker who surrenders themselves and their weapons by sunset tomorrow, along with all your hostages, unharmed. Supplies of food will then immediately be allowed into the city."

"Your Highness," broke in Pike. "We cannot allow traitors to—"

Orso silenced him with that raised hand, without taking his eyes from Malmer's. "I fear the alternative is that I order Colonel Forest to surround the city and let nothing in or out. I have quite cleared my calendar and can wait as long as it takes. When you surrender, which you surely must, it will not be to me, but to Superior Pike."

It hardly needed to be said that there was no comfort to be found in the Superior's melted face. Malmer slowly sat back and gave Orso weighty consideration. "Why should we trust you?"

"I can understand why you wouldn't. But in light of the circumstances, I believe this to be a generous offer. I *know* it to be the very best you can hope for."

Malmer glanced at Heron. Then at Teufel. Neither gave anything away. "I'll need to discuss it with my people."

"Of course," said Orso, standing. He offered his hand as Malmer got to his feet. The old Breaker frowned at it for a moment, then folded it in his big paw.

Orso held on firmly. "But I must insist on an answer by sundown today."

"You'll have it." Malmer considered him a moment longer. "Your

Highness." He strode weightily from the room, his twitchy friend at his back. Teufel's chair screeched on the tiled floor as she stood, gave Orso one last blast of scorn, then turned her back on the meeting. The door clicked shut.

"That was well done, Your Highness." There was the faintest suggestion of surprise about Superior Pike's hairless brows, and who could blame him? Orso had been diligently fostering low expectations for the past decade. "Quite masterfully done."

"I must confess, I had considerable help." Orso fished the list of demands from his jacket. "From the woman with the face like a pickaxe."

Pike blinked down at Orso's entire negotiating strategy, arranged in careful blocks of neat writing. "She must be the Arch Lector's agent within the city."

"I cannot see another explanation. It appears she has worked her way into a position of some trust among the Breakers."

"Impressive." Pike frowned towards the door. "A great deal now hangs on her assessment."

"It does indeed, Superior." Orso felt a sting of worry as he thought about Savine. Alone in the city. A hostage? A corpse? He grimaced. He had a bastard of a headache coming up behind the eyes.

Perhaps it wasn't too early for that drink after all.

Taking the Reins

Rikke's nose tingled with the chill before dawn, and the breath of the wounded men made plumes of smoke.

She wondered how many were laid out in that glade. Maybe a hundred. Maybe more. Hunched and bloodstained healers moved among them, stitching, bandaging, setting, giving food and water and what comfort they could. It wasn't much.

There was a low drone, like one of those flowering bushes the bees can't leave alone, but made of murmurs, whimpers, groans and sobs. A chorus of pain. Quite the downer, all told. Rikke shivered and pulled the fur tight around her neck with her free hand.

"Hold it higher, I said."

"Sorry." Her shoulder ached as she lifted the torch again so Isern could see her business, tongue tip wedged into the gap in her teeth as she stitched the red wound in a boy's shoulder. He had a stick to bite on, eyes closed and tear-tracks gleaming on his pink cheeks.

"Never really thought of you as a healer," said Rikke, wincing as Isern sponged blood away with a rag.

"No?"

"Didn't think you'd be gentle enough."

"Gentle? Ha! If you're wounded, a gentle healer's the last thing you want." Isern made the boy gurgle as she dug the needle back into his shoulder. "If you're wounded, a gentle healer could be the last thing you get. A great healer needs to be tougher and more ruthless than a great warrior. They're taking on a far harder job with far less reward."

One of the other healers grunted agreement around the little knife she was holding in her teeth.

Isern gave Rikke a significant look from under her brows. "A great healer, like a great leader, must make of her heart a stone."

309

The lad Isern was working on pulled the spit-slathered stick out of his mouth. "For the dead's sake, don't distract her."

"I can stitch you and talk to her at once, boy." And Isern plucked the stick from his hand, shoved it back between his jaws and carried on stitching.

Rikke looked wide-eyed across the groaning glade. "So many wounded."

"And these are the best-looking ones. The ones who might yet get up."

"You wonder why they keep doing it."

"What, war?"

"Aye, war."

"Maybe they wouldn't if all the Named Men came down here to have their faces rubbed in what's growed from what they've sowed, but they don't come down here, do they? Not very nice down here, d'you see? Not much shiny metal, except the bits we dig out o' the dying men. Women's work, isn't it, healing?"

Sounded a touch hypocritical in Isern's case, since Rikke had seen her kill at least five men with that spear of hers, but as a general principle it was hard to disagree. "They break," she murmured, "we make."

Isern shook her head, lips pressed into a hard line as she nimbly worked that needle. "All the effort it takes to make a person but it's the killers they sing about. When did you last hear a man sing a woman's name? Unless he was singing for his mummy when the Great Leveller had a hand on him."

"No doubt there's many ways in which the world could be better," said Rikke, with a smoky sigh.

"My heartfelt thanks for that revelation," said Isern, rolling a scornful eye towards her. "The one thing I've learned in thirty-six winters is the world won't change itself. You want some wounds mended, you'd better be ready to stitch."

Rikke felt even more than usually helpless in the midst of all this pain. "What can I do?"

"You? Rikke, with the Long Eye? Saw Black Calder's men coming, didn't you? Saved the army, maybe. Saved us all, maybe."

"Maybe." It was true folk were looking at her different since the battle. Like they respected her, which was a pleasant change. Like they feared her, which was less so. Like they hated her, a couple of 'em, which oddly was unpleasant and pleasant both at once. She'd never thought she'd be important enough to hate.

"You're not nobody any more, Sticky Rikke." Isern opened her eyes very wide. "The legend grows."

"Legend." Rikke snorted. "I'm nothing and no one."

"Ah, but isn't that how all the best legends begin? I'd hazard you're better equipped to lead us to a brighter tomorrow than most."

"I'm no bloody leader."

"How could you be, shuffling along at the back whining about how useless y'are? Hold that torch higher."

"Sorry. You'll have to find someone else to hold it soon. I've been called to a meeting at dawn." Rikke puffed herself up. "By Lady Governor Brock, in fact."

"Wants to use your womanly wiles to convince her son not to fight, does she?"

Rikke sagged back down. "If she's counting on my womanly wiles, she must be bloody desperate."

"Oh, I reckon you've more wiles than you realise. Talked the boy into fighting in the first place, didn't you?" And Isern gave her this sidewise glance, like they were in on some cunning scheme together.

"What?"

"With your lions and wolves and circles of blood."

"That's just what I saw, in the vision. You asked me what I saw!"

Isern paused in her work. "You can't choose what you see. But you can choose what you say. Moment ago, you were talking about changing the world. Now you can't even change one boy's mind? Let's face the facts, it's not the biggest mind around." She tore the thread with her teeth and reached for the bandages. "I know you like to think you're jolting about helpless in a runaway cart, carried off to who-knows-where with no say in the matter, but if you look down, you might see you're holding the reins." She gave Rikke another one of those looks. "Might be it's time to use 'em. Now hold that bloody torch up."

The Young Lion never looked bad, but being angry suited him, and being battle-scratched suited him, and even being a touch sulky seemed to suit him. Overall, Rikke was having some trouble imagining a better-looking man.

The trouble is that duels to the death aren't always won by the best-looking. If anything, history favours ugly champions. Maybe they spend the time training that the pretty ones spend preening in the mirror. Rikke kept that thought to herself, though, since everyone was rattled enough already. Leo had staked all their futures on a duel with one of the most dangerous men in the North, after all, and about the only person who didn't reckon that the worst idea since swords made of cake was Leo himself, known widely for his poor judgement.

Rikke's mood was by no means helped by the knight herald standing motionless in the middle of the tent, a letter from His August Majesty held out in one gauntleted fist. When she'd slipped through the flap and seen him standing there, she'd wondered where they found all these tall bastards. Then she'd wondered why everyone else was ignoring him. Then, during a particularly impassioned rant, the lady governor had walked right through him and back the other way, and Rikke had realised her left eye was hot and he wasn't actually there. Or wasn't there yet, maybe.

When she'd seen Black Calder coming, she'd started to reckon the Long Eye a blessing. Now it was looking like a curse all over again.

"I can't back out," Leo was saying, all sullen and scratched and beautiful. "What'll I *look* like?"

His mother stared in disbelief. She'd been doing that a lot. "There are bigger things at stake than *what you look like!*"

Rikke's father took a turn, easing himself between the two of them, putting a calming hand on Leo's shoulder. "Look, son, it's an irony of life that the older you get, and the less years there are ahead of you, the more you fear the loss of 'em. When you're young, it can feel like you're invincible, but..." He snapped his fingers under Leo's nose. "Fast as that, it can all be took away."

"I know that!" said Leo. "It was your stories of the Bloody-Nine that made me fascinated by duels in the first place! All his great victories in the Circle. The fate of the North hanging on a single—"

Rikke's father looked horrified. "Those were supposed to be warnings, boy, not encouragements!"

"Has it occurred to either of you that I might bloody *win*?" Leo angrily bunched one scabbed fist. "We're fought out! We've no help coming and Scale Ironhand has fresh men ready! This might be our only chance to take back Uffrith. To keep the Protectorate alive!"

Rikke's father folded his arms, and puffed up a slow sigh, and glanced at Leo's mother from under his bushy brows. "Can't deny he's got a point."

"I can win!" Leo came to stand right next to the frozen knight herald, the big seal on the scroll that wasn't there almost touching his face. "I *know* I can! Rikke saw it!"

Rikke's father and Leo's mother turned together to look at her. She stood frozen, mouth and eyes wide open like a burglar caught with her hand in a purse.

And it came to her then that Isern had been right. What she'd seen was one thing but what she said another, and there needn't be a straight road between the two, but any kind of maze she chose to put there. Sorry, Leo,

I made a mistake. Sorry, Leo, your mother's right. Sorry, Leo, actually the lion lost, and got his fruits ripped off and stuck on a pike.

Might be she was holding the reins after all. Might be she always had been. Might be she'd done this, and could undo it.

But somewhere at the back of her mind, in a dark corner she'd hardly known she had, she found she wanted to see Leo fight Stour Nightfall. To see him spill that evil bastard's blood in front of the whole North. To take her share of vengeance, for her father, for those wounded in the glade, for the dead already in the mud, for the shit she'd gone through out in the cold woods.

She could've said anything. She chose to tell the truth.

"I saw a lion and a wolf fight in a circle of blood, and the lion won."

Leo's mother pressed her fingers to her temples. "So you are going to risk your life, not to mention the future of the North, because this girl saw animals fighting while she had a *fit*?"

"She saw the Nail come from the woods before it happened," said Rikke's father, forced against his better judgement into defending her. "Weren't for that, we might all be in the mud already."

"For pity's sake, Rikke!" shouted Finree. "You're no fool! Tell him this is madness!"

"Well . . ." Rikke frowned at jingling footsteps outside, spurs on armoured boots, and she rolled her eyes up to the tent's ceiling. "Ahhhhh. I get it."

"Get what?"

"Hardly matters what I think. Or you."

"Might I ask why?"

Rikke nodded towards the tent flap. "Because of him."

It was swept open with a swirling of cloth and the knight herald stomped into the tent. He pulled the scroll from his satchel and stepped forward, coming to stand just exactly where he'd been standing the whole time, scroll offered out to Leo, great seal dangling.

"My Lord Brock," he said. "A message from the king."

There was a breathless stillness in the tent as Leo took the scroll and slowly unrolled it. He read the first few lines and looked up, eyes wide.

"The king confirms me in my father's place as Lord Governor of Angland."

Rikke's father let go a long, slow breath. Leo's mother took a half-step forwards.

"Leo—"

"No," he said. Not sharp, but very firm. "I know you want what's best for me, Mother. I'm grateful for all you've taught me. But I have to stand

313

on my own now. I'm fighting Stour Nightfall. Nothing anyone can say will change my mind."

And he turned and pushed his way out of the tent.

The knight herald nodded, somewhat sheepishly, to Lady Finree, then followed the new Lord Governor of Angland, thankfully taking his ghost with him.

Rikke's father rubbed wearily at his stubbled jaw. "Well. We tried." And he patted Rikke on the shoulder and made his own way out.

Lady Finree was left staring towards the flap. A few moments ago, she'd been in total command. With a stroke of the king's pen, she was cut down to some warrior's worried mother.

"It feels like yesterday I was feeding him, and dressing him, and wiping his arse." She looked at Rikke, voice turning harsh. "He's a bloody idiot who knows nothing about anything, but he was born with a cock, so he gets to decide for all of us!"

She looked old, of a sudden, and weak, and helpless, and Rikke felt sorry for her, and sorry for what she'd done, but there was no undoing it. You might see the past with the Long Eye. But you can never go there.

She shrugged so high her shoulders were tickling her ears, then let them flop helplessly down. "Maybe he'll win?"

A Fool's Weapon

"The bloody *fool*!" snarled Calder, stalking through the village.

"Aye." Clover sighed as he followed. "Bloody fool."

The muddy place was crawling with Scale's warriors, men armed and angry and used never to backing down. They soon scrambled aside, though, when they saw Black Calder coming with a face like thunder.

"I loved my wife, Clover," he growled. "Loved her more than my own life."

"Well...that's a good thing, I guess?"

"That was my great weakness."

"Ah."

"I loved her, and she died, and all that was left of her was our son."

"Oh."

Calder strode on towards the chieftain's hall the King of the Northmen had made into his temporary tavern. "So I indulged him, and I spoiled him, and on the many occasions when I should've given the bloody fool the beating he deserved, I saw her face in his face and I couldn't do it."

"Might be a bit late to spank him now," murmured Clover.

"We'll fucking see," said Calder, shoving the doors of the hall wide and storming through.

King Scale was drinking. What else would he be doing? He was drinking, and laughing lustily at stories of the battle, already bloating out with lies like so much watered beer. His nephew, the mighty Stour Nightfall, decorated with a few fresh cuts and bruises, grinned to hear of his own exploits, even more at the falsehoods than the facts. About these two heroes, old warriors and young basked in the sunny radiance of a victory they hadn't won yet.

They fell silent as Calder strode in, carrying no weapon but with his face sharp as a drawn sword. "Get. Out."

The old cunts and the young bristled, grumbled, looked to their respective masters, and Scale puffed his vein-threaded cheeks and gestured to the door. Up they got, out they filed, giving Clover his usual serving of scorn while he beamed back his usual good humour. The doors were shut on their performance, leaving only four in the room. King Scale Ironhand, his brother Black Calder, *his* son Stour Nightfall. And Clover.

Quite the party.

"My loving family, all together!" sang Calder in a voice rich with scorn.

Stour was all preening dismissal. "Father—"

"Don't 'Father' me, boy! You approve of this madness, do you, Scale?"

"We're at war, brother." The King of the Northmen looked calmly at Calder from under his grey-streaked brows. "And in war, yes, I approve of warriors fighting."

"It's how they fight and when that's the issue! You'd put all our gains at risk! All our work!" Meaning all Calder's work, since Scale had done nothing but drink at the back and Stour nothing but strut at the front. "You're our *future*, Stour! The future of the North! We can't risk you—"

"You said the same when I fought Stranger-Come-Knocking!" Stour waved his father away like a cobweb. "*He's too dangerous, we can't risk you, you're all our futures.*" He put on a parroting whine which was, to be fair, not too bad a match for Calder's prating. "But I *beat* him! Like the Bloody-Nine beat Shama Heartless, when no one said he could!" And his chest puffed and his eyes twinkled, like a cock that spies another in his yard. "This Union child isn't half the warrior Stranger-Come-Knocking was! Not one quarter!"

"The Young Lion, they call him, and my spies tell me he's formidable. How often have I said to you—never fear your enemy, but always respect him? Every duel is a risk and we don't need to gamble. The enemy are fought out and we have fresh warriors. Flatstone can come around on the flank and the ground is—"

"Enough *strategy*." Scale wrinkled his nose as if the word smelled. "Back in winter, you told me the war would be won in spring. In spring, you told me it would be won in summer. In summer, by autumn. Last week, you told me the war was won now. That you'd out-thought that Union bitch and outfought the Dogman. Seems the Union bitch is a sharper thinker and the Dogman a tougher fighter than you reckoned. What if you misjudge 'em again, and you can't finish 'em before the weather turns, and the sluggardly King of the Union wakes up and sends help? What *then*?"

Calder angrily waved it away. "If help was coming from Midderland, it would've come already. We can still finish them before winter."

"Don't worry," said Stour. "I can finish 'em before sunset tomorrow." And he laughed, and Scale laughed, and Calder very decidedly didn't, and Clover watched 'em, thinking this was no great way to run a kingdom. "The Bloody-Nine never backed out of a fight, nor Black Dow, nor Whirrun of Bligh, and nor will I."

"You've made a list of *dead fools*," hissed Calder, near tearing his hair. "Tell him, Clover, for the sake of the dead, tell him!"

Clover had been telling Stour for near half a year and made no mark, like shooting a quiver full of daffodils at a man in full plate armour. But one more daffodil could do no harm. He spread his hands as if he held out a platter covered in fine advice. "There's no bigger foolishness than to choose to face a dangerous man on equal terms. Look at me. Lost everything in the Circle."

Stour's lip curled. "Your fruits, too?"

"They're still there, my prince, if a little shrivelled. But I don't think with 'em any more."

"My nephew beat Stranger-Come-Knocking in the Circle," said the king, blowing some froth from his ale. "He can beat some Union fool."

"Who was it took your hand, brother?" said Calder. "Some Union fool, as I recall?"

Scale didn't anger, just smiled to show his missing front teeth. "You're wise, brother. You're cunning. Just like our father. What I have I owe to your wits and your ruthlessness and your loyalty, I know that. There are many things you understand far better than me. But you're no fighter."

Calder's lip curled with contempt. "You haven't fought a man in twenty years! You only want to watch him fight so you can relive your lost glories. You're fat as a—"

"Yes, I'm fat as a hog and twenty years past my best and I daresay quite the figure of fun for most. But there is one thing you're forgetting, brother." Scale hooked his thumb under his golden chain and lifted it so the great diamond dangled, sparkling with the flames in the firepit. "*I* am our father's eldest son. *I* wear his chain. *I* am king!" He let the chain fall, and slapped his good hand down on Stour's shoulder. "I name Stour Nightfall not only as my heir but as my champion. He'll stand for me in the Circle, and fight for Uffrith and all the land between the Cusk and the Whiteflow. That's the end of it."

Stour broke out that wet-eyed grin of his. "Perhaps you should leave the warriors to their talk, Father. We've the choice of weapons to discuss."

Calder stood quiet a moment longer, face a rigid mask. "Warriors," he hissed, like it was the worst insult he could think of, then turned on his heel and stalked from the room.

Stour lifted his ale cup. "By the dead, when the mood's on him, he can bleat like a fucking sheep—"

There was a sharp crack as Scale slapped him, knocking the cup from his hand and sending it spinning across the floor. "You'd be wise to treat your father with respect, boy!" snarled the king, his great finger shoved in Stour's shocked and pinking face. "Everything you have you owe to him!" There was a long silence, then Scale gave the golden pommel of the heavy sword he wore a fond pat. "Call me old-fashioned, but I still favour a sword. What do you say, Clover?"

"I say a sword's a fool's weapon."

Stour was rubbing his face with his fingertips, looking at his uncle through narrowed eyes. Now he turned them on Clover. "You carry one."

"I do." Clover picked at his own battered pommel with a fingernail. "But I try never to draw it."

Scale threw up his hands, the iron and the flesh. "You make your living teaching other folk to use one!"

"They pay me to learn. But I always start by telling 'em never to fight with one. Come at a man with a sword, he'll see you coming, and if a man you mean to kill sees you coming then you're going about it all wrong."

"There's no hiding in the Circle." Stour turned away from Clover in disgust. "In the Circle, the other man's always ready."

"That's why I'd stay even further from the Circle than I would from the sword," said Clover. "Money, land, fame, friends, even your name—lose them but keep your life, with time and hard labour you can always win 'em back." He'd lost his name, hadn't he? And won a new? He could still smell the sweet clover in his nose as he lay there in the Circle, waiting for the end. "But there's no beating the Great Leveller. No man comes back from the mud."

Stour gave a hiss of disgust. "Fucking coward's words."

"A live coward can find his courage another day. A dead hero . . ." Clover liked to talk, but sometimes silence says more. He let it stretch a moment longer, then smiled. "Still. I daresay you'll have it your way, Great Wolf."

And he followed Black Calder out of the hall.

Hopes and Hatreds

"They packed him in a box," said Jurand, staring sadly into the fire.

"Who?" asked Glaward.

"Barniva. To be sent back to his family."

Whitewater winced, prodding at a big bruise he'd picked up in the battle. "I guess that's what they do. With dead men."

"They packed him with salt, but I daresay he'll be ripe by the time he gets there—"

"Are you auditioning for his part as the war-weary one?" snapped Leo, not enjoying this conversation at all. Not wanting to think about Barniva's death. Not wanting to think about what part he might've had in it. "I've got a bloody duel to win. They might be packing *me* in a box this time tomorrow!"

"But they won't need to send you anywhere," said Whitewater, brow crinkling with puzzlement. "Your mother's in the camp."

Leo gritted his teeth. "My point is, I need to *focus*. It's a shame about Barniva. He was a brave man. A good friend. Always there when you needed him." He felt his voice quavering a little. "If he hadn't put his shield across me..." Perhaps he'd still be alive. All his tedious warnings about the horrors of war seemed wise words now. Leo never thought he might have missed them. "It's a damn shame about Barniva, but we'll have to mourn him later. Right now, we need to make his sacrifice worthwhile. Him, and Ritter, and all the others..." His voice was quavering again, damn it. He felt a surge of anger. "I need you all to bloody *focus*. I have to pick a weapon to take to the Circle. My life might hang on the choice."

Jurand straightened up. "I'm sorry. It's just..." And he sagged back down. "In a *box*."

"Spear," said Antaup. "It has the reach, the speed, the finesse—"

"Finesse." Whitewater chuckled. "The Circle's no place for finesse."

Glaward rolled his eyes like he never heard such folly. "And once Stour Nightfall slips around your pig-sticker, what then?"

"Your counterproposal?" asked Antaup with an urbane arched eyebrow. "A monstrous battleaxe, I daresay, heavier than he is, that he can swing twice before he's blown?"

Glaward looked slightly affronted. "They make small axes, too."

"Spear's too cumbersome for single combat in a small space." Jin grimaced as he rubbed at his bruised cheek again. "Axe is simple, sturdy, good close up."

"If you want close up, a sword's more versatile." Antaup mimed the actions. "Thrust, slash, lunge, pommel strike."

Glaward rolled his eyes. "Always with the bloody pommel strike. Sword is obvious."

"Sword is *classic*."

"You're all missing the point," snapped Leo. "You take a weapon, but you never know if you'll fight with it, or hand it to your opponent and fight with whatever he brings. What you need is something *you* can use but the other bastard can't."

Glaward frowned. "Such as..."

"I don't *know*. That's why I'm asking you!"

"Maybe you should ask someone clever." Jin was wobbling a tooth now, just behind the bruise, checking if it was loose. "Like your mother."

"We're not on the best of terms right now," said Leo, grumpily. "She's not too keen on the whole duel idea."

There was a brief silence. Antaup and Glaward exchanged a meaningful glance. Then Jurand sat forward, all open and earnest, flames reflected in the corners of his eyes. Leo couldn't deny it had an effect on him, when he did that. "Do you think...maybe...you should listen to her?"

"Really? Now?"

"Well, she's about the best tactician I know—"

"So you don't think I can do it?"

"No one believes in you more than me!" Jurand cleared his throat, glanced at the others, sat back a little. "More than *us*. But single combat... it's a gamble. Anything could happen. I don't...*we* don't want you to get...hurt." His voice failed him on the last word and became a croak. As if he couldn't quite bring himself to say "killed." They all knew it could only be victory or the Great Leveller.

"You any good with a whip?" asked Antaup.

Leo stared at him. "Seriously?"

"I once saw this Gurkish woman whip swords out of men's hands.

320

At a show. They came up from the audience, and, well, it was quite something. She whipped a girl's dress half-off without cutting her, too." And he grinned at the memory.

"So I should whip Stour Nightfall's clothes off?" asked Leo.

"No, but, you know, I was thinking of something he *couldn't* use, and—"

"I should whip the bloody lot of you." Rikke walked up, pushing chagga around her bottom lip with her tongue, as usual, and slowly shaking her shaggy head. Leo was glad to see her. Very glad. She always made him feel good. Long Eye or not, she always saw past the nonsense, somehow, and right to the heart of things. She helped *him* see to the heart of things. The dead knew, he needed some clarity then.

"We're talking of weapons, woman," grumbled Glaward.

"I heard, *man*," said Rikke, "and you're talking with your arses. What you take into the Circle in your hands matters far less than what you take in your head." And she tapped at the side of her skull. "Doubt you lot are much help with the former and you're a bloody hindrance with the latter."

"And how many duels have you fought?" complained Jin.

"As many as all you lot put together," she answered smartly. "Now lose yourselves, I need to talk to my champion."

Maybe they were used to being ordered around by Leo's mother, and Rikke seemed to have borrowed her air of command. Sheepishly, they stood, gathered their things.

"Don't go far!" she called after them. "He'll need you to hold the shields!"

"What's got into you?" asked Leo.

Rikke gave a haughty sniff and made the ring through her nose twitch. "Isern said I should be taking the reins."

"I'm a horse now?"

"Aye, and you need the spur."

"My mother usually gives me that." Leo felt a twinge of nerves, realising afresh he'd soon be fighting to the death. "When I need her most, she's bloody abandoned me."

"Makes for a sad story, but I daresay she'd see it differently. She's used to taking charge, Leo, now she's helpless. She's scared, I reckon."

"*She's* scared? I'm the one has to fight the Great Wolf! She should *be* here!"

"You've spent weeks moaning that she's always at your shoulder. Now you've stepped from her shadow you miss her? By the dead, the Young Lion shouldn't need his mother."

Leo took a long breath and blew it out. "You're right. All my life, I

321

wanted to fight in the Circle." He clutched at his head. "Bloody hell, Rikke, why did I ever want to fight in the Circle?"

She caught him by the wrists, pulled them down. "No one remembers how the fight was won, only who won it. Fight hard."

"I will."

"Fight dirty."

"I will."

"The lion beat the wolf."

"I know."

"No. You don't." She took his face now, with both hands. "The lion beat the wolf. I've *seen* it." Her big, pale eyes were full of certainty, and he took heart from that. Started to feel braver. To feel *himself* again. The Young Lion! She was just what he needed then. A spring of belief in a desert of doubt. It's like they say, every good man needs a good woman beside him. Or under him, anyway.

"I bloody love you," he said. Her brows shot up. Almost as high as his. Why had he said that? Swept off by whatever emotion blew his way, like his mother always said he was. "I mean . . . I don't mean *love* love," he stammered. What the hell did he mean? What did you call it, when a woman was your lover *and* your friend? It had never happened to him before. "Or . . . maybe I *do* mean that—"

"Then promise me one thing." She put her hand around the back of his head and dragged him close, so their noses were almost touching. "Promise me you'll *kill* the bastard."

He bared his teeth. "I promise. Killing the bastard is the whole point. For you. For your father. For Ritter. For Barniva . . ." He smiled. "Barniva's sword. That's what I'll take."

"Good choice, I reckon."

He felt another wave of sadness as he glanced down to the bridge, followed quickly by a shiver of nerves. "I just hope it brings me more luck than it did him."

"You don't need luck." Rikke twisted his face back towards her and kissed him, gentle and serious, and full of belief. "I've seen it."

Folk were already gathering at the appointed place. Seemed the rivers of blood spilled yesterday had only sharpened the thirst for more. Losing a duel himself had much diminished Clover's taste for the business, but he'd been asked to hold a shield for the heir to the North and that was reckoned quite the honour. Felt prudent to at least arrive in good time.

A patch of grass had been shaved to the roots not far from the bridge where the fighting had been hottest, the Circle marked out with pegs and rope, six good strides across. Carpenters had knocked up some seating on platforms so the big folk would get a good view of everyone's futures being settled. So Black Calder and Scale Ironhand, and the Dogman and Lady Brock wouldn't miss a drop of blood spilled. Be a shame for it to hit the dirt unnoticed, after all.

Good weather for it. Blue washing out to pale on the horizon as the sun sank wearily towards the hills. A great arrow of geese was honking off southwards, high up, not caring much for the doings of men. Not caring much who won or lost, who lived or died. Good to know the geese'd still be flapping regardless, though it would likely be scant comfort to whichever hero got a sword up his arse.

The men who held the shields around the Circle, making sure no one left till the business was settled, were meant to be the fiercest warriors either side could find and, to be fair, the younger ones were shooting some warlike glares across the shortened grass. The older ones had seen it all before, though, and saved their snarls for when they mattered. For all they stood on different sides, some of Scale's and the Dogman's Named Men were chatting like old friends. Clover knew most o' the names. Red Hat and Oxel, Flatstone and Brodd Silent, Lemun the Chalk from up near Yaws and Gregun Hollowhead from the West Valleys. The Nail, too, pale hair stuck up like thistle-fluff, bound all over with bloody bandages from yesterday's fighting.

Strange, in a way, for men who'd been fixed on killing each other a few hours before to be happily mingling, stamping and blowing and polishing their shield-rims, mulling over fights long past, the fight just done and the fight to come. But then warriors on different sides always had more in common with each other than with anyone else.

"Loneliest o' professions," murmured Clover to himself. Shepherds might not make many friends, but they weren't often called upon to kill the ones they had made, either.

"Jonas Steepfield." Clover jerked around at the whispering voice, the sound of that name frightening and oddly exciting both at once. A big man stood beside him with a battered shield on his arm, grey hair stirring in the wind about a grey stubbled face with a scar that put Clover's to shame. And in the midst of that scar, a bright ball of dead metal where an eye should've been.

"If it ain't Caul Shivers. I don't go by Steepfield any more. I learned a big hard name makes men want to take a blade to you just so they can cut off a piece of it."

Shivers gave the kind of weary nod that's born of hard experience. "The world's full of eager fools, all right."

"No call for me to be swelling their number. It's just Clover now."

"There was clover in that Circle, eh? Where you fought."

"There was. Whenever I smell it, I remember how being beaten feels."

Shivers gave that weary nod again, looking off towards the hills. "We should talk, sometime. One scarred old warhorse to another."

"You're the warhorse, Shivers. I'm more a crow, picking at the leftovers."

"Not that I don't like the act, it's a good one." Shivers glanced over towards Greenway, prancing around like he was the one about to face the Young Lion and was sure of winning, too. "Don't doubt you've got a lot of eager fools taking you for quite the figure of fun." He leaned close to whisper. Or maybe to whisper even more throatily. "But we both know what y'are."

Clover had heard it said Caul Shivers could see your thoughts with that metal eye. Horseshit, of course. But he'd seen plenty with the other. Few men more. Might be the hardest name in the North still casting a shadow. He didn't need a magic eye to make some sharp guesses.

Clover took a breath. "Aye, well, we all play the cards we're dealt."

"Some of us do. Some of us kill men with better cards and play theirs instead. What's this Stour Nightfall like as a fighter?"

"I wouldn't want to fight him."

"A sensible man does his best to avoid any fight."

"Any fair one."

A pause, and they watched the folk crowd in, from the Union side and the North. Warriors, servants, women, more and more of them until there was a gabbling crowd in every direction.

"What's he like as a man?" asked Shivers.

"About what you'd expect from someone they call the Great Wolf. Certainly no better. What about Brock?"

Shivers shrugged. "About what you'd expect from someone they call the Young Lion. Certainly no worse."

"Huh. Since we've got all the answers, I sometimes wonder why we follow these bastards."

The noise swelled up, cheers on one side and grumbles on the other, and Bethod's sons came through the press, as ill-matched a pair of brothers as ever there were. Scale Ironhand, huge and fleshy and flashing with gold, all smiles. Black Calder, lean as a spear and frowning like thunder.

"I hear a lot of talk about loyalty," said Shivers as the men who'd ruled the North for the best part of twenty years took their high seats above the Circle.

Clover snorted. "Since we've a dozen dead masters between us, and both had a hand in more'n one of the downfalls, I feel no shame in saying that loyalty is overrated."

"Helps to have someone worth being loyal to." The cheers and grumbles were reversed as a lean old man with long hair and a pointed face clambered stiffly onto the seats opposite.

"The Dogman?" He looked grey. Grey-clothed, grey-haired, grey-faced, like the life had leaked out of him to leave a wispy husk a sudden gust might whisk away. "The man looks a touch past his best."

Shivers cast a lazy eye towards Scale, and back. He had a way of saying a lot with a few words. "Least he had one."

"Aye." Clover gave a weary sigh. "Got a lot o' respect for the Dogman, as it goes. Only man won any kind of power in the North in my lifetime and stayed halfway decent. The rest—Bethod, the Bloody-Nine, Black Dow, Black Calder, well...between you and me..." Clover scratched gently at his scar and dropped his voice very low. "It's been quite the who's-the-biggest-cunt contest, wouldn't you say?"

Shivers slowly nodded. "A real arsehole's parade."

"But then the arseholes tend to win, don't they? Maybe I'm weak, but I'd rather be on the winning side, even if the losers smell sweeter."

"You should meet his daughter."

"Who, the Dogman's?"

"Aye. Rikke. I'll make no promises for her odour but she's worth talking to." He nodded towards the platform, where a girl was clambering over the back, all knees and elbows, to wedge herself between the Dogman and a pale, hard Union woman Clover reckoned to be the one-time Lady Governor of Angland.

She pushed her tangle of red-brown hair out of her face to show those big grey eyes and he'd no doubt it was her. The one who'd come tumbling down the hill and fallen at his feet. The one he'd let scamper off into the woods.

"We met in passing. Struck me as two-thirds o' nothing."

"Then you misjudged her."

No doubt she was fine-looking, but more than a bit mad-looking, too, wild and twitchy with a cross painted over one eye, a fat gold ring through her nose and a mass of rattling chains around her neck like she was learning to be some hillwoman sorceress but hadn't actually got to the spells yet.

"You sure?" he asked.

"Do I look like a man prone to fancy?"

Clover gave Shivers a quick glance up and down. "About as little as any living. And I was long ago cured of the misapprehension that I'm right on every score."

"The wiser a man is, the more he stands ready to be educated." There was a little curl at the corner of Shivers' mouth as he watched Rikke flapping her hands around. A hint of pride, maybe. The most feeling he'd let show the whole time they'd talked. Anyone who could coax some warmth from that face-shaped block of rock was someone worth watching, Clover reckoned.

Around the edge of the Circle, the shield-carriers were starting to form up, folk pressing in behind them, eager for the best view of the murder. "Let me know when you want that chat, then, Shivers, you old bastard." Clover hefted his shield and stepped away to find his own place. "My ears are always open to a better way of doing things."

Rikke had been hoping the hate would melt when she finally saw Stour Nightfall's face, because her hate for him was getting to feel like quite the weight to carry. She'd look in his eyes and see he wasn't the monster who'd whined his hopes for her horrible murder, who'd burned her father's garden and killed good folk she knew, but just a man with loves and fears like any other, and her hate would melt.

As so often with hopes, and hatreds, it didn't quite turn out that way.

The king-in-waiting strutted preening into the Circle to wild cheers from his side, lauded and clapped and slapped on the back, and stood there with a damp-eyed smirk like a wedding guest who'd pricked the bride the night before.

"That's Nightfall?" murmured Finree dan Brock, sitting pale and stiff beside Rikke and quite clearly trying to put a brave face over her misery.

"That's him." Rikke narrowed her eyes, wishing she could see through him. See some clue to what he'd do. See some weakness Leo could use. See his death coming.

But the Long Eye cannot be forced open, and all she saw was that infuriating bloody smirk, like he was the one who could see the future and for him it held nothing but victories. He glanced her way, and that wolf grin grew a tooth wider each side, and he sauntered over to her half of the Circle.

"You're Rikke, then?" he called out, giving her a slow look up and down with those wet eyes, his mouth open and his tongue showing. "You're prettier'n I thought you'd be."

She gave him the same sort of look, but with her mouth scorn-twisted. "You're about as ugly as I was expecting."

"I hear you can see what's coming. Did you see yourself sucking my cock yet?"

Jeering laughter at that, and Rikke clenched her fists. "Just you losing in the Circle."

He only grinned the wider. "I know you're lying about that one. Might be you're lying about the other." And he gave her a sly wink as he turned away. Winked at her, the bastard, and she felt the hate boil up hotter than ever.

"Don't worry about it!" she screamed, jumping to her feet and jabbing away with one clawing finger. "Once Leo's broke you in half, you can suck your own!"

Got some laughs at least from the folk on her side, and some ugly stares from Stour's shield-carriers. She recognised the Nail in their midst, staring right at her with his pale brows thoughtfully wrinkled, and she curled her tongue into a tube and blew spit at him, and he grinned, and gave a little bow.

"Easy," muttered her father, pulling her back down by the elbow. "Hard words are for fools and cowards. Stour might be both, but you're neither."

"Winking wanker," she growled. "I'll see him fucked by a pig, the bastard. I'll see him strung up with brambles and the bloody cross cut in him. I'll send his guts to his daddy in a box. With herbs. So they won't smell 'em till they open it."

She saw her father staring at her, and looking quite worried, too.

"What?" she grumbled, hunching her shoulders. "Didn't think I had it in me to hate a man?"

"Be careful, is all I'm saying. Hate a man that much, you give him power over you."

"Maybe. But it goes back to the mud with him." Her voice sounded hard in her own ear. "The Great Leveller cancels all debts."

The whoops and taunts from their side of the Circle became cheers as Leo pushed through the crowd, his friends at his back.

Her father leaned close. "Have it in you to love a man, too?" She looked at him, caught by surprise. "I'm old, Rikke, not blind."

Leo flinched as the wall of shields clattered shut behind him, like a prisoner might at the turning of the jailer's key. He'd said he loved her.

Wasn't that she thought he was lying. Just that she doubted he'd ever love anyone more than himself.

"There are things I love about him." Best stomach she'd ever seen, for instance. "There are things I don't." Biggest head she'd ever known, for instance.

"You can hate things about a person and still love 'em. Ain't easy, watching someone you love walk into the Circle."

Rikke bunched her fists until the nails bit at her palms. "Helps if you hate the other bastard more."

The noise started to fade as Isern-i-Phail stepped out onto the short-shaved grass, chewing slowly with her tall spear in her hand. When all that remained was a nervy silence, she wedged her chagga down behind her lip with her tongue.

"I'm Isern-i-Phail! My da, Crummock-i-Phail, judged the fight between Fenris the Feared and the Bloody-Nine. He was a well-known bastard." Some laughter and hoots of agreement. "But he was well known! And being a hillman, the closest thing to a neutral party anyone could find. I am as well known as he." And she lifted her chin and gestured at herself. "But for my piercing wits and haunting beauty." More laughter. "Seems it's fallen to me as a hillwoman to judge this bout." She grinned over at Stour. "Though I should declare up front that I hate this cunt over here, and might yet be prevailed upon to kill him myself."

The laughter only made Rikke more nervous.

"Have to admire your honesty," said Stour.

"I couldn't give a moth's cock what you admire, but the judging of a duel is a sacred trust and so on and bloody so on, and you can trust me to judge this one fairly, I'm sure."

"Wouldn't worry," said Stour. "Me standing over his corpse won't need much judging. You say start. I'll handle the rest."

"Whoa there, boy!" shouted Isern. "The moon loves a proper order to things, and there's the introductions, stakes and choice o' weapons to see to. Don't worry, I'll waste no time inflating your bloated names any more than I have to. Over here on my..." She thought for a moment, frowned at Leo, frowned at her hands, frowned at the sky, then snapped her fingers. "Left! On my left, we've got Leo dan Brock, son of Finree dan Brock, newly minted Lord Governor of Angland, who men call the Young Lion on account of his youth and heroic opinion of himself. If he's as skilful as he's pretty, we'll have quite the fight." She pointed her spear at Stour. "Which means this article must be on my right and it's Stour Nightfall, d'you see, son of Black Calder and heir to the chain of Bethod, that men call the Great Wolf 'cause of, who can say, the hairiest arse in the North, for all I know. He beat Stranger-Come-Knocking in the Circle but we're all aware the man was way past his best. Good enough?"

Leo said nothing, eyes fixed on Stour like they were alone in the Circle. Stour shrugged, still smiling. "Good enough."

"Bastard, bastard, fucking bastard," Rikke hissed through tight lips. She was biting on her chagga pellet so hard, her whole face was aching, willing her guts to turn sickly, and her eye to turn hot, and some ghost of the future to show itself. But nothing came.

"Your next question!" called Isern. "What are these two fools going to kill each other over? Mostly a matter of manly pride, as is proper in a duel, but there's also the rich, dark earth o' the North. The winner takes the patch of it men call the Protectorate, which stretches from the Whiteflow to the Cusk and includes the city of Uffrith. Stour Nightfall wins, it belongs to King Scale. Leo dan Brock wins, it stays with the Dogman in the loving embrace o' the Union. All happy with the terms?"

A quiet then. No one on Rikke's side looked too happy about anything.

"Dogman, Chieftain of Uffrith?" called Isern.

"Aye," said Rikke's father, wearily.

"Brock, Lord Governor of Angland?"

"Aye," snapped Leo.

"Scale Ironhand, King of the Northmen?"

"Aye," rumbled Scale, jowls quivering as he smothered a burp, like this was the third duel he'd watched that day. "Get to it, woman."

"Then I will, you hill of lard." Isern thrust her spear into the ground with a thud and snapped her fingers at Shivers. "Lend me your shield, handsome." He glanced over his shoulder like he thought she might be talking to someone else, then tossed it to her. She snatched it from the air, set it down on its rim. "Straps or paint, Brock?" Though Shivers' shield was so battered, only a few stubborn flakes of paint still clung to it.

"Paint," said Leo. Isern set the shield spinning, and men started shouting and whooping and calling, and beside her, Rikke felt Lady Finree give a kind of gasp, and she covered her eyes with her hands.

"He'll win," said Rikke.

"How can you know?"

Rikke took her cold, limp hand and squeezed it. "He'll win," she said, making it sound like a sure fact, for all her head was splitting with doubts.

Maybe she could've talked him out of it. But it was too late now.

There was a rattle as the shield fell.

"Straps down," said Isern. "Your pick, Great Wolf."

Stour caught Rikke's eye and shrugged, more careless than ever, like the notion of losing had never even occurred. "He can pick."

"Your pick, Young Lion."

Leo shook his head. "He can pick."

"Men!" And Isern rolled her eyes. "They never can commit. You'll fight with what you brought, then." She tossed the shield back to Shivers, plucked her spear from the ground and pointed it at the men about the Circle, shields all facing inwards now, rims grating as they locked them together into a wall. "You lot, keep these two in here till it's settled. And no more interfering than is seemly." She spat chagga juice, wiped her chin and nodded, like it was all set up to her satisfaction. "Let's get to it."

Where Names Are Made

Leo once heard someone say *attack is the best defence*. Couldn't remember who, but it struck him as a bold philosophy. Words to live by. So his plan was to be the whirlwind. Give Stour no breath, no space, no chance to think. Leo would overwhelm that smirking bastard, put him in the mud and look forward to feasts in his honour and songs of his prowess.

But plans often crumble when swords are swung at them, and Leo's lasted no longer than it took Isern-i-Phail to screech, "Fight!"

Stour came at him so shockingly fast, Leo had to twist his opening thrust into a clumsy parry, forced onto the back foot by a raking cut that jarred Barniva's sword in his hand.

A flash of Stour's grin and a flicker of bright steel and Leo stumbled back again, parrying, dodging, parrying, the quick scrape and clatter of their blades almost lost in the bloodthirsty roar of the crowd. He only just ducked a wicked cut that could've taken his head right off, but Stour gave him no clumsy backswing to work with, stepped scornfully away from Leo's counter and pressed in again.

Seemed Stour had heard that thing about attack and defence, too. But he was better at it.

"Kill him!" screeched Antaup.

"Come on!" shouted Jurand.

"Leo!" roared Glaward, shaking his shield. But Stour was already on him again, three cuts so quick, Leo only dodged the first two by the barest instinct. He reeled away from the third, fishing with his sword in a weak effort to keep his opponent back. Stour was the whirlwind. Leo was the leaf blown around the Circle.

The *speed* of him. He used a heavy Northman's sword—broad blade, solid crosspiece, weighty golden pommel—but he handled it nimbly as a Styrian rapier. Almost no backswing. Almost no recovery. Intentions masterfully disguised.

Apart from Bremer dan Gorst, who'd a fair claim to being the greatest swordsman of the age, Leo never saw a blade handled with such savage skill. He felt the doubt creeping cold up his spine. He was used to being swaddled in a blanket of self-confidence, and the chill as it was stripped away was all the worse for being unfamiliar.

But Leo once heard someone say *there are many ways to crack an egg*. Hadn't been entirely sure of the meaning, but it struck him as a workmanlike philosophy. Words to live by. Stour might have the speed, but Leo had the strength. He had to watch for his opening, pin the slippery bastard down and crush him like a walnut on an anvil.

Stour's next thrust came deadly fast, but Leo was ready. He twisted, forced it away, pressed forward instead of falling back, caught a satisfying glimpse of surprise on Stour's face. He cut and cut again, blows heavy with his fear and frustration, jarring the sword in Nightfall's hand.

Steel scraped as Stour caught Leo's blade on his, held it up short, the edge almost brushing the pointed tip of his nose. They snarled in each other's faces, straining for the upper hand, crosspieces grinding, knuckles almost rubbing together, shifting their stances in a bid to gain some hair of an advantage, locked together in a furious, frozen struggle while the crowd made a mindless thunder in which encouragement could hardly be told from insults.

The brief flicker of triumph went out as, ever so slowly, Leo felt himself losing the contest. He bared his teeth, growled, spat, but Stour forced him back, and back, until finally Leo was pushed off balance and had to stumble away, their swords ringing apart. He gasped as Stour's blade came hissing at him, dodged desperately, slipped and nearly fell, reeled back into a little space, breathing hard.

The crowd on the Northern side bellowed their approval. The crowd on the Union's murmured their disappointment. The Great Wolf gave a showy flourish of his sword and grinned. It was plain they were all coming to the same conclusion.

Stour was the better swordsman.

Still, Leo once heard someone say *there's always a way*. He'd had his doubts at the time, but now it struck him as a hopeful philosophy. Words to live by? If he couldn't beat the Great Wolf with speed or strength, he'd have to outlast him. Tire him with a dogged defence, a sullen determination, a stubborn endurance. He'd be the deep-rooted tree the hurricane can't shift. He had to wear the bastard down.

Stour thrust, but off-centre. It was easy for Leo to step around it, finally sensing an opening. But just as he pounced, Stour dipped his shoulder, whipped his sword across in a flicking cut. Leo gasped as he felt the wind of the blade across his face. He slashed back but the Great Wolf was already dancing away, grinning, always grinning.

The crowd roared. For a moment, Leo thought it was for him. Then he felt something tickling his cheek. Stour's point had scratched his face, so quick and so sharp he'd hardly felt it. It was blood the crowd were cheering for. His blood.

As Leo backed off, the cut began to tingle, then to throb. He wondered how bad a scar it would leave. Wondered if it was a Naming Wound. But as that cold doubt crept all the way up to his throat, he realised you had to live through the duel for that. The dead get no names.

Stour's grin grew a tooth wider. A tooth crueller.

"I'm going to bleed you, boy," he said.

Clover jerked away as the point of Brock's sword flashed past on the backswing not a hand's width from his nose. Stour darted in, all snarl and fury, thrust, thrust again. Brock gasped as he jumped back, knocking Stour's sword wide so it gouged into the shield just next to Clover's.

By the dead, the *noise*. The grind of steel, the growls of the fighters, the monstrous fury of the crowd.

By the dead, the *crush*. Shield-carriers straining, rims scraping against his as they shifted, shoulders squeezing against his as they shoved, the ring of shields twisting as the fighters danced close, boots mashing the dirt as men pushed back against the watchers behind, shoving ever inwards at the sight of blood.

Clover told himself he hated this fight between fools, watched by fools. A brutal waste of at least one life that appealed to all that was worst in men. But in some deep-hidden part of him, he loved it, too. Thrilled to the sharp metal swung and the hot blood spilled. A little piece of Jonas Steepfield, stuck in him like a splinter he could never quite dig out.

There wasn't much in the world to get your heart pumping harder than watching two men fight to the death. Only being one of 'em. He felt a guilty surge of excitement as Stour dashed forward again. Felt the eager grin on his own lips as Brock parried and fell back. No doubt he was a fine swordsman. But Stour was making him look ordinary. More so with every moment. He used that big sword nimbly as a dressmaker might her needle, all wrist and flick and effortless mastery.

Another flurry of blows, high and low, point and edge. Brock shuffled, blocked, but Stour caught him with the last cut as he whipped by. A slice across his left arm that sent a few spots of blood into the crowd. More than likely he could've left Brock's arm hanging off, but Stour hadn't become the Great Wolf by passing up a chance to pose, and he grinned as he showed the red edge of his sword to the crowd. He wasn't only a hell of a swordsman but a hell of a braggart. The two went together with depressing frequency.

Brock gritted his teeth, cheek red from the cut on his face, and came on doggedly. You couldn't fault his courage, but courage isn't a warrior's most valuable virtue, whatever the songs say. It's ruthlessness, and savagery, and quickness to strike that win fights, the very qualities in which Stour excelled. He jumped in now, laughing as he swung his red sword in great circles, sending Brock staggering into the wall of shields.

Clover caught the Young Lion on his as he stumbled, gave a little like a good feather mattress, then nudged him back up so he could dodge, catch a blow of Stour's and steer it wide with a screech of metal.

He doubted it'd change the result any. Looked like a black day for the Union. A black day for Leo dan Brock and anyone who loved him. A fine thing for Jonas Clover, you'd have thought. He did stand on the other side, after all, and winning was supposed to be meat and drink to a warrior.

Just sometimes he wished he had the bones to pick the right side, even if it was the losing one.

Someone had taken to beating a drum, slow and heavy. Rikke could've throttled the bastard.

By the dead, the *tension*. The long-drawn aching in her throat, worse and worse as the two of them circled, watchful, twisting like dogs after a scent, sniffing for an opening. Rikke's sore mouth tasted of vomit and fear while the men with the shields shouted, stomped, bellowed their hatred and their encouragement.

By the dead, the *helplessness*. She wanted to scream. Wanted to punch something. Wanted to rip the ring out of her nose. No one, however big an optimist, could've doubted Leo was getting killed in there and there was nothing she could do.

Most of the crowd were treating it like a feast day. There were children up in a tree, staring down with wide eyes. Scale, that great fat fucker of a king, was laughing, quaffing from his goblet, laughing again. The great fat mountain of blubber.

"How can they laugh?" whispered Finree.

"'Cause they're not the ones facing the Great Leveller," said Rikke's father, his face chiselled from grey stone.

The only thing worse than the fear of them coming together was the terror when they did, shocking as lightning every time, Rikke flinching at every movement, arse clenching at every flash of steel. She clung to the bench as if it was the saddle of a horse she was trying to break, clung to Finree's cold hand in her hot one so hard her wrist ached.

She knew with one twitch of a sword she might lose her lover, her home, her future. People can be so tough, survive so much hunger and cold and disappointment, take beatings you wouldn't believe and come out stronger. But they can be so fragile, too. One sharp piece of metal is all it takes to turn a man into mud. One little stroke of bad luck. One ill-judged whisper.

Had she done this? Had she made this happen?

She gasped as Nightfall came forward, switched direction in a blink. Steel rang once, twice, Leo lashed back, but too slow and Stour slipped around it, his sword catching Leo's leg and making him stagger.

"No." A kind of shudder went through Finree, and Rikke gripped her hand harder than ever. Tried to be strong for both of them though she wasn't halfway strong enough for herself. Tried to bare her teeth, and focus on Stour's smirk, and turn the sucking of fear and guilt into anger. Tried to make something from it she could *use*.

You cannot force the Long Eye open, no more than you can order the tide to come in. But where was the harm in trying?

She planted her fists on her knees and sat forward. Refusing to blink. Glaring at the grass like she could glare through it to what might come. Willing that heat into her eye.

Might be she saw what she wanted to. The dead knew there'd been plenty o' that going on the past few days. But for the briefest moment, she thought she saw ghosts there, in the Circle. Faint, they were, and flickering. Hints of figures. Stour and Leo, and their swords, torn apart like cobwebs on the breeze as the real men passed through them.

Rikke curled back her lips, and clenched her fists, and squeezed her jaw so hard it felt like her teeth might crack, and she stared at the Circle as if she was staring into a gale.

She *made* herself see.

Stour was laughing now. Giggling as if every contact was a brilliant joke.

Leo wasn't finding it funny. He told himself he was the Young Lion. The Lord Governor of Angland. The proud son of a proud line of warriors, with glory in his grasp. But in truth, he was scarcely even trying to hit back. Barniva's sword was getting heavier every time he swung it. He was scared if he attacked, he'd give Stour a fatal opening. But he was scared if he defended, things could only go one way.

It was getting to the point where he was just scared.

Stour jerked forward and Leo stumbled back. Just a mocking feint with the foot, a twitch of the hand, and Leo was sent scampering. Stour wasn't only aiming to win now, but to make a show of it. To teach a lesson. To show the whole North that the Great Wolf was a man to be feared. His sword flickered past Leo's tired guard. Stour could've spitted him, but he chose just to prick his stomach. Prick him then whip away again, laughing.

He was the Young Lion, but he was bleeding. Blood on his face, blood on his leg. Red streaks down his right hand, grip of Barniva's sword sticky with it. The idea of blood watering the Circle had thrilled him when he listened to stories of the Bloody-Nine. Thrills you a lot less when it's your own.

He was the Young Lion, but he was tiring. He panted, gasped, cold air raw in his throat, but he could never get enough breath. His knees were trembling, the snap going out of his arm. No way he could outlast Stour now. His only chance was to out-think him. Trouble was, he'd never been much of a thinker. If he had been, he might not have taken the challenge in the first place.

His eyes darted about the Circle, searching for some clue.

His friends, their shields drooping. Glaward chewing his lip. Jin tearing his beard. Antaup crestfallen. Jurand wincing as if he felt every wound himself. He caught a glimpse of his mother, stricken, pale, staring. The Dogman sat grim beside her, and Rikke, glaring into the Circle, fiddling with the ring through her nose.

Fight dirty, she'd told him. *No one remembers how the fight was won, only who won it.* A gritty philosophy. Words to die by.

Stour feinted and Leo fell back again, stumbled again, but this time he went down harder than he had to. He put a hand out behind as if to steady himself, tore up a handful of grass. Stour came on again, grinning, and Leo growled as he forced the snap into his legs, sprang up, throwing his grass in Stour's face, swinging his sword at Stour's neck.

Even blinking, spitting and off balance, Nightfall managed to parry, but Leo was already coming at him with all the strength he had left. He smashed his forehead into Stour's mouth with a glorious crunch, making the Great Wolf stagger back onto the shields of his men.

For a moment, his eyes were bleary, his bloody mouth wide with surprise. Leo took a great whooping breath, brought his sword whistling up and over, but the blade hacked into the shields where Stour had been a moment before, and Leo only just kept his grip on the buzzing hilt.

Stour danced back, spitting grass, showing red teeth as he grinned. "Oh, *now* we got us a fight!"

He darted one way, switched in an instant and whipped past on the other side, quick as the wind and as hard to pin down. Leo was left stranded, gasped as the edge of Stour's sword whipped across his thigh, left a cold line that soon turned burning hot. It was the most he could do to stay standing as the blood soaked into his trouser leg.

He wasn't a lion, he was a scared little boy who didn't want to die.

But it was too late to listen to Mother now.

Brock was cut bad. Red streaks down his face from the cut on his cheek, trousers dark around the cut on his leg, hand red from the cut on his arm. Watering the Circle with his blood, as the skalds have it. Not a pleasant sight, but nothing Clover hadn't seen before. Hadn't lived before. If pleasant sights are what you're after, the Circle's a bad place to come.

Stour was sure of victory. Grinning like a wolf, strutting like a cock. The kind that rules the farmyard rather'n the kind you piss with, but Clover reckoned both meanings fit the heir to the North pretty well. He laughed, arms spread wide, urging the crowd to ever-louder shrieks of admiration and delight. Some men take to applause like other men take to drink. The more they get, the more they need, until too much is never enough.

Scale was loving it almost as much as his nephew, shaking his iron hand at the Circle and roaring, "Play with him!" The admiration of one cock for another. Seemed to sting an effort from Brock, who lumbered in, sluggish from the bleeding, took a clumsy swing you could see coming ten strides off. Stour flicked it away with a contemptuous sneer, could've chopped Brock across the back but chose to let him stumble by.

"Finish him, damn it!" snarled Black Calder, as disgusted by his son's display as his brother was delighted by it.

Stour could've finished Brock five times now but he was enjoying hooking him so much, he kept letting him wriggle free so he could hook him again. Clover thought that ill-advised, to say the least. You take no risks in the Circle and give no chances, not with all you've got and all you'll ever have in the balance. It only takes a little twist of fate to land you back in the mud, and fate can be a twisty little bastard.

No one knew that better than Clover.

Rikke's head spun, sight swam, stomach churned as she stared down into the Circle. Her left eye was hot, burning in her head. She forced it open wider, staring, staring.

Leo bent, clumsy, hunched around the wound in his side, blood-streaked top to toe. Stour looked quicker than ever, surer than ever, prancing, dancing, only a short step from blowing kisses to the audience.

Rikke saw ghosts of swords and spears above the crowd. Of flags shifting with a wind that wasn't there. The battle yesterday? A battle yet to come? By the dead, she wanted to be sick. Her head was pulsing. The cold sweat tickled at her scalp, trickled down her face, but she didn't dare shift her eyes. Didn't dare blink. Didn't dare break the spell.

There were ghosts in the Circle, too. Shimmering and shifting. Ghosts of Leo and of Stour. Ghosts of hands and feet and faces. Ghosts of swords.

Leo winced as Stour's blade caught him across the belly. Not a killing blow. Just a kiss. A slash that spotted the shields beside him with blood. Leo stumbled, fell to his knees, sword slipping from his hand into the grass.

"No," whispered Leo's mother, tears running down her cheeks as she closed her eyes.

Nightfall turned slowly around in the middle of the Circle, stretching out the victory, sucking up the glory, and he looked over his shoulder at Rikke, and he winked.

By the dead, her eye was on fire. Like it might burn right out of her head.

Stour turned away from her, raising his arm.

She saw his sword.

But she saw it with the Long Eye.

And for an instant, like the water flooding in when the dam bursts, the absolute knowing of that sword flooded into her.

She saw the ore of its iron, ripped from the cold earth, made steel in the flame-spurting furnace and poured white-hot into the mould.

She saw Watersmeet the smith swing his hammer, face lit orange by sparks at each blow, his children working the bellows, his mother Drenna puffing plumes of chagga smoke from her pipe as she tugged at the binding on the grip.

She saw it gifted to Stour on his tenth birthday, Black Calder setting his hand on the smiling boy's shoulder and saying, "In war, it's the winning counts. The rest is for fools to sing about."

She saw it in the Great Wolf's scabbard, whipped free as the duel began, cut and thrust, the Circle full of the bright ribbons of its passing.

She saw it swung in a shining blur at neck height, Stour's teeth bared in a triumphant snarl. A great, heedless, showy sweep fit to take a man's head right from his shoulders.

She knew with utter certainty where that sword would be, always, but she didn't feel the joy she had when she knew the arrow, that day in the wet woods. For beyond Stour's bright sword she saw a crack in the sky, and beyond that crack a black pit yawned, a pit with no bottom and no end and no beginning in which there was a knowing not of a sword or an arrow but of everything. A knowing so vast and terrible that the merest splinter of it might rip her mind apart.

Leo dragged himself to his knees, groggy, bloody, clawing his own blade from the grass.

Rikke tottered up with him, moaning, gasping, gripping her throbbing head. The sky was opening, sucking her in.

Stour smiled. Began to turn. Rikke's eye was a smouldering coal in her skull.

Leo started to clamber up, head rising towards the shimmering ghost of Stour's sword.

She clapped her hands over her burning face and screamed out in the Union tongue, screamed at the very top of her lungs.

"Go low!"

Leo couldn't have said why, but it seemed important he die on his feet.

Hardly hurt any more. Just numb. Just weak. So heavy.

Took everything he had to heave himself up.

The world wobbled like jelly, all dark earth and bright pink sky and a swimming mass of painted shields and snarling faces and smoking breath.

He could hardly hear for his own thudding heartbeat, hardly tell the roaring of the crowd from the roaring of his breath. He'd clutched up a handful of grass along with his sword. Bloody grass. Bloody dirt.

His mouth tasted like metal. In battle, a man finds out who he truly is. He forced his legs straight, swaying, trying to focus.

He caught a glimpse of Stour turning away, a flash of his bloody grin. Then, over the din of the crowd, he heard a scream.

"Go low!"

So he dropped. Or just fell, maybe. Felt wind pluck at his hair and with a last effort swung his sword low. Far from his best swing ever. Clumsy and weak, grip loose in his sore fingers.

But sometimes a bad swing can be good enough.

There was a smack as the blade chopped deep into Nightfall's thigh.

Stour's eyes bulged, and he opened his mouth very wide and made a strange, high shriek. More shock than pain. He staggered a half-step, took a great whooping breath in the sudden silence and started screeching again. More pain than shock, this time.

Leo pulled his sword free and Nightfall tottered, spluttering bloody spit, rearing up on his good leg, raising his sword high so the blade glimmered red with the setting sun.

A slap as Leo caught Stour's fist in his and stepped forward, growling, jerking his other arm out hard so the pommel of Barniva's sword crunched into Nightfall's face, cutting his shriek off dead. His head snapped up, black blood against the pink sunset, and Leo caught the crosspiece of Stour's sword and tore it from his limp fingers as he toppled back.

The Great Wolf hit the ground hard, arms flopped out wide, blowing bubbles of blood from his broken nose with each snorting breath. Leo stood over him, by some strange chance holding both the swords. How had that happened?

The painted shields of the men around the Circle drifted down, limp, their mouths dropping open, and no one more shocked than Leo himself.

And now the noise of the crowd on his side rose up, louder than ever. Shock turned to stunned delight, and stunned delight to wild triumph.

"Leo dan Brock!"

"The Young Lion!"

And, loudest of all, "Kill him!"

No doubt Nightfall would've killed Leo, if he'd been the one lying there, helpless. Would've killed him in the slowest, most painful, most shameful way he could. Would've crowed his victory from the rooftops of Uffrith and laughed as the skalds sang the story back to him for years to come.

Stour tried to wriggle away, gave a bubbling moan as he moved his wounded leg, then cowered as the points of the two swords came to hover over his neck. He stared up, bloody hair stuck across his face, eyes wide and full of fear.

Not invincible, after all.

The shouts found a rhythm and became a chant.

"Kill him! Kill him! Kill him!"

Louder and louder, the smoke of the shouted words rising up into the chill evening all around.

"Kill him! Kill him! Kill him!"

Louder and louder, joined by the rattle of weapons, the clash of fist on shield, the thud of stomped boots making the chill ground shake, matching Leo's thudding heartbeat, echoing through him from his feet to his scalp.

"Kill him!" he heard Glaward roaring over his shield.

"Kill him!" he heard Antaup shriek, face twisted with fury.

"Kill the fucker!" snarled Whitewater Jin.

Leo saw his mother, tears in her eyes and a hand over her mouth. He saw the Dogman, caught halfway between sitting and standing with a disbelieving grin. He saw Rikke, stood up from the bench between them, her hands over her face, one eye gleaming between her fingers.

"Kill him! Kill him! Kill him!"

Leo took a long, cold breath, lifted Barniva's sword and Stour's, the growl in his raw throat growing to a throbbing roar as he brought them both stabbing down with a single thud.

Right into the turf on either side of the Great Wolf's cringing face.

"Stour Nightfall," he mumbled. Even speaking was a mighty effort then, each word a great stone to lift. "I spare...your life."

Dizzy as hell, and he dropped on one knee. Down in the Circle of turf damp with dew, damp with his own blood.

"Bit dizzy," he said, and flopped over sideways.

Best lie down.

The Poor Pay the Price

"Amnesty," said Malmer. "We give up our arms. We give up our hostages. We all go free."

Silence, while everyone thought over what that meant. It was a lot more than they'd expected that morning, maybe. But so much less than they'd dreamed of a few weeks before.

It was a sorry little meeting, in a looted warehouse with a chill breeze blowing through the broken doors. Fifteen Breakers, each in charge of a different district of Valbeck. As far as anyone was in charge of the chaotic warren of garbage the city had been reduced to. The gaunt and grim who'd stayed to the bitter end. They would've liked to call themselves the most loyal, but maybe they were just the ones with most to lose.

Broad took a breath. He should never have got involved. He'd known it then and he knew it now. But he'd told himself things might change. Smashed his face against the wall again, sure that *this* time it wouldn't hurt. For all his promises to be a new man, somehow he always made the same wrong choices.

"Full pardons?" asked a woman with a pinched-in grey face.

Heron nodded, though he didn't look all that convinced. "So His Highness tells us."

"What did that bastard Pike have to say?" asked Sarlby.

"He didn't like it," said Vick. "But he didn't disagree."

"You trust Orso?" asked Broad.

"Best never to make a decision based on *trust*," said Vick, like trust was some fantastic beast only children believed in. "Just on what's best for most."

Malmer gave a sigh that sounded like it rose from the very dregs of a well of weariness. "Coming to something, when revolutionaries pin their hopes on the crown prince. He seems decent enough, though, considering. Far better than expected."

"Expectations could hardly have been lower," said Vick, frowning, as always. She'd some frown on her, that woman.

Malmer gave a helpless shrug. "Guess I trust him more than most of the royal family. But then, I trusted Risinau. Look where that got us."

"Truth is, we've no choice," said Heron. "We're out of food. We didn't do this to starve our own people."

"Sometimes I wonder why we did do it."

Couple of months ago at those big meetings, folk would've fallen over themselves to list all the wrongs they'd die to put right. Now no one offered Malmer a reason. The causes had turned hazy, lately. Like far-off chimneys through the vapours, you could hardly tell if they were there or just a trick of your mind.

"Then that's it, I reckon," said Malmer. "Send word to everyone who's still listening. We pull down the barricades. We open the city. We surrender."

One by one, the others nodded their agreement. Mournful, like that nod cost a little piece of themselves. But no one could see another way. The uprising was done.

"Sticks in my gullet," said Sarlby, "giving up."

Broad clapped him on the shoulder. "Be thankful you've got something in your gullet."

There was still a tang of old burning on the air outside. Of old burning and new rot. Ashes blew down the street, settling on the rubbish like little drifts of black snow. Not far off stood the shell of a gutted mill, blackened rafters sticking naked into the pale sky, blackened windows gaping empty.

"And this was supposed to be our Great Change." Malmer slowly shook his white head. Broad could've sworn he'd turned whiter the last few days. "What a fucking disaster."

"I'm not crying for those owners lost their mills," snapped Sarlby. "I can tell you that."

"What about the jobs in those mills?" asked Vick. "Daresay the rich folk whose investments went up in smoke will muddle through. What about the poor folk lost their livings?"

"Thought we were doing good," said Malmer, worn face crunched up with wrinkled disbelief. "*Sure* we were doing good."

"Good and bad aren't as easy to tell apart as you'd think," said Vick. "Mostly it's a matter of where you look at 'em from."

"That's the sorry truth," grunted Broad.

Malmer frowned towards that burned-out shell. "It's the poor pay the price, again."

Broad remembered Musselia after the sack. The slums looted and turned into smouldering ruins, corpses scattered in the streets. But the palace untouched on the high ground above the smoke. He worked his mouth and spat. "Always the poor pay the price."

Folk poured out of Valbeck that night. Columns of them snaking past the abandoned barricades and across the fields. A few were Breakers, going to surrender their arms and take their chances at amnesty. Most were folk who'd heard there might be food.

The first to meet the wary queue of the filthy, hungry and dispossessed were smiling women, handing out loaves. You might've thought they had undiluted hope rather than bread in their barrows for the good humour they spread down the column. A few days before, folk couldn't have found language harsh enough to describe Crown Prince Orso. A bit of bread in their bellies and they were frothing over with praise for him. Broad was no better than the rest as he caught that heavenly smell of baking, mouth watering up a rainstorm. Seeing May and Liddy's smiles when they ate their share was a better gift even than the bread itself. Ardee didn't smile. Broad didn't think he'd ever seen her smile. Just chewed, staring at her shuffling feet, eyes big and damp in her thin, thin face.

Wasn't long after the taste of bread faded that Broad was back to the worried old killer he'd been that morning. The sun slunk down towards distant woods and the cold came on and they reached a knot of blank-faced soldiers collecting weapons. There was a mismatched arsenal heaped up on either side of the road—old pikestaffs, rusted swords, butchers' cleavers and gardener's hatchets.

"I'm a shoemaker," a man was grumbling as an officer looked over a set of gleaming blades. "How can I work without my knives?"

"You want something, you have to give something up. On you go."

Handing in a weapon had felt too close to an admission of guilt to Broad. He'd thrown his down a well before they left and been glad to see them go. Might be it's people who kill people, but you can't stab a man with a blade you haven't got.

"I've got nothing," he said to the officer in charge, shifting his lenses on his nose as if to imply he was a man of learning. "Wouldn't know what to do with a blade."

The officer looked him up and down as if that was a bit too rich for either one of them to swallow, but he jerked his head onwards.

Another hour of shuffling and the sky started to darken, the mood darkening with it. Folk muttered that the Inquisition were up ahead, asking questions. Pulling people from the column. Anyone who'd been tight with the Breakers. Soldiers on horseback prowled the fields to either side of the road, torches in gauntleted fists. Some wanted to think the best. Others were sure they'd all be hanged for treason on the spot. No one left, though. Like lambs queueing up for the slaughterman's knife, they only huddled tighter together and kept plodding towards the bleak unknown.

"Don't like this," whispered Liddy.

Broad didn't like it much, either. After what he'd done in Valbeck, and what he'd done on his farm, and what he'd done in Styria, could he really hope to wriggle free now? *It's coming to something when you reassure yourself with the thought that there's no justice in the world.*

A good score of soldiers were gathered where the road passed through a gate in a tumbledown wall, a good score of masked Practicals with them. All under the supervision of a black-coated Inquisitor, torchlight finding the hollows in his pale face and making him look quite the demon. While Broad was watching, two men were led away to the side and a kind of nervous moan spread through the column. He felt a sudden desire to run, glanced about for his best route of escape.

"Calm yourselves!" called the Inquisitor. "His Highness the crown prince has offered a full amnesty! There are some questions to be asked and some questions to be answered, that is all. No one will be hurt, you have my word, the word of Superior Pike and the word of Crown Prince Orso himself. There is soup for you all a little further on."

That was what it came to. You might die, but you might get soup. Shame was, it more or less worked on Broad.

"Got to trust 'em," he muttered. "We've come too far now."

"We could head back," hissed Liddy, forehead creased with worry.

"They'd see us, think we've something to hide. Might be best if you two move away from me." *Might've been best if they'd moved away from him a long time ago.* But May wouldn't hear of it.

"No! We're not splitting up. You've a better chance sticking—"

"What the hell?" While they'd been arguing, Ardee had stepped stiffly from the queue and walked straight towards the Inquisitor. "What's she doing?" *If that useless bloody stray drew the wrong sort of attention, they'd be finished.* But there was nothing Broad could do. *Dive from the column to grab her, he'd only make it worse.*

One of the Practicals blocked her path, stick gripped tight in his fists. "Get back with the others, girl."

"I am Savine dan Glokta!" she called in a ringing voice that seemed to carry for miles in the still evening. "Daughter of His Eminence the Arch Lector! I demand to speak to Crown Prince Orso at once!"

There was a pause while the Inquisitor stared at her. While the Practicals stared at her. While everyone stared at her, Broad included. He couldn't believe it. After all they'd done for her, she'd land them on the scaffold.

But there was something different about her voice. So pure, and smooth, and commanding. Something different about the way she held herself, stiffly upright with her shoulders back, her long, thin neck stretched out and her sharp jaw proudly raised. She looked half a head taller of a sudden.

"At *once!*" she snarled at the Inquisitor.

He stared at her for a moment longer, then bowed his head. "Of course."

The Practical looked as dumbstruck as a man could with a mask on. "We're just going to—"

"If this young lady is who she claims to be then she deserves our immediate assistance. If she is not...we'll soon find out. And the world feels like a brighter place if you believe in people's fundamental honesty." He offered his hand with extravagant politeness.

"Thank you, Inquisitor," she said. "These three are with me."

The Inquisitor gave Broad a doubtful look up and down. "I cannot exempt everyone—"

"Of course not," said Ardee. Or Savine. Or whoever the hell she was. "Just these three. I must insist."

"Very well." The Inquisitor beckoned them to follow. Broad looked at Liddy, but what could she do? What could any of them do?

"Better hope that girl's telling the truth," the Practical growled in Broad's ear as he followed them up the road through the gathering darkness.

"I'm surprised as you are," muttered Broad, then nearly bit his tongue as the man shoved him and his boot caught in a rut. He was sorely tempted to punch him in the head, but it would only have got him killed and perhaps his family, too. Fighting every fight you're offered doesn't make you a big man, it makes you a fool.

"Did you know about this?" he hissed out of the corner of his mouth at May.

"'Course I did. I arranged it."

"You bloody *what?*"

Liddy was staring at her from the other side. "What did you do, May?"

"What I had to." May stared straight ahead, jaw muscles working on the side of her face. "It's high time someone put this family first."

The New Woman

Savine chewed at her cracked lips. She fussed at the frayed hems of the horrible, over-starched dress they had given her. She picked at the peeling skin around her broken fingernails.

She used to take such particular care over her hands. Their elegance had often been commented upon. Now, however she tugged at her sleeves, there was no hiding the scabs, cracks, callouses. All she had been through, cut into her crooked fingers.

She was no longer Ardee, the little lost waif. But she certainly was not Savine dan Glokta, feared and fearless scorpion-queen of investors. She used to be drawn to her reflection like a bee to a bloom. Now she shunned the mirror, dreading what she might see there. But then, she dreaded everything.

She knew she should have felt overwhelming relief to no longer be hungry. Joy to finally be clean. Blubbing gratitude for all the unlikely chances that had led to her salvation. She knew few who had been trapped in Valbeck were anywhere near so fortunate.

But all she felt was a constant, nagging terror. More like a hostage taken than a prisoner freed. As bad as when she fled through the crazed streets of Valbeck on the day of the uprising. Worse, because then fear had made sense. Now, she was supposed to be safe.

She heard voices outside and spun, heart suddenly pounding. On some sluggish instinct from long ago, she thought of arranging herself to best advantage. A lady of taste should always be discovered in the midst of something more important. She reached up to adjust her wig, realised there was nothing there but her own shapeless, graceless, colourless fuzz. She ended up frozen, less a beauty arranged for a portrait, more a burglar surprised in a darkened hallway, one scabbed hand twisting the other as someone ripped the flap aside and ducked into the tent.

Orso.

The red and gold of his uniform looked impossibly vivid. In Valbeck, towards the end, everything had been the colour of dirt. He looked weightier than he used to. Or perhaps she was so used to seeing everyone famished that the merely well fed looked like members of another species. He had the strangest expression when he saw her. Horror? Pity? Disgust? He gave a kind of shudder and put a hand over his eyes, as though the sight of her was painful.

"It is you," he whispered. "Thank the Fates." He took a step towards her but stopped awkwardly mid-stride. "Are you...hurt?"

"No." They both knew she was lying, and not even with any conviction. She was mauled inside and out. She was torn apart and badly stitched back together.

"Good." He forced a crooked smile. "You look well."

She could not smother a bark of bitter laughter. "You always were a champion liar, Orso, but that one's a little too big even for you to lift."

"You look beautiful to me," he said, holding her eye. "Whatever you might think."

She had no idea what to say to that. She was a wretched understudy, kicked from the wings onto the empty stage and gazing horrified towards the crowd, not knowing her lines. Not even knowing the play.

When she finally spoke, it was a shock how calm she sounded. "There were some people with me. A family. I wouldn't have—"

"They are safe and cared for. You don't have to worry about anything."

"Not worry," she whispered. She was nothing more than a sheaf of worries, held together by a shitty dress. "I'm sorry...you had to come here," she managed to dredge up. "I know how much...you wanted to go North."

"When I heard you were in danger, I didn't think twice. I didn't think once. Not that your father or mine were going to give me any choice. Probably best I leave the North to men's men like Leo dan Brock. I think we can all agree I'm not really cut out to be a soldier."

"The uniform suits you."

"I may be a sheep on the battlefield, but when it comes to wearing the uniforms, I'm an absolute tiger."

There had been a time she could talk for hours and beautifully say nothing. Now it felt obscene. Swapping light-hearted pleasantries while one party is shitting themselves all over the floor.

She felt an entirely unreasonable stab of fury. Why hadn't he come sooner? Why had he sat out here waiting, the useless fucking coward? She wanted to tear at him with her nails. Instead, she vomited up compliments. "From where I stand, it seems you managed the whole business rather well."

"More by luck than skill, I rather think."

"Everyone's alive." A flash of blood spattering that guard's face as his arm was dragged into the grinding gears. Savine had to cough, swallow acid. "Most. Most are."

"*You* are. That's all that matters. I'm so sorry it took me so long. To get here. To find you." He looked into her eyes with an intensity she could not stand to meet. "To realise...what I feel for you. I don't see how things can carry on between us...the way they did before."

She almost laughed at that. "Of course not." How could anything be what it was before, ever again?

"That's why..." He looked ridiculously nervous. Crown Prince Orso, notorious for caring about nothing. How many women had he disappointed? Hundreds, most likely. He really should have learned to do it better.

"That's why..." He took a hard breath. As if readying himself for some great act of courage. Savine lifted her chin. As if to give the headsman an easier task. He looked up at her. Guilty. Haunted. Ashamed.

Her patience snapped. "Just spit it out!"

"I want you to marry me!" he blurted. "I mean...shit!" He wobbled awkwardly down to one knee. "This isn't how I planned it. I haven't even got a ring!"

She stared at him in cold astonishment. "What?"

He took her limp hand in both of his. They felt hot and faintly clammy. "It's mad, I know it's mad, but...I love you. It took this to make me realise, but...hear me out."

Honestly, she had no words to interrupt him with.

"I'm shit without you! Utter *shit*, everyone knows it. But with you...I have the *chance* of being a worthwhile person. I didn't come here to save you. The idea's fucking ridiculous. I came so that you can save me. I'm the last man you'd pick as a king, I know, but you...bloody hell, Savine, you were *made* to be a queen! There's no one I admire more. You have all the brains and the guts and the ambition I don't! Imagine what we could build together. Well, imagine what I could watch *you* build. Queen Savine." He gave that boyish, wheedling smirk of his. "It even rhymes."

"Queen..." It came out a strangled squawk. The sort of noise a goose might make when its neck was wrung. "Savine..."

He could have had anyone. But he wanted her. And not her money, not her connections, not her wigs and her dresses and her jewels. Not the idea of her. But her. At her worst. Even now. Even like this. Not just as his lover. As his wife. As his *queen*.

"I..." she breathed, but her voice failed her utterly and it came out no more than an acrid burp.

"Shit." He winced as he sharply stood. "You don't have to answer. You don't even have to think about it." He pulled one hand away, but clung on with the fingertips of the other as if he could not quite bring himself to let go. "I shouldn't have asked. I'm such an arsehole. Take all the time... you need..."

He had ridden to her rescue. With five thousand armed men. Men she had paid for, but even so. She had never thought she might need rescuing. She had never dreamed he might be the man to do it. It was as if she had never really seen him before. She had known she could laugh with him. But she had never imagined she might be able to trust him. To rely on him. She had been braced for rejection and disappointment. Sympathy and support she had no idea what to do with.

"Shit," he said, finally letting go of her fingers, leaving them strangely tingling. "I'm *terrible* at this. Is there something you need? Is there anything I can... Do you want to be alone? Do you want me to go?" He turned towards the tent flap.

She caught his wrist. It was trembling. His wrist and her hand both.

Then she was kissing him.

It was not elegant. He stumbled back in surprise, blundered into a pole in the middle of the tent and for a moment, she thought he might bring the whole thing flapping down around them. Their chins knocked painfully. Then their noses. She tried to twist her head to one side and he went the same way, then they both went the other.

She caught his head, gripped it with both hands, teeth scraping, ugly grunting, undignified slurping. Awkward and fierce and urgent, as if they were running out of time. Nothing like the neat routines they used to go through in Sworbreck's office, with all the polite back and forth of a formal dance, a dignified game in which they both kept their cards close. Now everything was on the table and it felt deadly serious, her heart thudding in her ears just as it had the day of the uprising.

She saw his bed behind a curtain, brass gleaming in the shadows, and she pushed him towards it. He blundered into a stove, still trying to kiss her, nearly fell right over it, then got tangled with the curtain until she tore it out of the way. How many people knew she was in here? How many might guess what was happening? She didn't care.

All the elaborate precautions she used to follow. The carefully laid alibis, the changes of carriage, the blinds lowered in Sworbreck's bloody office. Against her father finding out. Against his parents finding out. Against her ending up carrying a bastard. She had been so formidably organised. So overpoweringly sensible. Romance totted up and tallied in Zuri's book like a manufactory's accounts.

Now all she could think of was how easily she could have died in Valbeck. Beaten to death. Starved to death. Burned to death. Ripped apart by her own machines. Manners, and propriety, and reputation, and good sense... none of that seemed to matter beside the necessity to tear off this sack of a dress and have his skin against hers. Her face was wet. She might have been crying. She didn't care.

She twisted around so he could get at the fastenings. "Get this thing *off* me."

"Doing my best," he muttered, fumbling at her collar. "Fucking... damn it!" A ripping of stitches, a tap and rattle as buttons bounced away and she tore her arms free of the sleeves, dragged it down, wriggled out of it like a snake wriggling from its unwanted skin. She kicked it away, cheap petticoats and all, making the canvas wall of the tent flap and rustle.

There had been times, in Sworbreck's office, when she had not got as far as taking her hat off before they were done. Now she stood stark naked. Uncovered, unguarded. His hands were on her waist. Fingertips scarcely brushing her skin. As if he hardly dared touch her. She could hear his breath. Slid her fingers between his, wrapped his hands around her, guiding them, up onto her chest, down between her legs. She had her tongue between her teeth, biting, almost painful.

In the overwritten romances her mother pretended not to read, the prince would always ride to the heroine's rescue and whisk her from danger in the nick of time, and she would fall into his bed, swooning with gratitude, so pathetically predictable. Savine had always felt nothing but contempt for reading that nonsense, and here she was actually doing it. She didn't care.

He paused a moment, ragged breath tickling her ear. "Are you sure you want to—"

"Yes, I'm *fucking* sure." She reached behind to twist her fingers in his hair, twist his head down so she could kiss him over her shoulder, suck at his tongue. Clumsy, hungry, mouth-crushing kisses while her other hand struggled with his belt buckle behind her back, digging at it, twisting at it, finally dragging it clinking free. He gave a little gasp as she pulled his trousers open, found his cock, started to rub it, wrist painfully twisted.

"Damn it," he gasped, fumbling with the buttons on his jacket. "Bloody...uniforms."

When he finally ripped his shirt off, she closed her eyes at the warmth of his bare chest against her bare back, his arm slipping around her ribs, holding her tight against him, skin pressed to skin. His other hand slid back down between her legs again and she rubbed herself against it, backwards and forwards. She slipped one knee up onto the bed, clumsy, off balance, almost falling, had to grip the bedstead with one hand, the other still rubbing at his prick, feeling the end prod wetly against her backside.

No ambitions or manipulations. No fretting on what happened yesterday or what would come tomorrow. Just his breathless grunts and her whimpery moans, eyes closed and mouth open. By the Fates, she sounded like a cat crying to be let in. She didn't care.

She let go of everything.

Lost Causes

"**Y**ou can go," said Vick.

The Practical's eyes slid over to the prisoner, sly and cruel and very narrow. She wondered if they were trained to use their eyes that way, or if only people with a naturally threatening glare wanted to work as Practicals in the first place. Bit of both, maybe.

"I think I can handle him," she said. The prisoner's wrists were shackled behind his back, after all, and chained to the chair for good measure, the bag over his head shifting as he breathed.

The door shut, and Vick took the bag by one corner and dragged it off.

She'd liked Malmer from the moment she met him. She'd never have admitted it, because it could have become a weakness to exploit. But she liked him a lot. Respected him. Reckoned he was as close as men got to being good. So it hurt, his wounded look as he recognised her. But a look was all it was. Vick had met kicks and sticks and knives with a smile, and some of them from people she'd liked. A hurt look wouldn't shift her resolve any more than a breeze would shift a mountain. Or so she told herself.

"You're one o' them," he breathed, and he closed his eyes, and slowly shook his head. "Never would've picked you as the one. Would've picked you last of all."

"That's my job," she said as she dropped into the chair opposite.

"Well, you're damn good at it. Hope you're proud."

"I'm not ashamed. Folk who keep hold of baggage like shame and pride don't last a week in the camps."

"That much was true, then?"

"My family died there. All of them."

"Then... how can you work for these bastards now? After what you've been through?"

"You've got it backwards." Vick leaned towards him. "After what I've been through, how could I *not* work for these bastards now?"

Malmer's shoulders sagged. "We were promised amnesty. Is that true, at least?"

"That's true. But you must've known there'd be questions." She looked him full in the face, so she could judge every twitch or tick or movement of his eyes. So she could sense the truth. "Where's Risinau?"

He gave a weary sigh. "I don't know."

"Where's Judge?"

"I don't know."

"Just give me something I can give them. Help me help you."

"You think I wouldn't hand over Judge if I could?" Malmer gave a sad chuckle. "I'd cheer at her bloody hanging, the mad witch."

The answers she'd known she'd get. But the questions still had to be asked. "Who's the Weaver?"

"That's what Risinau called himself, when we first met."

"When was that?"

"I was arrested for agitating. Five years ago. Maybe six. All we did was band together to ask for a fair wage, but I got the blame. Seems I've a talent for that. Risinau came to me. In a room like this one. Said he saw things our way. Said he wanted to help. Strike a blow for the common man, that's what he said. Bring a Great Change." Malmer curled his lip. "Guess I believed what I wanted to. Guess I've a talent for that, too."

"Most of us do," said Vick. "You know what I think?"

"If I did, I might not be in this chair."

"Risinau was a fool. He might've presided over the chaos, but there's no way he planned that uprising." She eased a little closer, as if she was sharing her secrets rather than winkling his out. Nothing to make people trust you like pretending you trust them. "He said the Weaver was a name he borrowed from someone else. Someone who set him on this path."

It was thin, she knew. Nothing that might convince His Eminence there was some deeper conspiracy. But Vick had never been able to leave a loose thread dangling.

"What do you owe Risinau?" she asked. "He used you all. A blow for the common man? Don't make me laugh. Who's the Weaver?"

Malmer was frowning down at the tabletop. As if she'd made him think. As if he was picking through the past, trying things different ways. Then he blinked and sat back with a grunt, as if he'd suddenly made them fit.

"There was a man, at the first big meeting I went to. Risinau was so... respectful of him. Awestruck, almost. Like a priest who'd had God turn

354

up to his service. Risinau pointed him out while he was talking. Called him the founder of the feast. The reason we were all there. But he didn't say a thing. Just watched."

"Who was it?" growled Vick. She could taste the answer, dangling right in front of her.

"Never heard his name," said Malmer. "Never really saw his face, but—"

There was a clatter as the doorknob turned and Vick twisted around, ready to snap at the Practical to get out. The words never left her lips.

Superior Pike stood in the doorway, his burned face expressionless, two Practicals at his shoulders, even crueller glares than usual above their masks.

"Well, well," he said in a papery whisper, stepping into the narrow room. "This is cosy."

The legs of Vick's chair screeched as she stood. "Superior Pike. An honour."

"The honour is very much mine. That was remarkable work in Valbeck, Inquisitor. Both subtle and bold. Both cunning and courageous. Without you, this uprising might have had a far bloodier ending. But I should not be surprised. His Eminence has always had the trick of picking the right person for a job."

Vick humbly bowed. "You're too kind, Superior."

"Not many people would agree with you on that score," said Pike, his eyes shifting to Malmer.

"This man was one of the leaders of the uprising. I was asking him some questions about its origins."

"I thought we had our wayward colleague Superior Risinau to blame for that?"

"Possibly." Vick left it there. Never use more words when fewer will do the trick.

"I would love to watch you work. There are few people from whom I could learn something about interrogation." Pike gave a sorry sigh. "But His Eminence wants you to return to Adua. He wishes to congratulate you personally."

"It's really no trouble to—"

"Enjoy your rest." Pike laid a hand on her shoulder. The very lightest of touches, but it still made her skin tingle unpleasantly. "No one could say you have not earned it. I will uncover all that can be uncovered." And one of the Practicals placed a heavy box on the table, instruments rattling inside. "Trust me."

Vick glanced back at Malmer. Once, in the camps, while they were dragging logs across a frozen lake, a convict had fallen through the ice. Another two had slid on their bellies to the hole, hoping to drag them from the water. They'd gone through, too.

If you want to survive, you'd better get a good sense for lost causes. Then you'd better let them go. Let them go before you go down with them. She turned towards the door.

"We should talk at some point, you and I." Pike was one of those people with a nasty habit of calling you back, just to show he could.

"About what, Superior?"

"There are many people in the Inquisition who have spent time in the prison camps of Angland, but most of them held the keys." He leaned close to murmur, the tickle of his breath making the hairs stand on the back of her neck. "Those few of us who spent time on the other side of the locks should stick together. We should remind each other... of the lessons learned there."

She gave a queasy smile. "They're always at the front of my mind."

Malmer stared as one of the Practicals began to take instruments from the case, arranging them in a neat row down one side of the table.

Vick had liked him from the moment she met him. She didn't enjoy that scene one bit. But you'd better get a good sense for the lost causes. Then you'd better let them go. She hunched her shoulders and turned for the door.

"Now then. Master Malmer, was it? I think you were saying something about... the Weaver?"

And the latch dropped shut.

The New Man

Orso's eyes flickered open.

Pale light. The rustle of canvas in the breeze. It took him a moment to remember where he was.

Valbeck. And something to feel very pleased about...

The uprising was finished, and...

Savine!

He rolled over, ever so slowly, hardly daring to look, suddenly terrified that he had dreamed the whole thing and the bed would be empty.

But there she lay, beside him. Eyes closed, lips slightly parted, sharp collarbones gently shifting with her breath.

For a moment, he felt the prickle of tears, had to squeeze his lids shut. She was safe. She was with him. The smile spread across his face.

He had proposed. He had actually *done* it. And, true, she might not technically have given him an actual *yes*, but dragging him to the bed seemed a long way from a no. When he picked out a pair of boots, he changed his mind three times and was racked by doubts all day. About this, the biggest decision of his life, there was no question in his mind. Savine was the woman for him. The one he wanted and the one he needed. She always had been.

He shifted towards her. Reached out to touch her face.

He wanted to wake her. To hold her. To fuck her again, certainly, but it was much more than that. This was love, not lust. Or at any rate, it was both. He wanted to tell her about all the hopes he had. Hopes for them. Dreams for the nation. Plans for all the *good* they could do.

Then he paused, fingertips just shy of her cheek, the warmth of her breath on his palm.

She looked so peaceful. To wake her would be selfishness. For once in his life, he would put someone else first. He would make himself a pillar

357

of support rather than a dead weight of disappointment for others to drag from failure to failure. He pulled his hand back.

He would not do the easy thing and play the hero. He would do the work and *be* one. Ever so gently, he wriggled from the bed, fished up his trousers between two fingers and, holding the buckle to stop it clinking, pulled them on, wedging his morning stiffness dismissively behind his belt where it could droop in its own time. Wouldn't be needing *that* this morning. He would give her space. He would give her whatever she needed. He would help her *heal*.

He whisked his Suljuk silk dressing gown around his shoulders, unable to wipe his grin away. There were a hundred roles he had tried and failed at, often spectacularly. Husband was one of the few remaining at which he might yet achieve dazzling success. He would not let the opportunity slip through his fingers. Not this time.

He stood by the curtain to the main part of the tent for just a moment, looking back. He pressed his fingers to his mouth, almost blew her a kiss. He stopped himself, realising how ridiculous it was. Then he did it anyway, damn it, and let the curtain fall.

There had been a time—yesterday, being honest—when dawn would have found him searching through the bottles scattered about his bed for something he could suck the last drops from. But that man was gone, never to return. Tea was what he needed now. The dawn beverage of industrious achievers!

"Hildi!" he shouted, in the vague direction of the tent flap. "Stove needs lighting!"

He was beginning to feel exceedingly pleased with himself and he suspected that, for once, he might even deserve it.

True, the dangerous work had been done by Arch Lector Glokta's formidable double agent, but he felt he had played the hand of aces she dealt him rather well. He had made the hard call to wait and tread softly. He had handled the negotiations with regal authority. He had showed clemency, restraint and good judgement. He had saved lives.

Orso the Merciful, might the historians call him, looking back admiringly on his achievements? It sounded rather well. A great deal better than most of the names the public had for him, anyway.

This uprising had been appalling, of course, but perhaps good could come of it. It could be the moment he ceased to be a disappointment. To the world and to himself. With Savine at his side, he could do anything. *Be* anything. He strode up and down his tent, the ideas spilling over each other. Facing the day used to be an unbearable effort. Now he could hardly wait to get started.

He had to understand what was truly going on, not just in the corridors of power, but down in the dirt with the common folk. Speak to that woman Teufel. She clearly knew what was *really* what. Then, when he got back to Adua, interviews with the Closed Council about policy. Proper ones this time, with a real agenda. How he could *change* things. How he could free the nation of its debts and build. Get rid of those circling vultures Valint and Balk. Spread the wealth. What good was progress if it only benefitted the few? He had to make sure nothing like this uprising could ever happen again. And no bloody apologising for himself this time! Would Savine apologise for herself? Never!

The tent flap was ripped rudely aside and Hildi came stomping in, leaving a trail of muddy bootprints across the groundsheet.

"Morning, Hildi!"

She appeared to be a great deal less pleased with him than he was, not even glancing in his direction as she dragged a great basket of wood sullenly to the stove.

"Wonderful day, isn't it?"

Orso's mother had made him bloodhound sensitive to the particular character of punishing silences, and Hildi's was beginning to feel serious. She threw back the door of the stove with a bang and started shoving logs into it as though they were knives and the stove a despised enemy.

"Something bothering you, by any chance?"

"Oh no, Your Highness," her high voice close to outright collapse under the weight of sarcasm.

"And yet I sense the slightest *frisson* of hostility. Grievances are like a drunkard's bed, Hildi. Always better aired."

As she turned towards him, he was taken aback by her look of violent hostility. "I defended you! When folk laughed! I spoke *up* for you!"

"I...appreciate your support?" ventured Orso, baffled.

"You bloody *knew* this would happen!"

He swallowed, a sense of profound dread beginning to creep up his throat. "What would happen?"

She raised a trembling hand to point towards the flap, beyond which the sound of hammering and raised voices seemed to have taken on a suddenly sinister air. "This!"

Orso pulled his dressing gown about him and ducked into the chilly morning.

Once his eyes had adjusted to the brightness, everything looked rather ordinary. Officers enjoying their breakfast. Soldiers warming their hands at a fire. Others striking a tent as they prepared for the journey back to Adua. A smith some way off was hammering away at some wrought iron. No massacre, plague or famine that he was responsible for, as far as he could—

He froze. A tall pole, almost a mast, had been erected beside the road into Valbeck, a gib sticking sideways from the top. From the gib hung a cylindrical cage. In the cage was a man. A dead man, clearly, his legs dangling. A few curious crows were already gathering in the branches of a tree nearby.

An officer saluted him with a hearty, "Your Highness!" and Orso could not even bring himself to acknowledge it. He wanted very much not to approach the gibbet but he had no choice, the camp mud cold on his bare feet as he picked his way closer.

Two Practicals held the base of the pole while another thumped down the earth around it with a great mallet. A fourth was conscientiously hammering nails into its supports. A large wagon was drawn up beside them. On the wagon were more poles. Twenty? Thirty? Superior Pike stood beside it, frowning at a large map, pointing something out to the driver.

"Oh no." Orso's guts weighed heavier with every step, as though they might suddenly tear free and drop out of his arse. "Oh no, no, no."

The cage creaked as it turned slowly towards him, displaying its occupant, his face awfully slack behind tangled grey hair. Malmer. The man who had led the Breakers. The man to whom Orso had promised amnesty.

"What the fuck have you done?" he screeched, at no one in particular. A fool's question. The answer could scarcely have been more obvious. Their whole purpose was to make it as obvious as they possibly could.

"We are gibbetting two hundred of the ringleaders at quarter-mile intervals along the road from Valbeck," droned Pike, as though Orso's despairing shriek had been a straightforward request for information without the slightest emotional element. As though the issue was the precise positioning of the corpses, not that there *were* any.

"Well...*stop*, damn it!" frothed Orso, his majesty somewhat dimmed by having to hold his dressing gown up like a lady's skirts above the road muck. "Fucking *stop*!"

One of the Practicals paused halfway through swinging his hammer, a questioning brow raised at the Superior.

"Your Highness, I fear I cannot." And Pike nodded the man on, the hammer tap, tap, tapping at the nail. The Superior slid out a weighty-looking document, several signatures scrawled at the bottom, a great red and gold seal attached which Orso recognised immediately as his father's. "These are the express and specific orders of His Eminence the Arch Lector, backed by all twelve chairs on the Closed Council. Stopping now would do no good in any case. The two hundred traitors have already confessed and been executed. All that remains is to display them."

"Without trial?" Orso's voice had gone terribly shrill. Hysterical, almost. He tried to bring it under control and failed entirely. "Without process? Without—"

Now Pike turned his lashless, loveless eyes on him. "Your father has granted the Inquisition extraordinary powers to examine, try and execute the perpetrators of this rebellion at once. His edict countermands your feelings, Your Highness, or mine, or, indeed, anyone's."

"But I fear there was never really an alternative." Yoru Sulfur was lying on the back of the wagon, perfectly at ease among the hanging posts with one hand behind his head. His highly specific diet evidently allowed fruit, as he had a half-eaten apple in the other. He had different-coloured eyes, Orso noticed as he gazed up calmly at the gibbet, one blue, one green. "I have seen many cases like this and, take my word for it, justice must fall like lightning. Swift and merciless."

"Lightning rarely strikes those who deserve it," grated Orso.

"Who among us is entirely innocent?" Sulfur bared his teeth to take a bite from his apple and thoughtfully chewed. "Could you really have let these Breakers go? To scatter to the winds and spread chaos across the Union? To foment further uprisings? To teach the lesson that murder, riot and treason are small matters, hardly to be remarked upon and certainly not punished?"

"I promised them amnesty," muttered Orso, his voice getting weaker with every syllable.

"You said what had to be said to bring this unfortunate episode to a close. To ensure *stability*. A stable Union means a stable world, my master is always saying."

"You cannot be held to your word by traitors, Your Highness," added Pike.

Orso winced at the mud. He realised his cock was still painfully trapped behind his belt and hooked a surreptitious thumb through his dressing gown to let it flop loose, all trace of morning magnificence entirely wilted. Sulfur's arguments were proving hard to disagree with. Ruling a great nation seemed a much more complex business than it had a few moments

361

ago in the privacy of his tent. And what could he do about it anyway? Unhang the Breakers? His useless anger was already guttering out, replaced by equally useless guilt.

"What will people think of me?" he whispered.

"They will think that, like Harod and Casamir and the great kings of old, you are a man who does what must be done!" Sulfur nibbled away at the core of his apple and wagged a finger. "Mercy is an admirable quality in smallfolk, but I fear it does not keep kings in power."

"Feel free to use me as the villain again," added Pike. "I must accept that I am somewhat typecast." He bowed stiffly. "And now please excuse me, Your Highness, there is a great deal to be done. You should return to Adua with all speed. Your father will be keen to congratulate you."

Sulfur stripped his apple to the stalk and flicked it away, lazing back in the gibbet's shadow with one hand behind his curly head. "I don't doubt you will have made him very proud. My master, too."

Father would be very proud. Not to mention this fool's master. One of Malmer's trouser legs had ridden up to show his calf, grey hairs on the pale skin stirring faintly with the wind. One eye was closed, but the other seemed to peer down in Orso's direction. He had heard it said that dead men have no opinions, but this one appeared to hold an exceptionally low one of Orso even so. Almost as low as he did himself.

"Not quite the end to our adventure we were hoping for." Tunny had walked up, a steaming cup of tea in one hand. "But it's an end, I suppose."

Orso was not sure he had ever liked the man less than at that moment. "Why didn't you get me?" he grated out.

"It was my impression that you were *otherwise engaged*." Tunny cleared his throat significantly. "And what good would it have done?"

"I could've... I could've..." Orso struggled to find the words. "*Stopped* this."

Tunny handed him the cup and gave his shoulder a fatherly pat. "No, you couldn't."

Orso considered flinging the tea in his face, but his mouth really was very dry, so he took a sip instead. Above, the gibbet groaned and Malmer turned slowly away.

Orso the Merciful, might the historians call him, looking back admiringly on his achievements?

It did not seem likely.

Two of a Kind

"**H**ow are you?"

Leo winced as he stretched out his injured leg. "Still a bit sore."

"It could have been far worse."

He winced again as he pressed at the cut in his side. "No doubt."

His mother reached up and brushed his bandaged cheek gently with her thumb. "I fear you'll have some scars, Leo."

"Warriors should, don't you think? In the North they call them Naming Wounds."

"I think we've had our fill of Northern customs over the last few days."

"A break wouldn't hurt." Leo took a long breath. "Rikke hasn't been to see me."

"The outcome of the duel did not please her."

"She'd rather I'd died?"

"She'd rather Nightfall had. She was *quite* vocal on that point."

"She's quite vocal on every bloody point," grumbled Leo. Rikke might seem an ever-gushing spring of laughs but he was starting to see there was a well of deep grudges beneath. "And what do you think?"

"I think you spared Nightfall because you have a big heart."

"Meaning I have a little brain?"

"Stolicus said to kill an enemy is cause for relief. To make a friend of him is cause for celebration." Her eyes met his. That look she had when she wanted him to learn a lesson. "If you could make a friend of the Great Wolf... if you could build an alliance with the North..." She let it hang there.

Leo blinked at her. "Even now you're thinking of the next step."

"A runner who does not think of the next step will fall flat."

"If Rikke's sore at Nightfall being alive, how's she going to feel about him being a friend?"

"If you want to be a great lord governor, her feelings cannot dictate your policy any more than mine. Or even yours. You have to do the best for the most. Do you want to be a great lord governor, Leo?"

"You know I do."

"The Union has been at war with the North, on and off, ever since Casamir took Angland. We cannot beat the Northmen with swords, Leo. Not for good. We will always be fighting to keep them out." She spoke very softly. "Unless we invite them in."

"So...I'm a peacemaker now?"

"You're a fighter, like your father was. But what separates great soldiers from mere killers is that they know when to *stop* fighting."

Wincing at the pain in his side, the pain in his stomach, the pain in his thigh, Leo slipped his feet from the bed and swung them down onto the cold floor. "Got to admit, I don't much fancy fighting right now."

"I doubt we'll keep you away from the swords for long." Leo's mother had a dry smile as she slipped a folded paper from her sleeve. "You received a letter. A message from the king. Or from his lord chamberlain, anyway."

"Don't tell me, they're finally sending reinforcements."

"They've heard they don't need to. So, naturally, they overflow with praise for your martial prowess."

"Their praise will be quite the salve on my wounds, I'm sure."

"They offer more than that," she said, looking back to the letter. "You are invited to Adua for a triumph. A grand parade, to celebrate your victory over the Northmen! I suspect the Closed Council want the king and his son to bask in your reflected glory."

Leo rubbed at his slit shoulder through the bandages. By the dead, that smarted. "You're the one who deserves the triumph."

"For what? Retreating?" She put her hand on his. "You fought. You won. You deserve the rewards." She paused a moment, looking into his eyes. "I'm proud of you."

It was as if those words were another sword-cut, and he shut his eyes, and felt tears stinging at the lids.

He'd never realised how much he wanted to hear them.

It wasn't easy.

He walked with a stick, every step an aching effort, the Northmen scattered about the vale competing over who could give him the most threatening glare as he struggled past. One was sharpening a sword with a steady *scrape, scrape, scrape* that seemed to be applied directly to his raw nerves.

"I'm getting the feeling they don't like us much," murmured Jurand through tight lips.

"I'm getting the feeling they don't like anyone," whispered Glaward.

"They don't have to like us, as long as they don't kill us." Leo was starting to suspect this had been a very bad idea. But it would hardly have been his first. He put his head back and tried to walk as if he was looking for another duel right now.

It wasn't easy. But if changing the world was easy, everyone would be at it.

There was a house down by the sluggish stream in the valley's bottom, smoke smudging from its squat chimney. A man was just ducking from the low doorway, with iron-grey hair and an iron-hard frown. Leo recognised him from the Circle. Black Calder. Father of Stour Nightfall, brother of Scale Ironhand. The man who really ruled the North.

"You're bold to come here, Leo dan Brock." He narrowed his eyes as though he was a cat and Leo an especially reckless mouse. "Very bold or very foolish."

Leo ventured a winning smile. "Can't a man be both?"

It won nothing from Black Calder. "The two often go together, in my experience. Have you come to mock my son?"

"I've come to make a friend of him."

Black Calder raised his grey brows. "Even bolder. But if you want to stick your head in the wolf's jaws, who am I to stop you?"

"Which leaves only one thing."

"Yes?"

Leo nodded towards the glowering warriors. "Your men have no business squatting on the Dogman's land, specially with such warlike looks. High time they went back to their families and remembered how to smile."

Black Calder looked at him a moment longer, then gave a snort. "Defeat makes them surly." And he stalked off.

"You two wait here," said Leo to his friends. He'd have liked nothing more than to take them with him. But some things you have to do alone.

It wasn't much different from the room where he'd been lying the last few days. The sharp smell of healer's herbs and stale sweat. The smothering warmth from the overbanked fire. The one bed, the one chair. The well-used war gear heaped in the corner. A reminder that the man in here had been a warrior. A stubborn insistence that he would be again.

"Well, well. The Young Lion himself come a-calling." Stour Nightfall lay back in a shadowed corner, bandaged leg raised on rolled blankets. His lip was twisted into an epic sneer, as if to make up for the bruises around both eyes and the crusting of blood under his swollen nose. "The last bastard I expected to see at my sickbed is the bastard who put me here."

Leo hooked his walking stick over the back of the chair and sat down heavily. "A great warrior always tries to surprise."

"You speak good Northern."

"I lived a year in Uffrith, with the Dogman."

Stour's eyes gleamed in the half-light. Like a wolf's eyes in the darkness of the forest. "And I hear you poke his scrag of a daughter."

Leo held his eye. "When I'm not stabbing Black Calder's scrag of a son."

Stour's sneer grew more savage. "'Cause of your sword, they say I might not walk again."

Leo was too sore himself to find much sympathy. It would win nothing here anyway. "You're mistaking me for someone who cares a shit," he said. "I'm no nursemaid and no fucking diplomat, either. I'm a warrior. Like you."

"You're nothing like me." Stour squirmed back on his mattress, grimacing as he shifted his leg. "I could've put you in the mud a dozen times over."

"I daresay."

"I was the better swordsman, by far."

"I daresay."

"If I hadn't made a show of it—"

"But you did make a show of it, and you took me lightly, and you fucking lost." And Leo had to admit he greatly enjoyed saying it. "Now you owe me your life."

Stour clenched his fist as if he was about to strike. But you won't punch anyone too hard lying on your back, and they both knew it. He sagged down, looking away, like one wolf beaten by another, slinking off into the undergrowth. "A lesson learned." His eyes slid back to Leo's. "Next time, I won't give you the same chance."

"There'll be no next time. Even if you do walk again. You're not the only one can learn a lesson."

"Then why did you come here?"

"'Cause my mother says boys whine about what's done. Men decide what will be."

"You always listen to your mother?"

"I complain about it, but yes." He was no diplomat, after all. Bluntness would win the day, or nothing would. "She's a very clever woman."

"Sounds like something my father would say."

"I hear he's a very clever man."

"So he's always telling me. Let's look to the future, then," said Stour. "What do you see there, Young Lion?"

What indeed? Leo took a long breath. "The Bloody-Nine won ten duels in the Circle, but he let most of his opponents live. Rudd Threetrees. Black Dow. Harding Grim."

"I know the names."

"He left them bound to serve."

Stour curled his lip. "You want me to serve you?"

"The Great Wolf for a pet?" He saw Stour's face twist with anger, made him wait a moment longer before going on. "I don't need you for a servant. I want you for a friend."

Stour gave a disbelieving snort, bursting with pride and scorn. Everything he did burst with pride and scorn, even though he lost. "For a *what*?"

"I reckon we want the same thing, you and I."

"And what the *fuck* is that?"

"Glory!" barked Leo, voice clapping off the narrow walls and making Stour flinch. "You want men to whisper your name with *fear*. With *awe*. With *pride*. You want to hear it in the songs, in the same breath as the Bloody-Nine's, and Whirrun of Bligh's, and the great warriors of the age! You want *fame*." And Leo shook his clenched fist in Stour's face. "Fame in the Circle and fame on the battlefield! You want to strive against great enemies and put the bastards in the mud. You want to *win*!" He snapped that word out like a battle cry, and Stour's face twitched at it, like a miser's who's seen the glint of gold. "And you know how I know?" Leo smiled, or at any rate showed his teeth. "'Cause I do, too."

The room was silent again. Just the rustle as a log shifted in the fireplace. Stour had turned thoughtful, eyes fixed on Leo. Two handsome young heroes at the height of their strength. A lord governor and a king-in-waiting, ready to step out from the long shadows of their parents. A pair of champions, men of action, already with great victories under their belts, set to inherit the world and reforge it the way they saw fit.

"Maybe we understand each other after all," Stour said softly.

"We have to be neighbours," said Leo, sitting forward. "We could waste our strength fighting each other. Waste our lives watching for the knife in our backs, like our oh-so-clever parents have. But we're our own men, I reckon, and we can find our own way. The Circle of the World is wide. No shortage of other enemies. Might do better if we fought the bastards together."

"It's a pretty picture," said the Great Wolf, eyes shining, and Leo wondered if he might trust the thoughtful Stour even less than the furious one. "But do you really reckon a wolf and a lion can share the meat?"

"If there's enough meat to go around, why not?"

Stour slowly started to smile. "Then let's shake on it, Young Lion." And he thrust his hand towards Leo.

Leo wondered if he really was sticking his head in the wolf's mouth, but he'd come this far. There was no way back. So he winced as he stood, reaching out to take Stour's hand.

He gave a gasp as the fingers snapped tight around his and he was jerked forward, pain lancing through his wounded side. He found himself bent over Stour with a dagger-blade tickling his neck.

"Trot into the wolf's lair talking of friendship?" Stour clicked his tongue. "Not very clever."

"No one's ever accused me of being clever. But we've tried being enemies." Leo reached around the blade of Stour's knife to scratch gently at his bandaged face. "Look where it's got us."

The Great Wolf bared his teeth and Leo felt the knife's edge press against his throat, the tension in Stour's arm as he gripped the handle tight.

"I like you, Brock. Maybe we're two of a kind after all." Stour's snarl became a grin, and he rammed the knife into the wattle wall, much to Leo's relief. "The Young Lion and the Great Wolf together." The grin became a smirk as he squeezed Leo's hand even tighter. "*There's* a partnership'll make the world tremble!"

Empty Chests

The wind gusted up strong, whipping brown leaves from the trees and sending them chasing across the hillside, whipping Rikke's hair in her face as she stood, watching Leo limp towards her with Jurand and Glaward in tow, silently seething.

She'd been seething ever since the duel, and not always silently, either. Three times she'd gone to the house where he was lying wounded. Three times she'd prowled around outside. Three times she'd stalked away without going in. Wanting to see him, refusing to see him. She'd been hoping her silence would speak in thunder, but some men are wilfully deaf.

Leo bared his teeth as he walked, leaning hard on a stick. That sprinkled some guilt on her anger. He'd fought for them, after all. Risked his life for them on nothing more than her word he'd win. He stumbled, and she almost started forward to help him. But he glanced up, and saw her, and it was then he really started to look pained. As if he expected harsher treatment from her than his enemies. In that, if nothing else, he was wise.

"I'll give you pained," she muttered under her breath.

Didn't help her mood at all that, ever since the duel, she could still see ghosts. Misty figures haunting the corners of her vision. Misty after-images that followed faces. Folk preparing the Circle. Folk fighting and dying in the battle. One time a fellow taking a shit in the bushes. No pattern to any of it that she could see. Her left eye still felt hot, her nerves raw and smarting, her stomach squelching and bubbling. That morning she'd got out of bed and given a shriek as, looking back, she caught a glimpse of herself asleep. Now and again, she'd flinch at the thought of that crack in the sky. Shudder at the memory of the black pit beyond, that held the knowing of everything.

Maybe you can force the Long Eye open after all. But closing it again might be another matter.

"Rikke." As he came close, Leo tried a guilty smile which helped neither of them. "It's good to—"

"Antaup tells me you've been off chatting with Stour Nightfall."

Leo winced. "He wasn't supposed to say anything."

"So the problem's not that you did it, but that he admitted you did it? Tell me you killed the winking bastard this time!"

Leo sighed, as if talking to her was quite the trying task. "I think there's been enough killing, don't you?"

"I could stand one more grave for the right man."

Glaward was already edging away, no bones at all for such a big fellow. "I think I'd better...in fact, I definitely need to..."

Jurand loitered, frowning at Rikke, one hand out as if to catch Leo if he fell. "Do you want me to stay?"

"No," said Leo, as if he actually did. "I'll catch up with you."

Jurand backed reluctantly away. The looks he gave her, anyone would've thought it was him and Leo who were the couple. Rikke had meant to be firm but fair, the way her father always told her to be, but well before Jurand was out of earshot she ended up scolding.

"What did you and that murdering bastard have to talk about?"

Leo sighed. "The future. Like it or not, he'll be King of the Northmen. Better we talk than fight—"

"Is it?" snapped Rikke. "I'm surprised you didn't stay there. Hold hands while he heals, share a few laughs over how he burned my father's hall and chased me through the woods and killed my friends and yours!"

Leo winced like he was stepping out into a storm. "I'm not changing sides, Rikke, I'm just trying to build a bridge from one side to the other."

"No doubt. A bridge those evil fuckers can march straight across!"

"To kill an enemy is cause for relief," he trotted out pompously. "To make a friend of him is cause for celebration—"

"You make friends with your enemies when you see the mud heaped on top o' the bastards! You think Black Calder will just let this *go*? He wants all the North and he won't be happy till he has it. All you did was sharpen his appetite."

Leo had that sulky-child look he got around his mother. Rikke was feeling more sympathy with her by the day. "The heir to the North owes me his life now. He's bound to me. That's a valuable thing—"

"By the dead," she sneered. "You think the likes o' Stour Nightfall care a shit for debts or bindings? He'll turn on you quick as a snake. You promised me you'd kill him, Leo. You *promised* me."

"It's not that easy to kill a man! Not when he's just lying there, at your mercy."

"I'd have thought that's the perfect bloody time!"

"What would you know about it?" he snapped. "There's a *brotherhood* between two men in the Circle. A *bond*. You wouldn't understand!"

"Because I've got a quim or because I've got a brain?"

"My mother might treat me like a child but at least I bloody *am* her child. I'm lord governor now!" Half-angry and half-wheedling, like he was trying to convince himself as much as her. "I have to make the decisions."

"And your first one is to break your *fucking word*?"

He looked taken aback by how savage she sounded. Truthfully, she was a little taken aback by it, too. "I'd no idea you could be so . . . *ruthless*."

"Oh, aye, Ruthless Rikke, terror of the North. Seems none of the men in my life know me as well as they think. The fact is, being nice gets nothing *done*. You have to make of your heart a stone, Leo. You should've killed him."

"Maybe I should have." Leo lifted his chin. "But I won. It was my choice what to do with him."

By the dead, how had it come to this between the two of them? From a lot of bliss and a few niggles to all niggle and no bliss at all. She guessed you can only ride so far on a fine stomach. She felt a flurry of twitches chase up her cheek and the fact she couldn't get her own face to obey only made her angrier than ever.

"You arrogant *fuck*!" she snarled. "You were reckless, and stupid, and by some margin the second-best fighter out of two! You won because Stour was even more of a puffed-up fool than you and couldn't help showing off! You won because my Long Eye saw what he'd do and I bloody screamed it at you!"

Leo's bruised, bandaged face barely moved while she spoke. Once she ran out of things to hurt him with and petered off into silence, he took a small step towards her. Not angry. Not sad.

"What did you say to me? No one remembers how the fight was won. I won. No one cares how."

He brushed her shoulder as he stepped past, not quite barging her out of the way, but nearly.

Was only a day or two ago, he'd said he loved her. Seemed he shrugged his loves off as easily as his promises.

He left her on the hillside, in the wind. Silently seething.

"Leo dan bloody Brock," she snarled, and in case someone had somehow missed the point, added, "that preening dunce!"

Isern thoughtfully fiddled with the finger bones on her necklace. "I sense something hath come betwixt the young lovers."

"You've an uncanny feeling for these things," mused Rikke's father.

"He's a bloody bladder o' vanity!" snapped Rikke, rubbing at her eye. Still sore. Still hot.

"You know your problem?" Her father had that calming look that was always certain to enrage her more.

"It's Leo dan lying Brock, the faithless fucker!"

"You're prone to set folk up so high, all they can do is let you down…"

"It's a constant worry o' mine," said Isern, nodding away, "the way the girl worships me."

"…and when they do, it's a high peak to topple from."

"That's not true!" snapped Rikke. Then she wondered if it was, and quickly lost all patience with the exercise. "That's *shit!*"

"You've said all along he's prone to think of himself first, second, third and last," said Isern.

"And you're saying that's all right?"

"I'm saying it's a bastard of a shortcoming in a lover, but one your eyes were wide open to. If you build your boat from cheese, d'you see, you can't wail at the heavens when it sinks, for cheese is known to be a poor material for boat-building."

"You should only ask for promises you know are going to be kept," said her father. "And we're talking of the Circle." He gave a helpless shrug. "Things happen. You've got to try to look on the sunny side or you'll spend your life in darkness."

Rikke ground her teeth. The two of them had, as usual, many fair points. But it was unfair points she wanted right then. "So when someone kicks me up my arse, I need to thank 'em for not kicking me in the teeth, do I?"

"We got our land back, Rikke. Our city. Our hall. Our garden…" His mouth curled up in a faraway smile. "No doubt it'll all need some putting right, but—"

"How long for, d'you think?" sneered Rikke, not much comforted by thoughts of training a rose or two. "Will Black Calder just toss his father's dreams on the rubbish heap now, dump his ambitions with the fish skins? That greedy fucker's going nowhere. Moment we look away, he'll be back!"

Her father, as ever, refused to be goaded into anger and stuck with quiet resignation. "Nothing's for ever, Rikke. No peace and no war. All you can do is the best you can in the time you've got."

"Well, there's our answer then. Best you can! Wisdom to be proud of."

All that dug from him was a wistful wince. "Wish I had some wisdom to give you. Wish I had the answers."

Rikke felt guilty, then. She seemed to lately, whenever she wasn't angry. Lurching from one to the other like a bloody children's see-saw. The kind that smacks you hard in the arse. "I'm sorry," she grumbled. "You've given me plenty of wisdom. More answers than any child's got a right to. Ignore me." She couldn't resist adding, "Everyone bloody does," in a mumble at the end.

"Well, your faithless but finely proportioned lord governor problem is solving itself." Isern leaned back and put one boot up on the table, rolling a chagga pellet between finger and thumb. "Since he's off to the Union where the bloated fools who wouldn't lift a finger to help will call him the greatest warrior since Euz, and puff his head up with farts until he can't fit through a bloody door sideways."

"Huh." Rikke neatly swiped the chagga pellet as Isern lifted it to her mouth and stuck it up behind her own lip. "Some solution."

"Thought you hated him?"

"I do."

"But you don't want him to go anywhere?" asked Isern, rolling a new pellet for herself.

Rikke planted her elbows on the table and her chin on her hands and sagged unhappily into them. "Exactly."

Her father swiped the second pellet from Isern's fingers and stuck it down behind his own lip. "Just as well you're going with him, then."

Rikke looked up. "I'm going where now?"

"Adua."

"I need to go back to Uffrith, with you. Tend to the garden, and whatever." Though she'd never had much patience for it, and less than ever these days.

"Isern and Shivers'll go with you, make sure you don't get into mischief."

"Or that you do?" muttered Isern, eyeing them both carefully as she rolled a third pellet.

"You can pour a drink on my old friend Grim's grave." He gave a little smile. "No need for words over it. He never liked 'em. But there'll be deals done in Adua, and we need to be represented. After the battle at Osrung, we were promised six chairs on the Open Council. Never happened."

"Promises are like flowers," said Isern, stretching her arms wide. "Often given, rarely kept."

"Well, if Leo sticks by us, maybe it'll be kept now."

Rikke pushed her pellet sourly from one side of her lip to the other. "I haven't proved myself too good at making Leo stick to things."

"Try again. You might improve. And it'll do you good to see the world. There's more to it than forests, believe it or not."

"Adua," muttered Rikke. "The City of White Towers." She'd heard a lot about it but never thought to go herself. A year in Ostenhorm had been hard enough work.

"Just promise me one thing."

"Anything."

"Let go of it."

"Of what?"

"The feuds," said her father, and of a sudden, he looked so tired. "The grudges. The enemies. Take it from a man with a wealth o' bitter experience. Vengeance is just an empty chest you choose to carry. One you have to go bent under the weight of all your days. One score settled only plants the seeds of two more."

"So you're telling me I should just forget what they said? Forget what they *did*?"

"There's no forgetting. I'm hemmed in by the memories." And he flapped an arm about as though the shadows were full of an invisible crowd. "Besieged by the bastards. The hurts and the regrets. The friends and the enemies and those who were a bit o' both. Too long a lifetime of 'em. You can't choose what you remember. But you can choose what you do about it. Time comes... you got to let it all go." He smiled sadly down at the tabletop. "So you can go back to the mud without the baggage."

"Don't talk that way," said Rikke, putting her hand down on the back of his. She felt like she was on stormy seas and he was the one star she had to sail by. "You're a long way from the mud."

"We're all of us only a hair away, girl, all the time. At my age, you have to be ready."

Rikke realised she'd got swept away in her bitterness then, and she leaned forward and hugged her father tight, and propped her chin on his balding head.

"I'll let go of it. I promise." But it was starting to seem like she was no good at letting go.

Behind his back, Isern tapped her fist against her heart and mouthed one word.

"Stone."

Like Rain

"Home," said Savine as the carriage lurched to a halt. Broad never rode in one before and it had been a bone-shaking business. Like most luxuries, he was starting to realise it was more about how it looked than how it felt.

Savine's home would've been daunting as a fortress, let alone a house. An almighty box of pale stone, acres of dark windows frowning onto the Kingsway across gardens on fire with autumn colour. It had a great porch with great pillars like it was some temple of the Old Empire. It had a tower at one corner with slit windows and battlements. It had a pair of guardsmen holding ceremonial halberds, still as statues on either side of the sweeping marble steps.

Broad looked at Liddy, and swallowed, and she looked back, eyes wide, and neither one of them had a thing to say. Footmen helped them down from the carriage. Footmen with emerald-green jackets and mirror-polished boots and great flapping lace cuffs. May stared at the man when he offered her his spotless white-gloved hand as if she was worried her fingers might stain it.

"The bloody footmen look like lords," muttered Broad.

"One of them is a lord," Savine threw over her shoulder.

"Eh?"

"I'm joking. Relax. This is your home now." Which was easy for her to say, she was stepping through her front door. Broad felt like he was sticking his head into a dragon's mouth. Though few dragons could've had a maw half the size of the towering front doors.

"I don't feel too relaxed," he muttered to Liddy as he shuffled up the steps.

"Would sir prefer a cell in the House of Questions?" she forced through an unconvincing smile to one of the guards. "Or a gibbet over the road to Valbeck?"

Broad cleared his throat. "You've a point."

"Shut your mouth and be thankful, then."

"Always good advice..." The hall could've held a whole terrace of Valbeck's slum houses. A gleaming expanse of rare woods and coloured marbles imported from places whose names Broad couldn't even pronounce, most likely, and he twitched down his worn cuffs and twitched up his worn collar in a pathetic effort to make himself more presentable.

A fine-looking lady was waiting for them, dark-skinned, tall and elegant, with hands clasped and jet-black hair knotted tight. "Lady Savine—"

Savine stepped forward and caught her in a hug. "It's so good to see you, Zuri. I can't tell you how good."

The dark-skinned woman stood a moment, surprised, then lifted her arms and hugged Savine back. "I am so very sorry I let you down. I kept thinking...if I could have been there—"

"I'm glad you weren't. There was nothing anyone could do. Let's not speak of it again. Let's have everything...just as it was before." And Savine gave a brittle, queasy smile, as if that might be easier said than done. Broad knew how that went. "Were you able to help your brothers?"

"Thanks to you. They came back with me." Zuri beckoned two men forward. Both dark-skinned like her, but otherwise they could hardly have been more different. "This is Haroon."

Haroon was wide as a door, bald and bearded. He touched two fingers to his wide forehead, solemn as an undertaker, and spoke in about the deepest voice Broad had ever heard. "We thank God for your safe return, Lady Savine."

"And this is Rabik."

Rabik couldn't have been much older than May, slight and bright-eyed, glossy black hair to his collar. He gave a quick little bow, lots of teeth in an easy smile. "And we thank you for this refuge from the chaos in the South."

"I am very glad to have you with us," said Savine.

"Your mother would like to see you, of course," said Zuri, "and there is a great deal in the book to discuss, but I thought you might want to bathe first."

Savine closed her eyes and gave a ragged sigh. "By the Fates, how I've missed you. Bath, Mother, book, in that order."

"I will be up to help dress you as soon as your friends are settled. I... took the liberty of hiring a new face-maid."

Savine swallowed. "Of course. And could you get me some pearl dust, Zuri? I need...a little something."

Zuri squeezed her hand. "Already waiting for you."

Broad watched Savine sweep away up the stairs. They were wide enough she could've been driven straight up them in the carriage. His eye was caught by the chandelier. Nearly blinded by its glittering, in fact. An upside-down mountain of twinkling Visserine glass. Dozens of candles, and each a fine ten-bit wax candle, too. He wondered what it cost to make. Wondered what it cost just to light each evening.

"You must be the Broads."

Zuri was studying him, no longer so welcoming, her black eyes hard and cautious. Broad couldn't blame her. He and Liddy had lost the power of speech altogether. Fell to May to speak up for the family. That seemed to happen more and more.

"I'm May, these are my parents Liddy and Gunnar." She raised her chin in a little gesture of defiance which made Broad feel strangely proud. "We looked after Lady Savine in Valbeck. Made sure she was safe."

"She and her parents will be extremely grateful. And no one ever did this family a favour or a wrong without being repaid triple. I understand you will be joining Lady Savine's service?"

"We'd like to," said Liddy.

"She will make you work. She makes everyone work."

"Never been afraid of work," said May.

"The Prophet says it is the best way into heaven, after all." She said it with a funny sort of smile, as if she wasn't near so pious as the words implied, and led them through into a seemingly endless corridor. No gleaming marble, just whitewashed plaster and bare boards, but all orderly and smelling of soap. Even back here, Broad still felt a bit out of his class. A pair of girls walked past with armfuls of laundry, looking nervously at them as if they were animals got free of their cage. Maybe they were.

"How many servants are there?" asked May.

"Nineteen in this house, and twelve guardsmen."

Liddy's eyes were nearly as wide as Broad's must've been. "How many houses does she have?"

"This is the townhouse of Lady Savine's father, His Eminence the Arch Lector. Lady Savine spends much of her free time here, though she has very little." Zuri glanced quickly at a watch she wore on a chain around her neck and slightly upped the pace. "But she owns five houses of her own also. One in Adua which she uses for meetings of the Solar Society and other social functions, one in Keln, one in Angland, a small castle in the country near Starnlend and one in Westport." She leaned close to murmur. "But so far as I am aware, she has never actually been to that one."

"It's a *small* castle," squeaked May in Broad's ear.

378

They passed a kitchen where a woman was giving some dough a thorough pounding, another sawing away at some fish with a filleting knife. "How many people work for her?" asked Liddy.

"In her personal service, including you and my brothers and the new face-maid, thirty-four. In her various business ventures, well...hundreds. Thousands, maybe."

"What business is she in?" croaked Broad as they turned up a long staircase.

"It might be better to ask what business she *isn't* in. What experience do you have?"

"I can stitch," said Liddy. "Was assistant to a dressmaker once. I can wash, I can cook some."

"Lady Savine will always find work for someone who can use a needle. Her wardrobe provides labour for legions on its own." She turned a key and led them into a room flooded with light. Trees whispered in the breeze outside the three big windows, yellow leaves gently falling. Through one doorway, Broad could see a big old bed frame. He was wondering if they were there to clean the place when she held the key out to him. "You can use these rooms for now. Until we find you something better."

"Better?" muttered Broad, staring at a vase of fresh flowers on a fine old table. He'd always thought himself unfortunate. Now he wondered what he'd done to deserve all the luck. Why was he standing in these clean-smelling rooms while crows pecked at the corpses of better men on the road to Valbeck? All he could think was that deserving's got nothing to do with anything. Life just falls on you, like rain.

"What role did you see yourself occupying, Master Broad?"

Broad pushed his lenses up his nose and slowly shook his head. "Never saw myself occupying anything in a house like this one. I was working in a brewery, my lady—"

Zuri smiled. "No need to call me that. I am Lady Savine's companion."

"I thought you were friends," said May.

"We are. But if I ever forgot that I am also her servant and she is also my mistress, we would not stay friends for very long." She looked to Broad again. "What else?"

"My family were herders, going way back." She didn't care about that. He hardly even cared about that any more, it felt like a thousand years ago. "And...I was in the army...for a while."

Zuri's eyes came to rest on the tattooed back of his hand. "You have seen action?"

379

Broad swallowed. He was getting the feeling she didn't miss much. "Some. In Styria."

"You didn't learn anything on campaign?"

"Nothing that'd be useful in a lady's service."

Zuri laughed as she turned towards the door. A laugh with quite the edge on it. "Oh, you might be surprised."

Drinks with Mother

Savine had hoped that once she was home with her things about her, bathed, perfumed and safe in her armour of corsetry, she would be herself again. Better, in fact, because adversity builds character. She would be the deep-rooted tree that bends in the storm but cannot be broken. She would be the sword that comes through fire tempered and blah, blah, fucking blah.

Instead, she was a dead stick shattered. Pig iron, melted to a slurry. Valbeck was not behind her in the past, it was now, all around her. She jumped at whispers and startled at shadows, as if she were still hiding in the corner of May's sweltering room and the gangs were restless in the street outside. While she powdered the freckles on her nose away to pale perfection, she felt as if her slit guts were unravelling across the floor. She could hardly remember that easy confidence she used to have. She was an impostor in her own clothes. A stranger in her own life.

"Mother!"

"Savine! Thank the Fates you're safe!"

"Thank the Broads. I'd never have made it without them."

"I thought you'd come straight to me when you arrived." Her mother had that familiar lecturing pout. As keen as Savine was to pretend everything was the same.

"I wanted to get clean first. It seems like months since I was clean." She did not feel clean even now. However she scrubbed, the aimless dread still stuck to her like a clammy second skin.

"We've all been so worried." Her mother held Savine out at arm's length so she could look her over. Like an owner examining the damage to a fire-ravaged house. "Dear, dear, but you're so thin."

"The food was ... not good. Then the food ran out." Savine gave a shrill laugh, though nothing was at all funny. "We ate vegetable peelings. It's amazing how quickly you feel lucky to get them. There was a woman in the next house who tried to make soup by boiling the paste off her wallpaper. It...didn't work." She shook herself. "Could I get a drink, Mother? I need...a little something." She would much rather have been held but, since they were who they were, she could be drunk instead.

"You know I never turn down a drink before lunch." Her mother flicked open the cabinet and began to pour. "Lubricates the rough road through to afternoon." She handed Savine a glass, and she knocked it off right away and handed it back.

Her mother raised a brow. "You do need lubricating."

"It was..." Savine felt tears gathering in her eyes as she tried to put into words what it had been. Crawling through the grinding engines. Running through a city gone insane. Crouching in the stinking darkness. "It was..."

"You're safe now." And her mother pushed another drink towards her.

Savine jerked herself back from the slums of Valbeck. Sipped at her glass though she'd rather have swigged from the decanter. "Where's Father?"

"Working. I rather think he couldn't face you." Her mother sat with a rustling of skirts, wiped a streak of wine from the outside of her glass and sucked her finger. "He can send a hundred prisoners to freeze in Angland without batting an eyelid, but he lets you down and he can scarcely get out of bed. I'm sure he'll be along presently. To check that you're well." Her mother considered her over the rim of her glass for a long moment. "Are you well, Savine?"

"Of course." Splash of the bucket into black water, the stench of burning in her nose. "Although..." Creak of the chain as the body of the mill owner swung from the gib of his own manufactory. "It may take..." The feeling as her sword slid through that man's body. So little resistance. The look on his face. So surprised. "Just a little time..." The grinding, ripping, screaming as the guard's arm was dragged into the gears of that machine. "To adjust."

She drained her glass again. Shook herself free of Valbeck again. Forced the smile back onto her face. Again. "Mother, I...have some news."

"Bigger news than that you're alive?"

"In some ways, yes." Certainly Queen Terez would think so...

"Is it bad?" asked her mother, wincing.

"No, no. It's good." She thought. "It's very good." She hoped. "Mother... I've received a proposal of marriage."

"Another? How many is that now?"

"This time I'm going to accept." What man could suit her better, after all? What man could offer her more?

Her mother's eyes went very wide. "Bloody hell." She finished her glass with one long swallow. "Are you sure? Given what you've been through—"

"I'm sure." It was the one thing she was sure about. "What I've been through...only made me realise...how sure I am." Orso was the one thing that made sense, and the sooner she was back in his arms, the better.

"But surely I'm not old enough to have a married daughter?" Savine's mother snorted up a laugh as she went to the table and pulled the stopper from the decanter. "So...who's the luckiest bastard in the Union?"

"That's the thing. It's...well..."

"Have you fallen for someone unsuitable, Savine?" Wine gurgled out into the glass. "Marrying down isn't the worst thing in the world, you know, your father did it—"

"It's Crown Prince Orso!" Her mother's head jerked up, her glass, for once, forgotten in her hand. Savine had to admit it sounded absurd. The most unlikely part of some unlikely fantasy. She cleared her throat and looked at the floor, went halting on. "It seems that...in due course... I'm going to be Queen of the Union."

And she had to admit it felt fine to say it. Perhaps the snake of ambition twisted around her innards had not died in the uprising after all, only slept through it. At so heady a sniff of power, it jerked awake with twice its old hunger.

But when she looked up, her mother had the strangest expression. Certainly not joy. Not even surprise. One would have had to call it horror. The base of her wine glass rattled as she slid it onto the table, as if she could hardly hold its weight any more. "Savine, tell me you're joking."

"I'm not. He asked me to marry him. A lady of taste never answers right away, of course, but I'm going to say yes—"

"No! Savine, no! He's not...he's not at all your type. He's a wastrel. He's notorious. He's a drunk."

Savine almost gasped at the hypocrisy but her mother caught her, fingers digging desperately tight into her arms. "You can't marry him! He just wants your money. You just want his position. That's no foundation for a marriage, you must see that—"

Lectures on the proper foundation for a marriage? From her? Savine shook her off. "It's not about the money, or the position. I know everyone thinks he's a fool, but they're wrong. He will be a great king. I know he will. And a wonderful husband. I'm sure of it. He was there. When I really needed him, he moved mountains for me. People think he has no character but they're wrong. I am what he needs, and he is what I need. What I didn't even realise I needed." With him she could feel safe. Be the better person she had promised to become. With him she could turn her back on the horrors of Valbeck and look to the future. She gave a girlish giggle which was quite unlike her. "We're in love." Fates help her, she wanted to sing it and dance around the room like a child. "We're in love!"

Her mother was not dancing. She had turned positively ghostly. Now she sank down in a chair, one hand to her mouth. "What have I done?" she whispered.

"Mother...you're scaring me."

"You cannot marry Prince Orso."

Savine squatted in front of her. Caught her hands in hers. They were cold. Corpse hands. "Don't worry. He will speak to the queen. He will speak to the king. They've wanted him to marry for years, they'll be relieved he's marrying a human! And if they're not, he'll convince them! I know him. I trust him. He'll—"

"You cannot marry Prince Orso."

"I know his reputation's bad, but he's nothing like people think. We love each other. He has a good heart." Good hearts? She was blathering but she couldn't stop herself, going nervously faster and faster. "And I have sense enough for both of us. We *love* each other. And think of all the good I can do if—"

"You're not hearing me, Savine." Her mother looked up. Her eyes were wet, but there was a hardness in them, too. A hardness Savine had not often seen. She pronounced each word with stern precision. "You *cannot*...marry...Prince Orso."

"What aren't you telling me?"

Savine's mother squeezed her eyes shut and a tear black with powder streaked her cheek. "He's your brother."

"He's..." Savine stared, cold and prickling all over. "He's what?"

Her mother opened her pink-rimmed eyes. She looked calm, now. She slipped her hands from Savine's, took Savine's in hers, pressed them tightly. "Before the king...was the king. Before anyone guessed he'd ever be the king. We...he and I...were involved."

"What do you mean, involved?" breathed Savine. The king had always behaved so strangely around her. So curious. So solicitous.

"We were lovers." Her mother gave a helpless shrug. "Then everyone found out he was King Guslav's bastard, and he was elected king himself and had to marry where politics dictated. But I...was already with child."

Savine was having trouble getting a proper breath. The way the king had looked at her, at the last meeting of the Solar Society. That haunted look...

"It was a dangerous time," said her mother. "The Gurkish had just invaded. Lord Brock had rebelled against the Crown. The monarchy was hanging by a thread. To protect me...to protect *you*...your father," and she winced, realising that the word could not quite fit the Arch Lector any more, "offered to marry me." And she guiltily bit her lip. Like a little girl caught stealing biscuits.

"I'm the king's bastard?" Savine jerked her hands from her mother's grip.

"Savine—"

"I'm the king's fucking bastard, and my father's not my father?" She wobbled to her feet, stumbling back as though she'd been slapped.

"Please, listen to me—"

Savine pressed her fingers to her temples. Her head was throbbing. She ripped her wig off and flung it into the corner. "I'm the king's bastard, my father's not my father, and I've been sucking my *brother's cock*?" she screamed.

"Keep your voice down," hissed her mother, starting up from the settle.

"My fucking *voice*?" Savine clutched at her neck. "I'm going to be sick."

She was sick, just a little. An acrid, wine-tasting tickle that she managed to choke back down, hunched over.

"I'm so sorry," murmured her mother, patting her back as though that might do the slightest good. "I'm so sorry." She took Savine's face in her hands and twisted it towards her. Twisted it with surprising firmness. "But you cannot tell anyone. Not *anyone*. Especially not Orso."

"I have to tell him something," whispered Savine.

"Then tell him no," said her mother. "Tell him no and leave it at that."

Drinks with Mother

"When we heading North, then?" asked Yolk.

Tunny looked down his nose at him as if at a woodlouse turned over and unable to right itself. "You didn't hear?"

Yolk looked blank. His favourite expression. "Didn't hear what?"

Forest let vent two perfect streams of curling smoke from his nostrils. He was as accomplished a smoker as he was a hat-wearer and military organiser. "Our new Lord Governor of Angland, Leo dan Brock, won a duel against Stour Nightfall, son of Black Calder and heir to the throne of the North and by all accounts a most fearsome opponent."

"A manly duel, Northern style!" Orso thumped the table. "Man against man, in a Circle of men's men! Blood on the snow and all that. Men's blood, one presumes."

"Probably a bit far south for snow this time of year," observed Tunny. "Though not for blood."

"Tell me he got his damn fool head split doing it," said Yolk.

"He was by all accounts picturesquely wounded," grunted Orso, "but his skull remains intact."

"Truly, there's no justice," added Tunny.

"This comes as a surprise?"

"For some reason, I never stop hoping."

"War in the North is over," said Forest. "Uffrith is back in the Dogman's hands and the Protectorate just as it was before."

"Little singed, maybe."

"So the Young Lion stole all the glory?" moaned Yolk.

"Glory just sticks to some men." Orso glanced down at his hands and turned them thoughtfully over. "Others it slides right off."

"Like water off a duck," threw in Hildi, from her place on the settle.

"I've always been repellent to glory," observed Tunny, "and have no regrets."

"*No* regrets?" said Orso. "What about the two hundred people we left gibbetted on the road to Valbeck?"

"Not my fault."

"Not yours, either, Your Highness," added Forest.

"I suspect I will take much of the blame in some quarters."

Tunny shrugged. "The rich folk seem to like you more than ever." It was true that a polite crowd of well-dressed well-wishers had been gathered at the gates of Adua to welcome him. "And they can express their love financially."

"True," said Yolk, "I mean, what's the love of the poor actually *worth*?"

"Oh, indeed," said Orso. "All the best kings had utter contempt for the majority of their subjects."

He had intended his sarcasm to be withering but Yolk managed to miss it even so. "Exactly," he said. "That's what I'm saying."

The queen waited, perched with rigid discipline on one of her uncomfortable gilded chairs in the centre of her vast salon. Four musicians smiled radiantly as they sawed out soothing music in a distant corner.

"Orso! The conquering hero!" She rose to greet him, which was an almost unprecedented honour, gave him a chilly kiss on the cheek, then a chilly pat on the same spot for good measure. "I have never been prouder of you."

"I fear I have not set a high standard in that regard."

"Even so."

Orso went straight to the decanter and pulled out the stopper. It was hard to think of a good reason for the stopper ever to be in, really. "I find I can hardly compete with the victories of the Young Lion, however."

Queen Terez flared her nostrils magnificently. "You won without drawing your sword. Your grandfather always said that was the best kind of victory. He would have been proud of you, too."

Orso's grandfather and namesake, Grand Duke Orso of Talins, had by most accounts been a tyrant despised the length of Styria. But then he had been defeated, deposed and assassinated, and such men generally receive poor reports from posterity. "I tricked some peasants into surrendering then hanged them," he said as he poured. "That's what the history books will say."

"The history books will say whatever you order the historians to write. You will be a king, Orso. You cannot think of the few, but must consider the welfare of the many. I trust this little episode has quenched your thirst for glory for the time being, at least."

"I suspect it has quenched it for all time. In fact...I've been thinking about my dynastic responsibilities. Marriage, you know."

The queen's head snapped towards him like that of a hawk that has spotted a vole in the bracken. "You mean it?"

"I do."

She snapped her fingers. "The eldest daughter of the Duke of Nicante is coming of age and that family is almost indecently fertile. She is rumoured to have a wonderfully gentle temperament—"

Orso chuckled. "I'm not sure gentle temperaments are my type."

"You have a type, now?"

"Actually, I do."

Actually, there was one woman for him and the rest were all dross. The instant he had seen her in his tent, he had known he was hopelessly in love. The dignity. The resilience. The sheer *guts* of the woman, unbowed by all hardship. She needed no jewels, no powder, no wigs. She was more beautiful without them. He knew he didn't deserve her, but he wanted to deserve her, and in working to deserve her, he might come actually to deserve her. Or something. The weather was dreary outside, rain pattering on the great windows, gusts scattering brown leaves across the palace gardens, but as Orso thought about Savine, it was as if the sun came out and poured its warmth upon him.

His mother caught his blissful grin forming and narrowed her eyes. "Why do I feel you already have a lady in mind?"

"Because I have nothing on my mind but one particular lady." The queen would not be happy. But the time comes in every man's life when he must set his mother's opinions to one side. He took a deep breath and sat forward. "Mother—"

He was interrupted by a knock at the door. It creaked open a crack and Hildi's head slid through. She fumbled off her cap to reveal blonde curls for some reason cropped short. "I've got that message you've been waiting for, Your Highness." And she showed the letter. Just a square of white paper with a white seal. Such a small package to hold all his dreams.

"Yes, yes!" snapped Orso, nearly jumping out of his seat with excitement. "Come, come!"

It seemed to take her an age to shuffle nervously across the great expanse of gleaming tiles, then to stop and give the queen a wobbling curtsy. "Your Majesty—"

"Never mind that!" snapped Orso, snatching the letter from her hand. He could not remember ever being so eager for anything in his life. He fumbled with the seal but his hands were clumsy as mittens and he ended up ripping it wide in his haste. His heart was pounding. His sight was swimming with nerves. But it was brief, so it could only be a yes. Surely a yes. What else could it be?

He closed his eyes, letting the music soothe him, took a long breath, composed himself, and read.

My answer must be no. I would ask you not to contact me again. Ever.
Savine.

That was all.

His first feeling was stunned disbelief. Could she have turned him down? How could she have turned him down? He had been so sure this was what they both wanted.

He read it again. And then a third time. *My answer must be no.*

And now came a stab of hot fury. Did she have to do it so fucking *rudely*? So *savagely*? With a *note*? With a *line*? He had offered her everything he had, everything he was, and she had trodden on his cock while she kicked his guts out. He crushed the note up in his trembling fist.

"Bad news?" asked his mother.

"Nothing to worry about," he somehow heard himself saying in the usual bored drawl.

And now came a flood of cold loss. Like that, all his dreams were ruined. It was a note that left no room for hope. No room for wheedling, even by a veteran wheedler like him. *I would ask you not to contact me again. Ever.* There would never be another woman who understood him the way she did. There would never be another woman like her at all. She had never felt so dazzlingly desirable as she did now he could never have her.

"Is there a reply?" asked Hildi, frowning.

"No," he managed to say, "no reply." What reply could there be to that?

And now came the slow welling up of self-hatred, steadily becoming a flood of utter disgust. Familiar, at least. As the foul waters closed over his head, he did not even struggle. What was the point? He had been so sure this was what he wanted, he had hardly stopped to consider her desires. Everyone said he was epically self-centred, after all. It was no great surprise that everyone turned out to be right. Why would a woman like her want a man like him? Why would any woman? Aside from a crown, some bad jokes and a shitty reputation, what did he really have to offer?

"We must plan a grand triumph for you!" His mother's eyes sparkled at the thought of how right she would finally be proved in the eyes of the world. "The nation shall bear witness to the vindication of our family. I shall make *sure* of it."

And now he slid into a bog of depression. Savine had been the approaching dawn, and now the sun was snuffed out and he was plunged into eternal gloom. He watched the rain thicken outside. It wasn't only her that he had lost, but the better man he could have been with her beside him, the better Union they might have forged together. He felt himself wilting, melting down his chair into a sagging slump. He scarcely had the energy to lift his head. Scarcely had the energy to breathe.

He had tried, too little and too late, to make something of himself. The result was two hundred corpses gibbetted on the road to Valbeck and a dismissive note.

"And then we have a wedding to plan. As soon as we can find someone of your *type*."

Why did he bother? Why did he bother with anything?

He drained his glass. The best Osprian, but it was sawdust on his tongue. He heaved up a sigh that actually hurt.

He wanted to cry.

"Pour me another, would you?" he murmured.

Questions

"It's me," said Tallow, with his flair for stating the obvious. Vick had known it would be him. Wasn't as if she got a lot of visitors.

She took his shoulder and slipped him past into the narrow hall. Not much room but she was thinner even than usual after Valbeck and Tallow had always been a scrap of nothing. She glanced around the ill-lit yard outside. A habit from the camps, kept ever since the camps. But there was no one watching. The only sound was the dripping from a broken gutter, high above.

"You all right?" she asked Tallow as she shouldered the door shut and slid both the heavy bolts.

"You were the one stuck in the city," he said.

"Don't worry about me."

"'Course not," he said, giving his shoes a sad grin. "You're carved out o' wood. Nothing touches you."

He was more like her brother every time she saw him. Or maybe it was her memory that was changing. Making her brother more like Tallow. So she could save him this time around, maybe. How pathetic would that be? Memory could betray you, she'd seen it a hundred times. Chop things about until they suited you better. You have to be on guard all the time. Against everyone else. Against yourself.

She turned away, making sure he didn't catch any hint of what she was thinking. Show them a weakness, they'll find a way to use it.

"You see your sister?" she asked as she led him from the cramped hall into the cramped dining room.

"I saw her."

"She's well?"

Tallow nodded in a way that seemed to say *no thanks to you*. Or maybe she just thought it did. She nudged a chair out with her boot and he slipped into it, around the squares board. Wasn't easy, even thin as he was.

"What's this?"

She realised, with an odd little stab of annoyance, that he was looking down at Sibalt's book. *The Life of Dab Sweet*. Open at that page. The one it fell open at. That etching of a lone rider, looking out across the endless grass and the endless sky.

Felt decidedly unpleasant, having someone else look at it. Like they were looking inside her head, at her secret dreams. "It's the Far Country," she said, softly.

"Pretty."

She should've thrown the damn thing away. She reached out and snapped it shut. "It's a made-up picture in a book full of lies." And she tossed it on the dusty windowsill.

Tallow shrank down into his shoulders. "Guess so."

She felt a little bad, then, for snapping. "Can I get you something?" she grunted. That was what you were supposed to do, when you had a guest. However unwilling a guest.

"What have you got?"

She thought about that for a moment. "Nothing."

"I'll take a double serving o' that, then." Tallow glanced about her narrow, bare apartment with those big eyes of his, the walls mottled with damp around the dirty window. "So this is what you do it for?"

"What?"

"All this." He raised his arms and let them hopelessly drop. Had to be admitted, looking with his fresh eyes, it was less than impressive. Vick was only here when she had nowhere else to be.

"Would you feel happier if I was living like a queen?"

"I'd understand it, at least." He leaned towards her across the narrow table. If she'd leaned towards him the same way, they'd have butted heads in the middle. "They hanged two hundred people, you know. 'Cause of what we did."

"Two hundred traitors." She poked at the table under his face with her pointing finger. "Because of what *they* did. How many died in their idiot uprising? Don't fool yourself there was some right side to this. Don't fool yourself there was a noble path we didn't take. We took the only path there was. Regret it if you please, but I won't!" She realised he was sat back now, and she was sat forward, almost shouting. She lowered her voice with an effort. Less furious denial, more statement of fact. "I won't. Here." She slipped the coin from her pocket and put it down on the table between them with a deliberate *snap*. The head of Jezal the First frowned up from a freshly minted golden twenty-mark piece.

"What's this for?" asked Tallow.

"You did a good job in Valbeck. You moved quick. You took the initiative."

"I just did what you told me."

"You did it well."

He stared down at that golden coin. "Can't say I feel too proud of myself."

"I only care about what you do. How you feel about it is up to you. But leave the coin, if it bothers you that much."

He swallowed, sharp knobble on the front of his throat shifting, then he reached out and swept the coin off the table. Just like she'd known he would. She had to smile at that. Hell, but he was like her brother.

"We're not all carved out o' wood," he grunted.

"Give it a while," she said. "You'll get there."

"Inquisitor Teufel!" Glokta grinned as though her visit was a delightful surprise rather than a meeting he'd demanded and she couldn't refuse. He patted the bench beside him. "Do sit."

Sitting close to other people always made her uncomfortable. But then she'd slept next to strangers in the camps. Packed together in the stinking straw like piglets in a litter. Better that than freeze. Better this than offend His Eminence.

She sat, looking out across the park, tugging her coat tight about her. It was a clear, crisp day, the odd gust of wind sweeping ripples in the surface of the lake, bringing flurries of leaves down from the trees. Stirring them about the black boots of the watchful Practicals.

"I used to spend a great deal of time on this very bench." Glokta squinted into the autumn brightness. "Just watching the water. My physicians say I should get into the sun more."

"It's a very...restful spot," said Vick. Small talk had never really been her strength.

"As if either one of us will find rest this side of the grave." Glokta gave her his hollow smile. "You did an excellent job in Valbeck. You showed quick thinking, courage and loyalty. Superior Pike was most impressed, and he is a hard man to impress."

It wasn't lost on Vick that he was giving her the same compliments she'd just given Tallow. Some people you reel in by making them think they need you. More often, it's making them think you need them. People want to feel good about themselves. Want to feel needed. Vick wondered if she'd been reeled in already. Long ago.

She left it at a simple, "Thank you, Your Eminence."

"I am coming to rely on you more and more. You really are the only person I feel I can entirely trust."

Vick wondered how many other people the Arch Lector had fed that same lie to. The idea that he might entirely trust anyone was sugaring the pudding too much, but she let it go. She let them both believe they both believed it.

"You've earned a reward," he went on. "Is there anything you need?"

Vick didn't like rewards. Not even ones she'd earned. They felt too much like debts she might have to repay. She thought about saying, *Only to serve*, or some patriotic guff, but that would've been her sugaring the pudding too much. She settled for, "No."

"Let me get you some better lodgings, at least."

"What's wrong with the ones I have?"

"I know exactly what's wrong with them. I used to live in them. When I served my predecessor, Arch Lector Sult."

"They serve my purposes."

"They served mine, but I didn't mind getting better ones. There are people who take far more for far less."

"That's up to them."

He smiled as though he knew exactly what she was thinking. Had expected it, even. "Perhaps you somehow feel, if you do not take the rewards for your work, it is as if you have not done the work? Because we both know you did the work."

"I'll take new lodgings when the job's done, Your Eminence." She watched a gardener rake leaves into a barrow. A thankless task, every breeze bringing more onto the narrow patch he'd already cleared. "Things could've gone much better in Valbeck. Risinau escaped. Judge as well. He may be dangerous. She most definitely is. Many more left the city before the crown prince arrived, and I don't think the outcome will have made them any less eager for their Great Change."

"Nor do I. The Breakers have been ... *broken* ... only for the time being."

"Risinau was a fat dreamer. I don't believe he planned the uprising on his own."

"I am inclined to agree." The Arch Lector swept the park with his narrowed eyes, lowered his voice a cautious fraction. "But I am beginning to suspect the roots of our problem may lie at the opposite end of the social scale." And he shifted his glance significantly sideways. The gilded dome of the new Lords' Round peeped glinting over the trees.

"The nobles?"

"They were taxed heavily to pay for the king's wars in Styria." Glokta scarcely moved his thin lips as he spoke. "They demanded reforms to compensate, acquired a great deal of common land. Many lined their pockets handsomely. Nonetheless, most of the Open Council recently signed a letter of complaint to the king."

"Complaining of what?"

"The usual things. Not enough power. Not enough money."

"Demanding what?"

"The usual things. More money. More power."

"You're suspicious of the men who signed this letter?"

"Absolutely." Glokta reached up with his handkerchief to dab at his weepy eye. "But far less than I am of the ones who did not."

"Names, Your Eminence?"

"The Brocks I can excuse, they have been rather busy in the North. But the young Lords Heugen, Barezin and above all Isher smile entirely too much. They lost out when the king was elected, or at any rate their fathers did. They have the largest grievances, but make no complaints."

"You think one of them could have been behind the uprising?"

"It is the nature of men, especially ambitious men, to be unhappy. Happy ones make me nervous. And Isher, in particular, is cunning. He was involved in the drafting of these new land rules and they have made him exceptionally rich."

"Worries at both ends of the social scale," murmured Vick. "Troubled times."

Glokta watched that gardener struggle to clear the unclearable lawn. "They always are."

Civilisation

The deck creaked under her feet, the sailcloth snapped with the wind, seabirds wheeled and squawked in the salt air above.

"By the dead," muttered Rikke.

The city was a vast cream-coloured crescent, stretching around the wind-whipped, grey-green bay. A mass of walls, and bridges, and endless buildings crusted together like barnacles at low tide, rivers and canals glinting dully among them. Towers stuck up above, and great chimneys tall as towers, their brown smoke smeared across the skies.

She'd heard it was big. Everyone had heard that. If anyone went to Adua, they'd come back scratching their heads and saying, "It's big," but she'd never expected it to be *this* big. You might've fitted a hundred Uffriths into it and still had room for a hundred Carleons. Her eye couldn't make sense of the scale. The number of buildings, the number of ships, the number of *people*, like ants in an anthill. A thousand anthills. The thought of it was making her head spin. Or spin more, maybe. She looked down at the deck, rubbing her temples. She'd been feeling insignificant enough already.

"By the dead," she muttered again, puffing out her cheeks.

"Adua," said the man standing next to her. "The centre of the world." He was a thickset old fellow with heavy brows, a short grey beard and a bald head looked like it had been beaten out of iron on an anvil, all planes and knobbles. "The poets call her the City of White Towers, though they tend towards the grey-brown these days. Beautiful, isn't she, from a distance?" He leaned nearer. "Believe me, though, she stinks when you get close."

"Most things do," muttered Rikke, frowning at Leo. The Young Lion, grinning into the wind with his carefree friends, the bloody young lads together, the bloody young heroes, the bloody young pricks. She sucked some chagga juice out of her gums and sent it spinning into the churned-up water.

She kept thinking of things she could've said to him. Pearls of wit and wisdom like he'd never get from those idiots. He'd have died in the Circle if it wasn't for her Long Eye. And he treated her as if she was an embarrassment.

She was working up to being properly angry when he threw back his head and gave that big, open, honest laugh of his, and all she felt was sad they'd fallen out, and jealous he wasn't laughing with her, and let down by him and by herself and by the world. The truth was, she bloody missed him. But she was damned if she was saying sorry. It should be him saying sorry to her, on bended knees. But how could you hate a man with an arse like—

He glanced towards her and she made sure she looked away. Him catching her looking would be like he'd scored a point somehow. But looking away from Leo meant looking back to this bald bastard, who was still considering her as if he found her of quite some interest.

"Who the hell are you, anyway?" she asked. Somewhat rude, but her failed romance and her endlessly hot and smarting eye and a week or two of seasickness had worn down her patience.

His smile only grew wider. A hungry smile, like a fox at the henhouse. "My name is Bayaz."

"Like the First of the Magi?"

"Exactly like. I am he."

Rikke blinked. Perhaps she should've punched him for a liar. But there was something in his glittering green eyes that made her believe it. "Well, there's a thing."

"And you are Rikke. The Dogman's daughter." She stared at him, and he smiled back. "Knowledge is the root of power. In my business, you have to know who's who."

"What is your business?"

He leaned close, almost hissing the word. "*Everything.*"

"That's quite some area of responsibility."

"Sometimes, I admit, I think I should have aimed lower."

"Shouldn't you have a staff?"

"I left it at home. However big a chest you bring, it never quite fits in. And magic, you know, it's all rather..." And he squinted thoughtfully towards the city. "Out of fashion, these days."

"Speak for yourself," she said, shifting her chagga pellet across her mouth and chomping it on the other side. "I've been blessed with the Long Eye." At that moment, she glimpsed the faintest phantom of a sinking ship, its mast tipping towards them as it foundered on a stormy sea. She cleared her throat, doing her best to ignore the ghostly sailors toppling into the brine. "Or possibly cursed with it."

"Fascinating. And what have you seen?"

"Frustrating glimpses, in the main. Ghosts and shadows. An arrow and a sword. A black pit in the sky with the knowing of everything inside. I saw a wolf eat the sun and a lion eat the wolf then a lamb eat the lion then an owl eat the lamb."

"And what does that portend?"

"I'm entirely fucked if I know."

"What do you see when you look at me?"

She frowned sideways. "A man who could tell more truth and eat fewer pies."

"Ah." And he rested one broad hand on his belly. "Profound revelations indeed."

Rikke grinned. Had to admit she was starting to like him, even if she had no idea whether to believe a word he said. "What brings the First of the Magi to Adua?"

"I have been detained far too long in the ruined West of the world by the demands of some most unreasonable siblings. They are mired in the past. Blinkered to the future. But I like to stop off in Adua whenever I can. Try to make sure no one is destroying what I have built." He narrowed his eyes across the bay, crammed with vessels of every shape, size and design. "People's capacity for self-harm never ceases to amaze me. They love to find their own path, even if it clearly leads off a cliff. And the Union has many enemies."

Rikke raised her brows at the endless city. "Who'd be fool enough to make war on this?"

"The Gurkish, before their empire collapsed like an undercooked meringue. And Bethod, against my advice. Then Black Dow, against my advice. Then Black Calder. Against my advice."

"Seems your advice ain't as popular as you'd like," said Rikke, glancing sideways.

Bayaz gave a disappointed sigh, like the governess in Ostenhorm when she tried to explain to Rikke what deportment was. "People must sometimes be allowed to make their own mistakes."

She shielded her eyes against the spray as they cut through the mad confusion of shipping towards the swarming docks. She could hear the faint din of voices bellowing and wagons rumbling and cargo hitting the wharves.

"How many live here?" she whispered.

"Thousands." The First of the Magi shrugged. "Millions maybe, now, building upwards and bloating outwards every day. Eclipsing even the great cities of old for scale, if not for splendour. People from every land within the Circle of the World. Dark-skinned Kantics fleeing the chaos in Gurkhul, pale Northmen seeking work and people of the Old Empire seeking new beginnings. Adventurers from the new kingdom of Styria, traders from the Thousand Isles, people of Suljuk, and Thond, where they worship the sun. More than can be counted—living, dying, working, breeding, climbing one upon the other. Welcome," and Bayaz spread his arms wide to encompass the monstrous, the beautiful, the endless city, "to civilisation!"

Jurand stared towards Adua, eyes narrowed against the spray. "By the Fates, the city's grown."

"Hugely," said Leo. Yet it somehow looked smaller than the last time he visited. Then he'd been just the rural-mannered young son of a lord governor. Now he was a lord governor himself, who'd beaten a great warrior in single combat, saved the Protectorate and won a famous victory for the king single-handed.

No doubt Adua had grown. But Leo dan Brock had grown more.

He found himself glancing sideways. Where he was always glancing, against his better judgement. Towards Rikke. If she'd been beside him, he could've pointed out all the great sights of the city. Casamir's Wall, and Arnault's. The House of the Maker, the dome of the Lords' Round. The Three Farms with the plumes of smoke from its new manufactories. They could've been enjoying this together, if she hadn't been such a sulky, stubborn bitch. He'd nearly died in the Circle for her. And she treated him like a traitor.

He was cranking himself up to bitter outrage when he caught sight of her, waving her arms in that mad way she had while she talked to some bald old man, and all he felt was sad, and guilty, as if he'd wandered off the right path and couldn't find his way back. The truth was, he bloody missed her. Wasn't long ago he'd said he loved her, and he'd at least half meant it. But he was damned if he was apologising. It should be her begging forgiveness—

She glanced over and he only just looked away in time. If she saw him looking, she'd treat it like a petty victory. Everything was so *petty* with her. Why couldn't she just forgive him so they could go back to how things were?

"Looks like they've sent a welcoming committee," said Glaward, pointing towards the thronging wharves.

Leo perked up at that. A decent crowd had gathered on the quay under a great banner marked with the golden sun of the Union and another with the crossed hammers of Angland. Armoured men sat on horseback in a perfect row, wearing the purple cloaks of Knights of the Body. An honour guard from the king! At the front was a man with monstrous shoulders and an even more monstrous neck, his hair clipped to grey stubble.

Jurand was leaning dangerously far over the rail to see. "Is that... Bremer dan Gorst?"

Leo squinted towards him as the ship slid in closer to the harbour, captain squawking out commands and the sailors swarming to obey. "Do you know," he said, perking up further, "I think it is!"

When the gangplank scraped to dry land, Leo made sure he was first across, still walking with a stick, if only to remind everyone he'd been heroically wounded in a noble cause. A man with a balding pink head and a heavy chain of office started towards him. One weak chin had clearly not been weak enough, and he had opted for several spread across his fur-trimmed collar.

"Your Grace, I am Lord Chamberlain Hoff, son of Lord Chamberlain Hoff." He paused, as though expecting gales of laughter. None came. No doubt bureaucrats were a regrettable necessity, like latrines, but Leo didn't have to like them. Especially when bureaucracy became a family business. "And this is—"

"Bremer dan Gorst!" He would encounter important people now, of course, but there's something special about meeting a boyhood hero. Leo had listened for hours to his father's stories about the man's exploits at the Battle of Osrung, hanging on every word. How he turned the tide on the bridge single-handed and led the final assault on the Heroes, hacking through Northmen like a butcher through sheep. "I once saw you fight three men in an exhibition!" Leo brushed the lord chamberlain aside to seize the big man's hand and got a nasty surprise. *You can tell a lot about a man from his grip*, Leo's father always said, and Gorst's was shockingly limp and clammy.

"Not something I would advise on the battlefield." Gorst's voice was even more shocking than his handshake. Leo wouldn't have believed so mighty a neck could produce so womanly a tone.

"I think I once heard we're related?" he said as they began to mount up. "Fifth cousins or some such." Leo tossed his stick to Jurand. He was damned if he'd look like a cripple in front of a man he so much admired.

He insisted on dragging himself into the saddle in spite of the pain in his leg, stomach, side, shoulder.

"How is ... your mother?" came Gorst's odd squeak.

"She's well," said Leo, surprised. "Happy the war's over. She was leading the fight when the Northmen first attacked." He thought about the light that put him in. "Giving me some excellent advice, at least."

"She was always highly perceptive."

"I knew you saved my father's life at Osrung. He used to love to tell that story. But I'd no idea you knew my mother."

Gorst looked a little pained. "We were good friends ... at one time."

"Huh." Leo had spent more than enough of his life worrying about his mother's feelings. He abruptly changed the subject. "I would've loved to train with you while I'm here, but ... I fear I'm in no fit state. Maybe I could observe?"

"Alas, there will be so many demands on Your Grace's time," said the lord chamberlain, oozing uninvited into their conversation. "His Majesty is keen to greet you."

"Well ... I'm at His Majesty's disposal, of course." Leo gave his horse a nudge and set off at a walk after the two standard-bearers.

"As are we all, Your Grace. But first His Eminence the Arch Lector wishes to discuss your triumph."

"Since when do Inquisitors arrange parades?"

The lord chamberlain delicately cleared his throat. "Your Grace will discover there is little that happens in Adua without Arch Lector Glokta's approval."

One of the banners at the front of the Young Lion's grand column had got tangled with a washing line, so they all had to sit in their splendid saddles waiting for it to get untangled. Leo himself could hardly be seen for the fawning gaggle of overpriced arse-lickers. Even Jurand and Glaward had been demoted to trailing after, eased further back with every turn. Seemed the fake adoration of strangers mattered more to Leo than his friends, or his family, or his lover. If that's what she still was to him. If that's what she'd ever been.

Rikke raised her brows as a whole column of dark-skinned soldiers tramped out of a side street, gilded standards flashing and spears lowered. Wasn't until a wagon rattled right through 'em she realised they weren't there.

"By the dead." She held a hand over her left eye, hot and itching and aching right into her teeth.

"Still seeing things?" murmured Isern, jaw chomp-chomping happily on chagga. "Take it as proof the moon has marked you special, and rejoice."

It all made Rikke more than a bit nostalgic for a time when folk just thought she was mad. "If this is special, I reckon I'd rather be ordinary."

"Aye, well, we all want the things we haven't got."

"That's it? Thought you were here to help me with the Long Eye?"

"I said I'd work out if you had it, then help you ease it open. Plain to everyone at that battle or that duel you've got it and it's wide open." Isern grinned over. "Closing the bastard was never numbered among my promises."

"Fucking marvellous," muttered Rikke, nudging her horse on so she could find some space to get a breath. Wasn't easy in this damn place, though.

By the dead, the *air*. Close and sticky and full of odd smells. There was a catch and a scratch in her throat, a sting at her eyes, like far-off burning. And the *noise*. The babbling in a dozen languages she didn't know, pleading, shouting, fighting, everyone shoving on to nowhere as if they were all endlessly late for everything. Hammers clanging, wheels turning and fires burning, so many it became a low rumble that made the ground buzz. As though the city itself were alive, and tortured, and angry, and desperate to wriggle free of its infestation of human lice.

"All this *progress*." Bayaz again, glancing approvingly at vast building sites to either side, with their towering cranes and their cobwebs of rope and scaffold and their swarms of bellowing workmen. "You would not believe how much it has changed in so short a time. This district, the Three Farms? I remember when it *was* three farms, and far outside the city walls! The city burst those walls and they threw up another set and it burst those, too, and the Three Farms is so built over with manufactories, there's barely a stride of grass left in the borough. All iron and stone, now."

Rikke watched one of the horses in front lift its tail and drop a few turds. There was still plenty of that in the streets. "All iron and stone? That a good thing?"

Bayaz snorted as if the whole idea of good was a waste of his valuable time. "It is a thing as irresistible as the tide. A golden tide of industry and commerce. There is no limit on what can be bought and sold. Why, I saw a shop not far behind that was selling nothing but soap. A whole shop. For *soap*! When you reach my age, you learn to swim with the current."

"Huh. Would've thought famous wizards would ride up front with the big folk, rather than getting stuck at the back with the dross."

Bayaz smiled. He was a hard bastard to rattle, the First of the Magi.

"The figurehead goes at the front of the ship. Braves the terror of wind and waves, takes the risks and reaps the glory. But it's an unnoticed fellow hidden away near the back who does the steering." He smiled up towards the head of the column. "No leader worth a damn ever led from the front."

"Words to live by, I reckon," murmured Rikke.

"The last wisdom I can offer you for the moment, I fear." And Bayaz pulled his horse up at the grand front steps of a building. Vast, it was, somewhere between fortress and temple with huge pillars at the front and carved masonry all over but precious little in the way o' windows.

"What's this place?" She didn't much like its looks. Lots of serious people going in and out, stepping around some well-dressed fellow with papers dangling from one limp hand, the strangest horrified look on his face. "A school for wizards?"

"Not quite," said the First of the Magi. "It is a bank."

"Master Bayaz?" An ordinary-looking man had come up to hold the wizard's bridle.

"Ah! This is Yoru Sulfur, a member of the Order of Magi."

"I'm Rikke," said Rikke, "rhymes with—"

"Yes," said Sulfur, smiling up. "The Dogman's daughter. The one blessed with the Long Eye."

Rikke was caught between suspicion and satisfaction that her legend had come ahead of her. "Or cursed with it, I guess."

"I hope we might speak more later," said Bayaz. "Young women born with the Long Eye are rare indeed in these latter days."

"Almost as rare as Magi," she grunted.

Sulfur smiled wider, his eyes never leaving her face, and she realised they were different colours, one blue, one green. "We relics of the Age of Magic really should stick together."

"Can't see why not. I'm hardly besieged by admirers."

"Not yet, perhaps." Bayaz gave her one last thoughtful glance. Like a butcher assessing a shepherd's flock and judging what to offer. "But who can say what the future holds?"

"Aye," murmured Rikke as she watched him climb the steps with his curly haired sidekick, "that'd be a fine bloody trick."

Shivers was sitting in his saddle, turning that ring he wore on his little finger around and around, glaring up at the bank with a frown hard even for him.

"What's your problem?" asked Rikke.

He turned his head and spat. "Never trusted banks."

*

The man they called Old Sticks, the king's chief torturer, Arch Lector Glokta, hunched behind a giant desk loaded with papers, frowning as he signed one after another. Death sentences, Leo imagined, bloodlessly executed with a flick of the pen.

His Eminence made Leo wait an insultingly long time before he finally looked up, winced as he leaned to drop his pen into its bottle of ink, and smiled. On that gaunt, waxy, wasted face, etched by deep grimace-lines, a yawning gap where the four front teeth should've been, it was an expression as painfully unsettling as a leg bent the wrong way at the knee. If inward corruption expressed itself as outward ugliness—and Leo had always been sure it did—the Arch Lector was even more vile than the vilest things they said about him. And that was saying something. He held out his hand.

"Forgive me, Your Grace, I cannot easily rise."

"Of course." Leo limped forward, leaning heavily on his cane. "Not too sprightly myself right now."

"You, I trust, will heal." Glokta's revolting grin grew wider. "I fear that ship has sailed for me."

He looked as if a stiff breeze would shred him, but his bony hand, its liver-spotted skin almost transparent, gripped far harder than Bremer dan Gorst's great paw. *You can tell a lot about a man from his handshake*, his father had always said, and this old cripple's was like a smith's pincers.

"I must congratulate you on your victory," said Glokta, after studying Leo a moment longer. "You have done the Crown a great service."

"Thank you, Your Eminence." Though who could've denied it? "But I didn't do it alone. Lot of good men dead. Good friends...dead. And the cost to Angland's coffers was huge." Leo pulled out the weighty scroll his mother had given him. "The ruling council of the province asked me to present His Majesty's advisors with this accounting for the campaign. In the absence of any help from the Crown during the war, they expect —they *demand*—financial support in the aftermath." Leo had practised that speech on the trip and was rather pleased with how it came out. He could manage this bureaucracy business as well as anyone. But Glokta looked at the scroll as if he was being presented with a turd. His eyes moved up to Leo's.

"Your triumph will take place in three days' time. A parade of some four thousand soldiers, as well as foreign dignitaries and members of the Closed and Open Councils. It will begin at the palace, chart a course through the city around Arnault's Wall, and return to the Square of Marshals.

There His Majesty will give an address to the Union's foremost citizens and present you with a commemorative sword."

Leo couldn't help smiling. "That all sounds...marvellous." The stuff of boyhood dreams, indeed.

"Crown Prince Orso will ride alongside you," added Glokta.

"Pardon me?" asked Leo, smile quickly vanishing.

The Arch Lector's eyelid flickered and a tear rolled down his cheek. He wiped it gently away with a fingertip. "His Highness won a famous victory of his own recently, putting down a rebellion in Valbeck—"

"He hanged some peasants." Leo had been so pleased with himself all day that this sudden shock was doubly disappointing. "It's hardly the same!"

"True," said Glokta. "He is the heir to the throne, after all, and you the grandson of a traitor. Great generosity, on his part, to share the glory."

Leo's face tingled as if he'd been slapped. He bloody had been slapped, and in his pride, which was far more sensitive than his face. "I beat Stour Nightfall in a duel! I spared his life!"

"In return for what?"

"For his father and uncle quitting our land, keeping the Dogman's Protectorate alive and safeguarding Angland!"

"No further concessions?" asked Glokta, his eyes glittering in their deep, bruised sockets. "No ongoing assurances?"

Leo blinked, wrong-footed. "Well...there's a code of honour among Northmen."

"Even supposing there was, you aren't one."

"Among warriors! Wherever they were born. And I was raised with Northmen!" Leo curled his lip as he looked the cripple up and down. "You wouldn't understand."

"No? How do you think I got crippled? Codes of honour, I fear, aren't worth the paper they're not written on. You could have taken Stour hostage. Could have delivered him to the king to ensure Scale Ironhand's future good behaviour. Instead, you secured nothing but his *word*."

Leo wasn't sure whether he was more furious because Glokta was obviously wrong or because he wondered whether he might have a point. Perhaps there was more to this bureaucracy business than he'd thought. "I *won*." His voice had a hint of that whine it had when he complained to his mother. "I beat the whole bloody North! And without one soldier from Adua. I risked my life—"

"You risked not only your life, which is yours to lose, but Union interests, too, which most definitely are not. I am prone to be more generous, but some might call that reckless."

"I..." Leo could hardly believe it. "I made a friend of the next King of the Northmen! I'm a soldier, not a bloody diplomat!"

"You must be both." Glokta was implacable. "You are a lord governor now. One of the greatest men in the Union. One of His August Majesty's most important servants. You cannot simply think with your sword any more. Do you understand, Your Grace?"

Leo sat and stared, stunned by the disrespect, the injustice, the rank ingratitude. He'd been far from keen on the Closed Council when he arrived in Adua. One interview with this crooked desk-worm and he was utterly disgusted by them.

"By all the fucking dead," he whispered, in Northern.

The Arch Lector either took that for agreement or simply acted as if he did. "I believe the lord chancellor wished to talk to you next. Some concerns over the latest tax receipts from Angland. It wouldn't do to keep him waiting." He nodded towards the scroll, which Leo only at that moment realised was still in his clenched fist. "Perhaps you should present your war debts to him." Glokta plucked up his pen and slid down the next document in a heap. "It seems a lord governor must be warrior, diplomat *and* accountant."

A Natural

Broad turned the handle, swung the carriage door open and respectfully stood out of the way.

Savine raised a brow at him. "And?"

"Oh." He offered her his hand. "Er...my lady." He helped her down while Rabik grinned from the driver's seat, thoroughly tickled to see the business handled so badly.

So Broad reckoned he was a coachman now. He had the livery, anyway. Bright green jacket with brass buttons, better than most officers had got in Styria. Shiny new boots, too, though they were prone to pinch. He might've felt quite the fool in all the finery, if it hadn't been so clear that anyone within a hundred paces would be staring at Savine instead, and that included him.

He could still hardly believe this beautiful, masterful woman was the same ragged, helpless girl who'd hidden in his daughter's room. She seemed to come from a different species than the sorry rest of humanity now. Her clothes were a masterpiece of engineering as much as tailoring, twisting her into a shape no person ever was. She was graceful as a tightrope-walker, unstoppable as a warship's figurehead. Folk stood gaping at her, like one of the Fates had dropped from the sky and was taking a stroll through their building site.

"Should I stay here?" muttered Broad as he helped Zuri down, not that she needed it, she was deft as a dancer. Probably she should've been helping him.

"No, no." She had a smile that was hard to pin down. "It would be lovely if you came along."

They'd made a huge breach in the old city walls, rubble showing through a teetering mass of scaffolding and two cranes towering overhead. They'd knocked down a few rows of houses, too, and were digging a mighty trench through the midst of it all. Parties of men, some of them bare-chested even in the cold, thumped away with picks and shovels in time to a work song growled between gritted teeth. Women in filthy dresses, wet hair plastered to their faces, slipped and slid up the bank with yokes across their shoulders holding buckets full of mud. Further back, children swarmed in the bottom of the great diggings, smeared grey from head to toe, stamping clay down around the sides of the trench with their bare feet.

"What is this?" muttered Broad.

"It will be a canal," said Zuri, "floating cargo into the heart of the city. And out again, of course."

"What's Lady Savine's interest?"

"One-fifth of it. Or it should be. We are here to make sure."

They clattered up a stair and between two long rows of clerks. A narrow office at the end was crowded by a big, pudgy man with grey hair scraped over his bald pate and an oversized desk covered in green leather. He had to lean dangerously far across it to shake Savine's hand, giving the buttons on his waistcoat quite the test.

"Master Kort," she said as Broad shut the door.

"Lady Savine, I am delighted to see you well." Kort gave Broad a slightly troubled smile. Broad didn't return it. He was getting the sense he hadn't been brought there to smile. "Everyone has been... extremely worried."

"So moving," said Savine, pulling off her gloves one finger at a time while Zuri whipped free a dagger of a hatpin. "But in business, we must set sentiment aside." With the slightest twist, Zuri lifted Savine's hat away from a wig that must've cost more than Broad used to earn in a year. "I am delighted to see work on our canal progressing so well."

Kort winced, hesitated, winced again and finally leaned forward, clasping his hands. "There is no easy way to say this—"

"Take the hard way, then, I am not made of glass."

"Regrettably, Lady Savine, I was obliged... to come to a new accommodation."

"And who has been so accommodating?"

"Lady Selest dan Heugen." Savine's expression didn't seem to change, but Broad had the feeling it took a struggle. "Her cousin was kind enough to arrange for some permits—"

"We had an agreement, Master Kort."

"We did, but... you were not here to fulfil it. Thankfully, Lady Selest was able to step into the breach."

Savine smiled. "And you think you can just slip her into my breach without so much as a by-your-leave?"

Kort shifted uncomfortably in his chair. "The banking house of Valint and Balk was kind enough to act as her backer, and she was kind enough to act as mine. Lady Savine, I was really given no choice—"

"I recently spent several weeks living like a dog." Savine still smiled, but there was something brittle in it now. Something jagged. "And I do not mean that figuratively. Starving. Filthy. Hiding in a corner, constantly afraid for my life. It has changed my perspective. It has made me see how very *fragile* we all are. Then I have been involved in a...let us call it an affair of the heart, which did not end to my satisfaction. It did not end to my satisfaction *at all*."

"I have nothing but sympathy, Lady Savine—"

"Your sympathy is not worth a speck of *shit*." Savine fished an infinitesimal mote of dust from her sleeve and rubbed it away between finger and thumb. "It's your canal I want. Just what was agreed. No more and no less."

"What can I say?" Kort spread his big hands. "My canal is no longer available."

Savine's smile had hardened to a skull's grin. The fibres in her neck stood out as she bit off the words. "The thing is, so much of business is a show. It is about the confidence people have in you. And confidence is so fragile. I am sure we have both seen it a hundred times. Cast from iron one moment, crumbling like sand the next. Following my misadventures in Valbeck, confidence in me has been profoundly shaken. People are watching me. Judging me."

"Lady Savine, I assure you—"

"Don't bother. I am merely trying to make you understand that, whoever your backers might be, I cannot afford the luxury of letting you and Selest dan Heugen *fuck* me on this occasion." And she glanced over at Broad, and caught his eye.

At least there'll be no trouble, serving a fine lady, eh? Liddy had said. Broad had smiled. *Aye. No trouble.* He didn't smile now.

He knew exactly what Savine wanted. He'd seen that look in her eye before, on some of the men he'd fought with. The ones you had to watch. The ones you had to worry about. He knew he'd had the same look. A kind of mad delight that it had come to this.

He didn't understand business, or deals, or canals. But he understood that look. All too well.

So Broad took hold of the edge of Kort's great desk and moved it out of his way. There was no room to push it into, so he just lifted one end. Papers, ornaments, a nice letter opener, all slid down the green leather as it tilted like a sinking ship, clattering off onto the floor beside it. He hefted the great thing all the way upright, leaving Kort oddly exposed in his chair, eyes wide and plump knees pressed fearfully together.

Broad took off his lenses, and folded them, and slipped them into his jacket pocket. Then he stepped forwards across the suddenly blurry office, a loose board creaking under his new boot.

"I lost many things in Valbeck, Master Kort," came Savine's voice, from what sounded like a long way off. "Several investments and several partners, a lovely sword-belt and an irritating but very capable face-maid. I also lost my patience."

Broad stepped so close to Kort that their knees touched. He leaned down and put his hands on the arms of Kort's chair, their noses just a few inches apart, close enough that the blur of his face resolved into an expression of extreme fear.

"You displease me," said Savine. "And I am in a mood to see things which displease me broken. Broken in such a way that they will not go back together."

Broad gripped the chair so hard that every joint in it groaned, breathing through his nostrils, like a bull. Bull Broad, they used to call him. He acted like he was only just keeping a grip on himself. Maybe he was.

"Our agreement stands!" squealed Kort, face turned away and his eyes screwed shut. "Of course it does, Lady Savine, how could it be otherwise?"

"Oh, that is *excellent* news." And the bright tone of Savine's voice was like a hand letting go of Broad's throat.

"You are the partner I always wanted!" blathered Kort. "Our deal is forged from iron, just like my bridge—"

"*Your* bridge?"

As Broad hooked his lenses back around his ears, Kort was giving a desperate, quivery smile. "*Our* bridge."

"Marvellous." Savine pulled on one of her gloves while Zuri slipped her hat back on with masterful precision and slid the hatpin home. "I would hate to have to send Master Broad to see you without my restraining influence. Who knows what might happen?"

Broad pulled shut the office door behind them with a gentle click. It was only when he took his hand from the knob he realised it was shaking.

Zuri leaned towards one of the clerks. "Master Kort may need a little help righting his desk."

It seemed too bright outside as he followed Savine through the noise and bustle back to the carriage. "I'm not a coachman, am I?" he muttered.

"Much of what I do is to recognise talent," said Savine as she watched the workers struggle in the diggings. "I saw yours the moment you saved me from those men, on the barricade in Valbeck. Employing you as a coachman would be like employing a great artist to whitewash cottages. But don't you feel better for it?" She leaned close to murmur, "I know I do." And she glided off towards the carriage as if the whole world belonged to her.

"You're a natural at this, Master Broad." Zuri pressed something into his palm. A gold coin. A twenty-mark piece. More than he'd been paid for a month's work at the brewery in Valbeck. More than he'd been paid for the assault in Musselia.

Broad looked up at her. "You believe in God, right?"

"Oh, yes. Absolutely."

"Thought he was dead set against violence?"

"If he was set that firmly against it..." And Zuri smiled as she closed his aching fist around the coin and gave it a fond pat. "Why would he make men like you?"

Good Times

Leo felt a bit of an outsider at his own party.

It was staged in the Hall of Mirrors, the most amazing room in a palace full of amazing rooms, silvered Visserine glass covering every wall so the richest, noblest and most beautiful the Union had to offer stretched away in every direction into the dim distance.

Certainly the introductions went on for ever. Damp hands were shaken and powdered cheeks kissed until Leo's lips were chapped and his fingers raw. It was a flood of congratulations, admirations, well-wishes. An onslaught of long names and weighty titles scarcely heard and straight away forgotten.

The Ambassador from Here or There. The Over-Secretary for Whatever. The niece of Lord What's-his-Face. Some bald old smirker someone might've called the First of the Magi, who blurted some magical nonsense about defeating Eaters in a Circle of salted iron being just like fighting Stour Nightfall in a Circle of grass. Leo assumed it was a joke, and not a very funny one. His cheeks ached from returning all the beaming smiles, the promises of never-ceasing friendship which ceased with the next breath.

This was what he'd wanted, wasn't it? To be fawned over by the greatest people in the realm? But close up, it all felt so *false*. He'd much rather have been in a barn with the Dogman, and his warriors, and his friends. He caught a glimpse of Jurand, standing on his own across the room, and Leo felt himself smile. He made it one step towards him before he was cut off.

"It's an outrage, if you ask me," murmured a tall man maybe ten years older than Leo, though his carefully swept hair was pure white.

"What is?" asked Leo, never able to resist the bait.

"That you must share your triumph with the crown prince. You bled for the nation. What did our half-Styrian heir do? Hang some peasants?"

It was like this white-haired fellow had peered into Leo's skull and read out the contents. "I suppose taking credit for other men's work is why we have royalty," murmured Leo.

"I am Fedor dan Isher." If you could know a man by his handshake, then Isher was firm, cool and careful. "These are my colleagues from the Open Council—Lords Barezin," a heavy man stuffed into a braid-wreathed uniform, with pinking cheeks and a boyish riot of blond hair, "and Heugen." Small and handsome with bright little eyes and sculpted moustaches around a pouty mouth.

"Good to meet you all." It was pleasing to finally hear names Leo had heard before. These were the heads of three of Midderland's most powerful noble families. Men with seats next to his on the front row of the Lords' Round.

"My father knew your father well." Barezin's jowls shook with feeling. "Such a wonderful man, he was always telling me, such a man's man, such an exemplar of the noble virtues! They were close friends." As far as Leo could remember, his father had always written the Open Council off as a nest of vipers. But this was a new generation, and he reckoned you can never have too many friends.

"We all wish to thank you for the great service you did the Union," droned Isher.

"It was a disgrace that you had to manage the business alone," frothed Barezin. "A shameful business, awful!"

"New laws prevent us from keeping standing armies of our own." Heugen spoke with great pace and precision while constantly shaking his head, as though nothing ever met his high standards. "Or we would have *sprung* to your aid ourselves."

"Too kind," said Leo. Though actual aid would've been even kinder.

"Our ancient rights and privileges are under constant attack," said Isher, dropping his voice. "From Old Sticks and his cronies."

Heugen nodded away like a chicken pecking at seed. "The Closed Council are—"

"A crowd of bureaucratic *arseholes*," burst out Leo. He couldn't hold it in. "The *gall* of that bastard Glokta! Then the chancellor! Grilling me about extra taxes after we bled ourselves white winning their war! Good men gave their *lives*. Folk in Angland'll be..." He was about to say fucking incandescent, then realised how loud he was talking and settled for, "very displeased."

Isher looked quite delighted, however. "The Open Council must present a united front. Especially with all this unrest among the lower orders."

"Your place is with us," said Barezin.

"As the *foremost* of us," said Heugen.

"As our champion," said Isher, languidly clenching a fist, "just as your grandfather was."

"Really?" asked Leo, getting just a bit suspicious of their close-harmony flattery. "I heard he was a traitor."

Isher wasn't put off at all. He leaned closer to murmur, "I heard he was a *patriot*. He simply refused to be cowed by Bayaz." And he nodded towards that bald man, deep in a murmured conversation with Lord Chancellor Gorodets, who did, it had to be admitted, look thoroughly cowed.

"That actually *is* Bayaz?" asked Leo, baffled.

Isher's lip curled. "During the last war, he promised my uncles that they would be chamberlain and chancellor, then, when he had the crown in his pocket, he snatched the rug from under them."

"Loyalty is an admirable quality," said Barezin. "Admirable. But it must cut both ways."

"Loyalty to a corrupt regime," added Heugen, "is *foolishness*. Worse. Cowardice. Worse! It's *dis*loyalty!"

Leo wasn't sure he followed the logic. "It is?"

"We leading lights of the Open Council really must meet," said Barezin.

"Discuss the advancement of our mutual interests," said Heugen.

"To have a genuine hero among us would make *all* the difference," said Isher.

"It would certainly make all the difference to me." Leo looked around to find a very striking red-haired woman at his shoulder. "Your lordships really mustn't hog the man of the moment. Since you haven't the manners to introduce me..." Though she'd given them no chance and could clearly manage it herself. "I am Selest dan Heugen." And she held her hand out.

"Charmed," said Leo, bending to kiss it. And he really was charmed, as well. "The quality of the company's looking up," he said, and she gave a silvery laugh, and fanned herself, and he smiled, and she fanned him, and he laughed, and Isher, Barezin and Heugen melted away with a few grumbles about speaking later, but Leo wasn't really paying much attention any more.

Selest. Had a nice ring to it. And she had this breathless way of acting as though every word he said was a delightful surprise.

"Have you been enjoying our city?" she asked.

"A lot more since you came over."

"Why, Your Grace, I suspect you're flattering me." She brushed his wrist with her fingertips in a way that couldn't have been accidental. Could it? She leaned towards him, voice slightly husky. "You really should

414

take a tour of my new manufactory while you're in Adua." As if touring manufactories was a forbidden thrill. The way her eyes met his over the feathers of her fan made him wonder whether a tour of other things might be on offer.

"What do you—" His voice came as squeaky as Bremer dan Gorst's, and he had to clear his throat and try again. "What do you make there?"

"Money." She gave another giggle. "What else?"

Riding through Adua in a grand procession, Rikke had thought she couldn't feel more out of place. Now she discovered her error.

It was like they'd had a contest to dream up the circumstances she'd feel most horribly small, twitchy and ugly in, and this right here had been the winning idea. All she needed to complete the horror was to have a fit and shit herself across the pristine tiled floor.

Everyone was so *clean*. Everyone smelled so *good*. Everyone's shoes were so *shiny*. They all had these little smiles, worn like masks, so you'd no notion what they were really thinking. They all spoke in whispers, like everything was a secret meant only for particular ears and those ears certainly weren't hers. At least the Long Eye was leaving her alone for now. The only ghosts in attendance were her own awkward reflections, wincing at her, profoundly unimpressed, from the mirrored walls of the hall.

She felt as if her own skin didn't fit her, let alone her clothes. She wished she had some chagga to chew but she hadn't brought any 'cause it hadn't seemed the kind of place where you chewed chagga, and indeed it wasn't. Where would you spit? Down someone else's back? There were only a handful of people she knew in the whole vast room. Bayaz she could hardly call a friend, and the magus had as fine a suit of clothes as anyone, slipping through the crowds with bald pate gleaming, trading hushed secrets as though he belonged there. Jurand stood alone, apparently pining for Leo even worse than Rikke was, while the Young Lion himself was forever at the centre of a gaggle of fine new friends who'd no doubt stab him in the back the moment he turned it.

As if to rub salt in her still smarting wounds, some woman had floated up to him. Some pale and unearthly beautiful woman with hair redder than hair had any right to be, all scraped up with golden combs then swirling down her bare, freckled shoulders. Her tits looked on the point of popping out the whole time, but by some sorcery of tailoring never quite managed it. A fact which Leo was evidently not blind to. You'd have thought she had the secret of creation tucked in her cleavage, the way his eyes kept drifting back to it. She had a necklace of sparkling red stones, and a bracelet to match, and flashing crystals stitched into her bodice and by the dead, on her shoes, too.

Rikke had a ring through her nose, like a troublesome bull.

Summed it up. She wished she could pull the bloody thing out but there was no way to do it without ripping half her nose off. She doubted even that would've got anyone's attention. She hadn't the slightest notion how to play this intricate game of fans and eyelashes and hints dropped over the shoulder and not quite but oh-so-nearly out tits, let alone the tools to win.

She slurped down some more of the thin wine they'd given her. Didn't taste of much but it was already having an effect. Namely making the tips of her ears feel hot and sinking her ever deeper into jealous depression. They tell you drink makes you happy, but what they mean is it makes happy folk happier. They don't tell you that it makes unhappy folk more fucking unhappy than ever.

She gave an unpleasantly sweet burp and scraped her tongue on her teeth. "Men," she muttered, helplessly.

"I know," came a voice from beside her. "There's no reasoning with them."

By the dead, this one was even more beautiful than the other. Her skin had this sheen, like she wasn't made of meat but some magic alloy of flesh and silver, every gesture finished off right to the tips of her long fingers like it was part of a dance, endlessly practised and utterly perfected.

"Shit," breathed Rikke, unable to stop herself looking this woman up and down. "You have made some effort."

"Honestly, my maids made most of it. I only had to stand there."

"Maids? How many do you need?"

"Only four, if they know their business. I very much like your shirt. It looks so comfortable. I wish I could wear one."

"Why don't you?"

"Because there are a million different rules a lady of taste must observe. No one tells you what they are, but the penalties for breaking them can be most severe."

"That sounds a pain in the arse."

"You have no idea."

"Must admit, I didn't really know what to expect." Rikke plucked at her shirt. It had stuck around her armpits with the heat of all these people lying to each other. "I got new boots, too. Even combed my hair." She nervously twisted a stray tangle behind her ear. "But I slept out in a forest for a few weeks and it's refused to behave ever since. How d'you get yours to do... all *that?*"

The woman leaned close. "It's a wig."

"Is it?" Rikke stared at those shining braids coiled and piled and swept up like a nest of spun gold. "Looks like hair, just... more so."

"It is hair. It just isn't mine."

"Doesn't yours grow?"

"I clip it off."

"Or your maids do."

"Well... yes. Most of the women here are wearing wigs. It's the fashion."

She said that word, *fashion*, like it was an explanation for any kind of madness. "Everyone knows that?"

"Everyone."

"So why are we whispering?" whispered Rikke.

"Well... because everyone knows it, but no one admits it."

"So... you shave your heads so you can wear a hat made of someone else's hair, then lie about it?" Rikke puffed out her cheeks. "Puts my worries in some fucking perspective."

"Not all of us have the courage for honesty."

"Not all of us have the wit to lie."

The woman narrowed her eyes at Rikke. "I doubt you're lacking wit."

Rikke narrowed her eyes at the woman. "I doubt you're lacking courage."

She flinched a little, as if that somehow touched a sore spot, and changed the subject. "I very much like your necklaces, too."

Rikke tucked her chin into her neck to peer down at the mass of charms she'd collected over the years. Some Gurkish ones, some Northern ones, some shaman's teeth and this and that. She'd always felt you could never have too much good luck. Seemed a right lot of old junk now. She hooked the well-bitten dowel with her thumb and held it up. "This one's to bite on if I have a fit. Hence the tooth marks."

The woman raised her brows. "Beautiful *and* practical."

"These are runes. My friend Isern-i-Phail carved 'em. Supposed to keep me safe. Year I've had, though, I doubt they work."

"Well, they're lovely, regardless. I never saw anything like them."

She actually seemed to mean it, and she'd been kind, in a way. "Here." Rikke took the runes off and slipped them gently over the woman's head. "Maybe they'll work better for you."

"Thank you," said Savine, and for once she meant it. It was such a simple, forthright gesture, she found herself disarmed. She could hardly remember the last time someone gave her something without expecting double the value in return.

"I can get another," said the Northern girl, waving it away. "Looks much better on you. You've the shoulders for it."

"Fencing."

"What, sword-work?"

"It's fine exercise. Keeps me focused—" She was caught off guard by a sudden memory of her sword punching through that man's ribs, in Valbeck, in the gutter. The noise he made as she struggled to pull the blade out of him. She had to shake off an ugly shiver. "Though . . . perhaps playing with swords is a bad idea."

"Might be I'll try an axe instead. Axes are always popular, where I come from."

"I had heard." And they smiled at each other. Savine told herself she found this girl's artless ways endearing. The truth, as usual, was less sentimental. She did not trust herself to talk to anyone more important.

Whenever someone expressed their disingenuous condolences over her ordeal, or their unconvincing relief at her safe return, she wanted to knock them down and grind her heel into their eye. She'd been sniffing pearl dust all day. Just a pinch at sunup to chase off the nightmares. Then a pinch at breakfast to keep her head above water. Maybe a couple more before lunch. Only rather than keeping her sharp, the way it used to, it was making her twitchy and savage and strangely reckless.

"Here." She undid the clasp of her necklace. Red Suljuk gold and the most stunning dark emeralds from Thond, beautifully worked by her man in Ospria at a cost that had raised even her eyebrows. She slipped it around the girl's neck and fastened it. "I'll swap you."

The girl stared at it, nestling among that mass of beads, charms and talismans, big eyes bigger than ever. "I can't take this."

"I can get another," said Savine, waving it away. "It looks far better on you. You have the chest for it."

"It looks like a gold ring around a turd." The girl glanced down Savine's front. "And you've got twice what I've got."

"I have half what you have and some very expensive corsetry." Savine reached out with both hands, pushed the girl's unkempt mess of red-brown hair out of her face and studied it. Presumptuous, undoubtedly, but she was in that kind of mood. "Honestly, you have some remarkable natural advantages."

"I've a what?" she said, looking slightly scared.

Savine put a finger under her chin to tip her face into the light. "Fine strong bones. Excellent teeth. And your eyes, of course." Huge and pale and so very expressive. "I've never seen anything quite like them."

She flinched a little, as if that somehow touched a sore spot. "Not sure whether they're a blessing or a curse..."

"Well, I know women who'd kill for them. Literally. An hour with my maids and I could have every person in here drooling over you." Savine gave the girl's face a parting pat and let her go, frowning out at the oblivious gathering. "Just goes to show what a ridiculous lie it is. What a ridiculous fucking lie *everything* is." She realised she had spat that last phrase with sudden bitter fury. "Forgive me. I'm being terribly rude."

"You're being amazing, far as I'm concerned." The girl looked down at the necklace, blushing now, which only made her look better. "My father saw me wearing these, he'd shit himself."

"I don't know what my father would think, but he shits himself routinely."

The girl grinned up. "You're all right, you know that?"

And Savine felt, of all things, a sudden need to cry. She looked out at the Hall of Mirrors, blinking back the tears. There was some bald old man she could not quite place, staring right at her like a butcher at a livestock sale. She flicked her fan open as though she could hide behind it. "No," she muttered. "I'm not."

She had to stop herself flinching at the sight of Orso, draped against a pillar, looking drunk and despondent. It was as though there was a hook in her throat, and every glimpse of him was a painful tug on it. She was ashamed to admit it, but she wanted him no less. She certainly wanted to be queen no less. Her one desire was to go over to him and put her hand in his and say yes, and kiss him, and hold him, and watch the smile spread across his face...

And marry her brother.

The thought disgusted her. But hardly any more than everything disgusted her now. She took a shuddering breath. He was lost to her for ever, and the person she had been with him was lost for ever, and she could not even tell him why. How he must despise her. Almost as much as she despised herself.

"Lady Savine?"

She found, to her horror, that the king was standing right beside her with that haunted, fascinated expression he always had in her presence.

"Your Majesty." Savine dropped into a curtsy on an instinct, her face suddenly burning. Out of the corner of her eye, she saw the Northern girl clumsily trying to imitate her but, in trousers, abjectly failing.

"I so enjoyed my visit to the Solar Society," the king was blathering. She could hardly hear the words over the thudding of blood in her head.

"So impressed by what you and Master Curnsbick have achieved. The industry, the innovation, the *progress*. So proud to have...subjects... like you. Young ladies pointing the way to the future, and so forth—"

"Please excuse me," she managed to whisper, turning so fast she almost stumbled. She took a wobbling step or two, weak at the knees.

"I'm Rikke," she heard the Northern girl yammering behind her. "Rhymes with pricker."

"The Dogman's daughter, of course! He was a good friend of my good friend Logen Ninefingers, you know."

"Ah, you have to be realistic."

"Exactly!"

"Talking o' which, my father was saying we were promised six seats on the Open Council..."

Savine tugged at her corset in a futile attempt to let in some air. She felt buried. She was sure she was about to fountain vomit all over the pinnacle of society. It was only a sudden, sobering stab of cold rage that stopped her, froze the guilt and fear and left her icy.

Selest dan Heugen, that sly bitch. She was only twenty paces off, using every weapon in her arsenal on Leo dan Brock, fanning herself as if she was on fire.

Did she think she could worm her way into Savine's place? Steal her canal, her connections, her profits? It was precisely what Savine would have done in her tasteless shoes, of course, but that was only the more reason to make her pay for it.

Selest saw her coming, carried across the hall on a wave of poisonous fury, and darted to head her off. "Lady Savine! We are all so *very* glad you have returned to us unhurt."

"Lady Selest, you're such a treasure."

"It must have been a *terrible* ordeal, what you went through."

The temptation to bite her was almost overwhelming. But Savine only shrugged. "I was far from the only one who suffered."

Selest was pretty, clever and rich, but she led with her chest and smiled far too much. Smile all the time and you'll make them sick, like a cook serving nothing but meringue. Make your smile a rare treat, you'll leave them desperate to taste another. Savine let Brock see the corner of hers, just for a moment, almost hidden behind her fan.

"I'm Leo," he said, with that bluff, blunt Angland accent.

"Of course you are," said Savine.

Selest's voice dripped with tattletale venom. "Lady Savine was in *Valbeck*."

As if *Valbeck* was some awful secret. She thought to make Savine seem ruined. But all she would do was make her seem fascinating. Savine would see to it.

"It's true," she said, turning away, biting her lip as though at horrible memories.

Brock blinked. "During the uprising?"

"I was visiting a manufactory in which I am...in which I *was* a part owner...when it happened." She let it hang there for a long time, finally meeting Leo's eye. As if she would not tell just anyone, but could not hide the truth from him. "The workers turned on us. Several hundred of them. I am ashamed to say I locked myself in an office. I heard them overpower the guards, heard them set upon my business partner."

Brock stared, mouth slightly open. "By the dead..."

Savine caught a delicious glimpse of doubt on Selest's face. As she realised that her banal drivel could not possibly compete with this. "I found a loose board, broke my nails pulling it up. I had to crawl through the machinery to get away, while they smashed down the door above."

Brock was spellbound. "That must've taken some courage."

"Or lucky cowardice, in my case. I saw one of the guards dragged into the machinery. His arm was ripped off in the gears."

Selest preened and fluttered in an effort to recapture Brock's attention, but it was futile. Sometimes pretty lies win the day. But sometimes ugly truths cut deeper. She spoke on, relentless, imagining each word was a slap in Selest's face.

"I crawled through the guts of the building to the river and squeezed between a wall and a waterwheel. I found a filthy old coat washed up on the riverbank, disguised myself as a beggar and ran. The city was...going mad. Gangs on the rampage. Prisoners marched in columns. Owners hanged from jibs. I wish I could say I helped but I was thinking only of myself. Honestly, I was hardly thinking at all."

"No one could blame you," said Brock.

"I was chased through the slums. Through tenements where the husk-smokers lay twelve to a room. Through the filth of the pig pens. Two men cornered me in a blind alley..." She remembered that moment. Remembered their faces. Now she would turn her terror to her advantage. Even Selest looked gripped now, her fan hanging limp.

"What...happened?" muttered Brock, as if fearing the answer.

"I had a sword with me. A decorative thing but...sharp." Savine let the silence stretch an almost uncomfortably long time. A blabbermouth like Selest would never understand that drama is not so much a question of words, but of the silences between. "I killed them. Both of them, I think. I hardly even chose to do it, but suddenly...it was done." She took a breath, and it caught in her throat, and she let it go, jagged. "They gave me no choice, but...I still think about it. I think about it over and over."

"You did what you had to," whispered Brock.

"That makes it no easier to live with."

Selest's voice sounded slightly cracked. "Well, you're back with us now, and I for one—"

Brock spoke over her as if she wasn't there. "How did you get away?"

"I stumbled upon some decent people and...they took me in. They kept me alive, until Prince Orso delivered the city." Selest dan Heugen knew when she was beaten. She snapped her fan open and drifted off. The chill satisfaction of victory was the closest Savine had come to pleasure in some time. She might never be Queen of the Union, but she still reigned supreme over the ballroom. "And here I am."

"That's...quite a story," said Brock.

"Not compared to facing fearsome warriors in a Circle of shields, I daresay."

"Your ordeal went on for weeks. Mine was done in moments." He leaned close, as if sharing his own secret. "Between the two of us, Stour Nightfall's the better swordsman." He brushed the long scab under his eye with a fingertip and Savine realised, with a guilty thrill, that it must be a sword-cut. "He could've killed me a dozen times. All I did was survive long enough for his own arrogance to beat him."

She held up her glass. "To the survivors, then."

"I can drink to that." He had a fine smile. Open, honest, full of excellent teeth. Even though the fight was won, Savine found she was still talking to him. More surprising still, she found she was enjoying it. "Your name is Savine?"

"Yes...Savine dan Glokta." Say what you would for the name, you could always be sure of a reaction. Brock gave an ungainly cough. He really had no disguise at all. "You met my father, then?"

"All I can say is you got your mother's looks, and she must be quite the beauty."

She gave him a discerning nod. "Not a bad effort, under the circumstances."

All she had wanted was to crush Selest dan Heugen, now fanning herself wildly beside an oblivious Lord Isher. But with the fight won, the pearl dust and the drink closed back in on Savine and she found the prize was an extremely handsome man. There truly was something of the lion in his sandy hair worn long, his sandy beard cropped short, his confident, comfortable, obvious strength. With that healing cut across his face, he looked like the hero from an overblown storybook. So manly, and so popular, and so powerful. Indeed, the young Lord Governor of Angland was surely the most eligible bachelor in the Union at that moment. If you discounted Crown Prince Orso. Which Savine feared she had to.

"It must be difficult to be a celebrated hero," she said. Everyone wants to be sympathised with, after all, however little they deserve it.

"I'll admit it takes some getting used to."

"It must be hard to tell the genuine admiration from the empty breath. Surrounded by people, but all alone." She gave a theatrical sigh. "Everyone trying to make use of you."

"Whereas you've got my best interests at heart?"

"I wouldn't insult your intelligence by pretending anything of the kind. But we might be able to make use of each other." And she gave Leo another smile. Why not? His blunt, easy manners were the opposite of Orso's. He brought her no puzzles to solve. His words barely had single meanings, let alone double ones. And sometimes a beautiful fool is the very thing one needs.

Savine was tired of being clever. She wanted to be rash. She wanted to hurt someone. Hurt herself. "There is one place in the city you really ought to visit while you're here."

"Really?"

"The office of a friend of mine. A writer. Spillion Sworbreck."

Brock looked crestfallen. "I'm . . . not really much of a reader—"

"Nor am I, honestly. Sworbreck's away on a research trip in the Near Country." She touched Leo on the chest ever so gently with her fan, looking up at him from under her lashes. She needed . . . a little something. "I'll be there, though."

Brock cleared his throat. "Tomorrow?"

"Now," said Savine. "Tomorrow I might have changed my mind." She was probably making a fool of herself. She was probably causing a scandal.

But, safe to say, a smaller one than marrying one's brother.

Orso stood, and drank.

Well, to be precise, he stood, and drank, and watched Savine. Surreptitiously, to begin with. But less surreptitiously with every drink. Just watching her was torture. Watching her with that square-jawed oaf Leo dan Brock was triply so. A torture that for some reason he could not stop inflicting on himself.

People were dancing between the two of them, he rather thought, a whole floor full of sparkling, whirling figures, but they were just a drunken blur. All he saw was Savine and the Young Lion, laughing. He had thought only he was funny enough to make her laugh that way. It turned out she could do it for entirely unfunny people, too.

That she had turned him down was hardly a surprise. But that she would, by all appearances, start trying to snare another man—and that one widely thought of as his rival—within a few days of turning him down? That hurt. He finished his glass and snatched another from a passing tray. Who was he fooling? It all hurt. He was one tremendous wound. One that would never heal.

"And this is my son! The heir to the throne, Crown Prince Orso."

Orso turned to find his father in the company of a solidly built old man, bald as an egg and with a short grey beard.

"This is *Bayaz*," said the king, with great ceremony. "First of the Magi!"

He bore only a passing resemblance to his magnificent statue on the Kingsway. Rather than a staff, he held a polished cane shod in brass and crystal. Rather than an air of mysterious wisdom, he had an expression of hungry self-satisfaction. Rather than arcane robes, he wore the clothes of a modern man of business. One owed a great deal of money by an excellent tailor.

Orso gave a sniff. "You look more like a banker than a wizard."

"One must trim one's style to the times," said Bayaz, holding up his cane and admiring the way the light shone through the crystal knob. "My master used to say that knowledge is the root of power, but I rather suspect power has a golden root these days. We have met before, in fact, Your Highness. Though you, I think, cannot have been more than four years old."

"He's barely changed!" said the king, with a suffocatingly false chuckle.

"I'm afraid I've a terrible memory for anything that happened more than an hour ago," said Orso. "Bit of a blur."

"I wish I could have been here more," said Bayaz, "but there are always problems in need of solving. No sooner did I engineer a suspension of hostilities with a troublesome brother in the South than two siblings in the West chose to become...difficult."

"Family, eh?" grunted Orso, waving his glass at his father, who was looking less comfortable with every word exchanged.

"The seeds of the past bear fruit in the present," murmured Bayaz. "The wounds of the past, even more so. Then you can't turn your back on the North for an hour without at least one war breaking out. Never the *slightest* peace. Still, I hope my erstwhile apprentice Yoru Sulfur was useful in my absence."

"Hugely," swooned the king. "Now if I could just—"

"*Hugely*," echoed Orso, anger stabbing at him through the fug of drunkenness. "Indeed, he made himself useful in the hanging of two hundred innocent people. People I had promised amnesty!"

"Manners, Orso," murmured the king, through gritted teeth. He was always weighed down by cares, but Orso had never seen him look truly scared. What did the King of the Union have to fear in his own palace? And yet he looked scared now, his face had lost all colour and there was a sheen of sweat across his forehead.

"Let the boy have his fun," said Bayaz, mildly. "We all were young once, eh? Even if, in my case, it was a *very* long time ago. In due course, he will learn how the world really works. Just as you did." And with a smile, the First of the Magi turned away.

"You shouldn't indulge that old fool," grumbled Orso.

"You weren't *there*." The king's fingers dug painfully into his wrist. "When the Eaters came. You didn't see...what he is *capable* of." His eyes had the strangest, haunted look. "You must promise me *never* to defy him."

Orso tried to twist his arm free. "What are you talking about—"

"You must *promise* me!"

"A word, Your Majesty!" called Bayaz, and with one backward glance, the king hurried after the magus like a dog called to heel. Orso took another swallow of wine, then turned back towards Savine, still laughing with the Young Lion.

He would have been furious with her, but he could no more hate her than a drunk can the bottle. He would have been furious with Leo dan Brock, but he had done nothing wrong, the horribly but justifiably vain, magnificently manly, utterly superficial bastard. He was doing exactly what Orso would have done in his place, only looking like a hero while he did it.

The only person in this triangle of misery he could reasonably be furious with was himself. He had ruined it all, somehow. By being too backward, or too forward, too slow or too fast or too something. He knew most people scorned him utterly, but for some reason, though she was the cleverest, bravest, most beautiful woman in the world, she had not. He had let himself believe that she loved him. But it was just another trick. A trick he had played on himself.

"Women," he muttered, helplessly.

"I know," came a voice beside him. "Fucking bitches."

It was that Northern girl. The Dogman's daughter, Rikke. He had seen her from a distance and thought she looked interesting, with the wild hair and the twitchy gestures and the total lack of usual propriety. Up close, she was a great deal more interesting. She had, for some reason, a heavy gold ring through her nose, and some streaks of dark paint on her freckled face, and a beguiling hint of cleavage showing among a rattling mass of necklaces and talismans that included a rather wonderful and entirely incongruous set of emeralds. But most of all it was her eyes, big and pale and piercing. He felt as if she saw right into him, and wasn't repulsed by what she found there. Which was welcome, because he certainly was.

Hell, he was drunk.

"Is it wrong of me..." he said, mangling the words and not much caring, "to say I find you fascinating?"

"Not at all." She gave a haughty sniff, that thick gold ring shifting. "You're a man, you can't help yourself."

Despite his attempts to be the tragic hero of his own life, he could not help laughing. "It has been remarked upon."

He had always been the most wretched judge of what he needed, but what he needed right now might be the woman who was least like Savine in the world. And here, as if by magic...

"I sometimes think no one in this city can tell the truth for three breaths together." He waved his glass at the room and slopped some wine onto the tiles. "But you seem...*honest.*"

"And so funny."

"*And* so funny."

"Who the hell are all these bastards?"

"Well...*he's* the court clockmaker. And *she's* a famous actress. That bald idiot is a legendary wizard, apparently. I'm told that woman there is a Styrian spy. One of the ones we pretend not to know about."

Rikke sighed. "I'm like an angry chicken trying to pass myself off among swans."

"I've tried swan, as it happens. Thoroughly mediocre meat, once the feathers are off." She might not have worn lady's clothes but without doubt there was a woman's shape underneath, and one he found not the slightest fault with. "A good chicken, on the other hand..."

"A man of taste, eh?"

"It has been remarked upon."

"I'm told you're the heir to all this."

"A sad fact."

She puffed out her cheeks as she glanced about the Hall of Mirrors. "All this wealth and flattery must be...such a curse."

"It's made me the useless cunt I am."

"You can't argue with those results."

"I'm told you're a witch who can see the future."

"Witch, no. Future, sometimes." She winced, pressed a hand to her left eye as though it hurt. "A bit too much, lately."

"What's the ring for?" he asked.

"Keeps me tethered to the earth."

"Or you'll float off?"

"I'm prone to fits." She thought about that, then snorted laughter and blew some snot onto her top lip. "And shits," she said as she wiped it away. "I'm told you've bedded five thousand whores."

"I'd be amazed if it's more than four thousand nine hundred."

"Huh." She gave him a long, lazy, utterly shameless look up and down. A look that no one within thirty paces could have doubted the meaning of. A look that made him feel at once slightly embarrassed and rather aroused. "They teach you anything?"

He realised he had not even glanced at Savine since they started talking. He looked over now. Felt a sour pang of loss as she touched a grinning Leo dan Brock on the chest with her fan.

"I used to be with him," murmured Rikke. She was watching them, too, and looking more than a little sour herself.

"Fancy that," said Orso. "I used to be with her."

"Doesn't bother you? Being second-best to the Young Lion?"

"I'll confess it stings, but I'm used to being the absolute worst." Orso drained his glass and tossed it rattling onto a side table. "Second best is an immense improvement." He offered her his elbow. "Perhaps I could accompany you on a stroll around the palace gardens?"

She turned those bewitching grey eyes on him. "Long as it ends in the bedroom."

A Bit About Courage

The cold nipped at Leo's ears as they made their way through the darkened streets, but the fires of excitement were burning ever hotter inside. Jurand looked as eager as he was. A playful sparkle in his eye. A handsome flush to his cheek.

"Where are we going?" he murmured, his hand on Leo's shoulder and his voice a little squeaky.

"Somewhere far from prying eyes, I suppose." Leo nudged him in the ribs with his elbow. "Wouldn't want to cause a scandal, would we?"

"Honestly," said Jurand, with that grin at the corner of his mouth, "I don't care."

Leo wasn't listening. He'd seen the street sign. He'd seen the number. "This is the place," he whispered, breath smoking in the chilly night.

It was a tall terraced house, a little smoke-blackened, just like a dozen others in this street, which was just like a dozen other streets on the way from the Agriont. Not the most exciting building. But a chink of light shone between shutters in an upstairs window, and Leo felt almost as skittish looking up at it as he had towards that bridge on the day of the battle, ready to order the charge.

"Thanks for the directions," he said. "You're a good friend. The best. I'll see you tomorrow. At the parade." When he turned, grinning, Jurand had the strangest look on his face. Shocked. Dismayed. Let down.

"Who are you meeting?" he whispered.

"The Arch Lector's daughter. Savine." Leo felt a shiver of nerves as he said the name and lowered his voice. "Probably best if you don't mention that to anyone, though."

"No." Jurand closed his eyes and gave a disbelieving little laugh. "You're right. Of course."

"Cheer up." Leo hugged him roughly with one arm, looking back to the building. The one lit window. "There are plenty of ladies for all of us." Though he couldn't think of any close to Savine dan Glokta's class.

"Plenty of ladies," Jurand echoed, gloomily. "I hope you know what you're getting into."

"Sometimes it's better if you don't." And Leo handed Jurand his cane, gave him a parting poke in the stomach, then strutted across the street, trying not to let the pain show. They didn't call him the Young Lion for nothing, after all. He knew a bit about courage, and the secret is to dismiss the whole notion of choice and just do. He lifted his fist and gave four smart knocks, twisting his face into the kind of self-assured smoulder he imagined the great lovers of history might've used.

It slipped straight off when the door opened. There was a dark-skinned woman on the other side he'd never seen before.

"Oh...I was expecting—"

"You must be the Young Lion," she said in common that probably had less accent than his.

"Some people call me that—"

She snapped her teeth at him with a surprisingly lion-like growl and he jerked back in surprise, winced as his weight went on his wounded leg and tried to pass it off with a false chuckle as she let him past, leaning back against the door until it clunked shut. "Lady Savine is upstairs."

"Upstairs. Of course." He found he was blushing, which probably wasn't something the great lovers of history would've done. "I mean, not that, I just mean...I'm not much of a talker."

"No doubt God gave you other talents." And she turned away with the slightest smile.

It seemed a long way up that darkened staircase, his heart beating so loud they could've heard it in the street, the chink of light below the black door getting steadily closer, promising so much. He'd no idea what to expect. Wouldn't have shocked him to find Savine waiting with a loaded flatbow. Or stretched out naked on a tiger skin. Or both, for that matter.

He paused outside the door, trying to catch his breath, but it refused to be caught. Too cold outside, too warm in here. He thought about knocking, then realised it might be more masterful if he just swept in. They didn't call him the Young Lion for nothing, after all. Reckless charges were his trademark. He reached for the knob, paused at a rush of nerves, then bundled too eagerly through.

Savine stood, pouring wine in the light of one lamp, as precisely posed as if she was standing for a portrait. She didn't even flinch as the door opened, didn't even turn to look at him, just held the glass up to the light, frowning slightly as she checked the colour. "You made it, then?" she asked, finally turning towards him.

"Yes." He clutched for something witty to add but the cupboard was bare. She looked even more immaculate than he remembered. Her shape against the lamplight—almost impossibly—what? Where else would words fail you but in a bloody writer's office?

He looked around, hoping to find some inspiration. Shelves burst with books, a leather-topped desk was strewn with papers. What might've been a printing press stood in one corner, about the ugliest thing Leo had ever seen, all iron gears and handles, a blackened roller and one printed page lying in its open jaws.

"Sworbreck's latest tissue of fantasies," said Savine. "But you didn't come to hear about other people's adventures."

"Why did I come here?" he asked, pushing the door shut, half a weak effort at a joke, half actually wanting an answer.

"For an adventure of your own." And she offered him the glass.

She looked so composed, so poised, so totally in control, but as she glided closer, Leo caught something glimmering in her eyes. Some hint of hunger, or anger, or madness, even, that made him very excited and slightly afraid. Or maybe the other way around. He found himself shrinking back, ended up pressed awkwardly against the desk, the moulded edge jabbing him in the arse.

By the dead, even the most thick-headed man in Adua—and Leo counted himself in the running—couldn't have doubted what she was after. Probably there'd never been any doubt, but for some reason, he'd let himself think she might really want to give him a tour of a writer's office. Here the pens, there the ink, now we can all go back to our separate beds and have a lovely sleep, entirely untroubled by worries over one's abilities as a lover.

If anyone asked, Leo would always say he adored the ladies. But there'd been times when he worried that women didn't quite...*excite* him the way they should. The way they did other men. Now it seemed his problem had simply been finding the right one. Rikke had been such easy company. One of the boys. Savine could scarcely have been more the opposite. He'd never met a woman who was more...*woman*.

"Nervous?" she asked.

"No," he lied. His voice cracked a bit and she smiled. A hard little smile, as though she'd caught him out. Which she had, of course. He'd never been much of a liar.

The truth was, Leo had never been that comfortable around women.

But perhaps comfortable is the last thing romance should be. Perhaps it should have an edge. And every moment with Savine felt as thrilling and dangerous as stepping into the Circle with the Great Wolf.

"I...don't think I ever met a woman like you before," he said.

"Of course not." She threw her wine back in one easy motion, thin muscles in her neck fluttering as she swallowed. "I'm the only one." And she tossed the glass onto the leather top of the desk, where it rattled on its edge but by some sorcery stayed upright. She eased closer, pale chest rising and falling, soft skin gleaming with the lamplight and—

She was wearing a necklace that didn't fit at all with her flawless tailoring. A twisted thong with bone tablets threaded onto it, jaggedly carved. The kind of thing Rikke used to wear in a rattling mass. Even through the drink and the excitement, that gave him a twinge of guilt.

"Where did you get the runes?"

"From the North," she said, vaguely, her eyes on his mouth.

"What do they say?" He wasn't doing anything wrong, was he? Rikke had made it perfectly clear she wanted nothing more to—

Savine took him by the chin with a force that wasn't to be resisted. "Who cares?" Her thumbtip crept up his cheek, her narrowed eyes fixed on it, and the tip of her tongue showed between her lips as she found the fresh scar, stroked it gently, a little tickly, a little sore.

"Did Stour Nightfall give you this?" she asked.

"With a few other keepsakes."

"Does it hurt?"

"Only if you press—ah!" She very deliberately pressed it, her teeth savagely bared for an instant, and made him flinch away, twisted even more uncomfortably over the desk.

He could hardly believe how slight she was, how slender, the sinews twitching in her bare shoulder. He hardly dared to touch her in case she snapped in his hands. But she was stronger than he'd expected. Far stronger. Far warmer. He caught a waft of her scent, mostly summer meadow, but with some harsh animal edge in it. He might've been more scared than excited but without doubt his cock was the other way around.

His throat was so tight he could hardly speak. He found himself wondering how much older she was than him. Five years? Ten? How much more experienced..."Are you sure this is a good idea—"

"I'm sure it's a terrible idea. That's its appeal." She flipped open a little box, brought out a pinch of something between finger and thumb and lifted it to his face. She found a way to do even that gracefully. "Here."

"What is it?"

431

"Pearl dust."

"The stuff artists use to make them more sensitive?"

"What works for artists works just as well for the rest of us. They're really a great deal less special than they like to think. Just sniff it."

"I'm not sure I—"

"I thought you came for an adventure?" And she pressed that pinch of powder to one of his nostrils while she squeezed the other shut with a fingertip. He really had no choice but to snort it up. The time for choices had been in the street outside—.

"Ah, by the dead!" Fire burned to the back of his throat, out into his ears, down into his teeth, brought tears to his eyes. A horrible sensation. "Why the hell would anyone—"

"Other side," she hissed, twisting his head and near shoving her fingers up his other nostril. He hardly even knew she was undoing his sword-belt until he heard it clatter to the floor. Disarmed in every sense.

Bloody hell, he wanted to sneeze, stood for a moment with eyes closed, trying to smother it. When the urge passed, he found she was kissing him, gentle little nips at his mouth, then she twisted his face side on to hers, started lapping, sucking, biting at him.

He squeezed at her ribs but couldn't really feel her, just a fortress of corsetry, stiff as armour. The burning in his face was fading, his head pleasantly spinning. His mouth moved mechanically, numb and clumsy. Lips all fizzy. He could taste wine on her tongue.

Whether it was her, or the drink, or the stuff for artists up his nose, Leo couldn't say, but he'd started to feel bold. Wild. He was the bloody Young Lion, wasn't he? He'd come for a fucking adventure! He *was* one of history's great lovers, damn it!

He gave a lion's growl as he caught her face, thumb under her jaw, caught the strap of her dress and gripped it, twisted it, his knuckles pressing hard into her shoulder, making her gasp, turning her, until he was the one shoving her up against the edge of the desk. He caught his foot on his sword, staggered, and she kicked it away with one pointed shoe, blade half falling out of the scabbard as it clattered into the lion-carved feet of the printing press.

His face didn't hurt any more. Not one bit. He could hardly feel a thing from the neck up, but twice as much as usual from the waist down.

She grunted in her throat, lips curled back into something between a smile and a snarl as she nipped at him with her teeth. He felt her fumbling with his belt, dragging it open, felt his trousers sagging down until they were tangled with his boots. The air was cool on his arse, then her hand even cooler.

Any thought of saying no was long gone. Any thought at all, for that matter.

She wriggled nimbly back onto the desk, almost as if she'd had a lot of practice, skirts rustling as she pulled them up, pulled them up, and she dragged him after her, hand twisted in his hair.

Almost painful, but not quite.

Substitutes

"By the dead," groaned Rikke.

She propped herself up on her elbows, tried to blow free the hair tangled across her face and failed. She had to drag it back with her fingers, squeeze her stinging eyes shut against the light then bit by tiny bit peel open just the one.

She was lying with a sheet tangled around her hips, one leg sticking out, which she knew must be hers 'cause she could wriggle the toes. She was stark naked but for her shirt, the sleeve all rucked up around one wrist and the rest spread out limp across the bed like a flag of surrender.

She frowned past the shirt, towards the window, then jerked up, staring about.

Where the bloody hell was she?

The room was big as a chieftain's hall, acres of rich-coloured drapery stirring about the great windows. The far-off ceiling was all crusted with gilded leaves, the furniture all polished to a blinding sheen, the door high enough to be used by giants with a knob shaped like the sun of the Union.

It turned, and the door shuddered open as if from a kick.

Someone came in with a silver tray teetering on one hand, things sliding dangerously about on top. His crimson jacket, heavy with gold stitching, hung open to show a strip of pale and slightly hairy chest and belly. He turned slowly towards the bed, concentrating furiously on keeping his tray balanced.

It was Crown Prince Orso.

"Oh." Rikke felt her eyebrows go very high then, as that last part of last night suddenly came rushing back. "*Oh...*" She'd been about to cover up, but now there didn't seem much point, so she just flopped back, arms outstretched.

"You're awake," he said, grinning.

"So you say," she croaked out. "How much did I drink?"

"All of it, I think." He put the tray down proudly on the bed beside her. "I brought you an egg."

She lifted her chin a little to give it the eye. Her guts had felt far from settled ever since Leo's duel. They felt less settled than ever now. "Well done. Lay it yourself, did you?"

"There's no point being a crown prince if you mean to do all the hard work. But look, I carried it from the door to the bed." And he gestured at the path he'd taken. "As you observed last night, fucking a crown prince is no great distinction, even if you did it rather bloody well—"

She gave a humble shrug. "I've a gift, what can I say?"

"—but being brought breakfast by one, *that* is a rare honour."

She had to admit to feeling a little bit honoured. She wasn't sure anyone had brought her breakfast before. Leo certainly never bothered. The thought would never penetrate his thick skull that there were needs in the world other than his. She wondered where he was, now. With that hideously beautiful woman, more than likely, who she couldn't even hate on account of the absurdly generous gift of green jewels that were right now gleaming on her chest.

"What's this?" she asked, fishing a crumpled sheaf of papers from the tray. She was no expert on printing but she reckoned this a poor example.

"It's a newsbill. They tell you what's happening." Orso thought about that. "Or they tell you what to think about what's happening." He thought more. "Or the really successful ones just confirm what you already think about what's happening."

"Huh." There was a smudged etching on the front of Leo on horseback looking even more pompous than usual. There must've been half a page about exactly how he trimmed his beard. Then there was something about Breakers rampaging, trouble in the South, rivalries with Styria, how immigrants had ruined the tone of a neighbourhood, how everything was better during the reign of King Casamir...

She gave a disbelieving snort. "Hear this shit. 'His Highness was observed leaving the function in the company of the beautiful and mysterious Witch of the North...'"

"Now, that *is* poor writing." Orso ever so gradually leaned towards her as he spoke, eyes fixed earnestly on her face. "It should say beautiful, mysterious, shapely, cunning, talented, highly entertaining—"

She flung the newsbill fluttering across the room, grinned as she caught Orso by the ear, pulled him close and kissed him full on the mouth. A scuzzy and sour-tasting kiss, but if you hold off till everything's perfect, think of all the great kisses you'll miss.

"You're not quite what I was expecting," she said as they broke apart.

"Even more handsome in the flesh, eh?"

"Handsome, I expected. Kind, I didn't."

"Kind?" He gave a her a strange look. "That might be the nicest thing anyone's ever said about me." He peered up at the ceiling. "Now I'm wondering if it's the only nice thing anyone's ever said about me. I could show you the city!" He jumped up from the bed with an enthusiasm that made her head hurt. "Adua! City of White Towers! It's the centre of the world, you know."

"So I hear."

"The theatre! I can get the place cleared. Arrange a private showing, just for the two of us."

"Folk acting out silly stories? All magic and wars and romance? Don't reckon that's for me."

"Cards, then. Do you play cards?"

"Not sure it'd be fair. I've got the Long Eye, remember?"

His eyes went wide, like a boy who's found a fine new game. "Even better! I can finally wipe the smirk off that bastard Tunny's face at the gaming table!"

"Thought you had a parade to lead?"

Orso's mouth twisted. "I don't deserve a parade. Unless it happened to be stomping over me, I suppose." And he flopped down on his back, staring up at the gilded leaves on the ceiling.

"Thought you crushed some rebellion?"

"Oh, yes, the heroic crown prince. I talked some labourers into surrendering."

"Well, that's something to celebrate. Saved some lives, didn't you?"

"I did." He turned to look at her. "Then they all got hanged."

Rikke stared up at the ceiling herself. "Ah."

"I didn't make it happen. But I didn't stop it, either. Some hero, eh?"

"I'm told a leader has to make o' their heart a stone." Rikke sat up and plucked the egg out of its cup. "At least you know what y'are." And she bit the top off it.

"I'm no Young Lion. I think we can agree on that."

"Thank the dead." And she grinned, showing him a mouthful of egg mush. "Man's a fucking arsehole."

He grinned back. "Do you know, I don't think I ever met a woman like you before."

"And you've met so many."

"Honestly, my reputation in that regard is hugely inflated."

436

"Hugely inflated, eh? Perhaps you're more like Leo dan Brock than you think." She leaned over to grab a slice of bread off the tray, and there was a rattle as the door was flung carelessly open.

"For pity's sake, Orso." A strange, sharp accent. "Tell me you're not still—"

A superbly dressed woman glided into the room with all the majesty of a great ship under full sail and stopped, staring down her nose towards the bed. Didn't take long for Rikke to realise it was Orso's mother. Her August Majesty the High Queen of the Union. She gave a kind of helpless squeak. Might've done better if she hadn't just wedged a piece of bread in her wide-open mouth, but she doubted it.

"Who is this...person?" asked the queen.

"Er...this is Rikke. The beautiful and mysterious Witch of the North!" Orso attempted an ornamental flourish, as though she was being presented to the throne rather than caught in his bed, and Rikke coughed and almost blew bread out of her nose. "She is an emissary from the Protectorate."

Rikke wasn't sure whether he'd made her look better or the Protectorate worse. She took the bread out of her mouth, shut it, then pinched the sheet between finger and thumb and ever so gradually pulled it up over her tits.

The queen made an arch of one perfect brow. "When it comes to building close diplomatic ties with the future King of the Union, one cannot fault her commitment."

Rikke cleared her throat. "Well, it's a key alliance for us." Orso smothered a laugh. His mother didn't. Rikke thought about just keeping on pulling the sheet until it was all the way over her head.

"Tell me this isn't the girl you're thinking of marrying, Orso?"

Rikke stared at him. "You're getting—"

"No!" Orso gave a pained wince. "That was...all a misunderstanding."

The queen sighed heavily. "It says something for the scale of my desperation that I was entirely prepared to welcome her into the family." And she swept out, shutting the door behind her with a precise *click*.

Rikke puffed out her cheeks. "By the dead. Your mother's got a stare could curdle milk."

"I think she rather took to you," said Orso. "And it's a hell of a compliment. When it comes to naked women, she's quite the connoisseur."

"I'd best get dressed." Rikke sat up, peering about for her trousers. "In case your father comes wandering in next."

"I'm guessing it doesn't take you too long?"

Rikke glanced down at herself. "Get my boots on and I'm pretty much there."

"Wonderful." Orso was looking down at her, too, the ghost of a smile about his lips. He brushed her neck with a fingertip, then slid it down until it caught the hem of the sheet, and started to drag that down, too. "We may be able to fit in a brief round of diplomacy before the parade."

"Well...I *was* sent to improve relations with the Union." And she kicked the tray clattering off onto the floor, spat a bit of egg after it, grabbed a fistful of Orso's jacket and dragged him down on top of her.

No Expense Spared

"The bloody *people*," bellowed Leo over the cheering.

"There are a lot of them," Orso shouted back.

They crowded to the edges of every roadway, crammed every roof and window. The streets were canyons of humanity, the squares were seas of faces. Just when Leo thought there couldn't be any more in the world, they'd turn a corner and another avenue would open up, smiles stretching into the distance. His wounded side was sore from all the riding, his wounded arm from all the waving, his wounded face from all the grinning.

"Are they taking them from the back and rushing them to the front down side streets, or something?"

"Bearing in mind my mother organised this," said Orso, "I wouldn't be at all surprised."

The parade itself must've been several thousand strong. At the front rode magnates of the Open Council, garlanded with braid and medals. Leo got an approving nod from Lord Isher as he glanced over his shoulder. An energetically shaken fist from Barezin. A self-satisfied salute from Heugen.

Further back were lesser aristocracy, officers of the army and fur-trimmed bureaucrats. Wedged between them and the glittering ranks of tramping soldiers were a group of ambassadors, emissaries and foreign worthies with a daunting array of skin tones and national costumes.

Leo realised with a twinge of guilt that Rikke was probably among them. He wondered what she'd done after the ball last night. Probably sat on her own in the darkness, plotting his doom. He turned his eyes hastily forward, towards the magnificent standard flying at the very head of the column, its white horse rearing against a golden sun. Just the sight of it made the embers of Leo's patriotic fervour flare back into life. A relic of a better time, when the Union was ruled by righteous warriors, not copper-counting cripples.

"The Steadfast Standard," he murmured, in a voice hushed with awe.

Orso nodded. "The very piece of cloth that fluttered at the head of Casamir's conquering armies."

"Without him there'd be no Angland at all. Now *there* was a great king."

"Indeed." The crown prince sighed. "Makes one realise how terribly far the monarchy has fallen."

"I didn't mean—"

"Don't worry," said Orso, with a sad little smile. He looked sad in general, considering this was all partly in his honour. "*No one* has a lower opinion of the royal family than me, and that is with some savage competition. Makes you wonder, though, doesn't it? Whether Casamir and Harod and the rest were really the great men history paints them as. Or were they just yesterday's mediocrities, bloated up with centuries of stolen credit into today's towering heroes?" He gestured to the crowds. "I mean, it's you they're here for. You're the one defeated Stour Nightfall. Men are wearing their beards like you. Wearing their swords like you. There's a play about your duel, I believe."

"Any good?"

"I'm sure it's less exhilarating than the original."

Leo had to admit he quite liked the crown prince. He'd expected him to be a real wilting dandy and, yes, you wouldn't have called him a man's man, but there was no doubt he was a damn good-looking fellow, and he turned out to be really quite thoughtful and generous. A hard man to hate. Leo was learning that people and their reputations rarely had much in common. He found himself, ironically, joining the Arch Lector in trying to inflate Orso's achievements.

"You liberated Valbeck, Your Highness. Put down a bloody rebellion."

"I surrounded a city and had a very good breakfast, discussed terms and had a very good lunch, accepted a surrender and had a very good dinner, then found the majority of my prisoners already hanged when I got up the next morning. My own fault for being a late riser, I suppose."

"But you're the heir to the throne—"

"My parents might agree on nothing else, but they do agree on that. Being heir to the throne takes no effort, however. Believe me, I know. You, on the other hand, have risked your life." He waved a hand towards the scar on Leo's face. "Covered with the red marks of bravery! My most serious wound was sustained when I struck my head getting out of bed

440

dead drunk. The bleeding was quite spectacular, to be fair, but the glory was minimal."

Leo's eye was caught by a knot of dark-skinned beggars in the crowd. "Lot of *brown* faces around," he said, frowning.

"Troubles in the South. Refugees are pouring across the Circle Sea, seeking new lives."

"Fought a war against the Gurkish thirty years ago, didn't we? You sure they can be trusted?"

"Some can and some can't, I would've thought. Just like Northmen. Just like anyone. And they're not all from Gurkhul."

"Where, then?"

"All across the South," said Orso. "Kadir, Taurish, Yashtavit, Dagoska. Dozens of languages. Dozens of cultures. And they've chosen to come here. Makes you proud, doesn't it?"

"If you say so." Leo knew nothing about those places except that he didn't want the Union to become one of them. He took no pride in the watering down of his homeland's character. "Don't you worry there might be..." Leo felt a need to lower his voice. "*Eaters* among them?"

"I'm not sure cannibal sorcerers are one of our most pressing problems."

"Some of them can steal people's faces. That's what I heard." Leo craned around to frown at those Southerners again. "They can disguise themselves as anyone."

"Then wouldn't a pale face make a better disguise than a dark?"

Leo frowned. He hadn't actually thought of that. "Just...hardly feels like the Union's the Union any more."

"Surely the great strength of the Union has always been its variety. That's why they call it a Union."

"Huh," grunted Leo. Orso would think that. He was a half-Styrian mongrel himself. Something landed in his lap. A flower. Looking towards an upstairs window, he saw a group of smiling girls, tossing down more. He grinned and blew them a kiss. Seemed the only decent thing to do.

"Adua appears to be enjoying you," said Orso. "How have you been enjoying it?"

"Can't say I take to the vapours. And the politics is pretty murky, too. Since the Closed Council didn't help fight the war, I'd hoped they'd at least help pay for it."

"Easier to open a gate to hell, in my experience, than the king's purse."

"A royal waste of my time. But, on the other hand...I met a woman. Never met one quite like her before."

Orso gave a sharp little laugh. "Fancy that. So did I."

"Beautiful. Clever. Sharp as a dagger and fierce as a tiger."

Another laugh. "Fancy that. So did I."

"But so poised, so elegant…every inch the lady."

Orso laughed louder than ever. "Well, there we differ. Does your paragon of womanhood have a name?"

Leo cleared his throat. "Reckon I'd better not say."

"Went further than just a meeting, then?"

"She took me to…." No, no, that sounded too weak. "I met her, I should say, at the office of some *writer*." The prince's face gave an ugly twitch. Even less keen on books than Leo was, maybe. "But…she didn't invite me to read, if you take my meaning."

"I think I can deduce it." Orso's voice sounded strangled, but Leo had never been much good at finding the hidden meaning in things. He was a straightforward fellow. So he carried on. Straightforwardly. Was that a word?

"A night of passion…with a beautiful and mysterious older woman."

"Surely every young man's dream," grated Orso.

"Yes, except…." Leo wasn't sure if he should say more. But Orso was a man of the world. Infamously so. Maybe he could help make sense of it? "If the story got out, people might think I made use of her, but…I've a feeling she made use of me."

"We all want to be wanted," growled Orso, eyes fixed ahead.

"The way she *looked* at me." As if he was her next meal. "The way she *touched* me." With no gentleness and no doubts. "The way she *spoke* to me." Knowing just what she wanted and not caring a damn for what he might. The thought was making him stiff in his dress trousers. "It was just like…"

His eyes went wide. Bloody hell, it was just the way his mother talked to him! That thought made his trousers droop even more quickly than they'd risen. Could it be…deep down…he *liked* being spoken to that way?

"You know," said Orso, checking his mount, "I really shouldn't be here."

"What?"

"You deserve it. I don't." Orso clapped him on the arm and, without waiting for a reply, pulled his horse to the side and began to drop back.

Till then there'd been the odd false note in the applause. Boos, mocking calls of, "Young lamb," even outright screeches of, "Murderer!" But when Orso left, he took all criticism with him, and with Leo leading the parade alone, riding beneath the Steadfast Standard just as Casamir himself might've, the cheering was twice as loud. The flower petals fell in fountains. Urchins pointed fingers, eyes wide in dirt-smudged faces. There goes the Young Lion, saviour of the Union!

Leo smiled. It wasn't hard to do. Orso was right, after all. He *did* deserve the glory.

How many people can say they won a war single-handed?

Everyone had cheered for Leo dan Brock, up on his own at the front of the parade, a famous hero from head to toe. Things quietened down a lot as the great men of the Open Council followed.

"That's fucking Isher," growled Broad as he rode past with his chin in the air, great gilded cloak spread out across the hindquarters of his prancing horse. "The one who stole our land. Looks like he's done all right out of it, the—"

"Let it go." Liddy's hand was gentle on the back of his. Gentle but firm. "Your anger won't hurt him any, but it could hurt us."

"Aye," said Broad, taking a hard breath. "You're right." It had hurt them enough already.

Fur-trimmed worthies followed the lords, trying to steal a piece of glory they'd had no part in winning. Next came the officers, and Broad turned his head and spat. After what he'd been through in Styria, he liked those bastards no better than the lords.

"There's Orso!" called a child up on shoulders.

"Why's he back here?"

"Shamed to show his face beside a real hero," someone grumbled.

Broad saw him, now. Sat on a fine grey in this loose, relaxed way like he didn't know what guilt was, an odd little smirk at the corner of his mouth as he chatted to some old soldier in a fine fur hat.

"Shame!" someone roared. "Down wi' the crown prince!" A tall man with a thick black beard, standing on tiptoe to shout over the heads of those in front. Folk frowned around at him but he'd the light of madness in his eyes and didn't back down a step. "Murderer!"

Liddy shook her head. "Damn fool will only cause trouble."

"Got a point, though," muttered Broad. "Orso is a bloody murderer."

"Didn't Valbeck teach you any lessons at all, Gunnar? You can have a point and still keep it to yourself."

"Two hundred good men and women he hanged as traitors," grumbled Broad.

"They *were* traitors," said May, jaw tight. "That's just a fact."

Broad didn't like hearing it, specially from his own daughter. "We could argue that case, I reckon." Though arguing with May never got him anywhere he wanted to go. "Truth is, Leo dan Brock fought in a war. Orso just sat in a tent and lied."

"Cheer for Leo dan Brock, then," muttered Liddy, "and leave His Highness out of it. You've no idea who's listening. Inquisition are everywhere."

That bearded bastard didn't seem to care. "Shit on the Young Lamb!" he bellowed through cupped hands, and Orso looked over with that faint, bored smile, and gave a little bow, and there was some scattered laughter which Broad had to admit took a little venom out of the gathering.

Moments later, someone barged his shoulder and three black-clothed men shoved through the crowd. The bearded heckler saw them, spun about, but another two were coming the other way. The crowd surged back as if from a plague victim as the Practicals caught him, shoved him down, started forcing a stained bag over his head.

"No!" hissed Liddy. Was only then Broad noticed her hand on his arm. Both hands, dragging him back as hard as she could. "No more trouble!" Was only then he noticed his every muscle was stiff and his fists clenched trembling tight and his lips curled back in a snarl.

"Don't you *dare* fuck this up for us!" May had slipped in front of him, was stabbing her pointed finger in his face. "Not when we just got right!" There were tears glimmering in her eyes. "Don't you *dare!*"

Broad took a deep breath and let it shudder away. Watched as three Practicals manhandled that poor fool through the crowd. Could've been him, dragged off to the House of Questions. Would've been him, gibbetted beside the road to Valbeck, if it hadn't been for May and the biggest slice of luck an undeserving man ever got.

"I won't, May." He felt tears in his own eyes then, eased his lenses down his nose to rub them dry. "I'm sorry."

"You promised us," hissed Liddy, dragging him back towards the tramping men, and the high-stepping horses, and the flags and shiny metal. "No more trouble."

"No more trouble." Broad put his arms around his wife and his daughter, and held them both close. "I promise."

But his fists were still so tightly clenched, they ached.

Savine had always loved grand events. The bigger the crowd, the more opportunities to turn strangers into acquaintances, acquaintances into friends, and friends into money. They were a chance to be seen, and therefore admired, and therefore kept powerful. Because power is a mountain one is always sliding down. A mountain one must claw and strive and scramble always to keep one's place upon, let alone to climb higher. A mountain made not of rock, but of everyone else's writhing, struggling, grasping bodies.

Events came no grander than this one. A holiday had been declared for the working folk of Adua and the furnaces had been doused and the vapours cleared. It was warm for the start of winter, the sun shining crisp upon the revelling crowds. Those of the great and good who had not joined the famous victors on their parade were gathered here at the end of the route, along with a multitude of the small and bad, in the Square of Marshals.

Savine was at the heart of it, at one end of the purple-swagged royal box, along with most of the Closed Council, a legion of toadying footmen and stern Knights of the Body, not to mention Their August Majesties the High King and Queen of the Union. Terez stood painfully erect at the very pinnacle of power, honouring the crowd with the occasional scornful wave, unquestioned mistress of all she saw. For once, Savine did not need to make an effort to be jealous. That could have been her place. Should have been. Almost had been.

The king glanced sideways and, just for an instant, caught Savine's eye. That same sad, needy look, and she stared down at her very fine shoes. She had no idea why she should be embarrassed. She was not the one who had fucked her mother and abandoned the results. But still her face burned.

She had always loved grand events, but she hated everything and everyone today, and herself most of all. She missed Orso like an arm cut off. She would think of some observation only he would understand, and smile, and turn to Zuri to arrange a meeting...and then that sappy pang of loss all over again.

Leo dan Brock had been a pleasing diversion. From the neck down, he was astonishing. When she opened his shirt, she had spent a moment just staring. It was as if he was carved from flesh-coloured marble by a sculptor intent on exaggeration. There had been a moment when he lifted her clean off her feet so effortlessly, it felt as if she might never come down...

But in the end, what truly makes a man is above the neck. The instant she made a joke, Orso would have pounced upon it, unfolded and developed it, tossed it back delightfully changed. Leo scarcely realised a joke had been made. Like that new invention Curnsbick was always prattling about, he was a wagon on rails. Conversationally he went only one way, and that at no great speed.

She needed a little something. She bent as if to adjust her shoe and slipped the silver box from her sleeve. Just a pinch to settle the nerves. That first pinch, which was actually about the fifth that morning, did not quite do the trick, so she took a bigger one. A lady of taste never leaves a job half-done, after all.

She straightened up sharply and nearly toppled right over, the rush of blood to her head so savage she thought her eyes might pop from her skull. When things came back into focus, she realised Zuri was holding her firmly by the elbow.

"What?" snarled Savine, ripping her arm free. She felt guilty right away. "Sorry. I'm sorry. I'd be lost without you."

"Lady Savine..." Zuri glanced carefully about the royal box. Her stumble had evidently been noticed. They were always watching, the fucking vultures, hoping for fresh meat to rip at. "You do not seem yourself."

"Who am I now, exactly? Answer me *that*." She was close to shrieking all of a sudden, the pulse throbbing behind her temples, and she wiped her sore nose, and closed her eyes. "I'm sorry, Zuri. No one deserves being shouted at less than you."

"Do you need to leave?"

"And miss all this shit?" As she waved towards the thronging square, Savine noticed the finger and thumbtip of her glove were stained white with pearl dust and tried unsuccessfully to slap it off against her other hand.

"Sticky fingers?" murmured her father from the side of his mouth. Although, of course, he was not her father. Arch Lector Glokta, entirely unrelated by blood.

"Nothing you need to concern yourself with," she snapped.

"But I am concerned." He continued to gaze out at the crowd as the distant cheering grew louder, the happy parade approaching through the streets of the Agriont, but he crooked one finger to beckon her down beside his chair. "Might I ask what you are doing with Brock?"

"You know about that?"

"I imagine half of Adua knows about it."

"The last thing I need is a fucking *lecture*," she snarled, and suddenly, entirely unbidden, entirely inappropriate, a memory welled up. That dark-skinned little girl, wet eyes lit by flames, pleading with her in a filthy alley in Valbeck. Please, please, please, over and over, the crushing terror and the stink of burning.

Her clothes were too tight, far too tight, she could hardly breathe. She twisted and wriggled in a sweaty panic, fumbled pointlessly behind her

446

waist at laces she knew she could not loosen. No more than a prisoner could pick their shackles off with their fingernails.

Her father frowned up at her. "Whatever has got into you, Savine?"

"Into *me*?" Fury bubbling up again as she caught the arm of his chair and bent to hiss in his ear. "Do you know what *your wife* told me?"

"Of course I know. What kind of a fool do you take me for?"

She gave a snort of bitter, snotty laughter. "Not half as big a one as you and my mother took me for."

A flurry of twitches ran up the left side of his face and set his eyelid flickering. "Your mother was young, and alone, and she made a mistake. Since then, all she has thought of is what was best for you."

"That and draining a bottle—ah!"

Her father's hand gripped her arm, pulling her down closer. He forced the words through tight lips. "Put aside your *pique*, this is serious."

"Pique?" she whispered. "*Pique*? I'm a *lie*, do you not understand?"

Several people had evidently caught the anger of their exchange, curious faces turned towards them. One in particular. The First of the Magi stood beside the king, dressed in robes with a dash of the arcane now, for a public appearance. He smiled, a knowing little smile, and gave her a nod of acknowledgement.

Her father did not miss it. He scarcely moved his thin lips, but she could see a muscle working on the side of his head. "Has he approached you?"

"Who?"

"Bayaz," he hissed, gripping her wrist almost painfully tight.

"I've never spoken to him." Savine frowned. "Though...there was a man, at the Solar Society, who claimed to be a magus. He didn't look like one."

The cords in her father's thin neck shifted as he swallowed. "Sulfur?"

"He said some nonsense about changing the world. About seeking new friends—"

"Whatever they ask for, whatever they offer, refuse, do you understand?" He looked up at her now. She was not sure she had ever seen him look scared before. "Refuse and come to me at once."

"What the hell has Bayaz to do with anything—"

"Everything!" He gripped her even tighter, pulled her even closer. "I hardly think you have considered the danger of your position. Bastard or no, you are the king's oldest child. That could make you very valuable. And very vulnerable. Now pull yourself *together*. This sulking is beneath you." He let go of her, wiped a tear from his weeping left eye and began politely to applaud as Leo dan Brock rode into the square, smiling hugely, and the cheering was redoubled.

Savine slowly straightened, rubbing at the livid marks her father's fingers had left on her wrist. She wanted to punch him in his toothless mouth. She wanted to scream at the mad top of her voice, right in the king's face. She wanted at least to storm furiously away.

But that would only draw attention. And no one could know. Her father was right about that. Or he would have been, if he had been her father. Bayaz was still smiling straight at her. Less majestic than the statue which stood not far off on the Kingsway, but a great deal more smug. All Savine could do was turn her attention to the square, push her shoulders back, her chin up and her face into the blandest smile imaginable, and clap.

And fume like a boiling kettle.

Orso heard the cheering ahead as the parade reached the Square of Marshals. He heard the chanting of, "Leo! Leo!" The calls of, "The Young Lion!" There could be no doubt the manly bastard filled the role of hero spectacularly well. Far better than Orso ever could.

He had to admit to being pleasantly surprised by the new Lord Governor of Angland. He had expected him to be a humourless thug and, yes, he had the usual provincial prejudices, but he turned out to be rather winningly honest and generous. A hard man to hate. The poor bastard had no idea he was hammering nails into Orso's skull when he talked about Savine. He had no idea about a lot of things. Probably she would squeeze the hapless fool until his pips squeaked and leave him a pining husk. It would hardly be the first time she'd done it. All it took was the thought of her with another man to leave Orso wanting to puke out his eyes.

Then he caught sight of Rikke, and found he was smiling in spite of himself.

She slouched in the saddle, squinting angrily up at the sun as though she was taking its shining personally. He wasn't sure she'd changed a thing since getting out of his bed. Among that immaculately tailored, groomed and decorated company, he found her total lack of effort oddly attractive.

He had wanted to marry the best-dressed woman in the Circle of the World, after all, and look how that turned out.

"Your Highness," she grunted as he dropped back towards her.

"Your..." Orso frowned. "What's the term of address for an emissary from the Protectorate?"

"Rikke?"

"You don't stand on ceremony up there, do you?"

"We stomp all over it. What are you doing back here with the chaff? Not enough width on one street for two heads so swollen as yours and Leo dan Brock's?"

"I quite like him." Orso shrugged. "A great deal better than I like myself, at least. In which I think, for once, I am in tune with the public mood." Those commoners who looked in Orso's direction did so, in the main, with hatred. "No doubt I deserve it, though."

"Unpopular at home, you came down here to work on overseas alliances. You're not the self-obsessed rake I was expecting."

"I fear I'm even worse." He leaned towards her, dropping his voice. "There's only one alliance I want to work on, and it's the one between my prick and your—"

He caught sight of the man riding just behind Rikke. A towering old Northman with the most monstrous scar he had ever seen, a bright ball of metal gleaming in the midst of it. His other eye was fixed on Orso with an expression fit to freeze the blood. Though it must be hard to find warm expressions when you have a face like a murderer's nightmare.

Orso swallowed. "Your friend has a metal eye."

"That's Caul Shivers. Got a good claim to being the most feared man in the North."

"And he's...your bodyguard?"

Rikke shrugged her bony shoulders. "Just a friend. But I guess he's filling the role."

"And the woman?"

She watched Orso even more intently than Shivers, if anything, one hand blue with tattoos, her stony-hard face shifting rhythmically as she chewed at something. Without breaking eye contact, she turned her head and savagely spat.

"That's Isern-i-Phail. Reckoned most wise among the hillwomen. She knows all the ways. Even better'n her daddy did. She's been helping me open the Long Eye. And to make of my heart a stone. With mixed results."

"So she's...your tutor?"

Rikke shrugged again. "Just a friend. But I guess she's filling the role."

"For an easy-going woman, you have some fearsome retainers."

"Don't worry. You're safe." She leaned close. "Long as you don't let me down."

"Oh, I let everyone down." He grinned at her, and she grinned back, all the way across her wide mouth. It looked so wonderfully open and true, somehow, that he felt pleased with himself for having some part in it. He had proposed to the most manipulative woman in the Circle of the World, after all.

Look how that turned out.

No expense had been spared. They'd turned the Square of Marshals into an arena, like they did for the Summer Contest, banks of seating bursting with happy crowds. The buildings were decked with flags: the sun of the Union, the crossed hammers of Angland. Everyone wore their best, though their best varied depending on which end of the square you were at. Up at the other end it was jewels and silk, down here it was twice-turned jackets and a ribbon or two for the lucky ones.

Still, feeling is free, so there was no shortage of emotion as the glittering ranks tramped past. There was jealous admiration: of beggars for commoners, of commoners for gentry, of gentry for nobility, of nobility for royalty, all twisting their necks looking always up to what they didn't quite have. There was warlike enthusiasm, mostly from those who'd never drawn a sword in their lives, since those used to swinging them tend to know better. There was patriotic fervour enough to drown an island full of foreign scum, and righteous delight that the Union made the best young bastards in the world. There was civic pride from the denizens of mighty Adua, City of White Towers, for no one breathed vapours so thick or drank water as dirty as they did, nor paid so much for rooms so small.

When it came to feeding the people, or housing them better than dogs, there were always harsh limits on what government could afford. But for a royal triumph, the Closed Council would find a way. Someone who'd starved in the camps, who'd lied her way into the hearts and beds of good people, who'd tricked and tortured to betray a cause she halfway believed in for the sake of one she didn't at all, might've felt a little bitter at seeing all this money wasted.

But Vick had a harder heart than that, and for damn sure a harder head. Or so she told herself.

"Been looking all over for you." Tallow was at her elbow. No need for him to shove through the crowds. He was that thin, he could just slip through the gaps like a breeze under a door. He'd brought a girl, wearing a best bonnet that even Vick, who'd never worn a bonnet in her life, could tell had been out of fashion a century ago. "This is my sister."

Vick blinked. "The one who—"

"I've only got the one."

There was no telling how old she was. When children don't get fed properly, sometimes they look far younger than they are, sometimes far older. Sometimes both at once. She had her brother's big eyes but a face even thinner, so hers looked even bigger, like a tragic frog's. Vick could see her own stern, distorted reflection in the damp corners of them, and didn't much like the look of it, either.

"Go on, then," said Tallow, nudging his sister with his elbow.

The girl swallowed, as if she was dragging up the words from a long way down. "Just wanted... to thank you. It's a good place, I been living. Clean. And they feed me. Much as I can eat. Though I don't eat much, I guess. Just... our parents died, you know. We never had anyone looking out for us before."

Vick was hard. Ask anyone who'd tried to cross her in the camps. Ask anyone she'd sent to the camps since. Ask anyone unlucky enough to run across her. Vick was hard. But that stung. The girl was thanking her for being a hostage. Thanking her for using her as a tool to make her brother betray his friends.

"What did Tallow tell you?" muttered Vick.

"Nothing really!" Worried she'd get him into trouble. "Just that he was doing some work for you, and so you were looking after me while he was doing it." She glanced up, fearful. "Is the work done?"

"The work's never done," said Vick, and the girl perked up right away. Maybe she should've been happy that someone was happy about more work. But Vick had never been sure what being happy felt like. Maybe it had happened and she hadn't noticed.

There was an ear-splitting fanfare, hundreds of boot heels crashing down together as the soldiers found their final places and brought the parade to an end. For a moment, all was still. Then someone rose from among the great men of the Closed Council, from beside the king, sunlight gleaming on the arcane symbols stitched into his shimmering robes. Bayaz, the First of the Magi.

"My noble lords and ladies! My stout yeomen and women! My proud citizens of the Union! We stand at the site of a great victory!" And he smiled out at the Square of Marshals. A place that was still being painstakingly rebuilt after he'd levelled it no more than thirty years ago. They said it would be better than ever when they were done. But things are always going to be better, or were better long ago. No politician ever got anywhere by telling people things are just right as they are.

"Here the best the Gurkish could send against us were utterly crushed!" And Bayaz shook one meaty fist, calling up a patriotic grumble as a conductor calls up the percussion. "Here their great emperor was utterly laid low. Here the Prophet Khalul was utterly humbled, his cursed army of

Eaters sent back to hell where they belonged. We were told the emperor's soldiers were countless, the Prophet's children indestructible. But the Union was victorious! *I* was victorious. The forces of superstition and savagery were defeated, and the gates opened to a new age of progress and prosperity." Bayaz's smile was huge enough to be seen all the way across the arena. Clearly a magus could be as pleased with his own past glories as any other old man.

"To me—for it needs hardly to be said that I am very old—it still feels like yesterday. But the bright-eyed young heroes who fought the Gurkish here are old greybeards now." And he set a heavy hand down on the shoulder of King Jezal, who looked more queasy than pleased by the recognition. "The pages of history turn, one generation gives way to another, and today we have not one, but two new famous Union victories to celebrate! In the North, on the barren borders of Angland, Lord Governor Brock defeated enemies without!" There was widespread cheering, and a child on someone's shoulders frantically waved a little Union flag. "While here in Midderland, outside the walls of Valbeck, Crown Prince Orso put paid to rebellion within!"

Orso's applause was quieter, especially at this end of the square, and what there was had the overblown quality of coming from purse rather than heart. The prince had few friends among the nobility, even fewer among the common folk. From what Vick could see of his expression, he knew it, too.

"I feel bad for Orso." Tallow gave a maudlin little sigh. He'd a talent for maudlin, that boy. "Wasn't his fault those folk got hanged."

"Guess not," said Vick. Less his fault than hers, anyway. "Fancy a pauper having pity to spare for a crown prince."

"Pity costs nothing, does it?"

"You might be surprised."

"I have seen many battles fought!" Bayaz called as the last of the cheering faded. "Many battles won. But I have never been prouder of the victors. Never held higher hopes for their futures. We of older generations will do what we can. To advise. To inform. To give the benefit of our hard-won experience. But the future belongs to the young. With young people such as these..." He spread his arms wide, one towards the man they called the Young Lion, the other towards the one they were starting to call the Young Lamb. "I feel the future could not be in safer hands."

More applause, and more cheering, but there was grumbling, too, among the poor around Vick. Lord Isher had nudged his horse up close

452

to Leo dan Brock, murmuring something under his breath, both of them frowning towards the royal box.

Trouble at both ends of the social scale. Trouble all over. Vick frowned at Prince Orso, then at that Northern girl with the hair like a bird's nest blown from its tree. She was staring at her own hand with the oddest expression. From what Vick could tell, it was shaking. She scrambled drunkenly from her horse and took something on a thong around her neck and wedged it in her mouth.

"What's got into her?" asked Tallow.

"Couldn't say."

Like a tree chopped down, she toppled over backwards.

"Rikke?"

She prised open one eye. A slit of sickening, stabbing brightness.

"Are you all right?" Orso was cradling her head with one hand and looking quite concerned.

She pushed the spit-wet dowel out of her mouth with her tongue and croaked the one word she could think of. "Fuck."

"There's my girl!" Isern squatted on her other side, necklace of runes and finger bones dangling, grinning that twisted grin that showed the hole in her teeth and offering no help at all. "What did you see?"

Rikke heaved one hand up to grip her head. Felt like if she didn't hold her skull together it'd burst. Shapes still fizzed on the insides of her lids, like the glowing smears when you've looked at a candle in a black room.

"I saw a white horse prancing at the top of a broken tower." Choking smoke, the stink of burning. "I saw a great door open but on the other side there was only an empty room." Empty shelves, nothing but dust. "I saw..." She felt a fear creeping up on her then. "I saw an old chieftain dead." She pressed her hand to her left eye. Felt hot still. Burning hot.

"Who was it?"

"An old chieftain, dead, in a high hall lit with candles. Men gathered about the body, looking down. All of 'em wondering what they could get from it. Like they were dogs, and that dead old man was the meat." That fear grew worse and worse and Rikke's eyes got wider and wider. "I have to go home."

"You think it was your da?" asked Isern.

"Who else could it be?"

Shivers was frowning hard, sun gleaming on his metal eye. "If it is... there's no telling who'll seize power in Uffrith."

Rikke winced at the thumping in her head. "All shadows where their faces should've been. But I saw what I saw!"

"You're sure?" asked Orso.

"I'm sure." Rikke groaned as she pushed herself up onto one elbow. "I've got to go back to the North. And the sooner the..." She realised everyone was looking at her. And everyone was a hell of a lot of people right then. She wrinkled her nose at an unpleasant smell. "Ah, by the dead..."

My Kind of Bastard

"How's the leg?"

Scale laughed, and slapped his nephew's wounded thigh, and made him wince.

"Better'n it was," said Stour as he stretched it out under the table.

"You're lucky, boy." Scale took another swig from his cup, ale leaking out into his beard. Clover would've thought a man who drank as much as he did would've got better at it, but the bastard couldn't seem to stop spilling. "The Young Lion could've killed you."

"Aye." Stour frowned at the floor, still a trace of yellow bruises around his eyes. "I'd have killed him, if things had gone the other way."

"Daresay you would've." And Scale chuckled and beckoned for more ale. His old bastards had something smug about them now, and Stour's young ones something grudging. When their master lost, they'd all lost a little themselves. A little pride, anyway. It'd been a long time since Clover had seen pride as aught but a handicap, yet some men still loved it more than gold.

"The king seems oddly pleased about his champion's defeat," muttered Wonderful, almost without moving her lips.

"Aye," said Clover. "Maybe 'cause it gives him a chance to wag his finger and harp on the hubris of youth and go over all he's learned in a long career of draining ale cups."

"Even though he was every bit as keen on a duel as Stour."

"That's kings for you. The shit ideas are always someone else's." Clover watched Stour rubbing at his hurt leg. Seemed more tame puppy than Great Wolf now. Thoughtful. Subdued, even. "Looks like defeat might've finally taught our king-in-waiting some lessons, mind you."

"Like it did you?"

"Failure's the best schoolmaster, they say."

Wonderful nodded, looking out at the room from under her grey-flecked brows. "So the war's over."

"Seems so," said Clover. "A lot of men dead, and nothing much changed."

"That's war for you. Turns out best for the worst of us. No doubt we'll have another presently."

"I shouldn't wonder."

"And in the meantime? Back to teaching sword-work?"

"Can't think of aught else I'm fit for that I can do sitting down. You?"

Wonderful frowned over at Stour and let a breath sigh through her nose. "Long as I'm done babysitting this bastard, I really don't care."

"You could come join me."

"And teach boys sword-work?"

"You've more wisdom to pass on than most, I reckon."

She snorted. "More than you have, that's for sure."

"There you go. Like all good partnerships, we make up for each other's deficiencies. You can do the passing of the wisdom, I'll do the sitting in the shade." And Clover took a sup from his own cup and grinned, thinking about being propped up against his favourite tree. The rough bark against his back. The sticks going clack clack down in the field.

"You're serious," she said, eyes narrowed.

"Well...I'm not *not* serious. If I've ended up doing things alone, it's more through bad luck than preference."

"That and through killing your friends, anyway."

"This is the North," muttered Clover. "Who hasn't killed a friend or two?" And they grinned at one another, and tapped their cups together.

A few chairs down, Stour was frowning into his ale as if there was a riddle at the bottom. "I never lost before. Not at anything."

"Would've won if it wasn't for that fucking witch!" sneered Greenway, as bitter as if it was him who'd lost. "Fucking Long Eye, or whatever. Fucking cheating, that's what that was. They should all have the bloody cross cut in 'em."

"There's no rule against shouting out, is there?" Stour spoke soft, and with a musing sort of look Clover never saw him wear before. "And I reckon she did me a favour. Losing...it's made me see things a new way. Like putting a coloured glass to your eye and seeing the world in new colours, or...no! Like taking one away, and seeing the world as it is!"

Scale raised his brows at his nephew. He wasn't the only one doing it. Clover scarcely had room on his forehead for how high his had gone.

"Might be you're more like your father than I thought," said the king. "I knew you were a fighter, but I never had you marked down for a thinker."

"Nor did I," said Stour, his wet eyes bright. "But when you're laid up wounded, what can you do but think? Made me realise. The Young Lion didn't put me in the mud. But we're all heading there sooner or later."

"True, Nephew, the Great Leveller waits for us all."

"Made me realise." And Stour stared at his hand as he curled the fingers into a fist. "You only have a lifetime to make your name and a lifetime might not be that long."

"True, Nephew. No one'll hand you a place in the songs. You have to *seize* it."

"Made me realise." And Stour thumped the table. "You can't wait to take what's yours."

Scale smiled as he lifted his cup. "True, Ne—"

The word was cut off in a kind of sickly squelch, and the king puked blood and ale and Clover saw to his great surprise that Stour had buried a knife in his uncle's neck.

There was a click and something spattered Clover's face, and he saw the old warrior beside him just got his head split down to the bridge of his nose with an axe.

Another was shoved onto the table and had his head hacked off right there. Took two blows.

Another thrashed as Greenway cut his throat, kicking meat and cups off the table, ale spraying.

Another snarled curses, flailing with his eating knife, all tangled up with his own fur cloak before he got a sword through his guts. He swore and drooled blood into his beard then a mace stove in the back of his head.

One of the king's serving girls had been knocked on the ground, the other was clutching her jug to her chest like she could hide behind it. Scale himself had flopped face down on the table, eyes popping and his tongue hanging out, still weakly blowing red bubbles out of his nose while bloody ale dripped from the edge of the table with a tap, tap, tap.

One of his old warriors was underneath it, crawling, snarling, crawling, trying to reach a fallen sword with his one good arm. He stretched, and stretched, like working his fingers across that little space of stone to the pommel was all that mattered. One of Stour's boys hopped over the table and stomped down on the back of his neck once, twice, three times with a crunching of bone.

Didn't take more than a few breaths for the old cunts to be sent back to the mud, the young to stand over 'em with smiles on their red-speckled faces.

Clover cleared his throat, and carefully set down his cup, and pushed back his chair and stood. Realised he still had a half-eaten meat bone in his hand and tossed it on the table, rubbing the grease from his fingers.

He felt strange. Calm. The axe made a sucking sound as it was dragged out of that old warrior's head. Stour's men turned towards him, red blades in their hands. Wonderful faced 'em, on her feet in a fighting crouch, sword levelled and teeth bared.

"Easy, everyone!" called Stour. "Everyone easy!" And he sat back, the wolf smile across his bruised face wider than ever. "See this coming, Clover?"

"We don't all have the Long Eye." For all his high opinions of his own cleverness, he'd been as blind to it as Scale. But he knew if Stour wanted him dead, he'd have been stretched out with the others. So Clover stood there, and waited to see which way the wind would blow.

"You make out you're a silly bastard." Stour took a little sip from his cup and licked his lips. "But you're a clever bastard, too. The wise fool, eh? Always thought your lessons were coward's nonsense but, looking back, I see you had the right of it all along." He wagged his bloody dagger at Clover. "Like what you said about knives and swords. Spent twenty years training with a sword every morning and every dusk, but I won more with one knife-thrust. I'd like you to stick with me. Might be you've more to teach. But... I'll need a show o' good faith." He looked sideways, to Wonderful. "Kill her."

She turned, eyes wide. "Clo—"

She looked greatly surprised as he caught her in a hug, her sword arm trapped under his left while he stabbed her in the heart with his right, and the blood gushed hot over his fist and down his arm and spattered the floor.

You have to pick your moment. He'd always said so. Told everyone who'd listen. Have to recognise it when it comes, and seize it, with no care for the past and no worries about the future.

He held her as she died. Didn't take long. He told himself he'd want to be held when he went back to the mud, but it was really that he wanted to hold her. Needed to. What she felt about it, there was no knowing. The feelings of the dead weigh less than a feather.

No last words. Just a sort of grunt. And Clover lowered her to the ground and laid her in the widening pool of her own blood, her disappointed eyes fixed on some cobwebs high among the rafters.

"Fuck," said Stour. "You didn't have to think about that for long."

"No." Clover had seen a lot of corpses. Made a fair few himself. But he was having trouble thinking of Wonderful as dead. Any moment, she'd laugh it off. Make some joke about it. Cut him down to size with a raised brow.

"That was *cold*." Greenway shook his head while another of the young warriors gave a long whistle. "Cold."

"A man has to bend with the breeze." The Great Wolf's grin was wider than ever. "You're a bastard, Clover. But you're *my* kind of bastard."

Stour's kind of bastard. That was where all his cleverness had got him.

There was a bang as the doors were flung open, armed men spilling into the hall, painted shields up and swords and spears and axes ready. Black Calder strode in after them, eyes wide as he took in all the murder.

"Father!" called Stour, pouring some ale and holding up the cup. "Fancy a drink?" And he drained it, and set it down in the spreading puddle of the king's blood.

"What have you done?" whispered Calder.

"Chosen not to wait." Stour peeled Scale's fat head from the table by one ear and dragged the chain from around his shoulders, its dangling diamond red with blood. Greenway giggled and the others grinned, all well satisfied with the outcome.

Clover had never thought to see Black Calder at a loss for words. He looked to Wonderful's body, then to Clover, then back to his son, and bunched his fists. "We've got allies who won't stand for this! There'll be men who won't stay loyal!"

"Didn't you hear?" asked Stour. "I made a friend of the Young Lion! Won't find a stronger ally than the Union. But if folk want to stick with my uncle, that's fine." And he showed his teeth, wet eyes bulging. "They can go back to the fucking mud with him!" And Stour tossed the chain over his own shoulders, the red links landing skewed and smearing blood across his white shirt. "They're going to have to learn times change. And so are you. I'm King o' the Northmen now."

Calder's face was pale as milk, but what could he do? Kill his son for killing his brother? Stour was the future of the North. Always had been. And with all those old warriors lying slaughtered on the bloody floor of the hall, it seemed the future had come early. A man's worst enemies are his own ambitions, Bethod used to say, and here was the red-spattered proof. Black Calder had ruled for twenty years. With one thrust of the knife, his time was done.

"Your grandfather's dream—" he whispered, like all his grand schemes could be unfucked. Like King Scale could be unkilled.

Stour gave a hiss, somewhere between disgust and boredom. "Folk say a lot o' things about my grandfather, Bethod this and Bethod that, but I never even met the bastard." He winced as he lifted his wounded leg and propped it up on the murdered king's fat back. "I got my own dreams to think about."

Clover just stood there, the blood soaking his sleeve turning cold.

Long Live the King

Orso woke in the darkness and reached out, but she was gone.

He sat up, not sure where he was. Not sure who he had been reaching for. He rubbed at the bridge of his nose. Had he been dreaming?

Rikke had gone back to the North. Savine had gone for good. People still clambered over each other to be noticed by him, of course, to embrace him, to flatter him, to profit by him. But he was alone.

He could not remember ever feeling more so.

He was snatched from the comforting blanket of self-pity by a noise in the hall. A distant shout, muffled. Then another, closer, and the thumping of quick footsteps, past and away. He flung back the covers, swinging his bare feet to the cold floor. Shadows moved in a thin strip of light under his door, then the knob turned and it creaked open.

"Bloody hell, Mother, don't you ever knock?"

She looked regal as ever, face emotionless as a mask by the light of the candle she held. But she wore a dressing gown and her hair was down. Orso was not sure he had ever seen her leave her chambers without it elaborately pinned. It hung almost to her waist and seemed, somehow, a surer herald of disaster than if some other person had charged in on fire.

"What is it?" he whispered.

"Come with me, Orso."

There was a great deal of activity in the palace, considering it was the middle of the night. Everyone busy at nothing, running to nowhere, all with the same oddly panicked expression. A fully armoured Knight of the Body clanked past, sweat beaded across his forehead, the lamp in his hand bringing a glitter to the gilded panelling.

"What is it, Mother?" asked Orso, his mouth very dry.

She said nothing, only glided down the chilly hallway, decorated with

461

berries for the new year festival, so quickly he had to take the odd running step to keep up.

Three more Knights of the Body stood at the towering door of his father's bedchamber. They fumbled their way to attention as the queen swept up. One gave Orso the strangest haunted look before he turned his eyes to the shining tiles.

There was a press of people about the bed, in nightshirts and dressing gowns, grey hair in wispy disarray. Men of the king's household, lords of the Closed Council, shocked faces strange in the shifting candlelight. They parted wordlessly to let him through and Orso was drawn into the gap without choosing to move his feet. As if he was rolled along on a trolley, numb and dreamlike, his breath coming slow, slow, slow, until it hardly seemed to come at all.

He stopped beside the bed, looking down.

King Jezal the First lay flat on his back, eyes closed, mouth slightly open. The covers had been pulled down to his ankles, feet still making two little peaks in the crimson cloth. His nightshirt had been dragged right up above his chest, waxy pale body exposed, fuzzed here and there with grey hair, shrivelled prick flopped sideways and stuck flat to his hip. Orso's father had always said that dignity was a luxury kings could not afford.

The royal physician knelt by the bed, ear pressed to the king's chest. Someone pushed through the crowd to offer him a hand mirror and he held it to the king's mouth, fumbled for his eye-lenses and perched them on his nose.

"There was no sign he was ill," came a disbelieving mutter.

"I was talking to His Majesty just last night. He was in high spirits!"

"What the hell does that matter?" someone snarled.

The silence stretched.

The physician carefully put down the mirror and slowly stood.

"Well?" asked Lord Chamberlain Hoff, wringing his pale hands.

The physician blinked, then shook his head.

Bremer dan Gorst took a breath so sharp it made a strange squeak in his broad nose.

Arch Lector Glokta slumped into his wheeled chair. "The king is dead," he murmured.

A kind of groan went through the gathering. Or maybe it came from Orso's own throat.

Suddenly he felt that there had been so much he needed to say to his father. He had always supposed they would discuss the important things later. The profound things. But it would never happen. There had only been a fixed time in his presence, and Orso had pissed it all away talking about the weather, and there would be no more.

He felt a heavy hand on his shoulder, more grasping than comforting, and turned to see the First of the Magi standing beside him. He almost had the ghost of a smile at the corner of his mouth.

"Long live the king," said Bayaz.

Acknowledgments

As always, four people without whom:

Bren Abercrombie, whose eyes are sore from reading it.
Nick Abercrombie, whose ears are sore from hearing about it.
Rob Abercrombie, whose fingers are sore from turning the pages.
Lou Abercrombie, whose arms are sore from holding me up.

Then, my heartfelt thanks:

To all the lovely and talented people in British publishing who have helped bring the First Law books to readers down the years, including but by no means limited to Simon Spanton, Jon Weir, Jen McMenemy, Mark Stay, Jon Wood, Malcolm Edwards, David Shelley, Katie Espiner and Sarah Benton. Then, of course, all those who've helped make, publish, publicise, translate and above all *sell* my books wherever they may be around the world.

To the artists responsible for somehow continuing to make me look classy: Didier Graffet, Dave Senior, Laura Brett, Lauren Panepinto, Raymond Swanland, Tomás Almeida, Sam Weber.

To editors across the Pond: Lou Anders, Devi Pillai, Bradley Englert, Bill Schafer.

To champions in the Circle: Tim and Jen Miller.

To the man with a thousand voices: Steven Pacey.

For keeping the wolf on the right side of the door: Robert Kirby.

To all the writers whose paths have crossed mine on the Internet, at the bar or in the writers' room, and who've provided help, support, laughs and plenty of ideas worth the stealing. You know who you are.

And lastly, yet firstly:

The great machinist, Gillian Redfearn. Because every Jezal knows, deep down, he ain't shit without Bayaz.

The Big People

Notable Persons of the Union

His August Majesty Jezal the First—High King of the Union.
Her August Majesty Terez—High Queen of the Union.

Crown Prince Orso—King Jezal and Queen Terez's eldest and only son, heir to the throne and notorious wastrel.
Hildi—the crown prince's valet and errand girl, previously a brothel laundress.
Tunny—once Corporal Tunny, now Crown Prince Orso's pimp and carousing partner.
Yolk—Tunny's idiot sidekick.

Arch Lector Sand dan Glokta—"Old Sticks," the most feared man in the Union, head of the Closed Council and His Majesty's Inquisition.
Superior Pike—Arch Lector Glokta's right-hand man, with a hideously burned visage.
Lord Chamberlain Hoff—self-important chief courtier, son of the previous Lord Hoff.
Lord Chancellor Gorodets—long-suffering holder of the Union's purse-strings.

Lord Marshal Brint—senior soldier and one-armed old friend of King Jezal.
Lord Marshal Rucksted—senior soldier with a penchant for beards and tall tales, married to Tilde dan Rucksted.
Colonel Forest—a hard-working officer with common origins and impressive scars.

Bremer dan Gorst—King Jezal's squeaky-voiced First Guard, and master swordsman.

Lord Isher—a smooth and successful magnate of the Open Council.
Lord Barezin—a buffoonish magnate of the Open Council.
Lord Heugen—a pedantic magnate of the Open Council.

In the Circle of Savine dan Glokta

Savine dan Glokta—daughter of Arch Lector Sand dan Glokta and Ardee dan Glokta, investor, socialite, celebrated beauty and founder of the Solar Society with Honrig Curnsbick.
Zuri—Savine's peerless lady's companion, a Southern refugee.
Lisbit—Savine's rosy-cheeked face-maid.
Freid—one of Savine's many wardrobe maids.
Metello—Savine's hatchet-faced Styrian wig expert.
Ardee dan Glokta—Savine's famously sharp-tongued mother.
Haroon—Zuri's heavily built brother.
Rabik—Zuri's slight and handsome brother.

Honrig Curnsbick—"The Great Machinist," famous inventor and industrialist, and founder of the Solar Society with Savine dan Glokta.
Dietam dan Kort—a noted engineer and bridge-builder, losing money on a canal.
Selest dan Heugen—an admirer and potential rival of Savine's.
Kaspar dan Arinhorm—an abrasive expert in pumping water from mines.
Tilde dan Rucksted—the blabbermouth wife of Lord Marshal Rucksted.
Spillion Sworbreck—a writer of cheap fantasies.
Majir—an underworld figure, owing Savine money.

Colonel Vallimir—a failed soldier, now a junior partner of Savine.
Lady Vallimir—Colonel Vallimir's tasteless wife.
Superior Risinau—the sweaty-palmed head of Valbeck's Inquisition.
Lord Parmhalt—the somnambulant Mayor of Valbeck.

With the Breakers

Victarine dan Teufel—an ex-convict, daughter of a disgraced Master of the Mints, now striking a blow for the common man.
Collem Sibalt—leader of a cell of Breakers.
Tallow—a skinny young Breaker with a tragic face.
Grise—a Breaker with hard language and soft features.
Moor—a deep-voiced Breaker.

Gunnar "Bull" Broad—an ex-Ladderman wrestling with violent tendencies, just returned from the wars in Styria, married to Liddy Broad, father of May Broad.
Liddy Broad—Gunnar Broad's long-suffering wife, mother to May Broad.
May Broad—Gunnar and Liddy Broad's hard-headed daughter.

Sarlby—an old comrade-in-arms of Gunnar Broad, now working in a brewery.
Malmer—foreman of the brewery, a leader of the Breakers.
Judge—an unhinged lunatic, the leader of the Burners.

In the North

Scale Ironhand—King of the Northmen. Brother to Black Calder and uncle to Stour Nightfall. Once a great warrior and war leader, now... not.
Black Calder—Scale Ironhand's cunning brother, father to Stour Nightfall, and the real power in the North.
Stour Nightfall—"The Great Wolf," Calder's son, the king-in-waiting, heir to the North and famed warrior and arsehole.
Magweer—one of Stour Ironhand's Named Men, carries a lot of axes.
Greenway—one of Stour Ironhand's Named Men, expert sneerer.

Jonas Clover—once Jonas Steepfield and reckoned a famous warrior, now thought of as a disloyal do-nothing.
Wonderful—second to Black Calder, a Named Woman with a dry sense of humour.

Gregun Hollowhead—a Chieftain of the West Valleys, father of the Nail.
The Nail—Gregun Hollowhead's son, a formidable warrior.

In the Protectorate

The Dogman—Chieftain of Uffrith and famous war leader, father of Rikke.
Rikke—the Dogman's fit-prone daughter, blessed, or cursed, with the Long Eye.
Isern-i-Phail—a half-mad hillwoman, said to know all the ways.
Caul Shivers—a much-feared Named Man with a metal eye.
Red-Hat—one of the Dogman's War Chiefs, known for his red hood.
Oxel—one of the Dogman's War Chiefs, known for his poor manners.
Hardbread—one of the Dogman's War Chiefs, known for his indecision.

From Angland

Finree dan Brock—interim Lady Governor of Angland and a superb organiser.
Leo dan Brock—"The Young Lion," Finree dan Brock's son, Lord Governor in waiting, and a bold but reckless warrior.
Jurand—Leo dan Brock's best friend, sensitive and thoughtful.
Glaward—Leo dan Brock's exceptionally large friend.
Antaup—Leo dan Brock's friend, renowned as a lady's man.
Barniva—Leo dan Brock's friend, equivocal about war.
Whitewater Jin—Leo dan Brock's friend, a jovial Northman.
Ritter—Leo dan Brock's friend, easily led and with a weak-chinned wife.
Lord Mustred—an old worthy of Angland, with a beard but no moustache.
Lord Clensher—an old worthy of Angland, with a moustache but no beard.

The Order of Magi

Bayaz—First of the Magi, legendary wizard, saviour of the Union and founder member of the Closed Council.
Yoru Sulfur—former apprentice to Bayaz, nondescript but for his different-coloured eyes.

The Prophet Khalul—former Second of the Magi, now arch-enemy of
    Bayaz. Rumoured to have been killed by a demon, plunging the South
    into chaos.
Cawneil—Third of the Magi, about her own inscrutable business.
Zacharus—Fourth of the Magi, guiding the affairs of the Old Empire.